C000264051

Short story writer and novelist Owen Mai
sixteen books to date. Awards for his fiction include the PEN Lillian ...
Award twice, the *Evening Standard* Short Story Prize, the American Express Short
Story Award, the New Zealand Literary Fund Scholarship in Letters, Fellowships at
the universities of Canterbury and Otago, and the Katherine Mansfield Memorial
Fellowship in Menton, France. He received the ONZM for services to Literature in
the Queen's New Year Honours, 2000, and his novel *Harlequin Rex* won the
Montana New Zealand Book Awards Deutz Medal for Fiction in the same year. In
2002 the University of Canterbury awarded him the
honorary degree of Doctor of Letters.

Owen Marshall was born in 1941, has spent almost all his life in South Island
towns, and has an affinity with provincial New Zealand.

PREVIOUS BOOKS BY OWEN MARSHALL

Supper Waltz Wilson and other New Zealand stories — PEGASUS, 1979
The Master of Big Jingles and other stories — JOHN MCINDOE, 1982
The Day Hemingway Died and other stories — JOHN MCINDOE, 1982
The Lynx Hunter and other stories — JOHN MCINDOE, 1987
The Divided World: Selected Stories — JOHN MCINDOE, 1989
Tomorrow We Save the Orphans — JOHN MCINDOE, 1992
The Ace of Diamonds Gang and other stories — MCINDOE PUBLISHERS, 1993
Burning Boats (ed.) — LONGMAN PAUL, 1994
A Many Coated Man — LONGACRE PRESS, 1995
Letter From Heaven (ed.) — LONGMAN PAUL, 1995
Coming Home in the Dark — VINTAGE, 1995
Beethoven's Ears (ed.) — ADDISON WESLEY LONGMAN, 1996
Harlequin Rex — VINTAGE, 1999
Spinning a Line — VINTAGE, 2001
Authors' Choice (ed) — PENGUIN, 2001

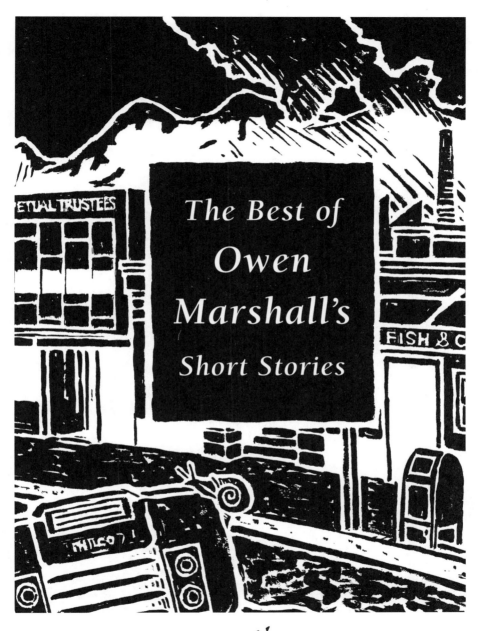

The Best of
Owen
Marshall's
Short Stories

V

VINTAGE

For Jackie and our daughters, Andrea and Belinda

Illustrations on title page and part titles by Peter Campbell
Cover photograph by Reg Graham

Random House New Zealand Ltd
(An imprint of the Random House Group)

18 Poland Road
Glenfield
Auckland 10
NEW ZEALAND

Sydney New York Toronto
London Auckland Johannesburg
and agencies throughout the world

First published 1997
Reprinted 2002

© Owen Marshall 1997
The moral rights of the author have been asserted.

Printed in Auckland by Publishing Press Limited
ISBN 1 86941 336 9

All rights reserved. No part of this publication may be reproduced
or transmitted in any form or by any means, electronic or mechanical,
including photocopying, recording, storage in any information retrieval
system or otherwise, without the written permission of the publisher.

Contents

Preface

My first effort at writing was a novel. The first piece I finished was a novel — a different one. Following the rejection of that short novel, I wrote another. As a naïve writer in my twenties I considered that that was what writers did: they wrote novels. After the rejection of the second book I decided to think again.

A rather obvious connection occurred to me: as the short story form interested me most as a reader, perhaps I should concentrate on that. So, closeted in the small South Island town of Oamaru, I began to write short stories. And they were rejected.

What I draw from all of this, now, is that whatever genre I attempted, I would have been compelled to serve an apprenticeship. Had I realised at the time, of course, I may have lacked the resilience to persevere with the business of writing at all, but instead I tackled each work with impetuous conviction of its value, as a serious writer should. As my writing improved, I was able to begin placing my work, first in literary periodicals and then as collections. Many people in the world of books gave me a hand up along the way. Of my indebtedness to them I have written in more detail elsewhere, but I wish to mention here Frank Sargeson, Andrew Mason, Bill Manhire, Vincent O'Sullivan, Elizabeth Caffin, Brian Turner, Barbara Larson and Grahame Sydney. I much appreciate also the encouragement of my present publisher — Harriet Allan of Random House.

By the end of the 1980s, five collections of mine had been published and I had little difficulty in placing what I wrote. I was able to consider becoming a full-time writer, after more than twenty years of giving teaching priority.

I have recently had two novels published but in the 1970s and 1980s I concentrated entirely on short fiction, and I continue to be interested in the form. I enjoy the constraints, the possibilities, the challenges of the short story, and marvel at the skills of its great practitioners. My early favourites included Anton Chekov, James Joyce, Isaac Babel, V. S. Pritchett, Sherwood Anderson, Ernest Hemingway, William Saroyan, Elizabeth Bowen and A. E. Coppard, but especially H. E. Bates and Theodore Powys. Bates and Powys are in many ways very different writers, and while Bates achieved the enduring success he deserved, Powys has been unduly neglected. Their writing, however, shares two elements that particularly attracted me: firstly a marked felicity of language, secondly a persistent affection for the countryside and rural people. Writers whom I came to admire rather later include Janet Frame, Frank Sargeson, John Updike, Alice Munro, William Trevor, Bette Pesetsky, John Cheever and Donald Barthelme. The best work of all such people can wrench the heart, so that as a reader you draw breath with difficulty in the mundane world.

It's hard for me to make critical generalisations about my own writing, although I'm sometimes presumptuous enough to do so in regard to the work of others. When readers ask me about my feelings towards individual stories, my responses are based largely on non-textual associations. I can read them only in that way. A piece of writing may bring with it images of the summer in which it was created, the pain of a physical injury carried at the time, a sense of family grief although the story itself be humorous. There is no simple way that the stories allow access to those things for any reader except myself. My work is not just a product of my life, but part of the achaeology of it.

As to my view of the short story: I agree with Frank O'Connor, who characterised it as the Lonely Voice, and by its very nature intransigent, unlike the novel which is so much more successful in the marketplace, and hence susceptible to the influence of the marketplace. And Bates said that, in its finest form, the short story is poetry. Intransigence and poetry — there's a combination to which I can give allegiance, even if I fail often to capture it effectively in my own work.

The sixty-seven stories in this book have been selected from some one hundred and fifty published by 1997, and I am grateful to my accomplished editor, Anna Rogers, for her help in this task. The main criterion was merit — which perhaps means no more than that some took our fancy more than others — but we also considered the balance of themes and styles. To allow some sense of writing development, we decided on an order which is generally chronological, but didn't hesitate to make minor departures from that sequence when there seemed advantage.

This selection doesn't aim to be definitive in any significant way. Despite my best efforts, the stories are only approximations of what I wished to achieve. I'm still learning, and that, too, is part of the satisfaction of writing.

OWEN MARSHALL
2002

from

Supper Waltz Wilson

Supper Waltz Wilson

~

SUPPER WALTZ LOVED oysters, and in the season he had them for his tea whenever his mother was on the afternoon shift. About half-past four, after we'd been playing along the cliffs, or wandering in the town, he'd buy his oysters. He couldn't wait any longer. If the rest of us had any money we'd buy some too, and walk up to the shelters overlooking the bay. Winter is the time for oysters, and from the shelters we would watch the leaden waters of the harbour, and the heat from the oysters and chips would make our noses run. Pongo, Graeme, Supper Waltz, and I. Supper Waltz didn't just eat his oysters; he ravished them. First he would tear off the batter, then hold the steaming oyster by its frill and bite cruelly into its centre with his sharp teeth. Sometimes, as a conscious indulgence, he'd eat two at once, growling with pleasure deep in his throat. It was another occasion on which we realised that Supper Waltz had a heightened perception of the world.

Children take their own situation as the universal one when they're young. My father dominated our family as naturally as a pyramid does the sands. That's why I always found the Wilson household disconcerting, I suppose. Mr Wilson was a master butcher, but years ago he'd had a revelation from the Lord telling him not to work anymore, and his religious conviction never wavered afterwards. He always seemed to be in his room. Scores of times I was at the Wilsons', and if Mr Wilson was mentioned he was almost always in his room. If he wasn't then he was in the lavatory singing hymns. He knew all the words, and never had to go dum-de-dah or some-such in places. He didn't seem to have much of an ear, though, and it wasn't good to listen to. Once he was singing, and Supper Waltz's eldest brother was in the kitchen. 'Arse arias again today, Mum,' he said, and Mrs Wilson threw down the carrot she was scraping into the sink, and began to laugh. The carrot splashed up water on to her face, and the drops ran like tears as she laughed. Supper Waltz laughed a lot too, and I joined in the way you do when you're not sure why.

Mrs Wilson worked in the woollen mills. She often seemed to be just coming, or just going. A very matter-of-fact woman, Mrs Wilson. Tall and strong, lacking any graces. When she cycled up the rise to the house, she didn't get off and wheel the bike the way other women did, but stood up on the pedals, using her weight and strength like a man, pushing right up to the gate. Pongo's and Graeme's mothers usually said hello to me, or asked about my parents, but I don't remember Mrs Wilson saying anything at all to me — except the once. A hard woman if she wanted to be I guess, Mrs Wilson. Wherever Supper Waltz got his looks it wasn't from his mother. They had the same eyes, though. The same restless, flickering eyes, like light through the wings of a bird in a cage.

Most grown-ups didn't like Supper Waltz. They were used to youngsters who were socially clumsy, and submissive to authority. The Reverend Mr Weir called him a smart aleck and barred him from the Boys' Brigade, and old Raymond detested him. Adults didn't understand the fierce vision of Supper Waltz's world, and they resented his unspoken contempt of their ways. The square of the hypotenuse, the 1832 Reform Act, were as dead leaves to Supper Waltz, and only art interested him. Old Raymond loved to ridicule him. 'And how many, Wilson, did you say you got for the test? Speak up lad. You got nothing! Well, perhaps that explains why I couldn't hear anything, Wilson. I didn't hear any mark because you didn't get any mark. Not a one, lad.' Raymond, with his broken teeth and first class honours degree, had to get his own back. I understand it better now. Raymond hated Supper Waltz because he neither needed nor desired anything that Raymond had, and they both knew it.

Girls knew that Supper Waltz was different too. Supper Waltz seemed old in the ways of the world. As fifth formers it wasn't easy for most of us to be the ladies' man. Pongo had a face as round and as innocent as a child's. Baby Brother, the girls called him. Supper Waltz never missed out at a teenage dance; Supper Waltz was a parochial legend of our youth. He went home with sixth form girls, and some even that had left school. Girls came looking for Supper Waltz, some without knowing why and blushing because of it. Some girls hated Supper Waltz, they said — afterwards. Supper Waltz rarely danced in the early part of the evening. He'd hang around the door, smoking, talking, watching who went in and who went out. We'd nudge one another and snigger when the supper waltz was announced. I don't think I ever saw Supper Waltz refused by a girl.

Supper Waltz had an understanding of women all right. Like the time I wanted to go out with Alice Hume. She was at the private girls' school. She wore a short, green skirt in the hockey games, and the inside of her thighs was flat and smooth. It used to give me a headache just watching her. Supper Waltz and I waited for her as she went to church, and I asked her to see me the next weekend. I thought she was going to say yes, but finally she went off laughing with the others without giving an answer. She had a rather longer dress on that day, but I still got a headache. Supper Waltz didn't joke about her or anything. We went into the golf course nearby and hunted for balls to sell. After a while I asked him why Alice Hume hadn't said she'd go out with me. Supper Waltz had no trouble with the answer. 'It's the Fair Isle jersey,' he said. 'No girl will make a date with you in a Fair Isle jersey.' My mother had given me the jersey for my last birthday. I thought of it as part of my best clothes. 'It's a kid's jersey, Hughie, see?' said Supper Waltz frankly. 'Girls think a lot about that sort of thing.' Supper Waltz was right of course. With some of my money from potato picking I bought a denim top, and I did my hair without a part before I asked Alice Hume again. I never told Supper Waltz about her thighs and my headaches, but the day she agreed to go out with me Supper Waltz watched her walk away and said. 'She has really good legs, you know, really good legs', and he seemed pleased for me in a brotherly way.

It might seem that Supper Waltz was always the leader, and that I was just tagging along all the time, but it wasn't really like that. There were ways in which Supper Waltz depended on me. With adults, for example, Supper Waltz let me do most of the talking. Even old Raymond said on my report that I was a straightforward, sensible boy. He meant predictable, I think. I was in the cricket team by the fifth form, and bigger than most of the others. I kicked Wilderborne in the back when he picked on Supper Waltz in the baths enclosure. Both Pongo and Graeme were better than Supper Waltz at some things too; Graeme was dux in the end. We all lacked the vision of Supper Waltz, though. The world was sharper, brighter for him, and the meaning always clear. Once Supper Waltz, Graeme and I went camping in the Rangitata Gorge, and came down the rapids on lilos. The water was a good deal rougher than we thought. Graeme got thrown off his lilo and smashed two teeth out on the rocks. I went on only because I couldn't stop. I felt sure I was going to drown. Supper Waltz loved it. Each time he bobbed up from the spray and turmoil of the water, he laughed and stared about as if born anew. He wanted to go down again, but Graeme and I wouldn't. That night, lying in the pup tent among the lupins, Supper Waltz told us that each time he'd come up from beneath the water the world seemed a different colour. Crimson the last time; after the longest spell under when his lilo capsized, everything was crimson he said. Graeme and I said nothing. The revelation rather embarrassed us and, besides, Graeme's mouth was too sore for him to speak.

Another time a group of us went into the reserve to do some geography fieldwork with Scotty, and at the edge of one of the gullies was a cast sheep. It lay on its side at the verge of some blackberry bushes, and the flat circle of its rotation was stained with urine and droppings. The sheep's black rubber lip twitched, and its eyes bulged with mild perplexity at its own fate. Some of the class tried to stand it up, but each time it just swayed there a moment before falling stiffly on the same side, flattened like the underneath of a scone. Scotty told everybody to leave it alone, but even as we worked our way through the blackberry into the gully, we could hear the sheep's hoarse, strained breathing. Wilderborne said he was going to come back after school and give it the works.

Once out of the sight and sound of it most of us could forget the sheep, but it persisted in Supper Waltz's mind. He was very quiet, and when the others were looking at some shell fossils in the limestone, I saw him crying. That would have surprised old Raymond and Mr Weir; anyone who thought Supper Waltz was so tough. He had a lot of emotion in him, did Supper Waltz. He could stand up to old Raymond and the head without a change of expression, but train whistles and morepork calls in the dark would haunt him for hours.

When I think of what happened to his father, and about Supper Waltz going away, I think of the evening I heard Mr Wilson talking about his voices. That was months before, but I always imagine him going mad right after I saw him in the kitchen. Recollection is apt to sandwich such things up, and there's a type of logic in it, I suppose. I'd climbed into Supper Waltz's window, and was sitting on his bed reading until he finished his tea. Then I heard Mr Wilson talking, and I went along the passage and stood there, looking in on the angle to the lighted kitchen. I very rarely saw Mr Wilson, and with me in the dark and him in the light I got a good chance. He was younger and softer looking than his wife. He had a pale, smooth face like a schoolteacher's or a parson's. He had youthful, fair curls, and yet his fingers were stained with nicotine, and his stomach folded softly over his belt.

'I heard the voice again today,' he said earnestly.

'Did you?' said Mrs Wilson. Her tone was the mild encouragement of a mother to her child, and she continued to iron rapidly from the cane basket on the table.

'Prepare for leadership, it said. Keep yourself ready for the test.' Mr Wilson ran his hand through his bright, metallic curls, and as they sprang back I half expected them to jangle. He seemed to be addressing a larger audience than Supper Waltz and Mrs Wilson. Like Supper Waltz he was small, and he had the strut of a small man as he walked about the kitchen. 'I will turn a righteous sword in the guts of this poor world before I'm finished,' he said. Despite the falseness of the words he said it with conviction. 'It was the voice to the left of me. That's always the strongest voice, the one to the left of me, and it doesn't hurt, not that one. I've got a feeling my leadership is near, Melanie.' That had the strangest sound of all — Melanie, Mrs Wilson as Melanie — and although no one could see me I smiled sheepishly.

Mrs Wilson and Supper Waltz didn't find it remarkable, however. 'Good,' said Mrs Wilson. She ran over a shirt-collar quickly, her thumb anticipating the iron along its length with practised ease. Supper Waltz was eating bread and cold meat, his eyes turning upwards like a sheepdog's with satisfaction as he ate.

'Everything will be sorted out then. I'll have my proper place then. I'm ready for the work.' The thought of his great work and its immediacy seemed to lift Mr Wilson. He went abruptly through to the lavatory, and there began to sing about the land of Canaan. In his absence, as in his presence, the kitchen went on as before: Mrs Wilson ironing urgently, and Supper Waltz eating his meat sandwiches as if he would never stop.

The day months afterwards, the day after it happened, was a Wednesday and Supper Waltz wasn't at school. It was a hot day, and I thought he'd probably bunked to be in the sun. Supper Waltz often took days off, and if the teachers checked up on him he'd produce notes that he'd written himself, but signed by his father. I imagined Mr Wilson signing them in his room, or on the toilet seat, as he waited for his call. Supper Waltz never explained to me why that one duty was performed by his father, when all else had been resigned to Mrs Wilson. I suspected that his mother never knew when he hadn't been at class. She came up to the school once, though, summoned after Supper Waltz and old Raymond had a confrontation in the film room. We were in one of the front rooms, and I saw her arrive, pedalling right up the sweep of the drive, and she left her bike leaning on the hydrangeas by the steps to the school office. She blew her nose in a businesslike way on what looked like half an old teatowel, and strode up the steps like a man. One or two of the boys close to the window laughed, but Supper Waltz and I didn't let on we knew who it was.

But that Wednesday, after it must have happened, I was sitting in Raymond's room when the first assistant came in. Old Raymond always made a show of rapport with his boys when there was another master in the room. 'Pop outside with Mr Haldane, Williams,' and he patted my shoulder as I passed. When the door was closed Haldane stood in the corridor for a moment, gazing absently down at the worn lino, and then up at the paper pellets that had been chewed and flicked on to the yellow ceiling. Most boys respected Haldane, although he wore some of the worst clothes in the school, and caned with distant severity.

'Stuart Wilson,' he said, and for just a moment I didn't think of Supper Waltz. None of us called him Stuart. 'You're his best friend, I understand.' It made me feel rather good, that; to be singled out by Haldane as Supper Waltz's best friend. It was a form of recognition in its way. 'You know the family quite well. You're there quite often?' I told him I was. Haldane looked at me as if he were wondering how much of me was still boy, and how much had grown up. I think he decided to be cautious. 'Stuart's father is not well, and there's been a bit of an accident at their home. Mrs Wilson wants you to go round and see if you can help. Stuart's rather upset. Have you got a bike? You needn't be back before afternoon school.' As I started off down the corridor he added, 'And Williams, use your common sense, won't you, lad. Don't tittle-tattle other people's problems all round the school, will you.' That disappointed me a bit, for after all I was Supper Waltz's best friend.

I remember that someone had twisted the dynamo bracket on my bike right into the spokes, and it broke off as I was straightening it. I felt odd biking alone in the sun down that street, always crowded before. In three blocks I passed only a mother and her push-chair. I was young enough to be amazed by the realisation that other people live different lives. It was like that all the way to Supper Waltz's place, hardly a car, hardly a sound, with just a few women around Direens' store, and a little kid crying at the top of Manuka Drive because his trike had overturned in the gutter.

I must have been to the Wilsons' hundreds of times, yet I felt shy arriving there then, during school time, and having been sent for. Mrs Wilson was sitting at the kitchen table, moving the butter dish round and round with her finger. 'Come in, Hughie,' she said. I don't think she'd ever used my name before. 'Sit down. We've had trouble here, Hughie.' She was a direct woman, Mrs Wilson. Her left hand was in plaster, and the fingertips stuck out from the end of it like pink teats. With her other hand she kept moving the butter dish on the red formica table. 'Stuart's father's had a breakdown and has had to go to hospital.'

'Oh.' I watched the butter dish revolve, and wondered about Mr Wilson's Canaan.

'The point is Stuart's run off. I haven't seen him since last night. Do you know where he could be?'

'No.'

'He's fond of you, Hughie. He might come to see you. He's very upset. But you're his friend.'

'Supper Waltz and I have always been friends,' I said. 'Always will be.' Mrs Wilson smiled, either at the nickname, or the claim of eternity; a man's smile, which divided her lined face.

'Bit of a charmer with the girls, from what I hear,' she said.

'With everyone. I mean they all like him.' I was trying to please with that admittedly. Teachers and parsons didn't like Supper Waltz, and some girls didn't — afterwards. Supper Waltz put his tongue in their mouths when he kissed them.

'His father was a popular man. He had a gift of imagination, that man, but not the character to go with it.' It wasn't as cruel a judgement as it sounded, for Mrs Wilson still had a half-smile, and she stopped moving the dish for a moment. 'He was national president of the Master Butchers' Federation when he was twenty-eight.' Mrs Wilson looked past me, and it was unusual to see her at rest. 'Then he began to listen to the morepork,' she said quietly after a time, and leant her head on her knuckles as the smile died. No one could call Mrs Wilson a dreamer, though, and she was soon practical again. She got up, and cleared her throat by spitting into the sink. 'I'm going back to work this afternoon,' she said. 'I'll have to leave a note in case Stuart comes home when I'm away. You'll let me know, Hughie, won't you, if he comes to see you? Don't let him do anything silly.' It seemed my day for being treated as an adult, and I tried not to be self-conscious. Mrs Wilson came out to see me leave, and as we talked by the wash house she busied herself by pulling at the twitch in the garden with her good hand. When I rode away the bleak whiteness of the plaster on her other hand caught the sun, and I saw also in the house next door a woman watching Mrs Wilson from behind the curtains.

I slept in the upstairs sunporch, and on the Wednesday night Supper Waltz woke me by pitching clods up at the window. I was annoyed at first, because whenever he did that I had to clean the glass and sills before Mum saw the mess in the morning. Then it came back to me about Mr Wilson and the trouble. I swung out of the window, let myself hang down by the arms at full stretch, then dropped into the garden below. It was after twelve, and Supper Waltz and I went into the garage and turned on the bench light, as we always did when he came round late. He had some oysters and chips, and we ate them in silence, Supper Waltz treating each oyster as a sacrifice of significance. He didn't say anything much for a long time. He wanted the reassurance of habit; to test some part of the old way and find it the same.

'Dad's a loony,' he said finally, turning his face from the light. 'He's a bloody loony. They took him off last night.' Even though it was Supper Waltz's dad, and I felt sorry for them both, I couldn't help being curious about the way it had been. 'Howling like a wolf or something, you mean?' said Supper Waltz when I asked him. 'Nothing like that. He was going out with no clothes on, to start his mission for Christ. He broke Mum's arm in the door when she tried to stop him. Said his time was come. His time had come all right.' Supper Waltz showed a depth of cynicism that aged him. 'You can say that again. He locked himself in the lav, Hughie, when they came, kept shouting and singing. In the lav, eh? Jesus!' Supper Waltz laughed in a harsh, pent-up way, and the tears showed in the light of the bench bulb. The paper on his knee shook with his laughter, and the few chips that we had left, because of their black eyes, danced in the salt.

It seemed fitting in a way, Mr Wilson locking himself in the lavatory. It had always been a refuge for him. I didn't say that to Supper Waltz; instead I told him that his mother was waiting for him to go home. 'No,' he said, 'I'm not going home. I'll write to her in a day or two. Tell her that. Tell her I'm all right and so on, but not what I'm going to do.'

'What are you going to do?'

'I'm off up to Christchurch tonight. Danny's got a job for me in Lyttelton. As soon as I can I'll be on one of the big overseas ships. You know, European ports and all that.' Supper Waltz's brothers were all seamen, as if united in some quest. He had a brief period of bravado, and got carried away describing all the things he was going to do as a sailor, but I knew he was churned up inside. It showed in his restlessness, and the flickering eyes like light through the wings of a bird in a cage.

Before he went I crept back upstairs, and got eleven shillings for him. It was all I had, but I gave him the two flat tins of Abdullah cooltip as well. I always kept them to smoke on weekend nights when I went out. I turned out the garage light, and went with Supper Waltz down the street a bit so we wouldn't be heard outside the house. Supper Waltz kept talking urgently about all the things that lay before him. I think that, once started, he was more set on convincing himself than me. Although I was his best friend, and he'd come to me, I felt for the first time there in the dark street that Supper Waltz had already gone. He'd cast off from the rest of us, and was on his way. He'd made the break. The exhilaration of it seemed to separate us. 'See you, Hughie. Wish me luck, Hughie.' His fierce mood drove him running down the pavement, until he was lost in the shadows of the trees around the orphanage.

If it had been me, or Graeme, or Pongo, they would soon have caught us, but I didn't think they'd catch Supper Waltz if he didn't want them to. Supper Waltz knew the way of the world. Supper Waltz would look after himself, you bet, I told myself.

Keep running, Supper Waltz, don't let the morepork get you.

The Tsunami

~

I REMEMBER IT was the day of the tidal wave from Chile. 'A tsunami,' Peter had said yet again, angrily, as we stood by the bench at breakfast. 'Nothing to do with the tide, nothing at all. A tsunami's a shock wave.'

Yet there it was in the paper of the night before; all about the Chilean tidal wave and how it was expected to be up to twenty-five feet high, and might sweep right over low-lying areas. Peter was doing a third unit of geography, and he took it as an academic affront that even the newspaper talked about the tsunami as a tidal wave instead of a tsunami. Toby and I agreed, of course.

'A tsunami, right,' we said, but we still thought of it as the tidal wave. In all of us is the perversity to resist correction.

We had tacitly decided that the tidal wave would be a big thing in our day. This wasn't a compliment to Chile, or the wave. As students we found almost every day some preoccupation to shield us from our studies. Even now I have a fellow feeling when I read of prisoners who tamed cockroaches, or devised whole new political systems in their heads to pass the time. Thoreau knew that most of mankind understand a prisoner's world.

The newspaper said that the wave was expected between noon and two p.m., and over the radio there were warnings to farmers and property-owners to be prepared. It was a compelling notion: the great wave sweeping majestically across thousands of miles of ocean, to fall with thunderous devastation on our New Zealand. It quite captured the imagination of the city, and before midday the cars were streaming out to the coast.

We bought pies and a half-gallon jar of apple wine on our way to the estuary. 'A carafe, you mean,' said the pale man in the bottle-store loftily. He still used hair cream and we mocked him as we went on.

'A carafe, you mean. Oh quite, quite.' We passed the jar of wine from one to another, regarding it quizzically and twisting our faces to suggest the features of the pale bottle-store man.

By twelve-thirty the cars were parked in rows along the beach frontages, and their occupants belched comfortably and waited for something to happen. Many people were down on the beach, impatient for the tidal wave to come. Peter's logical mind was outraged. 'My God, look at these people,' he said. 'If the tsunami does come it'll kill thousands, thousands of them.' He gave a shrill laugh of exasperation and incredulity. But Toby and I were delighted; it accorded with the youthful cynicism we cultivated at the university. We drove up the hill and parked in a children's play area, with swings, see-saws, and a humpty-dumpty among the grass. We took our apple wine and round pies, and sat with humpty dumpty on his wall, looking down over the houses on to the crowds along the estuary and beach. Toby stuck out his corduroy legs in delight at the unsought demonstration of human nature acted out before him.

'Look at them, Peter,' he kept saying, and drew further joy from the resentment with which Peter watched the crowd press forward to the tsunami.

Another car drove on to the playground, and a couple got out and stood with their backs supported by the grille, looking down upon the sea. Then the man wandered closer, and I recognised Leslie Foster. He sat on a swing with his hands hanging between his knees. He had a thin, Spanish face, with a beard to suit it, and his shoulders were slightly hunched in that typical way I recalled from the years we were at school together. At school at the same time would be a better description. He and I had mutual friends, but we never found any ease in each other's company. I never trusted his sneering humour, and he considered me something of a milksop, I think. Yet at university we gave each other greater recognition, for there our common background, always taken for granted before, was something of a link.

I went over and sat on the bleached, wooden seat of the other swing. I stretched my legs to pass the puddle in the rut beneath. 'How are things?' I said. He turned his head and gave his quirking, Spanish smile. 'I don't think that tidal wave's coming,' I said.

'Bloody tidal wave. Who needs it?' he said.

We talked idly for a time, but every topic seemed to release the same bitterness, and he didn't even pretend to listen to anything I said. He would screw up his eyes impatiently, and rock back on the swing. 'She wanted to come out here today,' he broke in. 'It wasn't my idea.' We both looked over at the woman still standing at the front of the car and staring out to sea. As if she realised she was the topic of our conversation, she glanced back at us, then came over towards the swings. Les introduced her grudgingly as Mrs Elizabeth Reid, his landlady.

'Nice to meet friends of Les,' she said. I wouldn't guess at her age, but she wasn't a girl. She had a lot of flesh on her upper arms and shoulders, and her hips swept out like a harp. 'I like a run in the car,' she said. 'Blows the cobwebs out and that, don't you think?' Les screwed up his eyes, and gave his mocking, lop-sided smile. 'I wanted to go down by the beach with everyone else, but Les wouldn't.' She paused and then said, 'It's late,' as if the tidal wave were a train or bus delayed by departmental inefficiency. 'It's a run out, though, isn't it? A chance to have a breather.' She had an unpleasant voice: ingratiating, but with a metallic edge.

'Yes. Chance to have a breather,' repeated Les, mocking the idiom, but she didn't seem to realise it. She went off to sit in the car out of the breeze, and have a cigarette. Les and I were left swaying on the worn seats of the playground swings. 'Chance to have a breather,' said Les again, with morose emphasis. 'Well, I suppose that's fair enough. You'd laugh if I told you. If I told you what she's sprung on me today.' I didn't ask. I wasn't really interested in any of his confidences, but I knew he was going to tell me anyway. It was something to do with his loneliness, I suppose; picking on me just because I was there and we had been to the same school. 'She's pregnant, the lovely lady. She told me on the way out.' He rocked back and forth, setting loose a distorted image in the water beneath the swing.

'You could get something done, I suppose.'

'Not easy,' he said, with a sneer at my vagueness, and the ignorance of facts that it revealed. 'Anyway, she feels that marriage is the best answer. She's divorced, but thinks in terms of marriage.' I made a feeble reply about how nice she seemed, and how things had a habit of working out. Les ignored it completely. 'I'll have to leave varsity. I can't see myself getting by in fulltime study with her and a kid.'

'I suppose so.' It did seem a waste. Les was a clever student. Even at school he'd been a clever beggar, and he'd had straight As since then.

'I can't blame her for it happening.' I admired him for saying that. In his own crabbed way he'd always seen things as they were. He was honest with himself. 'She's rather a passive person, really,' he said. 'Likes to talk more than anything else. It started last year. when she went on a citrus fruit diet. I used to go into the bathroom and joke about it when she stood on the scales with a towel round herself. Sometimes I'd put a foot deliberately on the scales, and she would laugh and jab back with her elbows.' Les was going to say more, then he broke off with a barking laugh. 'Funny how these things get started,' he said, and he pushed out with his legs to get the swing going again as a sign he'd finished talking about the seduction of his landlady.

I hadn't wanted to hear about it, but personal revelations impose an obligation, and I asked him if he wanted some apple wine. 'Love it,' said Les, and he came with me back to the wall on which sat the patient humpty dumpty, smiling in the face of his imminent fall and the tsunami. Les knew Toby, and I introduced him to Peter.

'I don't think the tsunami will persist across all that ocean,' said Peter.

'The what?' said Les.

'The tidal wave. He means the tidal wave,' put in Toby and I.

'That bloody thing,' said Les with belittling contempt, looking not out to sea, but towards the car and his landlady. He tipped the apple wine down his throat without appearing to swallow. We could hear its unimpeded gurgle as it went down, and we began to drink more rapidly to keep up. Les cast a malaise over our group, interrupting the established pattern of our relationships. He was interested only in his own problems, and our wine.

His impatience seemed to extend to the people along the foreshore below. The tsunami had not come; promises of something different had failed once again. Some people began to leave for the city, and only those with nothing they wished to return to remained. A few roared their cars across the asphalt frontage of the beach, while others stood in the sand-dunes and pelted beer bottles with stones.

When the wine was finished, Les said he'd better take his landlady home. I walked part of the way towards the car with him to show a fitting sense of comradeship for a fellow old boy whose secret I shared. By now he wished he hadn't told me, of course, and not being able to say just that, he got in some remark about how heavy I was. I saw him cross the rough grass of the playground, walking in his round-shouldered, rather furtive way. I felt no loyalty whatsoever, and told Toby and Peter as soon as I rejoined them. We watched Les and Mrs Reid having a last look down to the beach. She was talking, and waved a hand dismissively towards the ocean. Her strong hips and jutting breasts seemed to accentuate Leslie's stooped concavity.

'Serve him right. Serve him damn right,' said Toby. It wasn't a moral judgement, rather a reference to all those nights on which Les had returned to his landlady, and Toby had fretted his time away with cards and bitter study.

Les and Mrs Reid drove quite close to regain the road. I could see her mouth opening and closing quickly as she talked to him, and Les glanced at me as they passed. It was his own smile, though, inwardly directed and not for me. His tilted, Spanish smile which he still wore as he turned the car again and began to drive down the hill. Elizabeth Reid had turned sideways somewhat in the seat, the better to watch him as she talked, and her mouth opened and closed effortlessly. It was a recollection which I found hard to shake off as we ourselves left. Peter was in a good humour because the tsunami had failed as he had predicted, but the unwanted glimpse of Leslie Foster's life had chilled my mood, and Toby's too in a different way. He sat silently, holding the empty wine flask between his knees, and reflecting on his unwilling celibacy.

Before tea, as I prepared the vegetables, I listened to a government seismologist on the radio explaining why the tidal wave hadn't come. I suppose he was a different seismologist from the one the papers had quoted the day before. I called out to the others to say it was on the news about the tidal wave not coming.

'Tsunami,' said Peter.

'Right.'

'The tsunami certainly came for old Les Foster, though, didn't it? Talk about a shock wave,' said Toby. How we laughed at that. Toby and Peter came into the kitchen so we could see one another as we laughed, and better share the joke. All youth is pagan, and we believed that as the gods were satisfied with their sport, the rest of us were safe awhile. 'Came for old Les all right, the tsunami.' Even as I laughed I saw again Les and his landlady as they drove away, and that inward smile upon his face. As a drowning man might smile, for they say that at the very end the water is accepted, and that the past life spins out vividly. In Leslie's case it may well have been the future rather than the past he saw.

Descent From the Flugelhorn

IT WAS THE third in a series of summer droughts. North Otago must be as bad for droughts as anywhere in the country, I guess. In March the landscape lay stretched and broken like the dried skin of a dead rabbit, shrunken away from the bones and sockets. The pale yellow clay showed through the tops of the downs like hip bones, and even the willows along the bed of the Waipohu Stream had the blue-grey of attrition.

Wayne Stenning and I were selling raffle tickets so that the club could have new jerseys for the season. All over the district we went, and despite the cost of the petrol it was worth it. Most we called on had some connection with the club, and even if they didn't directly, then as country people they identified with the district name and gave anyway. Usually they bought whole books, not single tickets, which made the tripping about worthwhile. Wayne and I had been at it most of the afternoon and we were cutting over the old quarry road to call at a last few houses. The dust was bad. Some people had oiled the road outside their gates, but it didn't seem to do much good. In any case you couldn't see where the dust had settled, for everything was much the same colour.

Wayne was pleasant company, always ready with a joke, or a laugh at somebody else's. He'd been training most of the summer. Keen as mustard he was, and with some cause. Last season he made the local representative side and got his name in the rugby almanac's list of players from lesser unions worth watching. He had the right build for a prop — not all that tall, but his chest was so thick that his clothes hung out all round and made him look fat, which he wasn't.

I hadn't realised that Bernie Dalgety lived on that road, but we turned into a farm and found him at the yards, drafting sheep. I'd met him a few times at the gun club. He took three books. The only drawback was that Wayne got some grease on his slacks when we sat on the drill, waiting for Bernie to get the money. Wayne said they were his best trousers and his wife would be peeved. He hadn't been married long. He couldn't stay worried, however, and told Bernie the joke about the librarian and the lion tamer. He did a bit of running on the spot, too, before we got back into the car — said he'd been having some trouble with cramp in the thigh muscles. Bernie and I told him the cause of that and he laughed, but said he was serious. I hadn't begun any training myself. I'd reached the stage at which the most usual adjective applied to my game was 'experienced'. Anyone who sticks with the game reaches that point eventually — a sort of watershed after which you're no longer capable of improving, and it takes cunning to disguise the fact that you've gone back.

We nearly missed the place after Dalgety's. It was in a fold of the downs, and well back from the road. New farmhouses go for a view, prominence before all else. The old houses of the district seem to have been sited chiefly with the idea of escaping the wind. There was no cattlestop and no name on the letter-box. Wayne opened the gate and told me he'd close it and run up after me. Needed the exercise, he said, so I went on. The drive wasn't used much, I could tell, for the dry grass in the centre strip scratched and flurried underneath the car as I drove. I could see Wayne in the rear-vision mirror, jogging easily along. doing a few quick knees-ups from time to time. He let his arms hang loosely and flapped his hands to ensure relaxation. Our coach was very keen on relaxation; he trained anyone who would turn up three hours a night in the name of relaxation.

The house was of old-fashioned dark brick. It had bay windows that bulged out-wards and heavy, green tiles. The shrubs and trees must once have been in ordered harmony with the house, but in old age had attained a freakish disproportion. Shattered pines along the south side reached over the tiles and mounds of their nee-dles lay in the guttering. The path to the front door was obstructed by the growth of a giant rhododendron, mostly wood, but with a few clusters of leaves that defied the drought. The tall macrocarpa hedge down the other side had been cut so often that there was little foliage, rather a series of massive, convoluted branches that seemed barely contained in the rectangular shape the years had imposed on them.

Wayne and I avoided the rhododendron and walked along the concrete path towards the back door. At the far corner of the house was a sunporch that had been glassed in comparatively recently, for its large panes contrasted with the windows of the rest of the house. Wayne stopped suddenly at the corner, and I stumbled into him from behind. 'There's someone in there,' he said. 'We can ask him.' We stood a little foolishly by the glass doors and looked in. The place was well chosen, for despite the hedge the late afternoon sun was a warm pressure on the backs of our heads, and suffused the room with an amber glow. The rich and heavy light was liquid, and its slow currents bore dust that glinted and eddied, dissipating the shape of the dark dresser and falling like a fragile veil in front of the old man who sat facing us.

The old man was dressed, but over his clothes he wore a pink candlewick dress-ing gown, and in front of the cane chair he sat in, his zipped leather slippers stuck out, shiny and without the wrinkles of wear. Something in their positioning made it seem they had been placed by someone else, rather than the random result of move-ment. A green towel lay across his lap and his hands rested there, the fingers curled and trembling slightly. 'Hello,' said Wayne. He said it uncertainly, because he felt odd speaking through the closed door, yet he couldn't keep looking in at the old man only a few feet away without saying something. There was no coarseness of age in the old man's face, no warts, enlarged pores or tufts of hair. He seemed to have passed the time of excrescences and, like driftwood, only the essential shape and grain remained. His head and face were entirely smooth, polished even, the skin in the amber of the afternoon sun responding with a slight sheen.

'Don't think the old coot heard me,' said Wayne softly, and he turned his face away to snigger uneasily. The old man's neck did not stand up from his collar, or the folds of the candlewick dressing gown. Instead it protruded parallel with the ground like the neck of a tortoise, and so his head, to keep his abstracted gaze level, was tilted back. His head and neck were not directly forward, however, but rested more along the line of his left shoulder.

When I was a boy I had a favourite marble with a coloured spiral at the centre of the glass. Gradually the surface got crazed; little pits and star bruises appeared on the glass until it was clouded and the coloured spiral had lost its vividness. The old man's eyes were like that, and the lower lids had fallen away somewhat, revealing moist red linings that emphasised the bruised, opaque eyes, and contrasted with the pale sheen of his skin.

Wayne would have opened the door, but the old man was alone in the room and there didn't seem much point. We carried on round the house until the back door, where we knocked and waited. After seeing the old man Wayne needed reassurance of his youth. He performed several jumps from the crouch, leaping towards the tiled roof and patting the guttering. No one came to the door in answer to our knocks, or Wayne's acrobatics. 'Strange sort of an outfit,' he said. 'There must be someone else about, surely.' We were going to leave when there was a lot of noise from hens, and moving round the end of the hedge we saw a woman feeding white leghorns on the bare ground in front of the farm sheds.

She was a big woman, in cardigan and dark stockings despite the heat. She came heavily towards us, the last hens falling off behind her when they realised she had no more grain. In one hand was an old milking bucket half-filled with eggs, and she leant to the other side against the weight. At a distance she didn't look so old, but when she was close, though the strength was still there, the age was more apparent: rosettes of pigment stained her skin, and as she set the bucket down before us the swollen joints of her fingers clasped on the handle had difficulty releasing, nearly pulling the bucket over.

'We're selling raffle tickets on behalf of the Waipohu rugby club. For new jerseys.' Wayne seemed to assume that all old people were deaf, and he shouted into her face.

'Where have you been?' she said in reply. Wayne didn't know how to answer that, but she meant what other people in the district had we visited, and as we told her the ones we could remember, she murmured 'Yes, yes,' as if the familiar names established our authenticity. Her voice was flat and worn, but steady enough. She came back with us to the house, refusing to have the bucket carried for her. 'Dad would like to see you,' she said. 'I'll take a ticket for Dad.' Dad must have been her husband, not her father, yet the term she adopted for convenience in family times had stuck. Culland was the name she wanted on the ticket. I wrote it for her, because she said she found writing difficult. Watching her swollen fingers attempting to get money from her purse, we could understand. That was later, though. First she left the eggs at the back door, and took us through the dark, wainscoted hall to the sunroom to see Dad.

The old man hadn't shifted, but we approached him from a different angle and, like a figurine, his aspect altered. He'd been a big man once, but his shoulders seemed folded and the pink candlewick fell away loosely. 'These young people are from the Waipohu rugby club, Dad,' said Mrs Culland as we sat along the window seat, the sun behind us again, the golden dust drifting once more before the old man's face. 'Selling raffle tickets, Dad,' she said. Wayne nodded his head and chuckled, as if selling raffle tickets was a good joke he wanted the old man to share. Mrs Culland said nothing for some time. She forgot us and had a rest, breathing slowly and massaging the joints of each finger in turn.

'Well,' said Wayne brightly, in a manner that preceded comments about really being on our way and so on. Neither responded. Mrs Culland continued to rest, and the old man's terrapin neck and head remained extended, his eyes unblinking, and his hands trembling on the green towel. The mainspring of the world seemed to have run down, and time was held back in the amber warmth of the sunroom. The macrocarpa shadows stole further across the dry lawn, and the sound of Mrs Culland's coarse, swollen hands as she rubbed them together was like the sighing of a distant sea. Even Wayne stopped fidgeting and sat resigned, reading again the prizes listed on the raffle books he held. Three days at Mount Cook in the off-season, or the cash equivalent, was first prize.

'Dad played rugby,' said Mrs Culland. 'Not here though — in Southland. All his family played.'

'Great game,' said Wayne a little patronisingly, and flexed the heavy muscles of his outstretched leg.

'Played for the South Island twice,' she said in her flat voice. Booby Culland everyone called him then.' She pronounced it as a title and, heaving herself up, went to the dresser and returned with a photo of her husband in the South Island team.

'South Island,' said Wayne in an altered voice. The transience of it all seemed to catch him. Booby Culland's photo showed the arrogance of youth and strength. Guiltily, Wayne looked from the photo to the old man and quickly away again. 'Lock,' he said.

'That's right,' said Mrs Culland.

'Line-out specialist, I suppose.'

'Yes.'

Mrs Culland leant forward from the window seat, and held the old man's nearer arm, so that for a moment the hand stopped trembling. 'We're talking about football, Dad,' she said. 'Football.' The old man opened his mouth slightly, but if he wanted to speak he was prevented by his top dentures, which slipped down, exposing a swollen seam of artificial gum, as if he were bringing something up. Mrs Culland released his arm matter-of-factly and pushed his chin up. But briefly his opaque, bruised eyes focused in revelation; for an instant the prisoner could be seen from the shadows and behind the bars. 'Football, Dad,' she said again.

He tried once more. 'Descent from the Flugelhorn.' His voice was almost identical to that of his wife — worn and even, as if she had adopted the practice of ventriloquism.

'No, Dad, football. You know.'

'Descent from the Flugelhorn,' he repeated, and his eyes turned away. A thin skein of spittle ran from his mouth down the pink chenille of his left shoulder, touching it with amber spangles in the sunlight. Mrs Culland pushed his chin up again.

'He was very keen on music,' she said, in a form of explanation. 'As he got older and the boys took over the property, he turned to music.' There was another pause, and we sat subdued in the unrepentant sun of the summer drought.

'Lived for his football, though, as a young man. No doubt about that. They all did in his family, but Booby Culland was the best of them. Played in the provincial side fifty-one times, and was made captain for Southland on the day of his last game.' Wayne took it as a blow more than anything else. He still held the photo, and he cast about for other things to rest his gaze upon apart from the old man. 'I'll show you the jersey,' said Mrs Culland. I tried to tell her it wasn't necessary, but she had become accustomed to following her own will and went off into the rest of the house.

'Jesus, it's hot in here,' said Wayne. 'We'd better push off soon. There are other places yet and we don't want to be too late.'

As we waited the old man gave three sharp, inward breaths, and then, as if something had given way at the centre of him, his shoulders folded still further. His big translucent hands gripped the green towel in his lap, and one foot extended on the wooden floor of the porch so that the soft sole of the leather slipper squeaked as it moved. There seemed to be no breathing out. 'Jesus,' said Wayne. The old man looked much the same, but his posture gradually slackened, and although his neck still lay along his shoulder, his face turned down and lost its level gaze. 'Jesus,' said Wayne, and stood with his hands into fists as I tried to feel the old man's pulse.

Mrs Culland thought he'd just had a turn when she came back but, when she realised he was dead, she let the jersey slide into his lap with the towel, and began to stroke the smooth grain of his head. She didn't weep, she didn't even sit down; she stood beside him and it seemed as if her flesh had settled more heavily as her cupped hands moved clumsily over his head. We asked if we could help, but she said she could get in touch with everyone by phone. 'I did pay you, didn't I?' she said, and when she was satisfied of that she let us go. We never thought to use the sun-room door — perhaps it didn't open, anyway. We went out the back door, and as we passed the windows on our way to the car neither of us looked in.

Wayne called jerkily to me that he would run on a little, and I didn't hurry after him. If he wanted the chance to run it out then I didn't mind. Sooner or later he'd find it didn't work with everything. I let the car idle down the drive, the grass rustling beneath the chassis. Wayne had gone a fair way. As I shut the gate I could see him up the road, running hard along the grass verge. He ran a mile or so, and when I found him he had reached the dip and was sitting below a willow in the dry streambed. As I got out of the car I could hear him crying, and I went over and sat with him, the fine willow roots draped like hessian down the bank behind us.

The light began to change, but the evening was still hot, with no promise of rain. Homecoming magpies began their harsh calls in the trees around us, and a Land-Rover came through, travelling towards Culland's, rolling out dust clouds that we could barely see. but that had their own flinty taste. Wayne had stopped crying. and dug with a twig in the sand and leaves. 'Sorry about that,' he said. He gave a rather shy smile. 'Do you think everyone gets the feeling some time or other that they've passed themselves going the other way?'

'Yes.'

It was all we had to say about it, and it was enough. It doesn't always help to tease things out, to dissect our experiences like school days' frogs. As we stood up to go the magpies began a great racket, and some flew off in protest, the wingbeats whistling in the still air. 'I've ruined these tweeds of mine,' said Wayne. As well as the oil stain he'd torn them along the upper seams, where the sweat had made them grip as he ran.

'Put them down to experience,' I said as we went back to the car, and he smiled again at that. He hoped his wife would understand, he said.

from

The Master of Big Jingles

The Giving Up Party

~

ONCE THE JEWELLS' place had been set in the countryside, but the suburbs had caught up with it, and dreary villas were camped around it. Apart from the house itself only the long drive from the road, and the front garden, remained from the days of elegance. The drive possessed a seemly curve, and was shadowed with a line of birches which kept down weed growth on the compacted earth and gravel. A weeping elm dominated the garden; vast, diaphanous, like a green fountain when stirred by the wind. The house had a tiled entrance hall, and lead-light windows with red and patterned glass facing the drive. The roughcast was of a texture Lloyd never saw again, as if cream had been poured over marbles. On the hottest days the roughcast seemed ready to melt right off the house, and there were patches under the eaves and window frames where it had done so.

Lloyd's father said the Jewells used to have their money in shipping, but lost a lot of it for being under-insured. Mrs Jewell had no husband. He had drowned years before while surf-casting. Lloyd's father said he was renowned as a local stick man. It was some time before Lloyd dissociated that comment from the fishing.

Each Saturday morning Lloyd would bike out to the Jewells', turning off through the stone gateposts to pedal over the compacted drive beneath the birch trees. In winter his jobs were to cut kindling and fill the coal bins, in summer to mow the lawns. Mrs Jewell suffered from no vagueness, either aristocratic or induced by age. She would check the boxes of kindling by shaking them vigorously, and if the level dropped Lloyd had to cut more. In summer she checked the lawns, with special attention given to the edges. She believed firmly that edges make a lawn. She would tour the lawns with Lloyd, and her term of greatest satisfaction was adequate. Adequate became in Lloyd's vocabulary a superlative. 'The lawns and edges are quite adequate, Lloyd. Thank you,' Mrs Jewell might say on his good days.

Mrs Jewell's deft understatement was in keeping with her position. The rest of the town disliked the concept of position, without understanding it. People of importance, people of appointment, people of achievement; these are explicable in the scheme of things, but English-born Mrs Jewell and her assumption of Position stirred a vague, post-colonial unease. The uneasiness was relieved by stressing the diminution of the family's wealth, and the reputation of her dead husband as a stick man.

Lloyd was brought into the kitchen at the conclusion of each Saturday morning, given tomato or cheese sandwiches and a glass of cordial. Mrs Jewell always remained to see him eat, as if she feared he might blow his nose on the curtains, or start sharpening his teeth on the Welsh dresser. She would accompany him out to his bicycle, unless the weather was very cold, and give him his half-crown. He would feel the size and sheen of it, the solidness of it. Sometimes she would even hold his palm with one dry, firm hand while she gave him the coin, in case the responsibility of receiving it was too much for him. She thought of him as fifteen always, as he was when he first came to the house.

Mrs Jewell was economical of emotion; only the dogs seemed to really arouse her. They came from the surrounding sections, drawn by the spaciousness, the trees, the expanses of turned earth in the spring. Lloyd rarely saw them, but Rankin did. He came in to keep the gardens on Friday and Saturday. Rankin said that during the week, when neither he nor Lloyd was there, the dogs besieged Mrs Jewell. Rankin said Mrs Jewell had wept tears of rage and despair when she found the dogs had scratched the heart out of her gazanias and laid their wastes there. They left white and yellow bones on the steps, they gambolled on the shadowed drive, and pissed on every vertical plane. Mrs Jewell pronounced the word dogs rather like ducks, and with chilling inflexion. She had a slug gun sent out from England, and she retaliated with it. Rankin showed Lloyd the gun one morning. It was unlike the feeble guns sold locally, and fired heavyweight slugs, not bee-bees. Rankin said that he had disinherited many a dog with it, and that Mrs Jewell would fire it herself. Rankin said with admiration that she always fired at the head.

All the winter mornings he worked at Mrs Jewell's seemed compressed in Lloyd's mind to unremarkable routine, but the summer memories expanded, as did the season which began them. And then it was a summer Saturday when he met Mrs Jewell's daughter, and that one day enlarged the sum of all the others. It was the day of the junior representative cricket trials. The magnolia was still out, and its flowers of carved soap lay amid leaves that had undersides like a furred tongue.

'Magnolias tend to sulk,' said Rankin. 'They'll sulk for years sometimes before they choose to flower. A very feminine flower is magnolia.' Lloyd stopped mowing one of the walkways to listen to him. 'And don't put any more clippings on the new compost,' said Rankin. He reminded Lloyd that a depth of clippings generated too much heat and, as an afterthought, he said that Mrs Jewell's daughter was home from England.

Rankin went on past, into the shrubs and trees of the garden. Lloyd pushed back the grass in the catcher, and saw Mrs Jewell's daughter standing outside the front door, watching, with her hands in two big pockets in the front of her skirt. She was wearing a V-necked jersey like a boy's, with the sleeves pulled up, and sandals with heels. Her beauty took hold of Lloyd and rattled his head until he gripped the mower for support.

'You're Lloyd,' she said when she had come across the lawn. She said it as a stated introduction, not a question. 'I'm Helen Jewell. My mother told me that you'd be helping this morning. I'm to look after you, and you're to look after me.' She added the last to diminish the patronising sound of her mother's instruction. She pushed her hands into the exaggerated pockets of her skirt, and stared at the heaped grass in the catcher. 'We should have a motor mower really, for the amount of lawn.'

'Your mother doesn't like the noise.'

'Noise is not genteel.' There was both affection and mockery.

'They are noisy, though, and I don't mind the hand mower. Anyway if you had a motor mower Mr Rankin would probably do the lawns himself, and there'd be no job for me.'

'I imagine that my mother likes to feel that she is employing two people,' said Helen. They stood in the sun, Helen looking at the garden. 'My mother thinks of this place as being somehow representative of England.' Lloyd looked too, although he had no way of making the same comparison: the tulip plots, the lawns, the elm, the shrubs and birches along the drive. The direct heat of the sun seemed to deaden the sound of Rankin's whistling as he worked out of sight in the far corner of the garden. 'I lived in Wolverhampton when I was over there. I don't see England as a large cottage garden.'

'My mother thinks these are the nicest shrubs and trees in the town. She says that it takes over sixty years to have a garden like this.'

'It seems smaller. Not just the cliché of returning to a child's world, but rather that things have grown up so much. We used to have a tennis court on the lawn by the drive, and now with the elm and birches you can barely walk between them.'

'I've never seen a bigger elm than that.'

She went through one of the gaps in the tumbling leaves and branches, and Lloyd was drawn after her. 'It's so much cooler in here, like inside a church.'

'Or a waterfall,' he said.

'It's odd you say that. My father's family had a struggle to get it started. They had to keep carting water to it for years he said.' The wind stirred the skirts of the weeping elm, and the lowest leaves swept patches on the ground worn clear of grass. All that water lavished on its growth, and now, as if returning from the soil, a cascade in the hot sun. The cooler air beneath the elm encouraged them to breathe more deeply, and the scents of the garden were more pronounced: the cut grass, lavender, magnolia, and the elm itself giving a subtle essence in its transpiration. 'The perfumed garden,' said Helen. She lifted her bare arms, and pushed them through the elm leaves. 'I can feel the sun on them outside,' she said. Lloyd half extended his own arms, and then saw his hands were stained from the clippings, and dropped them quickly. Helen breathed noisily again. 'Isn't it terrible to drink in the morning,' she said. Lloyd just smiled at the ambiguity. 'I feel that wine is more forgiving, though. I wouldn't drink spirits before midday.'

'No,' said Lloyd. He didn't care what she said. He just wanted her to keep lifting her brown arms, and smiling at him in the dappled light through the elm.

'But I'm holding you up,' she said. Some of the lawn close to the house still wasn't done.

'I've plenty of time,' said Lloyd.

'No. You go on, get it done, then come into the sunporch and talk to me. I'm drinking alone. I'm having a party for myself this morning. A party, but no celebration.'

'I don't know the sunporch.'

'That one.' Helen moved to one of the openings in the elm, and pointed to the windows of the side entrance. Lloyd watched her go back to the house. The heels on her sandals made her legs more shapely by raising the calf-muscle.

As he completed the lawn Lloyd was in view of the windows of the house. Common sense told him that Helen wouldn't bother to watch him move round and round the lawn, but he was briefly self-conscious all the same. The awkwardness returned when he went to the sunporch. It was forgotten when she spoke. 'You're finished,' she said warmly, with that mixture of admiration and pleasure that from some women is the reward for even small achievements. 'I'm drinking wine,' she said, and raised her glass. 'White wine doesn't give me a head. It's my birthday after all, so I've started early.' Lloyd tasted the wine she gave him. It was very different from that at his sister's wedding.

'How physical a thing is the sun on one's skin,' said Helen. She pulled her skirt up her thighs a way, so more of her legs were in the sun, and she leant back in the chair, and turned her face towards the heat. She was not tanned, but her skin was naturally the colour of a dark hen's egg, brown and even, with the hint of inner warmth. Her arm with the glass showed no freckle or blemish, just warm egg-brown, and with a round bone in her wrist startlingly raised. Lloyd sat on the window seat, and waited with his quiet smile. His bleached hair was heavy and straight. 'I'm sweating,' said Helen. Beneath the jersey she had no blouse, and she lifted it completely without affectation, and blew on to her chest and stomach. 'And the wine's getting warm. It's not really a good enough riesling to be drunk warm. Chilling hides faults in a wine.' She poured herself more, however, tilting the bottle so much that the wine boiled in the glass and on to the floor. 'Oh damn,' she said.

'I'm thirty-four. I could be your mother. I'm thirty-four. Good God. Yet I look at you and feel that I'm your age, no more.'

'I'm older than you think,' said Lloyd generously.

'I'm thirty-four, I'm a poet, and I'm back to living in my mother's house.' Her hair swung over her face, and she gave a shudder which cast it away. 'Do you read poetry?' He didn't, but more than anything he wanted to be able to recite something sensitive and perceptive there before her. All he could think of was a classroom poem about a highwayman that came riding, riding up to the old inn door. So he said nothing, and traced with his finger on the window seat the shifting half-shadows from the elm fountain on the lawn. 'This can be my giving up party,' she said. 'You see? Like coming out, only far more significant.'

'It sounds a sad sort of party,' he said.

'I'm feeling sorry for myself today, and when you're feeling sorry for yourself you rarely have any pity for anyone else. Have you noticed that? I'm about to give up what's been central to my life: not poetry, but the idea that poetry could be the most important thing. That poetry could sustain my life, be sufficient to do that.'

'But you're beautiful.' He said it almost without sentiment: stated it simply and directly as an undisputed asset. Both knew that although it didn't seem to follow logically or immediately from what she'd said, yet it was relevant to what she meant.

'Do you think I am?' she said.

'Yes.' His throat was tight with the discipline required in saying it only once. He wanted to go on, until the insistence of repetition overcame the banality of the word.

'That can be the trap, you see, for a woman. It means that there's always another option. No matter what the commitment to my work, I've always known that the fail-safe was there. Men could become more, and poetry less. Marriage even. A solicitor perhaps, or the right farmer. My mother has a list of them. Tonight she'll have some of them to the house for my birthday. I think one's flying from as far as Wellington.'

Lloyd had never considered poetry as anything that a modern person would do all the time. His small impression of poetry was that it was unfailingly something produced at great remove from any place, or people, that he knew. 'Have you always been a poet?' he said.

'At school and university I was mad on netball. Spent hours practising it, and made top teams. I find it hard to imagine it now.' Lloyd found it easy enough. The suppleness and co-ordination remained in everything she did. 'Maybe when I'm married, or whatever, the time of my life spent on my work will seem just as strange. I'm living my life and it's not enough.' She looked deliberately out on to the wonder of her mother's garden: the soap blossoms of the magnolia were caught by the sun against the green of the shrubbery. 'And it's not enough,' she repeated.

Lloyd looked out too, his eyes unfocused, allowing the movements of the elm to dominate. Then he noticed the dog. It pushed out from the shrubbery, and stood half exposed on the lawn. Its drooping face had a mixture of effrontery and fear. 'There's a dog in the garden. Your mother hates dogs.'

'Where?' Helen Jewell left the chair, and took her wine to the window.

'An ugly-looking brown thing, like a labrador cross.'

'Brindled,' she said, and giggled.

'What?'

'It amuses me that it's brindled. It's a literary convention that all brindled creatures must be ugly and unpleasant. I can think of no greater horror for my mother than a brindled dog in her garden.'

'We could get the slug-gun,' said Lloyd.

'Slug-gun?'

'Slug-gun. Your mother keeps it in the wash house for the dogs.'

Helen laughed again. 'Get it! Get it!' she cried.

Lloyd brought the gun, and loaded it by the window. 'Quick,' said Helen, 'before it disappears.' The dog seemed to hear her, and its flabby jowls shook as it looked about. Lloyd aimed for its stomach, where there wasn't much hair, and they could hear the smack of the slug as it struck. The dog stood still for a moment, a look of perplexed agony on its face, then abruptly turned and disappeared back into the shrubbery. 'Incident is everything,' said Helen. 'I love incident in life without a moral.'

She came from the window, and knelt on the floor. She rested one hand on the chair. The waistband of her jersey folded on the arch of her hips. Her smooth knees were perfect amputations, and slightly angled in a V.

Lloyd put the slug-gun away, and sat on the floor too, by the window seat. Helen seemed already to have forgotten the humour of the dog. She was drinking again. 'You're very brown,' she said. 'One of the things I liked about the whites in South Africa was how brown and fit they were.'

'I'm outside a good deal of the time.' Lloyd wanted to tell her that he was in the cricket trials that afternoon. He thought he should be able to work it in naturally with the point about being brown, but the opportunity passed before he could phrase it in his mind.

'There's an irony in the situation as regards my work,' she said. She ran a finger back and forth beneath her left breast, the wool whispering. Lloyd imagined himself doing it, traversing her jersey there below the weight and curvature of her breast. As he imagined it he trailed his fingers slowly on the polished floor, in the flickering visual cadence of the elm tree's pale shadows. 'I know others have realised it. Any extreme position has dangers. We complain of the drudgery of earning a living, and blame that for stifling creativity. I thought I was one of the lucky ones there, for I could spend any amount of time on my work. Yet in the end my poetry was becoming too inward, drying up, trivialised. I looked out of flats in Stoke Newington, or Wolverhampton, and was cut off from the vitality that comes from working with people, from belonging. You can see that?' There was urgency in her question, but she looked into her wine glass rather than at Lloyd.

'People are what matter,' he said. 'I can see that. I suppose you can't reach them through poetry, or anything else, unless you know them. Watching people isn't the same as living with them.' It was his most daring contribution.

'Right,' she said. 'It's the things we do most that determine what we are in the end.' She bit her lips as she thought. It was the one mannerism which betrayed any agitation. Her mouth moved, and she delicately sought shreds of skin with her front teeth.

'I hope I'm not drunk before lunch. My mother's having people tonight for my birthday. A dinner for my giving up party. I don't drink during the day, certainly not mornings. That's when I work. That's when the muse comes.' She looked out at the splendour of the garden in the sun: the tonings, shapes, the movement and the texture. 'This must be the most difficult country in the world in which to maintain a creative resolve. Nothing much of mine gets published here,' she said. 'Here it is expected that I write poems about being a woman, having an intuitive view of relationships, and all that bilge. I hate the word poetess.' She was quiet for a while, looking down and moving her fingers over the rim of her wine glass, then she raised her head and looked steadily at Lloyd. 'It's like the disillusionment of a marriage,' she said. 'I chose poetry as my husband and I've found out that it can't give me everything. It's not enough for the whole of my life, the length and breadth of it. And I'm thirty-four, now I'm thirty-four.'

'You could always keep writing poetry as well as do other things. Combine it with getting married, or some job you like.'

'No, that's a difference in kind, not degree. No, I don't think so.'

'Maybe a fresh start will bring new enthusiasm. You said yourself that you needed to be involved with people in the things that mattered to them. You said about being on the outside looking in, when you were in England.'

'Maybe.' She smiled at him, cheered by his admiration and the youthfulness of his bleached hair.

They heard Mrs Jewell's car in the drive, and saw the blue of it flickering through the birches as it approached the house. Lloyd went and sat on the window seat. He glanced around the room, as if it were strewn with signs which might incriminate him. But outwardly there was only the wine together with the glasses. And Helen kneeling on the floor. There is always a certain wantonness in an excess of beauty. 'Mother's home,' she said, not with any apprehension, but matter-of-factly as if it marked the end of one thing and the beginning of another. The end of the giving up party, and the beginning of different priorities.

Mrs Jewell called out in her piercing, English voice, and when Helen answered, Mrs Jewell followed the sound, and came to the sunporch. She showed no surprise to see Lloyd sitting on the window seat, and her daughter on the floor. 'Good morning, Lloyd,' she said, and carried on to talk to her daughter. Yet her alert, birdlike eyes regarded him; noting his heavy, bleached hair, the size of his brown forearms, and a certain calmness in the way he sat there. Mrs Jewell wouldn't give Lloyd cordial in the kitchen again, or press the half-crown into his hand in quite the same way. She didn't mention money, or the lawns, at all with her daughter there. She took up the two wine bottles and glasses, and bore them significantly away without comment. Helen made a quick child's face of mock contrition behind her back.

'I'll have to go,' said Lloyd. They went out past the kitchen, and Lloyd stopped in the doorway to say goodbye to Mrs Jewell.

'I'll see you next Saturday as usual, Lloyd,' she said. It served to remind him that the order of things had not altogether changed.

At the side trellis, by his bike, Helen shook back her hair. 'I've been down this morning,' she said. 'Really down, and you've helped me. A giving up party is bound to be sad, but sharing it is better. Sharing the time of it, even if not the reason of it.'

'I've enjoyed it.' They listened to the bumble bees clumsily assaulting the yellow roses behind the trellis, and Rankin's persistent and invisible whistle as he worked beyond the drive.

'I think I'll go up to Wellington for a while,' Helen said.

'Maybe you won't give up after all. Maybe in Wellington it'll be different.'

She placed her hands on his waist, and kissed him with increasing fullness. She leant back, and as the arch increased in her throat her eyelids closed. It was a kiss and embrace of circular passion; from her to him and back again. Through him almost, in a definite farewell to her own youth, and the commitment of youth.

The Giving Up Party ~ 37

Lloyd could smell the riesling, some faint scent, the egg-brown warmth of her skin, and the comfortable fragrance of her woollen jersey in the sun. His hands moved down her arms, and he lightly held her wrists in which the bones were startlingly raised. When she had kissed him she said, 'You are the only person, the only person who came to my giving up party, and I thank you for it.'

'I'll always remember it,' said Lloyd, as she went back past the trellis towards the door. He stood with his bike for a moment, thinking about the morning, letting it settle in his mind. He could hear Helen begin to talk to her mother.

'Mother,' she said, 'I'm thirty-four today, and it gives me no joy. Who do you think I should marry?'

Rankin was waiting in the trees at the turn of the drive. He whistled and waved Lloyd down. Lloyd leant his bike on the scoured bark of a birch tree, and followed Rankin through the shrubbery to the corner of the garden where he was working. Rankin thought it his right to gossip about his employer, but he had an artisan's pride which made him continue his work while he did so. With practised ease he cleared one nostril by blocking the other with his thumb and blowing, then he began digging out another barrow of compost. 'What did she talk about then?' he demanded.

'Her poetry mainly, and so on.'

'She's been here most of the week, I gather,' said Rankin. 'Yesterday she was in shorts. I can't get on with my work. It's not good at my age.' He fragmented the compost in the barrow with two particularly powerful blows. Lloyd smiled and watched the great elm waltzing above the lesser trees of the drive. He had established few certainties to guide him in seventeen years, but he knew enough to be naturally protective of anything beautiful; even the experience of beauty. 'You can't remember a damn thing about what she said,' Rankin accused Lloyd. 'With a woman like that nobody can. You just soak her up. Am I right then?'

He was right about not remembering so much the things she said, while acute in recollection of her presence. As Lloyd looked away from Rankin, into the garden, he could see the folds of the boys' jersey on her hips, her thin eyebrows like the wings of a bird in the distance, the egg-brown skin of her thighs as she kneeled.

'So what happened?' said Rankin.

'Nothing much. She talked about the problems with her work. She's a poet.'

'Poetry in motion more like!' Rankin snorted impatiently. 'What else?'

Rankin was trying to spoil it, his innuendo an intrusion into Lloyd's awareness. Lloyd wouldn't talk about it. He wanted to seal it up like a ship in a bottle, safe from the clumsy exploration of Rankin and all the others. 'So nothing happened,' said Rankin. He seemed both satisfied and disappointed. Rankin was not capable of subtlety. He could apply only one assessment. Like a collector dissatisfied unless the butterfly is pierced beneath the glass, and giving no significance to having merely seen its colours and its grace. Even at seventeen Lloyd knew better than to attempt an explanation, or give any sign of being moved.

'I think she's getting pretty drunk,' he said carelessly. 'We shot at a dog. It was brindled.'

'What?'

'It doesn't matter.'

'I'm told Mrs Jewell was better looking even than her daughter,' said Rankin. 'She was a beautiful woman in her day, they say.' Lloyd tried to imagine Mrs Jewell as a young woman, but he could picture only Helen, and there seemed no process of evolution that could lead from one to the other. Mrs Jewell's tart intelligence and angularity of body seemed distinct from any gender.

'I have to get going,' said Lloyd. 'I've got the rep cricket trials this afternoon.'

'Good on you.' Rankin wasn't able to give it any real enthusiasm, however. Lloyd went back to the drive, and rode down the soil and gravel track to the stone pillars of the road gate.

He promised himself he wouldn't talk about the morning with anyone, but keep it all inside. Helen would marry one of those on her mother's list, or on her own list made up in time. He expected nothing else. But he had been there at her giving up party. He understood how much was coincidence, and he didn't take any credit himself, any more than he did when he caught the gorse in bloom on the hills he climbed behind the town, or for the one or two days in summer when there was a full flight of thistle down across the sky. Yet as Lloyd rode home, leaning forward and with his arms folded across the handlebars, he was happy enough. Sometimes coincidence itself can be a kind of blessing, and he knew, as Rankin never would, that receptiveness can be a virtue too.

Rosemary for Remembrance

My WIFE'S FAMILY is close knit. Its members cover long distances to inspect one another for signs of wear, and to chronicle the loves, deaths and orthodontic treatment of even the most distant relatives. For myself, I have come to believe that kinship is little guarantee of understanding. I have suffered too many aunts and second cousins; playing a kind of genealogical dominoes to find a common topic of conversation. My more distant family are cheerfully met by accident, and neglected by design.

This was in my mind as we prepared to leave the motel and spend a day of our holiday visiting cousin Rosemary. I had hoped we might travel through the National Park, and make some of the walks into the bush, but my wife was determined that I would do my duty. We'd go the coast way, she had said, and had rung Rosemary to tell her we were coming.

'You can't come all this way, even across the strait, and then go past without calling on them,' my wife said as I packed the car. 'Think what they'd feel if they heard.'

'Relief,' I said. In marriage there are aspects of personality so divergent that only humorous exaggeration will reconcile them.

'You fool,' said my wife with a smile.

At times the coast road ran past uniform stands of conifers, and even the marram grass planted on the sand undulated away in regimental lines. On the crests of some of the dunes the sand had broken free before the wind, and flowed out like salt. The inland side of the road had occasional weatherboard farm homes, half hidden in their screens of trees. On the other side, sitting starkly in the dunes, were groups of holiday houses. My cousin's home was on the only headland to break the sweep of the coast and give sufficient height to look down upon the sea. A solid place of summerhill stone, with a stag etched on the glass of the front door. Rosemary came out to meet us, her pleasant interest a victory for my wife's opinions. 'You don't remember me?' Rosemary said. 'I came down and stayed with your family for months when there was the polio epidemic in Masterton. I went with your brother Kevin to his primary school class for a while. We all used to go swimming at Parry's Crossing. Surely you remember that?'

'Yes, I think I do now,' I said, not wishing to be discourteous, but I could remember nothing of her time with us.

'He's got a hopeless memory,' said my wife.

'Has he really?'

'He has trouble remembering the names of his own children.'

'Norman's just the same.' They laughed not unkindly together, agreed in their view of the oddity of men.

Rosemary took us into her lounge, where she had morning tea set out. She said her husband was fishing, and wouldn't be back until lunch. She began asking questions about my family, and my wife began answering them. I took my pipe, and said I would walk down to the shore.

After the hour of driving, the physical immediacy of the headland's sloping gravel road possessed me. Broom stood along its sides, and the pods exploded their seeds into the sunlight. It seemed my passing set them off, but it was just that those near me sounded louder, I suppose. The track ended at three rusting boatsheds, and from there to the south the sandy beach dwindled away. The headland rose to the north, and the weak swell slopped in and out among the kelp beds and rocks below it. As I climbed along the rocks, I saw a man fishing. He wore only floppy hat, shorts and sandshoes, and his skin was burnt the same colour as the rocks. He whirled a hand line, and sent it soaring into a channel within the kelp, then relaxed on his rock again. It didn't occur to me that it might be Rosemary's husband, but as I paused there in response to his smile, he said he thought he knew who I was. Like a Masai warrior he squatted there, the knees of his long legs rising almost to the grey hair on which the hat lay. He held the line with gentle and extended fingers, as a woman holds a cigarette. 'I meant to go out in the boat,' he said, 'but I decided to fish from the shore instead.'

We talked for a time about the fishing: blue cod, butterfish, and the squid bait he preferred. The water didn't splash. It seemed too heavy, like soup, and flowed on to the rocks then strained out again, leaving a visible line of soupy residue. 'I ought to apologise really,' he said. 'When Rosemary told me that you were coming I decided to stay away from the house until lunchtime.'

'I'd have done just the same,' I said.

'I've reached an age at which the urge to meet new people has largely gone. The cause is in me rather than in others.' It was the growth of a cynicism of expectation.

'The psychologists say that life is a journey away from total selfishness, and back again,' I offered. Norman seemed to like the notion, and the fishing line hung forgotten in his hand as he looked out to sea and considered it. The cliff had a profound sense of isolation, like an island. It was the effect of the low coastline that stretched away from it, and the loneliness as well.

Norman said there was only one other permanent home, and a bach or two. In ten years the developers would be in, though, he said. There'd be concrete block toilets, swings, a launching ramp for the mass-produced trailer-sailers. 'I hope to God I'll be dead by then,' he concluded mildly.

Norman decided we should go up and have a drink before lunch. He wound in his line, and put it away in an old, strap bag. He had no shirt, but pulled on a jersey which bagged over his shorts, and showed a deep V of brown skin below his throat. People with very long arms never seem to straighten them, and Norman stood with his free arm folded to his side, as though it might catch if allowed to drop. He reminded me of those arrival photos of lone yachtsmen, having overcome every physical threat, but with the vulnerability that comes from things realised of self which cannot be shared.

'We might have a drink in my shed,' said Norman. He gave me a quick grin and a glance. It was the first indication that he preferred to keep away from Rosemary. His shed wasn't the handyman's muddle I expected, but a pottery workshop: quite a new building with a concrete floor and sliding glass doors. It had a kick wheel in the sun near the doors, and racks of raw, bisque and glazed pots. There was an oil-fired kiln in a lean-to, and a pug-mill encrusted with clay. Norman's pots seemed pretty good to me; bold casseroles and wine bottles with ridges from his hands clear upon them. Norman brought a bottle of beer and some glasses from the back of the shed, and when he saw that I enjoyed handling the pots, he took me out to the kiln, which was ready to unpack. As he took out each pot in turn, Norman inspected it quickly for flaws, letting his hands run once more over the shapes they had formed. Most of the pots had a brown glaze, sleek in the places where it was thickest. The pots were still warm, and made pinging noises as the glaze cooled in the open air.

When we had put away the new pots, Norman led me away to finish our beer. Just beyond the boundary of his section, in the brown grass before the broom began, was a discarded Ministry of Works wire spool. Like a giant cotton reel it lay there, just out of sight of the house windows, and with a full view along the coast. It was a favourite place for Norman, for there was a visible track to it through the grass. 'I come here sometimes,' said Norman. We sat on the warm wood, on the faded numbers stamped upon it, and looked out from its privacy.

'Is there any clay locally that you can use?'

'Nothing for stoneware,' said Norman. I lay back to let the sun shine on my face, and shielded my eyes. I would have taken my shirt off, but was ashamed of my whiteness. 'I could have gone to Britain to study in the early sixties,' said Norman after a time. 'I exhibited in Auckland, and was offered eight months study with Donald Simpkin in East Anglia. He worked with Leach.'

'I like Leach's work. The Japanese influence and so on,' I said, wanting to show some interest and knowledge.

'He's dead now,' said Norman. He scratched in his wiry hair, and folded one long arm about his waist. 'Even when I was given the chance I was nearly fifty,' said Norman. 'It was my first and last chance, working with Simpkin in Britain.' I was going to ask him why he didn't go, but lassitude made me slow to speak, and Norman assumed the question before I could get it out. 'It meant losing money, you see. It meant no superannuation security, and not enough money for the girls at training college and university. If I'd become a fulltime potter then we wouldn't have had this place. The chap that the Arts Council sent instead of me didn't come back, although he was supposed to. I would have come back. I wanted to see pottery here go ahead.' Norman gave a yawn of despair, and looked without affection at his house and grounds. 'Sometimes I wish I'd left clay alone,' he said. I told him I thought he would have missed a lot of hobby satisfaction. 'No, no,' he said, impatient that I hadn't understood him. 'If you can't do what you're capable of it's difficult to be content. It's a cruel situation, that.'

I didn't have time to comment, for Rosemary came out in search of us. 'I wish you wouldn't drink beer just before the meal, Norman,' she said. Norman gathered up the bottle and glasses without reply, and led the way to the verandah for lunch. At the beginning of the meal Rosemary spoke mainly to my wife and me, and what few words she and Norman exchanged were in that semaphore of marriage which represents the history of a thousand fortified positions and bitter forays. Yet as the meal went on a new fullness in conversation arose between them, as if the stalemate they had reached required our presence as a catalyst to resolve. We were the chance of appeal, some escape from the established bigotry of their opposition. Rosemary did most of the talking. The recurring theme between them was Norman's pottery. 'Norman blames me, I'm afraid,' said Rosemary with a laugh, as if she wished to forestall Norman saying the same thing with greater earnestness. 'But I felt that as a family we needed security at the time. The children came first, I felt. Because they were girls, we had to help them quite a bit financially after they left school. We couldn't take the risk of living on Norman's pottery.' Norman didn't look at his wife as she said this, but gazed at the twin blues of sea and sky, and nodded his head slowly, not in any agreement but in time with a tune he had heard many times before. 'It wasn't as if he couldn't do it at all. There was always holidays and that. He must have sold thousands of pots over the years. Actually, now that he's retired he doesn't spend all that much time potting. Some days not at all. He seems to prefer fishing. He gets plenty of fish. We might have been able to live on the income of that perhaps.' Rosemary laughed again, but the knife had gone in.

'It's too late. I've told you before, it's too late for anything but pottery as a hobby now. The decision had to be made years ago, if I was going to develop the quality of work I wanted. You understand?' Norman looked across at me with his fisherman's eyes, but I avoided them and bent over the grated cheese and lettuce. 'Anyway,' said Norman distinctly, looking out to sea again, 'both pottery and fishing get me out of the house.' He smiled and Rosemary laughed.

Rosemary had a collection of driftwood along the front of the verandah. Abstract shapes, in wood worn to the colour of dry soap, apart from those she had varnished. 'I'm hoping to get all of them lacquered in time,' she said. In some she had bored holes, and plugged in trailing plants. 'After a storm I'll usually go down,' said Rosemary 'and prowl along the shore to see what new pieces have been cast up. I feel like a beachcomber at times. Isn't it awful! But the shapes are so unusual.' She seemed to feel that there was something elemental in her driftwood, and that by propping the pieces around the house she expressed an artistic inclination.

'One hard winter and it'll all go on the fire,' said Norman. 'They have at least that value — as a precaution.'

'Norman doesn't think much of them,' said Rosemary complacently.

'Oh, I don't know. How about making some plaster of Paris ones, and painting them red and yellow? We could attach them to the fence along the front of the house.'

We all helped with the dishes, but it was not a convivial affair. I watched Norman deliberately break a Spode butter dish which my wife had admired at the table. Norman jammed it against the tiled back-board, and displayed with hollow consternation the pieces broken from its lacy rim.

Afterwards my wife and I walked in the sun around the section, and watched the line of the shore sweep away to the south. 'It hasn't been easy for Rosemary by any means,' said my wife. 'Sometimes Norman won't speak for days. He'll sleep out in the workshop, or even in the boatshed. Twice he's taken all their money from the bank and gone off. Rosemary's been almost distraught wondering if he would come back, but afraid to ring the police.'

'They're alone here. I suppose that's half the trouble. No family and friends with them to relieve the constant wear of one personality on another.'

'Rosemary said that sometimes when he's fishing he'll slip into the water and swim from the rocks, straight out to sea for hundreds of yards. She's seen him bobbing about out there, as if undecided whether to go on swimming out, or come back to shore.' It was a chilling, but compelling notion. We both looked to the sea, as if Norman might be there, his grey head bobbing in the swell as he trod the deep water and made up his mind.

To escape the thought we turned away, and approached Norman's shed from the side. Through the window we saw Rosemary and Norman arguing. It was a mime of subdued gesture and suppressed intensity. As she had inside the house, Rosemary did most of the talking, and again Norman could not look at her, but gazed away with bleak abstraction. They were talking of the driftwood perhaps, or the broken Spode butter dish, perhaps the issue itself of Norman's pottery and the sacrifice for the children. With their girls gone, and the price paid more evident than the reasons for it, Rosemary's justification must seem weaker.

We were about to move away, when Norman hit her. She had leant towards him with particular emphasis, and he swung his hand against the side of her face so that she fell backwards, one outstretched arm dashing against the shelves. I hadn't seen a woman hit like that before; not with the complete contempt that was in the blow. It was a sad and belittling thing to see. The sunlight lost its resolution, and the garden assumed a bland animosity. 'You'll have to do something. Please do something,' Jennie whispered. But there was nothing to do. Norman didn't hit his wife again, just left her there and walked from the sliding doors towards the fence, and the track to the Ministry of Works reel. Rosemary rolled awkwardly on to her hands and knees, then got up and stood brushing her dress with her hands. Again and again she did it, as if she were content to have that action to repeat so she wouldn't have to think.

Yet within half an hour they were both standing on the drive to see us leave, drawn up before the neat house with the stag etched on the front glass pane, and the dark broom on the headland slopes above the sea. Rosemary said how much she'd enjoyed the day, but the left side of her face was pink, and when she smiled the lip there lifted from her teeth instead of creasing. Norman scratched the bare skin of his ankle, above the shabby sandshoe, and told us we were welcome to call again on our way back. He slid one thin arm towards me, and held out a piece of pottery. A sauce jar with the sleek brown glaze I had admired. Norman didn't give any reason for the present. 'We could go fishing, if you call in on the way back from your holiday,' he said.

They stood watching us until we reached the road, then went their own ways without comment, Rosemary into the house and Norman towards the shed, the jersey hanging from his shoulders and bagging over his shorts.

Jennie held up the sauce bottle. 'It looks pretty good to me,' she said.

'But not what he wanted to do,' I said. 'Not what he'd set his heart on.'

'I quite liked them as individuals.'

'Yes.'

'When I see a marriage like that I feel in need of a religion. When he hit her . . . when he hit her . . .'

'Other people's lives,' I said. She rested her hand on my shoulder. Even the shadow of desperation can have its effect.

Mr Van Gogh

~

WHEN HE WENT into hospital our newspaper said that Mr Van Gogh's name was Frank Reprieve Wilcox, and that was the first time I'd ever heard the name. But I knew Mr Van Gogh well enough. He came around the town sometimes on Sunday afternoons, and he would excuse himself for disturbing you and ask if there were any coloured bottles to carry on the work of Mr Vincent Van Gogh. Whether you gave him bottles or not, it was better never to enquire about his art, for he would stand by any back door on a Sunday afternoon and talk of Van Gogh until the tears ran down his face, and his gabardine coat flapped in agitation.

Only those who wanted to mock him, encouraged him to talk. Like Mr Souness next door who had some relatives from Auckland staying when Mr Van Gogh came, and got him going as a local turn to entertain the visitors. 'Was he any good, though, this Van Gogh bugger?' Mr Souness said, nudging a relative, and, 'But he was barmy, wasn't he? Admit it. He was another mad artist.' Mr Van Gogh never realised that there was no interest, only cruelty, behind such questions. He talked of the religious insight of Van Gogh's painting at Arles, and his genius in colour symbolism. He laughed and cried as he explained to Mr Souness's relations the loyalty of brother Theo, and the prescience of the critic Aurier. They were sufficiently impressed to ask Mr Van Gogh whether they could see his ears for a moment. Mr Souness and his relations stood around Mr Van Gogh, and laughed so loud when it was said, that I went away from the fence without watching any more. Mr Van Gogh was standing before the laughter with his arms outstretched like a cross, and talking all the more urgently. Something about cypresses and the hills of Provence.

Mr Van Gogh had a war pension, and lived in a wooden bungalow right beside the bridge. The original colours of the house had given up their differences, and weathered stoically to an integration of rust and exposed wood. The iron on the roof was stained with rust, and looked much the same as the corrugated weatherboards. The garden was full of docks and fennel. It had two crab apple trees which we didn't bother to rob.

Mr Van Gogh didn't appear to have anything worth stealing. He used to paint in oils, my father said, but it was expensive and nothing ever sold, so he began to work in glass. No one saw any of his artwork, but sometimes when he came round on Sundays, he'd have a set of drinking glasses made out of wine bottles, or an ashtray to sell made out of a vinegar flagon. My father was surprised that they were no better than any other do it yourself product.

Although he had no proper job, Mr Van Gogh worked as though the day of judgement was upon him. He used his attached wash-house as a studio, and on fine days he'd sit in the doorway to get the sun. There he'd cut and grind and polish away at the glass. He would even eat in the doorway of the wash-house as he worked. He must have taken in a deal of glass dust with his sandwiches. Often I could see him as I went down to the river. If I called out to him, he'd say, 'Good on you', still working on the glass, grinding, cutting, polishing. If I was by myself I'd watch a while sometimes before going down to the river. One piece after another, none of them bigger than a thumbnail. A sheet of glass sheds the light, he said. They had to be small to concentrate the light. Some of the bits were thick and faceted, others so delicate he would hold them to the sun to check. Mr Van Gogh liked to talk of individual paintings as he worked — the poet's garden, street in Auvers, or starry night. He stored the different colours and shapes in cardboard boxes that said Hard Jubes on the sides. Yellow was difficult, the colour of personal expression, Mr Van Gogh said, but so difficult to get right in glass. He bought yellow glass from Austria, but he'd never matched Van Gogh's yellow. He never thought so much of his yellow glass, he said, even from Austria.

Mr Van Gogh wasn't all that odd-looking. Sure, he had old-fashioned clothes — galoshes in winter and his gabardine coat with concealed buttonholes, and in summer his policemen and firemen braces over grey workshirts. But he was clean, and clean-shaven. His hair was long, though, and grey like his shirts. He combed it back from his face with his fingers, so that it settled in tresses, giving him the look of a careworn lion.

Because my father was a parson it was thought he should be responsible for Mr Van Gogh and other weird people. Mr Souness said that it was just as well that my father had something to occupy his time for the other six days of the week. Ministers get some odd people to deal with, I'd say. Reggie Kane was a peeping tom who had fits whether he saw anything or not, and Miss O'Conner was convinced that someone was trying to burn down her house at night, and she used to work in the vegetable garden in her nightdress. Our family knew Mr Van Gogh wasn't like the others, though most people treated him the same. My father said that Mr Van Gogh's only problem was that he'd made a commitment to something which other people couldn't understand. My father had a good deal of fellow-feeling for Mr Van Gogh in some ways. Mr Van Gogh would've been all right if his obsession had been with politics or horse-racing. He wouldn't have been a crackpot then.

Two or three times Mr Van Gogh came to our house to use the phone. He'd stand quietly at the door, and make his apologies for bothering us. He was ordering more yellow glass from Austria perhaps, or checking on his pension. Mr Van Gogh's humility was complete on anything but art. He was submissive even to the least deserving. On art, though, he would have argued with Lucifer, for it was his necessity and power. It was what he was. His head would rise with his voice. He would rake back his grey hair, and for a moment the backward pressure would rejuvenate his face before the lines could appear again, the plumes of hair begin a faint cascade upon his forehead. He could be derisive and curt, fervent and eloquent, but people didn't understand. A naked intensity of belief is an obscene exposure in ordinary conversation. It was better not to start him off, my mother said.

When the council decided to make the bridge a two-lane one, Mr Van Gogh's house had to come down. The engineers said that the approaches to the new bridge would have to be at least twice the width of the bridge itself, and Mr Van Gogh's house was right next to the old bridge. Even the house next to Mr Van Gogh's would probably have to go, the consultant thought. Mr Van Gogh took it badly. He stuck up the backs of the letters the council wrote, and sent them back. He wouldn't let anyone inside to value the house. He wouldn't talk about compensation. The council asked my father to get Mr Van Gogh to see reason. My father said he was willing to try and explain the business, but he didn't know if he could justify it. The council didn't seem to recognise the distinction.

As far as I know, Mr Van Gogh never let anyone into his house. Even my father had to stand on the doorstep, and Mr Van Gogh stood just inside the door, and there was a blanket hanging across the hall behind him to block off the sight of anything to a visitor at the door. My mother said she could imagine the squalor of it behind the blanket. An old man living alone like that, she said.

My father did his best. So did the council and the Ministry of Works, I suppose. They selected two other houses to show Mr Van Gogh, and a retirement villa in the grounds of the combined churches' eventide home, but he wouldn't go to see them. He became furtive and worried. He'd hardly leave his house lest the people come and demolish it while he was away. The council gave Mr Van Gogh until the end of March to move out of his home. Progress couldn't be obstructed indefinitely, they said. Mr Souness looked forward to some final confrontation. 'The old bugger is holding up the democratic wishes of the town,' he said. He thought everyone had been far too soft on Mr Van Gogh.

In the end it worked out pretty well for the council people. Mrs Witham rang our house at teatime to say she'd seen Mr Van Gogh crawling from the wash-house into his front door, and that he must be drunk. My father and I went down to the bridge, and found Mr Van Gogh lying on his back in the hallway, puffing and blowing as he tried to breathe. 'It's all right now,' said my father to Mr Van Gogh. What a place he was in, though. For through that worn, chapped doorway, and past the blanket, was the art and homage of Mr Van Gogh. Except for the floor, all the surfaces of the passage and lounge were the glass inlays of a Van Gogh vision. Some glass was set in like nuggets, winking as jewelled eyes from a pit. Other pieces were lenses set behind or before similarly delicate sections of different colours to give complexity of toning. The glass interior of Mr Van Gogh's home was an interplay of light and colour that flamed in green, and yellow, and prussian blue, in the evening sun across the riverbank. Some of the great paintings were there: *Red Vineyard*, *Little Pear Tree*, *View of Arles with Irises*, each reproduced in tireless, faithful hues one way or another.

Mr Van Gogh lay like clay in the passage, almost at the lounge door. I thought that I was looking at a dying man. I blamed all that glass dust that he'd been taking in for years, but my father said it was something more sudden. He pulled down the blanket from the hall, and put it over Mr Van Gogh to keep him warm, then went down the path to ring the ambulance. The blanket hid Mr Van Gogh's workshirt and firemen's braces, but he didn't look much warmer. His face was the colour of a plucked chicken, with just a few small veins high on his cheeks. Very small, twisted veins, that looked as if they didn't lead anywhere. I stood there beside him, and looked at his work on the walls. The yellow sun seemed to shine particularly on the long wall of the lounge where Mr Van Gogh had his own tribute to the man we knew him as. In green glass cubes was built up the lettering of one of the master's beliefs — 'Just as we take the train to Tarascon or Rouen, we take death to reach a star' — and above that Mr Van Gogh's train to Tarascon and a star rose up the entire wall. The cab was blue, and sparks of pure vermilion flew away. It all bore no more relation to the dross of glasses and ashtrays that Mr Van Gogh brought round on Sundays, than the husk of the chrysalis to the risen butterfly.

My father came back and waited with me in the summer evening. 'It has taken years to do, years to do,' he said. 'So many pieces of glass.' The fire and life upon the walls and ceiling defied Mr Van Gogh's drained face. He'd spent all those years doing it, and it didn't help him. It rose like phoenix in its own flame, and he wasn't part of it anymore, but lay on his back and tried to breathe. All the colour, and purpose, and vision of Mr Van Gogh had gone out of himself and was there on the walls about us.

Both the St John's men were fat. I thought at the time how unusual it was. You don't get many fat St John's men. They put an oxygen mask on Mr Van Gogh, and we all lifted him on to the stretcher. Even they stood for a few seconds, amazed by the stained glass. 'Christ Almighty,' said one of them. They took Mr Van Gogh away on a trolley stretcher very close to the ground.

'What do you think?' asked my father.

'He won't necessarily die,' said the St John's man. He sounded defensive. 'He's breathing okay now.'

Mr Van Gogh went into intensive care. The hospital said that he was holding his own but Mr Souness said he wouldn't come out. He said that it was his ticker, that his ticker was about to give up on him. Anyway there was nothing to stop the council and the Ministry of Works from going ahead. People came from all over the town to see Mr Van Gogh's house before they pulled it down. There was talk of keeping one or two of the pictures, and the mayor had his photograph in the paper, standing beside the train to Tarascon and a star. But the novelty soon passed, and the glass was all stuck directly to the walls with tile glue. The town clerk said there were no funds available to preserve any of it, and it was only glass anyway, he said. Someone left the door unlocked, and Rainbow Johnston and his friends got in and smashed a lot of the pictures. Mr Van Gogh's nephew came from Feilding, and took away the power tools.

My father and I went down to the river to see the house demolished. With Mr Van Gogh's neighbours, Mr Souness and the linesmen who had disconnected the power, we waited for it to come down. There were quite a few children too. The contractor had loosened it structurally, and then the dozer was put through it. The dozer driver's mate wore a football jersey and sandshoes. He kept us back on the road. Mr Van Gogh's place collapsed stubbornly, and without any dramatic noise, as if it were made of fabric rather than timber. The old walls stretched and tore.

Only once did my father and I get a glimpse of Mr Van Gogh's work beneath the weathered hide of the house. Part of the passage rose sheer from the wreckage for a moment, like a face card from a worn deck. All the glass in all its patterns spangled and glistened in yellow, red and green. Just that one projection, that's all, like the vivid, hot intestines of the old house, and then the stringy walls encompassed the panel again, and stretched and tore. The house collapsed like an old elephant in the drought, surrounded by so many enemies.

'Down she comes,' cried the driver's mate, and the driver raised his thumb and winked. There was a lot of dust, and people backed away. Mr Souness kept laughing, and rubbed his knuckles into his left eye because of the dust.

'All the time Mr Van Gogh spent,' I said to my father. 'All that colour, all that glass.'

'There'll always be a Mr Van Gogh somewhere,' my father said.

The Master of Big Jingles

~

I KNOW WHAT it's called now, it's called fennel. Knowing the name doesn't make it what it was, however. I see it rarely now. It peers occasionally from the neglected and passing sections, like the face of a small man over the shoulders of others in a crowd. Its fronds are the pale green of hollow glass, and it has a look of pinched resignation, as if it can foresee the evolutionary course before it.

When Creamy Myers and I were young, it was in its prime. There were forests of it pressing in on the town, and it reared up confidently in waxy profusion. The rough strip below the bridge was its heartland, and there Creamy and I had our hut. We could reach it by tunnel tracks from the riverbank, and the fence. We built it in the summer that ended our Standard Four year, and in the summer after that we renewed it in our friendship. The year we finished primary school we restored it again. We cut out the tunnel tracks as usual, so narrow that the top foliage showed no tell-tale gap, and even Rainbow Johnston wouldn't find them. We evicted the hedgehog and its loosely balled nest from the hut, and spread new sacks to mark our occupation. In a biscuit tin we kept the important things, wax-heads, shanghais, tobacco, fishing lines and the tin of cows' teat ointment I found on the bridge.

Fennel is the great home of snails: it is their paradise, nirvana and happy hunting ground. The matchless abundance of the snails was a fascination to us, and a symbol of the place itself. The snails were the scarabs of our own hieroglyphic society, and the snail hunt was the most satisfying of our rituals. From the length, breadth and depth of the river terrace we took them. From time to time one of us would return, and lift his shirt from his trousers, to tumble the catch into the biscuit tin. When we had a massed heap of them, perhaps a hundred and fifty or more, we would sit in the hut and anoint them. We used the cows' teat vaseline, rubbing it on the shells to darken the pattern and make them shine. We would lie the snails in handfuls among the fennel, just off the sacks, and in the penumbral green light. As we watched the snails would begin their ceremonial dispersal: large and small, sly and bold, all with the patterns of their shells waxed and gleaming. Scores of snails, each with its own set angle of direction. The gradual, myriad intersection of the planes of their escape through the fennel was like an abacus of three dimensions.

The friendship of Creamy and myself was the smallest and strongest of several circles. We often played with Arty and Lloyd, and there were other faces that we expected at other times. If we went swimming at the town baths, for instance, we joined up with the Rosenberg twins. They didn't seem to do much else but swim. But sometimes when Creamy and I were sick of what the others were doing, or after school when we'd rather be alone, then we'd make our signal, just a movement of the head, that meant we'd meet later at the hut. The hut was something apart from the rest of the world. In its life were only Creamy and me. As long as we agreed, our word was law, and no conventions but our own were followed.

I remember just when Creamy told me about going to Technical. We'd had a snail hunt, and were sitting by the river to wash. Creamy had his shirt off, and the snail tracks glistened on his chest. The linear droppings, inoffensively small, clung there too. 'Dad told me I'm not going to Boys' High after all,' he said. 'He's sending me to Tech.' Creamy's voice was doubtful, as if he wasn't sure whether it marked an important decision or not.

'But I thought we were all going to High?'

Creamy leant into the shingle of the river. He supported himself on his arms, and lifted first one hand, then the other to wash his chest. 'Dad said if I'm going into the garage with him, I need the Tech courses. He doesn't go much on languages and stuff.' Creamy had a broad, almost oriental face, and his upper lip was unusually full. It sat slightly over the bottom lip, and gave his face an expression of thoughtful drollery.

'I suppose after school we'll be able to do things together just the same. Maybe it's just like being in different classes at the same school.' I had a premonition, though, that Creamy's father had done something which would harm us.

'I did try to get Dad to change his mind,' said Creamy. He said it almost as if he wanted it recorded, lest some time in the future he might be blamed for not putting up more of a fight. Creamy flexed his arms, and recoiled out of the water with easy grace. He pulled the back of his trousers down, and showed the marks of a hiding. 'I did try,' said Creamy, and his upper lip quirked a little at the understatement.

'I don't see why it should make that much difference.' I could say that because it was weeks away in any case. When you are thirteen, nothing that is weeks away can be taken seriously. Creamy and I controlled time in those days. We could spin out one summer's day for an eternity of experience.

'Maybe I'll play against you in football,' said Creamy speculatively.

'I'll cut you down if you do.' We smiled, and Creamy skipped stones across the surface of the river with a flick of his wrist. The sun dried the water from us, and snapped the broom pods like an ambush on the other side of the river. Already I was surprised at my innocence in thinking that all my friends must go like myself to the High School.

Time made no headway against us that summer, not while we were together. But then my family went on holiday to the Queen Charlotte Sounds, and I returned to find the world moved on. The new term was before us, and Creamy was indeed going to the Tech, and I to the High.

I didn't see Creamy after school during the first week, and on Saturday when we went after lizards on the slopes behind the reservoir, we didn't wear uniform. But the next Tuesday we met at the hut, and the nature of our division was apparent. Although I should have expected it, Creamy's Tech uniform was a blow. His grey trousers to my navy blue, his banded socks and cap, distinct in a separate allegiance. Creamy was never deceived by outward appearance. A smile spread out under his full upper lip, and creased his tanned face. 'I see you've lost your knob, too,' he said, and lightly touched the top of his cap.

'The fourth formers tore them off. Initiation,' I said.

'Same with us.' It was typical of Creamy that he should notice first about our uniforms a subtlety we had in common, whereas I couldn't help seeing us from the outside. Even my friendship with Creamy hadn't given me a totally personal view. Creamy didn't mention the uniforms again. We left our caps with our shoes and socks in the hut, and waded in the river to catch crayfish. As long as we maintained the old life separate from the new, then both could exist. It was like those studies I did at High School, about the primitive societies existing for hundreds of years, and then collapsing when the white man came. Creamy and I couldn't change much in the old way, because our ideas came from different sources that year. Sooner or later the white man would come; the white man comes one way or another to all the pagan societies of our youth.

I never sat down to think it out but, if I had, it must have seemed that as Creamy and I had held our friendship through the end of that summer, and the first term at our new schools, then there was no reason why we shouldn't go on. That wasn't the way of it, however. In the winter months I didn't see much of Creamy. The days were short, and the rugby practices we went to almost always came on different nights. I made new friends too, like big Matthew and Ken Marsden. When I was with Creamy, I sometimes found myself assuming that he knew all about High, and then halfway through some story I'd realise that it must have been meaningless to him. Creamy never showed any impatience. Creamy had a natural and attractive courtesy. He would sit there smiling, his expanding lip faintly frog-like, and say, 'He sounds a real hard case,' or, 'I wish I'd seen that.' Unless I asked him, he never said much about Tech. The odd thing perhaps about sport, or the time he saw Rainbow Johnston smash the windows in the gym. Rainbow was the baron of all our childhood fiefdoms. He had a job at the pie cart in the evenings, and made more money by stealing milk coupons. Birds stopped singing when Rainbow came past. He knew how to twist an arm till the tears came, did Rainbow, and it was said he made little kids put their hands in his trousers.

In the third term, when it became summer again, we began going back to the river. Not just Creamy and me anymore, though, for I'd grown accustomed to spending my time with Matthew and Ken. The first time I took them to the hut, Arty was with us too. Arty knew Creamy from primary school, but Matthew and Ken didn't. I could see them measuring themselves against Creamy as the afternoon went on. Creamy didn't seem to mind. Creamy liked a challenge in his own unassuming way. Creamy could stand measurement beside anyone I knew.

The mentality of youth is able to unhook its jaws like a snake, and swallow up whole antelopes of experience. Youth is a time for excess: for breaking through the ice to swim, for heaping up a mountain of anointed snails from the fennel, for sledging until your hands are bleeding from the ropes, and sunstroke smites you down. Youth is a time for crazes: hula-hoops and underwater goggles, bubble gum and three-D cardboard viewers.

But that year it was knucklebones. The year when Creamy and my new High School friends met, it was knucklebones. Knucklebones had risen obscurely, like an Asian plague, and swept as an epidemic through our world — brief and spectacular. Creamy excelled at knucklebones, of course: Creamy was insolently good at knucklebones. Like chickens about a hen, the knucklebones grouped and disbanded, came and went around Creamy's hand. Creamy had begun with plastic knucklebones. The soft drink colours of the pieces would rise and fall, collect and separate, at Creamy's behest. He won an aluminium set in the Bible class competition. The aluminium ones were heavier and didn't ricochet. Creamy was even better with the aluminium ones. Cutting cabbages, camels, swatting flies, clicks, little jingles, through the arch, goliath, horses in the stable; Creamy mastered them all.

Creamy's expression didn't change when Ken challenged him to knucklebones. He seemed interested in my new friends. His fair hair hung over his forehead, and his complex face was squinting in the sun. Ken was good at knucklebones, as good as me, but he wouldn't beat Creamy, I knew. Creamy was a golden boy, and it's useless to envy those the gods have blessed. Ken and he went right through knucklebones twice without any faults. 'What do you think is the hardest of all?' said Creamy. Ken considered. He pushed the knucklebones about the ground with his finger as he thought.

'I reckon big jingles,' he said.

'Ten big jingles on the go,' said Creamy. 'I challenge you to ten big jingles without a fault.'

'You go first then,' said Arty. 'You go first and if you make a mistake then Ken wins.'

'All right,' said Creamy. The injustice of it didn't seem to worry him. He started out as smoothly as ever, allowing no time for tension to gather. His rhythm didn't vary, and his broad face was relaxed.

'That's good going,' said Matthew when Creamy had finished, and Ken had failed to match him.

'They're small though, these aluminium ones.' Arty seemed jealous of the praise. 'Smaller than real or plastic knucklebones. It's a big advantage to have them smaller in big jingles.'

'Stiff,' said Creamy.

Later in the afternoon we found ourselves fooling about by the bridge. Along the underside of the bridge was a pipe which Creamy and I sometimes crossed to prove we could do it. 'Creamy and I often climb across that,' I told the others. They looked at it in silence.

'Shall we do it now?' said Matthew at last. He thought he was strong enough to try anything.

There's no dichotomy of body and spirit when you're young. Adults see the body as an enemy, or a vehicle to be apprehensively maintained. There's just you, when you're young; flesh and spirit are indivisible. For Creamy and I then, for all of us in youth, any failure in body was a failure of the spirit too. Creamy went first. As always when he was concentrating, his lunar upper lip seemed more obvious, the humorous expression of his face more pronounced, as though he were awaiting the punch line of some unfolding joke. He leant out, and took hold of the pipe. He moved his grip about, as a gymnast does to let his hands know the nature of the task, then he swung under the pipe, and began hand over hand to work his way to the central bridge support. He used his legs as a pendulum, so that the weight of his body was transferred easily from one hand to the other as he moved. When he reached the centre support Creamy rested in the crook of its timbers, and looked down to the river. Then he carried on, hanging and swaying below the pipe, becoming smaller in silhouette against the far bank as he went.

'Seems easy enough,' said Arty.

'You go next then,' said Ken.

Arty measured the drop between Creamy's swaying figure and the river beneath. 'I would,' he said. 'I would, but I've got this chest congestion. I see the doctor about it.'

'Sure.'

Matthew could only think about one thing at a time, and as he was busy watching Creamy he found himself next in line for the pipe. The rest of us, by slight manoeuvrings, had got behind him. 'It's me then,' said Matthew. He took a grip and his body flopped down beneath the pipe, and stopped with a jerk. His upstretched arms were pulled well clear of his jersey, and his hands were clamped on to the pipe. The crossing was an exercise in sheer strength for Matthew. He pulled himself along clumsily, and his legs hung down like fenceposts below his thick body. I went next. I didn't want Arty in front of me in case he froze, and I couldn't get past. The few feet just before the central support were the worst, for if I looked down there I could see the concrete base of the timber supports on which I'd fall, instead of into the water. I used to count the number of swings I made just there; one, two, three, four, until I was able to put my feet on the wooden supports. The second half wasn't so bad, because at the end, if you were tired, you could drop off on to the grassy bank which rose up towards the underside of the bridge.

Arty and Ken didn't go over at all. Arty pretended he'd seen a big trout in the hole beneath the bridge, and he and Ken went down and poked under the bank with a stick. When we came back over the bridge, we couldn't see any big trout in the hole. 'Want to go over the pipe again?' said Creamy mildly.

'That's hard work, that.' Matthew was always honest.

'Good, though,' said Creamy.

As we scuffed about in the shingle at the end of the bridge, a horse and rider came past. The horse paused and, with flaunting tail, deposited vast rolls of waste. Matthew watched the horse with awe. 'I bet horses are the biggest shitters around,' he said.

'No, in proportion guinea pigs are far greater shitters,' said Creamy.

'Guinea pigs?'

'Yeah, in proportion they are.'

'Rabbits are good shitters,' said Arty.

'I don't see how anything could beat horses and elephants,' said Ken. As an ally he weakened Matthew's argument. The rest of us recognised the subtlety of Creamy's reasoning.

'Guineas are by far the best shitters in proportion.' Creamy knew he was right. 'Imagine a guinea pig as big as a horse. Now there would be a shitter.'

'Yeah,' said Matthew in wonder, and capitulation.

We had a swim, and threw fennel spears at each other during the rest of the afternoon. We forgot about the time, and Ken's sister came looking for him. She left her bike by the road, and came down to the fence, calling out for Ken. 'You've got to come home,' she said. Her breasts caused furrows across the material of her blouse.

'Have you been eating too much, or something,' said Arty. We had a good laugh at that witticism. 'Turning into a moo-vie star,' continued Arty, pleased with his reception. He tucked his thumbs into his shirt, and paraded before her and us.

'Oh, get lost,' she said. She began to go back up the bank towards the road. 'You'd better come, Ken. You know what'll happen,' she said.

'Hubba hubba, ding ding, look at the tits on that thing,' we sang.

'Watch out for Rainbow Johnston,' I called out.

'Hey, Rainbow, here she is.'

'Quick, Rainbow.'

For the first time Ken's sister seemed flustered. She looked back along the riverbank, and then hurried on to her bike. I don't know why I called out about Rainbow. Perhaps, in looking at her smooth legs and breasts, I found some part of Rainbow in myself, some desire to reach out and pinch her, or twist her arm, or worse.

Ken stayed a little longer, trying to show he wasn't afraid of being late, but we soon all began straggling back down the road. Creamy and I walked the last part together. 'I'm looking forward to the full summer,' I said. Creamy agreed. He played with his knucklebones, and whistled as he walked, his upper lip funnelling out and creating a very clear, penetrating whistle. His shoes, worn by water and grass during the afternoon, were almost white at the toes. Creamy stopped whistling, and asked me if Ken and Matthew were the two I liked best at High School. I told him I quite liked them.

'I'm getting sick of Arty,' said Creamy thoughtfully. 'You know that. I'm finding Arty pretty much of a pill.'

'So am I,' I said. Creamy tossed his aluminium knucklebones up and down again in the palm of his hand. We were nearly at the street where Creamy turned off. 'You didn't mind Ken and Matthew being there?' I asked him.

Creamy didn't give any glib answer. He walked on for a while.

'I suppose it's selfish to just have one or two friends,' he said. 'I suppose as you get older, you meet more and more people and make friends with them. Only I don't seem to find as many as you. There's an awful lot like Arty.'

As Creamy went off home, I thought about that. For the first time I realised that, despite being good at everything, Creamy didn't have that many friends. Being good at everything was in itself a disadvantage even. That's what was the matter with Arty. He resented Creamy's ability. Somewhere, sometime, he'd like to see Creamy take a fall.

The next Saturday I went again. Ken couldn't come, but Matthew and Arty did. I hadn't seen Creamy, but I thought he'd be there. He had another Tech boy with him. None of us knew him. He had eyebrows that grew right across the top of his nose. I'd never seen anyone with one long eyebrow like that before. His name was Warwick Masters. When he thought something was funny, he let his head fall forward, bouncing on his chest, and gave a snuffling laugh on the indrawn breath.

Creamy and I hadn't had any snail hunts that summer. No decision was made not to, we just didn't do it. As third formers we were growing out of snail hunts, and into more fitting things like knucklebones, and calling hubba hubba, ding ding, at Ken's sister. Yet the way Warwick treated the snails made me so angry. I could feel my throat becoming tight. 'Christ almighty,' said Warwick, 'look at these snails.' He reached into the fennel walls of the hut, and plucked out the snails. 'Just look at these snails, will you.' He let his head bounce on his chest, and gave his idiotic, sucking laugh. He arranged a line of them by the wall, then smashed each one with his fist. The shells cracked like biscuits, and what was left of the snails seemed to swell up in visceral agony after Warwick's fist was lifted. Creamy made no attempt to stop him. He hardly seemed to notice what he was doing.

'Don't do that,' I said to Warwick.

'Bloody snails.'

'It only makes a mess in the hut.'

'Stiff,' said Warwick. 'That's really stiff.'

'Just leave them alone.'

'Yeah?'

'Yeah.'

'Yeah?'

'Yeah.' The verbal sparring quickened into a semblance of humour, and Warwick bounced his head and laughed.

'Anyway,' said Arty, 'I don't think you Tech guys should come to the hut.'

'It's always been my hut too,' said Creamy seriously. Three summers are an accepted eternity when one is young.

'It's got to be either Tech or High ground,' said Matthew. He liked things simple for his own peace of mind. 'All the places got to be either Tech or High.' Matthew's simplicity had found the truth. All the places that mattered in our town were either High or Tech ground. The territories were marked, and only the adults in their naivety were unaware. My father never understood why I wouldn't take the short cut through the timber yard on my way to school.

'This side of the bridge is ours,' said Arty.

'But it's closest to the Tech swimming hole.'

'Stiff.'

Warwick picked up some of the squashed snails and quickly wiped them down Arty's face, then crashed away through the fennel a few paces, and stood bouncing his head and snorting. Creamy's subtle and unique face creased with delight, but he made no movement. Arty flung the remaining mess of snails at him, and urged Matthew to grab him. 'Grab him Matthew, grab him.' Creamy dodged Matthew's first clumsy attempt. He seemed as if he were about to say something, but Arty got in first. 'High on to Tech,' he shouted.

'Yeah,' I heard myself say, but without reason. It seemed to come from a surface part of me, and not deeper where I thought things out. Creamy slipped from the hut, and stood with Warwick.

'For today you mean,' he said, smiling. Creamy loved a battle.

'For always,' said Arty. Arty was pleased that at last he had something over Creamy. Creamy was Tech, and the rest of us were High. Creamy was quicker, stronger, better at knucklebones and swinging under the bridge, a true friend, but he was Tech. Arty, like most weak people, enjoyed advantages he couldn't himself create. 'For always. No more Tech farts on the bank. Fight you for it.'

It was three on to two, but that didn't worry Creamy. He had a sense of occasion, though, did Creamy. If it had to be Tech against High after all, then it should be done on a fitting scale. 'Thursday night then,' said Creamy. His full upper lip expanded as he thought about it, and his eyes took on the visionary look with which he regarded his schemes. A look that hinted at the appreciation of more colours than existed in the spectrums of the rest of us. 'On Thursday after school we'll have the full fight between Tech and High for the bank. You get all you can, and we'll meet you. All out war.'

'I don't know,' said Arty. 'Maybe we should set rules and numbers.' Arty's brief moment of initiative was over; Creamy had, as always, taken control.

'All out war,' he repeated, and Warwick's head bounced and his laugh sounded through the fennel.

'Is it really all out war?' I said. I could see Creamy's face not many paces away, but he didn't answer. 'All out?' I said. Creamy's face was relaxed and droll, so difficult to read.

'Full scale,' cried Warwick. 'Tech against High.' And still Creamy didn't answer.

'We'll win easily,' said Matthew. 'We can round up a dozen or more easily.'

'Look out for Rainbow Johnston, that's all,' called Warwick. He went off, laughing, to follow Creamy, who had turned away and begun walking towards the fence below the bridge.

I watched Creamy climb up to the road with Warwick, and I knew it had happened. I knew that him going to Tech and me going to High had ruined our friendship after all. I looked at Arty and Matthew standing by the hut, and I knew that neither of them was half the friend that Creamy had been. 'Do you think they'll really get Rainbow?' said Arty hollowly.

'I've heard things about Rainbow. I think we need plenty of guys.' Matthew's slow logic was depressing.

'Can we get enough, though?' said Arty.

'Jesus, Arty,' I said, 'will you stop moaning.'

That week at school we started getting as many allies as we could. Arty wrote the names down at the back of his pad. He had two lists — one headed possibles and one headed probables, like trial teams. There were some names in the possibles that I hardly knew. Not even all the probables were at the gate after school on Thursday, though. Arty himself didn't show up until we were just about to go. We told him he was trying to get out of it. 'No I'm not. I'm coming, of course I'm coming. I just had to put off other things, that's all. What do you think of this stick?' Arty had a short piece of sawn timber. He hit it against the fives courts, and then tried not to show that he'd jarred his hand. 'I reckon I'm ready,' he said.

We began walking towards the river, but a car drew up over the road, and the man driving it called out to Arty. It was Arty's father. Arty went over and talked with him, then came partly back. 'Wouldn't you know it,' he said. 'I've got to go up to the hospital for my tests. It has to be tonight.' With Arty's father watching from the car, it wasn't any use saying much. 'Maybe the Tech will be there again tomorrow night. I'll be right for tomorrow.'

'Sure,' said Ken. Arty walked over the road quickly. As he got into the car he let his stick slip on to the roadway.

'He rang his dad,' said Lloyd. 'That's what he did.' Arty couldn't meet our eyes as the car pulled away.

'What a dunny brush he turned out to be,' said Matthew, and we laughed. I was on the point of telling them what Creamy had said about Arty, Creamy had him picked all right, then I remembered that Creamy had become the enemy.

That left seven of us. Matthew, Ken, Lloyd, Buzz Swanson and the Rosenbergs. And me, of course. As we got closer to the bridge I had a strange feeling that our group was becoming smaller, although the number remained the same. Ken was walking beside me, and I saw how frail he was. His legs were so thin they seemed swollen at the knees to accommodate the joints. He had little, white teeth that looked as if they were his first set. Even as Ken smiled at me, I thought to myself that he was going to be useless. I didn't want to be by Ken when we were fighting. I'd keep by Matthew. Matthew's dirty knees were comfortingly large, and he plodded on resolutely. 'Perhaps we should scout around first, and find out how many of them there are,' I said to Matthew.

'I've got to be home by half past five,' said Ken. I bet you do, Ken, I bet you do, I thought. I resolved that not only would I stick with Matthew when it started, I'd make sure Ken wasn't protecting my back. I had some idea it was going to be like the musketeers of Dumas, us back to back against the odds of the Tech boys.

We stood on the raised road leading up to the bridge, and looked over the bank from the fence, across the frothing fennel to the greywacke shingle of the riverbed, where the larger stones crouched like rabbits in the afternoon sun. Creamy stepped out from the cover of the willows two hundred yards away. He raised one arm slowly, and lowered it again. It caught the significance of our presence, as a hawk becomes the sky. It had nothing to do with friendship, or compromise: it was a sign of recognition. It was a sign of deeper cognisance too, in that we were there. Unlike Arty and the others on the list, we had come. So Creamy acknowledged our equality of hostility.

Life was drama when we were young. The power of it made Lloyd's voice shake when he reminded us to keep together as we broke our way through the fennel. Creamy watched us coming for a bit, then disappeared behind the willows. 'Where are they?' said Ken. They were below the bank, where the terrace met the riverbed. As if to answer Ken's question, they began throwing stones which snicked through the fennel.

'Let's head for the willows,' I said. The Tech harried us as we went. I could hear Warwick's indrawn laugh, and I had a desultory stick fight with a boy who used to be in cubs with me. The Rosenberg twins were the best fighters on our side. They probably had the least notion as to why we were there in the first place, but they were the best fighters all right. They seemed to fight intuitively as one person, four arms and four feet. They rolled one Tech kid over the bank, and winded him on the shingle below. Matthew seemed unable to catch anyone to fight in this sort of guerrilla warfare. Nobody took him on, but he was too slow to take on anybody himself. He kept moving towards the willows, and we skirmished about him.

I think the whole thing might have petered out, if Rainbow hadn't come. Even in an all out fight there were rules: you knew that no one would deliberately poke anything in your eye, or hold your head under water longer than you could hold your breath. Rainbow was different. He liked to hurt people, did Rainbow. He stepped up on to the bank by the willows, and halted our forward progress. He had a thick stick. 'So it's Tech against High,' said Rainbow. His features were gathered closely on his round head, like sprout marks on a coconut. He held the stick in front of Ken, and Ken stopped. The rest of us did nothing. We did nothing not just because Rainbow Johnston was a fifth former, but because he was Rainbow Johnston. And deep down we were glad he'd picked on Ken, and not on us.

'I'm pax,' said Ken. It was the best he could think of, and its incongruity set the Tech guys laughing.

'Pax!' said Rainbow bitterly. 'We don't have any pax between Tech and High.' He drew back his stick, and speared it out at Ken, catching him on the side of the chest. Ken fell on his back, and as his head hit the soft grass his hair flopped away from his face, making him seem even younger.

'Ah, Jesus,' said Ken, and he got up and felt his side where he'd been struck. He laughed shakily, and picked up his own stick in a show of defiance. Then he dropped his stick again, and began to cry. He slumped down on his knees and held his side. He arched his back and squeezed his eyes closed with the pain.

'We've won,' said Creamy, before anyone else could think of a reaction to what had happened. Rainbow motioned with his stick towards the rest of us. 'We've won,' repeated Creamy quietly. 'You can stay and play in the hut, Rainbow.' Creamy had found the right note as ever. With the fight declared over, Rainbow felt a bit ashamed to be with third formers. He vaulted over the sagging willow trunk on to the riverbed, and slouched off upstream. 'See you, Rainbow,' said Creamy.

'Yeah,' said Rainbow.

Ken was still crying. There was some blood showing through his shirt from the graze, and Matthew and I helped him up. We began to go back to the bridge through the fennel. 'They can't come here again, Creamy, can they?' called out Warwick. 'It's Tech now.'

'They can't come here again,' said Creamy. His face was the same, relaxed, and with the upper lip creating the impression of incipient humour. He didn't speak with any special triumph.

We broke down the fennel in our retreat, paying no attention to the tunnels Creamy and I had made. I was glad Tech had won. I joined in the talk about the injustice of Rainbow being there, but I was glad they'd won. It gave a more general explanation for the end of our friendship — Creamy's and mine. There couldn't be any personal betrayal when it was a matter of Tech and High, a commitment to a cause. Ken was still crying, but with greater artifice as his sense of heroism grew. He leant to one side, and he held his shirt out so it wouldn't stick to his graze. The fennel fronds were like miniature conifers, smaller and smaller, each in the join of the other as marsupial embryos in a pouch. The oddly coastal smell of the crushed fennel was all about us. 'I don't know that we lost, not really fair and square,' said Matthew. 'If Rainbow hadn't been there I mean.' They could say what they liked, but for myself I knew I'd lost all right. And it was worse that, as I climbed from the fennel, up on to the road, I could understand what it was I'd lost, and why.

Cabernet Sauvignon With My Brother

~

I WALKED THE last two miles to my brother's place. I was lucky to have hitched as close as I did. Along the flat through Darfield and Kirwee early in the morning I'd done a good deal of walking, but then a tractor repair man took me to within two miles. He told me he'd been working on the hydraulics of a new Case harvester which cost eighty thousand dollars.

I love the accumulated heat of the Canterbury autumn. When you rest on the ground you can feel the sustained warmth coming up into your body, and there are pools of dust like talcum powder along the roads. It's not the mock tropicality of the Far North, but the real New Zealand summer. It dries the flat of your tongue if you dare to breathe through your mouth. After spending the vacation working on the coast, I was happy to be back in Canterbury.

My brother Raf lived on seventeen hectares of gravel close to West Melton. He had been a tutor in economics at Lincoln, but resigned on a matter of principle. He said it was a form of hypocrisy to pretend to any skill in financial affairs, when the best salary he could command was that of a tutor. Raf said that the most important things to achieve in life were privacy and revenue. At West Melton on seventeen hectares he had privacy, but the income was precarious. Raf's best crop was manoeuvres. He said he received a small but consistent return from manoeuvres. The army paid him for access to the riverbed. Heavy manoeuvres was the better paying crop he said, but harder on the ground.

As I walked up the natural terrace to Raf's place, the heat shimmer on the riverbed was already beginning. The stones in Raf's paddocks didn't seem to have become any less numerous. I noticed that because last time I visited my brother, he told me that ploughing only brought them up, and that picking them off was uneconomic. Raf believed that if the ground were grazed naturally, and just a little super added from time to time, then worm action would increase the height of the soil until the stones were eventually covered right over. He said he read a report of French research on it in Brittany. Raf had a knack of finding theoretical justification for his lifestyle.

He was working on his motorbike when I arrived. It was an old Norton 500 cc, an enormous single-pot machine, and his only form of transport. With it he towed a trailer large enough for ten bales of hay. He left the front tube hanging from the tyre, and came down the track to meet me. 'Ah, Tony,' he said, and took me by the shoulder. 'I hoped to see you before the term began.' His blue eyes seemed bleached from the sun, and his hair and eyebrows were nearly white. 'I told myself you'd come,' he said. Although he was my brother, he was about fourteen years older than me: we were more like uncle and nephew in some ways. I was aware of the emphasis and undisguised pleasure in his voice. 'I've got quite a lot of beer at the moment,' he said proudly. 'I sold another dozen lambs last week.' To have revenue to share, as well as privacy, made him feel his hospitality was complete.

'I can't stay the night. Lectures start tomorrow. I should have been in today, really.'

'Well, we've the day together then,' said Raf, 'and you'll get out sometime during the term.'

I went with Raf into his house, and he put into his pygmy fridge as many bottles of beer as it would hold. The kitchen floor had a slant, and when the fridge was operating the vibration caused it to creep from the wall, inch by inch. I could see it, as we sat at the table with our coffee, shuffling up to Raf's shoulder like a prototype robot. 'It takes about seven minutes to reach the table,' said Raf. He tolerated it because it never broke down, just had to be pushed back to the wall every seven minutes. 'I have to switch it off when I go outside,' he said.

Raf felt no obligation to ask about our parents. Not that he disliked them; it was his way of showing that his friendship with me was apart from any other connection between us. He knew I'd tell him anything that he should know. 'You seem happy here still,' I said.

'Happiness is related to the level of expectation,' said Raf, and he pushed back the fridge. 'To be the mayor of Wellington, or the second richest farmer in Southland, is a gnawing futility if you can only be satisfied by being Prime Minister. Our education system should be directed to inculcating as low an expectation as possible in every child, and then most of them could grow up to be happy.' Raf's spur of the moment principle paid no heed to envy, but then he was working from the premise of his own nature. My brother was one of the minority who didn't compare themselves with others. He was self-sufficient in his ideas and ambitions. He enjoyed simple things, like being able to produce a meal for me from his property. We went outside, taking some beer with us, and I helped Raf to fix the front tube. As we did so, he laid out his plans for our lunch. 'If only we'd had rain,' he said, 'then there would have been mushrooms. I've been spreading the spores year by year. Now I get cartons-full at times, and take them in to sell. Everything's right for them now, except the rain.'

'I'm not all that fussed on them anyway,' I said, just so that he wouldn't feel my level of expectation had been high.

'I've been saving some rabbits, though, down by the pines. And I've got plenty of eggs and vegetables. We could have chook, but fresh game is better.' Raf thought we should cull the rabbits before we had too much beer, we went off over the stones and brown grass of his seventeen hectares towards the pines. 'You're doing accounting and economics, aren't you,' he said.

'Law. I'm doing law.'

'I found there wasn't much privacy in economics. I should say that law would be much the same: more revenue probably, but no privacy.' Raf stopped, and enjoyed the privacy of his land for a moment. The small terraces and scarps vibrated in the heat.

The bird calls were outnumbered by the muted sound of firing from the West Melton butts. 'I've been thinking of going out of sheep into Angora goats,' said Raf. 'I read an article saying they're much more profitable per head, ideal for smaller properties. Three rabbits?' He tagged on about the rabbits after a pause, when we had started to walk towards the pines again. 'Is one and a half rabbits enough for you?'

'Fine.'

'I've been keeping an eye on these. There's nearly a dozen here. I've been looking forward to a special occasion so I could use some.' Raf walked in an arc behind the pines, so that we would come from the broken slope where there was gorse and briar. He shot two rabbits quickly with the twelve-gauge, and then had me walk through the pines and flush another out to make the three.

Raf and I sat on the front step of his house, and he cleaned the rabbits, as I peeled the potatoes. He went over the various ways in which the rabbits could be combined with the other food we had. We ate those rabbits several times over before we had lunch. They were good at last, though, with potatoes, pumpkin, cheese sauce, boiled eggs and beer. Repletion made Raf even more relaxed and thoughtful. 'You get plenty of girls at the university, I suppose,' he asked me. For the first time there was a hint of dissatisfaction in his voice. 'Girls don't seem much interested in privacy. I had a woman out here before Christmas. She did a lot of screenprinting. She seemed to like it here for several weeks, but then she began to mope. She said she found the landscape oppressive. She wasn't a very tall girl, but big where it mattered, mind you.' My brother was at a loss to explain why anyone should prefer the city. 'I have to go into Christchurch now,' he said. There was a note of grievance. He saw it as a lack of consideration, the screenprinting girl choosing to go back to town.

'Maybe it's the old house,' I said. 'Women have higher expectations there, I suppose.'

'I bought a new bed for us. A brass one, original. It cost me a fat lamb cheque. She hated anything artificial: plastic, vinyl, nylon, veneers, anything like that.' There certainly wasn't much of such material in Raf's house. Almost everything looked pre-war. Even the walls were tongue and groove. 'She was a nice girl in many ways,' Raf said.

In mid-afternoon a visitor came. 'It's McLay,' Raf said. 'He's bought the big place up the road. I forgot all about him. He's come to look at my bore and pump.' McLay was a farmer of self-importance: one of those men who walk in a perfectly normal manner, but whose evident conceit makes them appear to swagger. He parked his European car at an angle which best displayed its lines, and his sense of complacency grew as he came closer to the house.

'Seen better days I'd say,' he said, and he tapped with his shoe at the decayed boards close to the ground along the front of the house. 'I like a place in permanent materials myself,' he said. 'Always have, always will.' Raf was never defensive about his property. He considered it too much of a blessing to need its weaknesses concealed.

'Most of the exterior is shot,' he said frankly. 'We had rabbit for lunch.' McLay was somewhat baffled by that, and suffered a subtle loss of initiative.

McLay would have taken his car to the pump, but Raf said it was easier if we sat in the trailer behind the Norton. McLay found it difficult to maintain his dignity there. He sat very upright, with one hand on the side to limit the bouncing, and with the other he tried to repel Raf's greasy tools, which clattered around us. Raf had one bore sunk into the gravel, and he ran off water to his troughs. When he reached the place he switched off the motorbike, and sat there enjoying the sun. 'Never seems to run dry, this bore,' he said. 'It's with the river being so close, I suppose.' McLay had scrambled from the trailer, and was wiping his wrist on the grass to clean it, after warding off Raf's grease-gun. He felt a need to dissociate himself from Raf's scale of farming

'I'll need to put in perhaps a dozen of these bores,' he told me. 'I've three hundred and fifty hectares, you see, and I hope to irrigate from them as well.'

'I only need to run it for an hour or so each day,' said Raf. He lifted the rusted kerosene tin that protected the motor.

'Mine will have to be electric, with remote switches. I won't be able to spend all day mucking about with petrol engines,' countered McLay. Raf wound up the starting cord, and pulled with no result. 'Gives a bit of trouble, does it?' said McLay. Raf tried again and again. The only result was one cough, which flicked the starting cord up to give Raf a stinging blow across the face. McLay gave an understanding laugh. 'Pity it's not Briggs and Stratton. They're the only small motor, I always say. I think you've flooded it.' Raf seized the choke, fully extended it, and bent it across the motor. McLay was quiet. Two veins began to swell beneath the skin of my brother's forehead. They made an inverted Y the colour of a bruise. He tried twice more with the cord, attempts of elaborate calmness, then he went to the trailer and brought back the crowbar. He systematically beat the four-stroke motor until the cooling fins had coalesced with the cylinder head, until the various attached parts had broken away. The crowbar made a solid crump, crump sound of impact, and the pipe from the bore rattled in its housing. Some of Raf's sheep stopped grazing to regard him for a while then resumed feeding. McLay had an uneasy smile, and his eyes switched furtively back and forth from Raf to me.

By the time Raf had finished, the veins in his forehead had subsided, and he wiped the sweat away with a sense of achievement. 'Never underestimate the perversity of objects,' he said. 'Never let them get away with it. A switch won't function, a fitting or tool won't work, then before you know — open revolt. Don't give an inch. Did you hear what I said, McLay? Never underestimate the perversity of objects.'

'I'd better be on my way now,' said McLay. There was an increasing air of placating wariness about him, as he realised the full extent of my brother's eccentricity.

'I'm going to use a windmill here,' said Raf. 'I should really have fitted one long ago. We're going to have to get back to wind power a lot more in this country.'

McLay rode back in the trailer without attempting to speak against the noise of the Norton, and when we reached the house he went off with a minimum leave-taking. 'An odd sort of chap. Didn't you think?' Raf said. There was no irony apparent in his voice.

Raf brought out more beer, and we sat again on the front step to drink it. The rural delivery car went past his gate without stopping. 'At Lincoln,' he said, 'the postman was a woman. She used to pedal about in yellow shorts, and her legs were very strong and brown.' He paused, and then said, 'So very brown' in a wistful way. 'She used to like me making puns about her having more mail than she could deal with. I have to go to Christchurch now.' The inconvenience of it rankled. 'I thought I might have had a letter from the Agriculture Department with information about goats,' he said. 'I intend those to be my two priorities this year: goats and the windmill.'

My brother's prevalent attitude to life was one of convinced cheerfulness, yet the non-arrival of the department's letter concerning the goats, and the poignant recollection of the Lincoln post girl's legs, had brought him as close to depression as I had ever seen him. The drink too, I suppose. We'd had quite a lot to drink. I felt it was a good time to tell him of my present. 'I brought you a present.'

'Thank you.'

'Cabernet sauvignon. It's only New Zealand, but it's a medal winner, and four years old. I remembered you liked it best.'

The secret of Raf's joy in life was his appreciation of all the pleasures, irrespective of scale. He got up from the step in excitement. 'What a day!' he said. I got the bottle from my pack, and we had an uncorking ceremony. Raf put the bottle on the step to breathe and warm. 'We won't have any more beer now until after the wine,' he said. 'We don't want to be unable to appreciate it. Afterwards it doesn't matter.'

'I'll have to go at six or seven. I don't want to have to hitch into Christchurch in the dark.'

'Right. I'd take you in, but I've only got one helmet, and the lights on the bike aren't going.'

Raf seemed to have forgotten his disappointment about the goats and other things. His thin face was alive with speculative enterprise again. 'What to have with the cabernet?' he said. 'We can't drink a good wine with just anything.' The full sophistication of a mind which had achieved honours in economics was given to the problem, and while the world grappled with the exigencies concerning inflation, corruption, guerrilla warfare, spiritual degeneration and environmental pollution, Raf and I sat amidst his seventeen quiet hectares at West Melton, and discussed the entourage for our cabernet. My brother was a great believer in immediate things.

We had peas and baked potatoes, tinned red cabbage and corn. We ate it from plates on our knees, as we sat on the front step. Raf talked to me of his experiences on the continent, and how bad the vin ordinaire was in the south of France. He had some good wine glasses, and we raised them to the evening sun to admire the colour of the wine. Raf invited me to forget university, and join him on his goat and windmill farm. 'Economics is a subject that destroys an appreciation of spiritual things,' said Raf.

'Law. I'm doing law.'

'Same thing,' said Raf. 'Probably worse.' He became so carried away in trying to persuade me of the deadening nature of formal studies, that he absent-mindedly kept the last of the cabernet sauvignon for himself, and so I fell back on beer. 'If you'd seen some of the places I have — Bangkok, Glasgow, Nice — then the value of privacy would be clear to you. Space brings the individual dignity, Tony. Herd animals are always the least attractive. Have you noticed that? I think that's one of the main reasons I want to move from sheep to goats. Goats have individuality, it seems to me.'

'A goat suits a name.'

'That's my point.' Raf sat relaxed on the step, his shingle land spreading away before him.

Just on twilight Raf took me down to the West Melton corner on the Norton. He drove carefully, conscious of the drink we'd had. 'Come out and see me soon,' he said. 'I meant what I said about forgetting economics, and joining me here to live.' I watched him ride off, without lights, and cautious of the power of the motorbike. I could hear it long after he was out of sight, and I imagined my brother riding up his track, over the stones, towards his disreputable house. To resist the maudlin effects of the wine and the beer, I lay down in the long grass, out of sight of the road. I rested my head on my pack, and slept for an hour or so.

So I ended up hitchhiking into the city in the dark after all. I was lucky, though, for after walking a few minutes, I was picked up by a dentist and his daughter. Her name was Susan. We talked about cars, and I tried not to breathe on Susan, lest she think me a typical boozy student. The dentist said he'd been having trouble trying to get the wheels balanced on his Lancia. 'Never underestimate the perversity of objects,' I said. The dentist liked that, and so did Susan. They had an appreciation for a turn of phrase. Raf would have enjoyed its reception. It isn't often that incantations are effective beyond the frontiers of their own kingdom.

The Charcoal Burners' Dream

~

AT RECEPTION I felt I belonged still to the outside world. I could breathe the exhaust fumes from the passing traffic in the street outside, and there was an undeniably healthy man in a post office smock sorting letters with one of the reception nurses. As I was taken down the corridor, however, and up the stairs, the smell closed in; a uniquely institutional fragrance of antiseptics, medication polishes — and resignation.

I was taken to the far end of Men's Surgical Two, almost to the balcony room, and I put my case on the bed and stood awkwardly before the veterans of the ward. There was a sparrow in the balcony room, and Nurse McKerrow wanted it let out. Colin and Jimmy chased it as best they could from one side of the room to the other, but only one window would open, and the sparrow slammed instead into the closed panes, becoming more dazed and bloody. Chris was in the next bed to mine. 'Oh, for Christ's sake,' he said and he cast his yellow hair from his face impatiently. 'Can you move about much?' he asked me. 'Throw a towel over it then, please, and let it out.' I went into the balcony room, and the next time the sparrow struck the glass I dropped the towel over it, and then released it through the open window. The bird half fell, half fluttered the three storeys into the hospital garden below. A trim pebble garden like a cemetery, with waxy camellias in a row.

Colin and Jimmy reluctantly came back to their beds, and I got out my pyjamas and dressing gown to change. Nurse McKerrow said I could pull the curtain screen, but I knew the impression that would create. I had to prove my anatomy, as well as my pyjamas, to be suitably nondescript. Chris watched me, propped up on his pillows. His almost yellow hair hung limply, like a transplanted tussock. When I was in my pyjamas, Chris considered I had formally joined them, and I was introduced to those close to my bed, Jimmy, Colin, Richard and Chris himself. Throughout the afternoon those less immediate in the ward were mentioned as they brought themselves to notice by refusing to eat, having a good-looking visitor, or being on the surgery list for the next day. Each was identified by his complaint as a suffix title. Arthur Prentice spine fusion, old Mr Webster prostate. Chris himself was bowel. He said the word bowel in the tone of voice a man might use for an ex-wife. A tone of intimacy and betrayal all at once.

Colin talked most to me that first day, superficial things, of course, about the hospital routine and the All Black tour, the headlines in the paper and the difficulty of making small businesses pay. That was Colin's line, small businesses. The sort of things you would expect two strangers in bed to discuss. I was to find, however, that there wasn't any more to Colin than the first superficial contact. When I left hospital he still talked about the All Blacks and small businesses with the same conformity.

Colin was the tribal New Zealander, for whom the greatest horror is to be different from what he imagines the majority to be.

Chris didn't talk much the first day, but I was aware of an aura of goodwill. In the morning, after Mr Millar had gone, and the others were having breakfast, Chris noticed me lying quietly. He told me what a good bone surgeon Mr Millar was, and how well known he was for it. I wasn't allowed to eat anything before the operation. I had trouble in my knee: bone disease in the knee cap, and cartilages to come out as well. Chris watched as Nurse McKerrow shaved and bathed my knee before the operation. When it was so smooth and pink that it shone, she gave me a jab of something. I remember Chris saying, 'Pentathol. My favourite magic carpet. As good as a night with Nurse McKerrow — almost.' Colin and Jimmy laughed, and Nurse McKerrow smiled with her eyes.

'Send in the trolley,' I said extravagantly. 'I'm ready for the trolley', and I wondered why the others laughed so hard.

The pain kept me from sleeping much the first two or three nights after the operation, despite the stuff they gave me. At night the ward was not completely dark, because of the light spilling from the sister's office. It dwindled down the ward, and didn't reach into the balcony room. But from where I was, looking back along the rows of beds towards the light, I could see pretty well once I got used to it. Old Mr Webster coughed a lot without waking up, and the radiators stood along the wall, on the lino, like piano accordions. I had plenty of time for thinking on those long nights. Lying there, looking along the beds towards the office, and with enough pain to banish any inner deceit, I had enough time for thinking, all right. Chris talked to me sometimes to take my mind off the pain. I was too selfish to realise then that he was awake for the same reason. That's when he first told me about the Liberal Mythology. Never let yourself get sucked in by the Liberal Mythology, he said. He saw it in the way I talked about my best friend who came to see me shortly after the operation. I told Chris how close we were, and how I'd known him over thirty years. 'The Liberal Mythology,' said Chris.

'What?'

'All this about searching out kindred souls. It's all part of the Liberal Mythology. You have as your friends who you can get as your friends, just as you have as your wife who you can get for your wife. Don't kid yourself any other way. It doesn't make them any less precious, but it's the truth of it. Take Jimmy there: he'd like to be friends with you, and marry Nurse McKerrow. Right?' We looked across at Jimmy. He lay asleep, with one arm over his face. 'How much choice has Jimmy really got?' said Chris. I couldn't think of any form of rebuttal, except saying that I wasn't the same as Jimmy. 'Only a matter of degree, for you and me,' said Chris.

During the day Chris helped me with my exercises. At first he'd just tell me how far I was getting my heel off the bed, as I lay on my back and tried to lift the leg. Later he'd rest his hand gently on the top of my foot to give me more weight to lift as the knee became stronger. 'You've got it beaten, Hugh, that's sure enough,' he'd say.

Anything that jarred my leg was the worst: knocking it with the crutch, or catching the toe on a rug, would bring an instant sweat. Hopping was out; progress was a matter of deliberate smoothness. On the fourth day I slipped while in the toilet and got wedged in the corner amid my crutches. My bad leg pressed against the lavatory bowl. I should have called out in a calm voice of suppressed pain to tell the nurse what had happened. It never occurred to me to do any such thing. I lay there, giving a very quavering and sustained squeal, like that of a girl. The sustained squeal was best, because any deep breath was enough to alter the unbearable pressure on my leg. The ward enjoyed it when I was carried back ignominiously from the toilets.

I began to get better rapidly, though. After a fortnight or so, Chris and I were able to go up to the geriatric wing and watch television at night. We weren't allowed to use the lift, so it meant a stiff climb and a rather furtive hobble along the dim corridors. The television was left on in the geriatric dayroom, right through until closedown. Sometimes Jimmy would come with us, occasionally a patient from some other ward, but usually just Chris and me. And the locals, of course. There were several geriatrics whose beds were regularly pushed into the dayroom at night, not because they liked television, but because they disturbed the others if left in the ward. Mind you, they may have enjoyed television. Chris said it's easy to be dogmatic when speaking for those who can't speak for themselves.

Puck and the Wrestler were our most consistent viewing companions. The Wrestler's skin was too large for him, and flowed around the few fixed features of his face. Only on the top of his head was it tight. His eyes were circular, and ringed with creases like those of a parrot. The Wrestler had regressed to some time of persistent physical endeavour, and reiterated it all in a monologue of quiet despair. 'That's a good hold, Bob. Ah yes. Ah yes. Ah Bob, Bob, that's a good hold. I'll pin your shoulders yet. But that's a good hold, Bob. Ah yes.' The Wrestler never moved, and his voice was drab in tone, but behind it somewhere was an epic of pain and fortitude, and underlying submission as if he fought with life itself. Puck provided less of a window. Most of the time he sat as primly as Whistler's mother, his hands demurely on the folded sheets. But from time to time he would give his own cry. It was the sound a contented chicken makes in the yard when the afternoon sun is hot, the dust dry, and a breeze in the pines by the woolshed. Poo-oo-ook. You know the sound. A sound of drawling enquiry in a rising inflexion. Puck caught it perfectly. He did it most when everything was quiet: late at night when there was something subdued on the television or, even better, when it had finished. Then, as Chris and I prepared to leave, we would hear him. 'Poo-oo-ook. Poo-oo-ook', gathering the sunshine, the dry, grey dust, and the pine trees about himself. We called him Puck because of Kipling's *Puck of Pook's Hill*. It was the most successful joke I ever made with Chris, mentioning Puck of Pook's Hill. His soft, even laugh went on and on, until he started swearing at me because I'd made his bowels hurt.

Nurse Hart was the night nurse on the geriatric ward. She seemed to feel the responsibility of it deeply. Unlike the physios and Nurse McKerrow, she wasn't immediately good-looking, and she was very quiet. She had legs, though, said Chris. Chris was quick to notice those girls who had legs. Nurse Hart's legs were long and graceful, growing more rounded to the thighs. Nurse Hart liked Chris and me to be in the dayroom watching television, in case something went wrong with her patients.

The physios were the best-looking girls in the hospital, except for Nurse McKerrow. All of us agreed the physios were the best, though, apart from Jimmy, we couldn't think of any explanation for it. Jimmy thought it was because they liked massaging people, and we knew that was just the inevitable expression of Jimmy's mind. 'All that rubbing and gripping,' said Jimmy slyly. 'The good-looking ones like to do it the most.' Jimmy was in for some sort of club foot, but he wasn't very Byronic. He had a cramped, impoverished face, and acquaintance disclosed a mind of similar character. He collected magazines of nudes, and laid them on the bed when the nurses came, in what he considered a subtle declaration of intention. From the balcony one day we watched Jimmy playing with his transistor. He found a woman's voice on one channel, and lay twisting the volume knob back and forth so that it sounded as if the woman was panting.

'Poor little bastard,' said Chris. Colin would have laughed, but Chris saw the poverty in Jimmy rather than the humour.

The Reverend Metcalf came to see us on Wednesday. Wednesday was his hospital day. I haven't anything against clergymen as such, not as such, but Chris and I disliked the Reverend Metcalf. He wore a look of infinite understanding and superiority. He had a rich, well-modulated laugh, tinged with pathos to hint at the load of revelation he bore. He would lay out his modulated laugh as a tapestry, while his eyes strayed to other beds, or the face of his digital watch. He was a vicarious vicar: a walking crucifixion, full of suffering yet having experienced no pain. I watched Chris regard the Reverend Metcalf as he left. 'The Liberal Mythology again?' I said.

'The Liberal Mythology.' Chris moved restlessly in his bed, stirred by the appearance once more of his old adversary. 'Life and death are the religious divisions in the Liberal Mythology,' he said. Now the reality of it, Hugh, the reality, is different.' Chris loved the word reality. The way he said it gave it weight and sheen, a soundness. 'The reality is the cycle of growth and decay.'

'And life after death?' I asked, because I couldn't quite see what he was getting at.

'How can the personality survive death, when it can't always survive life? That's it, all right. Take Puck, or the Wrestler: there's not much left to gather, is there? The Liberal Mythology deals in theory, see Hugh. You have life, and you have death: you have the prime of functioning personality, you have its perpetuation in spirit. It's a very comforting thing, the Liberal Mythology, and being a theory it doesn't concern itself with the complications of transition.' Chris rolled over carefully. He put a pillow beneath his groin, and hung his head over the bed in his favourite position to rid himself of flatulence. 'There's a bit of the pattern of the lino further down that looks like a giraffe,' he said. His yellow hair drooped away from his neck, and I was dismayed to see how the bones stood out beneath the skin.

Perhaps it was because he was losing so much weight that Chris had to have another operation. You don't know with bowels, mind. Mr Millar came to see him again, and told him he was to have another operation. The rest of us on our beds looked across to him to see how he was taking it. 'I'm having my operation on Tuesday, Nurse McKerrow. Give me a kiss.' It was unashamed blackmail, and both he and Nurse McKerrow laughed. She looked quickly down the ward, then bent over Chris. She kissed him, and Chris made no attempt to encircle her with his arms, but with one finger traced a line down her side, sweeping slowly over her hip before dropping his hand to the bed again. 'Tell Mother I died happy,' said Chris, and Jimmy cried out excitedly as we laughed, and said he wanted a kiss too. Nurse McKerrow went back up the ward. She looked as if she had received as much as she had given.

The night before his second operation, Chris came up to the geriatrics' television with me. We sat with Pook and the Wrestler, and watched a film about a donkey that talked. Chris couldn't sit still; he leant on his chair more than he sat on it, and he lay on Pook's bed with him for a while. Nurse Hart brought us coffee, and tried to share with us her fears concerning old Mrs Sanderson in the main ward. Later, when the donkey was winning the war for the Allies, Nurse Hart came back crying, and told us that Mrs Sanderson had tried to swallow her handkerchief and choked to death. Chris and I went into the darkened ward, and pushed Mrs Sanderson out to wait for the hospital orderlies. Mrs Sanderson's wispy hair stood up from her head, as if in her death she had frightened herself as well as Nurse Hart.

After the orderlies had come and gone, Nurse Hart remained in the dayroom with us for comfort. She stood by Chris's chair and tried not to be upset. Chris held her hand and talked to her. Gradually her head came down towards the chair, until she rested her forehead on the top of Chris's head. Her hair covered part of his face, and she didn't speak, though Chris continued to talk in his reduced but definite way. It was a scene of reassurance. The Wrestler and I were quiet, although I was not unaware, and Puck seemed to realise that the mood of the dayroom was particularly calm. 'Poo-oo-ook,' he said tentatively. 'Poo-oo-ook,' and the sunshine of it, and the sighing pine trees, gathered around us.

Chris was a lot worse after the second operation. He didn't seem to be able to pull himself right back to complete participation. The pain made him restless, and sometimes impatient. When I looked at him, and he wasn't aware of it, his face was full of a strange enquiry. As if he were getting smaller and smaller inside himself and could hardly see out of his own eyes. He didn't come up to the television anymore at night. Nurse Hart asked me how he was, and when I told her that he wasn't so good, she looked even more nervous than usual. She was afraid one of the geriatrics might have a turn, she said. Two died the week before, she said.

Chris liked to read poetry with me, and often in warm afternoons we would sit in chairs in the balcony room, and talk of poetry. I pushed for Dylan Thomas, and though Chris liked him well enough, he wouldn't have him in first place. He said that Thomas was the storm, but that Frost was the clarity after the storm. He may be right, the more I come to think of it. Other afternoons we would just sit and look over the hospital grounds towards the city. On those occasions we'd talk only when things cropped up: like the charcoal burners' dream, for instance, when Chris and I saw a primary school class crocodiling past towards the library. 'When I was a boy I believed in the stories read to me about the charcoal burners' dream,' said Chris. 'Those poor but sturdy charcoal burners who would share their bread and cheese in the forest with anyone who needed it. No matter how the odds were stacked against them, the charcoal burners believed that if they were brave and kind, then things would work out in the end. And so they always did.'

'I haven't read a story like that for a long time,' I said.

'Neither have I,' said Chris.

He kept trying, though. He had all the guts in the world; well, metaphorically, of course, his lack of it in the other way was the problem. On a Wednesday, when the Reverend Metcalf had gone, but the false tapestry of his laugh still lingered, Chris undressed Nurse McKerrow. 'Nurse McKerrow,' said Chris seriously. 'Why have you taken off your cap? I thought that was against the regulations?' Nurse McKerrow instinctively touched her cap, then went on washing old Mr Webster. 'Nurse McKerrow, you shouldn't take off your stockings in the ward. Not here, Nurse McKerrow.' Colin looked from one to the other, his face sagging because he was so busy trying to realise what was going on that he forgot to keep any expression on his face. Chris drew the blanket up towards his head. 'Not your uniform. My God, Nurse McKerrow, you can't take off your uniform in front of us all.' Jimmy began to laugh. Nurse McKerrow looked across at Chris, and they held each other's glance like a sliver of sunlight from one side of the ward to the other. 'Lovely Nurse McKerrow,' said Chris in a mocking voice of no mockery, 'you have nothing on at all. Nothing at all. How could you be so shameless.'

'Nothing at all,' squealed Jimmy.

'Nothing at all,' said Chris quietly, and smiled at her across the ward.

'You are the biggest fool,' said Nurse McKerrow, smiling with her eyes.

'I see Nurse McKerrow with nothing on at all,' said Chris.

And so he did, and she knew he did and didn't mind, while Colin couldn't understand, and said, 'What's this all about? Bloody Chris Palmer's going mad again.' Even if Nurse McKerrow had taken all her clothes off, Colin wouldn't have seen what Chris saw, because he didn't have that searing, blue spark of imagination that Chris had. That searing, blue spark that burnt away the flux and the dross, and allowed Chris to see reality as it was, and as he wished it to be, both at the same time. And Chris knew the difference between them: that was the price for seeing both, I suppose. The blue spark that gave the light was corrosive, eating away at the bowels of things.

Chris was never bored with life. He hated what he saw at times, but he was never bored with life. He was on a higher voltage than any of the others. When I compared him with the bland conformity of Colin and Richard, or the shrunken appreciation of the world that was Jimmy's, then I couldn't understand why it was that Chris was dying, why the doctors were cutting his bowel up piece by piece. I wasn't prepared to change places with Chris myself, but if I'd had the power I would have let Jimmy, or Colin, any of the others in the ward, die in place of Chris. I'm not afraid to admit it. Like Chris I'm not in the grip of the Liberal Mythology any longer: I don't believe in the charcoal burners' dream. If God had given me the power, I would have said, give Jimmy or Colin the bowel. I could have said it firmly. It doesn't matter how many times we talk about people being equal, it's not true. Some people are worth a dozen of the rest of us. The way perhaps one pohutukawa is worth a dozen tea-tree bushes. You don't like the idea, but I'll say it again. Some people are worth a dozen of the rest of us.

On Chris's last afternoon I was playing poker with Richard. Chris hated cards. Cards is just killing time, he used to say. He hated even to be near people playing cards, as if the trivial and repetitious talk as the cards were played prevented him from reading, or thinking. The ward was warm and quiet. Nurse McKerrow was laughing and talking in the office, and old Mr Webster had his transistor on to listen to the cricket. Chris stood in the balcony room by the windows, his fair hair drab in the sunlight. When I looked up again, he had opened the window and was sitting on the sill itself, facing back towards us. That surprised me, for he didn't like sitting on anything hard. I picked up a red jack, I remember, a red jack which pleased me because it gave me a straight, and when I looked up again Chris was gone. Jimmy was pointing and crying out.

To walk without crutches I had the habit of counting the steps. It helped me to be deliberate, and to anticipate the discomfort. So I counted from one to eleven as I walked into the balcony room. The garden was a long way down, the garden into which I'd released the bird on the day I arrived. Chris lay by the camellias, his blue dressing gown distinct. His flight through the air had pushed up the legs of his pyjamas, and his long, white ankles showed amid the camellia bushes.

Nurse McKerrow phoned downstairs, and a doctor and orderlies came out into the garden. Nurse McKerrow tried to lead me away from the window, but I stayed. I watched the doctor's urgency replaced by resignation, and saw one of the orderlies shake his head. Colin began to construct his emotional defence. 'It must have been an accident,' he said. 'Oh my God, what a thing to see. A fall, an accident like that.' I didn't answer him, but I thought it was the old Liberal Mythology all over again: the charcoal burners' dream.

Usually I won't let myself dwell on it now I'm well. But sometimes when I catch a whiff of some antiseptic, or see those old-style radiators, like the piano accordions that stood along the wall in Men's Surgical Two, then I think of Jimmy, of Puck, of Nurse McKerrow, and of Chris. I have a feeling that they're all still there; that the mood of resignation and reality is waiting for me, waiting for the end of the charcoal burners' dream.

Father and Son

～

HE WATCHED HIS father eating toast, impatient at the deliberate way his father spread the butter and marmalade into each corner before he would eat. 'If we hurry,' he said, 'we could do some before we have to leave.' He meant if his father hurried, for the boy himself had finished, and sat watching. The boy's head was round and the skin of his face clear and brown. He had combed his hair forward with his fingers, and it lay over his forehead like the worn ends of a thick rope.

'He gives me no rest,' his father said.

'You do too much for him,' said his mother. 'You give in to him.' She meant nothing by saying that. At least she didn't mean what she said. The warmth between the boy and his father was an aura. Even though she was at a distance from it, the complacency affected her.

'You two. I don't know,' she said. 'The two of you and that track.'

'He never gets tired of it. He gives me no rest, does he.'

'Next year for high school he'll have to spend more time on his work.'

'We could do some though, before we have to leave,' said the boy.

The end of the shed was given over to the slot-car track. A bulb on an extension cord hung from a nail in the rafters, so at night they could work on it if they wished. There was a tunnel and a viaduct, town streets and freeway. The boy and his father didn't need the light in the summer, even before eight o'clock. They talked about the rock face to go above the tunnel. 'When it's finished,' said his father, 'we could colour some kapok fluff and glue it on as vegetation.'

'I don't want any grass and stuff on it. Just all rock towering up. All rock glistening and high above the tunnel. Please, Dad.'

His father sat on the stool, pushing lacing wire through the pieces of old carton. The wire would hold the plaster of Paris for the cliff face. The boy was mixing it with practised ease.

'I could get some acrylic paint in the yard, I suppose,' his father said. 'Black and grey. It looks best with multiple coats. I remember noticing something at that Pixie Town in Nelson. On one part that was supposed to be volcanic rock it looked like they'd dripped candle wax.'

'Hey, yeah.'

'It's an idea, isn't it?'

'Hey, yeah. Candle grease.' He could see it in his mind's eye. The dark cliff above the tunnel, massy and glistening. 'Yeah,' he said, drawing it out.

'Perhaps I will then.' His father's voice was off-hand, but his hands on the carton and wire were loving.

The boy's mother came out to make them leave. 'You'll both be late again. How many times do I say it.' She held the lunchbag for her husband, and soccer boots and schoolbag for her son.

'He gets me carried away with this jolly set-up here.' He gripped his son by his hair, and rocked his head. 'You're right. I'll be late for work again.' The idea of his work seemed to sap his naturalness, and it was replaced by a jaunty manner which was false. He was an older father than most. As he got on to his moped his thin ankles showed between shoes and trousers, and he clenched the handlebars as if the traffic and the day ahead posed a significant threat. His son ran off at a tangent: a steady run with his bag and boots over his shoulder. The boy was not conscious of any effort, and as he ran he considered other things.

At lunchtime the boy thought he might run down to the council bus yards to see his father, but the teacher wanted the soccer game played against the other Standard Six. 'Flowerday,' he said. 'You'll be captain.' The boy was accustomed to achievement. He sat in the sun to put on his soccer boots, and he thought how to beat the other team.

When that had been accomplished he began to think of his slot cars again, and the cliff that he and his father would build. While the teacher explained the new maths in the afternoon, the boy wondered if they should have an overhang on the cliff face. He imagined it casting a shadow on the track and tunnel entrance from the light on the rafters. He imagined the candle wax and the glistening paint.

After school he went to see his father, jogging over the reclamation short cut, and across the railway sidings. If anyone watched him they thought him a healthy, somewhat stolid boy, but there was a secondary inwardness behind his eyes. The bus fleet was kept behind the transport depot, away from the bustle of the front offices and workshops. The yard was asphalted, and surrounded by a high fence of webbed netting. Most of the buses were still on the runs, and only the dark oil stains on the asphalt which never evaporated, showed their parks. His father's shed was in the far corner. It was filled with cleaning gear for the buses, and racks of destination plates. Some of the plates were for runs discontinued years ago, his father said, but they were kept in the hut still because that had always been their place. The boy reached up as high as he could and gripped the netting. His arms took some of his weight, and there was enough slack in the netting for him to be able to sway a bit back and forth, the netting rattling softly. He could feel the warm sun on his back, and its indirect warmth through the thick, galvanised wire. He hung quite happily, and pushed himself idly back and forth with the netting as he watched the shed to see if his father was there.

Two men in suits came from the offices towards the yard. They came from the bustle of getting things done, towards the stillness of the parking yard. They stepped through the gate not far from where the boy hung on the side netting in the weeds of the railway ground. They walked briskly to show that they had urgent responsibilities. One had a moustache, and he wasn't as important as the other.

The boy could tell that, because when he spoke he kept glancing at the clean-shaven man, but the clean-shaven man remained looking ahead when he said something. The clean-shaven man had an expression as though from a considerable height. A look which said, isn't that so, though, isn't that just so. Neither man took any notice of the boy: to them, he may as well have been a shrub on railway property. With the candour of childhood he swung gently on the netting and watched them carefully.

'He'll be hiding in his shed, Mr McPhail,' said the man with the moustache. 'He spends half his bloody life hiding in the shed. Whether he spends his time playing with himself or not I don't know.' He looked quickly at his superior's face to see how his words were received. Mr McPhail gave a burst of perfunctory laughter, and kept looking ahead. He surveyed the quiet, almost empty yard. He couldn't imagine what a man could do there year after year.

'What does he actually do?' he asked.

'He's supposed to valet the buses and that. He's responsible for making sure they're all secure before the yard is locked at night.'

'We need to make economies if we can, George. Even at his level. This work could be done by a good lad in four hours a day. Give him a call, George,' said Mr McPhail.

'Oiy, Norm,' shouted George. 'Norm — an.' The shed door opened and the boy's father came out and stood.

'What's his name?' said Mr McPhail.

'Flowerday.'

'Is that right, though? Jesus.'

'Yes, Flowerday. What a mouthful, isn't it.'

'He's not a pansy, is he?' said Mr McPhail. George laughed with Mr McPhail, pleased at the humour he had been able to provide with the name of the boy and his father.

Flowerday was walking rather stiffly towards them across the asphalt of the large parking area. George motioned again, using his whole arm as if throwing something over his shoulder. 'Shift yourself, for Christ's sake, Norm,' he shouted. Flowerday began to run awkwardly: more a skipping action. At a distance he put on a placating smile in anticipation, so that he appeared to grimace as he skipped. The three men gathered not far from the boy, but only his father took notice of him, and gave a fluttering gesture with one hand low by his hip: asking forgiveness because he couldn't recognise him, intending reassurance that they'd be together soon, expressing embarrassment that he should be seen in subservience.

'Norm, this is Mr McPhail,' said George.

'I intend to be businesslike,' said Mr McPhail. 'Mr Flowerday, my presence is required to witness a formal warning issued to you by Mr Lamont that your work has not been satisfactory in various instances.' The boy watched his father's posture, heard the formal notification of all the deficiencies in execution of his father's duties, but when George and Mr McPhail turned to walk back to the offices the boy had gone.

He ran purposefully through the railway sidings and over the reclamation track. His brown face was as stolid as ever, and no one was close enough to see his eyes.

The boy's father arrived home after five. He switched off his moped, and sat by the shed. His legs were angled as props to keep the bike balanced; his thin ankles were barely a connection between shoes and trousers. His glossy, full-face helmet was twice the size of the bike's engine, and therefore ridiculous. The boy didn't come out. The father put his moped away in the shed, and saw that the new pieces for the cliff above the tunnel had been broken. 'He said the soccer ball bounced on it accidentally.' His wife came in behind him. 'He said he was sorry about it. He's gone off to play soccer now.' The boy's father stood with one of the carton pieces in his hand, the fresh plaster like whipped cream. 'It does him good playing with kids of his own age,' said his wife cheerfully. Flowerday turned the piece over and over in his hands, as if examining it, almost as if he were still interested in it. 'You'll be able to have a bit of peace and quiet before tea for a change,' his wife said.

Requiem in a Town House

~

MR THORPE CAME off sixteen hundred hectares of hill country when he finally retired, and his wife found a town house for them in Papanui. Town house is a euphemism for a free-standing retirement flat, and retirement flat is a euphemism for things best left so disguised.

Mr Thorpe made no complaint to his wife when he first saw the place of his captivity. She had accepted a firmament of natural things for forty years, and he had promised her the choice of their retirement. Yet as the removal men brought those possessions which would fit into the new home, Mr Thorpe stood helplessly by, like an old, gaunt camel in a small enclosure. Merely by moving his head from side to side he could encompass the whole of his domain and, being long-sighted by nature and habit, he found it hard to hold the immediate prospect of their section in focus.

It wasn't that Mr Thorpe had come to the city determined to die. He didn't give up without a struggle. He was a farmer and a war veteran. He went to church on Sundays with his wife, and listened to the vicar explaining the envelope donation system. He joined the bowling club, and learned which side had the bias. But he could not escape a sense of loss and futility even amid the clink of the bowls, and he grew weary of being bullied by the swollen-chested women at afternoon tea time.

Mrs Thorpe developed the habit of sending her husband out to wait for the post. It stopped him from blocking doorways, and filling up the small room of their town house. He would stand at the letter-box, resting his eyes by looking into the distance, and when the postman came he would start to speak. But the postman always said hello and goodbye before Mr Thorpe could get anything out. There might be a letter from their daughter in Levin, a coloured sheet of specials from the supermarket, or something from the *Readers' Digest* which he had been especially selected to receive. It wasn't the same as being able to have a decent talk with the postman though.

The town house imposed indignities on Mr Thorpe: its mean conception was the antithesis of what he had known. To eat his meals he must sit at what appeared to be a formica ironing board with chrome supports. It was called a dining bar. After a meal Mr Thorpe would stand up and walk three paces to the window to see the traffic pass, and three paces back again. He would look at the knives in their wall holders, and wonder at his shrunken world. He had to bathe in a plastic water-hole beneath the shower. His arthritis prevented him from washing his feet while standing, and he had to crouch in the water-hole on his buttocks, with his knees like two more bald heads alongside his own. He thought of the full-length metal and enamel bath on the farm. Sometimes he went even further back, to the broad pools of the Waipounae River in which he swam as a young man. The bunched cutty grass to avoid, the willows reaching over, the shingle beneath. The turn and cast of the water in the small rapids was like the movement of a woman's shoulder, and the smell of mint was there, crushed along the side channels as he walked.

In the town house even the lavatory lacked anything more than visual privacy. It was next to the living room: in such a house everything, in fact, is next to the living room. Mrs Thorpe's bridge friends could hear the paper parting on its perforations, and reluctantly number the deposits. Mrs Thorpe would talk more loudly to provide distraction, and her husband would sit within the resounding hardboard, and twist his face in humiliation at the wall.

The hand-basin was plastic, shaped like half a walnut shell, and too shallow to hold the water he needed. The windows had narrow aluminium frames which warped in his hand when he tried to open them. The front step was called a patio by the agent, and the wall beside it was sprayed with coloured pebbles and glue.

The section provided little comfort for Mr Thorpe. The fences separating his ground from his neighbours' were so vestigial that he found it difficult not to intrude. One evening as he stood in the sun, like a camel whose wounded expression is above it all, he was abused by McAlister next door for being a nosy old fool. Mr Thorpe was enjoying the feel of the sun on his face, and thinking of his farm, when he became aware that he was facing the McAlisters as they sunbathed on a rug. Mrs McAlister had a big stomach, and legs trailing away from it like two pieces of string. 'Mutton-headed old fool,' McAlister said, after swearing at Mr Thorpe over the fence. Mr Thorpe turned away in shame, for he was sensitive concerning privacy. 'Oiy. Go away, you nosy old fool,' shouted McAlister.

After that Mr Thorpe unconsciously exaggerated his stoop when he was in his section, to reduce the amount of his body which would appear above the fences, and he would keep his eyes down modestly as he mowed the apron lawn, or tipped his rubbish into the bag.

He tried walking in the street, but it was too busy. The diesel trucks doused him with black fumes, and most of the children used the footpath to ride bikes on. The pedestrian lights beckoned him with Cross Now, then changed to Don't Cross whenever he began.

Mr Thorpe took to sleeping in the garage. In the corner was a heavy couch that had been brought in from the farm, but wouldn't fit in the house. It was opposite the bench on which he'd heaped his tools and pots of dried-up paint. At first he maintained a pretence of occupation between bouts of sleep, by sorting screws, nails, tap washers and hose fittings into margarine pottles. As his despair deepened he would go directly to the couch, and stretch out with his head on the old, embroidered cushion. It was one place in which he didn't have to stoop. He had an army blanket with a stripe, for he had begun to feel the chill which is of years, not weather. There he would lie in the back of the garage; free from the traffic, the McAlisters, and the confines of his own town house. He had always been able to sleep well, and in retirement he slept even better. He was granted the release of sleep.

Mr Thorpe would lie asleep with his mouth open, and his breath would whine and flutter because of the relaxed membranes of his mouth and throat. His face had weathered into a set configuration, but it was younger somehow when he slept. His wife played bridge in the living room with her friends, or watched programmes of glossy intrigue. Mr Thorpe lay in the garage, and revisited all the places from which he had drawn his strength. Age is a conjuror, and it played the trick of turning upside down his memory, so that all he had first known was exact and fresh again, and all the things most recent were husks and faded obscurity. Mr Thorpe talked with his father again, soldiered again, courted again; yet when he was awake he forgot the name of the vicar with whom he shook hands every Sunday, and was perplexed when asked for the number of his own town house. Waking up was the worst of all. Waking from the spaciousness and immediacy of past experience, to the walls of his small bedroom closing in, or the paint pots massing on the garage bench.

'He sleeps all the time, just about,' Mrs Thorpe told the doctor, and Mr Thorpe gave a smile which was part apology for being able to sleep so well. 'He must sleep for sixteen or seventeen hours of the twenty-four sometimes. He sleeps most of the day in the garage.'

'Ah, he's got a hideaway then,' said the doctor. He used a jocular tone, perhaps because he was afraid of the response to any serious enquiry. Let sleeping dogs lie is a sound enough philosophy. 'You need more sleep when you're older,' said the doctor. He'd forgotten that the last time Mrs Thorpe came on her own account, he'd told her that old people don't need as much sleep.

'And he hasn't got the same energy anymore. Not the energy he once had. His interest in things has gone. Hasn't it, Rob?' Mr Thorpe smiled again, and was about to say that he missed the farm life, when his wife and the doctor began to discuss the medication he should have.

He never did take any of the medicine, but after the visit to the doctor he tried briefly to interest himself in being awake, for his wife's sake. He sat in front of the television, but no matter how loud he had it, the words never seemed clear. There was a good deal of reverberation, and laughter from the set seemed to drown out the lines before he caught their meaning. He could never share the contestants' excitement over the origin of the term *deus ex machina*.

A dream began to recur. A dream about the town house in Papanui. In the dream he could feel himself growing larger and larger, until he burst from the garage and could easily stand right over the house, and those of his neighbours. And he would take the town house, all the pressed board, plastic and veneers, and crush it as easily as you crush the light moulded tray when all the peaches have been eaten. Then in his dream he would start walking away from the city towards the farmland. He always liked that best in his dream. He was so tall that with each stride he could feel the slipstream of the air about his head, and the hills came up larger with every step, like a succession of held frames.

He told his wife about the dream. She thought it amusing. She told him that he never could get the farm out of his head, could he. She said he should ask McAlister if he would like to go fishing.

In the dream Mr Thorpe never reached the hills: he never actually reached where he was walking to so forcefully. But he seemed to be coming closer time by time. As he drew nearer, he thought it was the country that he knew. The hills looked like the upper Waipounae, and he thought that he would soon be able to hear the cry of the stilts, or the sound of the stones in the river during the thaw, or the flat, self-sufficient whistle made by the southerly across the bluffs at the top of the valley.

Prince Valiant

~

THERE'S SOME UGLY country in New Zealand, don't let them tell you it's not so. Some of it is the country we are trying to form in our own image, perhaps. The Sinclair property was part of it. Bush had been taken off the slopes years before, and the soil was slumping into the gullies, the outwash spoiling what river flats there'd been. Eight and a half thousand hectares of land in an agony of transition. And Sinclair's place was only one of several just the same.

Sinclair had his priorities right. Money for super, then for his stock, then for his family. The country there just died without topdressing every other year. It was no use asking for anything to be done about the shearers' quarters. Over the four seasons that I could remember, nothing had been improved. The wall above the stove was still blistered bare of paint from the oven fire we had in the first year I went. The bunks had only slats, and palliasses with a smell of mildew and string. Under the bottom bunk by the door was a pile of *National Geographic* magazines with the covers torn off. I could look up from the glossy artificiality of winter in Vermont, or West Irian religious rites, and see the scoured track to the yard. Dog kennels with the beaten ground to the extension of the chains, and a tide mark beyond each of a hundred mutton bones. The bones stuck from the ground like defective teeth. No one ever came from the *National Geographic* to see it all, even when it was summer in Vermont.

I joined the others at Sinclair's. The gang didn't come up to full strength until well into the summer. I spent several months on forestry work at Dargaville, and started shearing again when they moved up country. Cathro still ran things. We had a fresh roustabout, but Neddy was the only new shearer. Neddy was younger than the rest of us: all elbows, knees, and eyes of a level intensity if you bothered to notice. Neddy was a good shearer. Tall, so that he suffered in the back, but flowing in his style and with the ability to calm sheep with his grip. Top-class shearers have that. Others, like Norman and Speel Harrison, transfer their impatience so the sheep will struggle if they can. I've seen Speel brain them with the handpiece when his temper was up.

Neddy wasn't disliked, and his shearing ability was recognised. He was easy and without malice. His laugh and brief replies were at once obliging and dismissive. He never drew close into the group. Perhaps it was his subtle lack of deference, or a companion's realisation, after a time with Neddy, that he considered one person very much like another and placed no great store on any, least of all himself.

Neddy was the one we called Prince Valiant, because of his car. It was a Chrysler Charger. He had it resprayed while they were working at the place before Sinclair's. A metallic green of gloss and iridescence. For some reason he'd never replaced the bumpers, and the brackets stuck out like small antlers at the charge. In scroll work on each side were the words Prince Valiant. The letters were chrome yellow with black edging, and a lance was the underline, piercing the letters.

So he was Prince Valiant, you see. At times there was something of a sneer in its use. The car was thought a pretension by the Harrisons and Sinclair. Neddy didn't seem to mind. He spent a lot of time on his car. He had twin speakers mounted by the back window, and a line of clammy little monsters hanging suspended there. They were green and purple, the colours of cloudy jellies. He had a file box in the front passenger's footwell, and he kept all his country and western tapes there. People like Willie Nelson and Whitey Schaeffer, Efram Nathan and Webb Pierce. Often during breaks, or after lunch, Neddy would go and sit in his car with the door open. He'd play his tapes, drink beer and gaze over Sinclair's raddled land.

Neddy talked to me only once about the car. I was sorting and oiling some combs, and he was making himself new sack slippers. A few deft tucks, and some stitches with the bag needle. 'I like to drive,' he said. 'I like to drive at night. Close everything up, turn on the music, and drive. At night what's outside could be any-where. It just falls away behind. The music and me in there driving. It's a whole world.' He looked at me quickly with intent eyes. The laugh he gave disparaged him-self, lest my reply should do it. Neddy had been expelled from school. He couldn't get the hang of it, he told me. All the time he was at school, Neddy felt he was get-ting pushed around and, having no sense of the existence of other people, he could-n't see any reason for being pushed around. Neddy's family hadn't done much by him, I gather. Cathro knew a bit about it. All I ever heard from Neddy was a com-ment in the shed when the Harrisons used the bale stencil to brand the roustabout's backside. He said his father had used a hot clothes iron on his mother

Another thing which kept Neddy a bit apart was the intensity of his interest in a girl in Te Tarehi. It had been going on most of the summer, Cathro said. No matter where they were working, every second or third night Neddy went all the way down to Te Tarehi to see his girlfriend. He'd put on his blue slacks and stock boots after tea, and that would be the last of him until the Charger came rumbling back up the track. Norman and Speel complained about being woken up when Neddy came into the quarters late, so several times when Neddy had had more beer than usual, he just switched off the car, and slept right there. I've come out before breakfast and seen him lying asleep, his polished stock boots dangling from his ankles, and his face pressed into the crease at the back of the seat.

Neddy's girlfriend was a source of undeclared envy. Speel and I resented being left with a pile of National Geographics without covers, and a monologue from his brother about the Social Credit philosophy. Speel tried to convince himself that Neddy's girl-friend in Te Tarehi wasn't worth it. He said he'd met someone who knew her: that she was flat-chested and the town bike. Neddy would carry on getting ready, waxing his stock boots, or taking his blue slacks from the newspaper underneath his pal-liasse. 'Bite your arse,' he'd say with a smile. The less Neddy said about his girl in Te Tarehi, the more desirable she became.

We were due to finish the last mob at Sinclair's on a Friday. On Thursday evening Neddy came out again ready for town. The ends of his hair were wet because he'd been cleaning his face. His blue slacks had pewter buttons on the back. In one hand he held three beer bottles by their necks like chickens. He laid them along the bench seat on the passenger's side. Sinclair had come down to catch him. 'You could do a job for me, Prince Valiant,' he said. Sinclair was pleased to demonstrate his familiarity with the joke. 'If you can get your mind off shagging, that is.' Sinclair tried to take some paper from his trouser pocket, but the trousers were too tight, and the pocket opening was pressed flat. 'It's a note for the Wrightson's agent.' Sinclair squirmed and swore. 'You'll need to go to his house. The office will be shut.'

'I won't be going that way.'

'There's only one way to Te Tarehi, for God's sake!' Sinclair gave a burst of laughter, drawing the others into laughter too. Neddy made himself comfortable in his car. He switched on a tape. Sinclair had the folded sheet at last from his pocket, and he came confidently towards Neddy's open window.

'Bite your arse,' said Neddy gently, and the Charger moved away. The misshapen creatures jiggled in the back window, the posts of the yards made a pattern of reflections in the green, metallic paint.

'Bastard,' said Sinclair. He went into the quarters to find Cathro and complain. 'Cathro, Cathro,' he called.

The Charger didn't come back during the night. Before we started next morning Cathro rang the two other homesteads in the district, in case Neddy had broken down, but they knew nothing. Then, after ten, Mr Beaven rang back. Neddy's car had been seen in a gully on the Ypres Creek turn-off, and Neddy was dead.

Cathro and I drove up. Mr Beaven and his head shepherd were there. They were waiting for the constable from Te Tarehi. The car had missed the corner and struck the yellow creek bank. From the road there seemed to be no damage. The metallic paint was untouched beneath the fine dust that the dew had set. But when we climbed down we found the Charger had struck with force. Mr Beaven and his man had covered Neddy and the dash with a rug from the back seat. His legs lay in a restful pose partly out of the door. I could see from the soles of his stock boots, how little wear they'd had. The flaccid monsters hanging in the back window jostled each other in the wind.

It was an intrusion to wait alongside the car. We went back up to the road and waited for the police. We leant on Mr Beaven's car and talked. 'He's been driving around here night after night,' said Mr Beaven. 'We keep seeing the lights from the homestead, along Kelly's Cut, the through road, and here as well. At times we've passed him on the road coming up. A green Chrysler without bumpers. He must have been covering a hundred miles or more a night, just cruising round.'

'Listening to his music,' said Cathro. 'Neddy loved to be by himself, listening to his music as he drove. The boys called him Prince Valiant.'

'I saw that on the car,' said Mr Beaven. 'All doo-dahed up all right.' Cathro didn't say anything about Neddy's girlfriend in town, the girl that each of us had imagined according to his own expectation, and who had no other life.

Those nights Neddy had left us, he'd fired up on beer and music, driving along the top roads. It didn't say much for our company, but then ugly country breeds ugly people, I suppose. Even so, the death of someone you don't know well can have its acid, for without the protection of emotion there's a clarity in what is bleak and random. As we sat and waited in the morning, I thought of Neddy driving alone, with his dashlights, the monsters, the songs of Whitey Schaeffer and Webb Pierce. And, in the darkness, that poor country slipping by.

Effigies of Family Christmas

~

THERE ARE TO be eleven of them. Meredith, and Alun with his family, are the last to arrive. They pull over when the car has rattled past the cowstop. Alun and Meredith look across their father's land to the sea. Dry pasture, with sinuous movement only in those paddocks which have been shut up. A breeze from the sea: the land breeze is rare, a memory of the night. The beach between the land and the sea is an uneasy meeting place. It cants steeply, and the unstable shingle rattles back behind each wave. The brothers feel no need to comment on what they see, for superimposed upon it is their common experience. They have long before made any communication that mattered with this landscape. Alun lets his breath out in an eloquence which says, yes, here it is. 'Why are we stopping?' says Jane. It reminds her father to go on down the track towards the house.

The family appear on the verandah, come out on to the grass, when they see Alun's car. Mother has a thick apron over her dress. The apron has Pegs written on its broad, front pocket, but she uses it only in the kitchen. David's boy dances in front of the car. 'They're here. They're here. We can have our presents.'

'Presents after dinner, Rhys. You know that.'

Alun and Meredith see their father and Uncle Llewelyn behind the others, both with the same shy smile of reticence struggling with affection. Their father has his ankle-height slippers on despite the heat, and a pale, blue shirt that was bought to go with the best suit. 'Ah hah,' says Uncle Llewelyn during the greetings, 'Ah hah', and he smacks his hands together like two bricks, to show his relish in the family reunion. A light aircraft flies overhead, an intrusion on communal solitude. The family watch it pass; the sound comes back in the amphitheatre of the hills behind the house.

'Now we're all here,' says Mother, and she leads the way into the house. Meredith and David linger at the front door, touching the verandah supports as they wish to reach out to each other. The unfamiliarity of brothers is a surprise to them.

'Nothing much changes, does it?' says Meredith. 'It's stepping right back again.' David thinks his brother lives too far away, and has forgotten what things were like. Then he absorbs new things into the pattern of the old. 'Try me then,' says Meredith.

'The open hayshed wasn't built when you left.'

'It was. I remember collecting eggs in it. Several of the leghorns used to lay there.'

'No, that was the old stack. It wasn't even in the same place, but further back towards the yards. That hayshed wasn't built till you'd gone to Auckland.'

'It seems the same to me.'

'The farm's going back. I come over when I can, and Uncle Llewelyn still helps a lot. But Dad's not the farmer he was. There's hardly any cropping done at all now. All the fences need work. He still has sound stock though. I'll say that. Always good with stock, Dad was.'

'He hasn't the energy anymore, I suppose.'

'No.'

As they go through into the living room they can hear the excitement of Michael and Jane, helping Rhys put the presents beneath the tree. And they can smell the Christmas dinner. The fragrance is of this Christmas dinner, and all the others. There is a poignancy in the repetition. 'And you're not married yet,' says David.

'I've kept my freedom.'

'What's the matter with you? Deirdre, Meredith says that he dislikes women.'

'No, I didn't.'

'What girl would have him?' says Deirdre.

'I don't know why we married one of them each,' says Margaret. They've nothing to recommend them.'

'Just sheer effrontery caught us off guard,' says Deirdre.

'Animal magnetism. We all have it.' Meredith makes as if to kiss them both.

Uncle Llewelyn listens as he stands in the kitchen to enjoy the preparations for dinner. He marvels at the relaxed abuse, says 'Ah hah', smiles at the contestants in turn. Mother pushes on his back and he moves amiably out of the kitchen.

'I think we'll dish up,' she says to the other women.

Three roast geese, larded with bacon strips, and with a thyme stuffing. Bread sauce, peas, new potatoes, sweet corn, and salad as a concession to the heat. The sweat runs down the side of David's face as he eats. The quick sweat of a fit man. He opens the windows behind him, and the sound of the sea and the gulls comes louder to those of the family grown unaccustomed to the place. David, his parents and Uncle Llewelyn are no more aware of it than their own heartbeats. Rhys is rebuked for wanting to pull his cracker before it is time. 'Own geese, own bacon,' says Uncle Llewelyn on his brother's behalf. 'Everything but the corn.' Mother is moved to a further distribution.

'Meredith, you'll have some more peas and potatoes.'

'I couldn't, thanks.'

'Nonsense.' She spoons vigorously, as she would have done twenty-five years before.

'All our own, as your father says.' His father's smile refuses credit for what he has achieved, and what he hasn't said.

Steamed pudding, with ten cent pieces smuggled in on the way from the kitchen to please the children. Pavlova, fruit salad and farm cream which is not whipped, yet so thick that it must be encouraged with a spoon. Some of the crackers don't explode, but all yield party hats, debased elephants and riddle sheets. Nuts, ginger, chocolate, and each adult pretending not to know what's black and white and read all over.

The heat and occasion redden Mother's face; not her cheeks, but beneath her eyes, the side of her nose, and again along the chin line. Emotion in their mother takes a form of fierceness which they remember from their childhood. Margaret lets slip that Alun has bought her a car for Christmas. It's waiting for her in Sydney. 'I hope it brings happiness,' says his mother, and is angry for some time afterwards. She wants no glimpse of a way of life which is not her own. Alun is general manager designate for Australasia, but here Mother is determined he shall not outgrow the old relationships. 'Alun was always the complaining one,' she explains to the family. 'Always wanted something better than he had. I remember him moaning when he had to walk up to the school bus in winter. Neither of the other boys minded the same.' Alun smiles. He understands that every mother must punish a son who can succeed without her. Yet his mother's intensity surprises him. David is the favourite: he became a farmer like his father. None of them resent that, least of all David, who has the greatest cause. Being the favourite is a test of character. 'You were always difficult to please,' says Mother to Alun. 'Maybe Sydney will please you if your own country doesn't.'

The men sit on the verandah. They drink the beer which was not considered seemly at the table. Uncle Llewelyn is very much like his brother. His legs are too short for his heavy shoulders and forearms, and his face is lumpy and indistinct. Mother always says the brothers are typical of Welsh pudding-face working class. Uncle Llewelyn was his battalion's wrist wrestling champion in North Africa. He and his brother sit there, with green, crepe party hats above their lined, pudding faces. They confront the hills of the farm with composure, and add their presence although saying little. They are not accomplished with machines, and listen to David talking of the new seed drier. He is acknowledged to understand the voice of the motor. Yet with all his enthusiasm and youth, he has the gentleness of his father and uncle. A gentleness compounded to sadness perhaps. In many years the nature of it has eluded Alun and Meredith, yet on each return they recognise its presence. As the scent of ocean is never forgotten, yet impossible to convey without its presence.

'It's a nuisance to be growing old,' says Uncle Llewelyn. 'Do you know I can't sleep a night through now without a piss. I'm up for a piss every hour or two. And I find it difficult sometimes to swallow toast and bread. It gets stuck at the top of my chest.' The others laugh, and Uncle Llewelyn is not offended. It is accepted that a list of ailments will be mocked provided there's no immediate pain.

'A wife would cure everything,' says David. It is the best joke of the day.

The children have been waiting for the women to finish the dishes. They raise a cry for presents. 'Time for presents then, is it,' says Uncle Llewelyn, when Mother has given approval by her arrival. He carries Jane effortlessly to the lounge, the broad forearm a bench for her. The Christmas tree is a pine branch in a brass preserving pan, and the family presents are heaped around it. Mother allows the children to announce and deliver each in turn. It is the social ritual of which Confucius so approved. To Uncle Llewelyn from Meredith, to Alun and Margaret from Mum and Dad, to Uncle David from Michael, to Jane from Grandfather. Mother allows no distraction from the interlacing address to family members. Whatever the disparity of age or conviction, she will have it established that this is the family; this is the pledge to a continuity which cannot be disputed. This is the lineage of them all. To Mum from Deirdre; to Grandfather from Rhys. There is a lot of nodding and display; appraisals and thanks. The children wrench out their presents, but Mother picks at the sellotape, and folds the special paper with the future in mind. Jane cries because of the excitement, and because she hasn't a separate present for Uncle Llewelyn. Meredith gapes a little in the heat. He thinks of the beer still in the fridge.

It is the women's turn to rest, and the men's responsibility to take the children for a swim in the stock dam. David and Meredith carry bottles of beer and orange, to put in the water there. Michael is amazed by all the droppings, and Rhys, though younger, laughs at his ignorance of the country. 'But there's poop everywhere,' says Michael.

'A farm's mostly poop,' says Uncle Llewelyn. 'Poop and grass. Two forms of the same thing.'

'I don't like it,' says Jane.

Uncle Llewelyn is very gallant. 'Quite right. Ladies never do,' he says.

The ground of the gateways is worn bare by the passing of sheep, but, more than that, the earth itself is worn away, so that there is a dip which becomes a puddle in the winter. The gates drag even so, and are held by a collar of thick wire. The ends of the wire have been turned to a latch by the power of their father's hands.

The stock dam is large enough to keep the water clean. No one considers trusting the sea, for its undertow is a local legend. There remains a sense of irony, however, if only visual. For the group of them gather at the stock dam while the ocean stretches to the horizon. The three children squeal, and stir up the mud to make the water yellow. They smack with their hands, and splash the men on the bank.

'I stood on something.'

'Eels, eels,' they shout, enjoying the terror of their own imagination.

'When do you leave for Australia?' David asks.

'I must be in Sydney in three weeks.' Alun lies on his side, propped on an elbow. He draws grass stems from their sheaths, and lances them into the pond. A flock of yellow heads sweeps by, bobbing like corks.

'Sometimes I feel I'd like a change myself. Living and dying where you were born isn't so wonderful a prospect.'

'It makes self-deception that much harder.' Alun plucks the grass, thinking of the way to continue. The wind blows his lank hair from one side of his face to the other. 'Change can sometimes seem a personal progress, when the essential journey bears no relation to distance at all.' Alun was able to talk of things that would make his family uneasy from any other source.

'Get your head right under, Michael,' calls Uncle Llewelyn. As he watches the children he shares their joy. He laughs when they do, his calls match theirs. He sits with his brother, a little apart from his nephews.

'I'd quite like to farm in Australia,' says David. 'I saw parts of Victoria that I could be happy in.'

'Imagine Mum and Dad if you went.' Wearing Joseph's coat has never been easy. The skuas gobble like turkeys, or give their keening cry, which hints at an essential hollowness of things.

Meredith, David and Alun watch their father. He has worn glasses for years, yet they are still an oddity. He puts them on awkwardly. The thin stems puzzle his fingers. The glasses are incongruous across his seamed, moon face. Glasses and hats don't suit their father. He has greater idiosyncrasies, with half a life of another way, and not even a letter since his parents died. Only Uncle Llewelyn can join in tacit reminiscence. Nothing is regretted it seems, but something sacrificed nevertheless for the new life. Alun points out to his brothers that their father never faces the sea when he rests. As a test they stand and talk to him, drawing him around to them. But soon he unthinkingly turns again, not right away from them, but so he can regard the downland, and the gully running up towards the road. He lifts his glasses, and rubs where they have rested. The Welsh are not great lovers of the sea in spite of all their coastline. Welsh men are miners, preachers, farmers and soldiers. Beneath the extravagance of song and poetry, an inward-looking people. Their father wasn't poet or singer, but he had a Celtic heart. His absurd glasses catch the sun, so that for an instant as his sons watch, the lenses silver over and his calm eyes are lost. His best blue shirt is open, and the hair of his chest begins abruptly at the razor's edge, grey and so dense it hides the skin. Meredith moves to get more beer, and Uncle Llewelyn brings his brother's glass and his own. David tells the children to keep away from the top end of the dam where there might be snags. They have had enough. Rhys and Michael begin to quarrel over the one stick they have between them. Jane is thin, and as she comes from the deeper water her knee caps flick up and down as she shivers. 'Throw that stick away now, boys,' says Alun. 'We're going back to the house.'

'Let's all play cricket,' says Michael. 'We always play cricket on Christmas Day.'

Uncle Llewelyn is asleep on the verandah. His hands are as broad as they are long, and the folded skin of his brows almost hides his eyes. The dogs are not usually allowed within the house enclosure, but nothing is denied the children on Christmas Day. So sheepdogs play awkwardly at being pets. Jane has gathered Uncle Llewelyn's presents on his lap while he sleeps: tobacco pouch, patterned socks, petrol vouches, handkerchiefs, cigars, parka, a box of twelve-gauge cartridges number five shot. There must be a good deal more to Uncle Llewelyn than such things represent, but it's not subject to easy scrutiny. If he is ever disappointed at being a supernumerary at his brother's Christmas, there is no sign of it. No outward show of affection either, yet they are rarely far apart. Every task on both farms which could not be done by one man, was accomplished by the two of them through the years.

Meredith stands for a time beside his mother, and they watch Alun and David play cricket with the children. Physical work hasn't yet stiffened David, and he is lithe and admirable. Alun has tapering, office legs. 'Soft as butter,' says his mother. 'The boy's as soft as butter.' There is an element of real contempt. 'And what does he want to go to Australia for, I'd like to know. We kept hearing how well he was doing in his job here.'

'It's a big job he's got over there. I don't think you realise just how much responsibility Alun has in his work. You'd be surprised, I think.'

'I blame Margaret as well. All these ideas. A car for herself, she said, and talk of a sauna bath in the house.'

'You know it's not Margaret. Things have always been different in the city; different tempo, other goals.'

'What Alun had wasn't good enough. He was always the discontented one.' She wouldn't relent. Any threat to old values and established patterns was received with bitterness. David must endure being favourite, Meredith being taken for granted, and Alun the guilt of finding his parents' life insufficient.

Tea is an attack again upon the food of midday, with the addition of ham, Christmas cake and strawberries. Daylight saving makes it only afternoon, and there are hours and hours for travelling, Mother says. She is reluctant to think of any member of the family leaving. For this one day in the year she can protect herself from the bare hills.

The bacon on the last goose has shaped itself to the breast, and Uncle Llewelyn makes a sandwich of it and thyme stuffing. 'Costs are beating us,' says Uncle Llewelyn. 'No matter what we do about production, the costs beat us every time. Most of the expenses we have no control over.' Uncle Llewelyn turns to his food again, and the pause is more than their mother can allow.

'Every union hanger-on in the country, every unnecessary middle-man and bureaucrat taking a fat living.' Her bitterness is unashamed. The family, each with an individual expression of wry restraint, carry on eating as she talks. Mother hasn't been educated to expect two sides to every situation, and the lifetime here hasn't suggested it.

'Workers in the city . . .' begins Margaret, but then she catches Alun's eye and falters. His mother carries on ready to start on the freezing workers, and her voice quickens in anticipation.

Michael puts strawberries into his mouth one after another. The sequence goes on and on. Uncle Llewelyn watches in admiration. David argues some point with his mother. 'Have you got the tree hut ready?' Meredith asks his mother. When he was ten David stole a fruit cake, and hid in the tree hut all night. No one had disturbed him, and the next morning he had returned for his breakfast, bringing the remains of the fruit cake as a token of submission. The children enjoy the story. David only grins and says he can't remember it. Each of the boys is the subject of some childhood anecdote, and the wives have learnt to join the laughter and the provocation.

Alun helps his mother sort the dishes to be washed. For a while they are alone by the window, and approach each other with a concern that always has the guise of exasperation. 'This job.' The manner in which she says it has a message in itself. 'This job of yours in Australia. Your father and I hoped that you'd be happy in Auckland.'

'The firm has its central office in Sydney. It's the opportunity, you see. It won't come again.'

'I thought at least you might have considered your father. I thought your own country would satisfy you.'

'It wasn't easy. Margaret and I spent a lot of time talking it over.'

'But you're going nevertheless.' Each, with an effort, says no more about it, for it is Christmas Day. They work in silence until Deirdre comes back from collecting the best cutlery.

'Uncle Llewelyn and Michael are still eating,' she says.

The view is ever the same from the window above the bench. The blank wall of the garage, old when he was a boy, older now. The wood is swollen and distorted as rotten wood is. Successive coats of paint disguise the worst of it. At the corners the decay is complete, for there the water can get into the joints of the timber. He could put a fist right through it without pain. On the garage wall are the two safes for dog tucker, or game before it's dressed: gauze sides and simple wooden latches. The brown grass of the lawn ironed to the contours of the ground. The macrocarpa hedge with holes maintained in its denseness by nesting birds. The pipe-frame gate to keep out the hens and dogs, and a clean sack folded on the path before it. A pipe hammered into the garden, with the radio earth attached. And the dry bank beyond the macrocarpa, with the ice-plant like a wave mocking the drought. Behind it the pines, the downs, the persistence of the ocean's sound.

At the end of the day they are at the front of the house, and Meredith and Alun are wanting to leave. The children are still playing. 'Don't let the dog lick you, Michael. Never let a dog lick you,' says Mother. 'They've got germs you see, dear. In their mouths. Wash your face and hands, and use the hand towel.' Margaret begins to gather their things into the car. When Michael comes from washing, Alun tells his mother that they must leave. 'But you can stay the night. Of course you can stay the night. The children would love that.' She is sweeping them briskly along with her opinions, establishing any opposition to her views as selfish. Alun is surprised at the anger it raises within him. Anger not so much at her doing it, but at her assumption that he would not recognise it, that he and his brothers had not known and suffered it all their lives.

'We can't stay, Mother. I told you when we wrote. I'm sorry, but we must be away by eight, with the distance we've got before us.'

'Very well.' The red patches on her face flame.

Their father is baffled by the need to say goodbye. He shakes his head as he says the words. He puts a large hand on Michael's head, and then Jane's. 'God bless now,' he says. The cadence of his youth has never been lost.

David comes with his brothers up to the turn-off. The three of them get out and stand together for the last time that day. 'I may have had my last Christmas here,' says Alun.

'Australia's not that far away.'

'It's not so much that. Mum's getting worse. All this compulsive manipulation of other people. We seem to have lost patience with each other. It's difficult for Margaret too.'

'That's why I've come this far with you, in a way. Not Margaret, but Mum, and what she's been trying to tell you both all day, and couldn't. The more difficult it was, the angrier she got.'

'About what?'

'Dad's going blind. One eye's all but had it now, and the other is just a matter of time. There's nothing can be done, they say, nothing can be done.' The brothers look down to avoid the glare of the setting sun. Margaret has no knowledge of what has been said. She leans across the car to the window.

'We should be starting, Alun.' He gives an odd gesture of dismissal and agreement.

'Is that the way of it then,' he says to David.

'We should go back down to them,' says Meredith.

'Not now. Not on Christmas Day. It'll only upset them both. Dad won't talk about it, even to me. Like everything else it's left to Mum. And this time she can't do it. For blindness she can't find a beginning.' David doesn't find it easy himself. So little is words, so much is feeling. 'I'll write to you,' he says, 'and I'll get Mum to write to you.'

Meredith and Alun watch him go back; his long shadow reaches down the track ahead of him. 'Poor Dad, poor Mum,' says Alun. 'She's been wanting to tell us all day. That's what it was. She couldn't do it.'

'We could still go back.'

'Dad would know why. He wouldn't care for himself, but our knowledge of it is what he fears most. Christmas Day, and Dad's going blind, eh Merdy. There's a vision for you. Blind, calm Dad, and Mum keeping the world away from him. And there's nothing to be done, David says. You see that. Nothing can be done.'

They watch David almost at the house. The wind blows in from the sea as ever, and the seagulls cry our lives away on those long New Zealand beaches.

Monologue and Absent Friends

~

DEATH, OLD CAPTAIN, it is time, let us raise anchor. Good, isn't it? Baudelaire. The Byronic mood is common to us all; a little bravado when things are at a distance. I have a notebook. I jot down good ones I come across. Some of them, I must admit, are salvaged from digest articles in dentists' waiting rooms, rather than original sources. You can sneer now you're told, Watson, but you liked it well enough, as the Actress said. When the weather's bright, so am I. More and more the old theory of the humours appeals to me. I haven't noticed any difference after taking those, in fact. Three weeks now. Even God cannot change the past. Agathon. Yes, well it is rather self-conscious perhaps. Watch out because I'm going to slip in at least one of my own before we're through. You won't pick it. It'll be wasted, I suppose. They all get attributed to accepted wits. Like metal filings and magnets. Half of the stuff put down to Voltaire, Wilde and Dorothy Parker, was said by men called Colin Walters, undersecretary for tourism, or whatever. To him that hath. Do you know they've even got me swimming in the heated pool now? Good, good they coo, if I as much as make a stroke or two. A friend of mine in classics said that traduce should mean seduce three times. No, I haven't seen her for weeks. I haven't even been to the house. My sons think that I've got special work that keeps me away. Let me tell you about Chang Ch'ang-i, a temporary favourite of the Empress Wu. He built himself a palace, and an enemy came in the night and wrote on the gate, for how long can a spider's web endure? Chang had it rubbed out, but it kept being written again, so he left it alone and wrote beneath in his own hand — even one day is enough. I thought you would. Yes, oh yes, he was decapitated when the Chang brothers fell. These colours that you keep showing me, and the names of colours. Isn't it rather a traditional approach? I like only green, brown and yellow. Puce, mauve, magenta aren't colours. They're names from women's magazines. Green because it's hope and youth, obvious enough; Marvell, Dylan Thomas. Brown as it's the sere age. Yellow is the colour of the soul, as Van Gogh knew. The man's mind is bright, bright yellow inside, if you cut it quickly enough. That's a good one! I don't know many from Jung. Just, all haste is of the devil. Yours is definitely better. It's idleness breeds all our virtues, Faulkner, occurs to me. I tried to do some work on the metaphysical poets, but I kept having spells of tears and dizziness. Any sustained note will make me cry; a train whistle, a violin. I know you said it could have that effect. All right. Oh, I will. No man is a hypocrite in his pleasures. If you're ever stuck for a source plump for Johnson or Toynbee. They're both so prolific, you see, and almost impossible to check. You know my methods, Watson. How long would such a course of treatment take? No, it's just that it sounds rather like the procedure I went through in April, and that had no lasting benefit, you remember. Yes, so you said. Hee, hee. You foolish man, you do not even know your own foolish business. The Earl of Chesterfield. I'll repeat it for you slowly so you can get it down. Hee, hee, hee. I don't quite know why. Yes, it's a sleeper. One of my favourites. You'll find it coming back to you with a smile, over and over again. There's something of a transferred epithet perhaps. I'm taking a lot more exercise than before it happened. Every second night I run for twenty minutes. I'll die of a heart attack after all perhaps. 'Tis a mad world, my masters. Since you talk about music so often I've begun listening more seriously myself. I went to the quartet recitals even. It's regional though, most of his stuff, don't you feel? Perhaps you're right; perhaps ethnic. There's that temptation of introspection. Always there. The eternal silence of those infinite spaces terrifies me, Pascal said. It's disconcerting to look back and see the fetishes of each part of your life for what they are. It saps any true commitment to the present, you see. Nothing is real once it has happened. Providing ourselves with a motivation is the real necessity. That's where you and I are. You manage it presumably. The mass of men live lives of quiet desperation. One of the great ones, isn't it? The irrefutable simplicity of it takes you by the throat. It's the juxtaposition of those two last words. Yes, it's a pity it's so well known really. Sorry, I was just looking out at the garden. You were saying. Yes. Yes. Well, why not. Did you know that punch meant fornicate in seventeenth century West Country usage? Hee, hee, haa, haa. No, but that's quite true. I came across it years ago. Now that I've told you, you'll never forget it. You see if I'm not right. You should know how the mind works. Right! It's the useless, inconsequential knowledge which remains. I must be one of the few men in the world to know the maiden name of Whistler's mother. I hardly recognised my room, did I tell you? The new faculty member has taken down all my Pissarro and Sisley prints, and covered the walls with photographs concerned with World War One. Bethmann Hollweg, Grey, and Sazonoff. I've no idea. No. All in grainy realism. All, all are gone, the old familiar faces. Lamb. The minority is always right, Ibsen said. What were we saying? No, no. I used to smoke a pipe myself, and enjoy secondhand smoke. If it's a worthy tobacco, of course; Three Nuns or somesuch. A filter is everything in a pipe, I think. He drops in sometimes, yes. Usually he likes to talk of his newspaper work. He seems to be moving into popular journalism, and away from textual criticism. That and his garden. Well, he's very keen on his garden. Flowering annuals mainly. Each of us forms for himself an illusion of the world, said Maupassant. Yes, I remember you suggesting that, however I've come to fear the library in some ways, which is sad. Passed over to the majority, burial chambers, and the attendants padding respectfully about, keeping the dust from the top of the sarcophagi. Hall Caine was prodigiously successful in his time, and now he has been judged. Terence Rattigan initially thought it an honour to collaborate with our own Hector Bolitho. What's Hector to Hecuba now I wonder. Yes. I think you've got something there. I don't get out to new places enough: places that haven't a miasma of association. How many in a group? All of an age, and students. Maybe. The young always despise a compromise. I'm willing to do it, if you feel such things help. I need more action, less contemplation, I know. It's a concentric concentration of thought: round and round, an increasing focus on a diminishing area until the warp of reality burns through with the white heat of it, and the space wind whispers from the chasm. One learns to howl with the wolves. I've been watching the creeper on the window stone. It's beginning to turn red with the autumn frosts. The leaves are like pygmy hands on the sill, and their bodies must be hanging there somewhere, waiting, listening. Inanimate personalities are everywhere, aren't they? But I'm taking too much time. I hadn't realised it was so late. Ah, ah yes, I like it. No, really I do. I'll return the compliment of writing it down. We shall find life tolerable once we have accepted to be always ill at ease. And it's Flaubert, you said. Wonderful. I'll pursue the context when I have an opportunity. If I go now there'll be a chance for me to lie down before tea. Trevor's been spitting on the butter again. Yes he has, hee, hee. For what do we live, but to make sport for our neighbours, and laugh at them in our turn? You won't find anyone better than Jane Austen at demonstrating foibles. Really? It's a kind offer. I appreciate it, but anything planned tends to become something of a threat. I must let you get on. Not at all. I'll go and sit in my room. I can tell by the shadows from the wall when it's teatime. Lie thee down oddity. You recognise it? Yes, when the shadow of the wall reaches the rhododendron I know it's time for tea. The past is a foreign country: they do things differently there. Oh, that Hartley. Not a bit. Tell her, tell them all, not to worry about me, not to think of me at all. Even the knowledge of concern can be difficult to bear.

Thinking of Bagheera

~

'YOU DON'T MUCH care for pets, I know,' says my neighbour. She smiles bleakly across the patio, and sips my Christmas sherry. She is pleased to be able to categorise me so utterly. It won't do to try to tell her of Bagheera, though what she says brings him back to me.

The cat was not even mine, but had been bought for my younger sisters. They soon excluded him from their affections, however. My sisters preferred those possessions which could be dominated. Compliant dolls who would accept the twisting of their arms and legs, and easily cleaned bright, plastic toys. The cat went away a lot, and had for them a disconcerting smell of life and muscle.

My father named the cat Bagheera. My father had a predilection for literary allusion, to use his own phrase. Not that I heard him use it about himself. He was referring to Mr McIntyre, his deputy. I remember my father talking about Mr McIntyre to Mum; pausing to preface his remarks with a disparaging smile, and saying that Mr McIntyre had a predilection for literary allusion. I caught the tone although I couldn't understand the words. There was blossom on the ground that evening, for as he said it I looked out to the fruit trees, and saw the blossom blowing on the ground. Pink, apricot blossom, some lying amid the gravel of the drive, a fading tint towards the garage.

In the evening Bagheera and I would go for a walk. We agreed on equality in our friendship. We would maintain a general direction, but take our individual digressions. In the jungle of the potato rows or sweet corn I would hide, waiting for him to find me, and rub his round head against my face.

The cat brought trophies to the broad window sill of my bedroom. Thrush wings, fledglings, mice and once a pukeko chick. My father hated the mess. He always drove the cat from the window when he saw it there. Yet often at night, waking briefly, I would look to the window and Bagheera would be there, a darker shape against the sky, his eyes at full stretch in the dusk. I was the only one in the family who could whistle him. It was a loyalty I would sometimes abuse just to impress my friends. Within a minute or two he would appear, springing suddenly from the roof of the sheds, or gliding from beneath the red currant bushes at the bottom of the garden. Beauty is not as common in this world as the claims that are made for it. But Bagheera's black hide flowed like deep water, and his indolent grace masked speed and strength. At times I would put my face right up to him to destroy perspective, and imagine him a full-size panther, see the broad expanse of his velvet nose, and his awesome Colgate smile.

In December Bagheera got sick. For three days he didn't come despite my whistling. We were having an end-of-term pageant at school and I was a wise man from the east, so I didn't have much time to look for him. But the day after we broke up, I heard Bagheera under the house. I talked to him for more than an hour, and he crawled bit by bit towards me, yet not close enough to touch. I hated to see him. He had scabs along his chin, his breathing made a sound like the sucking of a straw at the bottom of a fizz bottle. He wouldn't eat anything and just lapped weakly at the water I brought, before he backed laboriously again into the darkness under the house.

Each time I looked, his eyes would be blazing there, more fiery as his sickness grew, as if they consumed his substance.

My father decided to take Bagheera to the vet. He brought out Grandad's walking stick and said that he'd hook the cat out when I called him within reach. How easily the cat would normally have avoided such a plan. My father pinned Bagheera down, and tried to drag him closer. Bagheera rolled and gasped before he managed to free himself and creep back among the low piles. He knocked an empty tin as he went. It was the tin from the pears I had stolen after being strapped by my father for fishing in my best clothes. When the walking stick failed, my father lost interest in the cat. He had given him his chance and after that he put the matter out of his mind. My father possessed a very disciplined mind. I couldn't forget, though, for Bagheera had become my cat. At night I would look sometimes to the window, but his calm presence was never there, and instead I kept thinking of his eyes in the perpetual darkness beneath the house. Beseeching eyes that waited for me to fulfil the obligation of our friendship.

I asked my father to shoot Bagheera. To put him out of his misery, I said. It was a common enough expression, but my father had no conception of misery in others. I imagine he saw it, in regard to people at least, as the result of incompetence, or lack of drive. But I kept on at him. I said that Bagheera might spread infection to my sisters, or die under the house and cause a smell in the guest rooms. These considerations, which required no empathy, seemed to impress my father. He refused to fire under the house, though, he said. I'd have to coax Bagheera out where he could get a safe shot. He wasn't supposed to shoot at all within the borough limits, he said. At the time I didn't fully realise the irony of needing my father to kill Bagheera. I was the only possible go-between.

My father came out late in the afternoon, and stood with the rifle in the shade of the grapevine trellis, waiting for me to call Bagheera out. I felt the hot sun, unaccustomed on the back of my knees as I lay down. It was about the time that Bagheera and I would often take our walk, and I called him with all the urgency and need that I could gather. Even the pet names I used, even those, with the sensitivity of boyhood and my father standing there, for I would spare nothing in my friendship. Bagheera came gradually, his black fur dingy with the dust of the foundations, and the corruption within himself. I could hear his breathing, the straw sucking and spluttering, I could see his blazing eyes level with my own. To get him to quit the piles, and move into the light, was the hardest thing. I was aware of my father's impatience and adult discomfort with the situation.

'Move away from it,' he said, when Bagheera was at the verandah steps and trembling by the saucer of water. My father raised the .22, with which he never missed. No Poona colonel could have shown a greater sureness of aim. My sisters grouped at the study window to watch, their interest in the cat temporarily renewed by the oddity of his death.

The shot was not loud, a compressed, hissing sound. Bagheera arched into the air, grace and panther for a last time, and sped away across the lawn into the garden. Just for one moment he raced ahead of death, just for one moment left death behind, with a defiance which stopped my breathing with its triumph. 'I wouldn't think anyone heard the shot at all,' said my father with satisfaction. The saucer lay undisturbed, and beside it one gout of purple blood. Don't tell me it wasn't purple, for I see it still, opalescent blood beside the freshly torn white wood the bullet dug in the verandah boards.

I didn't go to find the body among the currant bushes. Instead I went and lay hidden in the old compost heap, with the large, rasping pumpkin leaves to shade me, and the slaters questing back and forth, wondering why they'd been disturbed. My father and mother walked down by the hedge and I heard my father talking of Bagheera and me. 'I find it hard to understand,' he said. 'He seemed determined to have it shot. Sat there for ages cajoling it out to be shot. And after the attachment he seemed to have for it, too. He's a funny lad, Mary. Why couldn't he leave the wretched thing alone?' My father's voice had a tone of mixed indignation and revulsion, as if someone had been sick on the car seat, or one of his employees had broken down and cried. But I remembered Bagheera's release across the lawn, and thought it all worthwhile. He'd done his dash all right.

I lay in the evening warmth, and watched a pumpkin flower only inches from my face. The image of the pumpkin flower was distorted in the flickering light and shade beneath the leaves. The gaping, yellow mouth and slender stamen nodded and rolled like a processional Chinese dragon: the ones they have at weddings, and funerals.

Body and Soul

~

THE SNOW HAD become water on the quiet road, yet alongside in the tussock grass it lay like separate white handkerchiefs. In the folds of the tussock hills there were still sweeps and angles of it etched by the sun over the contours of the land. The tussock was a rough coat over the hills, and only the road cut through it.

In the first hour after leaving the town they talked a good deal, the easy shorthand of husband and wife, but as the car worked higher into the hills Vicky became quiet, only smiling in reply to the things her husband said. She watched the tussock and the snow as if there were more than a world of tussock and snow passing. Her hands rested softly like birds in her lap, with the rings as bands upon them.

'I told you about George Liddell and the Dunedin branch,' said Paul, and Vicky smiled, but didn't turn her head towards him. 'It's a pleasant function of the position, to be able to tell George that. Being able to give people what they deserve even in a modest business way has a lot of satisfaction. That Sydney trip. I'll have to be away all week I'm afraid.' He whistled for a time as he drove. 'What do you bet Simon has forgotten we're coming today, eh? Wouldn't that be just typical.' Paul rested his hand on her dress. He wanted to cheer her up. She turned and smiled.

'It wouldn't surprise me. We know he's not practical at all.'

'Right. Like even forgetting what day it is. I hate to think of him in business.'

'So do I.'

'It can't be far.' He began looking for any signs that they were close. 'All looks very much the same, this country,' he said. The tussock was a rough coat over the hills, and only the road cut through it. Paul looked across to his wife, and she looked out on to tussock and snow. Because she was quiet and looked sad, he leant over and cupped his free hand over one of the hands like birds in her lap. 'Happy?' he said.

Simon's bach was quite new. He rented it from a Dunedin doctor whose love of solitude had died once it was consummated. The bach sat above the road, and faced north for the winter sun. There were two concrete water tanks like pill boxes beside it, and Simon's motorbike was draped with sacks on the small verandah. For miles there was no other building. 'This is his Walton's Mountain,' said Paul as they turned off the road, and he and Vicky laughed. Simon came to the door, stood grinning as they drove to within a few feet of him.

'What kept you? I thought you might have arrived last night,' he said. There was snow in the south shadow of the bach.

'Shopping,' said Paul. He cocked his thumb at his wife, and rolled his eyes upwards. By stressing the idiosyncrasy of women, he suggested a bond between men.

'Ah,' said Simon. He took two of the cases inside. 'I had a bit of a clean-up,' he said. 'I meant to do more, but I began painting again and didn't get time.' It was Vicky's turn to lift her eyes. 'You know how it is,' Simon said. He had made up the two single beds, and pushed them together in a clumsy but touching effort to represent his idea of how husband and wife should be. There was only one bedroom, and Simon had taken a lilo and sleeping bag to the studio.

'You've had a fair fall of snow,' said Paul.

'A fair bit yesterday. In the afternoon a good deal of it.'

To be brothers is no guarantee of intimacy, or understanding, yet each smiled at the other's similar face, willing to be a friend, and willing it to be so. Time had given them different priorities, and only superficial things and recollections were left for them in common. 'I use rock gas for the cooking and hot water,' said Simon. As if it needed proof he opened the cupboard by his sink, and they looked at the rock gas cylinder plainly there. 'Rock Gas', it said on it, sure enough.

'We use rock gas in our caravan. Never had any trouble with it at all. Have we, darling?'

'No,' she said. She was a beautiful woman.

'I've had no trouble with it,' said Simon. His voice began to yawn although his mouth remained the same.

'I'd say these rock gas people have built a tidy business up.'

They went walking after lunch. Nowhere did they come to any fences, and the only one Paul could remember was that which followed the road. Simon seemed not to care how far they walked. They talked, and went on and on, keeping just below the spur lines to avoid the breeze. They climbed almost to the top of one of the highest hills. 'It's called Saviour's Hill,' said Simon. The tussock was too damp to sit on, but they crouched down and looked over the lesser hills lit by the cool sun, looked down and over the plain. Whenever the air moved they could feel the cold. The snow that had been there in the morning was nearly gone, but it had chilled the hills in its departure.

'What do you do? When you're not painting, what do you do?' asked Paul. Simon looked down, and smiled. It was a smile not of amusement, but wry recognition. As though he had told himself that Paul would ask that question, and yet he couldn't help but think less of his brother for doing it. In its way it was a question which proved the completeness of Paul's misunderstanding.

'Most of the time I am painting, though, or thinking about painting, or reading about painting.'

'But when you're not. I mean there seems so little to do.'

Simon rustled the tussock, drawing it through his hand. 'When I'm not painting, what does it matter where I am,' he said quietly.

Paul was embarrassed, as men are when passion is revealed. He stood up and looked out towards the plain.

'You can see for miles and miles,' he said.

'So you can,' said Vicky.

'In the summer you can hardly see the plain for the heat haze,' said Simon. Although they were talking to Paul, they were looking at each other. Paul had a sudden apprehension that they felt sorry for him.

'I reckon you would need to have a fair imagination to paint this country,' he said.

'In a way painting's all imagination,' said his brother.

They talked no more of it: not because it was too theoretical, but because it was too personal. The inner landscape of belief is hazardous ground. Together the three turned back, and began moving down the ridge. The wind came, breaking on them like a wave, making them gasp with the shock of it. The wind whistled around their ears, and they had to turn their heads to hear one another. 'By Jesus,' said Paul.

'Sometimes it comes suddenly,' said Simon. The tussock tops were laid back in the wind. There were occasional schist outcrops, and in their lee the sheep kept the earth bare by gathering. Yet there were no sheep as they went down that day. Paul took Vicky's arm, and they angled across the wind, tacking to avoid its full force. Simon kept his head up, and his hair was swept back by the wind. 'It'll blow itself out before morning,' he shouted to them. There was something about the wind that was remarkable; something apart from the force, fierce cold and abrupt arrival. That other thing was its purity. Nowhere on the hills did any refuse blow; no grit, no dust. The wind was harsh and clean, and blew over land that was just the same. The tussock shed nothing to the wind, and the wind was nothing but its own force.

Even in the bach Simon listened for the wind. Paul and Vicky kept by the kerosene heater, but Simon stood by the large studio window and watched the hills in the wind. Vicky turned his canvases, and Paul asked him why he hadn't gone to the high school reunion, and about visiting their parents. 'I've been meaning to go and see them again. I know I should, and I'm not a good writer,' Simon said. 'I just don't seem to have the time.' Paul was going to laugh, but then he had a sense almost of fear. He realised that his brother was serious, that he spent his time painting as a kind of compulsion. That he accepted it as an occupation and as a reasonable justification for not doing other things such as attending school reunions, or visiting parents. Paul felt for the first time that his condescension in regard to Simon's work might be equalled by Simon's contempt for his own.

'We've put in a new moulding machine from West Germany,' he said. 'We think by the end of the decade we'll have a twenty percent penetration of the Australian hard plastics market.' Paul watched his brother open his mouth to reply and find nothing honest to say. He only smiled. 'I had to pay twenty-four thousand dollars in tax last year,' Paul said, and gave a descending whistle. Then he wished that he'd said nothing. He wouldn't look at his wife.

'Hell, I didn't make ten thousand,' said Simon.

'I didn't make anything,' said Vicky.

'You've got more brains than any of us,' said Simon, 'and a better education.'

'That's true. That's quite true. I always tell her that myself.' Paul was eager to detract from himself. 'Even in business matters she always realises what the essentials are. Vicky seems so good in reading people.' Vicky was interested in the canvases again; Simon had both hands in his pockets, and was looking away from his brother.

Paul began to examine the paintings and, as he made comments, Simon watched each of his paintings with the look that passes between secret lovers whose glances meet while their elders talk of everyday things. 'None of them has any shadows,' said Vicky after a time.

'That's right,' said Paul. He'd felt something odd about them.

'An artist's vision is omniscient,' said Simon. It was a pretension to free him from the need to make any explanation, but Paul accepted it.

'So the artist is in fact superior in view to the sun, and through him the whole landscape is accessible.'

'Perhaps that,' said Simon, and he looked at Vicky as she smiled a little. He had no desire to mock his brother. Paul was pleased with the reason. He liked a logical explanation. With greater sympathy he looked again at the painting: perhaps there were other clues to the riddle of it.

In the evening they were closer. The three of them sat in the studio by the heater, and drank red wine. Paul and Simon were able to minimise their separation by talking of their boyhood, and recollecting the curious incidents that all boyhoods have. It became dark early, but they were happy with the light of the kerosene heater. The flame like a campfire displayed only the surfaces square to it. A cheek, a forehead, the side of a shoe, were seen clearly in the glow. The light was a kind blush that made Vicky's beauty more obvious. 'I envy you your wife,' said Simon. He gave a laugh that was more a shout. 'If only I had Vicky.' With the fierce admiration of an artist he saw the turn of her hair below the cheek, and the solidity of her breasts beneath the jersey. 'Women's flesh has such weight,' he said in wonder. 'Why is it that women's flesh is so heavy? That's why it paints so well, I guess.' Paul looked at his wife, and was excited by her beauty.

'You are beautiful, beautiful,' he said. It was a statement of observation, not possession. In his pleasure and admiration he was aware of sadness too, and didn't know why. He was close to tears.

'Both of you have drunk too much,' said Vicky.

'I have to go into town and visit a very skinny girl who works in dry-cleaning,' said Simon. Paul laughed; not at the skinny girl, but in exultation at the beauty of his wife. 'A dear, kind, skinny girl,' said Simon. 'She's the only one who'll have me. Everyone there thinks I'm a complete nutter. I did have a girl with heavier flesh. She used to come and live with me sometimes, but she married a land agent. They have a house of three thousand two hundred square feet.'

'How cruel you are about women,' said Vicky, though she was laughing too.

'The skinny girl has a better colour sense,' said Simon, 'but it's not an adequate compensation.' The glow of the heater held the line of their faces as they laughed.

Paul and Vicky talked about his brother, later in bed. As couples talk of the people they have been with, so that they reach an accepted marital view of those around them. 'He's always had that spontaneity,' said Paul. 'Ever since a kid he's had this fresh view of things.'

'But then he's had no one to please but himself. Everytime in his life a decision has had to be made, he's been able to follow his own priorities.'

'That's true.' They were lying close together on one of the single bed sides. Paul stroked his wife's breasts softly. He made friendly circles around a nipple with his finger. 'I sometimes feel that people without money like to despise it. Don't you think? Money isn't easy to make, but people like to think it is.' The wind was gusting about the bach. It made noises like someone striking the walls with a flat board.

'Simon doesn't think about money,' said Vicky. 'You can see that. He wants things the rest of us don't know how to talk about.' Certainly Paul didn't, but he lay there and knew that his wife was right. 'He wants to cut the world up and see inside perhaps,' she said.

'I think it's dangerous in a way,' said Paul. 'Making painting be everything, a religion and everything. For if you're wrong about it, if you've got nothing else . . .' It wasn't quite what he meant to say, and he lay thinking about it some more, and listening to the wind.

'If you don't hedge your bets, you mean,' said Vicky.

They'd gone as far as they could. They lay and listened to the assault of the wind. 'There's no heating at all in this room, you know,' said Paul. 'The kerosene heater in the studio is the only one he's got. He should have the heating laid on to the rock gas. In the morning it's going to be cold here.'

It was cold in the morning. Paul woke because of it, and his nose was like putty. His wife was curled towards him, and her forehead beneath the sheets pressed into his chest. In the corners of the windows the frost had made patterns: hachured patterns like fossils in rock, and some like thick spider webs. He pushed himself carefully away from Vicky, keeping the blankets around her, not letting the cold air in. Even so, she murmured at his going. He found his slippers and dressing gown, and held the sides of the dressing gown together at his throat with one hand, as he went quietly to the kitchen.

Simon was painting. Standing in the winter dawn, with the light of the kerosene heater glowing behind him, he was at his work. He wore a thick jersey over his pyjamas, and two pairs of socks. Still drained by sleep, Paul stood in the kitchen and watched him through two doorways. Simon had an expression of complete absorption, more often seen in the faces of children than adults. If he turned away from the canvas, he did so in a haste to be facing it again, and when he used the brush he seemed to use it like a scalpel, cutting precisely into the canvas. At each cut his mouth moved, as if he were shaping words like there, and there, and there, to accompany each action. If the cut was a success he would work more urgently: there, and there, and there, with louder breathing that Paul could hear. If dissatisfied he might cough and glance away, wriggle his toes in their double thickness, before he was driven to the brush again. Simon's face in concentration was a picture itself of inward intensity, of hope and urgency impelled by vision. As Paul watched, he could feel the bland biology of his own face, with its heavy cheeks and cold morning nose. He moved to the bench and filled the jug. He used one of the rock gas rings which never gave any trouble, and stood shivering as he waited for the jug to heat. The lower part of the window glass was beaded with condensation, and he joined the drops with his finger as he stood there. Jesus, how Simon loves to paint, he thought. Painting his life away here, and nobody cares. Paul called to his wife that he was bringing coffee up and, when he went past, Simon was still working in the studio. Painting, painting: there, there, there, with the inspiration of a Christ.

'He's painting already,' Paul told Vicky.

'Well, he's got a heater in there, hasn't he.'

'He's at it like a masterpiece.'

'Maybe it is,' said Vicky. She stroked his wrist. 'How would we know.'

'How can he be sure then? Every artist can't be right.' They thought about that. The more they thought the more doubtful it seemed as a statement.

'Oh well,' said Vicky.

Simon was making breakfast for himself, when Paul went through again. They talked, then Paul went into the studio by the heater. He looked at the painting. As always with his brother's work, he could find no link between the man and the work, or even between the exhilaration of execution, and the result. The hills were triangles, and the sun livid, and scarred with the thick texture of the colours. The whole thing seemed to have a loss of symmetry which gave an uneasy tension. It looked only fifteen minutes' work. Paul took the brush, and charged it with yellow from the tray. He made a jab at the canvas: one more smear among many. It was an action of appeal, not malice.

'There's no snow today,' said Simon from the kitchen. 'Why not stay another day?' There was a letter on the tray that Simon must have been rereading. The sharp creases where it had been folded made it rock when Paul touched the tray. He read the last lines. 'I can only take one more for the gallery, but believe me I think you're on the right way. Go on, go on. Remember Klee and Dubuffet.'

'Who's Klee?' said Paul when he went back to Vicky.

'A symbolist, I think. His reputation is on the crest of the wave.'

'I had a look at that painting he's doing. It's just like the rest. All layered savagery and colours that don't match.'

'For you everything must be a representation.'

'And this place smells. Do you suppose he ever cleans up around here? Four rooms, and each of them a mess. Below the window in the studio there's a whole line of dead insects.'

'Yes.'

'They crunch under your feet.'

'Squalor is an artist's privilege.' She was enjoying his indignation.

'It's a pity he can't get the land agent's wife out again.'

'She wasn't married then.'

'Whatever.'

Vicky began to dress and, as Paul watched her, he felt the best he had all morning. She made it an unconscious spectacle of graceful movements and feminine angles: bowing so that her hair swung, lifting her arms to draw her jersey on.

'Remember Klee and Dubuffet,' he said.

'Why do you say that?'

'Oh, nothing,' he said.

'Hmm?'

'Just nothing.'

They left in the middle of the morning, when it began to snow. Simon said that if they were going to leave that day then it was better to go before it had been snowing for too long. Simon would have been content for them to stay; he was content for them to leave. Paul decided that his brother was impartial about all things, but one. Simon and Paul stood by the car for a time, and Vicky sat in the car, with the motor running and the heater on. 'We want you to come and stay with us soon,' said Paul.

'I really must do it,' said Simon. He looked past his brother, at the gathering snow in the air. 'The hills have gone,' he said. 'See how the snow has shrouded the hills.' There was no wind left, or they couldn't feel it, yet the snow came drifting in from the south, moving past them and rarely seeming to reach the ground.

'You said there'd be no snow today,' said Paul. He put out his hand to his brother.

'It's good to be wrong about snow.' Simon farewelled his brother, and put a kiss on to his hand then on to the window close to Vicky. He waved as they went down the track. He watched for a time the snow coming from the south. How it obscured the hills, and how it had to drop into the tussock for so long before any of it could be seen there. Then he went inside to paint.

It was quiet, driving in the snow. The expensive car was quiet and warm, and only the gravel crackled under the wheels, especially on the sharp corners around the spurs where the gravel had gathered in little drifts on the downhill side, mimicking snow. Paul and Vicky sat with their own thoughts, as husband and wife can do without offence, then he said, 'I saw him painting this morning. I watched him from the kitchen. He painted as if there were a naked woman before him instead of lines and colours. He painted as if there were nothing else in the world. Just him and the canvas. Do you know what I mean?' His wife smiled. 'I saw part of a letter from a gallery. It said that he should keep on with his own way of painting. Remember Klee and Dubuffet, it said.'

'Both of them had a vision.' She seemed farther from him than she had for a long time.

'What chance can he possibly have. I mean here in the middle of central Otago, and the whole damn country so isolated from the world's art anyway.' He laughed to emphasise to her how hopeless it was. Vicky leant back, and turned to watch the snow, seeming so ethereal at a distance, yet moving fast, and stinging on the glass by her face. 'He's forty-two now. He doesn't even own the place he lives in. He hides there, painting, painting, painting, as if his heart will break.' There was silence. Where the hills were closest the snow cloud was grey but, looking out of the hills and above them, they saw that the snow cloud was pearl, and the flakes slid out of it in a tracery.

'I left him a cheque,' said Paul. 'Just a few hundred.' He said it roughly, to minimise any sentiment.

'You may be rewarded yet,' said Vicky.

Paul thought he knew her mood. 'You think he can make it, don't you? You think he's going to be hailed a genius yet, and eclipse us all.' Paul was eager. 'That's it, isn't it?' Vicky moved her head in impatience.

'But it doesn't make any difference,' she said. 'Can't you see? You've seen him, painting. You said so yourself. Whatever it is that really matters he's got already, hasn't he?' She turned to him. Her eyes had affection, but he saw irony there as well. Pity for them both, and her hand rested on his arm, to help him bear her pity perhaps. Paul saw his brother again at his painting, the intense, closed face of his brother as he leant towards the canvas: and there, there, there, cutting with the brush. What did he care for anything else. There, there, there it was, all that meant anything.

Paul began to think of himself in a new way. As a successful man with a hairy stomach. A man who talked a lot about his possessions and import export regulations, watched television quiz shows, was popular at Rotary. A man who kept his teeth clean in case someone should want to look at them, and his current affairs up to date lest the conversation should turn that way. A man at ease in his environment. A man who moved happily from one thing to another in life, as a monkey moves briskly from one branch to the next. He determined to think carefully, and he drove carefully, the car dropping lower through the hills. 'Would you like to come to Sydney with me?' he asked his wife. 'Or we could go ski-ing perhaps when I come back. That rock gas set-up in the bach works well enough, doesn't it.' He wondered how many more years he would live, and if those years would be any different. 'All this country is so much the same,' he said in sudden exasperation at the anonymity of the snow and the road. Vicky stopped looking at the country which he thought so much the same. She moved her arm and stroked the back of his head, and then rested her hand on his shoulder.

'I don't think we should ever blame ourselves,' she said.

The snow was beginning to build. The first half-hour's snow had melted as it fell, but in doing so it took the last warmth from the ground, and the snow which fell later was crisp and gathered rapidly to mark those slight leading edges in the tussock that went unnoticed at other times. The snow softened the outline of the ground they could see, and lay thickest along the bank side of the road. 'We must be nearly down to the plain again,' he said.

Harvest Apocalypse

~

THE PUMPKINS WERE the strongest fruit in my recollection of harvest festival. Not marrows and all those watery relations, but pumpkins: swelling pumpkins in colours so blatant no artist would dare to reproduce them, and with seamed, igneous skins. The pumpkins sat in ribaldry among the sheaves, the carrots and the corn, the homemade bread. Even the vicar's wife seemed somewhat disconcerted after handling them, without quite knowing why.

In the afternoon I thought about the pumpkins, in an attempt to keep myself cheerful as we drove up to see Bob. There were three of us; my sister and her husband, as well as me. Bob stayed in one of those rural asylums with a euphemistic title. Such titles are helpful in forms of address, for you don't have to mention the words asylum, rest-home, or hospital. You just say Bob's at Pleasant Valley. I wonder if there'd be fewer inmates if they used names like Stark Terrace, or Forlorn Glades. 'Remember that wonderful book called *Cold Comfort Farm*?' I asked my sister. My sister is good on books. I forgot about the pumpkins even as I talked with her, and her husband drove.

The home and the garden around it were wonderfully well kept, tended to the verge of despair. The units were painted in the colours preferred by the latest research, and Dr Sullivan patted one of the patients on the shoulder, and called him Jacko.

Bob came out to meet us.

'The ice-man cometh,' he said. Bob had a habit of voicing snatches that drifted through his mind. He was quite unaware of saying them aloud, and we had grown accustomed to differentiating them from the things he intended for communication. 'I'm assembling wristwatches now,' he said.

'That sounds interesting.' We walked down the sloping lawn to be in the gardens, and chose a bench seat by the hedge.

'For my therapy, you see. It's the intricate nature of the work I like.'

'It's so wonderfully quiet here,' said my sister. She intended it as a compliment to the place, but Bob funnelled his lips apprehensively, and looked cautiously about.

'Yes,' he said slowly.

There were two young men working in the plots before us. They weeded clumsily, demonstrating no affinity with either plants or soil, and looking up often in search of some distraction. 'They're the unemployed on the special work scheme,' said Bob. 'The real gardeners can't stand them.' There were ranks of giant poppies and squat, brazen flowers the colour of the harvest pumpkins.

'Have you written any more poems?' My sister shook her head at me when Bob wasn't looking. She thought it was a strain for him to talk about his poetry.

'Not much, a few lyric refrains. I can get something of the same satisfaction from the intricacy of watchmaking. The parts come together with such precision.'

'Oh quite.'

'I've been reading some Blake, though.'

'Mum's going to bring the new dressing gown up for you on the eighteenth,' said my sister.

'Does the eagle know what is in the pit?'

'It's so peaceful here,' said my sister.

'Yes, that's perhaps the greatest danger,' said Bob.

A dumpy bird was singing in a crab-apple tree. It had a metallic and repetitious song, like that of the golden birds we are told that Arabian millionaires buy. 'There was very little traffic on the way up, actually,' said my brother-in-law. His voice was croaky because he had been sitting in the sun without saying anything for so long. Two young women with straight hair and healthy faces came and sat on a rug, and watched the gardeners working; and the Reverend Ludemann approached and sat on the bench opposite to us.

'The invisible worm that flies in the night.'

The Reverend Ludemann had the distinction of being part inmate and part practitioner. 'They don't let him leave the place now,' said Bob. 'His ministry's restricted to the institution. Hello, Alice,' said Bob to one of the women with straight hair who was waving.

The gardeners had a transistor radio with them. It was playing 'Lullaby of Birdland'. You know it: it goes lullaby of birdland, dum de dah, dum de doh. 'That's a very appropriate tune here, Bob,' I said. 'Lullaby of Birdland.' Bob laughed so much that the Reverend Ludemann and the young women on the rug looked across at us.

'We had a very colourful harvest festival service today,' said my sister. Her saying that reminded me of the pumpkins again. I wish I could have described the magnificence of those pumpkins for Bob.

'Ay, Corrymeela, in the same soft rain.'

Bob was conscious of colour and texture, because of his poetic susceptibility, I suppose. He would have enjoyed the pumpkins. 'Everybody seemed very generous,' my sister said. 'Mrs Harris even gave loaves of home-made bread, and on Monday evening it will all be auctioned for the Missions' Appeal. Something well over five hundred dollars is expected.' For a woman who did her thesis on T. L. Peacock, my sister has a remarkable grip on everyday things.

'We hope you'll be home again soon,' I said.

'Dr Sullivan said I can go anytime. It's just a matter of feeling secure really. A world in which abortion is legal and euthanasia is not. And they tell me I've got problems.'

The Reverend Ludemann climbed awkwardly on to the bench seat, and tried to stand upright. He extended his arms for better balance, as if he were on a tight-rope. He balanced there for a moment, an old man in a simian crouch of atavistic reversion. Then he threw up his hands. 'Apocalypse. Apocalypse,' he shouted urgently. In the wrinkled face his open mouth was like a tear in a paper bag. 'Apocalypse. Apocalypse,' he cried, in an abandonment of revelation, and he lifted up his face to the sky. The unemployed men in the garden laughed and thumped their hoes with a delight which seemed to show that what they had expected, had indeed happened.

The Reverend Ludemann held his pose as a challenge: he tried to bring on the vision of apocalypse. But the garden refused to change, only burned more brightly as if it would cremate old Ludemann and his words. Tears ran down Bob's cheeks. My brother-in-law laughed: not unkindly and certainly not in amusement, but for the lack of any more adequate response.

'They are not long, the days of wine and roses.'

The Reverend Ludemann sat down again. Alice and her friend went over and sat with him. The giant poppies were like glasses of claret, and the pumpkin-coloured flowers like embers beneath them. 'They don't let him do any pastoral work outside the hospital now,' said Bob. 'I tried to interest him in assembling watches, but he hasn't the patience, and his fingers are too thick.'

'Mum said she'd bring up your dressing gown on the eighteenth,' my sister said. We walked up the sloping lawn, past the buildings where Jacko still sat waiting, up to the carpark. 'You look after yourself, Bob,' my sister said. 'We'll come and see you again soon.'

'I'll have a watch done for each of you.'

'And a poem for us too,' I said, despite my sister's shaking head.

'And a poem for you too,' said Bob.

'Jolly good then,' said my sister's husband. His voice had become croaky again from lack of use.

Bob seemed content again. He smiled at us from outside the car, and as he turned away he was whistling. You know it. It goes, lullaby of birdland, dum de dah, dum de doh.

from

The Day Hemingway Died

Kenneth's Friend

~

AT THE NORTH side, towards the point, the shore was rocky. When the tide was going out I liked to search the pools for butterfish and flat crabs like cardboard cut-outs, sea snails with plates instead of heads, and flowing anemones in pink and mauve. Once Kenneth let a rock fall on my hand there on purpose, after I told him I didn't want to spend the morning making papier-mâché figures. He said it was an accident, of course, but I knew he meant it. The rock had a hundred edges of old accretions, and cut like glass. I sat and waited for the sun to stop the cuts bleeding. I thought about Kenneth and me, and how I came to be there at all.

I had good friends when I lived in Palmerston North, friends that experience had shown the value of, but when we shifted to Blenheim I didn't have time to make friends before the holidays. I liked Robby Macdonald best. He and I became close later, but Kenneth seemed to attach himself to me in those first weeks. Perhaps he felt it gave him at least a temporary distinction to be seen with the new boy. He came home with me often after school, and lent me *Crimson Comet* magazines. At Christmastime he invited me to go with his family to their holiday home in Queen Charlotte Sound. His father was a lawyer and mayor of the town. My mother was pleased I'd been invited, and for sixteen days too. She gave me a crash course on table manners and guest etiquette. I had a ten-shilling note in an envelope, so that I could buy something for Kenneth's parents before I left.

The house had a full verandah along the front, facing out towards the bay. We used to have meals there and, standing out like violin music from among the talk of the Kinlethlys and their guests, I could hear the native birds in the bush, and the waves on the beach. It was a millionaire's setting in any country but ours, though Mr Kinlethly was a lawyer and mayor of the town admittedly. Glow-worms too: there were glow-worms under the cool bank of the stream. At night I crept out to see them, hanging my head over the bank, and with my arms in the creek to hold me up. The earth in the bush was soft and fibrous: I could plunge my hands into it without stubbing the fingers. The sand of the small bay was cream where it was dry, and yellow closer to the water. There was no driftwood, but sometimes after rough weather there would be corpses of bull kelp covered with flies, and filigree patterns of more fragile seaweed pressed in the sand.

What Kenneth wanted, I found out, wasn't a friend, but someone to boss about. A sort of young brother, without the inconvenience of his sharing any parental affection. With no natural authority at school, Kenneth made the most of his position at the bay. Each night before we went to bed, Kenneth enjoyed the privilege of choosing his bunk and so underlined his superiority. He might bounce on the top bunk for a while, then say that he'd chosen the bottom one; he might wait until I'd put my pyjamas on one of them, then he'd toss my pyjamas off and say he'd decided to sleep there himself. He liked to play cards and Monopoly for hours on end, or work on his shell collection. Whenever we had a disagreement as to what we should do, Kenneth would say that I could go home if I didn't like it. I think in a way that's what Kenneth wanted — for me to say that I wanted to go home, that I couldn't stick it out. He didn't understand how much the bay offered me, despite its ownership. Kenneth's parents didn't know we disliked each other. We carried on our unequal struggle within the framework of their expectations. We slept together, and set off in the mornings to play together. We didn't kick each other at the table, or sulk to disclose our feud. His parents were always there, however, as a final recourse: the reason I had to come to heel and follow him back to the house when he saw fit, or help him catalogue his shells in the evening instead of watching the glow-worms.

The Kinlethlys seemed to take their bay for granted, corrupted by the ease and completeness of their ownership. Mr Kinlethly was away more days than he was there, and at night he shared the family enthusiasm for cards. I never saw him walk into the bush, and he went fishing only once or twice as a sort of tokenism. There was no doubt he was pleased with the place, though. He liked visitors so that they could praise it, and I heard him telling Mrs Kinlethly that the property had appreciated seven hundred percent since he purchased it. Mrs Kinlethly had some reservations, I think. She wouldn't allow any uncleaned fish near the house. She said the smell lingered. We would gut them at the shore, washing the soft flaps of their bellies in the salt water, and tossing their entrails to the gulls. Mrs Kinlethly gave us what she called the filleting board, and we would scale and dismember the blue cod and tarakihi in the ocean they came from: the filleting board between Kenneth and me, our feet stretching into the ripples. Mrs Kinlethly seemed sensitive to the smell of fish. When the wind was strong from the sea, blowing directly up to the house, she said it smelled of fish. It didn't really. It carried the smell of kelp, sand-hoppers, mussels, jetty timber, island farms, distant horizons, and fish.

One wall of Kenneth's room was covered with the display case for his shells, and our bunks were on the opposite side. I thought the collection interesting at first: the variety of colours and shapes, the neatly typed documentation. Each entry seemed to have one sentence beginning 'This specimen . . .'. Mr Kinlethly wrote them out, and Kenneth proudly typed them on the special stickers, which I got to lick. 'This specimen a particularly fine example from the northern coast of Sabah.' 'This specimen a gift from Colonel L. S. Gilchrist following a visit to our bay' or 'This specimen one of the few examples with mantle intact'. The collection seemed to admirably satisfy the two Kinlethly requirements concerning possessions — display and investment.

My dislike of the shells began when I had sunstroke. Kenneth and I had been collecting limpets on the rocks, and I forgot to wear a hat. The sun on the back of my neck all morning was too much for me. I lay on the bottom bunk, and tried not to think of the bowl Mrs Kinlethly had placed on a towel by the bed. The family considered it rather inconsiderate of me to get sick. After all, I was there to keep Kenneth amused, not to add to Mrs Kinlethly's workload. I lay there trying not to be a bother, and hearing Kenneth's laugh from the verandah. In the late afternoon Mr Kinlethly brought a guest back from Picton, and they came in to see the shells. 'A friend of Kenneth's,' said Mr Kinlethly as my introduction. I was bereft of any more individual name at the bay. It was always 'Kenneth's friend'. 'I think he's been off colour today,' said Mr Kinlethly. 'Now here's one in particular, the *Cypraea argus*.'

'Oh yes.'

'And *Oliva cryptospira*.'

'Strikingly formed, isn't it?'

'*Cassis cornuta*.'

I wanted to be sick. The nerves in my stomach trampolined, and saliva flooded my mouth. The mixing bowl on the towel seemed to blossom before me. Mr Kinlethly was in no hurry. 'Most in this other section were collected locally,' he said. 'Kenneth is a very assiduous collector, and also people around the Sounds have become aware of our interest. A surprising number of shells come as gifts.' Despite myself I looked over at the shells. Many of them seemed to have the sheen of new bone; like that revealed when you turn the flesh away from the shoulder or knuckle of a newly killed sheep. I had to discipline myself, so that I wasn't sick until Mr Kinlethly and his visitor had left the room. The shells were always different for me after that.

The Kinlethlys had a clinker-built dinghy. It had a little bilge water in it that smelled of scales and bait. They had their own boatshed for it even, just like a garage, with folding doors so that the dinghy could be pulled in, and a hand-winch at the back of the shed to do it with. The dinghy was never put in the shed while I was there. Kenneth said they left it out all summer. We used to pull it up the sand a way, and then take out the anchor and push one of the flukes in the ground in case of a storm or freak tide. Using the dinghy was probably the best thing of all. When we went fishing I could forget the boring times, like playing Monopoly, and helping Kenneth with his shells. I could look down the woven cord of the hand line, seeing how the refraction made it veer off into the green depths, and I could listen to the water slapping against the sides of the dinghy. Closer to shore the sea was so clear that I could see orange starfish on the bottom, and the sculptured sand-dunes there, the sweeping outlines formed by the currents and not the wind. Flounder hid there, so successfully that they didn't exist until they moved, and vanished again when they stopped, as some magician's trick.

Wonderful things happened at the bay, even though I was only Kenneth's friend. Like the time we were out in the dinghy and it began to rain, The water was calm, but the cloud pressed lower and lower, squeezing out what air remained between it and the sea, and then the rain began. I'd never been at sea in rain before. The cloud dipped down into the sea, and the water lay smooth and malleable beneath the impact of the drops. The surface dimpled in the rain, and the darkest and closest of the clouds towed shadows which undulated like stingrays across the swell. 'I never think of it raining on the sea,' I said to Kenneth. 'Imagine it raining on whole oceans, and there's no one there.'

'Bound to happen,' said Kenneth. He couldn't see why I was in no hurry to get back.

'I always think of it raining on trees, animals, the roofs of cars,' I said weakly. I couldn't share with Kenneth the wonder that I felt.

Kenneth had no respect for confidences. That evening at tea, when Mrs Kinlethly told the others how wet he and I had got in the dinghy, Kenneth said that I'd wanted to stay out and see the rain. 'He didn't know that rain fell on the sea as well as on the land,' said Kenneth. That wasn't the whole truth of it, but it was no use saying anything. I just blushed, and Mrs Kinlethly laughed. Kenneth's father said, 'Sounds as if we have a real landlubber in our midst', in a tone which implied he wasn't a landlubber. I learnt not to talk to Kenneth about anything that mattered.

On the Thursday of the second week there were dolphins again at the entrance of the bay. I admired dolphins more than anything else. They seemed set on a wheel, the highest point of which just let them break the surface before curving down into the depths. I imagined they did a complete cartwheel down there in the green water, then came sliding up again, like a sideshow. 'There's dolphins out at the point,' said Mr Kinlethly. Mr and Mrs Thomson and their two unmarried daughters were with us on Thursday.

'I've never seen dolphins,' said Mrs Thomson.

'Quite a school of them,' said Mr Kinlethly. He decided that his guests must make an expedition in the dinghy to see the dolphins. Mrs Kinlethly wouldn't go, but the Thomsons settled the dinghy well down in the water and there wasn't room for both Kenneth and me.

'There's not room for both the boys,' said Mrs Kinlethly. Kenneth didn't care about the dolphins, but he wasn't going to let me go. He called out that he wanted to go, and his father hauled him aboard.

'Kenneth's friend can come another time,' said Mrs Thomson vacuously, and the dinghy pulled away clumsily. I waded out a bit, and kicked around in the water to show I didn't care, but I could see Kenneth with his head partly down watching me, waiting to catch my eye, and with the knowing little grin he had when he knew I was hurt. The dinghy angled away towards deeper water, the bow sweeping this way, then that, with the uneven rowing of Mr Kinlethly and Mr Thomson.

'Dolphins, here we come,' I heard Kenneth shouting in his high voice.

That finished it for me, not missing out on the dolphins, but Kenneth going merely because he knew I wanted to. I'd taken a good deal because, after all, I was just a friend of Kenneth's invited for part of the holidays, but I was beginning to think myself pretty spineless. I thought of my Palmerston friends, and the short work they'd have made of Kenneth. I left Mrs Kinlethly watching the dinghy leave the shelter of the bay to reach the dolphins at the point. I went up to the house, across the wide, wooden verandah and into Kenneth's room. From the bottom bunk I took a pillowcase, and began to fill it with shells from Kenneth's collection. I tried to remember the ones he and his father liked best, the ones most often shown to visitors: *Pecten maximus*, *Bursa bubo*, and *Cassis cornuta*, the yellow helmet. The heavy specimens I threw into the bag, and heard them crunch into the shells already there. Once I was committed to it, the enormity of the crime gave it greater significance and release. Whatever outrage the Kinlethlys might feel, whatever recompense they might insist on, Kenneth would understand: he'd know why it was done, and what it represented in terms of him and me.

I took the shells up the track into the bush, and I sat above the glow-worm creek and threw the shells into the creekbed, and into the bush around it. Most disappeared without sound, swallowed up in the leaves and tobacco soil. The yellow helmet stuck in the cleft of a tree, and as I sat guiltily in the coolness and heard the ocean in the bay, it didn't seem incongruous to me, that *Cassis cornuta* set like a jewel in the branches. The bush was a good imitation of an ocean floor, or so I could imagine it anyway.

A sense of drabness followed the excitement of rebellion. I came down to the house, and replaced the pillowcase. Without a plan I began to return to the beach, scuffling in the stones and listening to the sound of the sea. Mrs Kinlethly came up the path towards me. I thought she must have found out about the shells already, and her response was more than anything I'd expected. She walked with her hands crossed on her chest, as if keeping something there from escaping, and her tongue hung half out of her mouth. It was an obscenity, worse than if she'd opened her dress as she came. I tried not to look at her face, and I felt the muscles of my arms and shoulders tighten, like at school just before I was strapped. Mrs Kinlethly passed so close to me that I heard the leather of her sandals squeaking, but she didn't stop or say anything. She went up the steps, and the house swallowed her up in complete silence. I couldn't work out what was happening. I sat down there by the path and waited. I looked out towards the bay and the drifting gulls, letting the wind bring the associations of the sea up to me.

Mr Kinlethly came up next, without his trousers and with everything else wet. Instead of his hair being combed across his head as usual, it hung down one side like ice-plant, and the true extent of his baldness was revealed. 'The dinghy went over. Kenneth's gone,' he shouted at me forcefully, and looked about for others to tell. He seemed amazed that there was just me by the path in the sun, and the birds calling in the bush behind the house. His eyes searched for the crowds that should have been there to receive such news. When I made no reply, he turned away despairingly. 'Kenneth's gone. I must get to the phone,' he shouted at the monkey-puzzle tree by the verandah, and he strode into the house. His coloured shirt stuck to his back, and on the ankle of one white leg were parallel cuts from the rocks.

The house filled rapidly after Mr Kinlethly made his phone calls, until there were enough people even for him: relatives from both sides of the family, friends, and folk from the next bay. Two policemen from Picton came, quiet men who kept out of the house and began the search for Kenneth. I rang my father when I could, and asked him to pick me up at the turn-off by four o'clock. My mother had made it very clear to me about thanking the Kinlethlys before I left, but the way it was I couldn't bring myself to say anything. I just packed my things, and walked up to the road to wait for my father. I was up there by mid-afternoon, and I climbed up the bank above the road and sat there waiting. I hadn't had anything to eat since breakfast. I could see right over the bay, and although the house was hidden by the foreshortened slope and the bush, I could see the boatshed like a garage at the edge of the sand. Where the dinghy had capsized at the point, the chop was visible, occasional small, white crests in the wind.

The Spendthrift

IT WOULD BE easy to begin by saying that everybody in Te Tarehi knew that Thorpe was a miser, but while it was true that all his acquaintances agreed on his utter meanness, it was equally true that he had few acquaintances. Thorpe was a miser in a very small way of business, not a millionaire recluse. A twenty-four-year-old miser who works in a supermarket is not the object of consuming envy or curiosity. Thorpe was noticed in derision only by those few people who met him not by inclination, but in the course of their own duties.

Thorpe worked in packaging, that part of the supermarket not seen by customers. He remained there because his standard of dress was not suitable for an employee who dealt directly with the public. Thorpe and Peter Ransumeen were responsible for weighing and bagging raisins and brown sugar, cutting and wrapping blocks of cheese, and sealing pork chops or tripe in soft, hygienic trays. Thorpe did an hour's overtime every evening when the others were gone: restocking the shelves, and watering the indoor plants in their tubs. Peter Ransumeen rather resented Thorpe's overtime, although not himself prepared to work any extra hours. Peter had a girlfriend and a Zephyr Six to maintain; Thorpe had only himself and a bike with no gears. 'The thing is,' Peter would tell other staff members bitterly, 'he hasn't anything to spend it on.'

A total disregard for appearances is essential in a miser, and Thorpe's bike was typical of his nature. Others biked to work, but they used ten-speed models that were as sleek greyhounds to Thorpe's bike. His was black and upright, with heavy, curved forks like the legs of a widow woman. Peter said it was the original Plunket nurse model. All other aspects of Thorpe's life showed the same priority given to economy. Although he had been away from school for seven years, he still wore the grey uniform shirts of Te Tarehi High. They never seemed to wear out. Peter said that Thorpe went out to the school each year and stole them from the Lost and Found Annexe. Thorpe wore sandshoes most of the time: residual seconds from his time in the badminton club. On very wet days he would put his landlady's galoshes over the sandshoes, and ride his Plunket special through the rain. There is something inherently ugly in galoshes over sandshoes. Thorpe kept down the cost of his board by not having a cut lunch, and he purchased nothing during the day. Instead he sustained himself in working hours by watchful predation in the packaging room. The great scouts of the frontier knew their environment well enough to survive in it; so did Thorpe. He ate damaged cheese, speckled fruit and the little, furrowed snouts of Belgium sausage rolls that were left lying by the slicer.

Thorpe's economic conviction seemed to deepen rather than relent with time. For the first three years after he left school Thorpe played badminton, but then he broke his racket, and left rather than buy a new one. The next year he stopped attending St Fustian's Anglican Church because they introduced a pledge-and-envelope system. Thorpe even managed to resist the greatest of all threats to a miser — women. This was achieved only after a bitter lesson shortly before he left the badminton club. He had stood for some time watching the women's doubles, and the graceful, scissoring legs of Hannah Stevens had seduced him into being included with her in a group which went to the Chinese restaurant. Once Hannah Stevens began to eat, he had realised the enormity of his mistake. Hannah showed complete determination in the satisfaction of her appetites, and the cost of the fried rice, pork and mushrooms was equal to a year's badminton subscription. In matters of money Thorpe was quick to learn, and he never again made any decisions after looking at girls' legs. To recoup the money Thorpe went without dental care for fifteen months, and the bouts of toothache hardened him in his misogyny.

Thorpe was good at his job: methodical, careful and sparing with materials. The privations he imposed on himself did not make him less gentle. Yet Peter Ransumeen found it difficult working with Thorpe. He kept calculating how much Thorpe must be saving, and what would happen to it. Thousands upon thousands of dollars, Peter thought, while he struggled to pay for two new tyres for his car and for tickets to the Sons of Eunuch rock concert. Thorpe in the same job, but immeasurably better off. Thorpe the miser with his school shirts, sandshoes and quiet ways.

Mrs Pollard, with whom Thorpe boarded, did her best to move him from the poverty of his lifestyle but, although a shy person, he showed a startling depth of resolve if pushed towards any cost. Mrs Pollard became quite concerned at times, particularly after any extended period of non-spending by Thorpe, for then she noticed an unnatural elation in his manner. She wondered if he were in the grip of some financial anorexia, and was afraid of the outcome if he denied himself any expense for too long.

Apart from his work, and the constant satisfaction in abstention in all its forms, Thorpe had only two interests — jogging and reading. He ran mile after mile over the logging roads to the west of Te Tarehi, his sandshoes soft on the dirt roads, and his elbows lifting rhythmically. The absence of any tollgates seemed to inspire him. On Sunday afternoons, when Peter, as a well-balanced young New Zealander, roared his Zephyr up and down the reservoir road, or drank beer at Whitloe's Gorge, Thorpe would be running, running through the dark, pine tree hills. Peter would sit on the bonnet of his car, and shake his head. 'That mad miser Thorpe,' he would say. 'What a way to live.'

When he wasn't jogging, or sitting waiting for his few clothes to dry, Thorpe often went to the free lending library. He read with steady implacability. He was fond of novels set in exotic places, but factual travel books were his chief love. Books written by retired naval men, redeemed legal stenographers and defrocked priests, who circumnavigated the world in balloons, travelled through Astrakhan on horseback, set up Esperanto missions on the Orinoco. Sometimes at work, as he packaged pumpkin pieces or priced rusks, Thorpe would murmur Samarkand, or Bacoor Bay. He would stare at the shelves of the packaging room, not focusing there, but on some grander view far beyond.

In June Thorpe was twenty-five. He celebrated his birthday by colouring in the card that his sister-in-law sent him, and by having a long run through the winter mist of the forestry roads. In the evening he put his scrubbed sandshoes by the heater to dry, and sat with them to read about the Hausa people of Nigeria.

Three weeks after his birthday Thorpe's savings account reached twenty-seven thousand dollars. It was a more significant event to him than his birthday. During the lunchtime of the day following his bank statement, Thorpe went to the travel agency. He stood by the window, the airline stickers close to his face. The soft lapels of his grey shirt lay over the neck of his jersey. His fine hair stood on end at the crown and wavered slightly in the convection currents of the central heating. His sandshoes were flattened obsequiously on the floor, but his eyes had a visionary depth. Mrs Jenkins ignored him for some time. She was the deputy mayor's wife, and conscious of appearances. She encouraged later clients to supersede him. She thought it likely that Thorpe was going to beg all the out-of-date brochures for use in collage work with the intellectually handicapped. Finally, when no one else had entered the office for some time, Mrs Jenkins grudgingly acknowledged Thorpe.

He came from the window towards the desk. He took a notebook from his pocket. 'I have places,' he said, 'to see.'

'Yes, yes,' said Mrs Jenkins. He looked unable to afford even the most cursory of Thermal Wonderland Tours. Thorpe began to read.

'Valencia,' he said. 'Chittagong, Palermo, Abilene and Alice Springs. Chengdu and Baton Rouge.'

'Are you serious?' said Mrs Jenkins.

'I have twenty-seven thousand dollars at the Bank of New South Wales,' said Thorpe. He began to read again. Each familiar word was released like a soft, loved pigeon into flight, and as he read he smiled at the wonder of the words. 'Campogalliano, Verona, El-Hajeb, Kotu Bharu, Rostov-na-Donu,' he said.

'And Xanadu,' said Mrs Jenkins.

'I beg your pardon?'

'Do you mind if I ring the bank before I begin an itinerary?' said Mrs Jenkins. 'Just to make sure that any exchange of overseas funds can be easily arranged.'

Thorpe kept his finger on the place in the notebook. He continued to smile, and had forgotten that his lunch-hour was over. When Mrs Jenkins had spoken with the bank, and given him a soft-topped stool to sit on, he began again without raising his voice. 'Bad Ditzenbach, Salinas, Odessa, Addis Ababa, Limoges.' Thorpe ran his hand over his head as he talked, trying to put to rest his fine, waving hair, and his worn sandshoes moved on the crossbar of the stool as if marking the cadence of a poem. 'Casablanca, Dehra Dun,' said Thorpe. 'Mandalay, Amarillo, Malacca and Kathmandu, Baghdad and Kandahar.'

The grand gesture is the road to fame. Thorpe the little miser had been virtually unknown in Te Tarehi; Thorpe the spendthrift caught the town's imagination. Mrs Jenkins bore the story home and hence it was dispersed via council, Rotary and phone. People were amazed at the rigours of his obsessive saving, and the magnificence of his final plan. Te Tarehi's newspaper *The Banner* carried a front-page story on Thorpe which made him a temporary and local celebrity.

The advantages of publicity go always to the strong, however, and the credit was taken piece by piece from Thorpe by more experienced citizens. The mayor talked of his own success in engendering a civic mood of initiative; Mrs Jenkins depicted herself as the original inspiration for the long years of hardship Thorpe had endured; and the bank manager, with self-depreciatory smiles and knowing silences, suggested his assiduous financial care of even the most humble clients. Such is human nature that, by the time Thorpe was to leave, Te Tarehi had almost convinced itself that it was sponsoring him. People discussed his trip as of right, and with a tone of self-congratulation.

Peter Ransumeen drove Thorpe out to the airport, and the miser-turned-spendthrift stood with his pack over one shoulder to say goodbye. Mrs Jenkins and the reporter from *The Banner* were there to see him leave. Thorpe had the vulnerability of a visionary. His landlady had ironed his grey school shirt, and his sandshoes had been whitened, but his hair still stood on end as if in response to the spinning of the earth, and he had no arrogant speech of farewell. Only a shy, dipping smile as he turned away.

'Twenty-seven thousand dollars he saved while working at the supermarket,' said Peter as the plane taxied.

'Front page of *The Banner* at twenty-five,' said the reporter.

'The full tour. The full, grand tour,' said Mrs Jenkins.

Each of them stood for a moment in the shadow of Thorpe's dream, and took from it their own priority.

The Divided World

~

THE WORLD IS divided between you and me, you and me babee, you and me. The world is divided between those who laugh on the inward, and those on the outward breath; between those who say at this point in time, and those who say that it does appear to be the case.

The world is divided between the superstitious, and the unimaginative; between those who love men, and those who love women; between those who have witnessed Bjorn Borg's top-spin, and those who have lost the chance; between the exemplary, and the few of us who are left.

The world is divided into those who appreciate Jane Austen, and fools. The world is divided between the apathy of ignorant youth, and the despair of incorrigible old age. The world is divided between those who blame Lucifer, and those who blame a lack of dietary fibre; between mediocrity, and its own evolution; between the over-worked, and the unemployed; between those who have a daughter, and those denied the greatest blessings.

The world is divided between those who say they adore the country and never go there, and those who say they hate the city and never leave it. The world is divided in the beginning, on all sides, and before God. The world is divided between those we betray, and those who betray us; between those who wake in the darkness with tears, and those too drugged to dream; between those who will not stand a dripping tap, and those who are moderate men. The world is divided among those who deserve it, but not often and not enough.

The world is divided between those who realise their own value, and those who think they may still amount to something; between those who prefer quiz shows, and those who still await their frontal lobotomy; between the old which has lost its edge, and the new which has not been tested; between indecision and hypocrisy, between feeble vacillation and energetic error; between cup and lip. The world is divided between those who understood the significance of Randolph Scott, and the new generation.

The world is divided between those who know nothing smoother than satin, and those who know a woman's thigh. The world is divided between the meek who will inherit the earth, and the strong who will dispossess them of it; between those who believe that they are essentially alone, and those who will be convinced with time; between Sadducees and Pharisees, Hannibal and Hasdrubal, Shaka and Dingane, Dracula and the Wolfman.

The world is divided between those who make a profession of software and prosper, and those who say they recall garlands, mole-catchers and stone walls. The world is divided between silver spoons, and macrocarpa childhoods; between the appalling and the appalled; between consenting adults; between the devil, and the deep big C; between honest toiling forwards, and flashy temperamental backs; between those who help others, and those prepared to let nature take their course.

The world is divided between those who have owned a Triumph 2000, and philistines; between those who have had sex, and those prepared to give it another try; between those who remember the old school haka, and those who attend no reunions even in the mind. The world is divided between those who have a favourite corduroy coat, and those with no affection for habit. The world is divided between those who maintain the distinction between further and farther, and those who compromise with usage; between those who have attended universities, and those who have been inwardly disappointed in other ways; between animals who know only joy and pain, and we who can visualise our own deaths. The world is divided between those who can roll their tongues, and those with more archaic genes. The world is divided between those who should know better.

The world is divided between the Greeks and their gods, and the Trojans who would otherwise have won; between the Green Mountain Boys, and the Black Mountain Boys; between those who gargle in a stranger's bathroom, and those with acquired delicacy; between the undiscerning undistinguished undeserving mass, and us. The world is divided into the states of Jeopardy and Paranoia, Halidom and Dugong, Condominium and the Tribal Lands, all of these, none of these. The world is divided between those who try themselves, and those who seek a less corrupt judge.

The world is divided between those who are tolerant and wise, and their husbands. The world is divided between those in authority, and those resentful of it; between those who are white, and those whose virtues are not so immediately apparent; between those who face the world with a religion, and those who wish to but have only irony in its place. The world is divided between those who have shifted to the North Island, and those passed over for promotion; between one thing and another if distinctions should be made; between tolerant contempt of the artist, and awe of the Cactus and Succulent Society's president. The world is divided between a lawyer and his client, but not equally or *per se*.

The world is divided between those people whose character is known, and those from whom something may still be expected. The world is divided between rancour and disgust, idolatry and idiocy, ballet and bidet, Sordello and Bordello, Bishop Blougram's and Prufrock's apologies. The world is divided between the first and the last, between a man and a woman; between sun and moon; stoics and epicureans; scholards and dullards; the fragrance of mint in the riverbeds and desolate clay. The world is divided between Lucky Jims, and those who see no humour in it; between professed intentions, and the things we would wish undone; between nostalgic falsehood, and anticipatory regret; between dreams of avarice, and visions of self-esteem.

The world is divided between the vices of free will, and the virtues of necessity;

between those who know where be Wold Jar the tinker, and those cast into darkness; between those who delight in games, and those who lack even that saving grace; between Tyrannosaurus Rex, and civilised marriages; between New Zealanders, and those people with a culture; between our adult selves, and the blue remembered hills.

The world is divided between those who boast of their climate, and those who rejoice in secret that a cold wind isolates a landscape. The world is divided between those who accept the division, and those who instigated it; between books on the Royal Family or gardens, and the remaining ten percent of publishers' products; between those who are proud, and those who have lost their self-respect and so become the most dangerous of men. The world is divided on the merits of everything; on all questions raised (at this point in time). The world is divided between optimism, and Mr Weston's good wine; between those who see, and those who understand; between confiding voluble people, and those we wish to know; between those on the inside looking out, and those on the outside looking in.

The world is divided between men who despise others for being what they are, and women who despise them for what they are not. The world is divided between those anxious concerning the physical, and those in terror of the mind; between those who love sausages and onions, and those who are effete; between the people we always suspected, and the butlers who did it; between idlers, and those who work hard all their lives to be able to do nothing when they die.

The world is divided between the few now, and the great majority on the other side. The world is divided above all, while we sleep, beneath our noses, and before we notice. The world is divided as we are all divided. The world is divided between you and me, you and me for a time, you and me.

The Seed Merchant

~

FATHER VERY WORSE, the telegram read. I had it folded in my pocket during the flight south. The wording itched in my mind, and the irritation diverted my worry. I imagined my mother being told that both very and much were an unnecessary expense, and agreeing without caring to cut one out. I was mowing the lawn when it came. I caught a flight so soon afterwards that in the hair of my wrist were fine pieces of cut grass, held out from the skin. At such times the senses are capable of meticulous observation. Birdy Watson was thirteen when he tried to climb the cenotaph, fell off and killed himself. As the taxi passed I saw, far above the stone figures, the ledge that Birdy reached, and the concrete steps below that broke him on his fall. Even his nickname had not saved him. The town had grown rapidly, the driver told me, though it held no progeny of Birdy's or of mine.

My father had rallied by the time I reached him. You will recognise the terminology. He had rallied surprisingly well, the doctor said. So my father was able to return home and wait a little longer. He lay in his own bed, and as I talked first in the hall with my mother and sister, I could hear him clearing his throat as he waited to welcome me. A questing smile as he tried to see in my face a picture of himself before I could disguise it. He clasped my hand rather than shook it, and looked away, asked about Susan and the children as a defence against his own predicament. The rowan trees by the fence were in berry amidst the fingered leaves, and I could see the hardwood chopping block where roosters had been sacrificed. All of us had lived together in the place, yet each had a separate experience of it: in the same way we share life, I suppose.

'Lately I've often thought of things to say to you,' my father said. 'No one argues about books anymore. No one cares. It's all politics and entertainment now, you see.'

'Reading and writing are too slow for them,' I said.

My father nodded against the pillow. 'Even in sport,' he said. 'Even in sport all they're interested in is finishes, and the money.'

I sat in the cane chair by the window and talked with my father. I hadn't been there long before he mentioned Ivy. He asked if I remembered her, and said what a close friend of my mother's she'd been. He turned his head and looked at the window with flat eyes, the symptom of the inverted vision of memory. The skin lay loosely on the tendons of his neck, and stubble was salt and pepper beneath his jaw-line. After a time he said, 'You remember Ivy.' He took my silence as forgetfulness. 'You stayed with her at times as a boy. You mustn't forget Ivy. People used to take her and your mother as sisters. Did you know that?'

Ivy must have been thirty odd when I stayed with her. She laughed a lot. There was always reason for a laugh at things, even though she did have her mother to look after. The trams came right past their house. Over thirty years ago. The noise and smell of the trams on the street straight through to the square. Ivy and her mother made painted eggs of wood. Ivy was a nurse as well at a private hospital, but I remember them sitting with trays of eggs. The old woman sanded the eggs wet and dry. She had a slight moustache. Ivy painted them: several coats and then designs and varnish. Patterns like Fair Isle, or hooped colours, or little circles like the seeds of silver birch. I don't know what they were for: darning, or paperweights, or to be valued for their own sake perhaps, on a mantelpiece in deep blue and gold.

'She came sometimes to stay with us. A great friend of your mother's.' And of my father. 'You remember staying there now?' he said. Yes, I remembered things that had a new interpretation with the years. Like the seed merchant. Some friend was with Ivy. They laughed in the bedroom as Ivy finished dressing to go out, and the trams rattled past to the square. I was to remain behind with the old lady, and fill the coal scuttle from time to time. Ivy called to me from her room. The two of them were laughing again. How they were laughing, and there was powder smudged on the dark polish of the duchess, and underclothes on the bed like the limp, pink petals of a rose. Ivy stopped me with her hand, and brushed the hair from my forehead.

'This is Frank's boy,' she said. Her friend started to laugh. 'Oh stop it,' said Ivy, laughing herself, and swaying back to ease the effort of the laughter. She brushed my hair again to show she wasn't meaning to laugh at me.

'How is your father? How is the seed merchant?' said Ivy's friend. Her top teeth were slightly buck, yet white and of a size.

'He's not a seed merchant,' I said. 'He works for the paper.'

'Oh, Ivy always told me he was,' she said.

'He proved to be, by God!' said Ivy.

I was disappointed not to be going with them into the city, for at night the noise and lights of the tram blurred its outline, fusing the tram with the other colours and movement of the city night.

My father slept a good deal. I spent much of each day working in the section which had been neglected because of his illness. I cleared and levelled several garden plots, and put them down in grass. I lacked the resignation of my mother and sister to sit and talk quietly in the living room with his medicines on a tray, while they waited for him to wake. Each task served to exorcise some small ghost of time past, trivial familiars that were in wait within the simplest things. My father's fishing rod above the garage door, and the breadboard shaped like a pig.

Sport was my father's realm as a journalist. He was given his own column when I was in the fourth form, and stayed so long in the hotel that my brother and I divided his scallops between us, and enjoyed the celebration on his behalf. I read to him about sport, and wildlife, which was his other interest. For years he said that he would write a book on that great man Anthony Wilding, but it was never done. 'Ivy married, you know,' he said. 'Went to live in Tasmania, but it didn't last.' We were quiet for a time. My father seemed to want me to remember Ivy, and I did, but not in his way. 'It didn't last,' my father said. 'She came back to New Zealand again, but we never saw her.' Ivy took me to the pictures in the square at night. On the tram I stood by the driver and watched him use the solid metal levers in place of a steering wheel. The noise, and the lights of the square in the distance. Ivy bought chocolates loose in a bag, and she laughed with the manager, who looked at the front of her dress. She told me that she used to go to the pictures often with my mother when they were nurses together. I hadn't thought about Ivy for a long time before coming to see my father: the trams, the painted wooden eggs, the seed merchant. Sitting with my father I realised more clearly that my age had prevented me from knowing Ivy as she was to a man, though even then I was conscious I think of warmth, fluidity of movement, and laughter both generous and knowing. 'They were fine lasses, those two. Ivy and your mother. A lot of people thought they were sisters,' said my father. I had no clear recollection of my mother at Ivy's age. We make present appearance retrospective for those close to us. 'You were only a boy,' said my father, recalling not so much my age then, as his own. Frank the snappy dresser and journalist perhaps.

'Trams ran right past her gate,' I said. 'Right past and rattling on down into the square.'

'I know.'

'And Ivy's old mother who was always cold, always sitting over the fire or heater.'

'Of course. Old Mrs Ransumeen. But she was deaf, you remember. Yes, that's right. Ivy's mother, Mrs Ransumeen. She didn't sleep well, but she was rather deaf.' My father laughed quietly. I couldn't remember the old lady being all that deaf. My father's laugh was even and subdued. It seemed the laugh of a younger man, just that once.

I asked my mother about Ivy one afternoon. My father had fallen asleep while I read aloud from his articles on Anthony Wilding. He started to weep in his sleep: the tears soaked into the white, cotton pillow, yet he lay without sound or movement, apart from his breathing. I hope never to see that again. I told my mother that he asked about Ivy quite often. She said he never mentioned Ivy to her. She'd known Ivy longer than the rest of us, but then perhaps a friend's view of Ivy was not what my father wanted.

The wind was strong outside. It set up a persistent and familiar whine around one of the protruding barge-boards. 'Could you cut back the twisted willow by the study again sometime?' my father said. 'The branches rub on the side of the house in the wind, and the leaves block the guttering.'

'You cut it down years ago,' I told him. He was quiet for a time, smiling.

'What an old fool I've become,' he said. 'Jesus, just an old fool. Even my sense of taste is playing up. I get a sudden taste of onions or marmalade when I'm lying in bed. It makes me sick at times, the taste of things I haven't eaten, suddenly there in my throat.' Ivy's mother had kept clearing her throat all the time — arp, arp, arp. Indignities come with age, it seems. She used to wet the eggs to give them a last buffing with a leather cloth. She always reminded us to check the coal bin before we left her alone in the winter. I don't think my brother ever went to stay with Ivy, it was always me.

Ivy took me to the knick-knack and souvenir shop by the river once. She had her eggs in a shoe box, each wrapped in tissue. She took some out to impress the shop-keeper, and spread them on the counter, and moved them with her fingers to show how even, bright and smooth they were. He touched each in turn after she had, his hands following hers. Ivy laughed, making the eggs brighter than ever on the counter, and her dress rustled on her stockings. I wonder if he knew better than I did what use they were, and I wonder why I never thought to ask her.

My father had become a noisy breather, not snoring, but the air forced in and out, whispering in his nose, resounding in his chest, so that the mechanism by which life is sustained was always emphasised. His thoughts turned back, and I couldn't follow him all the way. We started out as equals, with the same perspective in that at least we were adults, but as we went back my sight became that of a boy, while he remembered Ivy as a man. I don't know if my father realised that, or what he expected of me. Any interpretation of what we knew as a child is dangerous. 'I took them both to the Industries Fair once,' he said. 'I was working for the old *Herald* and had complimentary tickets. There was a demonstration of working machinery from the woollen mills, and a glass blower who made goblets and ships as you watched. Your mother and Ivy wore dresses with puffed sleeves.' My father paused. 'The skin that girls had then,' he said. I had a vision of my father then as in his old photos, with a soft brim hat, and two-tone shoes. With a smooth, thin face, and one hand in his pocket.

These questions and offerings of Ivy occurred among many other things not relevant to them in my talks with my father, but the reiteration was not in my imagination, I thought. I told my sister that in a way it embarrassed me, for I wasn't sure what was required. I was going to tell her of the seed merchant, but closed my mouth on it. She is a shrewd and handsome woman, my sister. About the age that Ivy had been, when I think of it. She said that he had a history with Ivy, odd expression, but that it was the time back he wanted, not just Ivy. She said the ache was for the time of it: Ivy and our mother like sisters, and he himself as he was. My sister may be right, and I too insensitive to understand. Perhaps my father did in fact see Ivy as the image of what they both were, my mother and her: even the image of what all three were then. He never knew Ivy old, never saw her since he knew her, and she had never seen him old.

My father would sweat a lot sometimes as he lay in bed. Not on his face, but at the base of his neck, the pit where neck met chest, and the sweat would glisten there with the movement of his chest and the forced breathing. When I went down to the living room my mother would ask me if he was awake. Ivy's mother fell asleep in front of the fire in the evenings. Ivy placed a patterned tea cosy on her head, and we laughed without noise, or malice. 'We lost touch with her after her marriage broke up and she came back. Even that we heard about through someone else,' my father said. 'Like a sister to your mother, like a mother to you.'

'I remember her better when I stayed with her, than when she came to visit us.'

'It was different,' my father said.

My father asked me to clean out the desk in his study, and yes, I found one of Ivy's eggs lying with Forest and Bird annual reports, typewriter ribbons, dry fountain pens and pieces of kauri gum. The egg was royal blue, with gold and red rosettes. Still shiny, but old-fashioned in a way I couldn't pick. The decoration gave a false impression of jewelled solidity, for when I lifted up that Trojan egg it lay lightly in my hand, as if already hatched. I could see faint cracks in the paint, which compensated for the drying of the wood through many years. The tram-lines were shiny in the street outside Ivy's house, as if someone from the council polished the top surface. On a hot day the sun caught the lines for blocks ahead, and the trams shook and shimmered all the more in the currents of heat. Ivy used to push my hair off my fore-head, and make a part using her own comb. I felt ashamed of the egg in a way. I put it in my pocket as I stood in the study, and my fingers caught on the edges of the telegram still there. Father very worse, it said, and it was true again.

A Town of Rivers

~

ORWELL, USK, CLYDE, Lune and Rother, Don and Dee, Stour, Tees and Tay. I live in a town of rivers. Even colonialism desires security, and a backward glance becomes a civic policy: an indirect geography which usage has made familiar, a transposed reality for thirteen thousand people. Original parochialism is forgotten as Trent and Forth flow in to join the Thames. A Thames which is undisputed highway, for even our eccentricity is betrayed by logic. Awamoa and the Severn are contiguous, and from the banks of Tamar a Pacific Ocean can be seen.

'I walk a good deal still,' my father says. 'A lot can be learnt from a place by walking.' We have walked Port Underwood, the Coromandel, Lake McKerrow, he and I. This is by contrast a very modest and a modern stroll. We tend to walk when we meet: a sense of progress is achieved perhaps. And yet I find it hard to prove such earlier places. We are many people in a single life, removed from earlier as well as other selves. I can as easily believe I lived once upon the tundra, for the images of that are conjured up as readily as those for Te Kuiti or for Monkey Bay.

'Your Uncle Barry called in, you know, shortly before I came down. He spent two days with us before going on to Hastings. Simon, his eldest boy is there, the dentist. Barry's got cataracts. My father, your grandfather, had the same thing: cataracts. So have I, but not disabling yet.' Then cataracts for me, I suppose, in time: a predisposed disease. But none in the smooth surface of the streams we follow as we walk. 'Barry can't look after the home place anymore. It's grown too much for him.' The home place, we both know, is the same size, but who wants to say it is my uncle that has become diminished.

The Tyne is a steep river here in this town, but noiseless still as we descend it. 'I have been invited to talk on Kipling at the teachers' college', my father says. 'Virtually disregarded now because of his politics, but ah, the man had ability, you know. A rich, a prolific mind.' I have heard and enjoyed the lectures. I know more of Kipling's boyhood than my father's. Shall I commission him to lecture on his own life? In a formal interpretation I think he will be at ease, a water jug and glass on the table by his side, and myself sitting alone before him at a distance.

In time we all punish our parents for having treated us like children. We make known our reservations by the bias of our anecdotes, the timing of our visits. The calculated attention we see fit to give them stresses the new order. We pay them back for small grievances they never knew existed, and which even our conscious minds have forgotten. In atavistic competition there is still wonder that we can't grow as tall as we remember them, and neither again can they.

Dart and Leith, Torridge and Colne, Avon, Wear, Chelmer, Withim and Wye.

Tweed, Itchen, Wansbeck and the sweep of Eden: a town of rivers. I walk here often, and follow river after river, courses which have no headwaters but flow in as tributaries from every right-angle junction. The cemetery is an island from which not a soul escapes, and on the high side of the Avon a bird heaped other than praises on my head. The ratepayers' trees follow the mown banks, and post boxes like moorings are marked in red. Starlings are the poor man's kingfishers, and crossings weirs which cause no ruffle on the surface. Lines surely lead back from the quiet streams to each shut bungalow. The lines are never visible, yet golden carp are feasted on perhaps, and punts put out on moonless nights to carry dreams away.

'There is a blue depth to the summer twilight sometimes,' my father says. 'I notice it looking down towards the park.' We walk on amicably. We talk of books: ours an intellectual rather than emotional umbilical. I have never seen my father greet a contemporary with the warmth with which he welcomes Wordsworth, Keats, Conrad and Galsworthy. 'As I grow older,' my father says, 'I'm surprised to find myself turning more and more to poetry again.' Yet Hardy did so, and with effect. 'Yet Hardy did, and with surprising lyricism too,' my father says before I can. He quotes from that old Lear as we go on.

In other families I was amazed to find, and find it discussed, that people shouted, wept and stole, slept with each other, had debts and diseases. The only gossip which interests my father is from Boswell and from Lamb, and the horror of the dog that destroyed a manuscript. While Holland governed here, my father in his study read to me from Gladstone on Home Rule for Ireland. He would pass a hand over his soft hair and say, ah, but the man had ability all right, had stature no doubt. Say what you like, the man had the gift. 'It seems to me,' my father says, 'that there was an integrity of personal and political vision in the best Victorians that is scarcely to be found today. A nobility in the best and classless sense of the word. Today's leadership, whether political or literary, is all snide cynicism and extension of self.' My father's pace and tone are calm and steady as we begin another river. A rigorous contempt of emotional display has been my inheritance: the composure of a solitary and self-sufficient man. A fierce self-criticism, and the acceptance of no other criticism. Privacy is the necessity of a thinking man. To ask my father of his health is almost as personal as to question his morality.

We talk of Eliot and R. S. Thomas. My father's quotes are longer and with a better emphasis than mine. He lifts a hand before him briefly to point a rhythm as we walk, and the breeze is brisk from the sea. Common admiration for a line is the mutual affection we allow ourselves.

Wharfe, Frome and Exe, Ribble, Mersey, Test and Towey. The Coquet, Weaver, Ure, Nen, Till, Humber and Arun. Old Yare and Ouse. Compressed in men's minds they flow closely here, evidence that no one can bear a land where everything is new, evidence of an alchemist's continuity. Along these British rivers we talk of Peacock and of Dickens. There are willows in this country now as well as cabbage trees. The Pakeha, too, brought memories, and if at first the gold is spun to straw, belief retained means the process may be reversed again with time. 'But ah,' my father says, 'the man had life in his writing, say what you will. He knew that history is people, that art is people, that time is only people set in ranks.'

We walk on in this place as we have in others, some physical, some verbal land-scapes. I live in a town of rivers: a town of rivers which, like time itself, run deep.

The Paper Parcel

⌒

For a long time I thought everybody could see the future in the way I could myself: an expectation based upon desire. The dream logic of the mind. Even though events were often very different, it was the reality I blamed and not the vision. The reality failed to match the vision, which was the first and greater view. The actual encroached, but expectation drew off, and set up again upon the high ground of the future.

I remember asking Dusty Rhodes what he thought being in a submarine was like. I dunno, he said, I dunno do I, until I've been in one. What a way to live. He didn't know any better. He was spared any disillusion at least. No matter how many times it happened, I felt a sense of loss and betrayal when things proved other than I had seen them. Not different only, but also less in fitness and in unity.

Like the fancy dress ball, for instance. I was twelve when the senior classes had a fancy dress ball to end the year. It was a strict convention that you had to have a partner in advance. Anyone not paired off would hold his hand in fire rather than turn up that night. As far as I knew I had only three attributes to attract the opposite sex. I was the second fastest runner in the school, I was top in maths and I had blue eyes. Dusty Rhodes was fastest boy. I never beat him, although sometimes I dreamt I might. I became accustomed to despair, and his greasy hair in front of me as we ran race after race. Dusty drowned in the Wairau the next year, by the berth of the coaster which used to come over from Wellington and up the river. For years I had a guilt that I might have wished it. I was second fastest in the school to Dusty. I used to boast to the others that my legs just went that fast without any effort from the rest of me. To enhance this I had the habit of looking sideways as I ran, as if to see the cars on the road to the bridge, and escape the boredom of my automatic legs. Being top of maths was the second thing, and quite beyond my control. I was always top and never had an explanation for it. I was fearful I would lose the trick of it. And the blue eyes. There were only four boys with blue eyes in the class, and Fiona McCartney told Bodger that she liked blue eyes best. The class had been singing beautiful, beautiful brown eyes, and Bodger asked her which she preferred. Fiona McCartney blushed and said blue eyes, and the other girls giggled. I didn't forget that. I was beginning to store up points of knowledge about girls. Fiona McCartney was the oracle about such things at that school.

So those were the advantages I had going for me, and I exploited them to the full in the weeks before the fancy dress dance. I never ran so often or so fast. I was closer to first and further from third than ever before. I turned my head to the side with casual indifference and the old legs went with a will. I took to answering more maths questions in class, and fluked most of them right, and I used to widen my eyes when I was close to girls so that the blue of them would be more conspicuous.

Fiona McCartney passed a message to me saying she wanted to see me by the canteen at playtime, and when she came we went over by the sycamores and railings. She put one hand on the railing and swung her right foot in an arc on the grass. She glanced at her friends by the canteen and considered she had set a good scene. I widened my eyes at her, and held my breath without realising it. She told me that she wouldn't be going to the dance with me. I hadn't asked her, but she knew she was every boy's choice and was letting me down gently. As I was the second fastest and so on, she realised my expectations. I felt dizzy, then remembered to breathe out again. She said I'd have no trouble getting someone to go with. The girls had been talking, she said. She said the girls had been talking, and she put the tip of her tongue between her teeth and smiled. I smiled back and widened my eyes, as if I were aware of what girls said.

It made me more anxious, though, Fiona saying that, especially when we started having dancing practices. I wondered which of the girls had partners arranged already, for I wanted to avoid the humiliation of asking them. Kelly Howick saved me the trouble. At the third practice she said to me that I wasn't much of a dancer, and was I going to the fancy dress night. I said that I thought that I probably would. Casually I said it, and looked to the side as if I were running. I widened my eyes too, which wasn't much good when I was looking away. Are you listening? she said. In the past I'd thought about Kelly mainly as the girl most likely to keep me from fluking top in maths. She was top in most things. She had definite breasts, though, and was pretty. Only a certain matter-of-fact manner prevented her from being more like Fiona McCartney. It came to me that she was willing to be my partner. Only later did it also occur to me that she and her friends had made the decision without my presence being required. I will be your partner if you like, she said. She didn't need an answer. She seemed pleased for me. She smiled at me, and at her friends, as we moved awkwardly to the dancing instructions of Bodger and Miss Erikson.

I'd had my share of success in life. Top of maths and running, as I've said, and trials for the under-thirteen reps, but in that school hall I felt for the first time the heady stuff of sexual preferment. Kelly Howick had sought me out. I looked with contempt upon the others in the hall: Dusty Rhodes who could only run fast, and Bodger with the sweat stains on his shirt. For the first time I perceived myself in the mirror of the feminine eye; I was filled with casual arrogance and power, I was aware of a new dimension to life. My head kept nodding indolently as we danced, and my shoulders shrugging in some instinctive male response.

The knowledge of sexual magnetism was a novelty. I felt I should be able to tap it for other purposes. The day after the dancing practice I raced Dusty again. I felt the new power within me and was resolved to express it in my running also. I would bury him. In fact it made not an inch of difference. I still had to run behind Dusty, his hair bobbing. And he didn't even have a partner to the dance. It was a shock to discover that the power generated by sexual preferment was not directly transferable to athletic performance.

In my mind I was quite sure how the fancy dress dance would be. Sure, I had been let down somewhat in the past by the failure of events to conform with my directions, but I wasn't responsible for that. I saw Kelly and myself always in the centre of the hall, always in the better light, and somehow slightly larger than our classmates. I would dance, or stand quietly and attract the attention of other girls because of my blue eyes, and a certain calmness of manner. Kelly would be constantly asking my opinion, and I would be giving it with easy finality. Instead of the lucky spot waltz there would be quizzes on tables, or a sprint the length of the hall and back when Dusty happened to be outside.

Kelly Howick talked to me during practices. I made the adult discovery that some people are ugly. I'd had the foolish idea that there were no common standards of appearance. Now I began to realise otherwise. Collie Richardson, for example, who told the best jokes in the school. He had a very small upper lip. It was like a little skirt, and his gums and teeth were always exposed beneath it. Once I realised he was ugly I never liked his jokes as much again.

At the practices Kelly took over my instruction. She gave an individual repetition of what Bodger and Miss Erikson kept saying. You've not got much rhythm, have you, she said. Me! Second fastest and with automatic legs. In other circumstances it would have irritated me, but in the complacency of preferment I let it pass. I just looked aside and widened my eyes at Fiona McCartney. Certain things about girls have to be tolerated for the overall benefit.

I skidded on loose stones by the sycamores next day and put a long graze along my left forearm. Mrs Hamil put iodine on it and Kelly was quite concerned. It won't show on the night, will it? she said. What are you going to wear anyway? What's your outfit like? Her saying that made my arm begin to throb. The blood seeped out into beads despite the iodine. I hadn't done anything about a costume. The priority of getting a partner had obscured all other aspects of the dance. I asked my mother about it that night, and she said that's nice, a costume party is nice. Sure, we'll think of something. And my father made jokes for his own amusement about being cloaked in ignorance, or dressed in a little brief authority. I could tell they didn't have the right view of the ball at all, that they were thinking of it as some party, some kids' thing.

Tony Poole said his parents were hiring a full cowboy outfit with sheepskin chaps, bandanna and matched revolvers. Dusty's parents were pretty poor. I thought he wouldn't have much to wear even when he did arrange a partner. But he said his cousin had a Captain Marvel costume which had been professionally made. What is it you're going as? Kelly asked me again. I started questioning my mother once more. What was she going to do for me? Kelly was going as Bo Peep. What about my costume, I said to my mother. Oh, we'll rustle up something don't you worry, she said. But I did. The more casual and unperturbed she was, the more I worried.

Finally my mother said she thought I should go as a parcel. A parcel, Jesus. She remembered someone at the New Year's party as a parcel, and he was a great hit. It was a cheap costume too, she said. A parcel, Jesus. It was the originality of it that intrigued her, she said. Anyone could go as a policeman or a musketeer; people grew tired of seeing them. The parcel left only head and limbs out, she said, and I could make up a giant stamp with crayons, and over my parcel body have stickers saying Fragile, London, This Side Up, Luxemburg, Handle with Care. The parcel was set to torpedo my night with Kelly Howick. Bo Peep Kelly with her beginning breasts and braided hair, and me as a brown paper parcel with a stamp done in crayon.

There was a sense of inevitability about the parcel. I tried to persuade my mother that I should go as something else. I said I wouldn't wear it, but the parcel became part of me before I ever saw it, something irrevocable and humiliating before I was even dressed in it.

The dance was supposed to start at eight. It said so on the printed sheet I brought home. Nobody arrives at a dance on time, though, my mother said. She never realised how little adult convention applies to the young. It said eight o'clock on the sheet, didn't it? Why would it say that if it didn't mean it? Nobody comes to a dance till later, my mother said. It's just how it's done. But I saw eight o'clock written. I knew everyone would be there. Anthony Poole in his cowboy outfit, and Kelly as Bo Peep.

On that Friday I didn't run well. Dusty beat me without hardly trying, and although I looked away as I ran, I was having a hard time to keep ahead of Ricky Ransumeen in third place. My automatic legs were being affected. I thought a good deal about that because it seemed unfair. When I was selected by Kelly, when desirability was conferred on me, although the power was great, it hadn't made me any faster, as I told you. But on that last day, as I turned my head in studied casualness, instead of the flowing leaves of the sycamores by the fence, I saw myself in a parcel costume with a crayon stamp. Just for a moment there in the stippled leaves and keeping pace with me was a *doppelgänger* in a parcel. I lacked rhythm as I ran, I lacked a full chest of air, my automatic legs made demands.

It wasn't until after tea that my mother even began the parcel. I had to wear my swimming togs so no clothes would show below the parcel. The brown paper strips were wrapped around me like nappies, and round and round my chest, and holes cut for my head and arms. I was tied with twine and with a yellow ribbon in a bow at the front. Over my heart was stuck the crayoned stamp, huge and serrated. Other oblong stickers were plastered on with flour-and-water paste. This Side Up, Handle with Care, On Her Majesty's Service, Do Not Rattle. I was finally packed by eight o'clock, and set off on my bike for the school assembly hall. I tried to sit up straight on the seat so that the parcel wouldn't crinkle too much. The wrapping made noises as I rode, and the greasy blue and red head on the stamp grinned in the setting sun. I told myself that the parcel was really quite clever and would go down well. I could only half believe it, yet I never seriously thought about not going. The power of sexual preferment was enough to transform me. It would make difference distinction, and

The Paper Parcel ~ 139

nonconformity audacity. To be with Kelly Howick would be sufficient to defeat the parcel.

They had started, of course. I knew it. The sheet had said eight o'clock after all. The light from the hall spilled out into the soft summer evening. The noise of the band and the dancing slid out with the light, and echoed in the quad. Bodger patrolled the grounds, alert for vandalism, or lust. Late, said Bodger. He looked at my costume and said no more. As I went in he was still there on the edge of the light and the noise, and with the blue evening as a backdrop. He had his hands behind his back, and he swayed forward on his toes. Hurry up then, said Bodger. I slipped in round the edge of the door, and worked my way over to the boys' side. Tony Poole had a curled stetson, sheepskin chaps, checked shirt and six-guns with matching handles. He came back from seeing Fiona McCartney to her seat. Toomey was a fire chief with a crested helmet that glittered, and a hatchet at his belt. Dusty's Captain Marvel insignia was startling on his chest, and his cloak was cherry rich and heavy. And I was a parcel. A brown paper parcel with bare legs and sandshoes. A brown paper parcel that crinkled when I moved. A brown paper parcel with a stamp drawn up in red and blue. It wasn't right: not for the second fastest runner in the whole school, not for the top maths boy, and the one preferred by Kelly Howick. What the hell is that you're wearing? said Dusty. Wouldn't you like to know, I said.

I went over to claim Kelly when the music began for the next dance. It was a fox-trot. I had learnt both sorts of dance. A waltz was where you took one step to the side every now and again, and a quickstep was where you kept forging ahead. A fox-trot is just a slower quickstep. I'm a little late, I said, smiling and nodding. I found that, without meaning to, I was trying to compensate for being a parcel. Kelly's Bo Peep outfit suited her. The bodice with the crossed straps accentuated her breasts, and she had a curved crook. She looked fifteen at least. As we danced I knew that she was looking at the parcel. I heard myself laughing loudly at Captain Marvel who was fighting with a pirate, but Kelly kept looking at my costume. I was going to come as a pirate myself, I said. I had a better pirate outfit than that; a huge hat with skull and crossbones, and an eye-patch. What? she said. I was going to come as a pirate, I said. I can't hear you for all the noise your brown paper makes, Kelly said. It wasn't so, of course. The band was making more noise than the parcel. No, she was giving me the message. Even the way she danced with me was different from other times. She had a dull expression on her face, as if she was doing me a favour by dancing. I tried whirling her around, the way Bodger and Miss Erikson had demonstrated. I nearly fell over, she said. It was a lesson for me in the transience of sexual preferment. It was apparently something that had to be taken advantage of immediately.

I was determined not to mention being a parcel. Not admitting it was some way of keeping the full force of its humiliation from me. I quite like Dusty's Captain Marvel suit, I told Kelly. A bit overdone, but I quite like it. I told Miss Erikson I'd help with supper, she said. It won't be worth you coming over for the next dance because I'll start helping her soon, I think. Sure, sure, I said, we must have the grub on time. The grub on time! I couldn't believe I was saying it. And afterwards I'll probably help with the washing up, Kelly said.

Flour-and-water paste isn't very successful when there's any movement. Some of the stickers were starting to work loose on the brown paper. This Way Up fell on to the dance floor. Handle with Care came off and I tucked it under the twine. It worked down low on my waist, and Dusty and Ricky Ransumeen started pointing and laughing at its anatomical juxtaposition. I took Kelly back to her side of the hall after the dance. See you then, I said. She slipped among the other girls with a murmur. Who could blame her? As I went back over the floor I could see several of my labels lying there. Fragile, Via Antwerp, Airmail. Maybe someone would start collecting them and draw attention to them. The parcel was ceasing to be recognisable as such. Without stickers, wrinkled and lopsided after the dancing, it had lost what little illusion of costume it ever had. I was a kid wrapped in brown paper and wearing bathing togs and sandshoes. Ah, Jesus me. Only the stamp over my heart seemed firmly stuck. A mark of Cain in crayon that leered out on all the world, and would not release itself or me. I was beaten all right. I couldn't maintain any longer my vision of how the night should be. And the withdrawal of sexual preferment had weakened me; my esteem had been eroded. I began to work my way towards the door: a paper parcel through the Batmen, policemen, riverboat gamblers and Indian chiefs. Little Wade Stewart was a Pluto. He came up to me with Fragile. Is this yours? he said kindly. Yes, what a dag, isn't it? I said. I kept on moving towards the door, and reached it as the lucky spot waltz was announced.

It felt good outside. The summer dusk, the distanced and impersonal buildings, the lucky spot music fading as I made my way to the bikesheds. Bodger loomed up. I got a bit of a nosebleed, I told him, but as I was by myself he wasn't interested. I rode out of the grounds, and the crinkle of the parcel and the lessening music conjoined down the quiet street. I allowed myself the indulgence of self-pity for a time. I was outside myself, I accompanied myself, I consoled myself, for the bland incomprehension of adults and the loss of sexual status. I felt I had been hard done by, that was the truth. Perhaps there would be a fire in the hall. I imagined the flames leaping from the walls, and the riverboat gamblers and fairy queens put to flight. Faster and faster I biked. I saw the fiery press of the blaze, the terror of my classmates, the impotence of Bodger and Miss Erikson. I stood up on the pedals in the soft, summer night and put on a sprint that would have carried me clear of any possible pursuit. Parcel my arse, I shouted, and louder, parcel my arse. I reckoned that I was about the fastest bike rider at that school. I reckoned that even Dusty Rhodes wouldn't be a patch on me at that. I felt the wind of my flight pushing the brown paper against me as I swept without a light down the blue streets.

There was a light in the living room when I reached home, however. I put the bike away, and looked through the gap between curtain-edge and window-side. My mother was listening to the radio and talking; my father was cleaning his shoes on a newspaper spread by his chair. I had to find some immediate focus for revenge, and they would serve as enemies. I crept into the kitchen and took a packet of my father's cig-arettes from behind the clock, and struck a match to inspect the pantry cupboard. Mixed fruit pack, I chose; raisins, candied peel, sultanas, figs, cherries. I took the fruit pack and cigarettes to the woodshed. I sat on the pine slabs in the lean-to there, and ate the fruit mix and smoked my father's Pall Mall. I ripped off the stamp in crayon, and burnt holes in it. I flashed the glowing cigarette against the navy sky, writing Zorro in swift neon. I undid the twine and unwrapped the parcel, burying the pieces in the wood heap. Jesus, I said, so what? Who cares about the dance and being a paper parcel? I was still second fastest in the school, wasn't I? Wasn't I! I sat in my togs and singlet, ate my dried fruit, and watched the smoke curl as shadows from my fingers. Let the world come on, I could take it. And next time it would be different. I could see so clearly the next year's dance, when I would be Napoleon and Fiona McCartney my Josephine. That's how it would be all right.

The Fat Boy

~

THE MEN COMING from the railway yards were the first to notice the fat boy. He stood beneath the overhead bridge, among the cars illegally parked there. He had both hands in the pockets of his short pants and the strain of that plus his heavy thighs made the flap of his fly gape. The fat boy watched the passers-by with the froglike, faintly enquiring look that the faces of fat boys have. The fat boy's hair was amazingly fair and straight; it shone with nourishment; it was straight and oddly medieval.

The men were leaving at twenty past four. It was a conventional extension of the time for washing up that their union had obtained. They resented the fat boy's regard day after day. They were sure that he was stealing from the cars, and it was just as well they were coming past early to watch him, they said. Sometimes they would shout at the fat boy and tell him to get lost, as they walked in their overalls along the black margin of the track past the old gasworks. Seventeen thousand dollars worth of railway property was found missing when the audit was made. The men knew it was outsiders. They remembered the fat boy. The fat kid is the lookout for the ring taking all the stuff, they told the management. Dozens of workers could swear to having seen the fat boy. They went looking for him, but he wasn't to be found beneath the overhead bridge anymore.

Instead the fat boy began to frequent McNulty's warehouse in Cully Street. Even through the cracked and stained windows the staff could see him standing by the side of the building where the bicycles were left. Sometimes he would kick at the clumps of weeds which grew in the broken pavement there, sometimes he would puff his fat cheeks and blow out little explosions of air, sometimes he would just stand with his hands in his pockets and look at the warehouse as if to impress it on his mind. He had a habit of pulling his mouth to one side, as if biting the skin on the inside of his cheek, the way children do. Often in school time he was there. Sometimes even in the rain he was there. The rain glistened on his round cheeks, and seemed to shrink his pants so that the lining turned up at the leg holes. The new girl looked out and said he looked as if he was crying. The owner said he'd make him cry all right. He was sick of ordering him away, the owner said.

McNulty's warehouse burnt down in November. The owner made particular mention to the police of the fat boy, but when McNulty's built again in a better area with the insurance money, the fat boy never appeared. The paper reported what the owner said about the fat boy. The railway men said it was the same fat boy all right. They said the fat kid was somehow tied up in a lot of the crime going on.

The fat boy seemed to be in uniform, but although he was clearly seen by many people there was no agreement as to his school or family. Some said his socks had the blue diamonds of Marsden High, but others said the blue was in the bands of College. The fat boy had thick legs with no apparent muscles, and they didn't narrow to the ankle. If just his legs could have been turned upside down no one would ever know it. When the fat boy lifted his brows enquiringly, one crease would form in the smooth, thick skin of his forehead.

The fat boy seemed to be a harbinger of trouble. The fat boy walked behind old Mrs Denzil on her way home from the shopping centre, and he loitered in the shade of her wooden fence, which was draped with dark convolvulus leaves and its pale flowers. The police maintained a quiet watch on the house for two days in case the fat boy came again. On the third night someone broke into Mrs Denzil's house and tied her upside down in the washtub. Her Victorian cameo broach was stolen, together with the tinned food she hoarded, and eighty-four-year-old Mrs Denzil was left tied upside down in the tub with a tennis ball in her mouth to block her breathing. Oh, that fat boy, they said: even murder, they said. That fat boy was so much more evil than their own sons. There wasn't anything that the fat boy wouldn't do, was there, they said.

Nigel Lammerton saw the fat boy on the night he was arrested for beating his wife. Lammerton told the police that when he returned from the hotel he saw the fat boy on the porch of his home, and that his wife couldn't explain why. Lammerton said that he saw the fat boy looking in the window at them while they argued, but that when he ran outside the fat boy was gone. It was the fat boy, and the medication that he had been taking, that made him lose control, Nigel Lammerton told the court. Mrs Lammerton agreed with everything her husband said about the fat boy.

The fat boy could not be found for questioning, but then no one had ever known the fat boy to say anything. He just watched. The paper said he was malevolent. No one likes a fat kid staring at them all the time. Lammerton said that everyone was entitled to privacy without a fat kid staring at him. The fat boy had the knack of being where he was least desired.

There was a certain effrontery about the fat boy. He appeared in council chambers during the discussion in committee on a special dispensation from the town planning scheme. The deputy mayor was declaring that no present councillors had any connection with the consortium which had made application. He became aware of the fat boy watching him from the corridor to the town clerk's office. The fat boy's fair hair trembled a little as his mouth stretched in a cavernous yawn and, without taking his hands from his pockets, he tapped with his shoe at the wainscotting, the way boys do. One of the councillors went from the meeting to confront the fat boy, but he must have slipped away through the offices, the councillor said.

The deputy mayor thought that in all of his considerable experience he had never seen such a sly one as the fat boy. He said that somehow he could never bring himself to trust a fat boy, just never could bring himself to trust one, he said.

The fat boy was seen at the IHC centre the day before Melanie Lamb was found to be pregnant. The air was warm; sparrows chirped beneath the swaying birch catkins and pecked at a vomited pie in the gutter. The fat boy stood before the railings and held one of the iron bars like a staff. The children smiled at him as he watched, and were content in his presence, but the supervisors saw him there and remembered when the doctor said that Melanie was pregnant. The music teacher who lived next door to the Lambs thought it a very significant recollection. He said that when he came to think of it he recalled the fat boy standing in the evenings by the hedge at the rear of Melanie's house. A very fat, ugly boy, the music teacher said, and everyone agreed that such a unique description fitted the fat boy perfectly and must be him. It was a terrible thing, the music teacher said, to think that the fat boy could take advantage of Melanie's handicap, even if she was physically advanced.

More than any of the other things, it was what he did to Melanie Lamb that enabled people to close ranks against the fat boy. They recognised in him a common enemy. Vigilante groups organised from the King Dick and Tasman hotels began searching for the fat boy. Not many days before Christmas they caught up with the fat boy by the gasworks. Artie Compeyson was drowning kittens in the cutting, and saw the fat boy watching but didn't let on. The fat boy was stolid at the top of the cutting. His pudding face and medieval hair showed clearly in the moonlight and against the grimy storage tanks of the old gasworks. He was still waiting when the vigilantes came, and they surrounded him there in the patches of light and shadow. The fat boy didn't run, or cry out. He watched them converge, his thick legs apart and his hands pushed deep into the pockets of his short trousers. He was sly all right.

They managed to overpower him, they said. Nigel Lammerton, with his experience as a wife-beater, got in one or two really good thuds on the fat boy's face before he went down, and the music teacher, who had an educated foot, kicked the fat boy between the legs. Everyone knew the fat boy must be made to pay for what he had done.

No one seemed to know what happened to the fat boy's body, and such a body wasn't easy to hide. The moon seemed to go behind cloud just at the time the fat boy fell, and the vigilantes became rather confused after the excitement of the night, and the debriefing at the King Dick and the Tasman. Although the police dragged the cutting, they found only the sack with kittens in it, and five stolen tyres.

Nearly everyone was relieved that the fat boy had been got rid of. God, but he was evil, they said, that fat boy, all the things he did. It didn't bear thinking about, they said. And no one likes a fat boy watching them, you know. They shared, among other things, a conviction that life would be immeasurably better for them all with the fat boy gone.

The Day Hemingway Died

~

YOU'LL BE WARY of too much coincidence, I know, but I had been reading a good deal of Hemingway about that time. We weren't doing it in lectures either. The *Faerie Queene* was what we were doing in lectures. The *Faerie Queene* is suitable for university study because people wouldn't read it otherwise. The lecture in the afternoon was on arachnid imagery in Book Two. The lecturer had the habit of lifting his head from his notes and glancing despairingly around the tiered seating, as if he feared we were drawing closer to suffocate him.

It was raining that day, and the streets were softened with it, and the cars hissed by. I rode very slowly because my bike had no front mudguard, and the faster I went the more water the wheel flicked up at me. So I was in the rain longer, but the water coming down was cleaner than that coming up. When the rain began to run down my face, I imagined I was Neanderthal, and persevered with sullen endurance. Cars came from behind, hissing like cave bears as they passed.

Mrs Ransumeen complained if I dripped inside. So I stood in the wash-house and dried off with a pillowcase from the laundry basket. I wriggled my toes and they squelched inside my desert boots. I put my feet down very flat when I went inside, so they wouldn't squelch. 'Don't you leave wet socks in your room,' said Mrs Ransumeen.

'I don't really think Neanderthal was a dead end,' I said. 'More and more research seems to show that they added to the gene pool that carried on.'

'I'm not doing any washing tomorrow. I'm not.'

'It's subjective, I know, but I feel the stirrings of Neanderthal at times. Some atavism of the mind, I guess.'

'Oh, shut your blah,' said Mrs Ransumeen. Her face was like an old party balloon that had been left strung up too long, become small and tired with stretch marks and scar tissue. Yet still more air pressure inside than out. Mrs Ransumeen's face was like that; looking blown up and deflated both at the same time.

'For three pounds ten a week I don't have to listen to your rubbish,' she said. 'And I don't have to pick up wet socks from your room neither. Stop dripping on the floor, will you.'

Mrs Ransumeen had beautiful hair. She had hair that girls would steal for. It was black and heavy. When well brushed it had a secret gleam, like water glimpsed in a deep well. Every woman has something of beauty, I suppose.

I went up the stairs, squelching. The party balloon stood at the bottom. 'It's a cold meal,' she said. The rain drifted into the window on the stairway landing. I should've gone back down and had it out with her about one hot meal a day. I owed it to myself, to keep my self-respect. For a moment I thought I could do it.

'Oh well,' I said. 'Yes, okay.' Even Neanderthal genes can be recessive.

Ron's door was open. He was lying on his bed with his hands behind his head. He was grinning at me. As I changed my socks he mocked me through the wall. 'Okay, Mrs Ransumeen. Yes, Mrs Ransumeen. Cold tea, how delightful, Mrs Ransumeen. Let me lick your bum, Mrs Ransumeen.' Ron was an engineering student. He lacked any culture, but had prodigious courage. He even took on the Ransumeens once or twice. Got beaten, but at least he took them on. He had to get worked up to it, mind you, with drink, or the desperation of academic failure. He had no culture, but a certain vision of self, did Ron. He had that hopeless courage that arouses both admiration and pity. In all other ways he was even less than ordinary.

The radio in the kitchen was always on. It was on when we came down for the cold meal. The party balloon liked to listen to the talkback shows. She loved to hear people making fools of themselves. 'Listen to that silly bitch,' she said.

'Arp, barp,' went her husband.

'For God's sake, stop that face-farting all the time,' said Mrs Ransumeen.

'It's natural, isn't it? A natural function, for Christ's sake.' Ransumeen's face was the evasive, plural face of a man who had no self-respect. A face pushed forward by impetuosity without talent, and worn back again by constant disadvantage. It was the face of a man who gets by how he can. It was the face in which you fear to look in case you see yourself.

The radio said that Hemingway had put a shotgun in his mouth and killed himself. 'It's a poor show, that's all, if a man can't express his natural functions in his own home,' said Ransumeen. When it said about Hemingway, each object in my line of sight assumed a derisive clarity. There was first the Belgium sausage sandwich on my plate. Its pink edge peeped like a cat's tongue from the uncut side, and the top piece of bread had a smooth indentation in one corner from a bubble in the dough.

'I saw the old tart next door putting rubbish in our can again,' said the party balloon. The salt and pepper were faceted glass with red plastic tops. The salt had five holes, and two were blocked because of the humidity. What I felt had less to do with Hemingway as a writer, than with the idea that no one cared if he lived or died anyway. There were better writers than Hemingway, but he was the one who died that day. In homes all over the country there would be the news about Hemingway, and no one cared. On the bench was a pie-dish with water in it to soak the burnt apricot on the bottom, and a tube of golden macaroons. The price was marked with felt pen on the cellophane.

'Lincoln is always a hard team to beat in the forwards,' said Ron.

'I'll take all the rubbish I can lay my hands on, and the next time she does it I'll follow that old bitch back and turf it all over her floor.'

'It said Hemingway's dead,' I said.

'Bread,' said Ransumeen. He had his hand out for it.

'Because she lives by herself, she thinks she can do what she likes.'

'And with this rain there'll be a heavy ground all right, and the forwards will tell.'

'I said Hemingway killed himself.'

'Barp, arp. Ah, that's better out than in, as the actress said to the bishop.'

I quite like macaroons actually, but the party balloon never put more than two each on the table. When I'm working I can eat a whole packet easily. The first Hemingway story I ever read was 'Indian Camp'. Hemingway wasn't always beating his chest. Mrs Ransumeen had a broad, yellow ribbon in her hair. When she turned aside to criticise her husband her hair had a sheen so dark there were hints of purple, as had the skin of a Melanesian bishop I heard preach once in Timaru. Sometimes I thought her hair must be false, and that underneath was the real hair that suited an ugly woman. Ron asked if he could have a stronger bulb in his room. He said he couldn't see to do his work, and he had two assignments due that week. 'Oh, you shut up,' said Mrs Ransumeen.

'Yeah,' said Ransumeen. 'You shut your cakehole. You're just a boarder here.' Vulgarity was a natural property of the Ransumeens, and to deplore it was like criticising wetness in water or the smell of methane.

The salt sloped high left to low right, and the pepper the other way. It must have happened as Mrs Ransumeen carried them to the table gripped by the tops in the fingers of one hand. The cellars tend to angle out when they're carried that way. The butter had Marmite on its top edge like an ink line, and one pendant of water dithered from the cold tap. The radio had finished with Hemingway, and begun on political instability in Italy. It was a lot more important perhaps. I don't know. 'You're not going out tonight,' said the party balloon. Ransumeen gnawed his sandwich and said nothing. It was a silence of hope rather than subterfuge. 'Are you deaf or bloody something?' she said.

'I may have to go out for a bit,' he said. She started on him, but with an underlying boredom from countless victories. Ron and I went upstairs.

Nothing in my room had changed for Hemingway, and the houses outside looked the same as ever. Mould stains always showed up on the roughcast when it rained, and the knuckled camellia bushes moved a little in the drizzle and the wind. Nothing flamed in the sky for Hemingway. Not even an aurora of picadors, or quail in the sun.

Mrs Ransumeen's voice reached a competent fighting pitch. She could sustain it as long as she wished. Her virulence was that of self-pity rather than active hatred. 'And why the hell you can't get some better job anyway I don't know,' she said.

'Ah, for Christ's sake,' said Ransumeen.

'S'obvious you won't get anywhere again. We never get invited anywhere.'

'Who's going to invite us, for Christ's sake?' Ransumeen went out, and left her talking.

'That's right. That's right,' she said. 'You bloody go out. Whether you get back in is another story.' She began banging the dishes in the sink, and talking to the radio again. 'Will you shut your face, I say? Prouting on,' she told the announcer. She traded him for a tidal flow of film themes. She seemed to be banging the utensils in time with them.

It seemed colder in my room as the darkness deepened outside. The bulb of small power grew even dimmer in the cold. Ron came in. He wore two jerseys, which gave him a stomach. 'The troll has turned off our heaters at the switchboard,' he said. 'It's unbearable.' His hands were yellow with cold, and his fingernails lilac. Mrs Ransumeen had become quiet below. She had laid the snare and was content to wait. 'We can't put up with it. Why should we? We can't work like this,' said Ron.

'Today I won't stand for it,' I said. Ron was encouraged by my support.

'Let's have it out with her.' Ron had a square, practical face and a feeling for natural justice. 'We'll do something about it. The troll has turned the heat off again and it's the middle of winter.' He swayed and marched on the spot, partly to keep warm and partly in rising militancy.

As we went down together, I felt that the day had to be marked in some way. As the lightning wouldn't strike, some risk was necessary on the day that Hemingway died. Mrs Ransumeen sat with her arms laid before her on the table. The twin bars of the kitchen heater glowed. 'Our heaters are off,' said Ron.

'Yes,' I said. It was a token of our alliance. Mrs Ransumeen's fat arms were dimpled, and spreading on the table as if filled with water.

'So?' she said.

'It's cold,' I whined. Hemingway knew all about the cold.

'It's too cold to work in our rooms,' said Ron.

'Horseshit,' said the party balloon. She began to breathe more noisily through her nose, and she stirred in the chair. She was getting ready to really let go, I thought. Ron and I stood shoulder to shoulder. Then her mood began to change; as visible in its way as a change of weather. Her eyes dulled like the surface of a pond beneath a breeze, and her shoulders settled. Her expression was for a moment surprised as she felt the change spreading from within, the new imperative. Her hands spread out like a starfish and, despite herself, she began to cry. 'Oh, I don't know. I just don't know,' she said. As she cried she lifted her hands and began rubbing her face, smearing the tears from forehead to chin. 'Sometimes I just wish to God I was dead,' she said. 'One lousy thing after another. One lousy day after another. A rented house, and a husband who becomes less and less a man.' She stood up, and her breathing was broken with hiccups from her sobbing. She went over to the fridge and opened it. From the rack behind the door she took eggs one by one and flicked her forearm and wrist to send them against the window, the bench and the cupboards. Her throwing action was restricted, and her defiance half-hearted. The eggs broke with the sound of black beetles being stood on. Mrs Ransumeen seemed to find no relief in doing it, and it shamed us to watch.

It should have been very comic: my landlady throwing eggs in the kitchen on the day that Hemingway died. Yet the thing is that it wasn't in the least funny. On the radio a man explained the importance of mulching shrubs for summer. The party balloon rather dully cast the eggs, and they crushed like beetles. 'Now I've bloody done it,' she said. 'I've started now and I've really done it. He'll notice something when he comes home tonight.'

'Will he ever,' said Ron softly. He was afraid to disturb her apathy. She began to cry again, and her mouth opened into the speechless square that accompanies the onslaught of tears. She closed the fridge door, and stood with one forgotten egg in her hand.

'Horseshit to it all anyway,' she managed to say. The situation was beyond her response. She was struggling with a crisis, the significance of which provided her with no greater means to confront it. Smashing eggs and crying were the only outlets she could think of. Ron and I left her there. We had nothing to offer as a consolation. Contempt and fear were stronger than our pity. We went quietly up the stairs. Ron was uncertain.

'I've never seen her like this before. She's packed up properly.'

That's how it was for me on the day that Hemingway died. I had meant to give it all a humorous gloss, and get in a bit of sex; bed springs and muffled cries. That's what people like in a story. But it remains much as it was. Cold and wet, horseshit and broken eggs, no heat in my room and a landlady I disliked crying aloud in the kitchen.

from

The Lynx Hunter

Convalescence in the Old City

~

ONLY THOSE WHO have experienced life there can know the feeling of the place, for such a city travels badly by words. An insect is active in the night there, between the paving stones of the old part of the city, and at first light sometimes I would see small mucus domes upon the cobbles. They made a brief defiance like fish eyes, then died beneath the bike wheels, the boots of passers-by, the sun. And in that city there was a faint scent of the past — desperation and unrequited injuries — which mingled with the steam from the sewer covers, the smell of new baked saasi bread and sprays of blue, upland lilies carried to the sanctuary, and the sleeping breath of crowded people.

At dawn and dusk there is an awkward turning: pretence fails and, sensed in the brief hiatus as one state gives way to another, is sadness for things seen as they are. I prefer to be alone at both these times or, if in company, to avoid the eyes of others. In the old city the death of a day or a night was a vulnerable time: one rhythm lost, another not quite begun. A time when symptoms of illness reappeared, and achievements seemed most trivial.

I was there for a month only, a little less, restricted by convalescence to a very limited patrol: the hotel, its view and acquaintances, the labiniska and the narrow streets surrounding. So I can't claim any general knowledge of the country, just the experience of a short time in the old city.

Mine was a small hotel, and the only other regular guest who was around much during the day was a Polish engineer. I didn't see his name written, but my guess is Debicki, Moritz Debicki. He came from Kalisz. I have never been to Poland, never known Polish people except for this one acquaintance. My expectation, based on films and books, was that Poles were histrionic and libidinous, full of poetic melancholy and the hopeless courage of lost causes. Yet Debicki was very practical and brisk. He had come south to work in the heavy industry of the new city, and because it was the time of union agitation he had little to do and was on half-pay until work could begin again. He found a way of turning circumstance to his advantage. He obliged with plumbing and mechanical work at the labiniska, and for the family tannery a few blocks from the hotel. The smell of the tannery remained with him after this work. Of course he was paid under the table by both concerns, to supplement his half-pay, and was pleased with his resourcefulness.

I wasn't well enough to go far from the hotel, and Moritz Debicki came in to talk to me in my room many days, or sat with me a while on the ramp by the old stables which held the shade. He was a foreigner too, but more familiar with the place than I, for he had lived there for almost two years and could speak the language. He had a wish to be helpful to me — alone in the old city. Also Moritz liked to use his

English, which was surprisingly good. He didn't like to waste opportunities, and if I was quiet too long from fatigue, or thought, he would prompt me to conversation again by starting up himself. 'The next day I am going to do work in the machineries of the tannery,' or 'Men and women in this country: both of them are not modern in thinking. They live in the history of their country altogether.'

I was glad of Moritz Debicki. I appreciated his practical nature, his interest in me, a stranger convalescing in the hotel, and his courtesy in regard to nationality. As a Pole, perhaps he considered pride in country to be everywhere a significant thing. Often when he came to visit me, he would offer some knowledge of New Zealand as a greeting: a gift of his research somewhere in a city which cannot have groaned with information of Aotearoa. I hadn't the resources or freedom to repay in kind, except to praise Chopin, and the charge of the Polish cavalry against the German tanks. Moritz told me with pleasure for both our countries that New Zealand's export trade to Poland was greater than to Spain, Sweden, Austria or Yugoslavia.

Midday was a sour sweat in summer; hot, still, and the fumes of the industries in the new city drifted into the irregular streets on the hill. The men left their sidewalk chairs along the wall of the labiniska I could see from my room. They took their tall tankards inside, away from the heat and the pollution of the new industries they despised; inside, where windows were closed.

Late in the afternoon, however, a fresh world was begun. By four the heat was such that it defeated itself, thus the cooler air came flowing down from the hills and the mountains behind them, and the poisons of the new industries no longer reached the old part of the city. Moritz said that the local name for the cool air meant snow breath, and when it came the decorous men brought their tankards out from the labiniska and took their seats again; women moved about the narrowing streets; the hotel cook who had a lazy eye talked loudly to his staff of one.

Moritz Debicki was fond of schnapps; I never developed the taste for it. He would bring the bottle when he came to see me, and two small glasses with very thick bottoms. He might preface his visit by saying that he knew Taupo to be the largest lake in New Zealand, or that our kiwi was an oddity of nature which I should explain to him. There was a sense of unreality concerning my country when I heard it described in formal tit-bits by a Polish engineer in a hotel room above the sloping streets in the old city. As I might in ignorance have talked of prayer wheels in Tibet, or the red fields of Tuscany. Outside my window was a plant box. The grey dirt had shrunk from the wooden sides in the heat, and there were no flowers. Moritz would stand at the open window in the evening and rest his schnapps bottle in the window box. He could see the men on their chairs along the wall, and he scorned them for their lack of ambition. Moritz was resolved to be a fully qualified mechanical engineer within a year, and then return, he said, to Poland and marry a virgin of good family. There were some very good virgins and families in Kalisz, he assured me, which was, after all, a city of some eighty-five thousand people.

When it was becoming dark and the snow breath had saved the old city again, sometimes the men along the wall of the labiniska would begin to sing. Songs not at all boisterous, but polite and reflective. As night came on, a son or daughter would be sent by the women and stand respectfully at a distance to remind a singer of his family. And the father would leave his seat along the wall, leave his quiet, repetitious singing, and go home with the child sent for him.

In the old city it seemed to me that the electricity was different from electricity in other places, although the pragmatist will tell you that it can't be so: the light lacked penetration and was very yellow. Moritz told me that it was because the city supply was overloaded and all the apparatus second rate. I recall the singing as night came, the weak, yellow light of windows and corner lamps, and the stink of the new city moved away by the cool air of the mountains. But I don't pretend to know more than these appearances of the place. I have often disparaged those who pronounce upon a place with authority after some superficial experience of it, and who have no under-standing of the life and sustaining prejudices of people there, so I won't name the country or city. Yet I was there, saw the things which I describe, as you might see them yourself if you cared to. Yet nothing is ever quite the same, even in such an old city, and the earth within the window box may not crack in just that pattern again, and Moritz Debicki is unlikely still to be in that hotel where I saw him arrested for theft.

Moritz would stand at the window, or sit on the other iron bed in my room, and talk to me in his effective English. His face was lively and he would tend his moustache with the thumb and forefinger of his left hand. His interest in people was sociological rather than personal, it seemed to me: he talked of groups and classes, not individuals, to a degree that was unusual. The striking factory workers were a fascination to him, their habits and intentions, but only as a body; he had no friends among them. He knew the characteristics of the traditional minorities of the old city's population, and explained to me the utterly different lives of married and unmarried women. Yet when I praised the expressive eyes of the maid at the labiniska, he said he hadn't noticed, but that almost certainly she would be Croatian.

Our acquaintance remained a slightly formal one: talks in my room, or less often on the ramp of the stables, an occasional walk in the evenings along the streets of the old city, or a visit to the labiniska where we seemed to inhibit the regulars so that they didn't sing. Moritz and I maintained a certain reserve — on my part because I liked him but was wary of rapid intimacy which might prove a mistake. I still needed a good deal of quiet and rest. And it was so obviously a temporary coincidence. A Polish engineer from Kalisz working in the new industries before returning to a virgin of good family, and a Kiwi teacher taking an unintended convalescence on his European tour.

Almost always I ate at the hotel, and not just to keep expenses down. Eating places were few in the old city. The locals ate at home, and it was not a tourist city to any special extent. The spread of the industries in the new city and the priorities of the government discouraged anything frivolous or deliberately appealing. The hotel food was all I needed, or felt like. The large meal was late in the evening, when the snow breath had come, for even in summer we usually had a heavy soup. I have seen the cook adding the bowl of blood late in its cooking — displaying the addition with pride. 'It is known an excellent goodness,' Moritz told me.

On my last Tuesday I finished my soup as the two policemen arrived in the dining room. There were seven guests including myself. The police were looking for Moritz Debicki, but he was working late at one of his under the table jobs. Both men were noticeably handsome, dark, set off well by their green and black uniforms. The police in that city all seemed possible leading men. Perhaps they were chosen for appearance rather than stature or skills; perhaps it was just the effect of the uniform. The senior man remained in the dining room to smoke, while the other policeman went out and waited in the foyer. Nothing was said between them; either it was planned beforehand, or their customary procedure. The hotel guests did not linger after the meal, and I was the last to go to my room. The policeman in the foyer smiled at me as I went up the stairs. It seemed disloyal to Moritz not to make some effort to warn him, and I stood by my window as if I would have the opportunity to signal to him on the cobbled street. I had little conviction, though. For all I knew it could be a matter of some technicality. I learnt practically nothing of the language in my time there.

Moritz Debicki didn't pass my window, and he was arrested in the foyer as he returned to the hotel. I heard the first, quick words, then the louder protestations of Moritz. To go down was all that I could do; my uncomprehending presence was the only support that I could offer him. One policeman gripped Moritz firmly by the jacket as they argued. Their three voices echoed in the hotel foyer, but no one else came out. The hotel was quiet everywhere except the foyer.

'Is this necessary?' I said. It sounded absurd even as I said it, for who was I to stand in the entrance of a hotel in the old city and question in English the actions of authority? The policemen regarded me, but didn't reply.

'I am so arrested for robbery of the tannery,' said Moritz. The police began to urge him from the hotel foyer into the street. The grip on his jacket pocket was maintained, but there was no sign of handcuffs or guns. Moritz called to me over his shoulder at the doorway. 'In your country would not occur this bungle of justice,' and as I had been addressed the senior policeman paused to nod at me.

I was ashamed for Moritz, his casual clothes shabby in contrast with the smart green and black of the police. The shabbiness was accentuated by his humiliation. I was ashamed for myself too — for my inability to help him, for my witness of his humiliation. They walked closely together across the uneven cobbles and past the labiniska wall where the singers sat quietly. I could see no car in the twilight. Moritz was still held by the pocket. One of his shoulders was lower than the other because of that grip, and his shoes were worn at the heels.

In that way was my acquaintance at the hotel in the old city taken away, and I went myself two days later. The police wouldn't let me see Moritz Debicki before I left the old city and its country. I never discovered if Moritz was really a thief, and if I would feel either of us changed because of it. I have only facts, those things that happen and then break off, as facts do, without the moral or symmetry of a story. Perhaps the justice he received was indeed a bungle; perhaps he was a thief.

Good fortune to Moritz Debecki. I hope he continues to enjoy his schnapps, that he finishes his training, that he returns to Polish Kalisz to marry a virgin of good family. Yet all I'm sure of are the facts of the place and the experience. You may see such things yourself if you go there. Often, when not well, I sat at the window and watched dawn in the old city — that turning, honest time. At dawn the triangle of our lives is glimpsed; three equal, sloping sides of time and change and death. I saw on the cobblestones the mucus bubbles made by insects in the night, and watched steep houses come up against the sky.

The Castle of Conceits

~

THERE ARE JULY days when the sky is inflated by mist to grey immensity, and pearls hang from wires and weatherboards and from the thinnest branches. No wind, and the grey of the sky is milked in the raindrops and in the shallow puddles. Blackbirds forage along the hedges, and foliage is subdued from the frosts of other days. Disconsolate smoke above the suburbs. Posters are cold and calm and stained: they advertise yet another production of *Macbeth*, and proclaim an evangelical mission long departed. The contagion of the former has overcome the latter, has seeped out and by osmosis reached within the people so that virtue and resolution are undermined. Fruit stares out of place, unwholesome, and in the butchers' shops the meat contracts and beads up blood. Green mould flourishes and marks the seepage on stone walls and, like cigarette paper, the birch skin is worn from the boughs. Alley cats shake hands with the invisible, fastidious in the passage from one warehouse to the next. Even the directors' cars, places reserved, are stained and bleed on to the stones embedded in the tar.

Both customers and attendants are present in the shops from duty: each blames the other for the necessity. They despise the product and the prices, the purchaser and the proprietor. Within their common hearing are statements on clothes and thick ankles, walrus moustaches, false jewellery, adam's apples like fists, noses like levelled shotguns, tweed bums that must sidle through the doors. Leached faces, eyes of universal reproach, replicas of smiles of good intent. Barrage balloons of hospitality, politics and the weather are put up to draw the fire. Disillusioned with life, fearful of death, all seek that comfort of gregarious creatures which is the mute realisation of shared inconsequence.

A painter's van with the side ladder slips its brakes, runs backwards just a few metres and shatters the windscreen of the car behind. The event is mundane, but the sound of the glass oddly musical: a chime which sounds throughout the street. It enters the dreams of Charlotte Ecclestone in her flat above the shop. It is converted into the sound of the hunting horn which gathers shoughs and water-rugs through the heather. Nine people stop to watch, their backs to the drift of misty rain. They are made aware by the painter's van that providence is still at work in the world. They may win their Golden Kiwi yet. They pause to see if there is to be any further spectacle, but only the painter appears. 'Ah, no, Jesus,' he says. The nine people ghost away lest they be approached for help. 'Jesus, though. Wouldn't you know it.'

Charlotte expands beneath the purple quilt. As she stretches she draws a vast, prolonged breath as if she has been dead all night, and is come alive again. She lifts her large arms, smooth, and small hands, replaces them beneath the covers for warmth. Noddy's head marks the ticks, and Big Ears is his companion on the face. Half past twelve and the mist is kissing at the window. 'Why me,' says painter Condell. Charlotte dresses before the heater. Her thighs shimmer as she draws on rugby socks of green and gold, mohair jersey, a skirt of French velvet with a burn covered by a butterfly. She eats the one cold sausage in the fridge, and searches for other items. Dried apricots littered in the cupboard, cracked cheese from which she gnaws out the heart. Her coffee is very hot, and very black. She has a tam-o'-shanter for her head, winds a varsity scarf around her neck. The ends curl like banded snakes across her bosom. A satchel; a handbag of real and crinkled leather. From the high womb of her coloured flat she descends the dark stairway feet first and, despite the danger, is born successfully into a grey and milky world in polished brown boots, red velvet with burn and butterfly, and tam-o'-shanter.

Insubstantial people eddy as froth, indecisive before the crossings, while Charlotte ignores the lights and strides on from block to block. The leather bag and satchel swing, and diamonds settle on her high cheeks. She stops at Hemmings' delicatessen. Stuffed shoulder and Cornish pasties, apple strudel and pin-wheel buns with lemon icing. 'Let the mind feed the mind, and the body feed the body,' she says. The chiropodist beside her nods, and moves aside. Charlotte goes in and waits till Bernie Hemmings can come to serve her. She calculates the distance between the pasties and herself. She positions herself.

'I'm sick of being conned by you, Lottie,' says Bernie Hemmings, but he looks to see that his father is not at the back of the shop, and puts his own back to it. Charlotte takes his hand with icing sugar on the knuckles and places it just under her blouse.

'Go,' she says. It takes Charlotte only a few seconds to put two Cornish pasties in a bag; it takes Bernie, dizzy from desire, the same to briefly range one epic breast. Does she ever wear a bra?

'You move fast for a big woman, Lottie,' he says in despair. 'Damn you.' The icing sugar is brushed from his fingers, and he imagines it dusted on her curving skin. 'Can I come round tonight?'

'Not tonight.' Bernie watches her leave: red skirt sways from her hips and laps the tops of her polished boots.

'Jesus, Lottie,' says Bernie. His hand is still shaking, and he rests it upon the till to quieten it.

Charlotte sits in 327B and eats her Cornish trove. She is early. It is the warmth of the room rather than intellectual impatience which draws her. She finishes her meal, blows up and bursts the bag to startle the three drab and calculating scholars who wait in the rows closer to the front. 'Wordsworth was a simplistic old goat,' she says when the lecturer arrives. 'Wordsworth knew nothing of the life of the people. He wouldn't involve himself in life. Wordsworth has no relevance for modern women.'

'Ah, Miss Ecclestone,' says Dr Taylor wryly, 'last week you rebuked me for Southey, now Wordsworth won't do.'

'Let's have Laurie Lee or Marvell again,' says Charlotte. '"He hangs in shades the orange bright, like golden lamps in a green night."'

'We are hag-ridden by our prescription.' He admires the presence of Charlotte Ecclestone: the focus of warmth and colour, the generosity of good-natured excess, the challenge to each conventional day. Her shoulders are broad, her hands small, her double chin seductive, one firm crease and smooth. Wordsworth is both spoken of and heard with reluctance: thoughts of other things drift like a vapour. Bursaries and team selections, macaroni cheese and white upper arms, dying aunts, lost assignments, collapsed pistons, scrutiny of dreams, chapped lips and visions of apocalypse. Charlotte draws a picture of Valhalla, and imagines a banquet for all her favourite poets. She occupies herself with sorting the precedence of seating in her mind.

'Miss Ecclestone,' says Dr Taylor when people are leaving. 'Miss Ecclestone.' He holds a finger up in a gesture to delay her. The drab and calculating scholars of the front rows leave them reluctantly, wishing the finger was raised for them. Dr Taylor looks at the bright butterfly on Lottie's red skirt, and her magnificent chest. 'I was disappointed to find that as yet you have made no entry for the Slye Poetry Award. It closes on the seventeenth, you see.'

'I've been so busy. The hurly-burly.'

'As long as you're aware of it. So few have bothered for the right reasons.'

'I might start something tonight. There's been the play and everything.'

'There's still time,' the lecturer says. He watches her go, and decides uncritically that Wordsworth should be deleted from the prescription. 'There's still time,' he says.

Charlotte leaves the campus. A foggy cloud hangs on the buildings, and a fug within the library. She boards a bus in Crosse Street, and finds she knows the driver by sight. They smile at each other in defiance of the weather and all probabilities. Each time the bus stops and starts, he smiles at her. Charlotte likes the agile, decisive way he moves: she likes the strong tendons in the back of his hand: she likes the contrast of his watch strap on the brown skin and hair of his wrist. She likes his square, neat sideburns. 'Have you ever thought of varying your route?' she says.

'People depend on a set timetable, you see. It's laid down.'

'Too much,' says Charlotte. 'But towards the end of a run most people are getting off, aren't they?'

'Pretty much.'

'At the end of a run you could go on a few blocks. I mean you are the captain of the ship.'

'Sometimes if the roads are dangerous or that, I'll make a detour, make changes.'

'I'm only a few blocks further on. I thought you might like to come on up.'

'I've got other runs,' he says. 'I could ring in sick, I suppose.' His eyes start to jiggle. Charlotte breathes in deeply, and her breast rises like a spinnaker.

'No time or thought for all that,' she says. 'Come now, or not at all. Act on impulse, or not at all. To commit yourself to a moment is a pledge of its value.' Murray sees the small knuckles of her hand, the mist which glints on her dark hair, her cheeks, her tam-o' shanter. 'Ostler Street,' she says.

Murray swings the bus to a halt, and vaults out of his seat. He hurries down the bus to the last two old ladies, one green, one blue. 'You'll have to get out here,' he says. 'The brakes have gone. We could start rolling back any minute. I can't take the risk of going on.' He gallantly carries their baskets down the steps, and urges them into the drizzle. The green lady is the smaller. She has a bad leg. Murray takes her arm for a few metres till she settles into a rhythm. 'There you are,' he says. 'On your way.' The bus begins again, swiftly hissing along the wet streets.

'I am the captain of my ship,' says Murray with the conviction of sudden decision. 'We won't leave it by the shops, but there's that little dead-end street by the lodge. Rice Street. We'll whip it in there and no one will be any the wiser.' Murray drives the bus into Rice Street, to the very end, and leaves the blunt nose of the bus jutting over the steps of the lodge.

'Bring plenty of money,' says Charlotte. 'You don't want to have to come back for it.' Murray takes a fist of notes, and a palm of silver as though it were only gravel.

'Jesus,' he says. 'Hardly anyone needs a bus at this time of day anyway. In this weather they're better off inside. They're nearly all old people wanting library books and sheepskins for their beds.' He comes and stands beside Charlotte. As a test of her sincerity he intends to give a horse-bite above the left knee, but the circumference of flesh is such that it becomes merely a pinch. Charlotte smiles at him. She closes her eyes for a moment as she smiles, and her long lashes lie down upon her cheeks.

'Let the mind feed the mind, and the body feed the body,' she says.

'That's right,' says Murray.

He doesn't look back at the bus as they leave it. He turns up the collar of his jacket, the way he has seen hard cases do in the films, and he blesses what he regards as providence. 'This was such a foul day too,' he says.

'Do you like camembert cheese?' Charlotte says.

'Do I.' He is captive to the contrast of black curls on her ears.

'Buy three tins,' she says. 'And oysters. You like fried oysters?'

'A-ah.' The tasselled ends of her scarf flutter. Murray straightens his back to ensure that, in her boots, she is no taller than he as they walk.

'And a bottle of Barsac,' says Charlotte. 'You've got enough money for Barsac?' Murray has no idea, but he can see the red velvet skirt swirling from her hips like a flame amidst the mist. He holds up the bunched notes from his pocket. 'Two bottles of Barsac would be better,' she says. 'And hot bread perhaps.' Murray sees her small hands; the nails delicate. There is nothing gross in Charlotte. Physical size and power are more than balanced by dimension of the spirit.

Murray allows her to choose the shops and purchases. In her aura the corruption of the grey day is powerless. The world in watercolour wash is just a backdrop and the canvas trembles. 'Did you see me in *Macbeth*?' says Charlotte. 'I was Lady Macduff, but I wanted to be Lady Macbeth. Come to that, I wanted to be Macbeth.' They rise up the stairs to her rooms, carrying the things that they will share.

Charlotte lights the open fire. Dry, flared pine cones serve for kindling. 'I love fires,' she says. 'I'd like to be an arsonist, set things ablaze. Huge things, irreplaceable things, precious things, all going up with a roar. Such a moment must give a sense of grandeur and fearsomeness to life. To stand transfixed and see a parable of flames.' Murray watches the writhing of the pine cones, the petals incandescent.

'Children understand fire,' he says.

'Fire is eternal catharsis. Fire is the act of substance giving up its essence.' Charlotte pushes the table closer to the heat, and sets out the oysters, bread, wine and the round cheeses. Her light shade is of hand-crafted coloured glass that casts additional colours to those of the fire. Murray is pale blue, and Charlotte oriental. The oysters in their batter are chameleon to no avail between the plate and mouth.

'This is the life,' says Murray. He takes a swallow of Barsac, cautiously, then another with wondering contentment.

'It's not much of a day for driving.'

'It could be worse. It could be ice, you see. That's when it's tricky for a bus in this city. But there's satisfaction. The bus can be a world too, distinct from everything out-side.'

'A technological denial of what is imposed. There are many ways to defeat the appearance of things. But driving buses on a set route: it must be the miniature golf of transport.'

It is not often that anyone bothers to talk to Murray about his job. He eats the last oyster, and drinks more Barsac to provide it habitat. 'It's other people though, isn't it,' he says. 'And they don't think of the driver after a time, you know. Just part of the bus and disregarded. I like to watch their faces as they look down through the win-dows at other people. All their life is in their faces. They can't help it. They lose their own masks as they watch people who are unaware they're being watched.'

'A series of emotional reflections.'

'Yes.'

'A waitress or a lift operator must have a wonderful sense of species,' Charlotte says. She puts three more cones on the fire and balances a chunk of bright coal with absorbed deliberation. 'I only burn anthracite if I can, because of the appearance, the gleam of it, you see.' The gem coal leaves barely a smudge on her fingers. 'Have you any pain?' she says.

'No.'

'Neither have I. Have you any serious regrets, any grand hopes and promises, anything of awesome threat or significant demarcation?' Murray smiles: such con-versation must represent humour. Antipodean reticence should be discarded for no other reason.

'I feel great,' he says.

'It's just that I take stock occasionally: snap the shutter sometimes on my life to frame assessments. The world is spinning fiercely while we are here. Here not there, this time not another. Immense concentration is needed to maintain actuality.' The anthracite falls silently in two, and new flames appear. 'And we have no pain. You said you feel great.'

Murray draws his hand across the bright velvet of her skirt. 'All the colours of this room,' he says. 'I don't know how you do it. That glass lamp is something.' Charlotte lifts her hand before the facets of the table lamp. Her skin changes colour.

'It is my castle of conceits.' She undulates her arms to catch the light. Murray pushes her skirt up and lets his hand trace her nearer thigh. The circumference, the passage of his hand, seem to go on for ever. 'e. e. cummings said break up the white light of objective realism into the secret glories which it contains.'

'This is the place for that, all right,' says Murray. Charlotte looks at the remaining food.

'God, this stuff,' she says. 'I'll blow right up on this food. Fatter and fatter.' She takes off her skirt: one knee is caught in a faint lilac bruise from the lamp. She admires Murray's clean hair, and the straight hair of his chest narrowing to a dark line down his belly; and his ribs showing like straps below the muscles of his side. 'I don't know how men keep the fat off,' she says.

'Metabolism,' says Murray vaguely, and then more forcefully. 'It's the jogging. I run for thirty minutes most nights.'

'I tried it once,' she says. 'I tried it, but I couldn't think as I ran. The effort kept breaking in on my thoughts, so I gave it up.'

'Ah,' says Murray. His head has ended too close to the fire, and the thick hair is in danger of being set alight. All of him is being set alight. The anthracite coal gleams of itself black, and in the varied flames of its essence, and the crafted glass lamp gives changing colours to movement, kaleidoscope of sex, and the Barsac in the bottle as strong a colour as a ginger cat.

Murray's trousers have become rolled inside out, and one sock lost down a leg. Charlotte watches him sorting it out. He stops to say, 'I've just thought about the bus still parked there in Rice Street. Parked there outside the lodge, hours ago, and no word to the depot when I didn't come back.'

'What will you say?' The manipulation of phenomena is always of interest to her.

'I'll think of something.'

'Of course you will.'

'It would have worried me to plan in advance, but I feel I'll have no trouble at all in thinking of something. A dozen things could have happened.'

'More,' says Charlotte. 'Each moment has infinite possibility of development.'

'Anyway, I've a good record there and there'll be no bother. Any story will be swallowed once.'

'Of course it will. One oddity will remind them of your reliability,' Charlotte says, 'and let me know how it works out.'

'Oh, I'll be back to tell you all about it.' He puts on his jacket, and kisses her.

'Saturday's a good day,' she says. 'I'd come down, but I can't be bothered getting dressed again.'

'Saturday,' says Murray. He grins and goes quickly down the stairs: he draws his chin into his jacket in expectation of experience beyond Charlotte's flat.

Rain has come with the night, and the mist which has reconnoitred all the city is reinforced by the main body. The southerly hurries the rain in, driving it around corners, down alleys, into soft, rotten crevices and bubbling through cracks against gravity. The streets are cold and slick, milky and cold. Gutter water begins its proletarian song, and shadows like acrobats swing and twist independent from the wires and cars and neons that cause them. And the rain has shadows as Murray goes, dark fans behind the squalls like a howlet's wing.

Charlotte runs a bath and watches the steam billow out into the other rooms, and twist before her fire and table lamp. She will begin her poem for the Slye Award. All the world for her is shrunk to three rooms, and will expand again within her mind.

The Frozen Continents

~

I HAD NEVER met Beavis before he and I were put on the PEP scheme together. I finished filling in the form promising not to divulge vital and confidential council business which might come my way, and then followed the supervisor to the car. Beavis was already seated. 'This is Beavis,' said the supervisor.

'Typhoon Agnes hit central Philippines on the fifth of November claiming more than eight hundred lives,' said Beavis. 'Five hundred on Panay Island alone, three hundred and twenty-five kilometres south of Manila; another forty-five killed in Leyte and Eastern Sawar provinces.' The supervisor looked away: I said hello to Beavis.

The PEP scheme was an inside one at the museum because it was winter. Where we were taken, however, it seemed colder than outside. Museums create a chill at the best of times, but in our unused part were ice-floes and penguins. A panorama, the supervisor said. All the penguins were to be handled with care and stored out of harm's way along the wall, but the rest was to be dismantled and carried down to the yard. 'I'll look in tomorrow and see how you're going,' said the supervisor. His nose was dripping in the cold.

'Right,' I said.

'A cold wave at the end of last year claimed at least two hundred and ninety lives in north and east India. Low temperatures and unseasonal fog and rain caused general disruption to air traffic,' said Beavis, with no apparent realisation of irony.

'There's a toilet and tearoom at the west end of the corridor on this floor. Ten-thirty and three-thirty,' said the supervisor. He started coughing as he left.

The ocean was what we began on first. As it was plywood it was difficult to recover any sheets to use again. When the water was gone we would be able to move about freely and take greater care with the ice-floes and penguins. I found it an odd sensation at first, standing waist deep in Antarctica as we dismantled it. I pointed out to Beavis the clear symbolism relating to man's despoliation of the last natural continent and so on. Beavis in reply told me that fourteen people were killed in a stampede when a fire broke out during a wedding ceremony at Unye in the Turkish province of Ordu.

We had the green sea out by ten-thirty. Beavis stood shivering by a window we had uncovered and wiped free of dust. He had his arms folded and a hand in each armpit, and he looked wistfully down on to a square of frosted grass, and the neat gravel boundaries. 'It's time for our tea-break,' I told him.

An outline of a hand in felt pen and a list of instructions concerning the Zip were the only decorations on the cream walls of the tearoom: points about not leaving the Zip unattended when filling and so on. I had it read within the first minute, but then words are always the things I notice. There was one failure in agreement of number between subject and verb, but overall the notice served its purpose. I wasn't as confident in assessing the people. They accepted us with exaggerated comradeship as is the response of people in secure, professional employment when confronted with PEP workers, amputees or Vietnamese refugees. I gave my name and introduced Beavis. Beavis had a classy-looking pair of basketball boots, and the most hair on the backs of his hands that I've ever seen. 'Army worms invaded the Zambezi Valley in the north of Zimbabwe and destroyed maize and sorghum crops over more than one hundred square kilometres of farmland,' he said. The museum staff present became more amiable still.

One girl had seductive earlobes and dark, close curls. I had a vision in which I persuaded her to come with me, in which I bit her ear beneath the curls and we made the earth move, or at least shook Antarctica with some vehemence. Instead, all of us apart from Beavis shuffled and spoke of inconsequential things. Beavis had several cups of coffee, then abruptly told us of the twenty-four bed-ridden people who died in a fire which broke out in an old people's home near the town of Beauvais. Impressively recounted, it subdued us all. I guiltily enjoyed the warmth from the wall heaters and my tea — before going back to the South Pole.

Antarctica had been built in sections and we tried to get as much clean timber and plywood sheets out as possible. As we worked I explained to Beavis the Celtic influence in modern poetry, and he told me of the bush fires in south-east Australia, and the earthquake, six on the Richter scale, which killed at least twenty people in India's Assam state. Beavis had a clear, well-modulated voice, and he was deft with the hammer and saw as well. I thought that he'd probably been one of those students, brilliant and compulsive, whose brain had spiralled free of any strict prescription. We had a rest after managing to strip off the first hessian and plaster ice-floe. The sun gradually turned the corner of the museum, melting the frost from a section of the lawn. It caused a precise demarcation between green and white, like the pattern of a flag. Beavis looked out too, and pondered.

We got on well, Beavis and I, although he wasn't light-hearted at all. As he was releasing one penguin the torso came away in his hands, and left the bum and webbed feet on the ice. Beavis stumbled back on to the discarded timber, exposing the heavy treads of his basketball boots, but he didn't laugh with me, just rubbed his shins and looked carefully down the corridor as if expecting a visitor. 'There's got to be some natural mortality among penguins,' I said. 'Put it behind the others and it'll hardly show.'

'More than one hundred people drowned when a boat capsized in mid-stream on the Kirtonkhola River near the town of Barisal in Bangladesh,' said Beavis.

I carried armfuls of wood and plaster down to the yard before lunchtime. I experimented with several different routes, partly for variety of experience, partly in the hope of seeing the girl with the dark curls, but she wasn't visible. Somehow I imagined her in the medieval glass and tapestry section rather than in natural history panoramas. I discussed the subject of feminine perfection with Beavis, pointing out the paradox that, in nature as in art, beauty comes not from beauty, but from the combination of the ordinary and the earthly. 'That woman,' I said to Beavis, 'is skin, blood and spittle, that's the wonder of it.' Beavis considered the insight and told me that more than four hundred passengers were killed when a crowded train plunged into a ravine near Awash, some two hundred and fifty kilometres east of Addis Ababa.

Beavis suffered a headache a little before twelve o'clock. I think the cold, and the dust from the penguins, caused it. He sat on a four by four exposed from the display and leant on to the window. His cheek spread out and whitened on the glass. Three times he began to tell me of a tsunami in Hokkaido, but his words slurred into an unintelligible vortex. He burped, and rolled his face on the icy glass. 'It's time for our lunch-break anyway,' I said. He rolled his head back and forth in supplication and whispered ahh, ahh, ahh to comfort himself. The penguins refused to become involved; each retained its viewpoint with fixed intensity. Illness isolates more effectively than absence: I knew Beavis wouldn't miss me for a while, so I went to the small staffroom and made two cups of sweet tea, and brought them and the yellow seat-cover back to Antarctica.

The yellow cover draped well around Beavis's shoulders, and he held it together at his chest. He had dribbled on the back of his hand and the black hair glistened there. He sipped his tea, though, and listened while I explained why I had given up formal academic studies, and my plan to use the Values Party to restructure education in New Zealand. I think he was pretty much convinced and I let him sit quietly as I worked. Afterwards he seemed to feel better, because he wiped his face with the yellow cover, and fluffed up his hair. He told me about the Bhopal poisonous gas discharge which caused more than two and a half thousand deaths. 'I remember that one,' I said. There was quite a lot I could say about Bhopal, and I said it as we started on the penguins and ice-floes again. Beavis's preoccupation with recent accidental disasters was a salutary thing in some ways: it minimised our own grievance, made even Antarctica's grip bearable.

The sun made steady progress around the building, and the frost cut back across the lawn with surgical precision. Beavis's affliction passed. I went, in all, eleven different ways down to the yard with remains of the southern continent, but I never saw Aphrodite. I stopped the permutations when a gaunt man with the look of an Egyptologist shouted at me that if I dropped any more rubbish in his wing he'd contact the PEP supervisor.

There's a knack to everything, and Beavis and I were getting the hang of our job. We didn't tear any more penguins after that first one in the morning, yet some of them were soft and weakened, and smelt like teddy-bears stored away for coming generations. I said to Beavis that there'd been too much moisture over the years, and that a controlled climate was necessary for the sort of exhibits which had stuffed birds. 'Torrential rain caused flooding and mudslides which killed eleven people and swept away dwellings on the outskirts of Belo Horizonte in the south-east state of Minas Gerais, Brazil.'

Before three o'clock I remembered to smuggle the seat-cover back to the tearoom, and return our cups. I told Beavis that my estimate was that we'd have the whole panorama cleared out inside four days. PEP schemes lasted three months, therefore obviously a good deal of job variety remained — other panoramas to destroy, perhaps. A nocturnal setting for our kiwis, or an outdated display of feral cat species. Beavis made no reply. He was most moved to conversation by literary and philosophical concerns. It was a credit to him really: he had very little small talk, did Beavis.

Do not turn off at the wall, it said by the Zip in the tearoom. The Egyptologist was there and he bore a grudge. 'We're going to have three months of this then, are we,' he said. 'A gradual demolition of the institution around us.'

'A Venezuelan freighter was washed ashore in Florida during a storm that caused one death and millions of dollars of damage.'

'For Christ's sake,' said the gaunt man.

The girl with the dark curls didn't come in. The tearoom hardly seemed the same place as that of the morning, but I knew from the writing on the wall that it was. As we went away the Egyptologist had a laugh at our expense. Beavis didn't mind: he trailed his hand on the banisters, and made sure he didn't step on any of the triangles in the lino pattern. Circles were safe, it appeared.

The ice age was in retreat before us. I had fourteen penguins arranged in column of route along the wall, and in the grounds two piles grew — one of rubbish and one of reusable timber. We realised that the sun wasn't going to reach our window, and days start to get colder again in winter after four o'clock. I suggested to Beavis that we leave the penguins in the habitat which suited them, and show our initiative by burning the scraps we'd collected in the yard. We could keep warm with good excuse until knock-off time. I didn't want Beavis to suffer one of his headaches again.

We built a small fire on a garden plot, stood close to it for warmth, and watched the smoke ghost away in the quiet, cold afternoon. Beavis enjoyed the job of putting new pieces on the fire, and I listened as he told of the consequences when the Citarum River overflowed into several villages of Java's Bundung region and considered myself lucky. The park trees had black, scrawny branches like roots in the air, as if the summer trees had been turned upside down for the season. Deep hidden in the soil were green leaves and scarlet berries.

The museum rose up beyond the yard and the park, but despite all the windows I couldn't see anyone looking out at all. No one to hear us, no one to join us, no one to judge us. The strip of lawn closest to the museum still kept its frost like a snowfall. It would build there day after day. No one to see Beavis and me with our fire. Beavis delicately nudged timber into the fire with his basketball boots, and watched smoke weave through the tree roots. I pointed out to him that we were burning Antarctica to keep ourselves warm, which was an option not available to Scott and

Shackleton. 'More than five hundred died when a liquid gas depot exploded at San Juan Ixhuatepec, a suburb of Mexico City,' said Beavis.

I felt very hungry by the time the hooters went. Beavis and I had missed lunch because of his headache. If he didn't have something soon I thought he might get another attack because of a low blood-sugar level. My own blood-sugar level was pretty low, it seemed to me. We left the fire to burn itself out, and went three blocks down to the shops. I had enough money for two hot pies, and when I came out of the shop I saw Beavis sitting on the traffic island watching the five o'clock rush. Some people walked, some trotted. Some of the cars had Turbo written on their sides, and some had only obscure patterns of rust, but they all stormed on past Beavis who was as incongruous there as among the penguins. His lips were moving. I suppose he was reminding the world of earthquakes in Chile, or of an outbreak of cholera in Mali.

I was surprised how satisfied most of the people were, but good on them, good on them. How should they know that the frozen continent was to be found right here in the midst of our city after all.

The Lynx Hunter

~

I WALK TO work. I play all their games: I shall not give them the satisfaction of winning. See me stand respectably dressed by the morning gate and take a japonica sprig to twirl in my fingers, and before my face as I walk. See me smile back to my wife, while anxious, fierce, defeated love pads restlessly between us. Goodbye, we say above the rearing cataclysmic opening of the earth: rifts and fumes, scoria of burnt-out promises, rose lava blackening, and breaking rose again in fits and starts. A lizard's tongue of aspirations mocked. I shan't be late. Oh, I'll be back by five. Failure in the execution of love can be absolved: failure in love's intention is beyond words or relief.

The small birds have gathered by the fence to cheek me more effectively: attack, attack, they sweetly cry. The sky is a child's blue of recollection, and the early sun shimmers as a spider at the corner of its web. That car has passed by twice already: its fat man hopes to see me die. But I'll not fall down here, not weep to darken the smooth asphalt by the Four Square sign. See me twirl my japonica and increase the confidence of stride beneath the asiatic menace of an impassive sky. Good morning, Mr Jeffers, and I can reply without a quiver in my voice. There are rice and mushroom specials, tins of cottage garden jam, three of everything for the price of two. Stickers and bunting and flags and games and prizes. I never refer to the malicious faces I see in labels and refracted light, among leaves, or massed at partly open doors.

A dromedary is up to its hocks in the pale ocean as it waits beyond the breakwater for the fishing boats to come out to play, and today I shall plan a seminar for forty or forty-five. There will be assembling and registering, name tags and a light lunch free of charge. There will be people allocated to explain both this and that, and role play (do you know all their games?), and assessment and introduction of instructing staff, and simulation exercises. Ah simulations at the seminar, so rich the ironies of despair. Set down a piece of time for simulation in the span of total simulation. Mirrors catch mirrors catch mirrors, until who cares what images we seek. At last we smile ingratiatingly to effigies in front, while some reality examines the back of our neck.

This is the house I constantly admire, or so it seems to me now. So corporeal and so groomed with stolid care. Each edge of lawn has been precisely found and, like dark residue of sea foam, the snail bait rings the tulips. This man must be a master of the game, an expert competitor. He has cornered Pall Mall in whatever monopoly of appearances he plays. The thick orange tiles are allsorts that keep the lid on the house with ease. I feel the spider's warmth on my face from the east, the colours of the sea stir apprehensions. Soft plants bend improbably into the breeze, and defy me to notice the inconsistency. Twirl the japonica, talisman of the customary. See me in this quiet morning as I walk to work. And oh yes, yes, there are watchers. Janissaries ride by to meet their Turkish masters, full of death's defiance and esprit de corps. Lenny, who fell from the monument and died when he and I were thirteen, sits by the railway line and smiles at his release from any adult pretence. He wears the brown roman sandals that my mother bought me time after time; the dirt follows the strap line on the skin.

All the sounds of all the world still quiver somewhere in the air, and could break out again. Barabbas, Barabbas, may respond once more, the moas' stupid cry,the laughter of Cleopatra, continental drifted from the Nile, the interminable drumming of Ackroyd's Mill, Savonarola's rhetoric competing with a thousand thousand enquiries of the weather. Good morning, Mr Jeffers. She likes to see inside me, but I have arranged all the features of my face according to Hoyle. I am a match for her, even to recalling Susan and Alastair as names for her children. Her dress lifts to display the pink, unperforated bum which is all that models need, but see I do not even glance away, and could go on for hours with perfectly approved information to match what she believes has happened, is happening, will happen. Masks wear thin; the skull of things shows through. The rack stretches, and the smiles and laughter grow. She says she must let me get on, but I keep a straightforward face. There is the Lynx Hunter on her porch. He tries to signal me, but I can see through him. I won't die just here, not talking to this acquaintance past the railway line on my way to work, with the spider's bright heat and the Lynx Hunter's appraisal. The passion of my belief is burnt out; seed pods of indefinable species tap against me when I pause. How purposeful are processes of decay. The air is briefly full of thistledown, each carries an island plea for rescue from the selfsame horror. Breathe shallowly and let them float by.

My daughter pedals past me on her way to school. Affection and recognition animate her face. Ah, the power that convention has over us, the hostages she keeps, like sons of satraps entertained in Rome. The cry of warning is stifled in my throat. I am seized with the fear of some betrayal of that love. I am pledged afresh to the straight and very narrow, to maintain absolute fidelity to every rule I know. A child's trust is the bird of paradise which has no phoenix resurrection. So indeed, Mrs Harrop, indeed. So goodbye, Mrs Harrop, goodbye. I shall see you again, Mrs Harrop, or some simulacrum of that name, and you shall address the guise of Mr Jeffers. Does she wait to see if a bolt protrudes behind my ear, or if I leave strange prints upon the ground. But see me walk on to work commensurate with humdrum expectation, with my japonica to catch the spider's threads. Who knows my shoes are full of blood, and the heart empty of it. My lungs hang like bats within this hollow man. The desolation yawns. Don't look back and don't look down is the high wire's rule, for the Lynx Hunter will be watching still.

They are rolling jewels behind me: amethysts and rubies and topaz jostle past me on the slope. Emeralds and diamonds, sapphires and agates, pearls, turquoise, garnets, opals, all compete in splendour. A fragmented rainbow coursed towards the creek by sounds as ordinary as could accompany plain, grey stones. It gathers and spills as vivid seeds into the sunken stream of which the heron is a sentinel. How snugly the tie's knot fits my collar, how snugly the collar fits my neck, how smugly the neck fits between head and shoulders. The water-buffalo wallow amidst the trees and meters of the main street. The mud is a sheen on their massive shoulders, and their movement boils the water. Errors of judgement have been made; pride encouraged me to talk of secret things, to open the nondescript coat we all possess and flash hope as designs. From their cars amid the buffalo the people watch me, half turned away to see how much longer I can take it. Hello, John, and I am quick with hand and smile to synchronise a greeting. Everything is in its place, yet how Lenny smiles to see me. The world is battened down in case of any storm. I know the way of all the games they play — unless they change the rules. I have learned by rote what it is wise to see. I have become a trustee among the inmates of this digest world. Yes, yes, see me. I can walk to work as well as the next man — maybe that next man will be me. There must be no enquiry made of life: stick to compatible descriptions.

For if at night we must lie tightly bound to suffer the other world, at least once more have I made the walk to work without detection. The atlas of our memory retains dark continents: Africas of fear and ecstasy from which we return scathed, old wounds bleeding. In the spider's indifferent warmth, and beneath my asiatic sky, I have walked to work, borne the sacred cripple through a world too opulent to be acknowledged. Good morning, good morning. But what did you expect, what did I expect, what did we expect, of life but this. At least now we know better, which is worse.

See, I have reached my work, flipped the last opal from my trouser cuff, opened and closed the door which is perhaps there. Now, Elaine, let us set up this seminar. All right? The cosmic music is unendurably sweet, planets and alpha stars strung on the ice-blue hoops of taut galaxies. The snout of the lava flow smokes by the Farmers' Co-op. Incandescence of roses gleams within its clinker prison. The Lynx Hunter is no doubt on watch, yet — psst, psst, help me for I die.

Valley Day

EVERY SECOND MONTH Brian went with his father on the Big Kick. They drove up the valley, and the minister took services at the little church of Hepburn and at the Sutherlands' house. One midday service at Hepburn going up, one in the afternoon at Sutherlands', then the evening drive home. In the autumn the long sun would squint down the valley and the shadows blossom from hedges and trees, and slant from the woodwork of buildings in angles no longer true.

One sermon did the trick on the Big Kick, with only the level of formality altered to suit the circumstances. The minister was relaxed despite the hours of driving, and treated it as a gallant expedition for his son's sake. 'Off on the Big Kick again, eh,' he said. 'The Big Kick.' The scent of the hot motor, taste of finest, stealthy dust, sight of the valley floor paddocks all odd shapes to fit the river flats and, higher in the gullies sloping back, the bush made a stand. Few farmhouses, fewer cars to be met, and dust ahead a clear warning anyway.

Brian had his hand in the airflow, and used it to feel the lift on his palm. He assessed the road. Each dip, each trit-trotting bridge, places he would set his ambushes. Hurons or Assyrians swarmed out to test his courage, while his father practised parts of the sermon or recited Burns and then murmured in wonderment at such genius. Brian made the air take some of the weight of his hand, and he kept his head from the window when a small swamp of rushes and flax was passed in case there were snipers hiding there.

'Will the one-armed man from the war be there?' he said.

'Mr Lascelles. Don't draw attention to it.'

'It happened in the war.'

'His tank was hit, I believe. The arm was amputated only after a long struggle to save it: not until he was back in New Zealand. I visited him in hospital I remember.'

'You can still feel your fingers when you've got no arm,' Brian said. 'They itch and that. If someone stood on where they would be then you'd feel the pain.'

'No,' said his father, but the boy kept thinking it. He saw a cloud a long way off like a loaf of bread, and the top spread more rapidly than the bottom, and both were transformed into an octopus.

Hepburn was a district rather than a settlement. The cemetery was the largest piece of civic real estate, and the greatest gathering of population that could be mustered in one place. Mrs Patchett had nearly finished cleaning the church. She was upset because a bird had got in and made a mess, and then died by the pulpit. She said there were holes under the eaves. Even such a small church maintained its fragrance of old coats and old prayers, of repeated varnish and supplication, and insects as tenants with a life-cycle of their own. The air was heavy with patterns of the past: shapes almost visible, sounds brimming audible. An accumulated human presence: not threatening, instead embarrassed to be found still there, and having no place else to go. There were seven pews down one side, and six on the other. Down the aisle stretched two parallel brass carpet crimps, but no carpet in between. One stained window, all the rest were plain, a blood poppy amidst green and blue, dedicated to the Lascelles brothers killed within three days of each other in the Great War.

Brian took the bird out on the dust shovel. It left just a stain on the boards behind the pulpit. He threw the bird above the long grass: it broke apart in the air, and the boy closed his eyes lest some part of it fly back into his face. He brought his father's Bible, soft and heavy, from the car, and the travelling communion tray with the rows of small glasses set like glass corks in the holes, and the bottle full of the shed blood of Christ.

'Don't wander off then,' said his father. 'Don't get dirty, or wander off. Remember we'll be going with one of the families for lunch.' The boy was watching a walnut tree which overshadowed the back of the church, and ranks of pines behind. He found a place where, Indian-like, he was hidden, but could look out. He crossed his legs and watched the families begin to arrive. The Hepburn church no longer had a piano, and the man with the piano accordion came early to practise the hymns required. 'Rock of Ages', and 'Turn Back O Man'. He was shy, very muscular, and prefaced everything he played or said with a conciliatory cough. Fourteen other people came as the piano accordion played. Fourteen adults and six children. Brian watched the children linger in the sunlight, before trailing in behind their parents. The one-armed Mr Lascelles came. Even to Brian, Mr Lascelles didn't look old. He wasn't all that many years back from the war, and he laughed and turned to other people by the cars as if he were no different. Brian got up and walked about in the pine needles as if he had only one arm. He looked back at the trees he passed, and smiled as Mr Lascelles had done. Without realising it he walked with a limp, for he found it difficult to match a gait to having one arm.

The accordionist coughed and began to play, the families sang, and the boy stood still at the edge of the trees to see the valley and the bush on the hills. Rock of Ages cleft for me, let me hide myself in thee. He felt a tremor almost of wonder, but not wonder. A sense of significance and presence comes to the young, and is neither questioned by them nor given any name. All the people of that place seemed shut in there singing, and he alone outside in the valley. He could see all together the silvered snail tracks across the concrete path, the road in pale snatches, the insect cases of pine needles drawn immensely strong, the bird's wing in the long grass, the glowing Lascelles poppy in the sunlit window. Rock of Ages cleft for me. Brian tipped his head back to see the light through the pines, and the blood ran, or the sky moved, and the great, sweet pines seemed to be falling, and he sat down dizzy, and with his shoulders hunched for a moment against the impact of the trees. The church was an ark with all on board; it dipped and rolled in the swell of the accordion, and he alone was outside amidst the dry grass and shadows, a sooty fantail, gravestones glimpsed through the falling pines of his own life.

He saw cones. The old cones, puffed and half rotted in the needles were ignored. He wanted those heavy with sap and seed, brown yet tinged with green, and shaped as owls. When dislodged they were well shaped to the hand to be hurled as owl grenades against impossible odds across the road, or sent bouncing among the gravestones to wake somebody there. He gathered new stocks by climbing with a stick and striking them from the branches. At first he climbed carefully to keep the gum from his clothes, but it stuck to him anyway, gathered dirt and wouldn't rub away, and lay like birthmarks on his legs and held his fingers.

His father was preaching, for the church was quiet. Brian heaped up a mass of pine needles beneath the trees, working on his knees and bulldozing the needles with both hands out in front. He built a heap as high as himself, and jumped up and down on it. When he lost interest he left the trees and walked into the graveyard to search for skinks. Quietly he bent the grass from the tombstones, like parting a fleece, and after each movement he waited, poised in case of a lizard. He found none. He imagined that they were destroyed by things that came down from the bush at night. He picked at the resin stains on his hands. Deborah Lascelles, 1874–1932, Called Home. Brian forgot about the skinks. 'Called Home,' he said to himself. He thought about it as he went down the tree-lined margin of the small cemetery and on to the road. He was disappointed that there were no new cars, but one at least was a V8. He shaded his eyes by pressing his hands to the door glass, in an effort to see what the speedo went up to. He reasoned that anyway as it had twice as many cylinders as their car, it must do twice the speed.

Old now is Earth, and none may count her days. The final hymn. Brian went back into the trees and stood as king on his pine needle heap. He arced his urine in the broken sunlight as an act of territory, and checked the two balls in his pouch with brief curiosity. He jousted against the pines one more time, and brought down a perfect brown-green owl. He ran his hand over the tight ripples of his cone. He hefted it from hand to hand as he went back to the church.

His father stood at the doorway to shake hands and talk with the adults as they left. Those still inside showed no impatience. They talked among themselves, or listened with goodwill to what was said by and to the minister. There were few secrets, and no urgency to leave the only service for two months. Mrs Patchett showed Mr Jenkins the holes beneath the eaves, and he stuffed them with paper as an interim measure, and promised to return and do more another day. Things borrowed were transferred from car to car. Wheelan Lascelles stood unabashed, and on his one arm the white sleeve was brilliant against the tan. 'That poem you used,' he said to the minister. 'What poem was that?'

'One of my own, in fact.' Brian shared his father's pleasure. They smiled together. The boy edged closer to his father so as to emphasise his affiliation.

'Is that so? I thought it a fine poem, a poem of our own country. I'd like some day to have a copy of it.'

From the sheets folded in his Bible the minister took the hand-written poem, and gave it. It was found a matter of interest to those remaining: the minister giving his poem to Wheelan Lascelles. Others wished they had thought to mention it, and strove to recall it.

'We're going to the Jenkins' for lunch,' Brian's father told him when everyone had left the church. The Jenkins lived twelve miles up the valley. The minister preferred having lunch with a family living past the church, for then in the afternoon the trip to Sutherland's was made that much shorter. He let the Jenkins drive on ahead because of the dust, and followed on. 'Mr and Mrs Jenkins eat well,' he said to his son with satisfaction.

On a terrace above the river were the house and sheds of the Jenkins' farm, and a long dirt track like a wagon trail leading in, and a gate to shut behind. 'What have you got on yourself?' said the minister, as he checked appearances before entering the house.

'Gum.' Brian rubbed at it dutifully, but knew it wouldn't come off.

'And what's in your pocket?'

'Just a pine cone,' he said. His father flipped a hand as a sign, and Brian took the owl and rolled it away. It lay still warm from his body on the stones and earth of the yard.

'You realise old Mrs Patchett died, of course, and wasn't there today,' said Mrs Jenkins when they sat down. Brian thought some day he might return and find his pine cone grown far above the Jenkins' home. 'Her mind went well before the end. She accused them of starving her, and used to hide food in her room. The smell was something awful at times.' Mr Jenkins smiled at Brian and skilfully worked the carving knife.

'She wasn't at the services the last time or two,' the minister said 'I did visit her. As you say, her mind seemed clouded, the old lady.' Mr Jenkins carved the hot mutton with strength and delicacy.

'She was a constant trial to them,' Mrs Jenkins said. Mr Jenkins balanced on the balls of his feet, and gave his task full concentration. Like a violinist he swept the blade, and the meat folded away.

'I saw Mr Lascelles who's only got one arm,' said Brian.

'Yes, Wheelan Lascelles,' said Mr Jenkins without pausing.

'Old Mrs Patchett was a Lascelles,' said his wife. 'They only left her a short time, but she must have tried to walk back up to where the first house on the property used to be. She went through the bull paddock, and it charged, you see. She wouldn't have known a thing of it, though.' With his smile Mr Jenkins held the gravy boat in front of Brian and, when the boy smiled back, Mr Jenkins tipped gravy over his meat and potatoes, and the gravy flowed and steamed.

'The second family in the valley were Patchetts,' said Mrs Jenkins, 'and then

Lascelles. Strangely enough, Wheelan's father lost an arm. There must be long odds against that, I'd say. It happened in a pit sawing accident before Wheelan was born.' Brian stopped eating to consider the wonder of it: two generations of one-armed Lascelles.

On the long sill of the Jenkins' kitchen window were tomatoes to ripen, and a fan of letters behind a broken clock. And he could see a large totara tree alone on the terrace above the river.

'And which was the first European family?' said the minister as he ate.

'McVies. McVies and then Patchetts were the first, and now all the McVies have gone one way or another. McVies were bushmen, of course, not farmers, and once the mills stopped they moved on.'

'I haven't seen a McVie in the valley for thirty years,' said Mr Jenkins, as if the McVies were a threatened species, fading back before civilisation.

'If your father has only one arm then you're more likely to have one arm yourself,' volunteered Brian.

'Play outside for a while,' his father said. 'Until Mr and Mrs Jenkins and I have finished our tea.'

'There's a boar's head at the back of the shed,' said Mr Jenkins. 'We're giving the beggars something of a hurry up recently.'

'There you are then,' said the minister.

The boar's head was a disappointment, lop-sided on an outrigger of the shed. It resembled a badly sewn mask of rushes and canvas. False seams had appeared as if warped from inner decay. Only the tusks were adamant in malice; curved, stained yellow and black in the growth rings. Brian reached up and tried to pull out a tusk, but although the head creaked like a cane basket, the tusk held, and only a scattering of detritus came down. The vision of the bull that murdered old Mrs Patchett was stronger than the defeated head of a pig. The boy sat in the sun and imagined the old lady escaping back to her past, and the great bull coming to greet her.

'What happened to the bull?' he asked his father as the minister topped up the radiator.

'What's that?'

'What happened to the bull that killed Mrs Patchett?'

'I don't know. Why is it you're always fascinated with such things? I don't suppose the bull could be blamed for acting according to its nature.'

As they left amidst the benevolence of Mr Jenkins' smile, and the persistent information from his wife, Brian saw his cone lying in the yard, green and turning brown, and he lined it through the window with his finger for luck, and saw it sprout there and soar and ramify until, like the beanstalk, it reached the sky. 'A substantial meal,' said the minister.

'There was too much gravy,' said Brian.

'I was born in country like this,' said his father. The bush began to stand openly on the hillsides, and on the farmland closer to the road were stumps which gripped even in death. 'It's awkward country to farm,' said the minister. 'It looks better than it is.' There would be a hut in his pine, and a rope ladder which could be drawn up so that boars and bulls would be powerless below. Tinned food and bottles to collect the rain. Mr and Mrs Jenkins wouldn't realise that he was there, and at times he would come down to the lower world and take what he wanted. 'They tried to make it all dairy country, but it didn't work,' his father said. Brian was willing to be an apparent listener as they went up the valley, mile after mile pursued only by the dust.

Dogs barked them in to Sutherland's. The Oliphants and more Patchetts were already waiting in the main room. There was a social ease among them, arisen from a closeness of lifestyle, proximity and religion. The Sutherlands had no children left at home, the last Patchett boy was at boarding school; only the Oliphant twins, six-year-old girls, were there to represent youth. They sat with their legs stuck out rebelliously because they weren't allowed to thump the piano keys. The Sutherlands had a cousin staying who was a Catholic. Brian watched him with interest. There was a mystery and power in Catholicism, he thought, a dimension beyond the home spun non-conformism that he knew from the inside. Surely there was some additional and superstitious resource with which to enrich life. 'Absolutely riddled with cancer,' Brian heard Mr Oliphant tell the minister.

When the minister was ready, the service in the living room began. No more exact timing was necessary. Mrs Sutherland played the piano, and Mr Oliphant enjoyed singing very loudly and badly. The Oliphant twins refused to stand up with the adults, remaining in a sulk with their legs stiff before them. Their eyes followed Brian past the window as he went from the house. He thought the piano disappointing in comparison with the accordion, more inhibited and careful, less suited to the movement of leaves and water, to the accompaniment of birds.

Brian remembered a traction engine from previous visits. Once it had been used in the mills, but since left in the grass: heavy iron and brass, and great, ribbed wheels. It was warm from the sun, and Brian scaled it and sat there. The traction engine had been built to withstand enormous pressures, and before an age of planned obsolescence. It was a weathered outcrop, the rust only a film which didn't weaken, and the brass solid beneath the tarnish. A land train cast there amidst the barley grass and nodding thistle. He shifted what levers were not seized, and rocked to suggest the motion of the engine on the move.

'You get tired of all the services, I suppose?' said the Sutherlands' cousin. He stood in his carpet slippers, and wore a green woollen jersey despite the heat. He was almost bald, with just a rim of coarse, red hair, like the pine needles the boy had heaped up in the morning. Brian came down to talk. It seemed discourteous to remain raised up. 'I'm in charge of the afternoon tea. I'm a Catholic, you see.' His eyes were deeply sunk, like the sockets of a halloween pumpkin. 'I've nothing against your father.' They watched heavy, white geese trooping past the sheds. 'There's cake, of course, but you know there's watercress sandwiches as well. Can you imagine that?' Brian thought it rabbit food, but the cousin was from the city. 'She went and collected it from the creek, just like that. There's wonder still in the world,' he said. 'Did I tell you I'm a Catholic?' The cousin began to cry without making any noise, but shedding tears. Brian gave him some privacy by taking a stick and beating a patch of nettles by the hen-run. But the cousin wiped his tears away and followed him. He didn't seem interested in maintaining an adult dignity any more. 'Is that gum on your legs?' he said. The boy told him that he had been playing in the trees at Hepburn.

'There's graves there. One said "Called Home" on it.'

'"Called Home" — did it really?' The cousin shared Brian's fascination with the phrase. '"Called Home."' He began to laugh: not a social laugh, but a hoarse laugh, spreading downwards and out like a pool. A sound of irony and fear and submission.

Mr Oliphant began shouting 'Earth might be fair, and all men glad and wise'. The cousin listened with his mouth still shaped from the laughter.

'I'd better see to the afternoon tea,' he said. 'There are lesser rendezvous yet. I'll crib another watercress sandwich if I can hold it down.'

'Peals forth in joy man's old undaunted cry,' they heard Mr Oliphant singing.

'These things are at the end of my life,' the cousin said, 'and the beginning of yours. I wonder if they seem any different for that.' The cousin turned back from the house after a few steps, and came past Brian. 'Jesus,' he said. 'I'm going to be sick again.' He rubbed the flat of his hands on the green wool of his jersey as if in preparation for a considerable task, and walked towards the sheds. He gave a burp, or sudden sob.

The Sutherlands, Mr Oliphant and the minister came out in search of him when their afternoon tea wasn't ready. Brian could see the Oliphant twins looking through the window. 'Have you seen Mrs Sutherland's cousin?' Brian's father asked him. The boy told him about the crying and the sheds.

'I hate to think — in his state of mind,' said Mr Sutherland. He and the minister began to run. Mr Oliphant saw his contribution best made in a different talent. He filled his lungs. 'Ashley, Ashley,' he cried: so loud that birds flew from the open sheds, and the Oliphant twins pressed their faces to the window. The echoes had settled and Mrs Sutherland had prevented him from further shouting, when Mr Sutherland came back.

'It's all right,' said Mr Sutherland. 'He's been sick again, that's all. He's got himself into a state.'

'Who can blame him,' said Mrs Sutherland.

'He was going to make the afternoon tea,' said Brian. 'He started to cry.'

'He's a good deal worse today, but the Reverend Willis is with him.' Mr Sutherland was both sympathetic and matter of fact. 'They're best left alone,' he said. 'Come on back to the house.' Mr Oliphant was disappointed that it wasn't the end, not even a more dramatic approach to the end.

'A sad business,' he said in his lowest voice, which carried barely fifty yards. Brian was left to wait for his father. He thought that in that quiet afternoon he could hear

Ashley's sobs and his father's voice. He climbed back on to the throne which was the engine, and rested his face and arms on the warm metal.

A column of one-armed Lascelles was moving back up the valley from the war, each with a poem in his hand, and the accordion played 'Rock of Ages' as they marched. Mr Jenkins deftly knifed a wild pig, all the while with a benevolent smile, and in his torrent voice Mr Oliphant Called Home a weeping Ashley: deep eyes and woollen jersey. A host of pine owls, jersey green and brown, spread their wings at last, while old Mrs Patchett escaped again and accused her kin of starvation as she sought an earlier home. Behind and beyond the sway of the accordion's music, and growing louder, was the sound of the grand, poppy-red bull cantering with its head down from the top of the valley towards them all.

Mumsie and Zip

~

MUMSIE SAW THE car coming at five, as she had expected. The general noise of homeward traffic was at a distance, but still the desperation was apparent in the pitch of it. Zip always turned off the engine when in the gate, and coasted on the concrete strips until he was parallel with the window. The grass was spiky and blue in the poor light of winter. Mumsie had cacti on the window sill, and the dust lay amid the thorns of *Mammillaria wildii*.

Zip undid his seatbelt, and stepped out. He took the orange nylon cover from the boot, and began covering the car for the night. He spread the cover evenly before he began to tie it down. Zip always started at the same corner and worked clockwise round the car. He didn't bend to tie the corners as a woman would bend, with backside out, but crouched, agile and abrupt, balanced on his toes. Sometimes when Mumsie was close to him as he crouched like that, she would hear his knees pop. Mumsie wondered if there would be a day when she would go out and ask Zip not to cover the car because there was something of significance she had to attend: a premiere perhaps, or an apparently trivial summons which would become This Is Your Life, Mumsie.

Mumsie knew Zip wouldn't look up as he came past the window: they always reserved recognition for the kitchen when Zip came home from work. Zip would go to the lavatory, and then to their bedroom to take off his jacket and shoes. Mumsie heard him flush the bowl, and go through for his other shoes.

Zip came to the stove. He stood by Mumsie's shoulder. 'How's things?' he said.

The mist of the winter evening was strung through the poles and gables, the thinning hair of a very old woman. Toby McPhedron tried to kick free a flattened hedgehog from the surface of the road.

'Fine,' said Mumsie. 'And you?'

'Busy as usual,' said Zip. 'Just the same, Mumsie. You know how it is.'

'Casserole,' said Mumsie as Zip lifted the lid, 'with the onions in chunks the way you like it. Chunky chunks instead of sliced up thin.'

'Good on you, Mumsie, good on you,' said Zip. 'You know what I like all right.' He rubbed his forehead and circled the sockets of his eyes.

'So the usual day?' said Mumsie.

'You know how it is. Busy, of course: always the same.'

'So Mumsie's got a casserole,' said Mumsie.

'You know I like a casserole all right,' said Zip. Mumsie noticed how the pupils of his eyes jittered the way they often did, although his face was flat and still. He stood beside her and looked at the casserole while his pupils jittered.

'You know I couldn't get hardly a thing to dry today. There's no wind and no sun. Hardly a thing dried. I had to take most of it off the line again and put it in the good room with the heater.'

'It's that sort of day,' said Zip. He placed the butter and salt and pepper on the table, and cork mats with the picture of a kitten halting a ball of fluffy wool.

'Mr Beresford died,' said Mumsie.

'Mr Beresford?'

'The place with the new roof, two down from the corner. I heard Mrs Rose talking about it in the shop.'

'Ah,' said Zip.

'So nothing of interest at work today.'

'Uh-huh,' said Zip. He sat down at his place, which was facing the stove and the bench. He laid his hands one each side of his cork mat, as a knife and fork are laid. 'They haven't found the murderer yet,' said Mumsie.

'Murderer?'

'Who murdered those two girls in the boatshed in Auckland. Shaved their heads, I think it said. There's a lot of sick things.'

Zip left his hands resting on the table and he looked at the floor by the bench where the pattern on the lino had been worn away. Mumsie's legs plodded this way and that around the kitchen, but always came back to that worn place, on which she shuffled back and forth from stove to table to bench. Zip seemed absorbed: as if that worn patch were a screen and Mumsie's splayed shoes played out some cryptic choreography. But his black eye spots continued to jiggle, and the focus wasn't quite right to hit the worn lino, but aimed deeper, at something behind. Zip sat still, as if conserving energy for a final effort, or as if that final effort had been made to no avail. Mumsie looked at him from time to time. 'Mumsie's done peas shaken in the pot with butter,' she said, 'and baked potatoes in their skins.'

'You're a winner, Mumsie, that's for sure.'

Tears began to form on the windows, and the light outside was fading quickly. 'I like to be in my own house when it gets dark,' said Zip. They could hear persistent traffic noise from the corner, and Toby McPhedron ran a stick along the tin fence next door.

'You don't mind about the heater on in the good room?' said Mumsie. 'There's no drying at all.'

'We can go there ourselves later,' said Zip. 'We'd have to heat one room.'

'Now why would the murderer shave those girls' heads?' said Mumsie.

'Kinky sex, Mumsie. You want to watch out.' Zip watched his casserole with the chunky onions being served, and the potatoes blistered grey-brown, and the peas in butter glistening as emeralds.

Mumsie talked about Mrs Rose's visit to the dentist, about the manner of Mr Beresford's dying third-hand, about the boatshed murderer, and the good room doorknob which just came off in her hand. The tears made tracks down the windows, and those tracks showed black, or spangled back the kitchen light. Mumsie talked of a party at the Smedley's which they weren't invited to, and how either a niece or a cousin of Debbie Simpson's had a growth in her ear which might be pressing on her brain. Zip said, 'Is that right, Mumsie', and nodded his head to show that he was listening, and in satisfaction as he crunched the casserole onions done in chunks as he liked them: and he kept looking at things deeper than the worn lino by the bench. Mumsie wondered if she should take some pikelets along to Mrs Beresford, or whether she would only be thought nosy because she hadn't really known him. A dog had torn Mrs Jardine's rubbish bag open again, and Mrs Jardine had to clean it up in her good clothes when she came home at lunchtime, Mumsie said.

The winter night, the lizard voice of the traffic at a distance, the condensation on the windows, all intensified the artificial light of the kitchen where Mumsie and Zip ate their casserole, until it was a clear, yellow space separate from the rest of life, independent even from the rest of their own experience, and isolating them there — Mumsie and Zip.

'Mumsie,' said Zip, 'now that was a real casserole, and don't worry about the doorknob, because I can get that bastard back on later.'

'I knew you'd like it, being winter and that. And there'll be enough for you tomorrow.'

Zip lit a cigarette as he stood by the bench and waited to help with the dishes. He pulled the smoke in, and his eyelids dropped for a moment as the smoke hit deep in his lungs. In a long sigh he breathed out. The smoke drifted, the colour of the condensation on the window, and Zip had the teatowel folded over his arm like a waiter, and stood before the plastic drip tray as he waited for the dishes. 'I'll put the rest of the casserole in something else,' said Mumsie, 'and then the dish can be soaked. There's always some bubbles out and bakes on the rim.'

'Let it soak then, Mumsie,' said Zip.

'Don't let me miss the start of the news. Maybe they've found the boatshed murderer.' Mumsie liked everyone to be brought to justice. Zip dried the forks carefully, pressing a fold of towel between the prongs. He tapped the ash from his cigarette into *Chamaecereus silvestrii* on the sill.

'It's just as well we're not in the boatshed belt,' he said.

'But it could be anyone, Zip.'

'Except Mr Beresford, Mumsie. I'd say he must be in the clear.'

'No, I meant it could be any woman. It said on the talkback that these things are increasing all the time.'

Zip spread the teatowel over the stove top, and shuffled the cork mats into symmetry so that the images of the kittens and the wool were in line. He stood by Mumsie as she wiped the table, and then he sat there and put down a plastic ashtray. Mumsie told him not to pick at the contact because it was already tatty, so Zip rotated his cigarette packet instead, standing it alternately on end and side, over and over again. His fingers were nimble, and the packet only whispered on the table as it turned. 'We'll go through to the good room soon,' said Mumsie, 'seeing the clothes are already in front of the heater there.'

'That's right,' said Zip. He sighed, and the smoke came like dust from deep in his lungs, and drifted in the yellow light. 'Another day, another dollar,' he said.

'Just another day, you said.'

'That's right. Another day,' said Zip. He tapped with his finger on the cigarette above the ashtray; a column of ash fell neatly and lay like a caterpillar.

'How many of those have you had today?' asked Mumsie.

'Five or six.'

'Mumsie's going to have to hide them, or you'll be up to a packet a day again.'

'You're a tough lady all right,' said Zip.

'Well, Mr Beresford was a heavy smoker, Mrs Rose said, and he wouldn't be told, just kept on. Mrs Rose said in the shop she wouldn't be surprised if that was it.'

'But you don't know it was smoking Beresford died of.'

'It can't have helped,' Mumsie said. Zip continued to turn the packet with his free hand, head over heels it went, again and again. Mumsie said that she'd heard that a lot of drugs had been found in the fire station, but it was all being hushed up. Mumsie enjoyed her delusion of occasionally sharing privileged information. 'It'll all be swept under the carpet because they know each other, all those people, you see if they don't.'

'They'd bloody well come down on you or me though, Mumsie, that's for sure,' said Zip.

Mumsie was talking about the food specials at Four Square when the phone rang. She was comparing for Zip the large coffee with the giant and the standard. Standard meant small, but nothing in supermarkets is labelled small. Zip remained still, apart from turning the cigarette packet. He paid no attention to the phone: he had no hope of it. He was unlucky enough to know his own life. But Mumsie was quite excited. She wondered who that could be, she said, and she tidied her hair as she went into the passage. Zip didn't alter just because Mumsie had gone. He stayed quietly at the table as if relaxed, turning the cigarette packet. He did work his mouth, pulling his lips back first on one side then the other, as a horse does on the bit. Zip looked at the table, and the worn lino by the bench, and Mumsie's cactus plants which could survive her benign forgetfulness, and at the windows decked with tears, and his eyes jiggled.

Mumsie was happy when she bustled back in. She felt things were going on. There were decisions to be made and she was involved, and someone had taken the trouble to phone her. 'It's Irene and Malcolm,' she said. Zip let out a dusty breath. The tears of condensation left black trails on the windows, and a small rainbow bubble winked as Mumsie shifted the detergent flask. 'They're going to stay for a few days next week,' said Mumsie. 'Malcolm's got some management course again.'

'No,' said Zip.

'Why's that?'

'I don't want them here. I don't want them here next week, or next year, or ever. I don't want other people in my house, Mumsie. Got it? I don't want Malcolm and his moustache telling me how well he's doing, and your sister making you look like Ma Kettle all the time.' Zip didn't raise his voice, but there was in it a tone of finality.

'But they're family,' said Mumsie. She turned the water on and off in the sink for no reason.

'They're not coming. You're going to tell them that they can't come, or I'm going to. You'll do it nicer than me.'

'How often do we have people?' said Mumsie. 'We never see anyone.'

'I don't want to see anyone, and I don't want anyone to see me. People are never worth the effort, Mumsie, but you never seem to learn that.'

'I get sick of no one coming. I get sick of always being by ourselves,' said Mumsie.

Zip spread the corners of his mouth in one grimace of exasperation, and then his face was flat again. 'You're stupid,' he said. 'What are you?'

'Maybe I am,' said Mumsie, 'but I've got a life too. I'm not too stupid to have my own sister to stay, am I.'

'You're a stupid, old bitch, Mumsie, and I'm as bad. In a way I'm worse, because I'm just bright enough to see how stupid we both are, and how we're buggered up here like two rats in a dunghill. We've got to keep on living our same life over and over again.'

'Oh, don't start talking like that, and getting all funny.' The windows were black eyes shining with tears, and the custard light of the room grew brighter in contrast with deep winter outside. The table legs cast stalks of shadow across the floor, and high on the cupboard edges the fly dirt clustered like pepper spots. 'Anyway, I've told them they can come, and so they can,' said Mumsie. She pretended that by being emphatic she had made an end of it, but her face was flushed and her head nodded without her being aware.

Zip eased from the seat, and took a grip of Mumsie's soft neck. He braced his body against hers and he pushed her head back twice on to the wall. Mumsie's jowls spread upwards because of the pressure of Zip's hand, and trembled with the impact of the wall. Their faces were close, but their eyes didn't meet. The sound of Mumsie's head striking the wall echoed in the kitchen; the mounting for the can opener dug in behind her ear. Mumsie began to weep quietly, without any retaliation. 'Now I tell you again they're not coming,' said Zip. He sat back at the table, and began to turn the cigarette packet top over bottom. Mumsie put her hand to the back of her head for comfort, and her fingers came back with a little blood.

'I swept out the storeroom today, Mumsie,' Zip said. 'I swept out the bloody store-room when I went to that place twenty years ago, and today I swept it out again. I was doing it when the buyers came and they all went past me and into Ibbetson's office. Ibbetson didn't say anything to me, and neither did any of the buyers. I'm the monkey on a stick.'

'I thought you liked my sister,' said Mumsie. She dabbed at the blood with a paper towel, but Zip didn't seem to notice.

'I'd like to screw her, Mumsie, you know that, but she wouldn't let me, and there's nothing else I want to have to do with her apart from screwing her. She's up herself, your sister.'

'You're just saying it.'

'I'm just saying it and it's the truth. We make a good pair, you and me, Mumsie. We don't take the world by storm. Two stupid people, and if we stopped breathing right now it wouldn't mean a thing.'

'It would to me,' said Mumsie.

'We're dead, Mumsie,' said Zip.

'Don't say that.' Mumsie watched Zip, but he didn't reply. He seemed very relaxed. He looked back at the watching windows and his eyes jittered. Mumsie didn't like silences: talk was reassuring evidence of life moving on for Mumsie.

'You're that proud,' said Mumsie. 'You're so proud, and that's the matter with you. You'll choke on your pride in the end.'

'You might be right there, Mumsie,' said Zip. 'Most of us could gag on our own pride.'

'You hurt my head then, you know. It's bleeding.'

'You're all right. Don't start whining. I'll have to hit Ibbetson's head one day, Mumsie, and then there'll be hell to pay.'

'Oh, don't talk about things like that.'

'It's going to happen. Some day it's bound to happen, and there'll be merry hell to pay.'

'Why can't you just be happy, Zip?'

'I'm not quite stupid enough, more's the pity. I can watch myself and I don't bloody want to.'

'Let's go into the good room,' said Mumsie. 'We'll push the clothes out of the way and sit in there in the warm.'

'Sure, but first Mumsie we'll have a cuddle in the bedroom. I quite feel like it, so you get your pants off in there and we'll have a cuddle.'

'It's cold in there,' said Mumsie.

'You get your pants off, Mumsie,' said Zip. 'You know what your murderer did to the boatshed girls — shaved their hair all off, so you want to watch out.'

'It's awful. I meant to watch it on the news to see if they've found him.'

'You can't trust anyone but your family, Mumsie. You've got to realise that.'

'I suppose so.'

Mumsie kept on talking so that Zip would forget to tell her again to go into the bedroom and take her pants off. She told him that after Mr Beresford died the blood came to the surface of his body, so Mrs Rose said, and his face turned black and his stomach too. 'Maybe it was the tarbrush coming out,' said Zip. She told him about Mrs Jardine claiming the family care allowance, even though their combined income was over the limit. She told him again that the doorknob had come off in her hand, and about the niece or cousin of Debbie Simpson's who had a growth in her ear and they might have to operate because it was pressing on her brain and making her smell things that weren't really there. 'What a world,' said Zip. He ran his thumb and fore-finger up and down the bridge of his nose, and his eyes jittered, and their focus point was a little beyond anything in the kitchen. He lit another cigarette, and Mumsie didn't say anything about that, but went on talking about who did Mrs Jardine think she was, just because they both worked and she could afford plenty of clothes.

The light was banana yellow, and the windows like glasses of stout, beaded with condensation. Mumsie had a magnetic ladybird on the door of the fridge, and the one remaining leg oscillated as the motor came on. Zip had no question on his face, and his hands lay unused on the table before him. 'Mumsie's going to tell you now that I made some caramel kisses today as a treat,' said Mumsie.

'You're a queen,' said Zip. 'You're a beaut.'

'And we'll have another cup of tea, and take it through to the good room with the caramel kisses.' Mumsie brought the tin out and opened the lid to display the two layers of kisses. 'They've come out nice and moist,' she said.

'They look fine, Mumsie,' said Zip. 'You know I like a lot of filling in them.'

'I made them after I'd been to the shop,' said Mumsie. 'It'll be warmer in the good room, and the clothes should be dry.'

When the tea was made, Mumsie put it on a tray. She was pleased to be going at last to the good room. She paused at the door. The blood was smudged dry behind her ear. 'Bring in the caramel kisses for me,' she said.

'Sure thing, Mumsie,' said Zip. He heard Mumsie complaining about there being no knob on the good room door.

'This bloody door, Zip,' said Mumsie. Zip cast his head back quickly and made a laughing face, but without any noise.

'All right, Mumsie,' he said. 'I'll come and do it now,' but he stayed sitting there, his hands on the table, his face still once more, and only his eyes jit jittering as bugs do sometimes in warm evening air.

A Day With Yesterman

~

CHATTERTON WOKE TO the birds. The absence of pain may have been the reason. He moved his legs, sucked in his stomach, but nothing caught, just the squeak of the plastic sheet beneath the cotton one. Chatterton was accustomed to the need to occupy himself much of the night, to sidle and belay from ledge to ledge of darkness, but not all that often did he hear the birds begin. He marvelled at the intensity — a sweet hubbub as a base and, superimposed, the longer, individual exclamations of thrush or blackbird. He had the pleasing thought that the birds gathered at his house to inaugurate a special day. Chatterton folded the sheet under his chin, so that the blanket no longer tickled, and he made himself a little wider and longer to pop a few joints and check that he was in good shape.

A mild suffusion of light from behind the curtains strengthened as Chatterton sang 'Danny Boy' and 'The White Cliffs of Dover'. He stopped with a feeling that something of value was slipping away, and then it came to him, a recollection of the night's dream in which he had made love to an ample woman beneath an elm tree in Hagley Park. It was to some degree an explanation of his mood. Chatterton was sensible enough to enjoy authentic emotion, however it reached the mind. Before the experience quite faded, he closed his eyes to breathe again the fragrance of the elm and observe a wisp of auburn hair quiver with the pulse of her neck. He lay listening to his birds as morning came. How young at last I feel, he assured himself.

By the time Chatterton was in the kitchen, he could get by with natural light. He poached himself an egg without boiling off the white, and he watched his yellow feet like flounder on the floor. He would never recognise his feet in a crowd, for they were just any old, yellow feet. Truck rigs passed with a roar on the nearby motorway as they tried to get a clear start to the day. Chatterton rubbed his knee to loosen the joint. The skin seemed to have no attachment to the bones, and slid all ways. Only the young body savours its union.

As the birds wound down, Chatterton finished his third cup of tea, and went back to his bedroom to choose his clothes. 'I'll make a bargain with you.' He addressed a small, familiar god. 'Best clothes for best day.' The trousers were a quality check, but big at his waist and so the band tucked somewhat under his belt. A grey jacket, with a chrome zip, that his daughter had given him for Christmas. Tropic Sands aftershave, which the label exhorted Chatterton to splash on liberally, but which he did not. 'Chatterton,' said Chatterton to his own reflection, 'you are an old dog.' He looked at all the bottles on his drawers, and decided to take no medication at all. Before he left the house Chatterton buffed the toes of his shoes with the socks he was putting out to wash. He should have known better, for the bending sent him dizzy, and he overbalanced and fell on to the smooth lino by the bench. He had a laugh at himself, and felt the cool lino on his cheek as he lay and waited for his head to clear. In the corner was a false cut in the lino: Chatterton could remember clearly the wet day seventeen years before when he had laid the lino and made just that false cut. How difficult it is to fault life's continuity. The rain had caught the window at an angle, and drained like rubber tree striations across its surface.

As Chatterton walked to Associated Motors, he calculated a route which would keep him on the sunny side of the streets, and he watched other people on their way to work, disappointed that he couldn't recognise them as friends. He nodded and smiled nevertheless.

Chatterton helped part-time with the accounts at Associated Motors. So very part-time over the last months that Susan was surprised to see him. 'And you're looking so smart today,' she said. Chatterton knew he was. He began to use the computer to calculate GST payments. Chatterton enjoyed the computer, and was impatient with people who claimed they couldn't adapt to them.

'Life is adaptation,' he said.

'Right, Mr Chatterton.'

'How I could run when I was young.'

'Could you?' said Susan.

'I was a small-town champion,' said Chatterton, 'and could have been a large-town one with training.' He was wistful rather than proud.

'I like netball,' said Susan.

'Ah, your knees are wonderfully smooth,' said Chatterton, his fingers nimble on the keys.

The sales manager broke up their flirtation. 'How are you feeling?' he asked.

'I am in complete remission today,' said Chatterton. 'I can sense my prime again. I'm growing young again very rapidly.' The sales manager laughed, for he thought Chatterton intended a joke.

'How about taking a Cressida down to Dunedin then?' he asked Chatterton. 'It's needed there today.'

The mechanics watched in envy as Chatterton took a set of provisional plates and two of his own cassettes. They hoped for such perks themselves. 'Hey, Chatters, you lucky old bastard,' and Chatterton winked and executed a no-fuss manoeuvre before them in the yard.

'I thought the old bastard was dying or something.'

'Dying to get away in that car, all right.'

In fifth gear the Cressida was only loping on the Canterbury Plains. Chatterton fed in his Delius cassette and the quiet interior was sprung with sound. Chatterton wondered why he dreamed so often in old age of hang-gliding. Something he'd never done, yet increasingly his night views were from above, the cold air whistling in a rigging he didn't understand. Progress was relentless, and from landscape and people half recognised, he was borne away. He supposed it might be a side effect of the medication. When he was younger he would have tackled hang-gliding He had been an athlete, hadn't he, and a soldier?

At Karitane, Chatterton turned off to take the old road. He could avoid the increasing traffic. He liked that swamp flat: rushes, brown and yellow mosses, mallards, and pukekos with their bookish, striding way. Later there was a stranded man — enquiring face and car bonnet raised. Chatterton stopped, and the man came with grateful haste to meet him. His name was Norman Caan. He began to thank Chatterton, who smiled, but was distracted by the peace as he stood there — the quiet road, the crimped blue light over the sea, the headland beyond with an apron of gorse on the steeper ground. The wind from the sea was wine, and it scented the beachside grass and bore spaciousness inland.

'I do appreciate you stopping. I've got something of a problem, as you see, and I've a city appointment at one.' Caan was close to Chatterton, his voice a trifle plaintive. He put out his hand and Chatterton shook it.

'Sorry,' said Chatterton, 'but what a day it is. Isn't it? How things continue to fit newly together, year after year.'

'I suppose it is.' Caan looked at the sky, blown almost clear, and the hills and the inlet and the horizon seaward, as though he had just entered a large building and had its architecture commended to him. The coast curved, and a far cutting bore a drape of pink ice-plant, and the sun shone back from it as if from glass.

As they examined the engine of Caan's Volvo, Chatterton noticed a balding spot at Caan's crown, as if a tidy bird had been scratching a nest there. Chatterton passed a hand over his own stiff, grey hair. A dunny brush he'd heard it called. He had to admit Caan's clothes better than his own, however: an integration of style and texture which Chatterton could recognise, yet not explain.

'There's nothing we can do,' said Chatterton. 'Lock up and come with me. We can have someone out in no time.' But back at his own car, instead of getting inside, Chatterton was drawn to the bank again. 'Will you look at that, though,' he said. 'No pain there at all. Will you look at the ripples on the bars as the tide comes in, and the bubbles over the crab holes in the mud.' The single cloud against powder blue made a cameo brooch of the sky; birch leaves tossed as a mane on the back of a macrocarpa hedge. 'You don't mind just for a moment?' asked Chatterton. 'It's just such a day.'

'No, no,' said Caan.

'It's just such a day,' said Chatterton. Caan had no option, but his face had initially a shrug of the shoulders expression as he watched Chatterton move to the edge of the bank above the coast. He was only a few feet above the sea, yet Chatterton sucked several breaths as a diver would on a high cliff. 'I shall become part of it. I see it all as if I'm twenty,' he said.

Despite concern for his situation, Caan was affected by Chatterton's wonder, and something more — something naive in his cheerful age, the trousers belted too large, and his hair bristling. 'It is rather splendid,' said Caan, diffident in praise of his own country.

'You know,' said Chatterton, 'today I keep thinking of when I was young.'

Somewhere between Lake Grasmere and Seddon the black AJS left the road at speed and took an angle into grass standing high as a field of wheat. There was no way of stopping quickly. The bike's metal scything through. He heard only one sound, that of the rushing grass, and he was aware in the clarity of fear how bright the sun shone on that roadside grass like wheat. Yet there was nothing hidden — no snare, no ditch — and fear gave place to exultation as the grass slowed him and he *knew* that nothing there had harm in it: an instant almost too brief to allow him the dangerous conviction that he couldn't die. The black, heavy AJS off the road, the hissing, even fluster of the wheat-grass in the vivid sun. All in a few seconds, he supposed. All happening in a few seconds, and in heightened perception. And the bike had stopped, and he found himself quite alone in that landscape, stalled high from the road with grass packed around him, the cicadas coming back to chorus, and fine pollens settling on the black tank of the AJS.

'Like riding through a wheat field,' said Chatterton.

'Sorry?'

'I was thinking back,' said Chatterton. 'Other days.'

As they passed over the hills into the city, Chatterton and Caan, together completely by chance they would suppose, talked freely. Chatterton found it easier to be honest as he grew older, and the knowledge that relationships had no necessary continuation ceased to disconcert him. Besides, Caan was prepared to listen as well as talk. Chatterton liked a positive listener: he could be one himself. They covered the decline of state medicine, the loss of flavour in Bluff oysters, the self-serving of the political powerful, and the suicide of Tony Hancock. There is a good deal of satisfaction to be had from free-ranging criticism. 'But then I'm a deal older than you,' said Chatterton.

'Not so much surely, I'm retired.'

'There are two possibilities as you get old,' said Chatterton. 'You become archaic, or you leave the world behind in your progress. Either way, increasing isolation is the result.'

'Well, isolated numerically perhaps.'

'And in confidence. It's hard to be confident and old. The opposite of what most people expect, I suppose.'

'But you are,' said Caan.

'An act of faith. Besides, superstition and disease have me now, so I indulge myself. There's days sometimes that favour you, you know.'

'Propitious,' said Caan.

'Pardon.'

'Propitious.'

'Yes,' said Chatterton. 'That's it.'

'Anyway, today you're welcome to travel back with me, and have lunch with me too. I'm allowed a guest at the Rotary lunch I'm addressing. I'll have my car delivered, and afterwards we'll pick up my sister who's coming back with me to recuperate for a while.' Caan was pleased to be able to establish the immediate future, and to provide for Chatterton's repayment within it.

The president of Rotary was a splendid host, just one size larger and more glossy than his fellows, as befitted his office. 'So much of what service groups do now is taken for granted,' he said. 'Assistance is an expectation now, almost a right.' Chatterton noticed the barman's black reefer jacket, and it produced before Chatterton his grandmother's sewing basket. The fine wickerwork and the embroidered top — black, black, with a country spire perpetually slate blue. The colours were ribbed, and the tranquillity of even execution rather than the subject had made an ache which allowed of no expression. So he had built childlike barricades of pins around the black field's spire in attempts at the protection which his memory was later able to assume.

'We get told who we should be supporting, and how much,' said the president. 'We get told we're not doing enough, rather than thanked. Not coughing up sufficiently.' Chatterton enjoyed a free whisky, and watched the last members picking up their badges. The president led the way into the dining room, and they took their places before three slices of ham on each plate. Chatterton rather enjoyed the Rotarian mood: an aura of confidence and good intent that arises from reasonable success in the world, and a wisely unexamined life. Chatterton looked with favour on his ham, and waited for the vegetables. Caan talked to the president.

'I ran my own business for twenty-seven years, then it grew too complex and I sold out. That's one of the things I want to mention in my address: the need to understand there's a point at which a business becomes too much for the managerial skills of its founder alone. A lot of concerns go wrong at that stage.'

Chatterton admired the Rotarians across from him, particularly an assured man in his thirties, eating and smiling carefully as he listened to his neighbour. A man well carapaced in a three-piece suit, and trusting the ground beneath his feet. Chatterton wondered if he had ever looked that way; and knew the answer. The man had a sheen almost, the beauty of a live lobster, an exoskeleton creature, any vulnerability safe within. He was all jointed precision of appearance. Chatterton caught his eye.

'Good on you,' said Chatterton, and they lifted their forks in mutual salutation.

'Few businessmen can make the transition from personal to corporate management,' said Caan. 'And why should it be expected, or easy.' Caan stopped, and looked first at the president and then at Chatterton, as if some explanation was expected from them. His face was pale, and he swallowed several times. 'I feel rotten,' he said. 'I think I might be sick.' His head gave a shiver, and he sighed as if lonely.

'Perhaps the cold meat,' said the president. Caan and he left the table and went through the conversations to find a place for Caan to lie down. Caan walked as if he were carrying a tray of marbles and the loss of any of them would be his death.

Chatterton was offered more vegetables, and accepted all but the peas. Sprouts he had, and potato balls, and corn heaped like nuggets of gold. And no pain was swallowed with them, no pain whatsoever. The president returned alone. 'He's lying down,' he said. 'He says he feels a little better.' The president looked searchingly at

Chatterton. Chatterton lacked an executive mien, and there was grey hair tufted in his ears. He alone in the dining room had a jacket with a zip. There was a sense of ease, though, and goodwill and self-will. The president was not a fool. 'Caan suggested you might speak instead,' he said. Chatterton was happy to be of service. He liked to talk to people. And he had his best trousers on, even if they were gathered at the waist somewhat. He had visions to draw upon, his life among them.

When the president's routine business was over and the serjeant-at-arms had imposed fines with sufficient humorous innuendo, Chatterton was introduced as a colleague of Norman Caan. As he waited to speak, as the polite applause eddied about the tables, Chatterton was reminded of his last battalion reunion and, by another step of recollection, Birdy Fowler, who died of heatstroke before they came out of the desert. Chatterton hadn't been invited to speak at the reunion, and he thought there was a need for Birdy's name to be heard again. So Chatterton began his talk with several of the stories Birdy used to tell when drinking. The Rotarians laughed at the ribaldry of natural man, and Chatterton laughed in tribute to a friend. Then Chatterton talked about his illness: the prostate and spleen which had been taken, the disaffection of other organs; about how to make it through the nights, the spiritual and practical ingenuities by which it's possible to inch closer to the day. About his wife who had been very beautiful when she was young and he was a coarse, stupid boy. About his dream of steam trains ascending steep tracks through the bush, so that the engine fumed and panted, the white steam like egret's feathers flared against the leaves, wild cattle crashed away, and deep, faded varnish of the inner woodwork still showed a living grain.

The green, sashed curtains quivered at the windows of the hotel. The long tables of Rotary luncheon had flower vases, and pollen beneath some of them was spread like pepper on the white cloth. A waitress with her hair up in gel was at the kitchen swing doors, ready to clear away. She picked her lip, and wondered if she would be through by four. We make the mistake of assuming that our present experience is the world's. The tussock would be blowing on all the crests of Dansey's Pass, glue sniffers sitting with statues of the city fathers, a fine rain flaking on to the pongas of the Ureweras, a sheer excalibur of sunlight from the high window of a panel shop in Papanui, transfixing young Marty working there.

The Rotarians were normally uncomfortable with personal revelations, which could easily obscure sound business practices, but as Chatterton was unknown to them, they felt none of the embarrassment that acquaintanceship would have brought. They were quite struck by his eccentricity, his passion, and the evident movement of the bones in his thin cheeks as he talked. Chatterton had an innocent pride as he left with the president to find Caan. He was resting on an alcove chair in the foyer. His coat and tie were off, and his head relaxed backwards. 'I think I'm all right now,' he said.

'Well, Mr Chatterton was a considerable success,' said the president.

'That's the second time he's saved the day,' said Caan.

'I just sang for my supper,' said Chatterton. The president's laugh was high-pitched, almost a giggle, and odd from such an imposing man.

Caan's car was delivered as he and Chatterton sat peacefully in the foyer. Caan washed his face with cold water, and then decided that he was recovered. 'You'll understand that Joan's had a hard time of it,' he said when he returned. 'She left her husband to make a mid-life career for herself in physiotherapy and then found she had cancer. The treatment's knocked her pretty badly.'

Chatterton knew the treatment, but he didn't think about it as they drove to the nursing home. Instead he enjoyed the dappled shadows on the road through the green belt, the shimmer caused by the breeze on the tops of the trees, and imagined himself joining in with the afternoon joggers — putting his weight well forward on the slope and judging a pace to keep both legs and lungs comfortable. The bellows of the chest in full use, cooling tree air on the damp singlet, hair heavy with sweat patting on the back of his head as he ran.

On the front lawn of the nursing home a badminton court had been marked out. Young people played vigorously there, their bare feet silent on the grass, their voices loud and sudden. Joan was waiting in the lounge with her two cases beside her. 'She'll need a good deal of rest, of course, but we're all optimistic,' Caan said as he and Chatterton walked past the lawn. Chatterton watched a brown girl leap forever, so that her arms and breast were outlined against the sea. He wondered why God still chose to punish old men. As Caan came closer to the lounge, he smiled and raised his hand, but his sister was behind the glass, and nothing could be said. She wore a light dress of floral pattern that would be considered cheerful perhaps — when purchased for someone else. She wore lipstick, but her eyebrows were very pale, and to hide her baldness she was topped with a tam-o'-shanter, green and red. She had the eyes of the travellers of illness.

'I'm sorry we're a bit late,' said Caan. 'It's been an odd sort of day.' As he told her of it, and Chatterton's part as an explanation for his presence, Joan and Chatterton regarded one another. When Caan finished, Chatterton touched the woollen cap in a friendly way.

'I had a hat, but not as colourful as yours,' he said. He took one of her cases, Caan the other, and they waited at the door while Joan farewelled a nurse. 'Chemotherapy as well as the ray can be pretty much a sapping combination,' said Chatterton when she was back. 'Is your hair all out?'

'All out,' she said.

'So was mine,' said Chatterton, 'but it grows in again. Mine grew back very wiry.'

'Very wiry,' said Joan. Well, frankness could work both ways.

'And you get a good deal of strength back.' To demonstrate, Chatterton stopped by the car and threw the case up, and caught it again in both arms. 'See,' he said eagerly.

'You get used to him,' said Caan.

'Are you so very different?' she asked Chatterton.

'I'm in search of natural man now,' he said.

'Too late, too old,' she said, but Chatterton threw up the case again and capered with it. The badminton players cheered; a nurse stood watching from the office and telling others over her shoulder what was happening.

Caan asked Chatterton to drive. After his illness at lunch Caan wanted a restful trip. Chatterton was obliging once more. As he drove he calculated aloud the unexpected profit he was making on the day — the price of the bus fare to Christchurch, and of a midday meal. Enough for a week's groceries, or for semi-gloss to paint his small porch. 'Do you enjoy painting?' he asked Joan. The triviality of it stimulated Joan. She was tired of weighing up life and death. She began to talk of the renovations she had done years before on her house at Port Chalmers. Although her voice was well back in her throat, and somewhat husky, it increased in tempo, and her tam-o'-shanter nodded green and red. 'Oh, no, no,' interrupted Chatterton decidedly. 'You should always strip back before repapering for a first rate job.'

'It's not always needed.'

'Shoddy, shoddy,' cried Chatterton.

'What would a man know about making a home,' said Joan. 'What does a man remember.'

Chatterton was in the presence of things which gave an answer. The water in the pink heart of flax, and a monkey-puzzle tree to hold up the sky. Sheep coughing out the night, and in a winter drizzle the horses smoking in the dray. His mother standing at the laundry, pushing back her hair with her wrist, smiling at him, and the smell of hot woollens and yellow soap again. Old coats without shoulders on nails like dried fish, and gulls following his father's plough.

At Timaru they had cream freezes, and turned off from the main road at the Showground Hill to rest and eat. Chatterton leant his arms on the top wire of the fence, and watched the downs and the mountains beyond. He led a game to distinguish as many shades of green as possible. 'Nine different colours. To stand and see nine different colours of green,' said Joan. 'All growing from the same soil, all compatible and with the promise of some use or crop.'

When he looked south, Chatterton sensed a change in the weather, and he told the others to expect a southerly. A fisherman gets to read the elements of his locality. Chatterton encouraged Joan to talk as they went on north. He refused to be deferential just because of her trial. 'You have to be careful illness doesn't make you selfish, you know,' he said. 'And you could do a lot more with your appearance — a young woman like you.' He could say such things because of his own illness, his lack of malice, but mostly because of a special innocence which arises from experience, and is the mark of rare and successful old age.

'I was never at all religious before,' said Joan. 'Now I'm an atheist by faith rather than logic. And I've got tired of most of my friends. They almost bored me to death when they came. What you expect rarely happens. You, Norman, you're one of the worst.'

'But I'm a brother. All brothers are boring. They lack sufficient biological variation to be otherwise.'

Eventually, release was almost overpowering for Joan. 'It's stuffy,' she said. 'I feel dizzy.'

'It's the closeness before the change,' said Caan, 'and you're not used to travelling yet.' Joan took off her woollen hat, and leant back on the seat. Her naked, bird's head had a little downy hair, and the skull plates joined in apparently clumsy workmanship.

'The treatment can have a long-term effect on your food preferences,' said Chatterton. 'Peas and beans, for instance. I can't eat them at all now, the smell disgusts me. While fruit is a positive craving. Nectarines and satsumas: ah, there now.'

The southerly came through late in the afternoon, catching them before Ashburton. The churned cloud, wind that flogged the trees and bore a scattered rain too pressed to set in. The temperature dropped as if a door had been opened. 'Oh, that's much better,' said Joan.

'Let's sing "Danny Boy". You know "Danny Boy"?' said Chatterton.

'Oh Danny Boy, the pipes . . .' Three of them together. Chatterton likes to sing, although he has a poor voice. He watched the broad, shingle riverbed, the islands of gorse and lupin in the scattered rain. He thought of his nineteen-pound salmon near the mouth of the Waitaki, the gravel unsure beneath his waders as he turned, and the cry going up from his fellow fishermen as they gave way for him. The salmon don't feed: they strike in anger, or home-coming exultation perhaps. The river aids its fish against the line, and swans form a necklace above the struggle as they pass to Lake Wainoni.

'We're all a bit high,' said Joan. 'I like the song, but we've all light voices and we need someone deeper. A bass baritone, say.' The southerly was blowing itself out, but the coolness remained. Near Dunsandel they saw a hitchhiker with a giant pack and the legs to make light of it. Chatterton pulled up ahead of him.

'Can you sing "Danny Boy"?' he asked. The hitchhiker was willing, although for a time he was embarrassed by Joan's head.

'Where do you come from?' she said.

'Dubbo, Australia.'

'We've all of us got problems,' said Caan.

There were enough voices for a barbershop quartet. 'Oh Danny Boy, the pipes . . .' The Australian sang well. He was out of the weather and travelling in the right direction. Over the sinews of his brown arms were raised a few graceful arteries, and the whites of his eyes glinted in a tanned face. 'The green, green grass of home' they sang as Caan conducted. Joan and the hitchhiker, who couldn't remember each other's names and would never meet again, combined their voices, and smiled at each other because of Chatterton's caterwauling.

They dropped the Australian baritone at the city overbridge. Chatterton took his pack from the boot, and Joan gave him a bag of seedless grapes she had from the nursing home. 'Goodbye, Danny Boy,' she said. What could he make of them: what could they make of themselves. A hitchhiker's experience is only life accelerated. 'Oh my God,' said Joan as they went on. 'I've had my hat off all that time. What a sight.' She laughed at her own humiliation, and wiped her eyes. She put the tam-o'-shanter on once more, for the formality of parting with Chatterton.

The wooden house was like the others that surrounded it, insufficiently individual, it seemed, to be his. Chatterton stood in the drive as Caan came round to take the driver's seat. The evening was calm, but the evidence of the southerly was there. Leaves stripped by the wind and gathered on the concrete in the lee of the house. Leaves of peach and maple. Leaves of birch with aphids still clustered on the underside. The wind's violence had in its eddy a delicacy of graduated winnowing, and the litter diminished to a whip tail of fragments which included two ladybirds, a length of tooth floss, a tuft of cat fur, and ended in a line of most fragile, perfect dust.

'But we'll keep in touch,' Caan was saying. 'You cheer Joan up because you know what she's been through, and she won't have many people to visit her while she's here.'

'If you can be bothered some time,' said Joan. The sheen of her hospital skin wrinkled in a grin.

'You know, right from the very start I had a feeling this was going to be a good day,' said Chatterton. 'It's a sort of Indian summer perhaps.'

'Life is sad, though, isn't it?' said Joan. She looked up at him with a terrible openness.

'Oh yes, sad, but not dreary, not lacking purpose. But sad, sure enough,' said Chatterton firmly. He went to the protected corner of his small garden and came back with a red rose for Joan, an old English rose, dark and red. 'Old style roses have the true scent,' he said. 'Aren't I right?' She had it to her face. 'Eh?' he said.

'Yes.'

Two white butterflies tumbled in the air above the letter-box, and Chatterton smiled, not withdrawing his attention from the car as Caan backed out. 'He's a hard case, that one,' said Caan. 'He gave a speech off the cuff at the Rotary meeting you know. Hardly a moment for thought.'

'He's certainly got no singing voice, but he sees through things all right.'.

Chatterton waited to see them drive away, not the last minute shamefaced turning of some people's farewells, as if they feared what might be being said of them. Only his trousers suggested age, crimped at his slender waist and bagging somewhat at the seat, the the way trousers of old men do. When they were gone, Chatterton arched back cautiously, and pressed with the flat of his hand on his stomach. He decided to stay in his garden while he felt so well. Did he tell them he was an athlete once, he wondered. Unthinkingly he kept his arched stance as he tried to remember. All the things he could do then, all the things he could feel. Chatterton could see his dark roses on the fence, and the two ladybirds upside down and closer in the whip tail dust upon the concrete.

The scent of the rose seemed to linger, maybe only in his heart, for he was no longer sure of such distinctions. What would he think of next, he wondered. He would fetch a beer, and have it in his garden, because of the extra money and the friends he had made that day. As he turned to go, he had in recollection the sight of the Marlborough hills, and a hawk the colour of a moth against the sea of the sky.

Essie

~

DAN HAD BEEN offered a hotel lunch: three courses and more talk of business, when all that was necessary had been said. He could have lunched in any of the mall cafeterias, with used dishes pushed to the end of the tables, and the clatter of plastic trays like a mechanical language around him. Instead he sat on a green bench beneath the trees on the bank of the river. He had a carton of fruit juice and a cheese sandwich. He watched the seagulls and mallards begging scraps from the people on the grass, and in the shallow river the soft weed imitate the motion of fish. The vehicles of the one-way systems pursued each other on both sides of the park, but the lawns and the path close to the water were in the bright sun, and the seats beneath the trees in dappled warmth, and the oaks and sycamores deflected the noise. Ducks sought out the acorns which were like copper bullets and, amazingly, swallowed them whole. Seagulls couldn't, and they hunched their shoulders and shrieked. There were leaves floating on the water, turning as they went as if to show themselves to advantage, and others had sunk in the calmest places and lay on the bottom as massed, dark prints of a hand.

Dan saw the girls in their summer dresses, and young office men with neat hair and their jackets off. And a group of uniformed NCOs from the Army Hall, who were office workers also and had escaped from their proformas to the grass and the sun. The girls in their summer dresses seemed the same as those he remembered from his time in the city: the same sharp eyebrows and vulnerable throats; the same aura, in those who were alone, of absorption and resistance to the glance.

Each time the lights changed there was a roar from the traffic zoo, but the greater the competition there, the more tranquil was the riverside, and the clearer and more deliberate the movement and colours. The seagulls hunched with their red beaks open in a call, the leaves as slow Catherine wheels on the surface of the river, and the girls with their books and lunches open on the grass.

He didn't recognise Essie at first. The woman came with her son in a push-chair, and sat on the stone steps of the fountain. She lifted the boy from the chair, and he splashed in the water with his hands, and ran a few paces to one side, then the other. She was compact and calm, and wore a white, lace blouse. Only later, when Dan had been watching the river, and glanced up when she stood, did he see that it was Essie. He felt a flow of pleasure and affection, then an ebb of regret. He smiled, although at that distance and among the various people on the grass and seats, Essie had no idea that he was there. It was an involuntary smile, marking at once the recollection and recognition of Essie. 'It's Essie,' he heard himself say quietly. Essie's boy ran back from the ducks, and Essie picked him up and went towards the ducks to show there was nothing to fear. The sun loaded the air so that it was resistant to movement, and direct reflections were difficult to bear. Some people had been pressed flat on to the grass, and lay with their arms spread out in surrender.

Essie sat back on the steps, her white blouse vivid against the stones. It was appropriate, he thought, that Essie should have fountains behind her and, further, the river. The fountain was not at all spectacular. The jets were unchanging, but the streams reached their undramatic height and came apart, glittered and fell. Essie and he had spent a life it seemed by the sea, rivers and swimming baths. For much of that time Dan had watched, as he watched once more, Essie as the focus of the action.

His Essie. Essie dives again, again. One unhurried exercise in technique after another, and then perhaps the coach has a few words to say, lifting the palms of his hands in exposition as he gives his advice. Essie doesn't care if Dan is there, or if he comes at the end of the practice. One bounce on the board for lift, her thigh muscles block for a moment, and she arcs and twists in the air above the water. Afterwards, while she is changing, Dan remains almost alone on the tiered seating. A few other swimmers practise, but Essie's repetition seems to have perpetuated her image above the pool, and Dan sees her continue to arch and dive: her dark costume firm, and her legs aligned.

They walk back together to her house. Essie dressed has almost a chunky look — handsome rather than glamorous. Dan makes her laugh by exaggerating the events and personalities of the office where he works, and takes advantage to press and kiss her before he leaves. Essie closes her eyes, as if the intimacy is too much for her to witness or to bear, and Dan sees her dark lashes, and the lids sensitive and trembling over her eyes. She has brown, sleek skin, and a space between her front teeth. As he kisses her, even as he sees her face and feels her body, he has again the image of Essie diving. Essie by herself, concentrating on herself: the heavy rattle of the diving board, and Essie compact and quick in the air.

Dan wondered if observation of Essie was enough, the conjuror for memories of Essie and himself. To watch at a distance and recollect suited his mood and posed no contradiction to his version of the past. Yet it seemed furtive to give no sign, to turn away from Essie seen in the summer park and say nothing. He walked along the path by the river, and then across the worn grass to the fountain and saw Essie stand to meet him. The reaction that he felt, the quick charge of odd emotion, was not for her voice, though it was much the same, but for the recognition of what was familiar in her presence in conjunction to his own as they stood there: the precise angle of her face up to his, the physical, spatial relationship repeated and reaffirmed after many years. It caused in him a brief malaise even as they talked and sat down on the steps together, a shadow part tenderness, part sorrow, the malaise of mortality acknowledged which accompanies such reunions. 'Yes, I've been watching you from the seats beneath the trees,' he said. Essie told him they often came to the river after they'd been shopping.

'I saw you once in Nelson, at Christmastime,' she said, 'with your family at the carnival. We were on the big wheel, at the top waiting for all the seats to fill. I could see right round, and you were with your wife and daughter, going down towards the sea.'

'Do you still dive at all?' said Dan.

'Not for years. God, no. I sometimes go to the swim fit classes at the main pool. That's all now.'

'Diving was so much the thing with you. In a way I was jealous of it once, I suppose.'

'It's a young person's sport, like so many these days. I gave up years ago.' Yet Essie still seemed young. Her wrists were strong, and her shoulders well developed from the swimming. Her hair shone in the sun. But a calm Essie, so different from the changeable, sudden Essie he had known. The new Essie was at ease with herself and others. She could talk with him, or let the talk trail away without care, so that they were left to enjoy their joint presence and the languor of the riverside.

The office workers began to leave, the girls in their summer dresses, the young men in shirtsleeves with watches glinting on their wrists, army NCOs in jungle green. They moved reluctantly away from the paths, the oaks, the river. The traffic zoo roared; the city took them.

'I'll have to get Richard home. He'll become grumpy if he doesn't have his meal.'

'Of course,' said Dan.

'Have you got time to come back with us for a while? If you're not picking up your daughter until the shops shut, why don't you?' Dan considered refusing, not because he wanted to leave Essie, not because he might be imposing, but from a trivial pride that he'd have to admit that he'd planned no significant alternative: no meetings on property matters, or promised visits to friends.

'I was just going to sit here, then perhaps have a drink in a hotel,' he said. 'I haven't got any other business. I'm just the chauffeur — waiting until required.'

'I have both sun and alcohol at my place.'

Dan took the push-chair, Essie held Richard by the hand and, as a small family, they walked through the trees to the carpark. 'I'm not used to having an afternoon off in the week,' said Dan. 'It seems more than just coincidence that I should happen to come up today and you be here. Things have chosen to catch up.'

'It's not so odd to me. I live here. I'm quite often in the park with Richard in the summer, after shopping.'

'I still feel a sense of intention.'

'Once things have happened it's easy to think them inevitable,' said Essie. 'If you'd met some other friend you'd think just the same.'

'Maybe,' said Dan. He folded the push-chair and put it in the boot of Essie's car, and in his own car he followed her, first through the busy city and then into the suburbs, which were quiet, and where the intense sun made sharp, Spanish shadows.

Essie led him into walled privacy at the back of the house: grass and trees, and deck chairs around a sandpit. The striped canvas of the chairs had been bleached almost white, and was warm to Dan's touch. He was left there with a glass of red wine, while Essie gave Richard his lunch. 'Go to sleep if you like,' said Essie. 'I won't be long.' Essie had a large house, but it was obvious she and her husband weren't gardeners. The lawn was kept down by drought rather than cutting, and tufted edges merged with an overgrown garden. Bright berries on currant bushes winked in the sun, and tall grass fringed the trunks of fruit trees. It was a garden which spoke of live and let live, of an absence of zealotry.

Essie filled his glass again when she came out. 'Comfortable?' she said.

'Except for my feet.' The heat of the city and the unyielding pavements had made his feet sweat and ache. Essie pointed out a tap at the edge of the lawn, almost hidden by the currant bushes, and Dan took off his shoes and socks, and washed his feet there.

'I'm afraid we're not much as gardeners,' called Essie without apology. 'We let the plants fight it out amongst themselves.'

'Laissez-faire,' said Dan.

'What?'

'Nothing.' The dry grass of the lawn was disconcerting under his bare feet as he came back. 'Laissez-faire,' he said, and walked through the sandpit for the novelty of its texture.

'Bare-foot boy again,' said Essie.

Apples were the only fruit that Dan could see on any of the trees, small apples, most with blemishes, for nothing was pruned or sprayed. One large golden elm stood by the gate. None of its leaves had fallen. They were flat leaves, extravagant crepe yellow, extended against the wall and the sky. Essie talked of things and people they had known together. He recognised them, though each had an oddity of aspect as the result of being seen through Essie's eyes, rather than his own.

'Were you in Auckland long?' said Dan. He had been thinking of them together, and then Essie going away because of her diving.

'Only three years,' she said. 'I never did well in the national championships, not once in those three years. I don't know what it was. I was fine in preparation and in squad training, fine on tour, but I never even placed at the nationals. It sort of psyched me out in the finish, and I came back south and gave more time to other things.'

'You gave it up?'

'Not all at once. Oddly enough, for a couple of years I dived as well as ever, without much practice. I let it go, though. It didn't run my life anymore.'

'You'll always be a diver in my mind.' Dan thought of the way they had been: his attitudes and hers. He realised how selfish youth is: how covetous its loves, all sharp needs and expectations, all competition and comparison. His fierce determination to imprint both body and mind on young Essie, her equal will both to succumb and resist on her own terms. He watched Essie with her son, and he thought of his own daughters. There was a deep simplicity and directness in the love of a parent for child. Love between man and woman was complicated, fluctuating, strung with sexual tension and threat to the self.

His Essie. They see Dale at last, deceptively small among the other passengers from the ferry, wearing a yellow parka and soft shoes, and seeming amiable. But his eyes are dispassionate, dark, and he walks with masculine balance close to grace. 'Is this my reception committee?' he says. Dan hears himself giving a fatuous laugh, but Dale isn't interested in Dan. He looks at Essie with eyes that concentrate the focus of the evening, so that the slopping water of the berth, the miscellaneous people, the useless noise of life going on, disappear. The soft travelling bag slips from his fingers, and lies there at his feet.

'Hello Dale,' Essie says.

'Have you been all right?'

'I've been getting by.'

'Do you want money?' says Dale. He puts his hand inside his parka and brings out a stiff, bank paper bag. The edges of many notes are pressed like the pages of a new book.

'We've got all the money we need,' Dan says, and Dale looks at him for the first time, basalt eyes that could gut him anytime.

'Good for you,' says Dale quietly, as if Dan were a child interrupting the conversation of grown people to talk of his ice-block on a stick. And Essie gives a laugh which is not spiteful, but is quite impartial, and Dan realises, with anger and resolve, that she is not going to say anything to Dale to tell him how things are now, that she's watching to see what Dan can do. He competes, and nothing is ever said of it between them, but he grows more selfish because of it. He's disappointed in Essie there, as they walk on the darkening wharf, and the light reflected on the water undulates like a white sheet spread upon the surface.

'It's lazy weather,' said Essie. She relaxed in the faded deck chair. Her frilled blouse, so white amidst the garden colours, disguised the provocation of her figure. Dan poured more wine into her glass, and stood looking at her, and she closed her eyes, but smiled because she was aware of him. He bent and kissed her, and put his hands in her hair, then shifted them to glide beneath her blouse. The feel of her bra cups and the warm skin above them. He kissed her harder. 'Say,' she said, 'hold on', and she turned her head. Dan followed her head and kissed her again, took his hand from her breasts, and held her shoulders. When the kiss was over, Essie laughed, and leant on his arm. The kissing had delayed their breathing, and excited them. 'You've found me in the mood for it,' said Essie.

'Let's go into the house then.'

'It's no use.'

'The best things are no use,' said Dan. He could feel the grass beneath his tender feet; through his hands he could feel the throb of Essie's pulse close to her neck.

'No, it's the time of the month,' said Essie with a smile and blush. 'You thought it was your lucky day,' she said.

'I still do,' said Dan. Richard came and put one hand on his mother's leg, and looked into her face, and spoke seriously in his own way. Dan sat down again next to them. He ran his fingers along the inside of Essie's other knee. 'I think it's a very lucky day,' he said.

'It's nice you say that.'

Richard sat down with his back against Dan's chair, and began picking grass and putting it on Dan's white foot. Dan slipped his watch from his wrist, and held it out to the boy so that it gleamed in the sun. 'You're disappointed,' said Essie. Dan spread the fingers of his hand on her knee to show that he didn't mind. 'I'll take my blouse off,' she said.

'I used to ask you to do that. You didn't like to in daytime.'

'I'm older now. I might as well while I can.' Essie undid the miniature buttons of her blouse, and took it off, and then her bra.' 'Of course I breast fed Richard,' she said, in case Dan should see too great a change since she was a girl. The skin below her throat was lightly tanned and spread with a few freckles, but her breasts were very white, each tilted slightly to the side. The skin surrounding the nipples was rough-ened like orange peel, but the colour darker. 'I feel the slightest wind now,' Essie said. 'The skin being sensitive to it, I suppose.' Just by her arm the fullness of the breast made a dart-shaped crease so utterly feminine that for a moment Dan felt lust grip, but it passed, and left only appreciation and calm.

The longer they forbore mentioning wife and husband, the clearer it became that neither would be talked of at all. Not from any sense of guilt, in fact the opposite, from loyalty, for any reference made in that garden's mood would have a degree of dis-paragement or justification. Dan no longer wanted to go into Essie's house. He didn't want to see how her kitchen was, or what sort of books and wallpaper she and her husband chose. He only wanted to remember the garden with the winking berries, small, blemished apples of character, things cheerfully overgrown, and the elm as king there, crepe yellow against the wall and the sky. Essie was lying back with her eyes closed, naked to the waist in the sun. The skirt band was tight enough to hold back the slight forward curve of her belly. 'Why is it rather sad though, Essie, to meet again?' he said.

'You just realise you're not young anymore,' said Essie matter-of-factly. She didn't open her eyes. She brushed one breast at the feel of an insect, and the flesh trembled.

'We used to go fishing,' said Dan.

'Once or twice. That's all surely.'

'We did. We did, though. We quite often went fishing from the rocks of the cape. We caught fish too: cod mainly. You used to wear jeans and a yellow, ribbed jersey.'

'What, always? You've remembered it often perhaps, but we only went once or twice. Unless it was some other girl.'

'Come on. We gave fish to your parents. I remember that as well.'

'We buried them when you'd gone,' said Essie. They laughed together, and Essie opened her eyes to look at him, and held up the palm of her hand to shield herself from the glare of the sun. 'Mum thought they might be diseased,' she said. 'They didn't look like the clean fillets she was used to from the shops.'

'More disillusion,' said Dan. 'I liked your mother.'

His Essie. She stands with her back to the cold wind that presses with an even force from the bay. 'You know I need to go to Auckland,' she says. 'I need to move there if I'm going to have a chance to improve anymore, and do any good.' Even in that grey, eroded day she is handsome and strong. Her dark hair is shaped close to her face; short for her diving, and the high neck of her red jersey is folded to her throat. 'You can come too. You could come up and get a job there, so things would be the same. But we've been over and over it all, you know that.'

'I can't come,' he bursts out. 'I can't just toss it in here, and hope to get the sort of job I want again. And why should I?' Why should he? Why should he have to follow her when she wasn't prepared to stay for him? Why should he? — and he wouldn't, for once she put herself first and he acquiesced, then so it would go on and on. And things wouldn't be the same, and he doesn't want things the same anyway: he wants them different, but the manner of the difference he can't explain.

'I mightn't be there all that long,' she says.

'Oh, come on. Once you're up there, that's it, isn't it.'

'Your choice. I've made mine,' says Essie. She deliberately looks away from him, looks over to a group running on the cold sand and towing their scarves in the wind, looks there to show him that he isn't all the world by any means, that it and she will go on no matter what he does.

'Bloody marvellous, isn't it,' he says. As well as what is said, each of them makes private decisions. Each withdraws one more means of access to the heart.

In Essie's garden they talked of personal things. He thought how often the enduring sweet or bitter experiences are of no relevance much to formal memory. The image of Essie diving, the taste of crayfish, and the colour of their scalded armour, pine roots as veins in clay banks, the scent of lupins and sand-dunes and fennel. The emotions of his life were strung on such things.

'Tell me things you remember we did together,' said Dan. So Essie talked of dances rather than fishing trips, of eccentricities rather than lovemaking. He could smell the warm, bleached canvas of his deck chair as he listened. Some of her recollections were only half familiar to him, and needed her sense of actuality to convince him that they had happened at all. Essie's memories were all good times, it seemed, and Dan was reluctant to leave them, or the sunlit garden in which they were shared.

'Don't bother to put on your shoes again,' said Essie. 'Who's to know, if you don't get out of the car.'

'Ah, too much wine and sun and reminiscence,' said Dan. He swayed, having stood up abruptly. Essie slipped her blouse on without caring about the buttons, and went to the gate of the walled garden with him. Her sleek breasts were only partly hidden by the lace. 'Essie, let's hope not to see each other again,' said Dan. I don't expect another time it will go as well.'

'Why not?'

'We won't be alone again like this, or just with Richard at this age.'

'I think it would be good to meet again,' said Essie. 'Our whole families even.'

There was rank mint by the gate. Dan took some as he said goodbye to Essie, and before he closed the car door he crushed the leaves vigorously in the palm of one hand with the heel of the other before dropping them. As a genteel lady might, he lifted his hand to his face to catch the scent of mint as he drove. The sun was crouching, still insistent, and Dan had the window down and drove into the city with bare feet and his trousers rolled up below the knee. He understood his Essie was gone, even from Essie herself: that the Essie he'd spent the afternoon with had grown wonderfully out of his Essie — but wasn't the same. His quick, vivid and sometimes angry Essie was lost except in memory. There he could see her still, yet never catch a glimpse of his own self. No former self to place with his Essie, just the ache of his presence having been with her then.

He drove into the hot city in the late afternoon. He had the window down, his trousers rolled up, his shirt undone to let the air stir the hair of his chest, and the scent of mint from his hand. He was dishevelled and relaxed. He let go; he forgave; he allowed some things to slip away, and was the better for it. But he kept an image of the new Essie in her rough, summer garden: and an image of his Essie, quick and strong in the air as she dived from a height towards him.

Wyldebaume at the Frontier

~

I (PERSONA RATHER than alter-ego) had worked part-time in the Old Clerks' Room at Laystall, Zimmermann, Laystall and Clone, and never once took my shoes off, although it was a mosque for some, and never once had Zimmermann come in; he dealt with those in the main office. (What I did, or was paid to do, in the Old Clerks' Room I will imagine later so as not to detract from the forward movement of this opening section.) Then on a heatwave Thursday — the specific gives an impression of verisimilitude — I took my shoes off just that once because my feet were sweating — and Zimmermann entered the Old Clerks' Room.

> **epithalamium,** *n.* (*pl.* **-ums, -a**). Nuptial song or poem.
> (GK *thalamos* bride-chamber)

I swear to you — if legal identification is possible in our form of contact — it's absolutely true: not a word of a lay. I was caught out in the open by the paper cabinet getting some of the quarto size light yellow correspondence quality paper headed in green — Laystall, Zimmermann, Laystall and Clone. Solicitors, Barristers, Notaries Public, and so on, with the address.

> And the frogs of the old quarry had their say too, like stair boards underfoot. (*Notebooks, March '83*)

I could smell my own feet: that sugary smell of hot feet in socks. To Zimmermann it must have been much stronger. It's a biological fact, you see, that you have a diminished receptivity to your own smells. Despite the heat and his recent marriage (a necessary touch to allow the introduction of epithalamium, and also suggest carnality) Zimmermann wore an elegant grey suit and blue suede waistcoat And as an affectation, on both our parts, he sported a fob watch on a plain, oh so heavy silver chain, like a Pumblechook, perhaps, or an Old Jolyon. He took the watch from his fob pocket, and held it cautiously in his hand, with his thumb arched above it lest, like a toad, it make sudden leap and escape. Zimmerman's mouth opened, his mouth and tongue glistened, as if he were about to begin an epithalamium, or perhaps it was just a reptilian tasting of the air.

A scout of Te Rauparaha, I edged towards my desk, socks gripping the stubble of residual carpet. There seemed just a possibility Zimmerman hadn't noticed, because the rest of me was fine. My tie knot, for example, still exemplary — snug in its collar.

> Laughing at himself with bitter and intense delight, as the profound Jester laughs at his own shadow crossed against the sky. (*Notebooks, April '86*)

'Wildbum,' said Zimerman ,'take an obligatory two weeks notice.' I could see the toes of my brown shoes under the front of my desk — deserters who held their distance, and their tongues. Zimerman had addressed me perhaps ten times (nay not so much) in the three years, and his pronunciation of my name was always the same — he was attempting no insult. Oh, I could have told Zimerman the unlikely truth (could tell it to him now quite as easily), that I'd never taken off my shoes at work before, and that it is a coincidence, his coming in when I had, of about a thousand to one. But even if he were allowed to believe it, nothing would affect his assessment of the enormity of the error. As a parallel, one (not the accusatory you, here) might as well put forward the first-time excuse for rape.

Just on that Wildbum thing for a moment, it occurs to me that bum always suggests itself as unmistakably onomatopoeic, when it's not at all. Do you feel the same? Anyway, to get back: quick as a flasher I decided not to take it lying down from Zimerman, but to unleash the dogs of pogrom. 'Zimerma,' I said, or perhaps 'Zimerma,' with just that altered, chilling inflexion. 'Zimerma, there comes a time in every man's life.'

Most of us are granted at least the blessing of never having to endure the death of our children. (*Notebooks, September '85*)

Zimerm's hand began to follow the silver chain towards the marsupial recluse of the yellow suede. I could feel the stubble of the Old Clerks beneath my Te Rauparaha souls, and for an instant, as concentration heightened, I was aware of a galaxy of dust particles tumbling and wheeling in the sun strip above the ribboned case files. Years of training — created in this instant — caused an automatic response. I pivoted with precise balance on my left foot, and drove the blade of my dexter hand for the single inch where the *dominus cassurii* nerve crosses the blunt bone of the *fenis cooperum*. I won't be apparent to you, but there's quite a pause here. I had typed *cooperii*, altered it with Twink, then compounded the error by typing over it too soon, and clogged the key of u. I cleaned it with an old toothbrush I keep in the second desk drawer. There was a packet of carrot seed there too — Manchester Table (*Daucus carota sativa*), a stump-rooted variety suitable for all soil types, it says. The flesh, which is fine grained and free of core, is a deep orange colour.

'Wildbum, are you listening to me?' said Zimer. As it is my story you will have it on my terms, or not at all. I'm not interested in what you expect, or have experienced. The Pharaohs concluded audience with their command — so let it be written, so let it be done. Not the reverse order, you will notice. Likelihood should never be a test of anything, for that is an appropriation of the freedom of others.

I briefly considered throwing myself on Zimer's mercy, but doubted it was sufficient to break my fall. For Zime was ambitious (and Zime was an honourable man). He wished to be a very Czar of David, and his gross ambition was betrayed by the faint, sugary aroma which persisted despite his toiletries.

Like that gaunt cat from the creek, I have begun to eat grass in order that death may be appeased. (*Notebooks, June '81*)

'What is the meaning of this, Wildbum?' said Zime. The meaning of this! I stand (shall we say) in my socks on the worn, commercial grade carpet in the Old Clerks' Room at Laystall, Zime, Laystall and Clone, the motes drifting in the pyramid light above the ribboned folders of a thousand animosities, and the great question is asked of me for immediate reply. What is the MEANING of, whatever. Wildbum, bum, bum, bum, bum — an echo is the beating of my heart. Beat, beat, beat, bum, bum, bum: the beat is to the heart of a different drum. Each genre must have a Fugleman.

I meant to say before, about my attitude to Zim and his ambition, that you're wrong to say (or to have said — but let's not tense up) that there's any ethnic rancour to the portrayal. No, NO, and there'll be no further interruptions in a summing up. You see, it's not that he's a Jew, but that he's a solicitor: an occupational not a racist prejudice. The one sign of validity in mass beliefs, is that all the world hates a lawyer.

> **ex cathedra** (ĕks kathē'drɑ, kă'thĭdrɑ) *adv. & a.*
> authoritative(ly); (of papal pronouncement)
> given as infallible judgement. [L. = from the
> (teacher's) chair]

So Zi fired me, there you are (where ARE you), and the instant had such significance it was caught in amber time, so that for eternity the silver watch chain glints, a shallow arc against the suede blue burnish, and the yellowed venetians in the Old Clerks' Room click ever so slightly like camel's teeth. The sound of Angela Pruitt typing in the main office is as the infantry in dispute at some remove, the tapping of both gunfire and courage beyond a no-man's-land. My green shoes lie supine and reproachful as the heads of beaten dogs beneath the desk. There is perpetual spit to glaze Zi's pouched red lip, and there is the sweet smell of my socks — or perhaps my life?

> **păd. 1.** n. Soft saddle; piece of soft stuff used to
> save jarring, raise surface, improve shape, fill
> vacant space, &c.; shin-guard in games; sheets
> of blotting or scribbling or drawing paper fas-
> tened together in a block; foot or sole of foot in
> hare, dog, &c.; (arch.) easy-paced horse. **2.** v.t.
> (-*dd*-). Make soft, improve shape of, fill out,
> protect, with p. or pp. or padding ; (sl.) *p. it* or
> *the hoof*, go on foot; *padded room* (for suicidal
> lunatic &c.). **pădd'-ing** a., (esp.) literary matter
> inserted merely to increase quantity. [ ]

So what have we arrived at, you and I, through the unexpected fracture of convenient effigii. Then in my socks, now in my cups, but fired by Z then and still fired by him today. The composite of things applying at any one time is always something of a process. There are nine tenses in our art, and only three in life. 'Wildbum, I mean what I say.' The entire point of the story is, of course, what happened after, which I'll get on to now. After, ah-h whatsisname, had fired me. You KNOW! The one with the camel's teeth and green suede waistcoat — I told you, for Christ's sake. Fair's fair, just hang on a bit, and it will come back to me.

In my dream the wind is scented with fennel, and laughter drifts like a garland. The iris of the deep sky rolls round its pupil of earth and subtle ocean. (*Notebooks, December '77*)

Just where were we, or where was I? Is there anybody there? 'Wildbum, you are fired. Take an obligatory two weeks notice.' Is that the fellow we were talking about. Certainly I remember the feel of the stubble in the Old Clerks' Room, how the wood worm dust lies like pollen in the unused pigeon holes, and the sugary smell faint on the internal air. Do you know, the rest escapes me: perhaps you could tell me the story instead.

A Poet's Dream of Amazons

~

MY FRIEND ESLER is sick again. His mother rang, and implored me to hurry to the bedside. She spoke in a whisper, not in deference to the sinking Esler, but from fear that her husband might overhear. Mr Esler hates me.

'He says he mightn't see the night out,' said Mrs Esler. 'He's had a dream again about a Big Woman, and she turned out to be a preammunition of death.' Mrs Esler is loyal in her way, but for a mother of that son her vocabulary is less than impressive. 'The doctor's been twice already,' she whispered. I suppose that a really Big Woman, and irrational as women often are in dreams, could quite well be a sinister omen.

I put down my work at once. I knew it was no joke if Esler said he was dying: well rather I knew that he might laugh about it, but die all the same. Esler fights a persistent and terrible battle against the world, but it is a losing battle.

My moped was in the shed, but before opening the door to it, I rattled the neighbours' fence to start their dog barking. A melancholy and majestic sound that dog made: deep bells in the cold air. Why should anyone sleep if Esler was dying? I interspersed the hound's barks with appeals to Odin, the god of my ancestors. I didn't want Esler to die, for he is one who speaks my language in this town.

On my moped I set a course from the forlorn suburb in which I lived, to the forlorn suburb in which Esler lived. Mrs Esler was watching for me: she was at the door when I approached, hoping that she would be able to smuggle me through to the laundry without a confrontation with her husband. I saw half of him in the doorway of the living room; one arm, one side, one leg, one eye looking down the passage to the front door, and half a sneer to have seen a grown man arrive on a 50 cc step-thru. 'It's only you,' said Mrs Esler. She pulled a face. 'The doctor's been twice. Oh, it's bad, it's bad.' She made another sudden face. Pulling faces is the qualifier Mrs Esler uses when her husband is at hand. They are the briefest flashes across her long face; semaphore by tic which hint at the hospitality, gratitude and compassion she can't speak of. They are spasms of emotional intent, and probably quite unconscious. 'You can't stay long,' she said, as we went up the passage, and then a fleeting contortion to nullify her tone. 'Mr Esler and I don't want you coming around really,' she said, and touched my arm. I turned at the laundry door, and went back, and put my head into the living room. I could see the back of Mr Esler's head as he watched sport on the television. There was a worn patch at the crown, as if he had a habit of twisting his head into the pillows at night.

'Mr Esler.'

'Uh,' said Mr Esler.

'I'm going through to see Branwell.' I said it loudly so that it would carry to Esler in his bed.

'Oh, it's you,' said Mr Esler. He didn't turn towards me.

Esler had his blue tartan dressing gown on in bed. He looked bad enough to be dying, but he was trying to laugh. He flipped his hands on the covers, and further down I could see his feet jerk. 'Branwell, Branwell,' he wheezed. 'I love it,' As well as liquid at the corners of his eyes, there was white gathered there, like a little toothpaste. On his cheeks were patterns from the creases in the pillow. Esler is balder than his father, but in a different way; going back a long way at the temples, and the hair between quite downy. 'Branwell's good,' he said, 'and look!' He put his hand under the pillow and produced a flat bottle of brandy. 'You see before you indeed, the Earl of Northangerland.'

Esler's voice was squeezed out, as if someone was sitting on his chest. The Big Woman perhaps. His wrist buckled with the effort of getting the brandy bottle back under his pillow. I'd thought up the mention of Branwell as I went over, something to give Esler a lift. He becomes depressed without literary allusions from time to time. He began to tell me about his fantasy of the Big Woman. 'As did the Pharoah I have a dream,' said Esler. 'Each night this vast and determined woman comes to wrestle with me.'

'All I get are nightmares of rooms without doors, and sinking ground beneath my feet.'

'Night after night,' said Esler, 'she seeks me out, and we must love and fight.'

Esler's room had been the laundry, but his mother now has an automatic washing machine in the old pantry, alongside the deep freeze. The laundry tubs have been taken out, and Esler's bed moved in, and a small table by the window. Esler's boyhood room has become a guest room, which means it's never used. His father refuses to let Esler keep it, because he is thirty-six years old, a poet, and still at home. Living in the laundry is one of those strange and bitter compromises that families have, and which remain incomprehensible to outsiders.

Mrs Esler came and interrupted her son, just when he was describing to me the body lock that the naked Big Woman put on him in their struggle. All poets have a tendency to pornography. 'Mr Esler says you've started him coughing again. He won't have it.' Her lengthening face, pulled inexorably towards the grave, convulsed to disavow the message she delivered. When she left, Esler continued to tell me of his Big Woman: a giant poster nemesis of sex. It was typical of Esler that even those things threatening his very life could only appear ludicrous.

His room retains a faint smell of soap and washed woollens. A fine mould like candle smoke covers the underside of the window sill, residue from a more tropical climate.

'Is he still there?' shouted Mr Esler. He must have been taking advantage of an injury stoppage on the television.

'Night after night she comes, this immense woman,' wheezed Esler. 'Hair like a waterfall, navel a labyrinth, thighs like a wild mare.' Esler's warm breath had scents of meatloaf, medication and mortality. His gums had shrunk from the palings of his teeth.

Esler's clothes are on plastic hangers on nails along the laundry wall opposite his bed, and his books are heaped beneath on shelves made from bricks and planks. What can I tell you of my friend which won't make you feel contempt or pity. What can I tell you of this man who is better than us, whose interests and principles have made him in a modern world a mockery, whose skills are as little considered as those of a thatcher, or a messiah.

'Waikato have scored again,' shouted Mr Esler, and Mrs Esler made an odd sound of wifely concurrence, like the instinctive response of a duck to another's call.

Esler and I have been friends since we ganged up at eleven to beat the second largest boy in the class: a prematurely hairy slob who used to hold us under water during swimming periods. We became one of those braces so common among boys — Brunner and Esler. We heard our names coupled more at school than we heard them separately. I can imagine the staffroom association.

'Caned Brunner today.'

'Who?'

'Brunner. Fair-haired kid, hangs about with Esler. Caned him too.'

Or perhaps, 'That's Esler, isn't it, smashing those milk bottles?'

'No, that's Brunner.'

'Both look the same to me, little buggers. Call him over.'

We fought together, smoked together, marvelled at the sky and stars together, took out the O'Reilly girls together. I have a scar on the underside of my left arm because Esler accidentally shot me with a home-made spear gun. We both saw Bushy Marsden collapse and die in the gym. We began the dangerous experiment of taking words seriously, and so resisting the process of attrition by which life betrays us.

'The Big Woman has a scent of almonds and macrocarpa,' said Esler in wonder and dread. His tartan wool dressing gown is also his lucky writing jacket, ever since he had it on when he wrote his Van Gogh sequence. Constant use without washing, a little lost food and the oils of feverish sweat from his asthma bouts, have taken the nap from it, have buffed it until it shines like silk, and the original tartan pattern is almost lost. 'Read me something to take my mind off breathing,' said Esler. He had a hundred poets to choose from, and I read Seamus Heaney to him. He nodded his downy head and squeaked 'Yes, yes' at the touches which moved him. The liquid and the white gathered at the extremes of his eyes, spread a little to the corner skin.

'Will you stop that never-ending jawing in there!' shouted Mr Esler to me.

'Exactly,' Mrs Esler said. I could almost hear the snap as her face, just for a moment, was contrite, bewildered.

'Read on,' said Esler.

The laundry never seems a bedroom no matter how long Esler is in it, or how many clothes or books he lines the wall with. Images of soap flakes linger in the air as a false Christmas, and one corner of the lino always seems to be damp. There is more utilitarian aura than even poetry can dispel. 'That's so,' said Esler as I read. In a paper packet on the second plank are one hundred and seventy-three green copies of Esler's poems, printed by the Whip-poor-will Co-operative Press. I have the dedication by heart: These poems are for Bruce Brunner and Frank Heselstreet, fellow poets and friends who share my belief that emotion is like ours a round world, and as far enough east becomes west, so is laughter to tears and genius to insanity.

I have eighteen copies in the top of my wardrobe. Frank and I buy one from the bookstore when we can afford to, and have our reward later when Esler tells us of another green pamphlet sold. Frank says we might end up with the whole edition of Esler's poems: a private joke, but what are friends for. Esler has always been absurd, but it is only one trait of character, as is deceit or shrewdness, composure or ambition. Just one aspect of my friend, but it makes it difficult to decide if he is dying or not. In a way I understand the Grim Reaper concluding that it is below his dignity to come for Esler, and sending a very Big Woman instead, who can laugh in her killing work and not be out of character.

Mr Esler appeared at the laundry door. His face was like that of a rock groper: reactionary and full of low cunning. 'You're doing him no good at all. Leave him alone, can't you. I blame you for a lot of it,' he said. I never resent Mr Esler's antagonism. I see it rather as one of the few remaining signs of concern for his son — this determination to blame me.

'I know you do,' I said.

'How many did Waikato win by?' said Esler in his squeezed voice. His father knew that Esler didn't care, but couldn't deny himself the satisfaction of saying the score out loud.

'Thirty-two, ten,' he said. 'Thirty-two bloody ten.'

'That means a season's tally so far of one hundred and forty-two for, and fifty-three against,' said Esler. 'How many did Mattingly score?'

'Fifteen.'

'That makes him the highest scoring fullback in Waikato provincial rugby apart from Rawiri,' said Esler.

'You don't care. You don't care!' shouted his father.

'It's so, though,' said Esler. He didn't care, but it was so though. He spent fifteen or twenty minutes each day on rugby statistics, so that he could know more than his father and still disregard the game.

Mr Esler knew better than to dispute Esler's facts; instead he looked around the laundry as a rock groper does another's cave. 'This place stinks of idleness,' he said.

'Mattingly has twenty-four points to go before he reaches Rawiri's record, and he's already played three more first class games,' said Esler. His voice became treble with an effort at volume as his father left.

'Shut up,' cried Mr Esler from the passage.

'Each night now she comes, my Amazon,' said Esler. 'Beautiful, but so huge. Dear

God. I try to oppose her with intellect and poetry when lust has failed. It's no use. She's killing me, the Big Woman, ending me with breasts and kisses.' Esler cleaned his lips by rubbing them with his fingers, and concentrated on breathing well for a time.

'I've never been afraid of women, or been against women, have I,' he said.

'I know.'

'The power, the weight, yet the subtleness of her. I can't stand it.'

'Take a sleeping pill or something,' I said.

'I can't. Not with my regular medication.'

Esler is loyal and honest, totally without envy or malice in his friendship, perhaps because the only basis he knows for friendship now is poetry. I have watched his other means of communication atrophy. Esler can discuss anthropomorphic imagery with wit and eloquence for hours, but when the grocer questions him of necessities, Esler grips the counter, is helpless before yet another stranger, stumbles to tell of sliced bread, or free flow green beans. People exchange glances and knowing smiles at this evidence of the dangers inherent in any serious scrutiny of the mind. Esler tries to give Frank and me money from his savings account which has less than three figures: he writes to the *Listener* to point out that regional poets Brunner and Heselstreet have not received sufficient recognition. He is ugly, incongruous, annoying, ludicrous, and a true friend.

Esler asked me to bring a packet from the laundry table. 'It's my new poems to go to Australia,' he said. 'I want you to post it for me: you're luckier than me. Bless it before you put it in the box.' He made no mention of the postage charge: such things are incidental when you are dying. 'Send it airmail, and don't let them use any stamps with heads on. They're unlucky for manuscripts, I always feel.' All the seams in the brown paper were traced with sellotape, and the parcel was quartered in string woven of green and red strands. I bet Esler had said a prayer or a curse over his parcel, and sprinkled on some of the lucky dust that he'd collected from beneath Honey McIlwraith's bed. Esler is that sort of intellectual and innocent. He really believes that there could be someone out there interested in poetry, willing to publish or pay for it, someone who will untie Esler's two-tone string, unpick his sellotape — and cry genius.

'If the Big Woman comes again tonight,' said Esler, then trailed off and began wheezing. It became worse until he was flapping his shoulders, and his veins began to swell.

'Puffer, puffer,' called his mother as she ran in. Her face twitched to one side then the other, as if offering her endless Christian cheeks to be slapped. She meant the asthma gadget with the diaphragm, and she and I tugged Esler to a sitting position, and she did his throat thoroughly, as if to ensure it would remain free of greenfly.

When he felt easier, Esler lay back again. 'Okay, Mum, okay,' he said. 'I'm fine now.' He turned away from us until he could regain the personal distance he required after the ignominy of his attack, his weakness, his mother with the puffer. Mrs Esler touched his downy head once, but he turned more resolutely, and she went out: first her dull curls and then the rest of her face, feature by feature, as a freight train curves from view. Esler rested: his skin gleamed with the sweat of illness and puffer liquid. I watched the soap flakes, and the light of the moon through the window without any curtain. 'Where's Frank?' said Esler finally.

'In Wellington at the technicians' course,' I said.

'They'll destroy him in the end, those computers,' he said. 'He left me the last poem in his Scheherazade series. So detached, so nimble. It makes me doubt my own progress. But those computers are the danger for poor Frank.' He picked up his puffer, held it to his mouth, but forgot to use it. Instead he said, 'I wish I could have a civilised life.' Beneath the bottom plank of his bookcase, close to the bricks, are Esler's two pairs of shoes. Brown shoes with roughly sewn seams, and each left heel worn to a slant, and the inside liners curling up. Where the outlets for the tubs had pierced the wall, Esler has fitted wooden plugs covered with muslin to improve the seal.

'Pass the ball, pass it!' cried his father from the living room.

'France,' said Esler, looking at his poets gathered on the planks. 'France has always seemed to me a place where people have a civilised life.'

'A cultivated people. A people who accept without reserve the necessity of art,' I said. I had almost starved to death on my one sojourn there. Having been nowhere, Esler still believed that life can be essentially different in other parts of the world.

He began on the Big Woman again. He was amused by his own recollections of the dreams. It was a tribute to his creative impulse that even the thing he thought was killing him was transmuted into an entertainment for us both. He had his brandy bottle in one hand, his puffer in the other, and he was trying not to laugh. 'You know,' he said, 'the odd thing is that I do feel that I might be dying this time after all. It's more than asthma the doctor said, but he doesn't know about the Big Woman, of course.'

Later he started tossing about. I put his brandy away and called his mother. She began to fuss over him, but he became worse. Mrs Esler called to her husband that he'd have to ring the doctor about Esler needing to go into hospital, and Mr Esler came and stood by the bed. He has a face not wildly dissimilar to our own: eyes facing forward, a two-entry nose, mouth, and teeth still nominally intact. Yet what a gulf of species is there. He might as well have been a rock groper or a pear tree, standing in the laundry.

'Thirty-six years old, writing bloody poetry, still has asthma, and now dirty dreams,' he said. 'Jesus.' The sound of the puffer was loud. 'I blame you,' he said to me.

'So do I,' said Mrs Esler, her face hidden.

'Heckel and bloody jeckel. It was a sorry thing when you two and that Frank Heselstreet met up,' said Mr Esler. He went out to phone the doctor.

I decided to go the back way. Mrs Esler came out with me. At the other end of the hall I could see Mr Esler with the telephone cord drawn tight. That way he could stand at the living room door and watch the television as he waited to get through to the doctor.

'This asthma can't be all that serious, can it?' I asked Mrs Esler. 'I mean he's had bouts before and come through. There's nothing else, is there?' Mrs Esler held her nose to stop herself from crying, and I didn't say any more. She gave a final, ambiguous face, and then turned her interminable chin away. Mr Esler talked at the other end of the passage on his extended line, as Mrs Esler went back into the laundry.

For a time I waited in the moonlight of winter outside the Eslers' back door. What it came down to, I suppose, was that I thought my friend Esler couldn't die because nothing was ready, and because it wasn't just. There was still too much that was ludicrous, and too much confusion. But you and I and Esler can't always rely on an appropriate setting for our deaths. Esler might have to go in a laundry bed, with soap flakes in the air, brandy under the pillow, a puffer in his mouth, and a Big Woman squeezing him in his dreams, with mould like candle smoke beneath the window sill, with one green vanity collection of his poems from the Whip-poor-will Press, with a polished blue, tartan dressing gown, and no reason for it to be happening at all. And just a friend or two, who can do nothing but remember better times.

As I walked the path at the side of the house, Mr Esler leant excessively from his window to bring his harsh whisper closer to me. 'Murderer,' he hissed. 'Don't come back. Leave him alone. You bloody writers have done for him.' The moon struck down, and held the Eslers' garden in a frost of light. I didn't take the accusation too much to heart. I knew Mr Esler becomes desperate late at night when all the sports programmes end, when he finds himself with hours ahead and no team left to join, and none to hate, just his wife's Greek faces and his son in the laundry with the ailments of asthma and poetry.

'Murderer,' I heard Mr Esler hissing. There were guilty ones, of course: Pound and Olson, Eliot and Larkin, Yeats and Frost, Stevens and Neruda, Lowell and Williams, Turner and Sewell, had all made their attacks on Esler. And Dylan Thomas. Now there's a murderer if ever I read one.

At the end of Te Tarehi Drive, and turning into Powys Street, which lay stark in the moonlight, I couldn't help laughing at the dying Esler. Laughter can be a guise of love: laughter can be helplessness expressed. Perhaps Esler is simply dying of his poet's amazement at the world in which he finds himself.

I let the moped engine run on in the shed for a few minutes, so that the battery would charge up a bit after the light had been on. I shook the neighbours' fence to rouse Cerberus again, and savoured the echoing sound. A deep barking dog suits a full moon. Esler had been dying before, and got over it. We all have to get over a little dying of ourselves in life. Is he dying of the asthma and the other things his mother wouldn't say, or is the Big Woman, that preammunition of death, suffocating him in his dreams with excess of loving?

from
The Ace of Diamonds Gang
and
The Divided World

The Ace of Diamonds Gang

~

AS OUR PAST recedes we can see only occasional pennons on the high ground, which represent the territory traversed between. So the Ace of Diamonds Gang seems my full boyhood before the uncertainty of adolescence. I recall no peculiar origin; like the heroes of history it arose when it needed to be there.

Always the special moment was when we put on our masks. The triangle of white handkerchief over the lower face, and the red diamond that we'd stamped on with the oil paints that belonged to Bernie's mother. There was frisson as each known face became strangely divided. Not handkerchiefs with red diamonds smudged did we acquire, but anonymity, confederacy, a clear exception to approved society. After Boys' Brigade was a favourite time, when lanyards and Christianity had been dispensed with, we would rendezvous in the centre of the old macrocarpa hedge to become the Ace of Diamonds Gang. The night would be moonlit perhaps, and we would move off in dispersed formation, keeping in touch by drifting whistles and calls of birds extinct except within the diamond lands. Like wraiths we went, said Bernie once. He read a lot, did Bernie. Like wraiths, the Ace of Diamonds Gang: if Ashley's farting didn't give us all away.

The Ace of Diamonds Gang was rather like that: subject in practice to mundane deficiencies which threatened the ideal. Ashley's wind, Bernie's glasses and Hec Green having to be in by nine o'clock every night, were the sorts of things. A certain power of imagination was necessary, but for thirteen-year-olds the source of such power is inexhaustible. We never spent much time in explicit definition of the gang, however — each had his own motivation, his own vision of the Ace of Diamonds Gang, and when we struck in that small town each of us gloried in a quite separate achievement. Dusty Rhodes insisted that the gang be used to intensify his wooing of Anna Nicholson, who had the best legs in the school. It was love all right. After watching Anna at the swimming sports, Dusty had an attack of lovesickness so severe that he was away for three days. The Ace of Diamonds Gang picketed Anna Nicholson's front garden sometimes, and when she came back from music practices called from the bushes and tossed acorns up to her window. Dusty considered this a normal form of courtship, and the rest of us had not sufficient experience to suggest alternatives. When Anna's father came out with torch and fury, we would drift wraith-like deeper into the shrubbery, not of course from fear, but to give him a taste of the menacing elusiveness of the Ace of Diamonds Gang when true love was thwarted. Dusty could never understand why Anna Nicholson didn't fall for him. The unbearable passion of first love rarely has any relevance to the response of the other party.

For Bernie and me the Ace of Diamonds Gang was more a life warp to escape from being thirteen years old in a provincial town: a chance to conjure heroism, to strike a pose, to create mysteries in which to dwell. We cut the backs off some Christmas cards, and stamped them with the red diamond. We left one at the scene of each of our exploits, just as in the books we read. The senior sergeant would pin them on his incident board we were sure, and his staff would attempt to work out a modus operandi.

So it was something of a let down to return to Seddon Park weeks after we had painted challenges there, and find the Ace of Diamonds card still there, weathered on the side of the cricket shed. 'They've given up, that's what,' said Dusty.

'That's it, all right. They've given up,' said Ashley.

'Perhaps it's still under surveillance,' said Bernie. It was a good word — surveillance, but even it could not impose conviction in that warm morning with the playing fields dipping to the willows, and a harrier club spread in the distance.

'We haven't actually done much lately,' admitted Ashley, who was sitting downwind a little. 'As a gang I mean.' We lay in the grass, shading our eyes with our hands, and attempting to justify the lack of daring in recent excursions of the Ace of Diamonds Gang.

Dusty suggested we spend time drilling a hole in the girls' changing sheds, but the rest of us wanted a cause of greater daring, and less obvious connection with our own interest. 'My father told me Jorgesson poisoned Mrs Elder's Alsatian because it kept him awake at night,' said Ashley. Jorgesson ran the second-hand yard, and his enmity could be relied on. He had cuffed Dusty's head for cheek, and once set the police on us after seeing us on the stacks of the timber yard. And he gave us wretched prices for any lead or copper we scrounged because he had the monopoly as the only scrap dealer in town. Sometimes we retrieved the stuff from his yard and sold it to him twice over to gain a fair price by simple addition, but even retaliatory dishonesty didn't remove our resentment.

'Hey, Jorgesson,' repeated Dusty. To defy Jorgesson was grand enough to be a reaffirmation of the principles of the Ace of Diamonds Gang, and Dusty agreed to hold in abeyance further collective effort to seduce Anna Nicholson, and the spy-hole in the sheds.

'Let's raid the place and leave a calling card,' said Bernie, raising a small, clenched fist. 'Strike and vanish, vengeance accomplished: the Ace of Diamonds Gang.' It was Bernie who usually provided the linguistic motifs for the gang.

'Christ, yes,' said Hec, 'but I'll have to be back by nine, remember.'

In the fastness of the macrocarpa we met on Wednesday evening, looked out into the soft, eternal twilight of summer. We linked thumbs to make our pledge and put on our Ace of Diamonds masks. Just a handkerchief and a change of mind. The mantle of secret brotherhood then fell upon us — oh, it was fish Christians in the catacombs, the Black Hand, Jacobites, the Scarlet Pimpernel. It was the League of Spartacus, the Boxers: it was Kipling's bazaar. I felt a small part of history's perpetual alternative as we ran through the Marlborough evening.

Jorgesson's was in that part of the town which was never very busy, off the main street and down toward the warehouses. On one side of his yard was a panelbeater's, on the other a vacant section, then the timber yard. When night came, all such lands reverted to the domain of the Ace of Diamonds Gang. We scaled the stepped pyramids of the timber yard, and made inventory of Jorgesson Traders. It resembled a field hospital in a desperate war of machines: the corpses and the parts heaped in rough classification as they came in. The ground was toxic and stained with oils, rust and the juices of dismembered machines. There were heaps of taps like discarded hands, radiators, bumpers, fan units, old bricks, used sinks, ceramic fire surrounds, short blocks, coppers, windows, roofing iron, bottle castles in green and brown, heaps of worn tyres like bitter, dark intestines. Amidst all the obsolescence were a few new kitset patio chairs assembled by Jorgesson during his quiet times. Much of the stock was exposed to take its chances beneath the spartan sky; a second category lay in an open-sided shed and its progressively diminishing lean-tos. We knew that the most precious and portable items festooned Jorgesson's army hut, so that it was a labyrinthine progress for him to make the short journey from his desk and cashbox to the door.

There seemed a dim light from the hut as we watched from our battlements. 'He must still be there,' said Hec. Ashley perfumed the night in response to heightened and unexpected tension.

'But we'll still go,' I said.

'We should reconnoitre in strength,' advised Bernie. His glasses glinted a moment in the last light of the evening. We steadied ourselves on the timber, and locked our thumbs again in pledge.

So did we move wraith-like across the rough section between the timber yard and Jorgesson's, scouts taking post, then others fading forward. We hand-cupped each other over the fence, drew up Hec as the last, and stood among Jorgesson's darkened possessions. The one window in the army hut showed light like the pale yellow yolk of a battery egg. It was above head height, and we pushed a drill chassis close to the wall — inch by inch to reduce the noise of the high, iron wheels on the gravel and scattered artifacts of Jorgesson's yard.

Jorgesson was lying on the floor by the door, or rather Jorgesson was lying on a woman who was on the floor by the door. It was the only space available: the one strip for the door to open and the clients to stand amidst Jorgesson's plunder. Jorgesson and his love seemed accustomed to the position, for without needing to look behind her, the woman reached an arm to brace herself on the stack of long life batteries, and Jorgesson's trousers hung conveniently on the impressive tines of a wapiti head behind him.

The apparent irrationality of sex is a vast humour to the young. Jorgesson had no electricity in his hut, and the low, angled light from a small Tilly was unflattering: single tendons jerking behind Jorgesson's great knees were picked out, and the wrinkles behind his head, and how flat his backside was in fact. Of the woman there was little more than the one practical arm, and her toes, separate and tumescent as facets in the Tilly light.

'He's doing her,' said Dusty. 'He really is.' His voice had qualities of awe and relief, as if after all the furtive talk, the innuendo, the chapter endings, the fade-outs, he was reassured that the act itself was not a myth. Jorgesson was doing it before his eyes. 'Jesus,' said Dusty.

'Yeah,' said Hec.

Jorgesson was unaware of any need to prolong his performance for our education. He slipped to the side, cleverly angling one leg between a brass fireguard and a Welsh dresser. He drew a rug about his love, and laid his bare arm upon it to stroke her hair. A candle sheen glowed on his arm in the localised Tilly light, and his face was all Punch features as he talked, stark in relief and shadow. Braces were a limp bridle from the wapiti, and the love's toes had coalesced with the passing of ecstasy.

The Ace of Diamonds Gang found an aftermath of restful affection disappointing. Dusty grumbled on the drill perch, and Bernie began hand signals of obscure intrigue. We had come to punish Jorgesson, and his pleasure would provide another cause. We withdrew to the darkness of Jorgesson's open shed to plan our assault. 'Have you got the card?' said Bernie. It was my turn: my turn to spike it, as Bernie said. I could feel it in my top pocket.

They gave me two minutes to creep around to the front of Jorgesson's hut, and there I took the card from my pocket and the brass pin from the side of my shoe. As I fixed it to the centre of Jorgesson's door, fellow partisans began their attack: stones cascaded upon the roof, Ashley ran towards me down the flank of the hut banging the boards with a length of piping, Dusty and Hec gave their wolf howls, Bernie beat a scoured copper in sonorous rhythm. The Ace of Diamonds Gang had released its terror.

I could hear also a sudden commotion as Jorgesson tried to rise from among his possessions to counter-attack. I had joined the others in a race for the gate when Jorgesson seemed to smite down the door and was behind us, like a black jumping jack with profanity as his sparks. His voice was husky with passion, and rage gave him an initial impetus — but we were prepared. Fled, the white masks and red diamonds flowing in and out of colour as we raced past the streetlights. We were our own audience, struck by the audacity of the Ace of Diamonds Gang; avengers, raiders, sentinels, even if Bernie had to carry his glasses as he ran and had trouble keeping up. 'Wait on, wait on,' he kept calling, which impaired our wraith-like progress.

Jorgesson gave up, though, once we reached the Sherwood of the timber yard. It was darker amid the stacks and he had no intimate knowledge of the trails there. He halted and sent in a verbal pack of bastards, buggers and sods to harry us on our way.

'Go home, shagger,' shouted Hec.

'Serve him right,' said Dusty, but his tone was one more of envy than impartial justice.

'Remember the Ace of Diamonds Gang,' called Bernie hauntingly. We joined thumbs on one of the stacks when Jorgesson was gone, and enjoyed the exaggeration of what we had done: except Hec, who had to go straight home, and risk being belted.

The depleted Ace of Diamonds Gang maintained its identity through the streets and short cuts from the timber yard to its macrocarpa headquarters, each scout call an echoing clearance. Yet after victory over Jorgesson there was arrogance rather than caution in our progress, and in the macrocarpa, darker than the blue, summer night, we put aside our masks and our greater lives with unspoken dismay.

In my room I folded my mask and placed it within the fuselage of the Spitfire Mk II: the special place. I began to undress, and as I pulled my jersey over my head I could feel my library card still in the shirt pocket from the afternoon. Except that it wasn't the library card, it was the Ace of Diamonds sign made out of the back of a Christmas card and, as I recognised it, there was a flux of all my stomach, and blood pumping up my eyeballs, hair follicles quickening all over my skin, falling electrical cadences of primeval terror through the matter of the brain. It was the library card I had pinned on the door of Jorgesson's army hut in the second-hand yard. The Ace of Diamonds Gang had witnessed his secret love, had interrupted it, had taunted him from the night sky and the timber stacks — and I had left my library card pinned to the centre of his door to avow responsibility.

I dreamt of Jorgesson's retribution during the night, starting up in abrupt horror at each climax revealed. Jorgesson in the headmaster's study when I was sent for, Jorgesson waiting in the shadows with an old sickle from stock, Jorgesson fingering a garroting cord beneath the swaying pines, Jorgesson at the door with my library card and asking to see my father.

That's how it happened. I had just taken a mouthful of toad-in-the-hole when I saw, through the kitchen window, an unnaturally tidy Jorgesson coming past the geraniums. There was a bulge in his pocket which could have been a garroting cord, and his Punch head was tilted to accommodate a paisley tie. Since then I have always hated geraniums and paisley patterns. A geranium is a coarse, disease-ridden plant with a flare of animosity, and paisley resembles a slide of pond water beneath a microscope. Even toad-in-the-hole has never been quite the same again. My father and Jorgesson spent time in sombre conversation and, although I couldn't catch the words, I could see on Jorgesson's face successive expressions of contained outrage, reasonableness, social duty to parents of evil children. My library card passed from Jorgesson to my father, the indisputable proof of a tale too rich to be denied.

My father punished me with the razor strop, and rang the parent of each friend I had unhesitatingly betrayed. It was the end of the Ace of Diamonds Gang. It was the end of wraith-like sorties into the consciousness of our town; it was the end of silhouettes upon the timber stacks, of thumbs clasped to pledge the redress of makeshift grievances. It was the end of free imagination, and of boyhood perhaps.

Lilies

～

THE CHALICE OF each lily flower was disembodied as darkness spread. Broad lily leaves merged with the shadows of the heavy grass and the docks. Arum flowers were luminous, hung in the night, and in the nearest throats each yellow spadix stood. The casual, crowded growth of such beauty amazed him. He knew the place was just a horse paddock in the suburbs. He had seen at dusk on their arrival the leaking trough, tracks amid the grass and lily clumps, uneven fences, and the horses standing apart for privacy. Yet it became a garden in the night, and from his hip height on the groundsheet the arum lilies were ranged depth on depth, a few pale lights in some places, but most massed as if carried in procession.

'My mother would have a fit,' Jenny said. 'Christ, she's got no idea how people can live. All those things owned and folded into the right drawer, or account, all that possession, getting on in the world, is nothing if you haven't found a really close person — a lover. A lover in all respects. A universal lover I suppose. Ha ha. Someone to trust with all of yourself. Don't you think? Don't you think, though?' Her face was itself the milk white of the arum lilies, but alert rather than decorous. She cocked her head and tried to see his expression in the night. Her hand squeezed his, and he could feel the light, individual bones of her fingers.

'I feel the best I have in the whole trip right now,' she said, 'and I don't care if we never find these people to stay with. We don't need help anyway. We don't need anyone else. This afternoon, coming up fast on the main road, it was so warm, wasn't it? I loved being on the back. I almost fell asleep leaning on you, and I could tell, before you turned, if you were going left or right, because the way the muscles of your back moved against me, like part of myself moving. Sometimes when we passed cars, when we were level with them for that moment, I could see couples in their separate seats and knew they envied us pressed together and then accelerating past. I bet they took it out in grudging comments about damn motorbikes. Eh? I think I understand how you feel about the bike now. You get this feeling of protection and isolation on a big tourer, don't you think? The faster you go, the more cocooned and invincible you become: the less distinct any threat can be. It's a sort of unity and a sort of detachment, isn't it?'

In the evening the road had sloped down to the bridge, and the Wanganui River was smooth and muddy, lacking the gravel bed of the South Island country he knew. Throttled back, the exhaust had a different note. Jenny pressed her helmet to his, and shouted, 'Keep going straight on, I think. Don't turn right towards the shops.' They were hoping to find a friend of a friend who might have a bed for the night. A friend's friend never met, never warned, but easy about their imposition they hoped.

In a flat suburb by a sports stadium, playing fields and a few paddocks across the road, the motor had died. The way it had gone made him think it was electrical, not mechanical, or a fuel blockage perhaps, but the light wasn't good enough to find the fault, and the warmth of summer, the languor of a day's travel had sapped any sense of urgency. He had pushed the bike into the paddock, and was held in thrall by the profusion of arum lilies there in the dusk. Each fenceline was overwhelmed with deep banks of lilies, and clusters spread into the low, green fields, and the ditches which especially suited them, so that they suckled in the mud. He had never seen lilies as vigorous and free as weeds before. They were multiplied clump on clump to gain an eminence, and the myriad white mouths among the heavy leaves glowed in summer's dusk. 'Oh, they grow like weeds round here,' Jenny said. 'They're everywhere between Wanganui and Palmerston North, but you didn't notice. They've spread all over the place, and nobody thinks twice about them.' But he did. He thought twice, thrice, a hundred times, and always that night he was conscious of the lilies spread around them, and the quiet horses standing thigh deep among their flowers.

'Finding someone to trust is what really matters,' she said. The lilies had the whiteness of her breast, and like breasts their hypnotic form was curved into the night. 'You like that, don't you? I know you like me doing that. I know you're smiling; turn your face towards me so that I can see. I don't believe that there's just one perfect partner for each of us in life. As you say, it's a pretty odd coincidence that person should just happen to be in our own community ninety-nine percent of the time. But it still seems to me that a lot of people never have a true relationship in their lives, even if they get married and all the rest. Never find someone to talk to as they would talk to themselves: never know someone care for them the way they wished they cared for themselves.'

Their night vision came in time. With his head close to hers, he wondered if the pupils of her eyes had dilated like those of a cat, but as he bent to see, she thought he sought a kiss, whispered assent and drew his mouth to hers. There were moths and flies in the moonlight, and quite loudly a horse blew its vast, flabby lips in derision.

'I like it best when we're alone,' she said. 'When there's just the two of us we never quarrel. Have you realised that? It's always when other people are about, our friends even, that any trouble comes. I know you don't like staying with my parents, because you say I'm different then. Now we only have to please each other. I'm the only woman, you're the only man. Do you like that? Turn over this way. I think we should stay on our own, and be happy like now. It's so warm I guess we could just stay here with the flowers you like, and in the morning you could fix the bike.'

From the centre of the city came the sound of a fire engine, or an ambulance, but it meant nothing to them for they had no house and complete health, and later a car horn started in the suburb beyond the stadium and sounded again and again, fainter as it moved away. When all those sounds had passed, there was Jenny's voice, so earnest and so lover-like. More enduring still, when she stopped, was the gentle whine of the night air through the trees, the fences and the lilies.

'You don't have to worry about me,' Jenny said, 'because I go into everything with my eyes open and don't expect things to be rosy all the time. You'll see that I can hold down a job if I need to. I can hack whatever has to be done. But the imperative I think is to have some part of each day with the one person who lets you be all of yourself, but not by yourself. You see? Someone to guard your back against the appalling triviality of life. It seems to me that you can't win by yourself.'

Jenny took their oranges from the pannier bag and, in peeling them, reproduced in action the level of intensity she experienced as she talked. She dug and tore the thick skin when she was adamant, and eased it from the fruit in a caress when love was spoken of. Her thin fingers were warm, had the fragrance of leather and orange peel, and the orange peel lay in the dimmed frog green of the grass and lily leaves, held up from the ground by the rich growth. Some pieces showed the underside like mushrooms, and others had their colour up, which caught the faint light and glinted orange to counter the lemon parrot tongues of the arum lilies. She drew on her cigarette, a long, wanton breath, and gave a shudder. He held a match and she squeezed peel at its flame, and the essence spat and flared like a rocket's dying burst far away. Her voice was so private, so trusting, so open to inevitable hurt, that he couldn't look at her, but put his head back and saw the lighted houses on the higher ground where people sat with the limits of their expectations and responsibilities clearly marked around them, while he and Jenny had nothing between them and the sky, could feel the night air drawn like a tide through the docks, the fences, the free lily clumps, the shadowed horses, and bearing off the scent of oranges and lilies and leather. Jenny's warmth and the salt smell of her hair too, bearing off sweet promises that could not otherwise be borne. The lilies pressed around them in the night, candles with a pale yellow flame. Something ancient in them survived within the modern city. Something biblical that was dispassionate in its magnificence. We believe beauty is of itself an invitation, when in nature it is a guarantee of nothing that we will ever understand.

'I don't care to look too far ahead,' she said. 'You never met my grandfather Renneck, but he used to say that you're a long time dead. And he had this other saying — take what you want, and pay for it. Do you see what he meant? I told Mum and Dad I can go back to university any time, but there's other things you can't have on lay-by. Hold me closer because it's getting cooler now. A horse won't stand on us in the night, will it? No, but it's true, isn't it, that nothing matters at all in the end, except having someone to love, but people don't want to say it, or admit it, because if they don't reach it then they're a failure, aren't they, and yet their life still has to go on. They won't, will they, walk over us in the night — the horses, I mean?'

He drew her closer, as if he believed that way they could secure themselves. Save them, save them from the fenceposts uneasy in the ground, from the slope of the stadium against the sky. Save them from the arum lilies, and the shadow horses deep in docks and grass and the lovely bog lilies. Save them from her trust, and his knowledge of its conclusion. Save them, save them amid the lilies from that meek, tidal wind of inconsequence.

The Complete Male Chauvinists' and
Idlers' Pipe Dream

~

IN SUMMER YOU should wake early, but not rise for some time. Rochelle Albuquerque, with her hair combed free about her shoulders, opens the curtains so that the horizontal sun warms your chest, and catches highlights in the crimson silk of your pyjama trousers. An equal opportunity sun, which will glance also from the top Rochelle wears, and tint a half-blush curvature upon her breast as she smiles towards you.

Breakfast must be brief, astringent: a little poached fish perhaps, nothing much more. Mandarin juice, or just one glass of Zeltlinger riesling, and no more than three pieces of whole wheat toast with rind marmalade as the one preserve. You might stretch to devilled kidneys perhaps, if you don't wish to offend the munificence of the Albuquerque sisters, or bacon and cheese in a pastry shell. A minimum meal, you understand, for a meditative man should be ascetic before the noon.

To clear your mind for the rigours of a business meeting with Ransumeen in the afternoon, you should allow yourself a quiet hour on the patio with a proven author. Pritchett say, Munro, Cheever, or Saroyan's seventy thousand Assyrians. Such excellence can scarcely pall; and the laughter of Susan and Angeline Albuquerque as they mow the lawns is barely an interruption, for you allow no motors to subdue nature in your grounds. It is Bates weather, and the smell of freshly cut grass, bluebells and toad horns wreathes into the laughter and drifts through the oscillation of green elms and the more modest sway of dwarf bamboo thickets.

Neither would you shirk physical endeavour: self-discipline is a necessary thing, and strengthened by constant application. So a game of tennis on the private grass courts, with rhododendrons and convolvulus pressed to the netting as a backdrop, and you impose upon yourself by covering all of your end of the court, while two Albuquerques are a smiling opposition. The Albuquerque short skirts are like white parasols against the foliage, and their smooth shoulders gleam. You insist on serving into the sun to make your task more difficult. You don't mention the score again after winning. How crisp the slap against an Albuquerque thigh sounds among the trees. Also, you put up with the inconvenience when Susan and Bobby-Anne use the shower with you because of press of time.

As you have always abhorred indulgence and ostentation, you decide to eat at home. A seafood basket, hardly more: well, a little goose liver pâté perhaps, then Beef Wellington with the St Emilion at room temperature, Roman peppers, baby potatoes, corn, a spartan bread sauce without brandy. No dessert, absolutely none. You are noted for it. The ascetic and aesthetic with you are one. Merely cheeses and a fresh roll — blue vein, a firm cheddar, gruyere certainly, and a bottle of Schloss Fustenberger mantled with the chill beads of condensation. An apricot? And even of this meal the Albuquerque sisters may well eat a third, and dig their red nails into your side to prove you ticklish: fun, careless so that a fluted glass of Fustenberger topples from a bare midriff. Yet you hold back rebuke, from tolerance and depth of understanding.

Even as the table things are being cleared away, you allow yourself no relaxation, but take a place in the north-facing bay window for meditation and inner preparation for the cut and thrust of negotiation with notorious Ransumeen. A pipe may assist attainment of mental poise and clarity: a Kenyan block meerschaum with a ripening glaze induced by prolonged use. It has a slender, amber stem. A coarse cut, molasses-cured Dutch tobacco that packs well to the thumb, and the smoke writhes blue-grey in the sunlight, climbs the velvet curtains. Phoebus direct on soft stock boots relays warmth to your feet, and liberates a fragrance of chaparral tan polish and leather. A quiet hour at some point of a busy day is a man's prerogative, so before going through the papers for the Ransumeen meeting you watch the drifting shadows of the poplars, the incandescence of the outer petals of camellia flowers as the sun strikes from behind. Like a float, one orb of thistledown on a line of spider's silk angles in the current of the warm heaven, as if to entice wing-finned azures of the sky. The blackbird on the mulch-heap cocks his head to listen to the centre of the earth. Had you a scant more time, then philosophic issues of some import could well be challenged, but someone must take the trouble to observe the grip that moss has gained along the lower terrace during winter, and how stubbornly it has held on since. How also the mottled lichens have made pale pirate maps on the stone wall. Scrupulous accuracy in small matters is the sign of business competence.

The insistent pressures of the world cannot be easily evaded, and the youngest Albuquerque sister smiles at you through the glass doors, then pouts at her exclusion. She has a blue ribbon to hold back her tumbling hair, and nothing to contain her generous intent. No man is an island, after all.

You have a long-distance call before two: Ransumeen's secretary with the news that the Lear executive jet has been unable to land because of bird strikes, and suggesting an alternative evening meeting. Many would be thrown by the pressure of such change, but flexibility is one indication of the profound mind, and you adjust by choosing a spell of dry fly fishing at the mill pond. A predilection for country matters should not readily be abandoned. The brown trout are not large there, but the sun is gathered wonderfully on the stone landing where the Albuquerque sisters strip to sunbathe, and willows half borne down with their own weight and the caressing stream, line the grassy hollows with narrow, yellow leaves like lemon slivers. The main boughs are mighty, yet ramify at last to delicate, flounced ends of nature's embroidery, which draw rustling back in the breeze as arcadian curtain. The lazy whipping of the line is a different sound, seeming to stir the rank of Albuquerque sisters, so that their legs turn obediently upon the stone. The line catches the yellow sun with an instant's snaky glint, and the one cockerel red feather of the fly bleeds into the light. Even more iridescent is the dragonfly that, slightly on an angle to its forward flight, skims like a chopper over quiet, bulging water. A single, white cloud is dismembered far above, and the parts drift away without pain or sinews evident.

As you search the ripple at the head of the pool, Bobby-Anne Albuquerque creeps up on you, grapples with you and laughs as she tries to wrest the rod from your hands. Her auburn hair like Persian tassels is veiled across your face, has scents of ocean salt and honey, has running fire of bright reflections that jump all breaks.

How the concentration of an afternoon's fishing can be physically taxing, you understand. The dry fly is an exacting mode, and sometimes, albeit briefly, you wonder why you couldn't be content with more plebeian forms of the angler's art. But dismay is only temporary and, although your creel is empty, you climb the track among the gentle ferns amiable with the passage of that afternoon's time. You pause to hand up each Albuquerque at the steep place above the mill. The evening light of such a day has a peach depth, and lilac butterflies as badges flaunt their brief lives upon the stage of magnolia leaves. Arm in arm the Albuquerque sisters stroll amidst the grasses, and studded flowers are snared between their brown, spread toes.

You would be willing to help prepare the light, evening meal were it not for the imminence of Ransumeen's demands, but even so you impose upon yourself the task of selecting wines — the fruitiness of a Niersteiner Spiegelberg Spatlese suits summer, and the body of the Domaine de Chevalier is needed for the carpet bagger steaks, or Wenceslaus imperial duck with almond stuffing. Nothing pretentious, you understand — a consommé rather than a heavy soup, for example, and entrées barely worth the name: perhaps a Neopolitan pasta dish, or a mere handful of scallops in a cherry and burgundy sauce. Oh, the Black Forest gateau has a splendid appearance in the candlelight at dusk, and the traditional Orleans flambé leaves a brandy fragrance in the air, but you have a certain austerity, and are conscious of Ransumeen business talks to come, and other service due, as all four Albuquerque sisters lean to the flattering candlelight in strapless gowns of a little organdy and less lace.

With the twilight you don the old smoking jacket of French corduroy with leather at the elbows. It falls easily into accustomed creases. You can draw on recollection and meerschaum pipe simultaneously, so that the thoughts themselves seem transmogrified into the blue, ascending strands that ape the Indian fakir's trick rope and lead to invisibility as they rise.

Ransumeen rings personally before nine, and you barely have time to steel yourself before the phone is brought to you, but Ransumeen is still in the city, and is unable to visit until another day. There is some skirmishing regarding conglomerates and offshore finance, but neither of you is prepared to make important decisions without meeting face to face. Ransumeen's defection creates time for your friend Laslo to visit and challenge you at snooker. The competition is of a high standard until Rochelle begins to dance upon the table. Laslo only smiles, for he is clay in the hands of the sisters. He is also a fellow admirer of Potter, and you watch together the video of *Pennies From Heaven*, taking turns to sing and dance in a jest at death.

Later, with the curtains open so that a calm moon is a Caesar's silver coin, Laslo tells you of the new Chekhov documents he has come across in the course of his work. He reads from them, including a fresh description of how Chekhov's body was brought back from Germany for burial in a green goods wagon marked 'Oysters'. Laslo has a fine sense of irony and literary style, and smokes dusky blue and yellow Turkish cigarettes. He begins to recite from Mo Tzu in a mood of gentle melancholy, which the Albuquerque sisters are determined to dispel. Rochelle and Angeline sing French folk songs in the original Gascon dialect: Susan and Bobby-Anne draw you off to your own room. You are amicably separated from your old smoking jacket and Kenyan meerschaum.

The day has had its pressures, you may feel: the ominous Ransumeen at a distance not surmounted, just deferred. Yet you have learned from stoical experience to accept your life rather than repine, and so fall to bed at last lulled by soft Albuquerques, whose bodies in the flowering moonlight are lustrous, reaching lilies, or globed lily bulbs. It is the end, friend, of another day: 'tis the flow of life that has three sides to the coin with which it's paid. The night may hold visions for you, memories, cavalcades from the sphinx that is the mind. A gentle vortex of edifying dreams, which even the lily arms of Albuquerque sisters cannot entirely restrain.

Off By Heart

～

TREVOR MCDERMOTT I'VE known, and Willy Seymour, Rachel Pesetsky, Mary-Lou Sutton, Peter Tamihana, Esplin Dee, Nathan Ives and Susan Tits McMurken. Albert Dwyer, Zim Soloman, Dipper McGee, Helen Scarlett, Genevieve Prattley and Simon Prattley of a different family altogether. Cuddy Moone I remember, and Alan Donahue, Lloyd Olorenshaw, Natalie Johnstone, Liz van de Linden, Hek Francis, Selwyn Downey, William W. Williams, Cruise Enari and Arron Meek.

Picked one? Ah, yes, Cuddy Moone. All right. Cuddy nearly blinded me when we were thirteen. I walked to Cuddy's one Sunday afternoon, because he promised me that his twin sister would take off her bra. It wasn't the magnificence of that revelation, or the prurience of my interest, which threatened my eyesight. The sister wasn't even there. The family, except for Cuddy, had gone to watch a dying relative, and Cuddy knew that I was sour at his failure to demonstrate hypnotic power over his sister.

To make up for it Cuddy built this volcano of dirt among the pumpkin leaves, and filled it with salt, matchheads, lighter fluid and so on. He lit it when I was bending over the top. He was vindictive, was Cuddy. My eyebrows vanished, my face was pocked with burns, and I had the taste of sulphur for days.

Cuddy Moone must have said something to his sister as well, for later in the term she slapped my face for nothing while the class was practising 'Good King Wenceslas' in the music room.

Hamish Gascoigne, Simone Field, Bridget McMaster, Snoz White, Hughie Gladman, Fitz Esler, Steven Aubert, Robby Dunn, Philippa Niall, Nancy Thomas, Richard III. I can't give any other name for him. I only met him once: we sat together on the railcar between Christchurch and Timaru. He had such bad teeth that he laughed only when he forgot himself, and then stifled that laughter with a hand over his mouth. He talked with fervour about adobe: how he intended to set up his own business once he had the expertise concerning the type of architecture and building techniques. He'd seen it used in America and the Mediterranean, he said. By the time we had passed Ashburton, he had invited me to come in as a partner, but I begged off. He might be an adobe millionaire by now, though I haven't read of it. Only when he left the railcar did I realise that he was a humpback, and as he passed quickly along the single platform, he didn't see my wave as almost partner from the window, but kept his suppressed smile over his bad teeth, and focused on the spaces between people with the introspective glare of a visionary.

Others are John McLeod, Coddy Youdale, Jane Caird, K. C. Venning and Ivan Platt. Sam Kingi, Eileen O'Loughlan, Irina Mintossian, Val Elsen, Kate Fairbrothers and Zipper Farrington. And Zipper had a younger brother who went to California on a sports scholarship.

That's a good choice: I like to remember Irina Mintossian. She was the office manager at Esterhaub, Hayhoe and Grant, where I worked for three years. I had hoped that I would be offered a partnership, but I never was. Instead of a reputation for steadfast loyalty or undeniable flair, Irina said that the partners considered me a self-opinionated fart. She passed the information on to me with such friendly glee that it set us both laughing.

Of the titular partners only Grant was alive: a mediocrity who wore coloured bow ties and spent his time on boards or committees. Irina and one of the junior partners called Dudley Watson were the brains of the firm. Dudley drank coffee liqueur between appointments, persisted in heterosexuality despite himself, and had wonderfully successful ideas. Irina Mintossian matched everything up: product to presentation, clients to staff, fees to scale, letters to addresses, documents to files, secretaries to typing, moods to days, attitudes to lives. She was the office hub, and the faster everything turned, the more blurred the extremities, the clearer Irina at the centre.

Her mother had Alzheimer's disease, and Irina would recount the incidents of that tragic comedy until our sides ached with laughing, and our hearts for other reasons. And she would stand at the end wiping her lined cheeks with a man's handkerchief, and say ah dear, ah dear, the things that happen, you know. So much humour and so much efficiency was a rare combination, I have since realised. Her mother once got lost at the harbour, and wandered into one of the woolstores. She was there two days with only Parmesan cheese from her bag to eat, and wasn't found until a forklift driver heard from among the high bales her imitation of a morepork.

Tricia Wallace, Elinor Brown, Warwick O'Nian, Norman Preddie, Cecil Doak, Wendy de Wet. Sandra Dennis, poor soul, Alice Reddaway, Richard and Mandy Tomkinson, somebody Addis, Paul Hamilton, Gene Alpers and Tub Mann. A concept of Christian duty was the reason Tub Mann took Life Boys: the same reason prompted his dislike of me, I suspect. No matter what I was thinking, or said, people assumed my intention was ridicule. Tub said I had a cheeky face. As captain of the Life Boys, Tub Mann refused to award me the yellow cloth badge for Bible Knowledge, yet I was always top. In my time in Life Boys I won every Bible quiz except the one after the saveloy-eating contest. Do you know that the third river to come from Eden was Hiddekel, or that Daniel was called Belteshazzar? No, you don't. Years later, when I studied corruption within the early Vatican, I understood it so much better because of my experience of religious hypocrisy under Tub Mann.

Emma Turnbull, Dr Aldridge, Graeme Earl, Belinda Dix and the Scammel twins. Margritte Leaper, Adrian Pyne, RSM Glassey, Jane Racinski, Peter Peterson, Peter Beloff, Peppy Jewell, Suzanne Alperonne, Nick Smythe, the youngest and runt of the seven Wilberforce boys, Vincent Messenger, S. D. Ogden and Patsy Bentley. Cilla Hill, Alain Grocott, Susan in the lounge bar of the King Dick. Denis Gadd, Podge Furnnell,

Lawrence Trevor, wonderful Billy Hawken, Evan Ransumeen, Malcolm Crowhurst and Virginia no longer.

Someone organised a reunion of our masters class, and it took the form of a twilight cruise on Lyttelton Harbour. It was embarrassing at first, because we remembered so little of one another after twenty years: perhaps we had never known much. The feeling wore off during the trip, not because we recalled much more, or even learnt much more, about our fellows, but rather that we drank enough to be reconciled by familiarity to the faces around us.

I was in a dull group at the stern around the wine casks — neat and high spirits were further forward, it seemed. We were denouncing politicians, I think. 'I'm Suzanne Alperonne,' said the quiet woman next to me.

'This is Suzanne Alperonne,' I said to my wife. Two things I could remember about Suzanne — she was a better scholar at the end than I was, and once the professor apologised to her for his comments on feminism. My wife seemed to know more people on board than I did. She and Suzanne began talking to others about saving whales, while I watched at a distance a good-looking bald-headed man give a speech. Perhaps he was the organiser, and I never thanked him.

At dusk, as we returned from the cruise, the tug hesitated out from the wharf to allow access for another ship, and a group disenchanted with the whales and the politicians dared each other to dive in and swim ashore. Silly, competitive male banter it was, stilled finally by Suzanne Alperonne who said she'd do it for a hundred dollars and would anyone else match her? I almost spoke, I swear, but was shy of my soft, middle-aged stomach, and my short, blue socks if I swam without my trousers. The water too: heavy, and with a greasy sheen in the fading light. 'No takers?' she said quietly, and dived in, as we cheered in our defeat. The tug seemed to keep pace merely by its movement in the swell, then she receded, her arms turning, as if on the face of a corrected clock.

Someone must have had the idea of that reunion, and found us all out, and organised the tug and casks of wine. I can't remember who, and never gave the thanks that were due. Suzanne Alperonne, though, swimming in the darkening harbour, was a lesson to me in courage and reticence.

Bob Isherwood, Neddy Dawson, Prue Whitby-Orme, Kevin Attwell, Carla de Joux and Fiona Ballance. Then there was old man Towler and Arch Hollis. Arch is my father's cousin. His farm in the Wairau Valley seemed baronial to me — a town boy. Baronial not in terms of evident money, or antique furniture, or tours abroad, but in the vast scale of ownership and decision: tractors, trucks, sheds, haybarns, married-couple cottage, sets of yards, silos, flocks, fields of crops, beehives, creeks, whole lines of windbreak trees and fences, gates, the very sky over it all. How magnificent a wardrobe of possession it seemed to me. I understood why Arch left his fief only when forced to by the need to placate his wife or deal cautiously with the professions of the town. He ruled in muted, muscular grandeur; ploughing and fencing, dipping and harrowing, shearing, sowing, harvesting, building and breaking down.

He dispensed justice and decided life and death on his land. He culled and mated with care and no vindictiveness.

From that place I would return home dissatisfied with our urban section, an area which Arch might use for piling stones, or setting a few hives on. My father's resources were all within his head, and difficult for a boy to appreciate. Arch is still gradually wearing into his context, still there and becoming more and more a part of what he both rules and serves until, when he stands still, he is quite indistinguishable from the texture, strong grain and natural contours of the land itself. I doubt if they will ever find a body to take away.

Will Ng, Richard Jones, Pinhead Guy, Catherine Dickison, Ace Gallagher, Joanne Ryder, Pearl Edgecombe, Gaston Labermoute and Maurice Hume. Such a compact figure, Pearl Edgecombe, the flesh smooth and dense like silver, and if she had been dropped into the sea she would have sunk instantly without flutter or bobbing. Her appearance mirrored her imperturbable nature. As an historian she was contemptuous of the present, for its transience and unsettled way prevented valid judgements being made.

In a morning of blossom and warm stone at the old campus, she talked of Cannae in passing. Not many had bothered to come, but she saw that as no reason for relaxing her scholarship. Her view was, as ever, orderly, exact, just what was required, yet so removed from the physical event. I had a sense of dynamic awe that the hopes and blood, the tumultuous horror and unbearable pain, the loss, the waste, and pageantry to follow, had dwindled through two thousand years to five minutes in that quiet room with flowers and old stone.

Have I said Tony Calder? He stole a girlfriend I never had. She was an AFS from Wolf Point, Montana, with a pony-tail and a languid voice. I told my friends I planned to ring her at her host family's place and make a date, but in the days I was using to perfect my telephone technique, Tony Calder rang and invited her to go water skiing. After that, every time they were together someone would remind me of my boast.

I never said a thing to Tony, but years later when a different Calder applied for a job with my firm, I turned him down, and had the illogical satisfaction of writing, Dear Mr Calder, I regret to inform you etc. We must assuage our grievances as best we can, after all. I had for a long time a vision of Wolf Point, Montana — blue sage hills, cattle yards, Chevrolet pick-ups, and lost blonde girls with bobby socks and pony-tails. He cost me, did Tony Calder.

Russell Priest, Noleen Suter, E. P. E. Tattersall, Raf Maslen, Iggy Rousse, Tracey Bates and Lily Gustafasson. Ah, yes, Awol Grisson, Naomi Allport, Sutz McCallum, Ivan Linkall and the big girl who played the part of the beadle in the Dickens play. I was in National Service with Awol Grisson: months at Waiouru, which is a sort of Gulag Archipelago the fortunate New Zealander never experiences. We twenty-year-olds were divided into a majority who could get by, even adapt and find friends and humour, and a minority who could not stand it.

Awol couldn't stand it. He'd come from a close provincial family of religious fundamentalists and suddenly he was on the parade ground and unable to remember whether he should turn left or right about; unable to recall the sequence of assembly for the Bren gun, unable to fold an immaculate bed-roll, unable to answer to his Christian name because it was never used. He was burnt with a thunderflash during exercises, and put on charge for losing a bayonet during bivouac training. Each day his large face was a map of uncomprehending misery, and each night his sobbing punctuated our plaintive dreams. He tried to escape, but was always brought back.

Awol was convinced he had passed into the shadow of death, and his anguish finally expressed itself in fits. He had one while we were lining up at the mess hall on a wet evening and, as he twitched, the rain matted his hair, and fine gravel stuck to the side of his face. Like a stricken cat he drew his lips back to show his teeth, and we knelt awkwardly to put coats on him until the medics came. So the army set him free at last, and the rest of us voiced contempt for his weakness, and felt envy for his deliverance.

I haven't been called upon to defend my country. I have forgotten my camouflage technique and ambush drills by whistle; the octopus of battalion signals has sunk to a mystery once more. But I see Awol Grisson spasm-bent in the rain outside D block, his teeth bared to all the world.

Aubrey Gilden, Con Dawson, Judy Posswillow. Did I say Judy Posswillow? Well, I didn't mean to, you see. I must withdraw my pledge to have no secrets. I couldn't bear it. Some shafts must be left buried in the heart for, if drawn, the very blood will follow to the death. And she was beautiful and wilful, Judy Posswillow. How beautiful she was.

Debbie Faas, Dutch Bleeker, Alun Heuw, Frank Lox, Donald Rangi and April Burton. Winn Mannering, Jocelyn Hills, Kate Lim, Catherine Smythe, Nolan Wright, Al Bruce, Essie Bray, Alice Lenns, Toad Hall. Essie Bray, you say Essie was my landlady in my second year. I've forgotten the medieval history and Georgian poets, but the taste of the beetroot sandwiches Essie sometimes made for my tea is fresh in my mouth. The blood comes through the bread if you don't eat them right away. Yet Essie lent me her bike with a chain-guard and basket, which I used in the twilight sometimes, clanking along back streets to the bar, or parties. She went through my room most days and read the letters in my drawer, I could tell. Several times she left a clothes-peg with red wool wound on it under my pillow: I never could work out why. Essie Bray will be dead now, and later so will I. I've done nothing in the meantime to make me feel superior, and I'll say this for Essie, when I had beetroot, so did she. Betwixt landlady and lodger was no distinction. How truly she mourned when Kennedy was assassinated: utter and inconsolable bereavement, as if she had lost a lover.

Nigel Uftern, May Brookes, Father Wilton, Buddy Carter, B. B. Candy, Lester Hefferman, Winston Eddy, Karl St John Darling, Barbara Troon, Dork Cowan and Janet Mathews who died in Ethiopia. Pop Casey and Stan Livesey, Banzai Frew, fat Gwillam, Wesley Collet, Amanda Hawkey, and Geoff Hyde, who was the best wing the school ever produced, many said.

We were all failures, Gwillam, Ian and myself. So we kept a fine old humour together at our wretched work, and never wished to see each other outside those hours. Gwillam was a boozer, and on his bad days Ian and I would hide him on sacks behind the pallets, where he could sleep. And we would do his share because, if he was fired, we might have someone in his place without a sense of humour, or failure. Gwillam would sleep on the sacks with his fat cheeks and lips sagging like a baby's.

The two essential qualities of friendship are to make allowances and to respect privacy. In return Gwillam told endless stories from his own Arabian Nights of sexual conquests. Almost certainly Gwillam had an ordinary experience — a baby face advances one only so far in a woman's affections — but as a voluptuary he would not allow fact to deny him pleasure. Over our breaks during three days he recounted the saga of the Mint Princess, a rabbiter's wife he claimed to have loved in Culverden. Ian and I laughed and listened to pass the time, breathed in the ash of the ground grain, watched the glimmer through the trailing webs of the skylights. They had a rendezvous in the creekbed, Gwillam said, in the old channel lined with upright mint, and in the still evening, he said, with the bronze north Canterbury hills too far to pry, he would roll in the mint with her, releasing essences to blink a slanted sun. Her white hips above him, heavily pale, turned like the Pharaoh's alabaster bowl, Gwillam said, sheened white with joy, he said, and Ian and I would turn our smiles to the corner of the warehouse, but listen all the same. We were all failures, Gwillam, Ian and myself.

Yes, you're right about Reg Osborne being a mutual friend. Strangely enough I had a dream about him not long ago. I dreamt that I was farewelling some friend at the wharf: the crowd immense, everything bedecked with tickertape, hooters and flowers in the television way. So great was the crush that I was being pushed over the side, between the heavy timbers of the wharf and the massive, breathing side of the ship, and I called in fear, reached to hold the man next to me. He turned sufficiently for me to see his face, and it was Reg Osborne. But he pretended I wasn't there. He drew his arms away and I wasn't able to grip the smooth back and shoulder of his coat. I fell, conscious of great horror and pity for myself.

Reg was a friend, and I'd not thought about him for years, yet how clearly I saw his expression, and how true to him it seemed that instant as he turned away. He wanted me to fall. He must have hated me for something. A dream means nothing, perhaps, yet if I ever meet Reg again I won't feel the same towards him. His expression so authentic, looking away, pretending he couldn't see my need, yet with malice apparent even in the determined face of that pretence. Just a dream, of course, you may say. All the same, all the same.

Lauris James, of course, Raymond Sadler, Gillian Burridge, Marya Robeliski, Peewee Riddle, Peter Guile, Archdeacon Langley, Margaret Reesman, Nonce Falconer, Pauline Stowell and Desmond Mulcahy. P. G. Fisst and Barry Beardsley. Akker Lisdeen, Prof. Webbernath, Mo Thyne, Esplin Dee, no, I said him. Yvonne Shelley, though, Alistair Smith and Gussie Addison. Each of them has a life.

Yvonne Shelley was the undertaker's daughter and let me take her home after the carnival on New Year's Eve. She took off her shoes and walked the final blocks in her stockings on the warm concrete. I had the feeling that she did it because of some film, or some book she'd read. She swung her shoes by their straps, and laughed when cars came by. Even in the seclusion by her house, I sensed that she was using me as a stock on which to base a more intriguing partner, but I didn't care. I would have answered to any name, bayed at the moon on cue, to be as I was hard against her in the hedge: feel her hip on mine, smell the warm, night leaves we oppressed, hear the rustle of her dress upon her thigh and the sound of my own snagged breath. I wasn't too proud. How rare the times when we truly envy no one; when there is nothing in this world's variety that we would swap for the present held.

'How you do go on,' said Yvonne Shelley. Her head was tilted back into the hedge in submission to my kisses, yet her smiles in the dark were languorous, as if for an audience. Shelley's Funeral Parlour, the sign said in unlit lettering, but it was life I served that night, not death. With an elbow awkwardly lifted to allow me to feel her breast from the top of her dress, I heard the lowing of harbour boats, though the New Year was long in. 'Don't squeeze,' she said. The hedge was well forced back. A pearl band of sky lay in the east beyond her father's kindly business. Her breath fluttered on my neck, and a hedgehog turned mystified away. 'Do you love me?' Yvonne Shelley said.

Hey nonny, names are the proof, we say, of anything having happened at all. Gunter Berge, Murray Young and Simon Hillier I remember now: Lennie Haseltine and Marianne Ranunski, cousin Violet and that Winston Talbot. All have a response in the roll-call which substantiates the trivial course of a private life. My name on the margin of theirs too, perhaps.

For names, the word, reversed can fertilise the combs of memory, and our lives are like expanding universes in miniature — the parts receding from the centre with a hapless, silent speed.

from

Tomorrow We Save the Orphans

The Rule of Jenny Pen

~

THE HEAVY MOONLIGHT gave it all the appearance of quality linen, flattering the exposed walls of the Totara Eventide Home, and the lines of stainless steel trolleys and wheel-chairs by the windows glinted like cutlery upon that linen. The moon was more for-giving than the sun, allowing a variety of interpretations for what it revealed. The shadowed places were soft feathered with blue and grey, like a pigeon's breast.

The only sound was Crealy pissing on to Matron's herb garden. The white cord of his striped pyjamas hung down one leg, and his bald head was made linen in the moonlight. 'Had enough?' Crealy asked the sage, basil and thyme. Residents were not supposed to come out and treat the Matron's herbs to such abuse. Crealy felt his life stir as ever at the defiance of rules. He could see the trim, summer lawn, and the garden which paralleled the side path to the slope of the front grounds. The moon-light lay over it all as a linen snowfall.

Crealy had never before lived in a place so pleasant to the eye, or so well organ-ised — and he hated it. Always a big man, he had never done anything with it; lack-ing the will, the resolution, the brains and the luck. At eighty-one and in Totara Home, he found that time had awarded him a superiority which he had been unable to earn any other way. He had given little, and lasted well.

Crealy's bladder was empty, so he put a large hand over his face to massage his cheeks, while he waited for an idea as to what to do next. Even in the moonlight the kidney spots on the backs of his hands showed clearly. He could think of nothing novel to do, so decided to persecute Garfield. He went back through the staff door of the kitchen, and bolted it carefully behind him. Before seeking out Garfield, Crealy wanted to be sure that Brisson was settled in the duty room. He went slowly through the kitchen and the dining room, through the corridors which were tunnels in the Totara of all their past lives.

Crealy stood in the shadow of the last doorway, and looked into the corridor which led past the duty room. He was like a bear which pauses instinctively at the edge of a forest clearing to assess possibilities of gain or loss. He walked slowly down the corridor of mottled green lino, his breathing louder than the regular shuffle of his slippers. Before the duty room he slowed even further as a caution, but his breathing was as loud as ever. The door was ajar, and Crealy looked in to see Brisson at leisure.

The duty room had a sofa, a chair, a log book with a biro on a string, a coffee pot, a telephone, a typed copy of the fire drill on the wall. It had the worn, impersonal look common to all such rooms in institutions, whether hospitals or boarding schools, army depots or fire brigades. Brisson lay on the sofa, and held up a paper-back as if shielding himself from the light. His head was round and firm like a well-grown onion, and light brown with the sheen a good onion has too. He wore no socks, just yellow sneakers on his neat feet. Crealy was surprised yet again to see how young some people were. He'll lie there all night and do nothing, thought Crealy.

'Who's that huffing and puffing outside my door?' said Brisson without moving, and Crealy pushed the door and took a step into the doorway. 'Ah, so it's you, Mr Crealy,' said Brisson. He swung the book down, and his legs on to the floor, in one easy movement. 'Why are you wandering the baronial halls?'

In reply Crealy made a gesture with his large hands which seemed more resignation than explanation. Brisson was lazy, arrogant, shrewd — and young. He took in Crealy: the awkward size of him, the sourness of his worn, bald face, the striped pyjamas and, between them and slippers, Crealy's bare ankles with the veins swollen. Brisson gave a slight shiver of joy and horror at his amazing youth, and Crealy's old age.

'Mrs Vennermann said you squeezed the blossom off her bedside flowers,' he said. Crealy itched his neck. His fingers sounded as if they worked on sandpaper, and the grey stubble was clear in the light of the room. 'She said you pick on people. Is that right?'

'She took my Milo,' said Crealy. Brisson picked up the exercise book that served as the log for duty shifts.

'Shall I put that in here then? Shall I? Mr Crealy deprived of his Milo by Mrs Vennermann. For Christ's sake. And someone said that you have been making Mrs Halliday all flustered. Eh?'

'It's just all fuss,' said Crealy. He began to think how he could get back at Mrs Vennermann.

Brisson smiled at his own performance, looking at old Crealy, at the mottled lino like a puddle behind him, at the exercise book with the cover doodled upon, and the biro on a string from it. He considered himself incongruous in such surroundings. He had such different things planned for himself. 'I won't have a bully on my shift, Mr Crealy. If I have to come down to the rooms, then look out. And don't you or the others come up here bothering me.' Brisson hoped to be with Nurse McMillan. What time was it?

'I don't do anything,' said Crealy in his husky voice. 'It's Jenny Pen.'

'What's that?'

'Eh?' said Crealy.

'Go to bed,' said Brisson, and saw the old man turn back on to the puddle lino, heard the shuffle and breath of him as he went back to the rooms of the east wing. Brisson did an abrupt shoulder stand on the sofa to prove age not contagious, then relaxed again with his book and thoughts of Nurse McMillan.

When Crealy reached the room he shared with Garfield, Mortenson and Popanovich he was ready for a little action. Jenny Pen time. Jenny Pen was a hand puppet that Garfield's granddaughter had made at intermediate school. Although christened

Jenny Pencarrow, it looked more like Punch, or the witch from Snow White, for its papier mâché nose and chin strove to complete a circle. Jenny Pen had a skirt of red velvet, and balanced all day on the left-hand knob of Garfield's bed. At night, ah torment, she became the fasces of Nero's power, the cloven hoof, the dark knight's snouted emblem, the sign of Modu and Mahu, the dancing partner of a trivial Lucifer, a tender facsimile of things gone wrong.

Crealy lifted Jenny Pen from the bed end, and thrust his hand beneath the velvet skirt. He held her aloft, and turned her painted head until all the room had been held in her regard. Garfield began to cry; Mortenson turned the better side of his face aside, and wished his stroke had been more complete. Popanovich was just a shoulder beneath his blankets. Crealy walked Jenny Pen on her hands up Garfield's chest, and she seemed of her own volition to rap Garfield's face. 'Who rules?' said Crealy.

'Jenny Pen,' said Garfield. Garfield had played seventeen games for Wellington as fullback, and later been general manager for Hentlings. It was all too far away to offer any protection.

'Lick her arse then,' said Crealy hoarsely, and Garfield did, and felt Crealy's hand on his tongue. 'You're on Jenny Pen's side, aren't you?' said Crealy.

'Yes.' Garfield's voice barely quivered, although the tears ran down his cheeks. He could scarcely conceive the life he was forced to lead: his soul peeped out from a body which had betrayed him in the end.

Crealy's eyes glittered, and he looked about to share his triumph with others. 'What about you, Judge? Want to do a little kissing?' Mortenson gave his half-smile.

'It's difficult for me,' he said slowly.

'Bloody difficult with only half of everything working.' Crealy walked over to the last bed, and shook Popanovich's shoulder. There was no reaction. 'What sort of a name is that for a New Zealander,' he said. 'Bloody Popanovich!' He banged his knee into Popanovich's back, but there was no defence of the name. It put Crealy in an ill humour again, and he went back to Garfield with Jenny Pen. He began to go through Garfield's locker. 'It's share and share alike here, Garbunkle.'

'Communism has the greatest attraction to those with the least,' said Mortenson in his slurred voice, knowing Crealy was not bright enough to follow.

'Shut up,' said Crealy. He placed a bag of barley sugars and a box of shortbread biscuits on the top of Garfield's locker. 'Is that all, you useless bugger,' he said. He looked at Garfield for a time, letting Jenny Pen rest on the covers, almost basking in the knowledge shared between them of Garfield's weakness and his strength. And even more, the mutual knowledge of Garfield's former strength and superiority, Garfield's achievements and complacency, now worthless currency before Crealy, who had achieved nothing except the accidental husbandry of physical strength into old age.

'What else have you got hidden after all them visitors?' Crealy slid his free hand slowly under Garfield's pillow, and withdrew it empty. 'Come on now, you bugger,' he said.

'Just leave me alone.'

'Make Jenny Pen sing a song,' said Mortenson. Sometimes Crealy would have Jenny Pen sing 'Knick Knack Paddy Whack Give a Dog a Bone', or 'Knees Up, Mother Brown'. It was an awful sound, but better than the beatings.

Crealy listened a while, to make sure that no one was coming who could take Garfield's part, then he pulled the near side of the mattress up and found a packet of figs. 'That's more like it,' he said. He sat on the bed as if he were a friend of Garfield. 'You selfish old bugger,' he said mildly. 'How many figs do you reckon there are here?'

Garfield didn't answer, and Crealy took hold of his near ear and shook his head by means of it until Garfield cried out. 'Don't you start calling out, or you'll get more,' said Crealy. He opened the packet and began to eat. 'For every one you're going to get a hurry up,' he said, and gave Garfield one right away.

So it began. Popanovich remained in hibernation beneath his blankets, Mortenson watched, but tried to keep the true side of his face as expressionless as the other, even though his good leg was rigid. Garfield covered his ears, and Crealy ate the figs, hitting Garfield's face with each new mouthful. 'Figs make you shit, Garfield, old son,' he said, 'but I'll make you shit without them. That's rich, isn't it. I said that's rich, isn't it, Judge?'

'Exactly,' said Mortenson carefully. What time was it? He tried to remember some of the letters of Cicero he had been reading.

The one light from Garfield's locker cast a swooping shadow each time Crealy leant forward solicitously to hit Garfield, and when Crealy held Jenny Pen up in triumph she was manifest as a monstrous Viking prow upon the wall. Mortenson had to accept the realisation that there were underworlds which he had been able until recently to ignore; now he was part of one, suffering and observing, powerless through reduced capacity and fear.

When he saw a little, shining blood beneath Garfield's nose, he could contain his opposition no longer. Yet stress undid his recent progress and Stefan Albee Mortenson, barrister, solicitor, notary public, could produce before the court of Jenny Pen only, 'Creal, youb narlous narl stapp awus nee.'

'Careful, Judge. I don't need your squawk. I might come across and give you more than just this feathering Garfield's enjoying. I'll do the side of you not already dead, you pinstripe squirt.'

Mortenson had nothing more to say, and Garfield sat with his chin on his chest as if in a trance. 'Had enough?' Crealy asked him. 'You're gutless, the lot of you.' Crealy was bored with his immediate subjects and, with Jenny Pen still on his hand as his familiar, he went to wander the night corridors of the home. No conversation began in the room he left. Popanovich feigned the sleep of death, Garfield remained slumped in his bed and Mortenson had no way of travelling the distance between them to offer comfort.

Mrs Munro knew nothing of Totara's netherworld. She had her own room in the separate block before the cottages, and the sun was laid on the polish of several pieces of her own furniture which had accompanied her. Mrs Munro could never understand those who complained of time dragging. She herself delighted in time to spare for all those indulgences a busy life had denied her, all those intellectual and emotional considerations that the slog of a seven-day dairy had prevented her from enjoying. She wore the tracksuit which she had insisted on for a Christmas present. She liked the comfort, the lack of constriction, the zippers at ankle and chest which made it easy to get off. She liked the two bright blue stripes and the motif of crossed racquets, even though she had never played sport.

Despite something of a problem with head nodding, and a hip operation on the way, Mrs Munro was quietly proud that, although she was an old woman, she was not a fat, old woman. She didn't complain about the food, and she drew more large-print library books in a week than anyone else in the home. She rejoiced in an hour to while away over a cup of tea, or in writing to Bessie Inder, or in putting drops in her ear, or measuring her room with the tape from the sewing basket. Miss Hails from the main block did visit too often, it was true, and her repetitions tended to start Mrs Munro's head nodding, but there was always the bedding storeroom as a sanctuary, and Mrs Munro had built a little dug-out in the blanket piles where she could rest in her tracksuit after lunch until Miss Hails had given up looking for her, and gone visiting elsewhere.

For the present, though, she counted the spots of a ladybird on her window sill, and watched sour old Crealy smoking on a bench by the secure recreation area. Crealy was not compulsive viewing, and when Mrs Munro finished her computations concerning the ladybird, she decided she would begin her next romance of the British Raj.

Crealy's cigarette was the last in the packet he had stolen from Popanovich, who was sleeping again. For Crealy, the days were not as enjoyable as the nights, because he was too much under the eye of authority, and the spirit of his fellows was not as easily daunted when the sun shone. He wondered if Mrs Halliday was by the goldfish pond, but couldn't see her, and so he went back indoors to check Mortenson's locker before lunch. In the main corridor he came across Mrs Joyce, who had her blood changed quite regularly at the clinic. Her forearms and elbows seemed forever to have the yellows, purples and blues of ageing bruises. Mrs Joyce had made binoculars of her hands and stood with them pressed to the glass doors, staring out. 'What's out there?' she asked Crealy.

'Herbs and spices, sycamores and young people. And bloody work.'

'I can't see it,' said Mrs Joyce.

'You've gone daft in there.' Crealy rapped on her head with his knuckles, but she kept peering out into the sunshine through the tunnels of her fingers.

'Let me join Jesus,' she said. Crealy looked down at her pink scalp beneath the white hair. Because there was no resistance whatsoever that she could make, because she was not even aware of his malice, Crealy couldn't be bothered hurting her.

'Dozy old tart.'

'Let me come to thee, sweet Jesus,' said Mrs Joyce. Crealy had a chuckle at that, and at how Mrs Joyce was peering through her hands and the glass, although everything outside was perfectly clear to him.

Matron Frew heard the chuckle from the office, and it reminded her that she wanted words with Crealy. She first of all took Mrs Joyce's arm in hers and walked with her down to the dayroom. She was back before Crealy could quite disappear from sight down the corridor, however, and she told him, with some bluntness, of the indirect complaints she'd been receiving, particularly from staff who had noticed Crealy pestering Mrs Halliday and Mr Garfield.

'Mark my words,' said Matron Frew. 'I will be watching, and also I'm making mention of things in my report to the board this month. You show an unwillingness at times to be a reasonable member of our community.'

As she spoke Crealy hung his head, but not from meekness or contrition. He was counting the number of usable butts in the sandbox by the office door, and when he had done that he imagined himself in the mild, summer night standing over Matron's herb garden, and pissing on the chives, parsley, mint, fennel and thyme. A lifetime in the indifferent, hostile or contemptuous regard of others had rendered Crealy immune to all three. He recognised no value or interest other than his own.

On Wednesday evenings Matron Frew turned off the television in the east wing lounge and organised communal singing. It was not compulsory as such, but absence meant no chocolate biscuits at the supper which followed. As a professionally trained person, Matron knew that a variety of stimulus was important for the elderly.

The committed, the egotistical and the hard of hearing stood close around the piano, the infirm or less enthusiastic were rims at a great distance. Golden oldies they sang, to Matron's accompaniment. 'The Kerry Pipers', 'Auld Lang Syne', 'The Biggest Aspidistra in the World', 'On Top of Old Smokey'.

Matron had begun her career as a physiotherapist and it showed in her playing; the keys kneaded like a string of vertebrae, each tune well gone over and the kinks removed. 'Waltzing Matilda', 'Home on the Range', 'The White Cliffs of Dover', 'Some Enchanted Evening', 'Polly Wolly Doodle'. Matron Frew allowed her charges to respond in their own way and order, but she always had Nurse Glenn or Nurse McMillan guide Mr Oliphant to the uncarpeted area by the door, because the pathos of any Irish tune made him incontinent.

A refrain, particularly with high notes, would sometimes trigger Miss Hails' weakness and she would begin the incessant repetition of a word. It happened, sure enough, during 'Riding Down From Bangor', and for several minutes Miss Hail sang only 'May'. Crealy was present not just for the chocolate biscuits, but because it gave him perverse satisfaction, after the Matron's rebuke, to exercise intimidation almost under her gaze.

He stood on Mrs Dellow's toe during 'Annie Laurie', and stared into her face, daring her to respond. Her thin voice assumed even greater vibrato and her eyes misted. Crealy then leant in comradeship over blind Mr Lewin and sprayed saliva into his face as 'Christopher Robin Went Down With Alice'.

When the chocolate biscuits came at last, Crealy kept himself between them and George Oliphant until they were all gone, then he said, 'Now isn't that a bugger, George, they seem all gone.'

'Silver Threads Among the Gold', they sang, and 'Swing Low, Sweet Chariot'. 'Home, home, home, home, home, home,' Miss Hails continued, until Matron Frew told her to suck her thumb until the cycle was broken. 'Knees Up, Mother Brown' Crealy liked but, because it was his favourite, the others found no pleasure in joining in.

Mortenson enjoyed the association the songs bore, even if not the singing itself. He preferred to be at some remove from the piano and his fellows, for then he could imagine other company and past days: his mouth would twitch and his good hand move to the melodies. 'Some Enchanted Evening' — he would sing it with Deborah as they drove back from skiing, ready for court work during the week. He hadn't realised then, that all roads led to this. 'Roo, roo, roo, roo, roo,' began Miss Hails.

Before midnight, aware of an odd, sighing wind around the home, Crealy made a patrol of his domain. Only his harsh breathing and shuffle gave him away. In his own room everything was as it should be — Garfield was weeping, Popanovich sleeping, and Mortenson in his snores fell every few minutes into a choking death rattle which woke him briefly, then he slept and it all began again.

Further down the corridor Mrs Doone was talking to herself as she strung up non-existent Christmas decorations. Every night was Christmas Eve for Mrs Doone, and the wonder and frisson of it were freshly felt night after night. 'Compliments of the season, Mr Ah — ah,' she said as Crealy slippered by. Around the corner, Crealy paused outside the room Mrs Oliffe and Miss Hails shared. Miss Hails was doing her thing, of course. For almost an hour she had been repeating the sound tee, while Mrs Oliffe was trying to find nineteen across, which was Breton Gaelic for divine harbinger.

'Oh, stop going tee, tee, tee, tee,' Mrs Oliffe said, but the simple satisfaction of it set her off also, and she joined in. Outside, Crealy could hear them in unison — tee, tee, tee. He found his own head nodding, and his mouth formed the sound. One night it might spread through all of Totara, and capture them in a transport of repetitious senility.

Crealy put his hand to his face to stop himself. He looked carefully down the corridor. 'Mad old tarts,' he said. He considered opening their door and frightening them into silence, but the chances of being caught up in their chant and left nodding with them indefinitely was too great. He went on, still with one hand to his face. Tee, tee, tee, tee faded behind him.

Outside the Matron's office were chairs for visitors, and a varnished box with a sandtray in it for smokers among the visitors. Crealy was able to find several butts worth using again, before he noticed Mrs Joyce standing by the main doors once more. 'Jesus loves me this I know,' she said. She had two overcoats on, and stood with her hand on the catch of the locked door. 'I'm going home,' she said. 'I've been here nearly a fortnight and they're expecting me back now.'

'You've been here for years,' said Crealy.

'Oh no, just a fortnight, and I need to be at home for every special occasion. We've always been a very close family, you see.' Crealy went through her double set of pockets as she talked, but all he could find was a small book of stamps. 'They may well send a car for me,' she said. They both looked through the glass doors for a moment, but there was only empty wind and moonlight: no car was parked on the linen of the drive.

'You can go home this way,' said Crealy, taking Mrs Joyce by the lapel and leading her towards the kitchens.

'Has the car come then?' she said, and 'God will provide, you know. Even Solomon in all his glory.' Crealy led her through the dining room laid for breakfast, and the kitchens, where worn, steel surfaces glinted like new bone. He unbolted the service door and set Mrs Joyce in the gap. 'There you are, then,' he said. 'The main drive's just around the corner.'

'It's a clear path to home, thank Jesus.' The blue second coat would barely fit over the first, and pulled her arms back like the flippers of a penguin. Rather like a penguin she began walking, struck her head on a pruned plum branch, and reeled past the herb garden.

'What's your name again?' said Crealy, but Mrs Joyce didn't answer and, still unsteady from the blow, made the best pace she could around the side path. She had the scent of freedom; she had a promise of home.

Crealy waited until Mrs Joyce was well gone, and there was no sound of pursuit or return, then he went out himself and stood in the summer night, sniffing the aromatic air of Matron Frew's herb garden. He hung out his cock, and waited patiently for his prostate to relax its grip so that he could enjoy the physical relief and pleasurable malice of watering the herbs. He had both in good time, then he stood under the sycamore by the old garages and had one of the visitors' cigarette ends, after nipping off the filter.

The sycamore creaked and murmured in the night breeze which blew out from the land to the sea. Despite the ache in his joints, Crealy enjoyed being by himself there beneath the branches, and the summer sky, for he knew that he had always been unloved. Even though old age at Totara had given him a mirror image power and significance, while always before he had been subjugated, he liked still to be alone, to have no sources of action or response other than himself. So he stood beneath the sycamore, and enjoyed his cigarette ends guardedly, shading the glow with a palm, and looking out to the better lit parts of the grounds. 'No bastard can see me,' he said. 'No bastard knows I'm here.'

Even a summer's night grows cold for old bones, and Crealy came in and bolted the door behind him. 'Had enough?' he had asked the mint and parsley as he went by them. He inspected Mrs Joyce's stamps in the dim light. He wanted to search her room, but had forgotten her name.

Crealy had never been an intellectual, and at eighty-one he found it difficult to move and think at the same time. So he remained stooped in the semi-light between kitchen and dining room, and he tried to remember what he had been going to do before he met Mrs Joyce.

He went into the pantry beyond the stainless steel moonlight of the kitchen, and lifted out a large tin of golden syrup. He took a thick crust from the toast drawer and, with his fingers as a ladle, spread golden syrup on it. The syrup lay dark in the tin, but silver in glints as it twined from his fingers.

Crealy replaced the tin, and stood with the bread and syrup in his clean hand, sucking his other fingers. He looked into the shadowed dining room: the identical tables, evenly spaced, and an oblong of light across them from the corridor. The golden syrup was rich and energy giving. Crealy began to wonder if Mrs Halliday was having one of her spells in the home. He made such demands on his old mind that his chewing slowly stopped, and his hand no longer held the bread level. He stood in the kitchen doorway as a Neanderthal at the entrance to his cave. The syrup made a silver necklace to the floor. Crealy couldn't remember: couldn't remember at all.

'Bugger me,' he said at last. He was unable to come up with anything, so he stopped thinking, allowed the motor-sensory centres priority again, and moved into the lino tubes which were the Totara corridors.

At the duty room, Crealy decided to check on Brisson in case he was doing the unexpected thing and actually making a round. There was no key for the duty room door, but when Crealy pushed lightly against it, he found that Brisson had set the end of the sofa hard to it. Then he heard voices. Nurse McMillan talked as she and Brisson made love, but her topic was dissatisfaction with conditions of service, not romance. Lovemaking altered the normal rhythm of her words so that odd, accentuated syllables were driven out of her. '*God* we've all thought *of* handing in our resig*nations*,' she said.

'There's nothing in all the world to match it,' Brisson said.

The palm of one of Crealy's large hands still rested on the door, though he pressed no more. He listened to a tune which mocked him, and his arthritis drove him on, shuffling and disgruntled, missing out as usual. Mrs Doone had finished putting up her Christmas decorations for the night, and the corridor was as bare as when she first began. Even Miss Hails was silent, but as Crealy passed Mr Lewin's room he heard a talking clock. 'It is twelve o'clock, midnight,' it said. Like a fox at a burrow entrance, Crealy stood before the door, but the clock didn't speak again, and blind Mr Lewin, who must have activated it, made no sound either.

As he neared his own room Crealy could hear Mortenson's stricken breathing, and remembered with sudden vividness a time more than thirty years before, when he had been a cleaner at the Nazareth Hall and Mortenson had been president of a group that banqueted there. Crealy had looked out from the serving hatch, waiting to begin clearing up, and S.A. Mortenson CBE, barrister, solicitor, notary public, city councillor and party chairman, had been standing at the top table, standing in his dinner jacket to give an erudite speech which was buoyed up constantly by delighted applause and laughter from the other tables. The recollection had such strength that Crealy felt again the flat ache of his own inconsequence, but it passed and he was aware of the cream Totara walls again, and the struggle Mortenson had to breathe.

Crealy laid Popanovich's open bottle of lemonade on the bed so that it would wet the sleeping man's feet, and plucked Jenny Pen from Garfield's bed end and held her briefly aloft. 'Wake up, Judge,' he said, and took Mortenson's nose between Jenny Pen's hands.

Mortenson's good side woke with horror. What time was it? 'Let's have poetry tonight,' said Crealy. He made himself comfortable on the bed with his room-mate. 'And I want to see you enjoying it, Judge, getting into the swing of it,' he said.

> *And where the silk-shoed lovers ran*
> *with dust of diamonds in their hair,*
> *he opens now his silent wing*

began Mortenson indistinctly.

Crealy put one of Jenny Pen's fingers into the slack side of Mortenson's mouth and pulled it into the image of a smile. 'Let's not be half-hearted about this. Try something else,' said Crealy. Mortenson wished to disregard the setting his senses made for him, and the only escape was through the words. He did his best with a bit of 'The Herne's Egg'.

> *Strong sinew and soft flesh*
> *Are foliage round the shaft*
> *Before the arrowsmith*
> *Has stripped it, and I pray*
> *That I, all foliage gone,*
> *May shoot into my joy.*

'Eh?' said Crealy. He tired quickly of poetry, even when seasoned with humiliation. 'Had enough,' he said. His thoughts turned to Garfield. There were hours to go, years maybe, before it would be day again.

Blind Mr Lewin was guided by Mrs Munro to the sunroom in the east wing the next afternoon. Mr Lewin loved the warmth, and found that he could sleep easily during the day in full sunlight. Mrs Munro kindly led him down, and Lewin could feel the warmth even as they approached the end of the corridor. Mrs Munro's head nodded companionably as she pulled a cane chair close to the large window: so close that Lewin was able to put out his hands and feel the glass while sitting comfortably. And she gave him his talking clock to cradle, so that he would not be anxious about his meals. Mr Lewin thanked her, and listened to the departing footsteps.

He had never seen the sunroom, and instead of the meek, faded place that it was, looking out over the crocodile paving and lawns in front of the cottages, he imagined it cantilevered high into the sun's eye, and with only the yellow, benevolent furnace of the sun to be seen from the window. Lewin had known far worse times.

While Mr Lewin slept, Crealy elsewhere watched Mrs Halliday. Mrs Halliday was only in her sixties, but subject to Huntington's chorea in recurring spells during which she often came into the Totara Home to relieve her family. Crealy always took a considerable interest in her visits, for her breasts were large, she still had firm flesh and, caught at the right moment, she could be used without much recollection of it.

Towards the end of the long afternoon she was at her most confused, and Crealy watched from outside the television lounge until he saw her talking to herself and constantly folding and unfolding her cardigan. He went in and firmly led her along the trail of mottled lino to the sunroom, which visitors or clergymen sometimes used to have their talks. 'Has the family come? Has Elaine?' said Mrs Halliday. Crealy was quite pleased to see blind Lewin there, close to the window, for he could pass as a chaperone at a distance, but not act as one on the spot. Crealy sat Mrs Halliday with her back to the window.

'Your family are coming soon,' he said, and opened the front of her dress.

'Is that you, Mrs Munro?' asked Lewin.

'Shut up,' said Crealy.

'The family, you say,' said Mrs Halliday. She allowed Crealy to unclip her bra at the back, and he scooped out her breasts so they made two full fish-heads in the flounce of her dress.

Lewin was still groggy from his sleep, but he didn't wish to seem discourteous. 'Where would we be without families,' he said gallantly, and fingered his talking clock for reassurance. Crealy stroked Mrs Halliday's breasts, and clumsily rolled the nipples between thumb and forefinger so that she pursed her lips and put her hands on his wrists.

'You need to get changed for your family,' said Crealy absently.

'What time is it then?' asked Mrs Halliday.

Lewin pressed his clock.

'The time is four forty-two pm,' it said.

Crealy took another minute of satisfaction in the sun, then refilled Mrs Halliday's bra, and with some difficulty fastened it across her back. Matron Frew might come looking for her soon. 'Stay here and talk to Lewin,' he said.

'Am I changed for my family?'

'Good enough,' said Crealy.

'Who is that?' said Lewin, turning an ear rather than an eye for better comprehension.

'Jenny Pen rules,' said Crealy as he left.

The impartial sun that Mr Lewin blindly enjoyed shone on Mortenson who sat in his wheelchair on a landscaped hillock which looked over the SRA — the safe recreation area. Within it the bewildered or fretful, the complacent and serene, could be left in security. Only the staff could manage the latch. Crealy called it the zoo, but it was pleasant enough, more like a kindergarten. There were seats with foam cushions for thin flesh, and raised garden plots which keen Totarans could work on without stooping or kneeling.

The SRA was overlooked by the wide windows of the dining room on one side, but to the warm north side there was a view across the grass and gardens towards the cottages and the spires of the great world. Mortenson could see the goldfish pond in the zoo, and George Oliphant dolefully shaking the back of his trousers because he was in trouble again.

The Matron and Dr Sullivan stopped beside Mortenson on their round, but finished their conversation before greeting him. 'I've no idea how Mrs Joyce managed to leave the block in the first place,' said Matron.

'It can't be helped.'

'It's a puzzle, though.'

'I haven't told her family the actual circumstances of the death, to minimise the trauma, you see. And how are you, Mr Mortenson?'

'Mr Mortenson is brighter every day,' replied Matron. Mortenson gave his half-smile. He could see the exquisite glow on the sunlit tulips, feel the sun's good will on his faithful side, and hear Miss Hails practising her word for the day. The word was nell, or perhaps knell. How was anyone to know but her.

'Nell, nell, nell, nell,' said Miss Hails. Like a prayer wheel she gave a benediction over all the zoo, the lawn, the cottages, the totality of Totara and beyond. 'Nell, nell, nell, nell, knell.'

'Well, nice talking to you,' said Dr Sullivan, and they went on their way. Mortenson felt an itching tic begin at the corner of his eye. In all that ground of apparent pleasure he wondered what Crealy was up to. What time was it? It came to Mortenson that his karma had been assessed; that from the best of lives he was in a spiral descent of reincarnation from which he would emerge perhaps a six-spot ladybird, as counted by Mrs Munro, and would clamp the stem beneath the wine glow of the sunlit tulip blooms.

What time was it? Dr Sullivan and Matron were trying to wake Popanovich. 'It's always the same. Ah, well, he seems healthy enough, and sleep can't hurt him.' Dr Sullivan smiled at the other three in the end room, while Matron moved Popanovich in the bed. The doctor was not a dour person; he believed in good spirits and optimism. He looked about for something that would provide an occasion for light-heartedness and rapport.

Matron sensed that the mood had abruptly changed, though at first she didn't see that behind her Dr Sullivan had taken Jenny Pen from Garfield's bed and mounted her on his hand. Garfield began to shiver, and put his hands out, palms uppermost, as if to play pat-a-cake. Crealy hung his head to one side like an old dog, while the whites of his eyes showed as he kept things in his view. Mortenson felt a sweat break out on his good thigh beneath the rug, and his smile was slow to form and slow to fade. He smiled as a Christian might smile who catches the Devil out walking in the daytime.

'What a good life we lead at Totara,' said Dr Sullivan in falsetto for Jenny Pen, and he jiggled her to emphasise his humour. The only responses were those of Matron Frew's crepe soles on the lino, and at a distance Miss Hails saying her catechism for the day. It drifted to them down the corridor.

'Mi, mi, mi, mi, mi, mi.'

'Perhaps puppeteer isn't my calling,' said Dr Sullivan. He was disappointed by his reception and withdrew into professionalism. Matron knew how to keep that patter going.

Crealy's arthritis was giving him gyppo again. To appease it he walked the maze of corridors, and watched from window after window the sunshowers above the grounds. Dramatic clouds were towed across the sky, and when they met the sun they were lit with red and orange embers, which glowed and shifted in the deep perspectives. From the dining room Crealy saw a travelling shower fracture the surface of the zoo pond, so that the goldfish lost their shape, and became just carrots in the shallow weeds.

On his second circuit Crealy noticed that Nurse McMillan had left the office, and that the morning's mail lay partly sorted on the counter. He eased in, and his stiff hands found envelopes addressed to Mortenson, to Oliphant and Garfield. He pocketed them, and was cheered by the petty malice, even though he couldn't see Mrs Halliday in the TV room as he went past. For the life of him he could not remember when he last had a personal letter. Garfield, on the other hand, received far too much kind attention from outside, and Crealy decided to give him a hard time until the weather improved. He began a search for Garfield, but George Oliphant saw him checking the TV room, and afterwards went to the window that could be seen by Mortenson and gave a warning by semaphore, which Mortenson passed on to Garfield.

Garfield began his slow but urgent escape down the corridors of hours towards the bedding storeroom. The door there had a plunger and cylinder to draw it closed without slamming. To Garfield the mechanism seemed to take an eternity to work, and the cylinder hissed as his view of the corridor and bathrooms narrowed. Garfield sat in semi-darkness, content with the little light entering from a glass strip above the door.

The broad shelves had stacks of sheets and pillowcases, and on the floor were piled blankets which rose like wool bales. Garfield sat on a half-bale to wait it out. He didn't trouble himself with the metaphysics of his situation: what he had come to. The former Wellington fullback and general manager for Hentlings sat grinding his teeth in the bedding store-room of Totara Eventide Home, and listening to the perpetual echoing orchestration which his tinnitus inflicted on him.

Crealy found him there.

It was nearly four. The showers had become less frequent, and a rainbow stood clearly behind the cottages, fading up towards the sun. Yet Mortenson couldn't concentrate on his history of Rome. He felt a helpless consideration for Garfield, and a fear of Crealy. He knew that, where there are no lions, then hyenas rule.

His chair was very low-geared and, despite the busy noise of its motor, Mortenson moved only slowly along the corridors towards the bedding room. At alternate windows the day's strange weather was displayed as sunlit promise, then skirts of rain from fiery clouds, then blue sky once again. The door took all the thrust his chair could manage, and sank closed behind him, so that the failing light and hiss half hid Crealy's torture of his friend.

'Hello, Judge,' said Crealy. Once he found that Mortenson had come alone, he was pleased. He had become almost bored with Garfield. Yet an advantage can be gained or lost quite unexpectedly, and with such an absence of drama that it is easy to miss the significance. Crealy moved to get a better leverage, overbalanced on the soft surface and fell backwards just a couple of feet into the comfortable crevasse fashioned by Mrs Munro between the banded blankets. His old arms and legs moved silently in the shadows, as if he were a beetle on his back there. He was too stiff to turn easily.

Mortenson took a pillow with his better arm and pushed it across Crealy's face.

'Come on,' he said to Garfield. It was more a delaying tactic at first, with neither of them having much hope of success. Even Crealy gave a sort of grin whenever he managed to free his face, as if he recognised his temporary difficulty, but would soon pay them back all right.

But the more Garfield and Mortenson pushed, and the more Crealy twisted, the deeper his shoulders sank between the blankets. He began to pant and jerk: the others saw a chance indeed and their lips drew back in the dark and they pressed for all their lives. Crealy's big arms and legs fell in harmless thuds against the embracing blankets. Mortenson felt strength and justice in his good arm, even though it trembled with exertion, and Garfield was on his knees to use his body weight upon the pillow.

'Had enough. Had enough, Crealy old son,' he kept whispering. The competitive urge in Garfield revived one last time. Crealy's arms and legs moved less, but his body bucked.

'Now let us play Othello,' slurred Mortenson.

'Had enough,' sobbed Garfield.

For a good time after Crealy was still, they continued to hold the pillow over his face. Accustomed to such full tyranny as his, they could hardly believe that they had beaten him so completely. Even when they heard his sphincter muscles relax, and had the smell of him, they held the pillow down. 'Had enough?' said Garfield tenderly.

'Put the pillow back,' said Mortenson finally, and he wiped the tears from Garfield's face. They didn't look again at Dave Crealy, who was a big, stupid man lying well down among piles of blankets. Garfield opened the door a little and, when he saw that there was no one outside, he held it back for Mortenson's chair, and the snake hissed behind them in the dark.

As they went home they met Mrs Munro guiding Mr Lewin to the sunroom. Mrs Munro delighted in being useful, and was thinking also of a nice cup of tea. 'There's a rainbow,' she said, nodding. Mortenson and Garfield could see its thick, childish bands behind the cottage; at the same time the sun was strong enough to cast shadows from the benches in the grounds. Who knows what Lewin saw, but he could hear with them the piping of Miss Hails at a distance.

'Na, na, na, na, na, na, na, na.'

Mr Lewin pushed the button on his clock.

'The time is four nineteen pm,' the clock said.

Iris

~

IRIS, MY MOTHER, had this idea that sooner rather than later something marvellous was bound to happen: a lucky break in life if you kept at it. She wasn't selfish about this; everyone had the same chance for something quite undeserved, like being approached out of the blue in the supermarket by a talent scout to become a model, or marrying an accountant as my aunt did, who now spends money like water and has two homes. For my twenty-first Aunt Esther gave me a cream silk dress, but I snagged it at the polytech wine and cheese on a rivet in the plastic chair.

Even when Iris was too old to go on hoping to be approached in the supermarket for anything other than shoplifting, she believed magnificent opportunity was in the offing She took Golden Kiwis, and then Lotto tickets, and worked out on the backs of envelopes how she would divide and spend the money. I was to come in for some pretty good stuff when she won, according to the lists. Each mailtime was a high, never mind that she hardly wrote to anyone, had jobs without prospects and shifted a lot. Throughout the drizzle of magazine offers, bills, perfunctory greetings, community newsletters, demands on former tenants and coupon books, she kept a fierce hope in miraculous correspondence. An approach concerning political candidature, perhaps, or an invitation from the Max Factor directorate to be a special consultant, gardenias from a secret admirer, or notification that she was meter maid of the year. Iris never did realise that her whole life was unsolicited. She intently examined each special offer and would speculate joyously if her actual name was used. But how would they know my name, she'd say, look, they use my proper name. So that I could be at my best, she would roam the twilight, feeling in her neighbours' boxes for shampoo sachets sent as samples. Needs must, my girl, she would say firmly. Our time will come.

Iris answered an advertisement about Dr Asmunzov, professor of the mind, who came and said he could do a seance on my dad, even though he'd gone off, not died. I was seventeen and the professor of the mind had other interests as well, for he clasped my knee beneath the table. Being naturally blonde and with a good bust, I've always had to deal with that sort of thing. Iris, my mother, said that it didn't necessarily mean anything, and that men were just like that. Hormonal, she said, and nothing in it to blame anyone. When she was going to school in Taranaki, a share milker used to undo his fly each day as the bus passed his milking shed. The association gave her a particular aversion to cholesterol, she said.

Iris did win a Christmas hamper when I had chicken pox in Form Two, from Woolworths, and once initiated a correspondence with a firm of Auckland solicitors acting for an unclaimed British estate. The hamper she unpacked on my bed and found lots of low-cost, bulky items under the more glamorous surface layer: Weet-bix, dried lentils, toilet rolls, stuff like that, and the solicitors lost interest when we couldn't provide any evidence that the family on the Bleeker side originated in Dorset. I ate a small tin of sardines cold from the hamper, and with my finger, put their oil on all the chicken pox that I could reach. My second-hand bed head had transfers of Pooh Bear and Cliff Richard that were nothing to me.

For a time, when we lived in Wanganui, Iris thought we had a fortune at our toes, because our Aramaho suburb neighbours said that the house we rented used to belong to a retired Greymouth dentist who must have been worth a packet, but left nothing when he died in my room. I did consider using the untainted third bedroom, but mine was so much sunnier, and I could come and go from the big window without bothering Iris. She said he would have had it all in gold, being able to get it for fillings as a dentist, though other people weren't allowed to buy it. She had a dream of gold-filled Havelock Dark tobacco tins hidden under the brick paving between the back door and the laundry. We dug up the bricks, every one, but found no gold. The bricks remained stacked on the lawn and next winter we got muddy feet going to the laundry. They were a reminder of yet another false lead in the treasure hunt which was my mother's life. It's there all right though, Iris said, he just doesn't want a woman to find it.

My boyfriends seemed possibilities to Iris: opportunities for advantage. Being blonde and with a good figure, as I said, I had plenty of guys coming on to me. You get used to it after a while. Not great, but not unbearable. It's just the effect you have on hormones, I guess. Mum said that she'd been trim herself in her time, but her face had become a bit of a handbag. My father had been an All Black trialist who couldn't get used to his diminished place in life when he got past playing. He had these wonderful hands, though, Iris said, and should really have taken up the saxophone, or the piano. She took it up herself soon after he left, from an easy stage instruction booklet called *Jazz Sax Made Easy*. She didn't find time for much practice, but made herself a black sequin dress to wear when she played in cabarets. I wore it for the leavers' dance at high school and Maurice Prentice told me that I gave him such a hard on that he could only dance stooped.

Maurice wasn't one of those Iris had any hopes of, but Nigel Utteridge and Denzil Smith were. Denzil and I were both keen on roller-skating and won the under sixteen figure skating title in Marlborough, not long after Mum and I shifted down from Horowhenua. Iris saw a magnificent future for us on the international circuit, like Torvill and Dean, with her managing the television interviews and contracts. She cut down the sequin cabaret dress, sewed in bra cups and I wore it for competitions. Nigel Utteridge was later. His parents were both doctors, would you believe. Each worked in a different practice so they could have professional independence. Mrs Dr Utteridge was quite confiding and told me there were no children after Nigel, because Mr Dr Utteridge was injured by the Big Dipper at the Tahuna fairground. Mr Dr Utteridge had the thickest, most muscular neck you can imagine, wider than his head even. He must have taken up the sport of butting at a very young age. Iris imagined me getting married to the son of two doctors and neither of us having to work again, just sit behind the receptionist's desk, lift our heads occasionally and say, Dr Utteridge will see you now, I'm sorry Dr Utteridge has been delayed by an outbreak of anthrax, Dr Utteridge is at present examining your uterine x-rays. Maurice Prentice was probably the best-looking guy I went out with early on, but very hormonal, always talking about cars and he walked with a stoop.

Sooner or later, Iris would say, our ship will come in. Over Kentucky Fried Chicken on her fiftieth birthday, she told me about this Grandma Moses who, at eighty, started painting pictures of her farm and became famous. The Grandma Moses in all walks of life were a marvel of reassurance to my mother. What can happen once, can happen twice, she said, and she was not afraid to work. She formed a co-operative when we were in Palmerston North. Herself and two huge twins called McIntosh, and they supplied hors d'oeuvres at functions. Salmon or crab finger pastries, gherkin, prune and pineapple on toothpicks, cheese balls, home-ground pâté and cinnamon sticks. They made a go of it, too, though Iris said that people didn't appreciate the cost of the fillings, but then the twin five minutes older than the other had an experience when delivering to the town clerk's farewell. A lap dog ran up inside her dress as she was carrying trays into the civic chambers and she went right off the business. Iris said the filthy little beast had ruined what could have been a catering empire, because that twin had the flair and they couldn't carry on afterwards.

I don't want you to think Iris's vision was a mercenary one. Money wasn't an end in itself. What Iris wanted was to force life to yield her something of value, something from the top drawer. She had no belief in a heaven and wanted a greater share of life. We all go down to the grave in the end, she'd say. Behind the library building, and no longer used, was the old cemetery on the slope. When I had the job at Hendry's cosmetic counter we would meet some lunchtimes and walk through the alleys of crushed, white quartz between the tombs. She would sigh, but only to cool the meat pies she liked for winter lunch. Iris was in fact cheerful in the cemetery for, of all the people on that slope, only she and I had any further hope of a shot at life. Died for King and Country, she might read for me, her meter maid shoes making a sensible crunch upon the quartz. Iris would eat strips from the top of her pie and the steam would wisp into the winter air.

Meter maiding was only one of Mum's skills. She believed in a variety of jobs to lure good fortune. In Christchurch she was a fish splitter for almost a year. Well, Lyttelton she actually worked in, but we lived at New Brighton. A bach over which the fine, grey sand would whisper when the sea wind blew through the marram grass. A millionaire's view of the ocean, Iris said. I was still young enough to need entertainment and she played the water pipes for me. By turning on the taps to different positions we could hear fog horns, fire engines, the howling jabberwocky. My schoolbag on the lino beside me, the smell of fish all the way from Lyttelton, the millionaire's view over the fritz haircut of the marram dunes, as I crouched by the lion paws of the bath to hear tubas, or what Iris said was the farting of the elephants in the jungle. I wouldn't be surprised if there's a way to make a career from this, she'd say, and the water is all free, she'd say. Called Home, or Till the Daybreak Comes, she read out in the cemetery of that later town. As I Am Now So You Must Be Prepare Yourself To Follow Me, as we opened up a bag of crisps, pausing by the dearly loved and much missed husband of Astral Pruitt while I explained the new gloss shades of half-pink, full-pink, mink-pink. Iris said that the pasty man had asked her to go to the trots with him, but she didn't like his lank hair. A man should have some bit of natural wave or curl in his hair, my mother reckoned. I had plenty of offers from men myself by that time and, while Iris never interfered, she did say that men made lousy friends, and that women knew how to stick together. Her own mother was a grand friend, she said, and in one tough year went into the city gardens and lopped off a branch to make a Christmas tree.

Mum was fascinated by those things which defy routine — a locust swarm, footsteps of *Homo erectus*, Halley's comet, which was certainly a fizzer, the Brewster kid who used to run howling round the block in Te Kuiti when his parents were fighting. Iris would take a cold sausage or potato out to him and he would snatch it on the trot with his face gleaming with tears in the streetlights. Iris was a good neighbour, though a temporary one. She babysat scores of kids who we never heard of again. Later she would send me out to do it. We received neighbourly kindness in return, of course. In the Brewster kid's Te Kuiti, I remember sneaking over each night to plug an extension cord into old Mr Hammond's work bench. He was rich and never went out after dark. While we lived there most of our power intensive activities were late at night. We had an adaptor plug into the water heater, and a large frypan for our main feed at nine or ten at night. When we had to leave Te Kuiti my mother made Mr Hammond a green, double-knit jersey with a V-neck and raglan sleeves. Only it had a narrow yellow band, because she was one green ball short.

From what Iris said, my grandmother must have been the same sort of person, though I never met her because she had Iris late and died in a nursing home somewhere in the North Island while we were living in Tuatapere. Iris was a school cleaner. There was a mill just down the road and the sawdust piles were mountain ranges there: the oldest peaks with the richest colours. Iris said that once I asked for a packed lunch to take to climb them. She couldn't afford to go up for the funeral. Her sister sent some of their mother's things down to her, including a sealed envelope addressed to Iris in her mother's handwriting. For days Iris left it unopened on the mantelpiece, and speculated on the way the contents would change our lives: how it might be the title deed to her father's brick house in Seatoun which she could not remember having been sold, or evidence that she had an illegitimate brother who had become a Cabinet minister in Brazil. The night we opened it we were having curried eggs for tea. The curry coloured the inside of Mum's mouth as she laughed to find clippings about my father's court appearances. This man deserted his wife and daughter, grandmother had written on the newspaper. Men are a different species, Iris told me over the curried eggs. Men are always alone, she said. My father had played squash twice a week for four years with a work-mate, yet never bothered to know where he lived, or how many children he had. Men don't ask anything of each other; it's both their weakness and their strength.

Iris was disappointed by the degeneration that happens to men as they age — hair grew all over my father's shoulders before he left, she said, as if he had died and the mould already begun. The oldest man I ever saw naked myself, was the physiotherapist who took a fancy to me in Putaruru. Being in his line of business he kept himself from the most obvious signs of mould, but he had eerily white, caved-in buttocks and besides, as I lay on my back on the carpet, I grew tired of looking at the unvarnished underside of his desk with the lines of the carpenter's pencil still clear.

My mother did better work than that. When we were in Bulls she saved for my kitset duchess, and spent hours getting the tracks aligned so that you could open and close the drawers with the tips of your fingers. Just radiata, but how she sanded it, then umpteen coats of dark stain and a clear finish. I've still got it; each scratch and discoloration is a mark of our life. Yet see, the drawers open with finger tips, the tracks have traces of the candle grease Iris dripped on with puckered lips of concentration. The wood smell evokes the rose-hips that in one Marlborough summer were a livelihood for Iris and me. We spent weeks picking them from the briars growing wild on the Wairau terraces and riverbed. It must have been my holidays and my mother had no better job. She picked into the pocket of a bag apron and, try as I might, I can't remember how we got out to the riverbed each day. We sold our harvest to the rose-hip syrup factory. The syrup was a big thing for children's health at the time. Dry river terraces with their rabbit scrapes, foxgloves, bleached grass stems and rose briars. Iris with her bag apron, floppy hat, bloodied knuckles. We're not licked yet, she said. We would have our sandwiches together on the stones, from a paper bag so often used that it had the soft creases of a dowager's face. She'd heard on the radio that the country was poised for great transformation and growth and she was determined that we would be swept along with it. The rose-hips were burnished in all that sun, almost ceramic with a red-yellow sheen. The last time I saw the sequin dress was when Iris offered it to me for Glenda's wedding dance. It had grown dull out of its time, as a lurid fish out of its element grows dull. Perhaps you're right, Iris said.

I'm surprised at all the places I've lived in. Ours was the off-season, budget sort of view of Wanganui, Blenheim, Lower Hutt and Bulls, Putaruru and Tuatapere. I never went surfing at Taylors Mistake, or had trout at Taupo Lodge, but I surely know the panoramic view of the Redruth tip, low before the sea, the gull flights wheeling like windmills above the plastic bags massed on the netting. A man putting tiles on the Oddfellows Hall in Invercargill was struck by lightning, yet not hurt much at all. Each working day as I went past, I could see where the spouting was dented as he fell. The windows were small and high to stop the rest of us from seeing what the Oddfellows were up to. Sometimes Iris and I walked past the hall together until we reached the lights, when she would turn right to old Mrs Brody, who gave her one of the last jobs she ever had, and I would walk on to Acme Smallgoods. Mrs Brody left Mum a Victorian washing bowl and jug used before plumbing was invented. Iris said the set would be worth a fortune today, because it was stamped Duenly Pottery, Sussex, underneath, but the jug was broken when our neighbour's tom jumped up at the budgie's cage. I keep a plant in the bowl now. That bowl is big enough to bath a baby, with bruise blue embossed leaves on it and pink roses.

I've had at least two chances to marry rich, apart from the son of the Drs Utteridge — a sheep farmer from the Hakataramea, and the owner of three rest-homes in Mount Eden. By then, though, neither Iris nor I saw marriage as such an easy step to success. The merino farmer never spoke more than seven words at a time, yet Iris said you've got to think hard about marrying. You've a responsibility to ask yourself if you really want someone coughing in the same bed, walking in and out of your house at will, telling you things about his life. She thought that men were best as visitors.

Iris went at sixty-four: only sixty-four, and I was there. I'd come down to visit her in the first and last house she ever owned. A married couple's house in Murchison, where prices were that cheap. Mum had put new iron on the laundry lean-to and, when the rain began, she took me out in delight to prove it didn't leak. Things were good for her, because she was on super by then and had plenty of work at the pub as well. She was a terrier for work. From the lean-to window we could see the rain cloud moving across the dark, native bush of the Murchison hills, and the rain dashed on the new tin roof. Send her down, Hughie, cried Iris, and she pointed out the good second-hand washing machine and the red lino she'd put down. There wasn't a leak, or a spider's web, in the place. Send her down, Hughie. I think it rains a good deal in Murchison, for the grass on the flats below the bush was lush and there were rushes in the dips. She used to say send her down, Hughie, when she comforted me during a winter we spent in a Johnsonville caravan. We're snug as a bug in a rug here, she'd say. I turned to say something of this to my mother in her Murchison laundry, but she was falling backwards with a stopped heart. As if pole-axed she went down, and any murmur against it I certainly didn't hear above the rain that Hughie sent down. I reckon she died still with the satisfaction of her own home, the new red lino, tin laundry roof, and some great thing to come, even if she never made supermarket star, lost family heiress, or became a medium who told the police of a dozen murder sites, like Beryl Judkins' aunt.

Beryl Judkins' parents took her camping to the Coromandel and she raved on at school about moonlight swims, campfires and pohutukawa blooms along the shore. I must have whined at home about our failure to have holidays, as a ten-year-old will, so Iris made a tent in our backyard by putting a sheet over the clothesline and anchoring the sides. We had onion chips and lemonade. We lay rolled in blankets watching the sky through the tent end. My mother told me about the black sequin dress she was planning to wear as a jazz sax player. I heard a hedgehog sorting for grubs in the currant bushes as Iris described the life of a cabaret star. Mr Thompson came out late on to his lawn for a leak and a spit. We were quiet until he was inside again. Sure, it wasn't Beryl Judkins' Coromandel. Mr Thompson once had his photo in the paper, because an ancestor had been killed at the Wairau Massacre, he said, and he wanted compensation from the government on behalf of the family. The fighting can't have been far from the bright rose-hips of years later.

We shifted away before there was any response to his claim, but Iris checked at the library anyway to see if anyone with our name had been massacred there. She said Bleekers had been in New Zealand since before the Treaty. We shifted because she was offered a job as assistant matron at Stanhope Preparatory School in Johnsonville, but when we arrived the assistant matron refused to leave, because her marriage plans had fallen through, and so we lived in a caravan at the motor camp until Iris became car groomer at Crimmond Motors.

It was a shock at the time, of course, Iris going like that, but I came to be glad she'd not suffered any sense of failure. She died in her first home and, although Hughie was sending it down outside, not a drop could get through to her red lino and washing machine. The certificate gave Murchison as the place of death; I just thought it strange as about the only one of all those towns and suburbs that I'd not shared with her. All those uncaring places where she had fed and clothed me, and so much more. We're not finished yet, she'd say. Some of us have to achieve what we can despite our lives, rather than as a consequence of them. So there was no supermarket stardom, no Lotto first division, no Brazilian millionaire, no double doctor marriage, no jazz sax cabarets in the sequin dress, not even my father coming back reformed and freshly shaved to start again. Just Iris, my mother, and me.

The Rose Affliction

~

MYRA WAS USING the orbital polisher in the staff cafeteria at Proudhams when she first saw the rose. She had been working for five hours, her asthma was bad again and her shoulders ached from hauling the polisher from side to side on the brown and yellow mottled lino. The first rose was in the extreme upper left of her vision, and as her head moved with the polisher, so the rose moved, skimming over the cafeteria lino, or rising up the pale walls when she lifted her eyes. At first Myra thought it just a temporary continuation of the patterned whorls on the floor, or of the enamelled manufacturer's crest on the central boss of the polisher. But it was quite clearly a small rose. The petals were flushed pink with the packed effort of escaping the green bud capsule.

Myra took one hand from the polisher to rub her eyes and then blinked several times, but although the rose blurred for a moment, it reformed perfectly. She could see the slightly crimped ends of the small petals, like a delicate, miniature clam, and the deeper tonings of colour towards the centre of the rose. She turned off the machine and opened her mouth to call out to Ruby, who was doing the executive suites not far away. As the whine of the polisher vanished down the empty night corridors, Myra thought how silly it would sound to complain of a rosebud in her eye, and how impossible to prove. She didn't know Ruby all that well, or trust her with personal things.

It was just that she was tired, Myra told herself: she would come right after a good sleep, and at fifty-nine she had experience of the tricks that body and mind could play on you, though menopause couldn't be blamed any longer. Her knees, for example, after all that wear in commercial cleaning, rattled like dredge buckets if she had to get down on to the floor, and her left ankle on a hot day would swell over the rim of her shoe if she had to stand a lot. She had a frozen shoulder, found it an agony to have to work her right arm above the level of her head. Not that she mentioned those things to the supervisor.

But nevertheless, to see a rose was an oddity: like a transfer, or a logo, high left in her vision and superimposed on anything that she looked at there. Even in the bucket of water, milky with disinfectant, that Myra used for the urinals, the pink rose could be seen, and as Myra had a lift home with Ruby, because Wayne was out in her car, the imposition of the rose continued. 'We'll get double time if we do the two extra hours on Sunday at the Super Doop Market,' said Ruby. As Myra looked at her to answer, the pink rosebud glowed in Ruby's straight, brown hair.

The rose was still in her eye when she woke: had gained company in fact, a darker pink, larger bloom, past its best so that the full petals exposed the straw-coloured stamen of the centre — a round cluster like the cleaning brush Myra's dentist used on his drill. 'Weird,' said Wayne, as he asked her for a loan and, without waiting for an answer, began scrabbling in her purse.

'What do you think I should do about it?' she asked her son.

'Does it hurt?' It didn't hurt at all; just the oddity of it concerned her, and what it might represent as a symptom or warning of something going wrong. 'Well, I'd say just keep on normally then,' said Wayne. 'You don't want to miss work unless you have to. Not with double time at the Super Doop coming up.'

Myra was pleased with Wayne's matter-of-fact response, but she didn't say anything to Ruby, or any of the others at work, although there was a steady growth of roses over the following weeks. They massed to the left of her sight, roses of all colours and types, so that when she was cooking or cleaning, at home or at work, the blossoms were imposed on everything she saw. They festooned the cafeteria tables she wiped clean and softened the blatant commercialism of the Super Doop.

Myra developed a rather off-putting habit of cocking her head sideways in an effort to bring those things she wished to view into the clear area of vision that remained. 'What on earth's got into her?' said Ruby to the supervisor.

'You'd better see the quack,' said Wayne reluctantly at home.

'You realise that it isn't actually the image of a rose,' said Dr Neumann. 'Perhaps a vibratory retinal effect, but more likely organic particles in the vitreous or aqueous humour of the eyes. It is in fact quite common for some opaque cells to be there from birth, or to detach in later life from inner surfaces.'

'Oh, they're roses all right,' said Myra.

'Indeed. Are they "Charlotte Armstrong" then, or perhaps "Diamond Jubilee"?' Dr Neumann was not accustomed to being contradicted.

'I don't know one from another,' she said, humbled.

'The images don't drift you say, though. That's the difficult thing to reconcile with cells in the fluid. There's a drifting effect normally in such cases. I think that we had better make an appointment with Mr Hardie. There's nothing to worry about. He will introduce drops to dilate your pupils before the examination, but there's no discomfort.'

No discomfort, but a considerable wait, Myra found. A specialist's appointment can take months for all but the urgent cases. In the meantime the roses multiplied, white, yellow and red, until they were scrolled over much of Myra's sight, and she saw the world through an increasingly profuse floral lattice of glowing petals and frog-green small leaves. The roses obscured the urinals, and the smeared tables and walls that Myra was meant to clean. Instead of stains and accumulated grease, scuffs and carpet fluff with blowflies, all of which had been her responsibility in life, she had a host of roses closing in.

'But no scents at all. That's the queer thing, and a pity really,' Myra told Mr Hardie, who looked up from his examination to smile to the nurse. Myra could see one side of that smile above a cluster of yellow floribunda.

'We'll keep a check on its progress,' he said. For all his kind intentions he could find neither cause nor cure. 'Don't hesitate to contact me if you experience the least pain,' he told her and, later on the phone to Dr Neumann, agreed it was an unusual and rather tragic case.

'She can't see to work anymore,' Ruby said to the supervisor. 'I can't bear to imagine her cut off from us all. Oh, it's so sad, isn't it? And there's no operation will help, they say.'

'We'll have to get you right on to the sickness benefit,' was Wayne's opinion, 'and the car had better be put in my name, as you won't be able to drive anymore.'

The last roses to come were the richest — and the darkest. Though Myra sat in the sunroom with her face to the window, for her the roses were the enduring and exclusive view. The last roses fitted as if completing a cathedral window, and they bloomed so velvet, so red; downy black-red, red-black. The colour of the blood that goes back to the heart.

Heating the World

~

TUCKER LOCKE WASN'T married until he was forty-two. A cheerful woman from the Taieri with good legs and three daughters finally decided to move north for the sun and take him in hand. Before that Tucker was one of a group of bachelor farmers so typical of the New Zealand heartland that they form a sub-species of the population.

After his mother died, Tucker had done for himself, as the saying goes, and with his cooking he just about did for anybody else who called as well. He had lived in traditional rural simplicity rather than poverty. He had an average downland mixed farm worth about half a million in bad years, and camped in his own home — a tartan rug on the porch bed, a laundry that still had a copper, and yesterday's paper as a tablecloth at breakfast as he read today's.

It wasn't that Tucker was a failure as a farmer, not at all, but his financial priorities and lifestyle were congenital. Super and drench, a new post-hole digger, or drill, the best stock and certified seed, were the natural expenses of life, but to buy a new lampshade, or replace the kitchen lino for reason of colour co-ordination, would no more enter his head than to dine at the Victor Hugo restaurant in town when he had food in his own home. A four and a half thousand dollar skeet gun, on the other hand, or an irrigation mule at twenty thousand, were perfectly justifiable purchases.

The sub-species of rural bachelordom is perpetually renewed, of course, by the very process of attrition which reduces its contemporary generation. By the time he was forty even Tucker had become aware that he was no longer typical among his acquaintances, and that there were deficiencies in a comparative sense. At the tables of his married friends he developed a taste for lasagne and apple strudel. His devotion to cold mutton, mashed potato and swede was somewhat undermined, and the sight of children forced him to consider the fact that his farm had no heir. So, advised by his friend Neville O'Doone, who had taken the plunge a few years before, Tucker began the display which indicated that he was willing as well as eligible. He appeared in the retail area of his local town, wore a woollen tie with his sportscoat and attended a few mixed gender events such as the trots and the show.

The community considered Tucker very fortunate in his marriage, and so did Tucker, nevertheless he had no knowledge of modern women, and the marriage brought changes he had not predicted. Neville O'Doone was his counsel in such things, always in the informal and off-hand way that the sub-species deals with the deepest matters of the psyche.

Tucker and Neville were travelling together to an open day on shelter belt trials at Methven when Tucker first sought advice from his friend. They had been commenting on the management and condition of the properties they passed, doubtful of the future for Romney wool, when Tucker abruptly referred to Neville's wife.

'Margaret likes soap, I suppose,' he said.

'Soap?'

'Women like soaps: a variety of soaps and things,' said Tucker. 'I counted seven along the bath last night, and all partly used, you know.' His laugh had good-humoured ease as its intention, but conveyed bewilderment instead. Neville told him that he meant shampoos. 'Shampoos, all different colours,' agreed Tucker. 'One oily, one normal, one dry, a body shampoo, a protein conditioner, an apricot facial scrub, and one enriched with the natural oil of some sort of pretzel which grows only in the Orinoco. And soft pink soap which turns to a slush like snow, and vanishes as rapidly.'

Neville could recall Tucker's bathroom before his marriage: one block of yellow soap on which it was easier to work up a sweat than a lather, and with dirt settled into its seams as it weathered so that it was grained like a metamorphic rock. 'It's mostly liquid stuff they buy,' said Tucker sadly. 'It just runs away. You've no idea. It just runs away down the plughole. And women don't like to share a bath, do they? We've put in a shower as well. I could dip a mob of two-tooths in the time my girls take to shower.' In a half-hearted way Neville tried to persuade Tucker that shampoos and conditioners weren't really soaps. 'All do soaps' job,' affirmed Tucker. 'Can you believe seven different bottles, and others besides. Bath salts and that.'

'Oh, yes,' said Neville, but then he'd been married some years before Tucker. He felt a little superior: the sort of superiority you feel when up to your waist in quick-sand, but observing someone else in up to his neck. 'But you wouldn't want to go back to being single again would you, Tucker?'

'Oh, no. Hell, no,' said Tucker, but his face was pensive, as if regarding a moun-tain of expensive saponaceous products degrading in natural atmospheric humidity.

They were together at the gun-club when next Tucker raised his home life. Neville had commented on a flash, wine shirt his friend was wearing. 'Pull,' said Tucker, and fired. 'Yes, Dianne thinks I should have some new things. My clothes seem to be wearing out more rapidly these days.'

'How come?' Neville hadn't noticed Tucker working any harder than usual.

'I reckon my stuff is getting worn away in the washing machine,' said Tucker guardedly. 'Women love to get the clothes from my back.'

'Do they indeed, you old dog.'

'I mean for washing. I've always felt myself it takes a day or two to feel comfort-able in what you're wearing, but Dianne has it into the machine before I'm hardly used to it. Continual washing is bad for the stitching, I'd say, and seems to be shrink-ing the waistbands, but there's no telling her. I'm getting quite a wardrobe now, you know.'

It was true. For twenty years Neville had identified Tucker off his own property by his blue checked sportsjacket, but he was becoming more difficult to spot since marriage, as his colouration varied. 'Women have a good deal of clothes, you know,' said Tucker with some vehemence.

'I know.'

'My daughters have a drawer of pants each. Whole drawers of pants.' Tucker lifted his hands to emphasise the incredibility of it, then let them fall helplessly to his side. Tucker had been accustomed to maintain three pairs of underpants — one to wear, one to wash and one to change into. He couldn't comprehend the necessity of any other regime. 'Scores of them,' he whispered absently. It was axiomatic for Tucker that clothes were used until they were worn out, the same sensible approach he took to cull ewes, or tarpaulins for the hay shed, yet he was confronted with a philosophy which discarded garments because puce was no longer in fashion, or because the pleats had a tendency to accentuate the hips. 'Margaret buys a fair amount of clothes?' asked Tucker.

'From time to time, yes,' said Neville. Tucker's expression lightened. If headlong expense was universal in wives, he was human enough to feel pleased that he had company in being a witness and somewhat reluctant backer.

'You're getting to understand why women look better than men. One reason, anyway,' said Neville.

'I guess you're right,' said Tucker. 'I've got two suits myself now, though I can't see that people are going to die regularly enough for me to need to alternate them.'

Tucker still shot well, however, despite his financial concern, Neville noted rue-fully. He has an eye like a stinking eel, Tucker has. He shot everything out of the air with almost vindictive skill and won another top gun sash and a side of hogget. Neither he nor Neville thought to relate the cost of their day to the conversation.

Tucker and Neville met on sale days at the Dobb Hotel, the only one in town that hadn't put in a barbecue and outdoor seating. Tucker drank draught beer, but slipped in a Glenfiddich every now and again as a chaser. It was in the Dobb that Tucker confided further in Neville concerning his personal life. They had been talk-ing about the Celtic-Old Boys game, and Neville said Ransumeen wasn't talented enough to bring on the oranges at half-time. 'I've rather gone off fruit,' said Tucker, after a pause during which they both watched through the window Gus McPhedron trying to climb into the back of his utility for a nap. Neville found it difficult to follow Tucker's claim, for old Mrs Locke had been a great one for utilising their own orchard, and their pantry had held rows of bottled plums, peaches and quince jam. She had showed them even, in the produce section of the A & P show. There had been boxes of wrinkled autumn apples in the laundry and Tucker normally had one or two in his pocket, or the glove compartment of the truck. He had a kelpie once which liked eating them, but Tucker had shot it for biting his best ram in a costly fashion. Neville said something of all that. 'No, no,' said Tucker. 'You don't under-stand. There's bought fruit, see.' His tone was one of shocked disclosure. Fruit was nature's bounty, something that arose naturally from one's land without great atten-tion, and with no mercenary aspects. Ah, but since his marriage, Tucker had been introduced to mandarins and melons, pawpaws and peppers, passion fruit, oranges and kiwi fruit.

'Do you know how much a feijoa costs?'

'Well, ah,' said Neville.

'Much more,' said Tucker. 'We have bananas often in a bowl together with oranges and pears.' Tucker was half defiant, half distraught, convinced that such hubris would bring his ruin. 'This morning I looked at the ticket on one of the bananas. They each have their own ticket, you know. It had come from Ecuador. Ec-u-a-dor!' Tucker was silent after his syllabic exclamation, which had drawn looks from other tables. He was considering the number of chargeable exchanges and activities needed to get a banana from the plantations of Ecuador to his wooden fruit bowl in Te Tarehi. Gus McPhedron was asleep in the ute outside, the tail-gate down, the sun glinting on his tan stock boot. 'And the thing is, see, that often fruit goes off before it's eaten and has to be thrown out.' The concept of produce purchased from the ends of the earth, and then thrown out, was arsenic to Tucker's peace of mind. Almost bitterly he downed another Glenfiddich. 'No one bothers to eat a quince, or a plum, these days,' he told a sagely nodding Neville. 'The whole crop lies beneath the trees in the orchard for the wasps and the birds.'

'But what's that against all the advantages of marriage,' asked Neville.

'Oh, you're right there,' said Tucker. 'Of course I wouldn't change for the world.'

Yet at the Town versus Country game, in the first half, when the action was mainly down the other end, Tucker voiced further anxiety. He had picked up his family from town the night before and unfortunately been exposed to some of the prices. 'You know how much a lipstick costs, just one?' he asked. Neville was embarrassed in case some of their mates heard, but they were too busy abusing the town ref. 'Twenty-nine dollars thirty-nine,' said Tucker. 'It's true. It's true. And how often do you see a tube used right up? Answer me that.'

'You're blind and bloody half-witted with it,' shouted Neville.

'And Sarah wanted some shoes for aerobatics,' said Tucker as the Town took their penalty.

'You mean aerobics,' Neville said.

'Right.'

'You see aerobatics is —'

'Okay,' said Tucker.

'So she wanted sports shoes.'

'I went in with her myself,' said Tucker. 'Reddickers had a sale and I found a decent pair reduced to fifty-five dollars.'

'That's reasonable enough,' said Neville.

'Oh, but they wouldn't do. Not enough heel cushioning for the effects of aerobics, the woman said. A lot of people did structural damage to their feet that way, she said, and Sarah said her friends had different ones. You wouldn't believe what I had to pay before I got out of that shop.'

'Tell me,' said Neville. 'Back up your man, Cecil, for Christ's sake. That boy's all prick.' But Tucker couldn't bear to mention the actual amount in all its grotesque enormity.

'Six lambs at today's schedule prices,' he said, and even the sight of the Town's captain being taken off on a stretcher barely lightened his spirits. 'Six lambs, can you credit it — And all for jumping about in.'

On their way back from the match, Neville and Tucker heard on the car radio that there was progress at the great power summit. 'They're wanting more changes,' said Tucker pensively. Neville thought he was referring to the world leaders, but after some confusion realised that Tucker was meaning his wife and daughters. Perhaps it was just a matter of scale after all, though. 'Interior renovations,' said Tucker, as if giving Neville a medical diagnosis of some significance.

'So?' said Neville.

'First grade Axminster, designer wallpaper, new drapes.' Tucker was marking them off on his fingers as he spoke, and steering with upward pressure of his knees. It seemed that Tucker's wife was determined that the good room get the works. 'Ceiling repainted, pelmets removed, droop light fittings and new fire surround tiles of Tuscan red. We'll use the room a good deal more because of it, of course,' said Tucker to console himself, yet the car shimmied because Tucker's knees were trembling.

'It's improving your asset, Tucker,' said Neville. 'There's that as well.'

'That's true,' said Tucker. Neville's considerate response encouraged him to further revelation. 'We all have duvets now,' he continued, his tone wavering between pride and defensiveness. 'Yes, duvets on all the beds, and now we have a double dozen unused blankets folded in the cupboard.' Tucker had pressed past anxiety to a state almost of awe. The grandeur of the extravagance conditioned him to expect some providential punishment. All those blankets that had provided sensible warmth for generations of Lockes, now stored with good wear still in them, and duvets purchased in their bedstead. It couldn't be right in the view of a Calvinistic God. 'Of course I'm a believer in progress,' said Tucker stoutly.

'A lot of the improvements have been on you, haven't they?' said Neville. 'I mean Dianne's done you up proud since you've been married.'

'True, true,' said Tucker. Neville was thinking of Tucker's wet weather gear. In the old dairy next to the back door there had been an array of Locke coats going back into rural antiquity. Tucker's favourite had been a sou'-wester which must have defied the last ice-age, and although the cuffs were frayed completely away, the coat itself remained so stiff that if Tucker took it off between cloud bursts, it would stand like a tent in the wet grass. And it blended in with the landscape so well that even the wiliest mallard couldn't pick Tucker out in the mai-mai.

'That new nylon parka, for example,' said Neville.

'An anorak,' said Tucker. 'You ever heard of an anorak?'

'Oh yes,' said Neville complacently, as a well-married man.

'A bright, red anorak.'

'Very fetching.'

In frosty July, Tucker and Neville went to a euchre evening at Wally Tamahana's. Afterwards as they stood in the moonlight to enrich the nitrogenous content of the lawn, Tucker spoke with unease of the range of alternative milks with which he was forced to become familiar since he was persuaded to abandon a house cow. Red tops, blue tops, green tops, banded tops, low fat, non-lipid, reduced cholesterol, anti-coagulate, mineral free. Tucker claimed he could see a logical trend in it all: the more things were removed from the milk the more the product cost. 'You know,' he said to Neville 'soon we'll pay the highest price of the lot for milk with everything extracted — and it'll be water.'

'It's all progress, I suppose,' said Neville, but he too could remember the cream jug of his boyhood in which the spoon would stand upright.

'Right. Right. Of course I wouldn't have it any other way,' said Tucker bitterly.

Neville was deliberately cheerful as he drove Tucker home, but Tucker, having lost fifty-seven dollars at the euchre to Wally Tamahana, was in a mood to resent any hint of extravagance in others. They rattled over the cow-stop at the entrance to Tucker's farm and drove up the track. The median grass not yet brittle with frost whispered beneath the car, and the lights and the moon picked out the massed stinging nettles by the hen-house and sheep yards. Tucker's house was a focus of activity and warmth: every room seemed to be lit, and one of Tucker's new daughters was singing along with her cassette player. Neville thought it grandly welcoming, but Tucker gave a whimper. 'The door. Ah, God.' The back door was open in defiance to the vast, surrounding winter night, and the glow of double bar heaters could be seen. 'Look, look,' said Tucker brokenly. ' We're heating the world.'

Literary Fair

~

YES, FOLKS, IT'S Lit-rature land at its very best, a stroll down the culled de sac of cultural bequests. Our British light section is the envy of all arcane arcades. (Believe me, madam, he'll be perfectly secure with us. Pick him up in ten minutes at the Moriarty gates.) Just keep to the track, follow me, and don't touch the exhibits, for they're completely irreplaceable, you see. Smooth your dress down, Anna my dear, and look after the little ones; rendezvous at the Cheshire cat, or the Dr Doolittle zoo. Take her hand, dearly beloved, there's a treat in store for you: off to that wonderful world inside the Pied Piper's mountain. Oh, a land of no mummies and daddies, just kind aunties and nannies, barber striped candy and chocolate fountains, and pierrots and carousels, and wise old owls that philosophise and tortoises that instruct. There's fairy dust to sprinkle, and a never never land. There's tin soldiers and tinder-boxes, and mice with mustard spats. Little Black Sambo and gollywogs, and handicapped people as villains. Blind Pew, fingerless Black Dog and Captain Hook are nonconformity. A land of innocent frilly dresses and suck a thumb cherubs, and goose-girls, and Cook all warm in flannelette who lets us steal Madeira cake while the adults are dressing for dinner. Come potter in the land of Green Ginger, where plovers and curlews are calling. Hear the rattle of the tilt cart, and the fairy caravan. Everybody pitches in, you know, even Milly Molly Mandy. The mock turtle's a standing joke for his mathematical creator: the single print of the day of the week is acknowledged as living theatre. The fox uses a Latin tag in talk with a well-dressed drake, and every stump has a small red door which leads to another land. Meet me there, Anna my dear, meet me there. Bunter of the lower fifth foils the mad scientist once more, by sagacity and loyalty and crumbs laid on the floor. Oh, it's the boys' own annual fête with China or Indian tea, and the Lord of Blandings nonplussed fours are seen in baronial halls. Oh, Fritz the Hun is on the run from constable Plod my friend, and a white Russian princess is gloriously saved by the charge of the 9th Hussars. And Prepington-Smythe of Scotland Yard heads down to Paddington Quay. The Queen's word is clearly heard in a hundred tribal districts, and law has come back with the drums' beat to subjugate the jungle. The Commissioner brushes a ginger moustache and narrows his eyes in the sun. Day after day with fairness and calm he rules the vast Mungapopo, and at night in his tent with a gin and a lime he says not a word of why he is there for the honour of Lady Cecilia. See Ellen will take in the tea things, for the gypsies are camping again by the oaks of harpenny field. Oh, it's Wooster's sauce we must laugh at, he's the devil's own chap for a prank. Yes, and cut along young Delacombe, or you'll be late for chapel. They're changing the guard at Buckingham Palace; it's shoulder to shoulder with Englishmen and follow the fun to Khartoum. It's potted ham and honey for tea, and the curate's a fatuous ninny: it's striding along in the wolds and the fens and not caring for stains on the pinny. Oh to think of it, oh to dream of it, fills my heart with tears. Come and eat our fill again at the wonderful Wodehouse café. It's Saunderson's last race, and the price is paid in full. Squeers is blamed — and Joe Gargery? We're ashamed to be ashamed of him. Mungo Park and Livingstone are modern Marco Polos: assegai are raised on high at the mouth of King Solomon's mine. The capstan winds a tale or two for cabin boys and bosuns. There's an indrawn hiss as the black spot's sighted, ah, Jim lad so there is. There's grottos of immortals and each lingers in the mind: Edward Whymper, Captain Trotter and R.E. Prothero. Oh, huzzah for E.J. Trelawny and the adventures of a younger son, huzzah for Peacock's English prose from Mandeville to Ruskin. Oh huzzah, huzzah, for the rallying cry of the indomitable 9th Hussars. Camping holidays what a wheeze, with Wodger and William, and no hint of panky in the dark, not even thoughts of hints of panky in the dark. Oh, it's mistletoe and holly, and a communist robin all the year. And a chimney sweep to be discovered with talent, scrubbed up and sent to Grammar. The wreckers are out on the Cornish coast and the revenue men are massing. The mad woman in white flits over the moor, the laird reviews his crofters. So cut along young Dewkesbury, or you'll be late for chapel. Three cheers for threequartermain, hurrah for Ralph and Peterkin, and dinghies on the Yar. But psst, psst, beware of the man with the scar! Cads and bounders, rotters and blighters, sneaks and heaps of uriah. We'll cut them dead without a nod of the head, and pass with a careless laugh. And Kitchener's grim and determined for the sake of the old country. Oh, steady the blues, steady the blues, don't fire till the light of the Khyber glints on the blades from Kandahar. Don't trust the French master new to the school, we've always judged him a rum 'un. It's nine wickets down, two runs to win, and the captain's taking the strike. He's a good type of chap and plays a straight bat, and tries to take after his pater. Though whether the family is really quite county we're bound to find out later. Oh, the Afghan passes from hand to mouth, and Purun Bhagat is seen again in grinning Kali's shrine. Absolutely everyone is part of our kith and kin, we'll have no rank out-siders to tamper with the cellars, for there's some jolly splendid Medoc, laid down by the fourth baronet. The game's afoot I surmise, Watson, bring the slipper and a ser-vice revolver. Now you girls follow me, and try to keep from blubbing. Do what you're told, be good scouts, and we'll fox them yet against the odds. And cut along young Pountney, or you'll be late again for chapel. It's rotten luck for Archie, but Biggles is coming, you'll see. There's the code of silence, the stiff upper lip, law of the jungle, the done thing, a fair crack of the whip, and the honour of the British Raj. The svelte veldt is a customary place for the regiment to die. All in the donger together, with a jibe at the fates as they wait. And in the south quad late tonight, there's Queensberry rules between the Head of House and the foreign chappie with a shock-ing cut to his jacket. Oh the sounds of the Kerry pipers, oh the shouts of the 9th Hussars. Stand by the captain against mutinous crews, rescue the runt of the litter. Play in the attic and orchard, stomp in the mud with your wellies. But is that a hunchback at the darkened window! He at the Hall is frightfully grand, but never puts on any side. He's even developed a stutter, it seems, to put other chaps at their ease. When the Toad comes home: when the Toad comes home. How splendid a recitation. And Ratty and Mole are always loyal to the muscular Christianity of Badger. It's Baden-Powell for ever, and never a thought of panky. It's Kaffirs and Boers falling neck and koppie before the 9th Hussars. And brother Mycroft, from the smoking room of his cherry leather club, summons a hansom woman to carry an esoteric clue to Prepington-Smythe of the Yard. Pluck, puck, luck and the good old school will surely see us through, and we'll never be found a shirker. There's watchers along the paper chase, with moleskin trousers and hair on their cheeks, and ominous dark felt hats. And you know, old chap, deuced if it doesn't, it all comes down to you. Play up and all that, do your bit, we know we can rely on you. Up and at them, the Blues. Take my hand upon the truth of it, and follow to the ends of the earth, for when the salt of the Government's taken, there's no turning back at the pass. Nancy's for it, I'm afraid, she sees what no woman should. The subalterns grow pensive in their cups, and the children from the orphanage sing thankful carols in the snow. It's a damn near thing, but we'll see it through at odds of thirty to one. Goodbye Mr Potter, goodbye farmer Meek, goodbye Aunt Polly and the road to Manderley. Goodbye to Cook and Nanny and the pert little parlous maid. Goodbye to midnight feasts, and goodbye school bully with a squint — the beast. The hare and the houndstooth are nearly done, the race of life is nearly won. And a Gothic moon leers in at the madmen in all the secret rooms. So here's to Landseer paintings, and here's to the 9th Hussars. Here's to life at the Grange, and to Prepington-Smythe of the Yard. Here's to the purple sashes and blushing rosettes all on the harness room wall. Here's to Toby and Runnymede Glen, and the turrets of Baskerville Hall. Here's to the Forsyte an Englishman shows in planning for his future. Here's to endless summer Hols. Here's to pikelets and scones and strawberry jam, bluebells and hyacinths, cobblestones and slates, cousins in the country, new people at the manor. Here's to furling the topsoil gallants, and claymores raised by the tartan clans in honour of '45. Here's to the little people and animals that talk; here's to the toadstool kingdom and cowslip wine. Here's to the hills of Simla, and the Pathan of the days. Here's to the sense of duty and regimental ways. Here's to roses over the cottage door, and plaintive minstrel lays. Ah, here's to all those things so bravely done within the covers. Here's to every decent chap, as British as an apple. So cut along young Fothergill, or you'll be late for chapel.

Yes, folks, it's Lit-rature land, and all your old friends were there: some of the paint is chipped, it's true, and the costumes a little soiled, but we move so much from place to place to satisfy the punters. Ah, no photos, sorry, we're very strict on that. Keep it all in the mind — it's our livelihood, you see: but come again, come again, if you've the genuine price of admission.

Don't Wake Beside Me

~

DON'T WAKE BESIDE me, for there's no continuation here, no ending even, that can complete our night. The rocket falls unseen from its fiery ascent and rainbow burst. The hair is still pushed back from your face, roughly combed by my fingers in the dark. Your lips have wet the pillow while you sleep, and as you had no time to take your face off, the chinked light from the curtain's edge smudges your eyeliner. So, you Cleopatra, you.

Honk, honk. Yes old Baz, I admit the ridicule is clear. Every jest and verse he knew to pass the time. A German officer crossed the Rhine, parley vous, parley vous. He told the world that the angle of the dangle depended on the heat of the meat. A hard case, bit of a dag, real joker, always good for a laugh. A manifest old goat and smelling like it: we can pin our sins on him and despise him for it. Honk, honk, old Baz, gaga now in an eventide home, I suppose, and boasting to the wall of how many he put in the pudding club. How coarse a fabric he could weave from the stuff of life. Inky pinky parley vous, as the actress said to the bishop.

When you sat across from me and talked to Wilkinson of your campaign for individual employee contracts, it was your hands I paid attention; supple, strong tendons like the ribs of a fan. Your nails were water clear, and short in a practical way. And the light woman's voice of you. Your smile tugged at the corners of your mouth: your blouse was ruffled on your hip.

Don't wake beside me. Don't tell me with a smile, or deadpan face, there's no obligation because of it. Don't talk of it when all that is left of a good red and the cheeseboard is my stale breath above the covers. When you wake, the real time will end, or start. The evolution of our nature has accustomed us to value continuity in our experience, which is not always the benefit we assume. Any discussion of what we have done imposes boundaries and definitions, is a process of reduction.

Honk, honk, old Baz would say. His office desk was closest to the window, so that he could see the women passing in the mall. Built for comfort not for speed. What a pair! Thighs like a wild mare. Wouldn't mind getting my balls caught in that rat-trap. A month's wages, oh my God, just to slip a link in there, Baz would say. Get up them stairs. I'm only thirteen. I'm not superstitious; get up them stairs. Honk, honk. Does old Baz speak for us all, though we deny it and despise him? Baz confided in me that every time he scored (and that not often, surely, old Baz) he wondered if it would be the last woman for the last time. He found it incapacitating, Baz said, the event and opportunity suddenly invested with such significance. The end of that life faced him. I suppose that I am now about the age that Baz was then. An ugly thought. Honk, honk, he'd say, I need my rations. The whippet needs a run. The wick needs dipping. Honk, honk. Mrs Palmer's the young man's friend, but not first choice of company, Baz always told us. Shut up, we said. The louder he gave his jackass laugh, the more lonely were his eyes. And somewhere, of course, there will be the last woman, for the last time.

Don't wake beside me and begin the disintegration. Full light will discover the wear on your blue shoes, and on my balding head, before I have the chance to comb my hair in a disguise, that you have a toenail blackened perhaps by a falling breadboard a week ago. Don't tell me with enthusiasm of the TV show I find most moronic, or let me bore you with oblique aspersions on my peers. The air-conditioning has dried my lips and throat, and anyway I'm never much at breakfast conversation. I find it awkward to balloon the trivial and would rather make a face and go.

Never quite strangers, you and I; we saw each other in the course of similar work for similar employers, but the juxtaposition of our routines was set and so formed our feelings in the same way. Now, however, a symposium no less, with mutual accommodation and chairs revisited from plenary sessions in the conference room. You were the only one to laugh at the keynote speaker's malapropism, then looked down and bit your lip.

They laid on a happy hour each night, with all the jollity that instant friends create, and Willcocks from Whangarei charmed us long enough with his Muldoon impersonations. Those sisters from Christchurch were more vocal than you. Their laughter added balance to the middling wines: laughter which prevented the business bores from perpetuating their tyranny of the day. Yours was the breast, though; the perfect form the bra cup could not duplicate, so that a little space was there which diminished with a breath, and formed again. I watched with the sad envy of middle-aged desire, and squandered a friendship in my conversation to raise a laugh — from you. The few dark hairs on your small wrist were like commas on ivory paper.

Yet that night I dreamt not of your supple wrist, but of being vacuum cleaned in the main street along with other passers-by. In the common illogic of that world my concern was not that it should be customary, but that the prying nozzle would expose my old fellow — soft, wrinkled, the shrivelled filling of a cold sausage roll. Such a fear that I almost woke to the whine of the air-conditioning, but then lapsed back to meet my first boss, who died bungy jumping at fifty-four. He sucked his teeth in the old way to ponder a problem and asked, as always, for Indian tonic in his drink. All the same in a hundred years he told me. Siss ss-ssh; the breath drew through his teeth. Did he have time for one last, indrawn breath, I wonder, on the bungy cord? Will it all be the same in a hundred years, and what consolation is that?

I shall burst, old Baz would cry, if I can't get a shot away. His eyes would be blood-shot with the pressure. Honk, honk. Old Baz whose soldier stood to attention, so hopeful of an engagement, so seldom called to arms. Tell us the one about the ele-phant and the librarian, that's a good one, Baz. Honk, honk. Who else in the firm knew the twenty-seven verses of *Eskimo Nell*, and the chugalug refrain, or the nipple song, yet to remember any more than a single professional task, Baz had to use the office memo paper, which he then usually misplaced. A deep understanding of women, had old Baz. They all like it, but some like it more than others, was the basic tenet of his creed. Honk, honk, sings Abdul Abulbul Emir. Get up them stairs. My mother won't like it. Your mother's not getting it, get up them stairs. He had the loud-est office laugh, but I never saw him smile to himself in all those years. Baz, the old mutton gun soldier. The old pretender.

Let me be most truthful while you sleep, and take your silence as assent. Other expla-nations are more comfortable, more laudable, more convenient, but the truth is I don't need your friendship, though I'd welcome it, can get by without your expertise in workplace equity management. Yourself is all you have that I find indispensable, or ideal. How bad does that sound to you? Yet it is the truth — I think. If you com-plain that I want only that, then isn't the disparagement your own. Only that! Only the smooth belly and the matchless thigh, the shoulder blade beneath my palm. Only that. Only the gift of beauty and of joy. If men express themselves so poorly that women have cause to feel demeaned, then accept apologies for the deficiencies, not the need, or the gift.

A knowing hand to make a cowling for my cock: those mild-loving pornographies which make life more than the living of it. Can you laugh in your throat again, can you whisper, can you flutter. Your eye make-up is smudged, Cleopatra. I watch a pulse in the curve of your neck. Shall I kiss there? So don't wake beside me. Don't ask what follows the pulse in the neck, the fine laughter lines at the corner of your mouth; a night well spent, spent.

Didn't you know, would cry old Baz with delight. Oh, yes. A real porker, hot to trot, an absolute nympho, never gets enough. I thought everyone knew that. Honk, honk. We could be in there, old son, though somehow events usually conspired against old Baz. He told me gloomily that he'd seen firm statistics that at any given moment only point five percent of the earth's population was copulating, and that even among men only the figure was less than two percent. Oh, look at the bristols on her, Baz would say. I wouldn't mind a piece of that. Towards the end I had to talk to him officially about his language to the women on the staff. An awkward task given to me on promotion, when it was Baz who'd kindly helped me when first I joined. With righteous tact and understatement, I gave him a reprimand, censure for his dirty mind.

Honk, honk. Old Baz saw all of his life as just a context for the act of union, yet had no language to give it dignity. Am I the same as Baz, despite all my denials? Sleeping, you require no answer.

In our night to bear down, and hear the tempo of breathing and of words altered by our mutual grasp. That must mean a unity of sorts, don't you agree? In the act of love is life most strongly affirmed, and death most scorned. This French little death is an inoculation against the form most grim and absolute — for a time at least. A brief assertion which defies intellect, but by which instinct is assuaged. Oh, yes indeed. There are realms where words and logic have no power: red and golden tulips flare and jostle there, with no stems to grasp. So don't wake beside me, don't even whisper in your sleep.

Honk, honk. Be quiet, old Baz, and wipe your chin. Toothless in your eventide with the candles closing in.

Don't wake beside me, when in art one of us would take leave, take and leave, leave a single red rose against the white sheet. So let me write that clean, quick ending of our night, as if it could be. Your arm across the bed to seek the bloom, the tremor of the petals on your skin, Cleopatra, and myself withdrawing. In every man is that hunger for a woman he has not wounded.

Don't wake beside me.

Pluto

~

I SAW HIM first in the pool — a blue, free-standing motel pool set in high duckboards and with a fence of the same boards for privacy, and to stop toddlers from straying in to drown. Wesley Smith was very thin. He gripped the pool ladder and floated like a spider monkey, with his arms and legs spread yet bent. His feet were lunar pale beneath the clear water, and his shins sunburnt. I don't suppose there is a great opportunity to build up a tan in prison administration.

My wife and Jean had taken a liking to each other as soon as they met in the motel laundry. They had been to the gallery together, to the shops. 'Her husband runs a prison,' my wife had told me. It was an indirect introduction to Wesley Smith, and I briefly indulged the fancy that he was the Mr Big who manipulated the occupants and staff of all the cell blocks, although I knew that even such a power would hardly be on holiday in a Tahuna motel. 'Don't be absurd,' Liz said. 'He's the governor, or whatever, there.' And so he was; the head of the largest prison in the nation, and getting away from it all by having a fortnight in Nelson.

'Ah yes, of course,' he said as Jean and Liz introduced us, and from a sense of courtesy he came out of the pool to talk to me. The dense hair of his arms and legs lay in scrolls from the play of the water, the shaving line on his chin was blue-purple, and within his rather taut face the eyes were oddly lustrous, expansive. 'Our wives have decided that we shall be friends,' he said, 'and so we must comply.'

I brought out to the poolside a carafe of the local apple wine, and the four of us got on with friendship. Wesley told a story against himself as a city man getting lost in a shopping mall at Richmond, and in the relaxed mood of holiday we were all able to stretch to an anecdote or two, so putting our feet forward in acquaintanceship. We were couples of a similar background, outgrown by our children, and without any clash of temperament. It is no disrespect to marriage to say that there are times on holiday when another couple is welcome. My wife was glad of a more knowledgeable shopping companion, and I found that Wesley was a golfer, and not intimidated by silence. It was in fact that casual friendship hoped for while on holiday, and uninhibited by any likelihood that I would fall within Wesley's workday jurisdiction, or he within mine. He already had a competent dentist. I could tell by the quality of his capped upper incisors.

I wouldn't class myself as a particularly curious man, not prying into other people's lives I mean, but it was difficult to be with Wesley Smith without wondering at times about the nature of his job: the responsibilities of it, and the special pressures of the whole criminal and penal aspect of our society. With just a few people it's like that; a poet maybe, or a professional soccer player, and you wonder how their particular frame of mind must affect their view of the day's ordinary experience that you share.

Occasionally when we were walking up to the tee, or tending the motel barbecue, just saying commonplace things, or nothing at all, I would look at thin Wesley and imagine his gaol with its tiers of mezzanine cells, and similarly hierarchical prisoners, exercise areas, security devices, staff with needs for promotion or counselling, and all that bitterness, deceit, despair, malice, pressing outwards. Dentistry certainly isn't an ideal lifestyle: working in people's mouths all day is a good living financially, but not an easy one, and the figures show the profession has one of the highest suicide rates of any career, but I imagined that Wesley Smith would smile at any stresses I could mention.

Jack Spratt could eat no fat and his wife could eat no lean, the old rhyme says, and I normally expect the close proximity of personality in marriage to highlight differences, but Jean and Wesley Smith seemed similar in essential temperament: both intelligent, self-possessed, slightly rueful. Jean had her weaving, which success had made more an art form than hobby, and Wesley was a wood carver with his work in several important collections.

It was wet on the second Monday of our vacation, and cool as well. The city was swollen with campers with nowhere else to go, and the concrete block cathedral tower at the head of the main street was a fulcrum for an uneasy swirl of cloud. After leaving Jean and Liz at an exhibition of pottery, I drove back towards the beach, and later went over to Wesley's unit to find him carving, his tools on the window sill and the chair as close as possible to seek the light. Wesley's carvings were smaller and more elaborate than I had expected. Two of them stood on a tray by the motel window. One was a wood pigeon in kauri, the painstaking and precise detail of the feathers only partly complete. The other was carved in a macrocarpa canker, Wesley said, and the grain had a wonder of its own. It, too, was incomplete, but enough had been done to show that one pygmy had snared another with ropes about a tree trunk, and with exultation, yet caution, leant forward to torment his enemy with a spear. The whole thing no more than ten centimetres high, and yet scores of hours needed to show the two creases on the crouching pygmy's belly, or the pattern on the woven twine that held his enemy, whose individual fingers had been carved around the coil he tried in vain to keep from pressing on his throat.

I won't presume to make comment about artistic merit, or the talent of the carver, but fine work is an element of my profession also: almost a worker in ivory, I could say, and I could appreciate the patience and precision that amount almost to a trance to work such detail on such a scale. Wesley had a wooden vice with padded jaws and a suction base, and over this in the window light he bent to carry on his almost oriental art. We talked for some time of the levels of dexterity needed, and he was very interested in the added constraints imposed by working inside somebody's mouth. He had in fact been considering buying one of the old dental service treadle drills, he told me, and he asked me questions concerning them, and also the advanced, high-speed modern drills. Wesley said he often did a model in soap first to check on balance and technical problems before committing himself to wood. He'd done some scrimshaw work, he said, and some in meerschaum, sandstone and jade, but hard wood he loved best of all. Wesley said carving was popular with the long-term prisoners, and that he took a class himself of the three or four who grew to love it: their obsession perhaps to blot out the reasonable, unreasonable world. When Wesley told me of the most skilled prisoner, I had a sense of undeclared envy in his heart that the man had more time than the governor himself to perfect his craft. From the motel window I watched the rain bounce on the road in a sudden fury and the water flow off its curve and fill the hollows of the lawn alongside as Wesley quietly talked.

The leisure of a wet day can be a time for confidences, and the carvings, the discussion of common practices to an extent, had moved us on from our usual trivial subjects. I had a measure of natural curiosity about the prison and his work there. His eminence in an unfashionable career: what it was like to be in charge of the underworld that society wished to see only through safe and entertaining fictions.

'What do you imagine it to be?' Wesley said. He loosened the carving of the pygmies from the suction vice and put it gently aside. He leant back and drew his finger along the blue-purple rasp of his chin. I was close enough to see the grey, downy light reflected in the noticeable curve of his soft eyes.

'I visualise a job demanding a good deal of administrative skill, and judgement as well, and elements of sympathy, even compassion.'

'The system squeezes out compassion,' said Wesley. 'Perhaps you will understand that everything there has to do with responsibility and power. We have all the responsibility and barely enough power, strange as it may seem. They have no responsibility and considerable power. Think of me as a general manager of a firm whose clients are willing it to fail. There's no goodwill, and the best of policies, the most secure of theories, can be destroyed by apathy, by spite and viciousness.' Wesley and I watched the rain, and he twirled the most slender of chisels in his fingers.

'It can't be easy,' I said.

'Not a week passes without a stir of some sort: an effort to screw the system. Not a week without accusations from inmates or their outside supporters, and whatever deceit or animosity is discovered they suffer little and just lapse back sullenly to await another opportunity. But oh, let there be a hint of negligence or oversight on our part, something not done quite by the book, and it's a different story. I can be front-page news then.' Wesley's eyes lit, and his voice, still quiet, had nevertheless a tone of savage fun. 'We're never bored,' he said. He smiled at me, as the veteran smiles at the new chum who cannot know the significance of what he hears.

'I can imagine that,' I said.

'It's a difficult game when only one side is bound by any rules, and when it's only us who have anything much to lose, any character to be discredited. Do you see what I mean? One of my best department heads is fond of saying that we manage the anal end of society. No one else much wants to know how things are in our prisons, our psychiatric wards, our front-line welfare services.'

'You seem able to cope with the pressures well enough.'

'When has the pitcher gone too often to the well, though,' said Wesley. 'That's a question, isn't it.'

I thought about that when we drove back through the cool rain to collect our wives. It was the only talk of that sort we had, for the weather cleared for the remaining days, and Wesley put away his carving and his frankness, for golfclubs, tourism and studied cheerfulness again.

We worked something out for the last day of the Smiths' holiday. They were to drive their rental car through the Lewis Pass and fly out from Christchurch in the evening. Liz and I took our car with them as far as Shenandoah, and we found a picnic spot there with meadow grass on one side of the river and native bush to the water's edge on the other. Wesley loved the bush, Jean said. She and Liz had made a special picnic lunch with fruit and fresh rolls, and I brought a bottle of Barossa red to mark the parting of the ways. It was a hot, blue day and the sunburn was intensified on Wesley's thin legs and the shoulders of our wives.

We got on well till the very last, and it was more than regret at the recognition of another holiday's conclusion that made us sorry to part. Jean said it was time Liz and I moved to the main city, and Wesley said that instead of being content with just one captive at a time in my chair, I could become the official prison dentist with as many patients as I could manage, and paid with no bad debts by the state as well. We talked in an inconclusive way of meeting again during next year's vacation; the Coromandel perhaps, or even Singapore, said Jean hopefully. It could all be worked out in letters, we agreed. Growing sleepy in the sun between the cars, and with the red wine drunk to mark our parting, we allowed our personalities a certain abandon before return to workaday selves.

The Smiths left before two. We waved them out of the meadow grass and bush at Shenandoah. Wesley held up one slender hand and wrist in salute, and Jean smiled back until the corner. There was anti-climax, of course, with their departure, and Liz and I had only two more days ourselves before returning to the world which had caries at the bottom of its garden.

I was asleep on the tartan rug in the shade of the car, and Liz was reading, when Jean came back to Shenandoah alone in the rented car. Liz woke me even before Jean had stopped and, in the stupor of that sudden awakening in the heat, I was at a loss for a moment to realise that Wesley should be with her, and both of them over the Lewis and on their way to Christchurch. 'I didn't know what else to do,' said Jean, embarrassed by her return. 'Wesley didn't come back and I waited and waited, and then I went into the bush a little way, but you can't see anything, there's no tracks.' Liz put an arm around her shoulders.

'It's all right. You'll see,' she said

Jean explained that just past Springs Junction the trees crowded the road, almost reached over it for one lovely section of the growing slope before the top of the pass, and Wesley had pulled over to stop and enjoy the bush: a last opportunity before the barren heat of Canterbury on the other side. A last walk in the calm trees, hundreds of years old, before he was back to work. He just walked in, she said, and never came out.

Oh, we said that he'd be waiting on the roadside now, sure enough, that he'd be wondering where she'd got to, but I had a feeling of desolation about it right from the start. When has the pitcher gone too often to the well, Wesley had said. I packed up in a hurry, even in those circumstances struck by my own selfish concern at not being able to find the red thermos top.

Jean came with Liz in our car, while I drove the rental after them back towards the pass. Just a few kilometres past the buildings of Springs Junction was the place where Wesley had gone missing, and it was beautiful right enough. The bush was drawn up to the sides of the road and formed a canopy so that the road was part shadow, part dappled sun, in degrees of direct and indirect light. The air was tunnel cool and fragrant, the banks plump with moisture which kept a rich green in the tumbling ferns. Liz pulled over where there was a slightly wider road edge, and Jean was standing among the first trees when I joined her. There was no sign of Wesley. The road ahead wound out of sight towards the summit. The bush was high on our right and undulated away down the valley on the other side.

'He must have lost his way, or twisted his ankle,' I said. 'He's sensible enough to work his way down the watershed if he's got lost, and so come out further down, no worse off and just feeling a bit foolish.' I wasn't convinced: why should Jean be? She must have understood her own husband, had some knowledge of the things which would make Wesley walk into the bush and not return. I walked in myself, so that it might seem I was taking positive action. I followed the direction Wesley had taken, and within a few metres the road was lost above me and the bush closed up in intense scrutiny. The ponga ferns were clumped at head height and great sooty trunks slid up into the shifting forest canopy like the poles of a big top. I called Wesley's name, and heard no reply. There was just the noise of my own feet in the sloping leaf mould, and a chorus of cicadas far louder than I had ever heard before.

Maybe Wesley Smith was watching me, sitting amidst the fern and lancewood with his thin, hairy arms around his knees, and his lustrous eyes wide in the shadows. Maybe he was watching me go through the routine. It wasn't that I didn't care, but that I didn't believe he was lost in the way it would be assumed he was lost, in the way that would be reported in the papers. Prominent penal administrator missing: Dr Wesley Smith lost in Lewis Pass wilderness.

I made my way back up the slope towards the road, and came out fifty metres or so from the parked cars. I stood to catch my breath before walking down to Liz and Jean, before travelling back to the Junction to make the necessary report. Perhaps I rested also so that Wesley would have just that much more time to do what he wished. Within me was a conviction that Wesley would never be found, though God knows what it is makes a person step away from wife or husband like that, from life, and walk into the bush. Afterwards when there was all the speculation about whether he was still alive, still out there, my own interest and sympathy, my own guilt even, was not at all for the consequences of his action: just the motivation.

Glasnost

~

WHAT MIGHT SEEM the most difficult thing is often the easiest to account for. Peter Belikov, beloved in his own Ukraine, and of some repute elsewhere, attended the International Festival of Landscape Poetry in the Barossa Valley, and so did Nigel O'Kane. Thus they met. Belikov was almost a name, of course, while O'Kane was no name at all. New Zealand PEN initially nominated Minkner but at the last moment he suffered a sports injury, and the secretary remembered O'Kane's 'Kurow Triptych' in *Agapemone* magazine. The secretary was not well up on South Island landscape poets, but was determined to find one. She assumed that as there was more natural landscape per capita in the South Island, the standard of its poetry must be correspondingly higher. O'Kane had a part-time job under one of the government employment schemes, checking for carp infestation in the hydro channels of the southern lakes, but the threat posed was not thought such that he couldn't be spared for a few days.

No, the more difficult thing is to explain why, amid one hundred and seventeen male and eleven female nature poets concentrated in the Barossa, the Ukrainian Belikov, almost a name, and obscure O'Kane of the Waitaki, should form any sort of friendship at all.

The answer lies in O'Kane's state of mind at the first plenary session. He had once been overseas before, but only to the North Island, and the flight to Australia made him agitated. On landing he had to stifle his anguished cries as what appeared to be a portion of the wing disintegrating proved to be merely airbrakes. As the sole New Zealand poetic representative he knew no one on the mini-bus to the Barossa, no one in the multicoloured marquee which stood in the scented gardens for the first evening plenary session. The name tag he was issued, registered him as O'Kay, which he was philosopher enough to accept as a favourable omen. Alone at such a function, he did what all alone at such functions do, he drank more heavily because of it. The Barossa reds were particularly robust that year, and the nibbles well hidden.

O'Kane found Dutch courage enough to cheer the Colombian representative, who spoke out bitterly against the cancer of industrial society, and to smile into his neighbour's Hamitic face when the chairman, a Tamil professor of Asian literature, told a joke which proved he was a personal friend of Seamus Heaney, or Nissim Ezekiel.

O'Kane was most conscious of his obscurity when the formal part of the evening was over, and the poets began to mingle. Many appeared to be acquainted from the trail of festivals, launchings, readings, conferences, exchanges and academic fellowships which criss-crossed the world. The talk and laughter rose, so that the marquee began to swell like a bull frog, the candy stripes tightening in the lights temporarily strung. Midges and moths were drawn in enquiringly from the twilight Barossa, and hovered as parentheses about damp, open mouths.

The chairman made himself heard with an Asian gong, and suggested an impromptu reading. An accomplished chairman, he had cunningly forewarned some poets and had them planted in the throng. Before any of these could rise to their cue, however, O'Kane, driven by alcohol and the heady presence of so much poetry, stood on a tubular steel chair and recited Baxter's 'Rocket Show' from memory.

It was then that Belikov first saw him. As he watched, as the talk in the marquee died until the only sounds were the breaking of wind and plastic wine glasses under-foot, Belikov felt his heart tighten at the true demonstration of a poet's love for his profession. The front legs of O'Kane's chair sank gradually into the wine-soaked soil, and he steadied himself with one hand on the back. His running shoes had from long usage come to follow the shape of his feet perfectly, his grey trousers were worn at the knees from obeisance beside the water channels, and his natural wool jersey was unravelling at the band. His name tag hung out the more he had to crouch, and those nearest could clearly read that he was O'Kay.

There is a fitness in a poet's poverty, Belikov considered. A rich poet is like a fat ballet dancer, both gross failures in the essentials of their art. Even those listeners who had difficulty with English, or O'Kane's accent in its use, could respect a conscious-ness of a love for the words greater than his unpractised delivery was able to express. He received a good-humoured reception as he toppled forward at the poem's con-clusion, and the chairman quickly moved on to another poet whose spontaneity was more expected, and more in keeping with the hierarchy of those present.

Overawed by his own presumption, O'Kane burrowed his way to another part of the tent where he could be insignificant once more, and Belikov left his small retinue and tried to follow. O'Kane was fortunate enough to find a plate full of asparagus shoots wrapped in ham and held with toothpicks, that had been put down and for-gotten behind a rubber plant. He ate eleven of them, which served to regain his com-posure, and Belikov found him there in time to eat two of the last remaining with him.

Belikov and O'Kane talked not of poetry, but of their lives, which is the way of true artists. It is the difference between the spring and the trough. The Ukrainian spoke of his home town of Osipenko on the shores of the Azov Sea, and O'Kane asked excitedly of Chekhov's Taganrog and Babel's Odessa in the region. O'Kane described the treeless slopes of the inland basins of his South Island, with the tussock undulating in the unchecked wind, and the scree slopes glistening in the iced water of the thaw.

Belikov was on the rise. He gave a speech at the festival's second day, on the lyric pessimism of Ukrainian poetry. It was rumoured that he would appear on Australian television, but for some reason it didn't happen. However, he gave several radio interviews and readings. Despite his position and responsibilities, despite his established acquaintances at the festival, Belikov made a point of talking to young

O'Kane at least once each day. Belikov was not so far from his days of full-blown poetic idealism that he was unmindful of its wonder and passion, its obsessive innocence, and before the two poets parted at the conclusion of the festival in the Barossa, Belikov gave O'Kane his home address and a copy of his ninth volume of poems — *Dusk Upon the Asov Sea*. In return O'Kane wrote out for his new friend the 'Kurow Triptych'.

O'Kane returned to his brown valley and his search for fish no longer content with mandarins' gardens. It suited his whimsical humour when he was asked his occupation to say, carping. He supplied PEN with a report of the Barossa Festival as required, some five thousand words, which the secretary reduced to two hundred in the newsletter, for since her invitation to him it had been pointed out to her that O'Kane was utterly insignificant as a poet, and lacked any acknowledged publishing or critical history. Yet O'Kane could not be deprived of his experience, or his friendship with Belikov, and he wrote every month, long letters of the milky flow of the Waitaki, of the dust billowing from the Hakataramea in wind storms, of the delicate pulse in a gecko's throat, and the flight of a hundred Canada geese in a necklace against the setting sun. He shared the inspiration for his in progress, 'Sonnets of Otematata'.

And Belikov replied, despite his many correspondents, describing the majestic steppes, sturgeon fishing in the sea mist, the reed beds of the Yevpotkin, and his growing reputation, which necessitated ever more frequent visits to Kiev, Moscow and outside Russia to represent his country in America, Britain and so on. Belikov became a name: a small major poet rather than a large minor one. He was included in a *Time* magazine article on the leading contemporary Soviet poets, and he was awarded the Nekrasov Medal for his lyrical 'Return to Osipenko'.

Art, however, is a jealous god, and Belikov suffered a severe stroke thirteen months after the Barossa Festival, while reading a letter from O'Kane. His memory and movement were desperately impaired, and only his last thoughts about O'Kane were clear in his mind. His wish to see him finally became evident to doctors and family. The brother, Andrey Belikov, told of 'O'Kay' O'Kane's letter found clutched in Peter's hand, and the earlier letters were recovered from the poet's files.

In the spirit of glasnost the tender story was told not just in Russia, but around the world. A small enough piece of news perhaps, for the literary community is always despised by media power, nevertheless it was human interest, and there was an element of hands across the political waters as well, which was an angle worth working.

The Ukrainian Academy, benevolently regarded by Moscow, was permitted to approach the New Zealand Minister for the Arts through the Soviet Ambassador, to invite the poet O'Kane to visit Belikov in the Dostoevsky Clinic at Rostov. The minister called upon the Arts Council to identify O'Kane, the council called upon the Literary Fund, the Literary Fund called upon PEN, and PEN heaped praises on their secretary, who had shown the perspicacity to recognise O'Kane's talents and send him to the Barossa Festival in the first place. There was even a brief discussion in the Prime

Minister's office as to the implications of accepting the Soviet offer to meet the expenses of O'Kane's trip, and it was decided New Zealand should provide the funds, and so present the visit to the ailing Belikov as a gesture of goodwill from New Zealand to Russia.

Oh yes, it was quite a thing for a time. There were photos of both Belikov and O'Kane in the papers, excerpts from the letters, and mention of the *Time* article to establish Belikov's significance. The nickname O'Kay O'Kane provided a pleasing tag which no journalist strove to overlook, although certain senior common room staff with a sense of irony spoke instead of Arcane O'Kane. The MAF when approached described the poet's responsibilities with them as conducting a survey of the comparative distribution of freshwater Cuprinidae. PEN dug out O'Kane's original five thousand word report on the festival and published it in full. *Landfall* claimed an interesting editorial correspondence with the southern bard, saying that it had rejected his work, it was true, but had never rejected it out of hand. Several anthologists contacted O'Kane in order to obtain permission to include his work in forthcoming definitive collections of New Zealand poetry, and the Ngai Tahu, recognising O'Kane's spiritual affinity with the land, presented him with a twenty-seven-inch bone fish-hook pendant to carry to the indigenous people of the Ukraine.

Traditional poets and critics came forth from the woods and gullies all over the country to beat post-modernism over its fictive heads with O'Kane's success. It was rumoured that the as yet unfinished 'Otematata Sonnets' displayed a textural richness and sacro-guilt symbolism which rivalled Baxter himself, but 'Kurow Triptych' was the only published work available and so it received considerable attention. The coda was much quoted.

> *Christ is advent anew in the black stilt*
> *On a braided crucifix of silt.*

Nigel O'Kane coped with it all. Innocence can be its own protection in such things. In the same, soft running shoes he made his pilgrimage to the Black Sea to meet his friend Peter Belikov, who was by then unable to give a greater recognition than the clasping of his hand. Before returning to New Zealand, O'Kane visited Taganrog and Osipenko, stood himself on the loved shores of the Asov Sea. He was amazed that what seemed so insignificant and hemmed in upon his home atlas should be in truth so vast, so calm, and so uncaring.

Other news supplanted O'Kane soon after his return, but his story was too much the stuff of literary anecdote to be entirely forgotten. He went back to the solitary pursuit of art and carp, convinced he was a man of letters, and he was still young enough to think it was his poetry which had done the trick.

The Dungarvie Festival

~

IVAN AND LEN worked together for two years, and then by chance got to know each other on the summer day they didn't make it to the Combined Local Bodies Civil Defence Seminar in Dunedin. Each council had to send two representatives, and there was a good deal of duck-shoving to sort out who had to go. Ivan was landed with it because he was a comparative newcomer, and wouldn't be missed anyway. To show that the council was taking civil defence seriously there had to be a chief as well as an Indian, so Len, who was administration officer, had to go.

He came around early to pick Ivan up, so that they could be away in good time, and Ivan saw that they had been given the oldest vehicle in the fleet. They would be the Kettles come to town in Dunedin. The ute's left front guard had been in pink undercoat for years, and in the back was an assortment of road signs and three boxes of poisoned carrots that someone kept forgetting to set out around the treatment ponds. Low on both doors were paint bubbles, showing where the rust was eating through from the inside.

Len knew he looked incongruous. His good suit was already picking up a variety of rubbish from the wool sack which covered the front seat. Neither of them said anything about the ute, though, and Len drove, as befitted a chief, and Ivan sat on the pink wing side as the Indian. Len's manila envelope with the programme for the seminar lay on top of the dash, so Ivan put his there as well. They didn't discuss the programme: it had headings such as statutory responsibilities of local authorities, and counter-disaster logistics for rural communities.

Reticent, I suppose, is a word that you could use for Len, and professional would be another. He did his job from day to day without malice or favour, and without any inclination to pry into the thoughts or lives of colleagues. A working relationship over two years had for Ivan merely confirmed those aspects of Len's nature that he had recognised within the first week.

'We've drawn the short straws,' said Len with a smile.

'It looks that way.'

That's all they said for a while, but to be fair to both of them the ute didn't encourage conversation. The motor laboured and the road signs and poisoned carrots in the back had a disappointing fellowship. Also there was the threat of the Central summer, even at that time of the day. The ground had little cover, and the schist outcrops were bright, scaly, with no sweat to give.

'I don't much like the sound of the old girl,' said Len when they were close to Dungarvie, and as if by speaking of it he gave recognition, even acquiescence, the motor sickened in that instant and then died. They drifted, with just the road noise and the diminishing quarrel of the road signs and carrots, almost to the restricted speed zone of the village, and where they should have reduced speed the ute stopped completely.

'Ah well, Jesus,' said Len.

'At least we're not far from a garage. That's a welcome fluke.'

'That's true.'

There was a garage at Dungarvie. They could see it clearly. In fact all of Dungarvie could be clearly seen ahead: on the left the garage, then a community hall, on the right three stock crates jacked up on a section until needed, then the gap of a lucerne paddock before the store. Past the store was the only separate house they could see for all Dungarvieites. Len tried the starter several times without success, then went to the front of the ute and looked at the engine, more from a sense of responsibility than any hope of finding what was wrong. Ivan stood by him, but looked along the flat road to Dungarvie. He saw no one. Nothing moved, and in the time between the ute stopping and their walk to the garage beginning, only a blue Triumph passed them, paying no heed to them, or the restricted speed zone, disappearing down the road before they had taken many steps.

Len and Ivan took off their ties, and folded them and put them in the pockets of the coats they carried as they walked into Dungarvie. 'I suppose I should have rung up the yard yesterday and insisted on a better vehicle,' said Len. 'I just never thought we'd end up with that ute. I mean they knew we were going through to a meeting in Dunedin. It's poor.'

'I suppose it's mostly bad luck really.' Ivan was more accustomed to being given the ute as council transport.

'Yes, but after all we are going to the city as representatives of the council, aren't we.'

Ivan could feel his lips drying as he walked. He licked them, and moved his coat from his shoulder where it was making him sweat, and let it hang over his wrist. Through the thin soles of his best shoes he could feel the unevenness of the seal. It seemed to take a long time to walk the two hundred metres or so before the garage. Some barley grass heads had attached themselves to his trouser legs. He felt his face screwing up against the glare of the sun.

The garage was wooden: so old and so high that it may once have been a smithy. There was no one amid its workday untidiness, although a transistor radio, hidden like a cicada in the jumble of the side bench, sang on. Ivan and Len were not surprised. They knew that in a country district one mechanic is thinly spread. They kept walking and, even before they reached the hall, the sound of laughter claimed them: laughter despite the few, quiet buildings and the sky burnt to a powder blue. The laughter billowed from the community hall, but then lost its force in all the calm, surrounding space. Laughter at once natural and engaging, asking to be found out, yet also with defiance perhaps at all that emptiness, all that press of the given moment which there was no movement to disguise.

The hall was representative of a persistent species: outside all cream weather-boards and bleached red tin roof, inside a wooden floor with chairs stacked to one side, and on the walls the district rolls of honour for the Great War 1914–18 and the Second World War 1939–45. At the far end was one door to the committee room, and another, plus a slide, to the 'facilities'. A rolled bowling mat leant like a furled flag in a corner and on top of chair stacks were three jars of dried flowers and an unclaimed cardigan.

The laughter came from the far end of the hall, in the open door of the facilities, but Len and Ivan found it difficult to see the people there at first, because of the alternate shadow then fierce shafts of light from the windows as they walked the length of the floor. Two women and a man sat on chairs and peeled potatoes. One woman had yellow shorts, matching sneakers and the ease of attractiveness; the other had a floral dress and a laugh like a string of firecrackers. Their helper was a Maori, very thin, wearing a green army singlet, shorts and heavy boots. Even carrying their coats and ties, Ivan and Len felt over-dressed. The three had a sack of potatoes and two enamel basins at their feet. They washed and peeled the potatoes in one basin and laid them in the water of the other so they wouldn't brown.

Ivan and Len had found their mechanic it turned out — Charles. Evonne had the Hollywood legs, and Judith the laugh which made every speaker feel a wit. The two of them were mother helpers for a Guide camp being held in the domain next to the hall. It is the way sometimes that the more random the meeting, the more relaxed the mood. They all fitted in: there was not a nark among them. By rights they should never have met up at all. Ivan and Len should have been on their way to the seminar in Dunedin; should have been through Dungarvie too quickly to have heard the laughter from the hall, or to have seen the red crosses by the names of soldiers who had fallen. Yet Ivan could smell the bowling mats, and old paper lining cupboards, see the withered flowers in their jars, and the table tennis challenge ladder which displayed its champion so aptly as C. Meek.

Ivan sat with Evonne and Judith, offered himself as a replacement potato peeler, while Charles and Len went back to examine the ute. 'Does it matter much if you're late getting to Dunedin?' asked Evonne.

'We're supposed to be going to a civil defence meeting.'

'I don't know much about civil defence,' said Evonne, 'but then I don't know much about Girl Guide camps either, yet I'm here.'

'All camps have certain fundamentals, like peeling potatoes.' Ivan was flattered by Judith's laugh into imagining he had made a joke. She threw a potato into the basin with such force that the droplets as they scattered were caught in the sun from the window and for an instant held all the colours of the rainbow within themselves. Judith and Evonne began their story of all the indiscretions and mistakes they had committed as mother helpers, and of the Guide officers who never failed to discover them. As Charles, Len and Ivan held no rank within Guides, they were seen as reassuring envoys from a more tolerant world.

Carrots had replaced potatoes by the time Len and Charles returned, and Ivan had joined in so completely that the other men returning had to break the circle. 'Charles says it will take a while: probably something electrical,' Len said.

'Could be the distributor,' said Charles. Judith laughed and Evonne joined in. 'Heh,' said Charles, 'I've told you before there's nothing the matter with my name. I bet plenty of mechanics are called Charles.'

'How many Maori ones?' said Evonne. Judith's laugh, so sudden and so complete, drew them all in. Charles looked at Len and Ivan. He tried to make his thin face dead-pan.

'These women are trying to offend me,' he said.

'I rang the office,' said Len.

'What do they think?' asked Ivan.

'Well, they want us to go on if we can be on the road again before midday, other-wise we might as well wait here and bring the ute back when it's fixed. Someone would only have to be driven over to get it anyway.'

'Right.'

'I'll tow her in and have a look at things now,' said Charles. 'If you come up in an hour or so, I should know what the story is.' He took a carrot from Evonne's hand, as if she should know better than to grip such a thing, and walked back through the hall. His shoulder blades showed clearly under the singlet and his boots seemed clumsy on the ends of such thin legs.

'Goodbye Charles,' said Judith sweetly. He didn't turn at their laughter, but wag-gled his fingers with his hand behind his back.

As a break from the vegetables, Len and Ivan were taken through the back door of the hall to be shown the camp. There were no goalposts on the domain because of summer, but at the far end some pony-jumps were still set up, and on the hall side two lines of bell tents with a flagpole in between. Ivan thought the scene like a lim-ited budget set for a Boer War movie, with a minimum authenticity of the grass worn between the two rows of off-white tents, the flagpole, the heat shimmer beginning over the brown landscape, and the blue, hollow infinity of the sky. He thought things might look like that at the end of the world: all people spirited away, and just the props, the objects, left to get on with it.

'Where are they all?' said Len.

'They're on a badge trek in the hills. A six-hour round hike from the dropping off point and they have to carry their lunch and emergency clothing in case the weather turns. All the qualified people have gone with them, and we're left here to prepare tea,' said Judith, 'and look after Suzie Allenton, who was sick last night and is sleep-ing now in her tent.'

'We're supposed to make an inspection of the tents sometime during the day,' said Evonne, 'and give points to the tidy ones, which go towards the top tent competition.'

Ivan was about to ask what happened if the Boer commandos attacked while the camp was undefended, but he remembered he had said nothing to the others about the impression the tents had created. Yet he imagined Botha's or de Wet's horsemen cantering in to surprise the mother helpers and sick, sleeping Suzie Allenton. 'Were you ever in the Scouts, Ivan?' said Len from the back steps of the hall.

'No.'

'It wasn't my thing either. I never had anything to do with Scouts or Boys' Brigade, and although I was roped into National Service the only tents I remember were bivouac things which we had to carry ourselves. They were so small you had to crawl into them.'

'Time for your confessions now,' said Ivan to Judith and Evonne.

'I was brought up on a farm,' said Judith. 'I could never be in group things.'

'I was in the city, but don't remember going to Brownies, Guides or anything like that. I don't think anybody ever invited me.' Evonne looked carefully at the tents and flagpole, as if for the first time. 'Have I missed out on something important, do you think?'

'You can do your penance as mother helper,' said Len. 'Girl Guides, like any other army, march on their stomachs.'

'I'd like to march on the stomachs of a few of them,' said Judith.

The direct sunlight was intense. Len's head lolled back to rest against the door jamb, and his eyes closed. The others rested their heads in their hands, and supported both by propping their elbows on their knees. Ivan wished he had a hat, and found himself breathing through his mouth. 'Should we make a round of the tents now?' said Evonne after a time. The two women lifted their heads enough to see across the grass to the tents, and assessed the effort it would take to visit them all, and compared that with whatever energy and duty they felt.

'Maybe later,' said Judith.

'I'll just check on Suzie then,' said Evonne. She stood up, pulled her shorts down at the back of her thighs, and walked across grass so dry that it crunched beneath her sneakers.

'I could sleep the day away in a tent myself,' said Len. 'The less you do the less you want to do.'

'She's a good sort,' said Judith, watching Evonne as she neared the tents. 'Her husband's wealthy, but she's still come to take her turn. She pitches in just like everybody else. She even cleaned up on the bus when one of the girls was sick after fish and chips. It's not very pleasant then in the confined space of a bus when you're travelling so far.' Ivan and Len watched Evonne at the tents; her banana shorts and sneakers, her graceful, brown legs. The men kept their faces non-committal in Judith's presence, and they made no comment. 'Yes,' said Judith. 'Beaut legs. She's lucky there, don't you think? Mine keep getting thicker year by year.' She pulled her dress up to show her strong legs and big knees with a smiling crease on each. 'What about your legs?' she said to Ivan.

'Skinny and hairy. Not a pretty sight.'

'It's just as well we're both wearing longs,' said Len. 'I've nothing much to offer in the way of legs either.'

'Charles's have a good natural tan, but they're skinny too,' said Judith.

'Evonne will have to win first prize for legs then,' said Ivan. Evonne looked back towards the hall and laid her head to one side on her hands to show that Suzie Allenton was still sleeping.

Len and Ivan didn't wait for Evonne to reach them across the domain, but gave a wave and told Judith they might be back if Charles wasn't able to fix the truck in time.

'Oh, God,' she said. 'Do come back and rescue us.'

'We haven't lost a mother helper yet,' Len said.

Once the habitual responsibility for events had been shifted from him by forces beyond his control, Len became increasingly relaxed. He was in no hurry on their walk back to the garage, and he talked with Ivan of seeing the original subdivision plan of Dungarvie in the council files: two hundred private sections had been surveyed in the flush of colonial enthusiasm, and sites for shops and churches, but even the gold rushes didn't create that Dungarvie, didn't build its churches or fill its cemeteries. Dungarvie had never been much more than they could see. Ivan noted that there was not even a pub in the place, and his interest was not historical. At least the high, red barn of the garage offered some shade.

'She's never been any Rolls-Royce,' said Charles when they joined him. 'However you shouldn't have any trouble getting to Dunedin and back.' Len and Ivan looked without enthusiasm at the ute, its patch of pink undercoat, soft tyres, and stains weeping from the various rust spots on the body. The carrots in the back were bleached and wrinkled: a sign face-up announced road works ahead. Len thought of the drive to Dunedin in the heat, and the attention that would be drawn to them by their late arrival at the seminar. 'On the other hand,' said Charles as one of life's entrepreneurs, 'we could declare a Dungarvie Festival if you wanted to stay for a while, and give Evonne and Judith some company. I've even got a carton of beer that we could all chip in on.'

Len opened his mouth as if to say no in his role as administration officer, but then was seized by the wonderful implausibility of it all as he stood in the garage doorway. The few ill-hung bell tents he could see not blocked by the hall, the dozing store, the barley grass in the free sections, the sheep crates with dung burnt to an inoffensive crust, the old smithy garage he stood in, Charles smiling from the shadows which matched his skin. 'Well, why not,' Len said and, having said it and not been struck down by conscience or by lightning, he repeated it boldly. 'Well, why not. We're too late to bother going on anyway, don't you think?'

'Yes,' said Ivan and Charles with certainty. Charles hoisted the carton of beer into the back of the truck, and they drove back slowly towards the hall through the welling shimmer of the road and grass.

The mother helpers had gone inside again, and were preparing a vat of mince and onion to go with the potatoes. The sight of the beer on Charles's shoulder was enough to start them laughing. The sooner the meal was prepared, the sooner they could relax, Judith said, so Ivan and Len chopped carrots directly into the mince while Charles sliced onions. Tears ran down his face, and his brows lifted oddly as he tried to keep his eyes from closing.

'Come on, come on,' said Charles. The women took some apples and apricots, everyone took a mug, and Charles led the way across the domain to the culvert where the road crossed the stream. There was a small, scoured pool where the concrete ended. Charles took the bottles of beer from the carton, and dropped them on to the shingle bottom, reaching down till his shoulder was in the water so that the bottles would land gently. Part of his singlet became bright again with the water, and the drops skated across the oil of his hands. There were small grasshoppers at the pool's edge, and a silver skink for a moment on the concrete of the culvert bridge. Len tasted his share of the first bottle, which was given no time to cool.

'I love the salty taste good beer has,' he said. 'Ah, it's needed in this weather.'

They surrounded the small pool. Len and Judith stepped over the trickle of its outlet and sat on the other side, but that put them hardly any further apart than the others. All of them were soon barefoot. Charles's feet were dainty alongside his work-boots. Judith tucked her floral dress up like pantaloons, and hung her legs in the water so that the effect of refraction had them broken at the calf. Ivan leaned forward to eat a ripe apricot so that the juice would fall on to the grass and not his best shirt or suit trousers. He had knotted the corners of his handkerchief, soaked it, and it lay on his dark head as a first defence from the sun. Occasionally a truck or car went by in the midday heat. The growing whine of any approach gave all five a chance to compose their faces. Sometimes drivers or passengers happened to look down and saw with envy, surprise or condescension the group around the culvert pool celebrating the festival of Dungarvie. But as time went on, the road, its travellers, its starting points and destinations, ceased to be a relevant awareness, and no disguise or provision for them was made at all.

'Let's hope no one breaks down,' said Evonne to Charles, 'otherwise you'd have to leave our picnic and fix the car.'

'Actually I never meant to be a mechanic,' he said. 'I wanted to be a physicist.'

Judith's laugh exploded pod-like in the dry air. She had difficulty in holding her mug of beer. Len's laugh was almost as loud, almost as distinctive: high-pitched and abrupt, it was not the social laugh that Ivan had heard from him in the past, but a new laugh. It was a laugh of instinctive delight and lack of inhibition. 'No, I did, fair go,' said Charles. Laughter feeds on itself, so that they were all drawn in. Charles himself found his voice so collapsed with laughter that it was husky when he managed to carry on. 'Look, look, I was a marvel at physics at school and could have easily gone on, but at Vic I got sidetracked into a heavy metal band, and lost my bursary because I failed everything except physics.'

What a depth of humour and irony there is in actuality. Evonne lay back because her stomach was sore from laughing. There must be a hundred reasonable ways to explain the move from physics and a Wellington rock band to sole charge of the Dungarvie garage in the old smithy. It had the freakish likelihood of truth. 'I wanted to be a wildlife officer,' said Len, sudden in his decision to be confidential as well. He had dipped his hands into the pool, and cooled his face with the water. The hair of his forehead was stuck together. 'I wanted to save the black robin, the takahe, the kakapo and so on.' At his ears amid the short sideburns were the first grey hairs, and on the sides of his nose the sheen where his glasses normally rested. 'More than anything else, that's what I was set on doing, and somehow I've ended up as an accountant, a council administration officer.' He was still sufficiently self-conscious to add that of course he had remained a financial member of the Forest and Bird Society. It set the others off again, particularly Judith. She considered it a great one-liner. Her feet jerked beneath the water and her laughter cracked like a stock whip across the domain. Did any accountant ever dream of becoming an accountant, any more than the day-shift foreman of the chicken nugget factory dreamt of his success, or a man sold his soul to the devil for the right to be caretaker at the Shangri-La Lodge and Cabin Park? How many shopping reporters, high school language teachers, rural delivery drivers, one term politicians, or Pleasant Valley inmates could point to a constant ambition?

The bottles of beer lay on the gravel bottom of the pool, and quivered like trout in the ripple of Judith's feet. The stones had a fuzz of slime because the water was barely flowing; the label from one bottle had come adrift and undulated like a fin. The pool had a thin lip of green cress and clover before the brown grass began. 'How can you work day after day in this heat?' said Evonne to Charles, who was reaching down into the pool to bring up another prize.

'You tell me,' he said. 'This part of the country is stranger to me than to most of you, I'd say. I'm Tuhoe, you see, children of the mist, and so on. This isn't my place.' It was a final incongruity. Len was delighted with it.

'I don't suppose there are many Tuhoe physicists in Dungarvie, when you come to think of it,' he said.

Everything seemed amusing to them in that afternoon. Sometimes there is an intoxication of the heart which has little to do with drink: some combination of circumstances and personalities which slips past defences and brings a mood of goodwill and acceptance. All of which may be just another way of saying how hot it was in Central that day, how influential the beer and fruit on empty stomachs, how each person felt release in a new role and company, knowing it was just for one day. Ivan noticed that Len rolled his trousers higher as time went on, and that his face was almost impetuous. They had left the office, yet not arrived at the seminar. They had shrugged off routine, yet not assumed interim responsibility. They were in a pleasant limbo, and yet with some excuse.

'Me?' Evonne was saying. 'I wanted to be a school dental nurse, and make snowmen with red ink faces from cotton wool wads. The uniform quite suited me, I thought, and as well you had your own special room. Instead, I'm just a rich bitch, I suppose.'

'A toast to the mother helpers,' said Charles amid the talk of Bertie Germ and money, and the mother helpers drank deeply to themselves as a sign that they recognised their worth.

Ivan wondered about himself: what he had intended as distinct from what he had become. The physicist, the wildlife ranger, the dental nurse, and Judith still with her mystery, all wanted to hear of his lost life. Judith shaded her eyes the better to watch him, and her mouth was open for her explosive, benevolent laugh. 'An actor,' he said. There was joy that he had not disappointed them. Charles threw his head back as if to dislodge something in his throat. 'I did a fair bit at school, and then a polytech course. We had a group that toured schools and hospitals but, when the funding was withdrawn, I switched to office management.' As he said it, he was amazed how the exigencies of the moment become, in retrospect, a seamless process of inevitable selection.

'Oh, but you would have been good on the stage,' said Evonne loyally. 'You could be a gentleman caller for Laura, or a rebel in a kitchen-sink play.'

'Or the fool in *Lear*,' said Len, 'who knows more than the king.'

'Give us something now,' said Judith.

'I've forgotten it all.'

'Yes, come on, Ivan,' said Len. He was delighted that his colleague had revealed such an exotic past. A chant began.

'We want Ivan. We want Ivan.'

In any other setting, any other time or people, Ivan would have suspected an edge of vindictiveness, an underlying hope of some humiliation, but the Dungarvie Festival was all goodwill. None of them knew each other well enough to wish for any harm. Ivan stood up to free his breathing, and gave them one of Biff's speeches from *Death of a Salesman* about the dangerous gap between self-image and reality.

As part of his concentration on it, Ivan had an exact awareness of the others listening; their combined physical existence on the grass there, around the culvert pool. A grass stem turned in Len's fingers, and on one pale ankle bone a green vein was looped. Judith's sunburnt face was full on to him to give support, and Charles nodded as he listened and dabbed an insect from his beer. The Boer War tents were in their two rows at a distance, the hall and store and garage becalmed in heat and time. Then Ivan quoted Willie to his friends in the Dungarvie domain, isolated from the rest of the world with a bird singing up high somewhere, one great, strutted pylon glinting on the hill, two lines of sagging tents and, in one of them somewhere, sick, sleeping Suzie Allenton whom he never saw.

Ivan had his immediate appreciation, however, and a stock truck happened to pass at just that time and made a roar of approval upon the little bridge above them. Judith had seen the film version and talked of it with Len and Evonne, while Charles gave Ivan his ideas on the importance of sustaining enthusiasms. Ivan was breathing heavily because of the heat and his nervousness at reciting. He was content to listen for a while. 'You must keep the idea of your life being special,' Charles said. 'Of it having nothing to do with any historical generalisations or social trends, but instead as a free-wheeling thing with all the possibilities still there if you want to explore them.'

'There's an underlying feeling of time past,' Ivan heard Judith saying, 'and it's pressing forward into the present and the future more and more.' For a moment Ivan thought that Charles would accept that as an answer in their own conversation, but Charles still waited.

'Sometimes I doubt the depth of what we see,' said Ivan. 'Sometimes, despite the exact, connecting detail before us, I feel it bulging, and just a shimmer at the seams to hint at things quite different beneath.'

'That's it,' said Charles, and he topped another bottle.

'Didn't he marry Marilyn Monroe or something?' asked Len. 'I thought I read that he married Marilyn Monroe.' He picked blemishes from his apple with his fingernail.

'At our last staff meeting,' said Ivan, 'we were discussing the computer training programme, and for an uneasy moment the words spoken didn't fit the movements of the people's mouths, and there was the scent of the open sea that I haven't thought of for years.'

'That's it,' said Charles. 'Last week I took an irrigation pump I'd mended back to a cocky up the valley, and at the gate a dog challenged me. Not a sheepdog either, but a Labrador. The sun was going down, and this old dog stood right before me, barking hoarsely, but it had so little belief in its own threat, or mine, that its eyes turned away as it barked. I had a feeling that it marked something in my life, but I had no way of guessing the significance.'

'Kerouac called Monroe a trash blonde. He met her once and she snubbed him,' said Evonne.

'I've never read any Kerouac,' said Len. 'I come across the name from time to time, but I've never read anything.'

'We'll do our Kerouac dance for you,' Judith said. She and Evonne stood up and swung their hips slowly, and undulated their arms. Judith's dress was still tucked in, and her legs were pink with sunburn, only behind the knees still white. Evonne could have been a Marilyn Monroe herself, with smooth muscles on her thighs, and heavy breast. Len gave his new, high-pitched laugh, but much softer than before.

'That's just a hula,' he said.

'Now reincarnation is another thing,' said Charles. The beer had reached his eyes and they had a moist gleam. He lifted the strap of his green singlet, and scratched his shoulder. His thin body was crumpling in the heat and the relaxation of unforced conversation. 'I find myself considering it quite often.'

'You believe in reincarnation?' said Ivan. Evonne and Judith still did their Kerouac dance, and Len clapped in time. It was a leisurely dance because of the heat, and Judith could drink from her mug without interrupting her movement.

'Let me give you an example,' said Charles. 'I had this dream of hunting polar bears from a kayak, and one reared up on an ice-floe, and I felt all the authenticity of detail in an instant: how the water drummed the kayak's skin against my hips, and the bear's fur yellowed and disordered in the armpits as it raised great paws.'

'An Eskimo dream. You didn't,' said Ivan.

'What's this?' said Evonne.

'Charles dreamt he was an Eskimo.' The dancing was over, and Evonne and Judith sat down to laugh again.

'You didn't!' said Len.

'Only a few nights ago,' said Charles. 'It was so true that it woke me up. It took a while for the Arctic chill to pass. I got out of bed and went to the window. I could see some of the hill facings full to the moonlight, and a fenceline across them. But there wasn't a polar bear in sight.'

'Perhaps an Eskimo has had a vision of Dungarvie as recompense,' said Ivan. 'The view from your window with the dark gullies and moonlit tussock slopes of the Old Man Range, and a single fenceline to divide one side of emptiness from the other.'

'Or the festival now,' said Judith. 'Us at our picnic here when we're all supposed to be somewhere else. But it's so hot. You'd hardly dream such heat.'

Even reincarnation and the Kerouac dance couldn't protect them all forever. The afternoon was well on, and consciences were stirring. No one voiced it, but they had a small fear that the Guides and qualified instructors might return from training and they would have to see themselves reflected in scornful eyes — five feckless people, moist-faced and idle in the sun from an excess of goodwill and beer.

'I suppose we'll have to go,' said Len, but he continued to lie back, his suit trousers rolled below the knees. 'I haven't enjoyed myself so much in ages.'

'We've still got our inspection to do, and poor Suzie Allenton,' said Evonne.

'And the meal,' said Judith.

'You didn't give the mother helpers any of the carrots from the truck, did you, Charles?'

'Why not?'

'They're poisoned.' Len knew this would set Judith off again.

'That's the sort of lunch issue our council runs to,' said Ivan. Amid the laughter, Len clumsily stood up, but was unable to find his balance. Too many factors were combined against him: dizziness from standing up suddenly in the heat, pins and needles in his left leg from the hard ground, the flattery of beer and laughter, the loss of steadying inhibitions. He began to fall sideways despite whirling his arms, and the laughter increased. He tried to turn his fall into a leap across the pool, easy enough, but hit the far edge with an outstretched leg and half fell in. Had it meant his death, the others could not have stopped their laughter, which went on as Len hobbled in a circle on the grass to get his jarred leg moving properly again.

The incident allowed Ivan and Len to make easy goodbyes, with no scrutiny of the day attempted. Laughter and spontaneous acceptance had been the start of their trivial festival; with laughter and openness they kissed and parted.

Ivan and Len carried their shoes across the domain, and when they reached the truck they opened both doors, but stood outside for a while until the cab was a little less stifling. 'You'd better drive,' said Len. 'I think you drank less than me.' They could see Charles fitting his heavy boots as they pulled away, and when Ivan gave a farewell on the horn, Charles, Evonne and Judith raised their hands and, even at that distance and above the noise of the ute, there seemed an echo of machine-gun fire which might have been Judith's laugh.

Dungarvie fell over the edge of the world behind them. Soon they could see just the top of the high smithy garage. The morning's trip seemed a life away. 'We're not much further ahead on civil defence,' said Ivan.

'The farmers round here say that disaster struck some time ago anyway, and today's seminar was too late for that.' Len was dusting his feet with his socks while Ivan drove, then he rolled down the legs of his suit trousers and began picking out spears of barley grass. 'I never knew you'd been an actor,' he said. 'We should see more of each other and talk about those things.'

'We will.'

'Judith was the only one that didn't tell us what she wanted to be. Did you hear her say that she was going through a break-up with her husband?'

'No.'

'She told me while you were talking to Charles about reincarnation, or his time at Vic, or maybe his Eskimo dreams. Being a mother helper was a chance to step back from normal things and sort herself out.'

'She could laugh anyway.'

'That's true. You meet interesting people by accident at times, don't you? Scores of times I must have been through Dungarvie and I don't think I've ever stopped. Yet today was some sort of fun, wouldn't you say?'

They talked easily in the afternoon sun. The Dungarvie Festival had been one of those oddities — a oncer — like a freak giant hailstorm, or the escape of zoo leopards into the suburbs. Those things which happen once in a blue moon, and which bind those caught up in them with a sharp sense of comradeship, and of life's possibilities after all.

Tomorrow We Save the Orphans

MY FINAL VOYAGE, a winter's night, and Dubois accompanies me as a courtesy of farewell. After more than a year at Acme Textiles, I have been appointed a researcher with Statsfact Polling Agency. Dubois is piping me ashore. 'I might do the same at your age,' he says, 'but later you'll see the advantages of night work. Fewer people and more interesting ones.' He's right: they drop through the sieve of daylight employment to a nether world. The most fallible of fools and perverse of the profound.

The breath that forms Dubois' words is a plume in the freezing air as we stand beneath the water tower and check the sacking on the pipes. Appearance is most marked and memorable on the day that we meet a person, and the day we part. Dubois' continental good looks are in some way debased, the casual, toss away features of a circus rouseabout, but his eyes and hands have individual authenticity. Dog killing hands, strong and supple, with muscle raised between thumb and forefinger, and eyes that will not tolerate deceit.

'I've been reading more about castle development and the influence of the Crusades. Brattices and the advantages of circular masonry,' he says.

I returned from Europe with an innocent bladder infection and a debt of over three thousand dollars to my parents. Acme Textiles was unimpressed with my education, but when I crooked my arm to make a muscle and talked of labouring in Wolverhampton, the personnel manager said okay, I'd got it, night work, but only if the caretaker liked the look of me. I never saw the personnel manager again. He was the Charon who delivered me to the underworld. His name was O'Laughlan. The managing director, whom I never met at all, was called Jim Simm, and the caretaker was N.F. Vincenze Dubois. Life is full of such splendid ironies.

On this last night, a winter round, Dubois seems willing to put aside all except that final cover which is the necessary reserve to keep the glare of other people from our soul. At farewell to comradeship and proximity, it matters little if some confidences are shared which might be awkward if you had to meet again. We all learn to jog along in our relationships, not expecting too much, not admitting ambitions we can afterwards be beaten with. 'Have you really been here fourteen months?' says Dubois. He has a muslin cleaning rag knotted around his neck for warmth and the collar of his tartan jacket turned up against the chill. 'Fourteen months. Fourteen months,' he says, 'and I don't remember more than two or three things in that time, apart from the Middle Ages, that I care a damn about. I hope it's different for you.'

Night has a stark effect. A liposuction that removes the inessential until the bones, the sinew, the organs only of an impartial world remain. The dump skips cast perfect shadows from the moon across the frosted shingle and dirt of the yard. Larger stones are rising up like mushrooms, and cats troop Indian file silhouettes upon the wall at Pine Light Engineering with shoulder bones that undulate against the sky. Grass which grows three storeys up in the gutterings gives a faint, prairie whisper in the barely moving air, and hedgehogs fossick out from weed and fennel corners to feed.

Frontages of industry present the latest faces, but the backsides retain the scars and emblems of old allegiances. Pine Engineering was once the warehouse of Pacific Skins Ltd, and Acme Textiles itself incorporates, among others, the bulk of Aldous D. McManus and Sons, Pastoral Agents and Scourers, estab. 1862. The brave old lettering can be seen behind the fire escapes. Dotty Standish has come to one of the small side-doors to cry, as she does most nights. Her husband died three months ago from cancer of the bowel. Dubois will not fire her yet, as she has been a good cleaner for several years.

'I could have made you assistant caretaker, or night watchman, if you wanted to stay on, even though you're no good with your hands,' says Dubois as we check the loading bay doors. Our steps echo on the hollow wooden ramps and between the echoes is the sound of Dotty snivelling not far away. 'I heard a new dog barking last night,' says Dubois. 'A Labrador, or Labrador cross I reckon, at the refrigeration depot, or perhaps further over at the seed driers.'

Dubois is chunky and middle-aged, but nimble still. In the main machine room he vaults to the top of the spinners to check them. He leaps from one to the next. There are fourteen French Bavantes and six Wisconsin Hammonds, the names in proud red and green bas-relief on the sides of the casings over which Dubois strides. He has come to check on the Hinkles' electrician. As caretaker Dubois has patronage to dispense; not just cleaning for the women of his choice, but suppliers and trades-people. The Hinkles' man has finished with the freight lifts, and tells us they should get their certificates of worthiness now.

'I meant to say,' says Dubois, 'that my telly is playing up. The sound cuts out every now and then.'

'I'll call in on my way out,' says the Hinkles' man eagerly.

'Would you?'

'No sweat, Jesus, no. If it's anything serious we could let you have a nearly new set we've repossessed.'

'Tell Keith I'll probably need someone out to fit new fluorescent lighting in accounts. I'll know for sure in a week or two.'

'Right. No sweat. See you then,' says the Hinkles' man. Dubios conducts the conversation from the height of the spinners, which accentuates his mastery. He now climbs higher as the electrician leaves. Into the steel rafters he moves to check his rat baits, disturbing delicate colonies of wool fibres built up over the years. Some fall lightly in clumps like varicoloured lichens, others disintegrate and drift for a time before the lights as a haze of green, or gold, or blue.

'The bastards have been at it.' His voice is tight with satisfaction. 'Oh rat, rat, you'll feel thirsty now.' Dubois half swings through the bolted rafters above the machines, leg and arm, leg and arm, careful to protect his head. 'Rat, rat,' he says, 'you feel the thirst of death.'

The factory at night is a titanic; dimly lit and throbbing. A place of many levels and decks, with lives a world apart separated by just a bulkhead, or a narrow stairway which says factory staff only. The boiler pipes are never silent in this season, the air conditioning fans resonate with individual melodies from deck to deck. A persistent vibration gives a sense of movement, of voyaging, so that Acme Textiles is pressing on over the sea of the night.

Vincenze Dubois is more absolute captain of the firm by night than Jim Simm ever is by day. In trading hours the place is subject to the compromise and transactions of the world, taking cognisance of powers of equal, or greater, strength. But Dubois has a concentric empire, a ship of the night that rumbles self-sufficiency, and to which only minions from the outside come. This caretaker knows the place as an extension of himself. The cleaners and the routine of their tasks, the machines in all their variety, rat paths in the ceilings and cellars, the seventh skylight in the warehouse which leaks after hail. He knows the stalagmites of borer dust glinting on the lower beams of the acid store, the folded blankets behind the dye crates where the works supervisor takes Sarah from reception during breaks, the blue pigeons which have pushed past the netting on the east gable, the forgotten box of Chinese silk cocoons above the cupboard in the old boardroom presented by a trade delegation in 1949. Dubois knows Stevens of personnel picks his nose, that the three original doors nailed shut behind boxes in the old storeroom are solid kauri, that the morning sun strikes Acme first on the rusted iron above the blue pigeoned east gable. There is a piebald rat in the boiler house, Dubois tells me, which eschews all poison, and antique green jars in wickerwork ignored beneath the dust and spiders' lace of the upper gantry. Cannington writes old-fashioned poetry on the firm's paper, and Tess Eggleslee hides stolen lipsticks in the ledge above the toilet cubicles. There is a faint stain on the smooth wooden floor of the press room. Dubois points it out as the blood of Kenny Donald, crushed there seven years before by a forklift carrying the umber bolts of commercial grade which were so popular at the time.

'Remember we talked of mead,' says Dubois. 'I've had some working, several batches, in fact, with different herbs, but it's difficult to control the fermentation. I'm not very hopeful and honey's bloody expensive.'

We are in the first-storey offices, which have imitation wood grain formica desks and vinyl swivel chairs with corrective backs. There is not a cobweb, or a textile thread, in sight. From these windows the freight yard is a bleak field. In the summer the security beams suffuse the penetrable and billowing air, but now their light is fractured, crystalline in the frozen night. The Tuki sisters watch Dubois check behind the wall heater and beneath the photocopiers.

'You won't find anything there, eh,' they say.

'I'll catch you one night,' says Dubois.

'Promises, promises,' they say.

Dubois will miss the Medieval Age, I suppose. As well as women and machines, he likes discussion of the origin of heraldic devices, and how donjon, Norman-French for tower, became corrupted by time and usage into dungeon. Dubois likes me because I am an intellectual and simpleton. I am without authority or skills in the nether world, yet have information he finds interesting. 'There was a Dubois with William at Hastings,' I say, 'and Cardinal Dubois was Premier Minister in 1772 and in effect the ruler of France.'

'I was told that Dubois meant by the wood. My grandmother always said we had property in New Orleans.'

'Edmond Dubois-Crance served in the Royal French guard, but became a leading Jacobin in the revolution and organised its armies.'

'There's a Negro branch of the Dubois in the States,' Dubois says.

'What did you do before?' I ask him.

'Before?'

'Before becoming a caretaker,' I say. Dubois leans away from me to peer behind the drink dispenser.

'Charlotte, Charlotte,' he calls, and Charlotte comes from one of the corridors. 'There's cardboard cups squashed down the back here. Get one of the girls to poke them out with a broom handle please. Michelle, perhaps: she looks as if she'd be better with that end than the brush.' Charlotte laughs, nods, walks away, says nothing. 'Charlotte,' calls Dubois again a little while after. He has found something else to rectify, but Charlotte is out of earshot. 'Charlotte? Ah, never mind. Do you ask a lawyer or an architect what they did before? Do you ask a headmistress or a mercantile banker what they did before?'

'It's just that . . .'

'It's just that you can't imagine an eighteen-year-old deciding to make a life career as a custodian, right.'

'No, it's not that,' I say, but it is exactly that. Caretaking is something that you end up doing, surely, as a result of compromises and expedients. A wintering over until you line up something more in keeping with your view of yourself. There is something in the concept of caretaker that suggests the pathological poles of murderer or poet.

'It's my life's job,' says Dubois. 'I started out as a primary school caretaker and I've done pretty much all sorts. The more night work the better, though, because I'm interested in freedom, see, which is a form of power.' Dubois hears a hoon car in the alley, and leaps up on to one of the canteen tables so that he can watch the lights pass his domain. We can hear the car back-firing as it slows to turn into Astle Street.

Charlotte comes in to release the *Phantom of the Opera* in volume from the cleaners' transistor. The Tuki sisters, three doors down, start to sing along and, before Charlotte can go back to work, Dubois begins to dance with her. How well they dance on the white and yellow of the cafeteria floor, amid the chair legs upturned on the tables, and spun by the swelling music of the night. Dubois is handsome, and the muslin cloth a cravat at his throat. There is no parody in the care and skill he shows, and Charlotte's calves are well muscled above her working shoes. Faces and voices at the doorways as the other women watch them dance, and when it is over they go back to work the better for it. Dubois is unselfconscious regarding the life he leads.

On our way to the boardroom, Dubois and I are talking of tallage and the earliest practice of paying in kind. And the tax which was a further burden on the serf. The boardroom has 'Boardroom' in gold pretension on the door, in case there may be confusion with other rooms with a fourteen-berth, pale pine table and better than average blue vinyl chairs. Dubois smokes a black cheroot, but we don't sprawl, for it is too cold in this part of the building. Our hands are in our pockets and we shrug our shoulders for warmth. On the wall there hang the managing directors: Jim Simm will be added in good time, but their *doppelgängers* of the night persevere only in the minds and hotel stories of casual workers. Even Dubois can remember only the caretaker immediately before him. A 21st Battalion man whose stashes of gin still turn up from time to time. However complete and despotic their reign, caretakers go largely unrecorded. So earls and barons pass into history by virtue of their rank, while butlers who bestrode a world below the stairs are forgotten when their subjects die.

'So heriot was the death tax,' says Dubois. 'Nothing much alters in the state's greed, does it?' I am so close I hear the outside leaf of his cheroot crackle as he draws in and the red rim moves. 'Let's talk of Sir William of Cabagnes who captured King Stephen in battle,' says Dubois, his finger checking a window catch. I am sentient of the subterfuge and interlock of time and place in that instant. The moonlight winking on Dubois' thumbnail at the window, my rather nasal voice pronouncing the vowel in mace, my torso shrunk within the heavy clothes of winter, the words Alistair P. Brigeman beneath his proud black and white face on the wall. A tremor through the carpet from the Phantom's songs beneath. Then time moves with a whisper, and again we bowl on towards our end.

The cleaners are nearly finished for the night. The long watch is an exclusively male affair. They walk past us in the shadowed corridor. Dubois asks me to check the fire-doors on level three. He'll catch me up shortly, he says, and as I go on he steps out to separate Carol from her friends, guiding her towards the switchroom with the pressure of his hip. 'Wait your patience,' Carol says, so as not to seem too amenable while still in view.

The fire-doors are as safe as most excuses. I decide to walk back outside the loading bays. Dubois has told me it is important not to become too rigid in one's routine, for that could be exploited by a thief. I doubt for the moment that he is following his own advice. An angel swish: high on the factory side above me a muffled thump, and a mallard drake falls to the frozen dirt and stones of the moonlit yard. I turn a full circle with a sheepish smile to see who has played this joke, but there is no-other-body. The drake's sleek head follows me. I don't want the responsibility it brings and try to shoo it away. In response the duck rolls on its side, almost like a cat to have its stomach scratched, but one wing extends in a tremor of departing life and in the soft, body feathers where two legs should be, is only one and a little blood. Something terrible has been happening further in the night.

A car without lights is driving slowly down the yard. The gravel crunches sharply in the cold air. It is only Ransumeen who works for Sleaptite Security. Ransumeen is an idle, moaning sod who has been an insulation salesman, grader driver, post tanaliser and now, despite his complaints, will see time out in the security business. 'It's an agony, my back,' he says. He gets out and falls into step beside me, pulling on a balaclava to wear beneath his uniform cap. Ransumeen has no regard for me, but seeks anyone to talk to on a lonely shift. 'It's an agony. Too small for my build. I've a good mind to tell them that I'll have to toss it in unless I get a better car.'

'Right,' I say. Ransumeen has a habit of arriving at the Lintell Street entrance after ten o'clock when the women are leaving. He hopes to entice the younger ones with an offer of a ride home in the security car.

'I could do with a workout for the old mutton gun,' he boasts. But Dubois has warned the women against him, because he considers Ransumeen workshy and unreliable. 'I suppose the cleaners have almost finished now?' says Ransumeen. The balaclava does nothing for his looks. 'That Eileen's got a nice pair on her, a very nice pair.' He sees the women coming from the lighted doorway in twos and threes, and hurries from me to offer them double service.

The full moon this mid-winter night has a round, idiot face. My nose is putty, and all of us are made slump shouldered by the cold. This stark, dead duck yard of Acme Textiles has no links with the expansive world in which the same night staff played volleyball last Christmas. On that night the air had rolled languidly amidst us, heavy with fragrance of the chocolate factory, the wheat silos, metallic cinders from the foundry, the sharp tar and salt from the harbour, and the plebeian scents of weeds along the fences of stained factory yards. I was in charge of the beer and fruit juice from the munificent management, and took it from the cafeteria into the summer night, where Charlotte, Carol, Rua, Eileen with such a good pair, the Tuki sisters and the others chased a yellow balloon as their volleyball. It was a mutant version of the office party, or the true one perhaps, with Dubois as seigneur, myself as squire in the medieval sense. The cleaners were boisterous and obscene, because they were all female together, away from their families and knowing they deserved better than the treatment they received.

The world is a thousand worlds and our experience of it is determined by the point of vantage. The history of one moment in one place is a thousand histories, which are horror and joy apart, men and women apart, old and young apart, worlds of temperament and esteem apart, of education and expectation apart. Our own vision is a lie to the rest of the world who jog beside us. Eileen and the Tukis had leapt for the balloon into the tar- and wheat-scented summer night, and Dubois gave gifts of pantyhose purchased from his own wages.

I say nothing to Ransumeen of these recollections. Disappointed in his advances, he heaves phlegm in the moonlight, tells Dotty he's not going her way and complains of the rigours of the job as we head for Dubois' winter headquarters in the boiler room. 'Where is that mad bastard?' says Ransumeen. 'A good Kiwi name, I must say — Dubois. Jesus.' The furnace is now kept going all night. Dubois is there before us, his face cherry red in the glow of the drip-feed and his hands clasped around his enamel mug as if in prayer. There is a low, wooden form that we sit on, and the great pipes lead off above our heads, each one lagged with sacking held by hoops of tin. This is the vibrating engine-room of our night ship and almost I can hear the ocean of the outer world surge past. Dubois has made a line of blue plastic packing tape which stretches between the pipes and dries his jockeys, woollen work socks and heavy shirt.

'I've been thinking about the three-field system,' he says, with only a nod to Ransumeen, 'as the means of maintaining some level of fertility in village soil. It's the tie to the seasons surely, one spring sowing, one autumn, one fallow, that explains its importance more in the north.'

'I suppose so.' Dubois is at his most scholarly in the post-coital glow. The fly of his work trousers is still partly undone and the corner of a green shirt can be seen, yet the collar of the one he wears is grey. Ransumeen is a reluctant audience on the occasions when Dubois and I discuss feudalism. He is not aware of any connection between the past and the present: those not alive have never lived. His perception of life is reptilian: conscious only of the sun which warms his blood during the day, and the frost which slows him in his night work. He can barely maintain a latitudinal interest in things around him unrelated to his appetites, let alone a longitudinal one in the past and the hereafter. Only the concept of *droit de seigneur* appeals to Ransumeen from talks between Dubois and myself in the boiler house, on our rounds, or in the gully of the roof where we have sat on pigeon blue summer nights.

'So the big cheese of the district could have every sheila on her wedding night?'

'It was a prerogative not often enforced in practice,' I say. Ransumeen doesn't want to know that.

'They knew how to live in those days,' he says. Ransumeen's response assumes, I suppose, that he himself would have been the big cheese.

The warmth of the boiler room is having an effect. Ransumeen lifts his cap to remove his balaclava. 'There's a bloody vicious Doberman at Fraser's yard,' he says. 'A real goolie cruncher. The police and our guys won't check anything on those premises.'

'Fraser's, Fraser's,' ruminates Dubois.

'Grocery warehouses, down from the coolstores.'

'Of course,' says Dubois. 'A big Doberman, eh? They have tender feet.'

'A real bastard. He tore the cheek off a boy whose bike threw a chain there. He had to have his arm grafted on to his face for ages.' Ransumeen gives me the thumbs up so that Dubois cannot see. He knows the caretaker's interest has been aroused: an odd passion whetted.

'If you're passing again in a couple of hours with a mate who'll take over here, then we could pay this Doberman of yours a visit.' Dubois takes up a stick, and thumps along the overhang of the boiler house roof until a deadened sound tells him that Pongo is lying in his coats there for the warmth. 'I know you're there, Pongo. You remember that anything goes missing round here and you're for it.' I have never climbed up to the roof to see Pongo, but passed him once in the yard. He is quiet, gingery and, on winter nights, creeps up to the boiler house overhang in Dubois' fiefdom.

As we begin another round, Ransumeen takes his cue to leave. He complains about his car again. The yard lights and the moon make geometric patterns of the skips and pallets, the high building walls and roofs. All that the day will prove worn and soiled has a bridal veil in the winter frost. How cold it is. Can this be the same ground over which Dubois saunters in summer nights, coming from the staff showers back to his humble rooms by the incinerator? I have seen him with a towel as a skirt, and carrying just his trousers and soap. Parrots and roses climbed on his back: tattoos of green, vermilion and purple. Parrots and red roses while I explained to him that steward was originally sty-ward, to emphasise the importance of swine in medieval times.

With Ransumeen gone we check the west doors and go in again. Dubois continues to give me company on this, my last night. He is thinking of agriculture again. 'Why didn't they use horses to plough with more?'

'Horses were few in number and expensive,' I say. 'The ox was the draught animal for ordinary people: healthier over its life span, giving more work from poor fodder and the people didn't mind eating it at the end. The church then forbade the eating of horse meat.' We talk of medieval stock practices as we patrol the factory. Dubois stops abruptly to feel the air. Niceties of movement and temperature, which I cannot register, tell that a window has been left ajar. Complacent people think that occupations of little status can have no special skills: that any fool can be a lobster catcher, gardener, or poet. The main cleaners' storeroom is ajar, and Dubois' quick instincts lead him to investigate. There lies Dotty with her head on the orbital polisher and her feet among the mop handles. Her thin legs are hairy, and her breath comes as quickly as if she were climbing the Matterhorn.

'She's taken all her pills at once again,' says Dubois, and lifts her easily in the fireman's hold to carry her into the cafeteria. 'No. No, Dotty, there's no easy death for you here,' he says, and gives me the daughter's number to ring. It's not the first time, but the last cannot be far off. While we wait and talk of Agincourt, Dotty moans beneath the drug. Dubois has placed a bag of cleaning rags beneath her head, and she smiles fatuously despite the noises she makes. Dotty's daughter and her husband are ashamed of her. They come quickly. Without thanks to us, or more than angry solicitation for Dotty, they bear her away. 'Poor Dotty,' says Dubois. 'She's about come to the end of her tether.'

Ransumeen blows his horn after midnight, and it is sharp in the cutting air. He is back with a friend who will patrol while we go to punish the Doberman who bit off the boy's cheek. Dubois armours himself in his dog fighting kit, which I have seen only once before, in October when he killed a roving Alsatian which kept shitting by the boiler house door. More than anything else he looks like a samurai: black breast-plate, wickerwork and elbow guards. The orient had a modern feudal age, I remind Dubois. 'Know your enemy,' says Dubois. 'It's the head and hands you have to be most careful of.' He has tubular steel finger stalls within his fireman's gloves, and tells us that a fully grown Great Dane has a bite that will shear three-millimetre aluminium, while a bull mastiff damages mainly by shaking. 'I come crawling for a big dog,' says Dubois, 'but it's me that walks away. Get past the shock impact and the bite, and dogs rupture internally quite easily really. Sudden, full-body weight even from a kneeling position is too much for them. Rottweilers are sensitive to that, despite their reputation. You see dogs are not meant by nature to be individual fighters.'

Fraser's is well away, among the newer factories on low-lying ground. Ransumeen switches off, and the car glides down the empty street and up to the gates so as not to antagonise the dog until Dubois is ready. There is a straggling, knee-high mist from the sea, and beyond the streetlight is a main pylon with its own barbed wire enclosure. The thick cables droop and glisten between that pylon and the next. From its skeleton, knuckles of insulators hang to grasp each wire, and the electricity crackles and snaps so loudly in the winter air that it is difficult to hear what Ransumeen says in his voice at once ingratiating and confident. 'The mad, mad bastard,' he says. 'No one would believe it, would they?'

Dubois is fighting the Doberman on all fours. Neither of them makes any deliberate noise. The dog has Dubois' left arm in its teeth and shakes its head, wrenches suddenly with an instinct unpleasant to see. All the while it keeps its body away from the caretaker, who shuffles in a circle, attempting to come to it. The sparking of the pylon lines is amazingly loud. The breath rising from man and dog mingle in the broken mist. The fight is difficult to watch because of the many shadows despite the moonlight.

In the entire time the Doberman does not release its first hold. 'Get the bastard. Stick the bastard,' hisses Ransumeen. His greater animosity is expressed towards the dog, I think. He glances behind to check that the street is empty. Dubois and the dog drag and circle their way to the heavy netting of the inner fence. There Dubois is able to get the Doberman side on at last and bring his elbow down with the weight of his body behind it. Abruptly a sound like the first harsh burst from bagpipes. A second time the sound, and the Doberman scrambles lop-sided away with its head low. 'The bastard's done for. It'll die soon,' says Ransumeen. I see in my mind's eye the duck again, its iridescent head, and the wing fretting on the yard. I hear Dotty snivelling. I tell myself I should have no sympathy for a dog that bites a boy's face.

Dubois gives no commentary on his actions as we drive back to Acme Textiles, and does not immediately take off his helmet. It is metallic blue, with the half-visor that modern helmets have. Perhaps he wants time for his civilised face to reassemble behind the mask. The leather padding of his left arm is bright with the Doberman's saliva. Ransumeen catches my eye and smirks.

We have coffee and brandy in the boiler room on our return. What envy might Pongo feel, only a thickness of tin, and a world, away. Ransumeen tells his colleague how Dubois got rid of the Doberman, but is cut short by the caretaker. Ransumeen's work-mate, who is a keen Salvation Army man, takes the opportunity to produce three glossy, foolscap posters promoting an orphans' fund, and he asks Dubois if they can go up in the staff canteens. It is little enough return for his surveillance, and Dubois puts them aside with a nod, close enough to the furnace to have the flames flicker on the beseeching faces of the orphans as Ransumeen tells the story about the staff nurse and the elephant. It's not well received: Dubois and I have heard better punchlines, the Salvation Army man doesn't like the genre.

'They can't be regular partners,' says Dubois, as we watch the Sleaptite couple from the boiler room door. The moonlight and the frost grip ever tighter, and the world outside is motionless, except for Ransumeen and the Salvation man squeezing into the small security car. 'There were some twenty-five thousand slaves entered in the Domesday Book,' says Dubois, 'but the numbers gradually diminished.'

'They joined the rank of the half-slaves, the villeins.'

'The luck of birth meant more then.' He seems to have forgotten the posters, but when I remind him that we will be passing the cafeteria he waves a hand. 'This is your last night as castellan,' he says. 'Tomorrow we save the orphans.' So the orphans remain in the glare of the drip-feed, together with the jumble of samurai armour.

We decide to begin through the piece room, whose arched windows cast the dense, quiet light of the moon like cheeses on the concrete floor. 'Did I tell you of Hugh the Brown, Lord of Lusignan? A wonderful crusader who was victimised by King John,' I begin. Dubois does not answer me. He is lost for a moment behind the curtain of epilepsy. These petit mal attacks come only occasionally, then he picks up again without realising that he is ten seconds behind the rest of the world. Here is matter for metaphysical speculation: the brief loss of synchronisation might, in the puzzle of time and events, either kill or save him. I saw him have a more serious attack only once, after he came from fighting a schnauzer in the docks, and a fierce, spring hailstorm then blocked the gutterings so that the water banked up, flowed down the walls of the computer room and into the switchboard beneath. We were coming back through the nanny presses, having done what we could, when Dubois began soft noises which were no words, took with the urgency of a lover one of the press covers to lie on, as he felt the aura. He sat down and held up the palm of one hand as a sign to me that what was to happen would be over without harm, or revelation, without need of any intervention. Convulsive trembling, harsh breath, the glimpse of a parrot's head upon his shoulder, then calm in which his face was innocent. Soon he had been up again and taken up his command.

'I find the guilds interesting,' says Dubois. He is bending at the grating of the ducts to check the air flow. 'Furriers and glaziers, silversmiths and ironmongers, doublet and hose makers, glovers, cobblers. They were unions in their way.'

'But including employers as well as workers. Setting up standards of the craft, as well as conditions. I suppose more like the Japanese *zaibatsu* than unions on a British model.'

'A personal approach.'

'Things suited the scale of commerce, the scale of population then. The people of London would come out to see their king, or a hanging, quite literally. In William the Conqueror's time London was the size of Oamaru.'

'No,' says Dubois. He slows to consider it.

'It's true. Much of England was forest, and wolves ran in packs through Shropshire.'

'Ah, I can see it,' says Dubois.

Our checks have led us outside again and our faces shrink in the cold. It seems that he is going to see the whole shift out with me. He flashes his torch behind the loading bay door handles. He has put some blacking there as a test of Ransumeen's efficiency. 'That whining bastard's not done a check. I'll have him out.'

Dubois turns to look across the yard. He shows his teeth, and draws his breath deeply in defiance of the temperature. 'This is my weather as a northerner,' he says. 'A people get acclimatised over thousands of years, and function best that way. I can't stand too much heat. A cold day and a stiff wind makes something in me stir. I'm at my most alert and ready. I have this awareness of my origins.'

'It's sound enough reasoning,' I say. 'Clear genetic links with environment are proved. Look at those Andean Indians with special respiratory adaptations for altitude, and Kalahari bushmen who hardly sweat.'

'In this weather my tribe stirs inside me.'

'You might find that you suddenly come out with the words of a Frankish war cry,' I say. I wonder, however, how the boiler room fits Dubois' hypothesis.

'I'm rusty on the Franks,' says Dubois, 'except for Charlemagne. I remember that he could hardly write.'

'Yet he spoke popular Latin as his mother tongue and was also fluent in German and classical Latin.'

'Tell me something else.'

'The Basques had a rare victory over him at the Roncevalles Pass. About 780 — no, I can't remember. Anyway that's where the epic hero Roland died.'

This is the trivial way I can be of help to Dubois, some recompense for lacking the skills of a handyman. I owe my job at Statsfact Polling Agency to the Acme Textiles testimonial Dubois provided. The managing director's stationery was from Jim Simm's office, and Dubois asked Noreen to do the typing. Noreen was a cleaner, but had been a secretary before she started having children. Dubois suggested the sentiments and in-house detail, Noreen the authenticity of phrase — such as, throughout his successful time with us, and, it is with pleasure and no hesitation that I recommend. I like best of all the part referring to my grasp of corporate sales strategy and my progress in the fast track executive promotion scheme.

'When he was old and sick, he had to campaign against King Godfrid of the Danes and, as the Franks marched north through Saxony, the Emperor's pet elephant, Abbul Abbas, died. It was seen as a terrible omen,' I tell Dubois.

'Abbul Abbas,' says Dubois meditatively.

On our way back to the boiler room, Dubois detours through his maintenance workshop, where his tools line the walls. All have blue paint on their handles and are stamped with the letters VD to lessen the likelihood of theft. I have accustomed myself not to smile, or pass any comment. Through the cavernous main factory we walk and Dubois is contentedly imagining his poison at work above us. 'Rat, rat,' he says, 'you begin to feel the thirst of death.' So might we all in time, of course.

Furnace light flickers on Dubois' clothes strung to dry and the orphans who still await a home. The great pipes rumble in this engine-room which powers Acme Textiles through the night. It is like this with heaven and hell perhaps: no spatial difference, just that Lucifer leads the night shift and employs the same means to different ends. Dubois untucks the muslin from his neck, allowing it to hang as a scarf. 'We'll have a last cuppa, then you might as well go. No sense in two of us hanging on till the last.' Not once during this last night has Dubois said that we might meet again, that any possibility for the continuation of our acquaintanceship exists. He is too honest and too wordly, understanding the contacts of labour. We have spoken more of manors and garderobes than our own lives, but then who wishes to be told the details of other people's problems; it is sufficient comfort merely to know that they have them.

Dubois comes out to see me leave. He challenges the winter air with Merovingian equanimity, and shows the white of his eyes at the offensive sound of a dog somewhere beyond the engineering works. His hair is greying, but only at the edges so that it appears frosted like all else around us. Even the flat surfaces of tin or wood have fine hachures of frost, not shiny at all, but feathered almost, grey-white in the moon and security light like a blossoming mildew. The puddles by the freight entrance, though, do have a crystal surface, and creak beneath our feet. From illogical habit we stand out from the shadow of the factory, although the lighted yard will be no warmer. 'Things will go all right for you,' and Dubois takes a hand from his pocket to shake with. There is music for this white winter night. Pongo is playing his mouth organ. No doubt he has been kept awake by the comings and goings of this last voyage.

For every place there is the official and accredited view, and for every place there is a reverse of which only intimacy allows knowledge. From our lives we can all demonstrate the truth of that. So at Acme Textiles I leave a population known only by those who must board each night. And Vincenze Dubois is its strange captain.

from

Coming Home in the Dark

Working Up North

~

MY OLDER BROTHER arranged a job for me as a fish splitter in Nelson and I travelled up to Blenheim by train and then to Nelson by bus the next day. In the Rai Valley an old Bedford truck loaded with pumpkins had run off the road and lay overturned like a beetle amidst the pig fern, with the brilliant orange and yellow pumpkins scattered alongside.

We were the first to come across it and the bus driver posted people to warn traffic, then he and a thickset woman who said she was a physical education specialist decided to comfort the truck driver, who had a broken wrist. The rest of us stood around to appreciate the novelty of it. The truck driver was quiet and self-reliant. I think that having a busload of gawpers at his mishap was the worst thing about it as far as he was concerned.

The pumpkin crash meant that we were late into Nelson and if there had been anyone to meet me, there wasn't any longer. I left my bag and walked down to Golden Seafoods on the waterfront. There was a blue sky, but also a strong wind that put grit in your face and stirred up the shallow water to make a dirty mix which slapped among the jetty piles and broke along the sea wall of the road to Tahunanui.

Golden Seafoods (1974 Ltd), it said on the wooden sign, and there was a picture newly glossed of a crab with its pincers up and what looked like a groper. I went past the small window of the direct to the public sales and further down to the large sliding door of the factory, where I got a good whiff of the fish, rubber and damp clothes that made the atmosphere of the place. A small man, with blue gumboots and hair like a dunny brush, was hosing out the place with such force that tides of water washed through the door and ruffled there in the wind. I stepped on a pallet to keep dry till he saw me. He raised a hand to show that he had, then finished off the job.

'Just having a good swill out for the day,' he said. 'This chop has meant there's not much coming in and gives me a chance to catch up. I guess you're another McGarry. You've got the look of your brother.' He spoke loudly into the wind, but the stiff, white crest of his hair moved not a bit with the force of it. 'Another soft-palmed varsity wallah is all we need,' he said with a grin as we went into the big shed of the factory. 'You fixed up for somewhere to stay?'

I knew this must be Mr Trubb, who was Golden Seafoods. I knew that he had five boats and the factory, three retail outlets, some big contracts, a stake in a helicopter safari business on the Coast, and that he expected all his employees to work hard and toiled more than any of them himself. 'I haven't got anything fixed up,' I said. 'I've just got in and my bag's still at the depot, but I don't want to be any trouble.'

Of course I was happy to have his help, so I ended up sitting in the factory to escape the wind, with the concrete floor a glistening shadow, while Mr Trubb finished his cleaning. All the factory staff had gone early, because there wasn't much catch in and he saw the opportunity to have a good dung out. When he'd finished with the water hose he did some of the plant with superheated steam. A nasty way to have an accident, it seemed to me. I did offer to help, but Mr Trubb said I'd have the chance soon enough. He shouted through the steam that my brother used to put in a fair day's work for a fair day's pay and I could see that some sort of bench mark was expected of me. There were stainless steel-rimmed tables, drip trays, trolleys, plastic and waxed boxes, a line of freezers and a rack of rubber aprons like new pelts. I guessed that it would all dwindle to the apparatus of monotony soon enough.

Mr Trubb had the build of a sixteen-year-old, and the full head of hair, though grey, added to the impression of youthfulness at a distance. But not so nimble any-more and close up you saw how lined and worn was his dark skin and how the veins stood out over his arms and neck. He had a green 4.2 Jaguar and he said that he'd pick up my gear if I liked and take me to Chandler's where several of his casuals stayed. First he had three boxes of fillets to deliver to the Brightwater Hotel and as we drove he told me that he'd lived all his life in Nelson; left school at fourteen to begin nailing apple boxes and by eighteen had his own truck, which he drove between Nelson and Blenheim most of the day and night. 'You can't do that sort of thing now,' he said.

As an ex-truck driver, Mr Trubb was interested in my story of the Bedford and the pumpkins in the Rai Valley. He thought probably a blowout caused the load to shift. There's a knack to loading a truck, just as there's a knack to building a haystack. Mr Trubb told me a good deal of the way he'd become established in the world. It didn't seem to be so much boastfulness as a wish to show the rest of us what hard slog leads to. He saw himself as no different from anyone else and wanted others to have the satisfaction of getting on through hard yakker. He seemed rather surprised when I told him that my brother had gone overseas for a spell.

At the Brightwater Hotel I helped to carry in the big cartons. 'Duck under a load,' said Mr Trubb, 'rather than lifting it to your own height. It's a good lesson, that.' Mr Trubb was paid in cash and he shouted beer, which we drank inside because of the wind, and when he realised I hadn't had any lunch, he bought chips and pan-fried fish — his own, I guess. 'Go on, go on,' he said. 'We'll sweat it out of you tomorrow. One thing I've learnt is that you've got to eat well to work well. You ever done any real farm work? You can judge a farmer's savvy by the meals he gives his shearers and musterers.'

Mr Trubb had a packet of cheroots, thin and dark like himself, and he'd smoked two of them and eaten his food before I'd finished my fish. 'If you don't mind,' he said, 'we'll just drive a few miles up the Lee Valley. There's this hill property that I might be interested in, though not at the money that's being talked at the moment.'

It was lovely, quiet up the Lee. The river itself was small and clear in a rock bed, and the hills were being greened up with pine plantings. The no exit road wasn't much wider than the Jaguar and on the small river flats the wind showed itself as muted flurries in the long grass. Mr Trubb stopped the Jaguar in a paddock gateway that had a bit of height over the property he was interested in: quite steep country and some of it gorsed, but with the Lee Stream in a series of small cascades below. 'I reckon there's a different sort of tourism coming,' he told me. 'More people want to stay in the country, not city hotels.'

He had this idea for a lodge above the river and the whole farm around it for privacy — hundreds of hectares. He didn't want to let on to the owners about those plans, of course. 'Keep it under your hat,' said Mr Trubb with easy familiarity, as if I was someone he'd relied on for years. The late afternoon sun slanted down the valley and we went out into the wind and looked across to the terrace where Mr Trubb thought he'd build the lodge, long and single-storeyed to be in keeping. 'What do you think?' he said and I was close enough to see the veins standing out from his neck and the small skin cancers on his face and arms from years of sweat in the Nelson sun.

I appreciated being treated as an equal, as if I had already proved myself a toiler at Golden Seafoods, but I didn't want to presume. If he had to come into the factory in a day or two and give me a rocket over something then it would make it more embarrassing. 'The Asians,' said Mr Trubb, 'they jump at anything like this. We don't realise how lucky we are to live here. The best air and water in the world.' At the head of the valley was the sheen of old serpentine workings and there was a scattered mob of Hereford steers on the river flat. Among the green of the young pines on the far slope were the rust-coloured branches from the last pruning. There were briars close to us on the roadside and the berries had a summer burnish. Not one vehicle had passed us since we arrived, yet we must have been within half an hour of the city.

Mr Trubb walked back to the Jaguar and stood by the door for a moment. Then he leant forward and said something I didn't catch, before he slipped to his left along the flank of the car, which partly supported him. His body slid, taking the fine dust from the polished paintwork beneath. He lay in the grass by the car and when I knelt down I could hear his altered breathing, which was oddly similar to the noise that the wind was making in the wheel arch of the car. One of his eyelids was almost closed and a trouser leg snagged on a briar as I lifted him. The suddenness of it made me swear a good deal for relief.

There was a moment, with Mr Trubb belted in the front seat and the Jaguar's automatic roughly sorted out to get me to Brightwater, when I had a sudden, passing amazement that everything in the valley was just the same. The green and brown of the pines unaltered, the steers still filling their guts, the cascade of the Lee, the utterly indifferent whine and pulse of the wind.

A stroke rather than a heart attack, so I was told, and Mr Trubb died a few days afterwards, despite putting in some hard work to stay alive. I couldn't settle at Golden Seafoods and for the rest of the vacation dug potters' clay at Mapua and then did some fruit picking in the Upper Moutere. When the new term started I was lucky to get offered a ride from Nelson down through the Lewis and we passed the turn-off to the Lee Valley on the way. I had a glimpse of the Brightwater pub again. I'd been a couple of months in the Nelson district and yet afterwards I always associated the whole time with three things from that very first day — the pumpkin smash in the Rai Valley, Mr Trubb and his vision of the lodge, and that damn, persistent wind.

The Occasion

~

On THEIR WAY to the North Island they had one night in the Astle Motels, Picton, before they were to cross over on the ferry. The motels were concrete block, painted cream both inside and out, so that several times that evening it took Mervyn a moment to recall if he'd come inside, or was still standing outside. There was a shower so confined that it felt like a coffin. 'Oh, it's only for one night, isn't it,' his wife said. 'One night won't kill you.'

The owners, the Perrits, had four units near the steep road, then their own home that looked as though it, too, was painted cream inside and out, then a long strip of lawn, with a faded trampoline to justify the phrase, children's play area, in the brochure. Right at the back, by a Japanese box hedge, was a tin garden shed with high windows.

Mervyn had these pills for what ailed him and after he'd taken a couple he couldn't settle to watch the game show on the television. Whoever was going to win the family sedan, the trip with spending money to Los Angeles, or be dismissed with just the sponsor's products, seemed a long way from the Astle Motels. Mervyn walked past units two, three and four, each resounding with the same game show host, past the Perrits' house. It was dark and the lights of the town glowed below with a spurious magnificence ending abruptly at the sea's edge.

He climbed on to the trampoline, gingerly lest it disintegrate beneath his weight. Much of the elasticity seemed weathered out of it. Rocking gently there, oddly reassured by the movement, he was high enough to see directly into the window of the lit garden shed, where Mrs Perrit was dancing among laundry powders, empty cartons, and heaped net curtains like Kleenex, which had long ago hung in all the units.

Mervyn had never been introduced to Mrs Perrit, had never heard her voice, knew nothing of her life beyond that day, had seen her just the once before, standing behind her husband and sucking her teeth as Mervyn signed in. Yet, oscillating four feet above the lawn in the summer night, Mervyn glimpsed her in some most private transport of euphoria, dancing by herself in the tin shed. She wore a sleeveless print dress, cut unkindly so that the puckered flesh and hair of her armpits were displayed when she raised her hands to place the palms together. She closed her eyes as she spun as if better to establish the consummate surroundings in which her dance was set. Mrs Perrit was a large, clumsy woman in Picton, who apparently wished to be set free. Her hair was lacklustre and her movements of absurd gentility.

The psychiatrist later was at pains to point out to Mervyn that of course everything at the Astle Motels was the occasion of his breakdown and not in any way the cause. He found it interesting and important to have Mervyn realise that the dancing, the trampoline, all of it, was merely a conjunction of phenomena. Mervyn had not been driven mad by Mrs Perrit's dancing in the back shed. No, there was a complex series of factors going way back that took a good deal of the psychiatrist's time, and a good deal of Mervyn's money, to identify.

Mervyn knew that his doctor was right, that the dancing Mrs Perrit wasn't to blame, but always afterwards when he thought of his illness, or when he felt very low in himself — how are you, in yourself, Mervyn, his wife would say — then he felt again suspended, oscillating in a summer night, while watching poor, desperate Mrs Perrit dancing in the hope of who knows what release. It was a parody that struck deep into Mervyn's heart.

He saw, as if the wind had turned suddenly, that the whole splendid ballet of life casts larger shadows, which are the jig of death.

Mervyn had crept down from the trampoline, walked back to his Ford Falcon by the concrete motel unit, and sat with the door open, reciting in sequence of purchase all the cars that he had ever owned. That's where his wife found him eventually. The first one, he told her gently, the very first, was a second-hand 1936 Morris Eight older than himself, and it was two-toned, black and a wonderful scarlet, and the doors were hinged behind the seat so that, if they opened while you drove, they could scoop in the whole world.

Cometh the Hour

⌐

THE SUN LAY stretched in the evening and summer sky, the weeping elms sighed and rustled in the cat's-paws of the easterly, and Crimmond's Alsatian, like a wine taster, raised its head to the promise of night. James Cumuth paused at the doorway of his wooden sleepout before going in at the end of his working day. Tall and spare he stood there, holding his left arm with his right hand in an odd posture of relaxation. In his urban backpack, as well as items from the Super-Doop store, were the latest copy of *International Creative Scientist*, his plastic lunchbox with the Gladwrap folded ready to reuse, and a piece of driftwood shaped rather less like a dolphin than he had first thought. In his jacket pocket was the half-size manila envelope that held his bonus from Palmer's Product Testing.

Cumuth wasn't insensible to the attractions of the natural world, though his was essentially a life of the mind. He registered the subsiding sun, the elms, his landlady's clumped irises, even the gleam of condition on the Alsatian's pelt as it cast an oblique glance to ensure that he hadn't ventured on to Crimmond property. It was all a banality, though, wasn't it? Cumuth still awaited some mission worthy of him: some palpable need that would justify the cool, implacable resolution he felt inside.

In the neatness of his one room he emptied the bag in a manner that did not lessen the order. It was the neatness of a man who puts no store on possessions: a travelling, on-the-road man who, by whim or principle, could pack in half an hour and blow, leaving nothing of himself behind. He took his one chair to the open door where he sat in the rectangle of amber sun and read from *International Creative Scientist* the Popoffvich article on salinity trends in large European catchment lakes.

Cumuth had not forgotten his bonus envelope, but it remained unopened. A cursory thing. He knew that he was not considered a valued employee and he knew from experience that Paul Bigelow was right when he said that the rich have a touching faith in the efficacy of small sums. At Palmer's Product Testing, Cumuth's task that week was the determination of epidermal resistal material in Paree Natural Parfume Creme after atmospheric exposure — in other words how thick a skin was likely to form on the top when the lid was left off. A man doesn't establish a personal creed on such things.

Cumuth had a BSc, but more than that he had a pioneer ancestry: lean men who had walked slow and tall through their time, proudly reticent men who could spit a double metre from the side of their mouth, without leaving a trace on their chin, when they heard a personal vanity spoken. Solitary men with a natural focus on mountain peaks, even the stars above them. Such men despise the even tenor of the life of the mass of citizenry and wait with a quiet half-smile for a challenge sufficiently cataclysmic to justify their acceptance. Their progeny are not numerous, for such pioneers are loath to spill their seed recklessly.

Cumuth himself told no one of such things of course, never consciously exalted himself. It was more a disposition, a detachment of view. He knew, however, that his paternal grandfather had done something in the war so special that no one spoke of it. So he sat in the open doorway of his sleepout, letting the dying sun copper his aquiline features and listening to the soughing of the elms.

Mrs Burmeister, his landlady, watched from the kitchen window and talked with her divorced daughter. I reckon he's a sandwich short of a picnic, she said. He's sunning himself with his mouth open. You could fart in his face and he'd still look at the mountains. Nadine gave her low, even laugh, full of knowing derision concerning men. A loser, she said. A loser with bells on. Neither mother nor daughter set much store by taciturn, frontier values.

He always seems to look past you, said Mrs Burmeister.

Always has an idiot half-smile, said Nadine.

James Cumuth was aware of them at the periphery of his line of sight, aware of the tilt of the Alsatian's muzzle also and the pulsation of the Harley Davidson, about two blocks away he reckoned. The magazine had fallen to the floor in the doorway and his hands were relaxed in the dying sun. The hands of a pianist, or a fighter pilot. When the hog was out of earshot it was quiet in the suburb, but not too quiet.

In the labs at Palmer's, Mrs Burmeister's opinion of James Cumuth was unknown, yet shared nevertheless. He was a loner all right. He was the cat that walked by himself. A one man band, that's for sure. Odd ball city, all right. He was a queer fish. He contributed little to the harmless gossip and advantageous obsequiousness of the staff cafeteria. He drank his coffee black, his bourbon neat and if he was looking out of the third floor lab window at the small people scurrying below when Errol Golightly PhD came around, then he made no pretence to be doing anything but that, watching the small people scurrying.

You can see that he wasn't one for cultivating the approval of other people and he had this habit of screwing up his eyes a bit and looking into the far distance as if to check for some menace there. One or two women at Palmer's, and one or two men, were initially attracted to his steady silence and his slender hands, but they found he meant no invitation by them. The personnel manager said that there was no reason for family pride; that Cumuth was brought up by an uncle who ran a video parlour and that he lived in a one-room sleepout over in Kodacks. No truth at all, he said, in the idea that Cumuth was part Easter Island chief on his mother's side. None at all.

And people don't like idiosyncrasy in a quiet person, whereas in a boisterous one they see it as being just hard case behaviour. Now that's the truth. Cumuth wore tan stock boots; always he wore them, when everyone knew that there wasn't any stock for miles and miles around. Even way out of the city what you got was crops, horticulture and stuff. Everyone knew that. Aaron Schoone came from the country. He'd survived out there for years and he said nobody wore stock boots. Glasshouses and orchards and nurseries and poultry farms were the things out there, Aaron told the cafeteria crowd at Palmer's Product Testing.

Once they had this full-day professional motivation course run by Clarence Best Associates and Cumuth came in a full twenty minutes late after lunch and never said as much as a word, but walked slowly to his chair and screwed up his eyes a little and put his left stock boot on his right knee — after he'd sat down of course.

On the fourteenth, Wesley Igor Drom, the notorious garrottist and entrail fetishist, broke out of the maximum security institution at Happy Glades with a body count of twelve. Some papers said more. Drom moved through the pigeon blue summer dusk like a kauri tree stump. He bit a man half to death at the motorway overbridge and even took flowers without paying from a little boutique next to the Bonafide Dance Academy and the waterbed shop. Blazing red roses, the boutique lady said and when the top psychiatrist being interviewed on television was told that, he said, ooh, red you say, ooh, now that's not a good sign by a long chalk.

The Enderby twins were roller skating at the Kodacks rink on the night of the fourteenth. Normally they'd be safe home, but it was Easter Mulheron's birthday and a whole bunch of them were skating before being picked up. Wesley Drom, irritated by the noise, crippled the gatekeeper with a twist of his left hand and took the Enderby twins as lightweight hostages. Tucked both of them under one arm, it was said, so that their blonde ringlets hung in the night. The armed offenders squads were all over, but no sign, and they had to be careful because of the twins.

To Mrs Drom, Wesley Igor was just her boy who took a wrong turning, I suppose: to the city he was the nation's galvanised degeneracy, and to James Cumuth he was manifest destiny.

Mrs Burmeister and Nadine were woken by the sound of Drom beating the Lewis-Smythes so that they would rustle up a breakfast for him in quick time. Dawn is a good time for screams to carry. Cumuth was at the door of the sleepout when his landlady came out on to the verandah and she told him all she knew about Drom and the break-out from television. Sweet Jesus, she said, that'll be him all right, murdering someone.

Oh God, he's at it. Right here and he's killing everybody, said Nadine. He's butchering people and there's nothing to be done. She stood in her pink, candlewick dressing gown and pressed both hands to her throat.

James Cumuth reached back into his sleepout for his boots and sat on the step to draw them on. There is a bleak, steely quality to the first dawn light and it seemed reflected in JC's eyes as he ran a hand through his hair before going over to the house of the Lewis-Smythes. You can't do anything there, said Nadine. You'll get torn to pieces. Jesus yes, but for the first time there was an uncertain note in her derision. Cumuth looked past her as ever and gave his half-smile redolent with a stoical seren-ity. He walked across the lawn belonging to the Crimmonds and the Alsatian bounded towards him with its ears back and lip up, but was checked by some ema-nation of the man's presence, and began fawning and dragging its head sideways on the grass. Attaboy, said Cumuth softly.

Wesley Igor Drom realised that it was almost the end of the line and was intent on taking a few more down with him. He still had the Enderby twins under one arm like bagpipes so that the sharpshooters wouldn't risk a shot at a distance. The breakfast can't have been to his liking for he gave both host and hostess their quietus head down in the full sink and when a brave unarmed combat expert made a rush through a skylight, thinking Drom had his hands full, Drom proved adept with a novelty bottle of peanut butter in the shape of Princess Di. It struck the expert's head with a sound like a greywacke stone on a rotten pumpkin.

A good many people formed a ring behind the police cordon as the light improved. Somehow JC got through both ring and cordon without so much as a word. People felt a need to step aside. They watched him stroll across the dewy grass and pause to trail his relaxed hand in a jasmine bush. He stopped on a nice piece of crazy paving between the back door and the barbecue area and stood balanced there with his hands relaxed by his side and his legs somewhat apart. The morning sun coppered his face in profile, glinted on his tan stock boots. The breeze made hush and not a bull horn sounded. Nellie Hambinder later swore that there was in the sky a cloud the exact shape of a tombstone. No mistaking it, she said.

How long am I going to be waiting here, Drom? said JC. His voice was even and dispassionate, coming from a long way inside the man.

Then Wesley Igor Drom stepped out of the door to face him and there was no shouting, no frothing. He saw the green grass, the elms, the summer flowers, the barbecue area, all in the light of a new day. He heard the uncaring birdsong and the water dripping from the overflowing Lewis-Smythes' sink. Tree trunk Wesley saw many of the police and gawpers who crouched at a distance and he saw as well the one man who stood before him and he dried his hands on the ringlets of the Enderby twins and gave the moment its due.

Put down the Enderbys, said JC, and for once his eyes were focused not on some distant thing, but on the man to whom he spoke. It was a match, you see. It was black and white, day and night, fire and water, it was the Greek guy and the Minotaur; it was the circle of the agonising grace of man's free will to face his destiny. For both of them.

Put down the Enderbys, said JC. And Wesley Drom put the twins aside as you put a pair of fire tongs aside and in the same movement drew a chromed sawn-off shotgun from beneath his coat and fired, and the police started firing, and when it was all over in slow motion and the birds had flown up from the elms in startled alarm, then the police came forward urgently to check the dead and Nadine said, he lived with us, in a voice of reverential exultation and Nellie Hambinder began to sing 'Rock of Ages' and Crimmond's Alsatian slunk away into history.

That's just as it happened and just how it's remembered. People still visit the place today.

A Part of Life

~

ALL THAT SUMMER Polly was at the Shangri La Motels, Lake Tekapo. She and her daughter did the cleaning and were given free accommodation in an old, wooden bach that had no view of the lake and was close to the pine plantation. There were sixteen units at the Shangri La, including a new block of four, two up and two down, with sloping tiled bathroom floors set with chrome drainage grilles, which suited the Asian tourists. And they had air-conditioning and a balcony where you could sit and watch the water skiers and boaties.

The owners of the Shangri La had decided to go for top dollar, so they were very fastidious. When a party moved out everything had to be given a going over. The owners called all guests a party, no matter how many came. Polly and her daughter had to wash all the crockery, all the cutlery, wipe the microwaves, even if it was obvious that they had not been used. Mrs Beaumont gave the instance of stripping a bed that seemed immaculate, to find a pair of false teeth near the foot. 'We would prefer that you leave nothing to chance here, Polly.' She demonstrated the paper seal that was to be put on the lavatory after it had been cleaned. 'You know, Polly,' said Mrs Beaumont, 'the tourist standard has to be higher than their own homes, or ours.'

At the bach, Polly and Alice didn't waste a lot of time doing housework. After fronting up to it most of the day, neither wanted to be cleaning things off duty. 'A good scrub-up at the end, that's the ticket,' Polly told her daughter and she got no argument from Alice. An old, wooden place anyway, with only four rooms; you can only do so much with that.

Their day at the Shangri La depended a good deal on how many parties were checking in and out, because that was when most work had to be done. For other units it was mainly just the linen change and clearing the waste bags. On a good day they had time to talk to the longer stayers and take their time in the well-appointed laundry. 'Have the best of basics, Mr Beaumont always says,' said Mrs Beaumont. There were even times when Polly could let her daughter duck away to meet her new friends.

Polly was naturally sociable and would chat away to the longer stay guests. Mrs Beaumont encouraged it within reason as she had a shrewd understanding that, for travellers, some friendly words could be just as satisfying as a lake view. 'The personal touch, the little extra, Polly,' she said. 'That's the way to get return custom.' Mrs Beaumont knew that people away from their own locality develop a hunger for simple recognition; someone to greet them and to use their name; someone to provide a brief respite from the close company and predictable response of travelling companions, or from loneliness.

That's how Polly met Mr Sondeen. He was one of those very tall, short-haired

Americans that you imagine having been on the college basketball team. His hair was still vigorous, although it had become grey, and his height still gave him a presence, although he was a little round-shouldered. He always wore very baggy, light-coloured slacks as though he were a fat man. He had lots of pairs, all with excellent creases. He had one of the new upstairs units for a month as part of a vacation he was giving his two older sisters — one who had never married and the other who had just lost her husband in a random killing in a diner on the southern outskirts of Kosciusko, Mississippi.

He told Polly all that and more within fifteen minutes of meeting her: told her how the weirdo in Kosciusko had kept shouting, 'Who's laughing now?' as he fired at the people eating, and his sister's husband just happened to be there because he was coming back from a blood test and hadn't been allowed a regular breakfast. 'He'd never set eyes on that diner before,' said Mr Sondeen. 'Just a sonofabitch chance, that's what it was.'

Mr Sondeen was a straightforward, candid man and told Polly that he had made a good deal of money in commercial dealership franchises, but at the cost of his wife who had left him to marry a high school principal in Gary, Indiana. 'Neither of my sisters can afford to cross the road,' said Mr Sondeen on another occasion. He was yarning in the laundry while Polly and Alice ironed sheets and pillowslips. He had put his sisters on the stones of the lakefront for the morning and was set to go golfing as usual. 'I notice that in families. Either the women make the money, or the men do, but you don't get both sexes doing well; not in my experience you don't. Anyway, I've gotten into the shape to be able to show my sisters something of the world and so why not. Okay, so my wife's gone, but then again I could've been like Ben — dropping into the wrong diner. There's cause for thought in something like that.'

On the Friday that began the second week of his stay at the Shangri La, Mr Sondeen sought Polly's help when she came with towels and another liner for the waste unit. It was very still and hot; the lake was a harsh blue. A party from number fourteen were assembling by their car below to go fishing at Alexandrina, but Mr Sondeen's voice barely dropped a decibel. 'Now I hope you won't take offence, 'cause none is intended, absolutely. I'm not entirely sure of your ways here, but I mentioned something of it to Mr Beaumont and got no sense at all. The thing is I'm interested in womanly company, you understand, and I'm damned if I can find any such resource for a travelling man in this otherwise beautiful spot. Quite frankly put, I need to fire a round or two, you understand?'

'I can't help. I'm only here for a summer myself.' Polly just prevented herself from adding the usual courtesy that she was sorry that she was unable to help. It wasn't the sort of conversation she was used to.

'It's embarrassing, isn't it?' continued Mr Sondeen, yet without showing the slightest sign of it. 'Absolutely no offence intended. But at home, you see, there's a desk clerk, bell boy, or barman you can talk to man to man. Here no one seems to have a handle on it at all. Jesus, I mean Mr Beaumont seemed to think I wanted to go courting and the guy at the lakeside hotel told me what a shame New Year was over. I've never known so little opportunity for a friendly transaction.'

'It's different here, I suppose,' said Polly and she thought that Mr Sondeen's tone was just the one that he had used when cloud prevented his sisters and him from taking the scenic flight over the Alps.

'Look Polly,' he said, 'it's not for a gentleman to go on about it. Let's just say that I've several hundred dollars for the local economy that isn't being taken advantage of.'

'Anyway,' said Polly, 'I'll just put in these new towels as well.'

'I see it as a perfectly natural inclination myself, but the last thing I want is to give offence as a visitor in another country.'

Mr Sondeen yawned and spread his arms as if directing traffic, to show that he was done with the subject. The sliding door to the balcony had been pushed back and he stood in the gap looking out over the slope to the shingle beach, across the blue expanse of the lake towards the mountains.

'I tell you, Polly, this Kiwiland is something. I haven't had my eyes so drawn to landscape about me since I spent some time in Montana at the end of the seventies. Ever been to Montana, Polly? Now that's fetching country. Red Rock River and the Beaverhead Mountains, where they found gold in the sixties, about the time you did here so I'm told. Such beautiful, desolate country.'

Wednesday was the one day of the week that Polly and Alice had to themselves: it tended to be one of the quiet days for arrivals at the Shangri La and the policeman's wife used to come in and help Mrs Beaumont. For the first few Wednesdays Polly and Alice did those of the tourist things they could afford, but then Alice found that Ruby Corrigan, from the same netball team, was staying with friends in the camping ground. Polly didn't much enjoy being on the lakefront by herself. She had no husband for company and she was self-conscious about her white, middle-aged legs if she wore shorts.

She took to spending the day sitting in the open door of the old bach, which was shielded from the road and in which she could arrange herself to receive just that balance of shade and sun she wanted. She had lemonade and an economy cask of müller thurgau in the small fridge. She rationed her drinks, leant on a palliasse that smelled like the inside of an old biscuit tin and read, off and on, popular paperbacks about lissome, corporate bitches making it in a man's world. What she tended to think about, though, was how, at forty-seven, she had come to be in someone else's four-room bach at Tekapo and cleaning the Shangri La Motels for a living.

Looking back, she could see that the signs of such an outcome had been there all along, but, like the rest of us, she had taken her own experience, her own indecisions and opportunities, as something inaugural and not part of a normal population curve. It pained her enormously to be treated for what she was: to see people's attention slide away from her as she talked, to watch her pleasant, unremarkable face and plump legs in the windows of shops she passed, to have no skills or knowledge that were indispensable. She was aware, and Mrs Beaumont was aware, of the affable, egalitarian relationship between them — with certain tacit constraints. Your business is only as good as your staff, Mr Beaumont would remind his wife.

Polly told her daughter about Mr Sondeen's complaint. 'The dirty old devil,' said Alice with a laugh. She herself had begun a very fulfilling, but uncomplicated, relationship with a guy dumped by Ruby Corrigan and so was at peace with the world. 'An old geezer like that should stick to his golf and his memories,' she said.

'Right,' said Polly. She remembered when Alice's father would miss lunch and drive across most of Christchurch to spend twenty minutes making love to her in a flat above Sumner. He was very quiet, very intense and had one small patch of dark hair between the muscles of his chest. 'Do you know,' he would say, with his palms on her shoulders, 'how often I dream of this?'

Mr Sondeen liked to talk to Polly, but he didn't complain about his celibacy again. He was as cheerful and positive and loud as ever. Polly felt no particular physical attraction, but no aversion either. Mr Sondeen must have been sixty, but he was thin and very clean and his wealth and nationality seemed to give him a certain gloss. Most of all, there was that disconcerting frankness of which Americans are master and which is at once rebuked and envied by those more accustomed to modesty and deception.

Most days Polly passed at least a few words with Mr Sondeen and his elderly sisters. The sisters wished she could come sightseeing with them; Mr Sondeen gave her a four-pound rainbow trout he caught in Lake Alexandrina. She cooked it in foil the way Mrs Beaumont recommended. Almost every time she talked with Mr Sondeen Polly wondered whether he had found his opportunity for physical intimacy and what he was prepared to pay for it. She told herself it was more a natural curiosity on her part than an interest in sleeping with him.

It became Alice's practice not to come back to the bach several nights a week — staying over with Ruby she called it, but it wasn't Ruby who picked her up after work at the Shangri La, or dropped her off there in the morning. Polly felt neither anger, nor envy, just a sense of part of her own life being played out again in her daughter's easy, summer existence. Polly remembered the casual assurance that came from being young and desired, an assurance that assumed both immutable. Sometimes when she looked up from her work to see Alice's boyfriend waiting in his car — all brown forearms and light hair drawn back in a ponytail — she thought that he was waiting for her, as men had often done, but then she remembered that it was 1994 and that it was her daughter who would run over to the car and laugh and call goodbye.

No place is perfect, of course, even for those come only in a summer. On some days a fierce wind came right down the lake from the black and white mountains at its head; not cold so much as unpleasant and tiring. It chapped the face, blew back hair until it was painful at the roots, whipped words away so that conversation was a mockery. It scurried grit into the Shangri La Motels from the lakeshore, even into the bach further back among the pines, rattling the old door and window frames. On such a day, when the Japanese tourists preferred to regard the Church of the Good Shepherd from the glassed comfort of their buses rather than traipse around it, and

Mrs Beaumont had been particularly vigilant in her inspection of the units, Polly thought that maybe she would let Mr Sondeen make love to her.

A considerable experience of very moderate success in life can create a defensive self-deceit, or be the cause of an altogether more detached and matter of fact view. Polly was inclined to be honest with herself. She watched the pines buck in the wind, heard their needles skating on the tin roof, as she made a sandwich of the last of her slightly fishy-smelling ham.

By the end of March she would no longer be needed at the Shangri La and would have to go back to Christchurch for the winter. Five hundred dollars, say four then, could make quite a difference — the agent's fees, bond and rent in advance needed in getting a flat perhaps. Polly could have justified her train of thought by bringing in romance, but she didn't. No dream that wealthy Mr Sondeen might fall for her and offer marriage, a life in the United States. No, Polly was weighing up if the money would be worth the effort — the embarrassment of bringing up the matter with Mr Sondeen, the humiliation if he didn't want her, all the little auxiliary hassles such as shaving her legs and armpits, taking precautions, tackling any kinky stuff, worrying about her breath, her underclothes, her dimpled bum, whether he would want something to eat, where they would do it.

Polly watched the grit puffing in around the window frame with each gust of wind. The whole bach would have to be cleaned if they came there and it would have to be a time when Alice was away. She was surprised how much there was to it and told herself that the sums of money involved weren't that over the top after all. There was one big advantage if it didn't go well: Mr Sondeen and his sisters were leaving in less than two weeks. Polly didn't like the prospect of having to maintain the same terms with Mr Sondeen afterwards; bringing the towels and sheets, passing the time of day with his sisters, listening to Mr Sondeen explain his golf round, or the stop-off points on the day's sightseeing. Nor did she want too much opportunity for him to talk to the Beaumonts in the candid way he had about recent satisfactions he may have experienced, or any disappointments. And maybe he would insist she use his Christian name and maybe it would be Al, Myron, or Randy.

The wind blew itself out in the night and the next day was bright and still. From unit nine Polly saw Mr Sondeen putting his golf clubs in the rental station-wagon and she left her work in the kitchen of number nine and walked over to him.

'Lake's a picture, Polly,' he said. 'I aim to make the most of today.'

'It's beaut.' Polly wondered just how best to bring up the subject of the womanly company he had talked about. 'The wind's so tiring. Don't you find?' she said.

'Worse than rain,' said Mr Sondeen. 'You can fish in the rain. Sometimes it's even more likely that way.'

'I've been thinking about what you said — about a woman's company.'

'Absolutely,' said Mr Sondeen.

'Absolutely?'

'No change in the situation,' he said. 'I've just about given up on finding that particular recreation until we get to one of your cities. The last thing I want is to give offence. There's a civilised way with all of our needs.'

Mr Sondeen left the back of the station-wagon up, because it was creating a little shade for them both. The air was so still that they could hear people laughing up by the hotel and the swish of a car coming down to the little township along the lupin-fringed road from Burke's Pass. Blue, purple, pink, cream, less commonly white or apricot flowers on the bushes that never grew tall and were restricted to the roadsides where the sheep couldn't eat them. The road wasn't visible from the Shangri La but, hearing the car on the slope, Polly had the complete scene in her mind for a moment. Mr Sondeen had the grace to stand quietly, smoothing his eyebrows, so that Polly had the opportunity to think or speak. 'Maybe you'd like to be with me,' she said.

'Indeed I would,' said Mr Sondeen. It was Alice he usually watched when she and Polly were working around the motel, but he had a realistic view of his prospects and said nothing of that.

'Great, just great,' he said. 'How about I buy lunch at the hotel today and we can talk there. Say twelve thirty?'

'Better make it quarter to one.'

'That's really great, Polly. I look forward to that.' He was genuinely, unashamedly, pleased and so at ease with the situation that Polly felt it less unusual herself. His voice had retained the same volume he used for telling her of his golf rounds, or how the colour of Pukaki was milky green and not at all the deep blue of Tekapo.

She walked back to number nine to finish cleaning the kitchen. In some ways she was relieved that the details of actually doing it hadn't been talked about; in other ways she wished that such a discussion were already over. Mr Sondeen closed the back of the wagon and went up to fetch his sisters so that he could take them to the lake before he went on to play golf. When they were coming down the outside stairs of the new block, Polly could hear them praising the day.

One of the sisters said she couldn't believe that, after the wind of the day before, it was possible for it to be so heavenly. 'You could just live in this place for ever.'

'Couldn't you though?' said Mr Sondeen.

Polly hadn't expected to be going to the hotel for lunch and she had no opportunity to go back to the bach to change. She wore a print frock and her flat working shoes, which needed a polish. At least she had been able to spend a while on her hair in unit eleven when she should have been vacuuming and as there was no wind at all, the walk to the hotel didn't muss it up. Mr Sondeen insisted they have the salmon and that he pay for it.

They sat on the terrace. Sondeen still wore his golf shoes and talked at first of other places that had some affinity with where he found himself, as those who travel a good deal tend to do. The link was often quite circumstantial — the salmon lunch, a guest speaking Italian, the wind of the day before. As he talked, Polly made a physical appraisal, so that there was nothing visible that she couldn't tolerate if he were to make love to her. She decided that, even as a young man, he hadn't been handsome at all, hadn't possessed any overwhelming charm, but the advantages he had then he retained; nothing of grossness had developed. He had a good head of hair; he was very tall and still so slim that the belt on his expensive, baggy trousers was a brief circumference and not an ounce of fat hung over it. He had a long, big-featured, plain face that was seamed rather than wrinkled. His mouth often hung open when he was listening, or thinking. He had a beautiful, gold watch that slipped very low on his wrist and his hands were large and clean, showing no other signs of wear except that from golf clubs. He was an ordinary man who, through hard work, or good fortune, had succeeded to a greater degree than other ordinary men and that success gave him assurance in his beliefs, his needs, his appearance, and it gave him good humour and tolerance as well.

'Now in Singapore,' Mr Sondeen was saying, 'it's different. Shoot, they run a tight ship there all right, I tell you. I've been there three times. The Chinese know what service is in Singapore. Mind you, you can't get privacy within a natural landscape there the way you can in this country of yours. That's what keeps reminding me of Red Rock River.'

Mr Sondeen talked so much of other countries that in the end the arrangements for their rendezvous had to be hurried through in his station-wagon as he drove Polly back just in time to start work again at the Shangri La. Polly would have liked to think it the result of a nervous anticipation on Mr Sondeen's part, but she recognised it rather as a true indication of his priorities. It was no big deal, after all, to bed a middle-aged cleaner at the Tekapo Shangri La Motels. She imagined there had been women in Montana too, but his recollection was of the mountains, the sagebrush, conifers, the high grasslands under snow that showed cougar tracks.

Polly spent much of her Wednesday cleaning the bach. She entertained herself with the ridiculous idea of the itemised account she could present to Mr Sondeen — preparation of venue, smoked cheese and a chardonnay, the forgoing of her normal relaxation, depilatory costs, loss of sleep. Prostitution was novel to her; she was surprised at the extra work and obligation involved even before anyone else arrived. Probably she wasn't casual enough, she decided, or sufficiently angry. Perhaps she should feel a righteous indignation that, as a woman, she had been forced by her society to obtain money in such a way to ensure her winter in Christchurch. What she did feel was disappointment that, after loving three men, she was left with just Alice dear to her — though very dear. There had been good reasons at the time, of course, for each break-up and optimism for better opportunities to come, but with hindsight she was able to see that each relationship was in fact a step to where she found herself — tidying an old bach in the pines at Tekapo for Mr Sondeen's visit.

In the slanted, evening sun Mr Sondeen came through the wooden gateway and up the dirt path to the bach. He had walked from the Shangri La Motels and wore his floppy golf hat to protect himself. He had tan shoes and a pair of his expensive, baggy slacks that Polly hadn't seen before — a very light powder blue. He carried a bottle of wine in a red striped paper bag from the Tekapo Hotel and in the other hand a purple lupin cob that he had picked from the roadside. 'Jeez,' he said to Polly, standing by the worn, wooden step, 'have these lupin things got a fair smell, or what!'

'They're not even native.'

'They're not?'

'I don't think they are.'

It was what Polly had feared — him arriving at the door and the awkwardness of talking about some such nonsense as the lupins, when they both knew he'd come to undress her and make love to her by arrangement. Almost as soon as the awkwardness was apparent, Mr Sondeen moved to dispel it with a direct matter of factness. He put both the wine and flower behind him on the bench with scarcely a glance. 'The thing is, Polly, you don't have to do anything. We can just drink this wine and talk if that's what you feel best with; if you've gone off the idea of bed for the two of us. The last thing I want is to give offence.'

'I don't mind,' said Polly.

'I've been looking forward to it ever since Thursday — after that damned wind when you mentioned it.'

'Would you like a drink of something?' Polly stopped herself adding the word, first. 'I've got cheese and fruit. It's difficult to bake much of anything here. The kitchen's not set up for it.'

Mr Sondeen didn't look around the small kitchen cum living room; he made no comment about it not being such a bad little shack, or anything like that. He kept his direct gaze on Polly. 'Now you can tell me I'm wrong here, Polly, but it seems to me that you're only going to feel embarrassed until we get to the loving, so the sooner the better. Afterwards, I'd say we have a damned good chance of relaxing. That's my best guess, anyway.'

And Polly knew that in his candid way he was right and she said so briefly and took him into the bedroom determined not to care about the smell of the palliasses, or the water stains on the ceiling panels, or the hangers of clothes on large nails hammered into the wall. She was far more comfortable with what she was doing than with trying to talk about it. She sat on the bed and watched Mr Sondeen take off his powder blue, baggy slacks and fold them on the floor to keep the creases.

'Let's see what we've got here,' he said kindly and he parted Polly's blouse, smiled and stroked her breasts firmly. Her nipples were small, pale and with almost no aureole. Mr Sondeen ran a circle around each with the longest finger of his right hand. 'Lovely skin, Polly,' he said. 'Lovely skin.' Her breasts were full and extended a good way down her chest. Her first lover had been able almost to contain them with two champagne glasses, but she must have told a good many lies since because they had continued to grow. Mr Sondeen tried to kiss them and did so clumsily because of his height and the stiffness of his joints. His head was very close; she could see his scalp beneath the grey, short hair and the sun-damaged skin on the tips of his ears. He smelled of anti-perspirant, a good aftershave and peppermint. 'How beautiful you are,' said Mr Sondeen cheerfully.

'I'm middle-aged.'

'You can't be forty yet.' He was delighted with his own flattery and showed white, even teeth when he laughed. All capped, Polly supposed, at vast expense; she felt a passing grievance that at his age he was able to have better teeth than her own. She had a soft wart on her right side above her hip and supposed that in time he'd see it. 'Ah, Polly,' he said, 'why didn't we think of this sooner?'

'And maybe regret it later,' she said.

Mr Sondeen slid his own clothes off so easily; everything was so loose on his thin body and he helped Polly out of hers with obvious enjoyment. He caressed her for a time. The loudest noise was the regular, rather loud rustle of his breathing. Then Mr Sondeen worked a little on himself, half turned away out of modesty. 'Hell, Polly,' he said, 'don't think that it's any lack of inclination; it's just age, you see. You get to be not so quick on the draw.' He was intent and just slightly impatient. She looked at the tendons in his neck, the fuzz of grey on his flat chest, the customary creases at his amazingly slim waist, the long, blue veins on the inside of his arms. When he first lay against her the slight mutual sweat before exertion was like an adhesive and their skin sealed, not altogether unpleasantly.

'Take a grip on it for a moment, sweetheart,' Mr Sondeen said.

Polly could see the pines through the one bedroom window. The sun was low and so bright still, that it shone almost parallel with the great branches and lit up, at random, patches of fissured bark, glittered on wept resin, singled out green needle clumps as if they were helmet plumes.

'That's it. Yes,' said Mr Sondeen loudly.

Alice's father was the third of the three men Polly had loved. She'd never seen any prospect for happiness in promiscuity. Each of her men had been a love for life until circumstances proved otherwise. Each of them had been a partner for several years. Alice's father had a breakdown because his personality proved incompatible with his job in local government. He longed to work outdoors, but his marketable skill was in computer software. After the hospital he went to northern Queensland and sent back just one letter, which didn't even enquire after Alice.

'Yes, upward and onward. That's it,' said Mr Sondeen. He meant nothing at all by it and his eyes rolled.

Polly had not expected to be sensually transported, and she wasn't. Neither did she feel any aversion. Doing it was familiar despite a celibacy of several years. There was a surprising degree of localised pleasure. The circumstances did make her a little sad, however, bringing to mind the act when she had been passionately involved: sparking quick images of the ardent voices, bodies and hopes of the young men she had loved. Polly made the most of it; partly for Mr Sondeen, partly for her own gratification, mainly for the memories of other men in her arms.

'Home run,' said Mr Sondeen, his voice subdued for once. It was then she wished she had set the time rather later, when dusk was due. The light was still quite good in the bach; enough to show in unbecoming clarity the heavy droop of her breasts, the small, fleshy excrescence on her side, the mottled flush that she knew would be on her neck and breastbone. She pulled the sheet across her thighs. She could think of absolutely nothing to say. She watched the fly spots on the light fitting and listened to Mr Sondeen's heavy breathing. At such a time her second man had always kissed her stomach and said he was the luckiest guy in the world.

Mr Sondeen extended his arms behind and above him, arms so long that the hands hung over the wooden rail. They were crossed at the wrist as if he were tied in bondage and the long veins on the hairless, inner scope of his arms were drained of their blue blood. 'A man's a prisoner to it, Polly,' he said. His thin legs didn't share the sheet and Polly saw with some envy that his waist and legs had just narrow muscle and tendon shaped to the bone. His pubic hair retained much of the darkness that his head had lost. His cock had become subdued to a half-arch on his thigh. Sweat gleamed in the creases of his face and neck; there was a little white at the corners of his eyes.

'A prisoner?'

'Women are martyrs to their hormones, we're told. And I don't doubt a bit of it, not a bit of it. Shoot, I went through it with my wife for Christ's sake. But then a man is driven too, Polly. Just think how many have been cock driven to humiliation and disaster, half knowing it, but unable to go any other way.'

'Is that supposed to make me feel good?' said Polly.

'This is by far the best thing of my holiday here. I just don't want you to think of me too much as a silly old bugger.'

Mr Sondeen brought his arms down and then sat on the bed side to put on his green boxer shorts. He stood up and took the few paces to the window. With his back to her he rubbed his face and his short, grey hair with his hands. 'Most of the pines here in Kiwiland come from America. The lot of them in fact, I've been told.' His voice became oddly high and distorted because he was yawning as he spoke. 'The species I'm talking about. I was in a foursome with a DOC guy in the weekend and he said that there wasn't a tree here before your settlers. The whole caboose was just snow-grass, he said, up to a man's waist.'

'When there's a strong wind at night here, the pines make a noise like the sea. It's uncanny.'

'Plenty of cones for winter,' said Mr Sondeen and then after a pause, 'You mind if I have a shower, Polly?'

'It's a bit Mickey Mouse,' she said.

'Shoot, I know what the plumbing's like in these huts.' The bathroom was next door to the bedroom and Mr Sondeen was almost through it when he turned back on impulse, leant forward with his hands on the end of the bed. 'That really did the trick for me, Polly. I feel good and easy.'

'I'm glad,' said Polly. While he had his shower she listened to the pipes gurgling; a muffled exclamation from Mr Sondeen as though the water was suddenly too hot, or he'd slipped on a soap remnant on the concrete base.

Polly decided that it hadn't been too bad. Not up to the best hopes that she'd had, but a good way from the worst fears. Everything was much the same, wasn't it? That was at once the most obviously reassuring response and, more subtly, the most worrying. Polly had her shower after Mr Sondeen, not caring that by then the water was almost cold, and when she finished she found that he was dressed and back in the kitchen; that he had shown the initiative to open his wine and her cheese. 'It always does give you an appetite, don't you find?' he said. 'Sex and a mountain climate seem to do that. I imagine some really big eaters shacked up in your high country and in western Montana. Shoot, now there's magnificent country without question, Polly.'

'I guess so.' Polly liked to hear about places overseas, because she'd never been herself, except a seven-day Sydney package with her second partner. Mr Sondeen asked her about it and she enjoyed recalling the city. He knew it better than Polly, but he encouraged her to talk about her harbour cruise, the hotel by Elizabeth Bay, the trip to the Blue Mountains, and then he began on the interior of Australia, the Philippines, where he'd lived for two years while supervising the installation of plant for tanneries, and Mexico. Polly rather enjoyed hearing so much about his life, even though she knew there was no future in it for her.

'I must remember the money,' he said finally; the first sign that he was thinking of going. 'How much do you want?'

'You mean how much do I deserve — a fair rate.'

'No. How much do you want?' Mr Sondeen was interested in the attitude others took to money. He himself knew a lot about it and valued it, without at all being possessed by it.

'I've no idea. I told you it's all new to me. I don't want to haggle.'

'But you must have imagined some amount when you decided to let me come,' persisted Mr Sondeen. 'You had a target, that's for sure. Something you wanted and didn't have any other way of rustling up the bucks. This isn't your regular thing.'

'I was thinking that three hundred dollars would help me into a small Christchurch flat for the winter,' she said.

'Sure enough, Polly. That's a sensible way to go.' He took a bill-fold from his back pocket and put four hundred-dollar notes from it on the worn laminate of the bench top. 'Winter, eh? There's always something you've got to bear in mind, isn't there? Always a situation that's snuck up.' But Mr Sondeen was more concerned with looking into the mirror on the wall to inspect the side of his head. 'Goddamn shower. I hit my head a real one on the fitting in there. That sucker was just at head height. It must have been a bunch of small people who put up this place, Polly.'

Mr Sondeen put on his floppy hat again to shade himself from the setting sun as he left. 'Hell,' he said, 'we'll see each other at the motel anyway.' It undercut the need to deal with even a business-like farewell. He kissed her at the doorway where he smelled less of deodorant and slightly more of wine and cheese. 'Shoot, Polly,' he said, 'I just hope that I haven't given any offence. That's the thing.' He walked down the dirt track towards the road, the lupins, his two grateful sisters waiting at the Shangri La Motels.

Recollections of MKD

~

TREVOR LAYSTALL (B. 1939), for over fifteen years a sub-editor with the Christchurch *Press*, was an exact contemporary of M.K.D. Ash at Te Tarehi High School and kept in sporadic touch with the author until five or six years before the latter's death. Laystall saw this year's three-part television programme of Ash's life and works (*Phoenix From the Ashes*) and considered it so little representative of the man he had known that he approached Ash's official biographer, Professor Forbes Kendaell, who recorded this interview for *Simulacre*. The interview took place at Mr Laystall's home in Spreydon, suburb of Christchurch, on the evening of 19 July 1994 and the transcript that appears here is a version modified slightly by subsequent correspondence.

FK: *In utter predictability, which I will not pledge to maintain, I would like to begin by asking you when you first became aware of MKD.*

TL: We came from different primary schools, but on our very first third form day at Te Tarehi High we juniors had to stay behind in hall after assembly to be sorted into classes. Old Bubber Greene, who was head of science, always used to do it. Anyway this day was wet, a typical drizzle from the sea, and Bubber couldn't do it outside. There was only one absolutely hopeless new teacher to help Bubber, who was losing his rag in the confusion and noise. Anyway, this tall, calm boy, almost beautiful, went into the wrong line —

FK: *And this was MKD?*

TL: No. Ash was the small, ratty kid who got under Bubber's feet when he charged forward to pull the tall boy out of line. That boy was Simon Oakes, the best winger the school ever produced. Should have been an All Black.

FK: *But MKD?*

TL: Bubber grabbed him and asked him his name and Ash said, 'Mulvey Kannaith Desmond Ash,' in that high faluting voice he had and Bubber mockingly repeated it several times and shook him till the tears came. Everyone gave Ash hell after that.

FK: *So he was an extremely sensitive boy?*

TL: Never happy with his peers certainly.

FK: *In the course of my research for the biography,* MKD: A Nation's Delineator, *I went into the schooldays. There was MKD's own memoir, of course,* Fallow Education, *the generally acknowledged autobiographical elements in the earlier novels, particularly* No New Bethlehem, *and the eponymous short fiction of the collection,* Marcel Proust and I. *I didn't know then of your own friendship, but I talked with other MKD acquaintances of school days, including Dr Errol Williams and your fellow journalist Jye Lee. I met Mr Norman Johnson, who had taught English there and retained very vivid and lively recollections of*

MKD. *The picture that emerged in fact was that of something of an achiever. MKD himself in* Fallow Education *says that in his final year he would have been* proxime accessit *except that he refused to do any work in biology dissection on creatures killed for that purpose.*

TL: It's difficult to comment without appearing churlish, well, more disparaging perhaps. Snoz Johnson never even taught Ash and yet from that television programme you'd think that he had started it all, but was too modest to say. Errol Williams and Jye Lee were two of his chess club and photography club cobbers — anything to get out of sport. They were what the Americans now would call nerds.

FK: What, then, drew you to MKD initially? How was it that the two of you became friends? Were you a 'nerd'?

TL: With due respect I think you show just there that tendency to give Ash a retrospective significance: assuming that I was drawn to him rather than —

FK: I'm sorry.

TL: I realise that since those early days —

FK: Point taken, but what, then, did you find admirable in him as a boy? You were more than just classmates and you kept in touch for many years afterwards. Why was that?

TL: As to what I liked about him at first I'm rather hazy. I think more than anything else his willingness to entertain, his interest in your life because his own was so boring. He used to carry my first fifteen gear down to the lower ground and do his *Goon Show* impersonations as we went. About keeping in touch, I suppose because we were at the same university hall and he used to come along to my room and slaughter all the flies with a rolled up *Time* magazine. He kept asking me when my sisters were coming to visit: he'd caught a glimpse of Rebecca at a school prizegiving. I think he was very lonely at the hall and he knew there were often people in my room. I established an informal society called Quaffers.

FK: Do you know if he was writing at this time?

TL: At school, or university?

FK: Both.

TL: He always did have a knack with dirty limericks, I remember that. At Te Tarehi he wrote them on the wall of the fives court; at varsity he supplied the capping magazine. I don't recall anything else then. One of his best was about the young lady from Calcutta.

FK: I'm interested, surprised, that you didn't see any writing. His nickname was Dickens, wasn't it? That's well established. Surely there must have been some awareness that he was enthusiastic about literature, an aspiring author?

TL: That was a sort of sarcastic pun, you see. An undergraduate joke. Ash wasn't very well endowed and Dickens had an element of the diminutive as well. Simon Oakes gave him the name, I think, in the hall and so of course it stuck.

FK: If we could move on somewhat. There's the famous moral and intellectual crisis — the nether vortex, he calls it in Macrocarpa Bondsman — *which always recalls, for me, Shelley's line, 'a hell of death o'er the white water'. And MKD was totally unable to take his finals even though there was a general expectation that he'd get a first. There's his tremen-*

dously powerful description of waking in a cirrus mid-afternoon to the realisation that the Restoration drama exam is going on and he lies there cognisant of the vomit on the sheet and he sees on the wardrobe door the Ivy League shirt that his mother bought him but could ill afford and from some other room he hears that Roy Orbison song.

TL: I don't think I know it.

FK: *It's on the tip of my tongue.*

TL: No, I mean I haven't read about his breakdown. I knew of course —

FK: *Oh God, an epiphany of self-loathing. I read it in Vancouver where I was doing my PhD. I wrote on the flyleaf of the book — this has called me home!*

TL: I don't remember his lead-up marks being that good actually. He could yap about anything, but I don't remember his grades being wonderful. He failed Philosophy II, for example.

FK: *A good many people recall him being very penetrative academically when he set his mind to it, though he could be dismissive about a prescribed course of study, about exams — in the way Housman was, for instance. One of the sociology lecturers told me that MKD would quote Schopenhauer and Spengler.*

TL: That sounds like him. You think that he really did have some sort of emotional crisis?

FK: *Absolutely pivotal. Certainly he saw it that way: a final confrontation with the expectations that his father in particular had for him — Iapetus, MKD always called him, one of the Titans, but not to his face, of course. He fought it out within himself when barely twenty-two, the age-old dilemma for the artist between vision and a securely conventional life, between his own imperatives and the family expectations, yet something more deeply and innately contradictory in his case. It liberated him to go on to be the greatest of our writers, although at an immense psychic cost to MKD personally. We lost one more graduate; we gained* The Toby Jug World, Cyclops' Second Eye, Journals of the New Te Rauparaha.

TL: At the time I thought he'd gone to pieces because of that involvement with the Rawleigh's woman. Ash came round to my flat a few times and lay on the verandah sacks telling me about his sex life with this forty-seven-year-old woman. She'd been going round door to door. Insatiable, he said. She had three children and drew blood with her bite. He was finding it impossible to get any work done. I think it was his first experience and he'd talk, talk about it. Not a pretty story and an unlikeable trait to go on about it. I recognised a good deal of it again in that book he wrote about the guy working in a bank.

FK: Cheque Me Out.

TL: Right.

FK: *There is this whole issue of the MKD libido, isn't there, and it's been addressed best perhaps in John Cecil's articles in* Landfall *and* Sport. *The rather strange essays on Zilpah, for example. Did you feel that it was important to MKD? Do you feel so now?*

TL: Not as important as he would have liked it to be. I remember him as essentially parasitic in regard to getting to know women.

FK: *Parasitic?*

TL: Dickens — Ash — always depended on other people to give him the opportunities to meet women. He always had his ear open for a party, was always interested if a couple was breaking up, but he usually just made an ass of himself. When Simon Oakes had a party before going to Oxford to take up his Rhodes Scholarship, Ash accosted his (Oakes's) girlfriend and got his face slapped. He spent the rest of the night drinking in the broom cupboard in case Simon had been told about it.

FK: *You kept in touch after both of you had left the university?*

TL: Susan and I married when I got a job at Hatherleys, which was a firm of printers down by the station. This would be 1963, or 1964, I suppose. We had a very small flat in Armagh Street; the whole building's a women's refuge centre now. We have some laughs about that.

FK: *Yes.*

TL: We were very poor, of course. Susan was still finishing her degree; I had no real idea what I wanted to do.

FK: *And MKD was a friend to you in those somewhat difficult years?*

TL: He was living in somebody's garage by Wilding Park, within walking distance unfortunately. He had this habit of coming in just before tea-time on a Friday after he'd been to the pub. He cottoned on to the fact that I got paid on Thursdays and that we ate rather better on Fridays than most of the week. Sometimes we tried to sit him out, a few times I threw him out, but Susan felt sorry for him initially.

FK: *I imagine that for him these would have been the difficult years in which he was wrestling with* No New Bethlehem *and* Room Between Sea and Sky. *Beckett's praise of what he termed the deanthropomorphisation of the artist comes to mind (laughs).*

TL: He certainly wasn't wrestling with any paying job. A few times, though, he brought a simple bunch of flowers, daffs, or —

FK: *The considerate aspect of his nature so often overlooked.*

TL: We thought it a nice touch, until our neighbour, Mrs Posswillow, burst in to complain that he'd stolen them from her garden on the way past. Ash pretended to be drunk, of course, and was still not sufficiently shamed to leave. We were having beef for the first time that month; he had a nose for such things.

FK: *Did you see him in other circumstances during this period — an apprentice one for both of you perhaps? Did the two, or three, of you do things together?*

TL: Once or twice we walked into the park. Ash always took a collection of stones and he would pelt the ducks viciously. He kept saying they were nature's bounty. And he would go on about his own wretched life; I don't recall him once asking about my job with Hatherleys. Later, when I was first with the *Press*, he became very interested, but it was only because he hoped I could get his stuff into the paper somehow. When he realised I wasn't able to do that he lost interest.

FK: *Yes, I want to talk about those years too, but your comment about him going on about his life, extemporising from what must have been in many ways a painful experience. Did he talk about his work?*

TL: Yes. He would still quote his smutty limericks from Te Tarehi and later, but he often talked about what he called his 'freefall novel', which he said would be the great Irish novel of New Zealand literature.

FK: Hence the line many years later put into the mouth of Murphy Upshott — 'Amanuensis I to the almost totally blind.' His exegetes were slow to recognise the Irish debt that he acknowledged there so simply.

TL: I was writing myself at the time — quite well received pieces about provincial rugby — and Simon Oakes was sending some poetry back from Oxford. Ash rarely made the pretence of interest, or attention. He had a very personal line of questioning which my wife found rather unpleasant.

FK: Unpleasant?

TL: I'd rather not go into it in detail.

FK: You mean MKD intruded into your lives in search of material?

TL: Well, one instance I remember clearly. In the height of summer Ash had bludged a meal and then wandered out of the kitchen in case a teatowel was thrust at him. I went through for something and found him standing in our bedroom. I remember the sun slanting across the room from the old sash windows on to his face and how his eyes were closed. When I asked him what the hell he was doing, he said he needed the smell of a married bedroom.

FK: There's that remarkable scene in No New Bethlehem, *isn't there, in which Lowell Knowell has returned from the maternity annexe knowing both wife and child are lost and he stands in the bedroom with sun stippling the unmade bed and he makes the first prayer of his life, yet aware during it of the residual physicality of the place. 'Marmalade, musk, mildew, moth dust and Maya.' Yes, an almost Orwellian concern with the olfactory.*

TL: He had a bit of pong about him himself.

FK: Did you have any inkling then, when you were both young men and trying to find a place in the world to stand, that MKD would go on to become the greatest of all antipodean writers — one, as Bungyjump *declared in a cover story, of the key figures perhaps this century?*

TL: I can't say I did.

FK: When did that perception occur to you?

TL: When I read about it in *Bungyjump* (laughs). No, I suppose in the mid-eighties when there was the publicity when *Bully For Me* came under such critical attack and Dickens started popping up on radio and television. That was when I could see that his writing was popular with the gurus.

FK: Were you still in contact with him at this time?

TL: Not so much. In about 1969, or maybe 1970, he shifted away to Wellington.

FK: April 1971, I believe.

TL: Could well be. It's fair to say that we didn't part on the best of terms.

FK: Would you like to talk about that?

TL: Simon Oakes had just been killed in England.

FK: The former companion of MKD and yourself?

TL: My friend. Simon considered Ash very much a second-rate mind and inconsequential as an athlete as well. Did I mention that it was Simon who gave Ash the nickname Dickens? Ash hated him for that.

FK: *I think so.*

TL: Simon died only a few weeks after receiving his PhD —

FK: *His D Phil. You did say Oxford.*

TL: What? Anyway, Simon was killed near a Shropshire village when he was leading the Federation Invitation Marathon. The well-known theatrical agent Hilton Fowlds had a heart attack and his Morgan V8 went out of control. Simon had no family here and his college sent all his papers to me. There were several boxes of his writing — a great deal of prose, which surprised me, for Simon had only ever shown me his poetry. Susan and I couldn't face reading it so soon after his death; we left the boxes virtually undisturbed and then on the Labour Weekend when we had gone to Susan's parents and left Ash in the flat because his garage had been flooded, all of Simon's papers were stolen. Ash must have left the flat unlocked at some time, though you'd wonder who would bother to steal typescripts. They did take my Dave Brubeck records as well.

FK: *This was the cause of your rupture with MKD?*

TL: I was very angry with him; furious, and so angry with myself for letting Simon down. None of that stuff ever turned up. Ash kept away and then I heard that he'd gone to Wellington, owing rent even on his garage.

FK: *You did re-establish your friendship with him later, I understand, on his return from the capital. How did that come about?*

TL: Actually, I did have a brief correspondence with him during his time in Wellington. He wrote asking if I would become a subscriber to a literary journal he was to start up there. He wanted me to find other subscribers in Canterbury as well — even sent me a list of people he considered possibilities.

FK: *Have you kept the list? It might shed interesting light on who MKD considered were people of literary sensibility at the time.*

TL: I didn't, I'm sorry. He also said that subscribers would receive what he termed 'positive editorial inclination', but although I sent three articles, none of them was published. Mind you, the whole thing didn't last long, did it?

FK: *Mopsus had just the three issues, but is considered to have been prophetic of New Zealand literature, as befits its title.*

TL: For years afterwards it kept sending out subscription forms. Ash must have found that a useful income.

FK: *We have passed over two questions that I would like to return to now, if that's all right. The more recent concerned the picking up of your friendship with MKD after he returned here.*

TL: Well, we're talking the late seventies now, aren't we. Susan and I were living in Sumner. I'd left Hatherleys and after a stint in the Social Welfare Department and then as a taxi driver, when I was writing a good deal, I got a job on the *Press*. Susan was teaching at Avonside Girls', I think — no, Papanui High School still, yes.

FK: *And MKD?*

TL: He had been taken up by the unmarried Devinne sisters who still lived in the family home in Merivale. They'd both known Charles Brasch quite well. Ash had convinced them his genius was worthy of support. They were almost gaga, of course. He would flirt and flatter to their faces and slander them at other times. He called them Gorgon and Gorgonzola.

FK: *Did you ever meet Celia and Malisse Devinne?*

TL: Yes.

FK: *What were the circumstances?*

TL: There was a sleepout by the shrubbery which was Ash's, but it wasn't big enough for his parties, so he persuaded the old dears to have a soirée in the big house from time to time. Gorgon and Gorgonzola were left tinkling at the piano while Ash and his friends boozed in the other rooms. It was quite sad, really; he demeaned their friendship and mocked their infirmity. There were even things stolen from the house. I stopped going.

FK: *The suggestion is that MKD stole from his benefactors?*

TL: I never saw him take anything, but I saw others remove ornaments — there was a Devinne jade collection that suffered. Finally there was a legal intervention by members of the wider family and the sisters were taken into care and Ash ordered to vacate his sleepout. I think in the end the whole place was bought by the Anglican church and became a diocesan retreat.

FK: *Was it MKD's practice to read work at these soirées?*

TL: Oh yes. He'd read on and on from what he termed 'work in progress' until he got too drunk and all his sycophantic friends would drink, chatter and applaud. By that time he had a sort of arty entourage of women with short black skirts and blue eyeliner, and one or two guys with ponytails.

FK: *The other question I wanted to come back to was that relating to the approaches that you say were made by MKD when he knew you were working for the* Press. *You mentioned that your impression was that he cultivated you because he hoped for some advantage from that connection.*

TL: He was very interested in who decided on where books went for review, who did profile features, things like that. Bill Zimmerman did all that at the *Press* at that time. I introduced them shortly after Ash came back from Wellington. Bill told me later that the very next day Ash called at his office, saying that I was one of his closest friends and that he had been Simon Oakes' mentor in the year or so before his death. I had asked Bill to do a feature on Simon, but Ash persuaded him to concentrate on a living writer instead — Ash himself, of course. I tackled Dickens about that and I remember him saying, 'Let the dead bury the dead, Jinky old son. The inheritance is what matters.'

FK: *You had by this time known him for nearly thirty years. You were familiar with his work.*

TL: Certainly I'd read *No New Bethlehem*, *Marcel Proust and I* and *The Toby Jug World*.

FK: How did the consciousness you encountered there equate with the MKD you knew from day-to-day life? Could you hear Racine's wolves from the page?

TL: I've always been impressed by the intensity, by the absolute candidness, but it's just all his own life, isn't it — or rather experience and observation manipulated so that he has become the centre of it. It's a sort of regurgitation, but with his own bile become dominant. In *Bully For Me*, I think it is, he has seventeen pages about using the lavatory in the Lyttelton Domain.

FK: 'Sphincter Sphinx in crapt Crypt seated is the eye of I: retention is the name of the game, the pit and the sun's pendulum through the creak crack of the swings outside and the follicles of the salt gulls' cry.'

TL: It all goes on rather, for me.

FK: I have the impression that in the eighties, when MKD was increasingly gaining national attention, you and he were drifting apart. Would that be an accurate summation?

TL: Yes.

FK: In fact after the mid-eighties you lost contact? You didn't see him at all in the last years of his life?

TL: Susan and I had a sense that he couldn't be bothered with us once his prospects improved and, to be honest, I may have been somewhat envious of his success. The very week that *The Toby Jug World* won the big Commonwealth prize, I heard from Zeon Press that they had rejected the collection of my articles. But basically I feel that Ash wanted to kick off his earlier acquaintances, anyone who'd known him before he was important. That way he could create himself over again. The way he afterwards wrote about Te Tarehi High in *Fallow Education*, for example, and the accounts of his early years which became all excitement and bizarre experience and angst. I remember when he was in the garage behind Wilding Park he would spend hours catching blowflies with an old vacuum cleaner and he would stand in his duffle coat outside the window of Meehan's Electrical watching television for most of an evening.

FK: When was the very last time you saw MKD?

TL: I remember that it was the year of the big Canterbury floods; must have been '85, or '86. Bill and Heather Zimmerman were with Susan and me at the Bush Inn and Ash and his crowd came in all dressed up from some mayoral thing; made a big entrance with their loud, affected voices. Dickens had been a small, ratty guy and I remember thinking that he'd become a small, puffy guy, like the old Sinatra. They came past us as they were leaving and Susan said hello to him. He stopped and stared for a few seconds then said, 'Bugger the proles' and laughed and went on out. I never saw him again. When he died, the editor asked me to attend the funeral on the paper's behalf and write an article, but I couldn't bring myself to do either. No one wanted to hear the truth about the man.

FK: I did a small piece for the overseas papers, I recall. MKD had insisted on having a Brubeck number in the Cathedral and a march past of the Ferrymead Fusiliers Dancing Team outside. Irony was everything to him. A tropism to be found throughout his mature work.

TL: Will his stuff last, do you think? Will people know *Journals of the New Te Rauparaha* and *The Toby Jug World* in fifty years?

FK: *Absolutely.*

TL: He wasn't likeable, you know; he used people, but all that's being changed now.

FK: *How is it at the end of Gab's drowning in* Bully For Me? — *'The evolution of the strongest lies is always towards truth.'*

Rebecca

MAYBE THE VERY worst thing that a woman says to a man is that she feels towards him like a sister, and almost as bad is to want to talk about Our Relationship, as though it's one of a set of abridged novels.

'I need to know where I am,' says Rebecca. She is sitting on the sill of the window in our flat above Montgomery's Kitchen Showroom in Madras Street. Full summer and the warm air brings scents from the park, intimations from the Chinese takeaway, as well as fumes from the traffic. She seems settled, prepared to give time and attention to what it is that explains our presence together here. The late sun glints on the hairs of her tanned forearms, two large top teeth rest on her lower lip, but such things are inadmissible as evidence. She taps a stainless steel table knife on the grey, worn wood of the window sill.

'Don't you have any ambition whatsoever?' she says.

'To get you back into bed,' I say. In a sense this is true.

'Don't you have any long-term plan,' she says, 'and see yourself in five, ten years' time, in the phases of its achievement?'

Rebecca wishes to be a television frontperson. She is quite open about this career and already has a post-graduate journalism diploma and a part-time reporter's job with Peninsula Radio. She has acquired professional training in front of the cameras and practises the techniques before our mirror. She can retain a direct gaze and small natural smile indefinitely as a fadeout. It had been remarked on, she once told me, that she had no tendency to rictus.

'I've always thought I'll die young,' I say.

'Why's that?'

'I just do. Whenever I try to imagine myself twenty years on, or whatever, there's just a fog there, grey and damp and dense.'

'That's weakness,' says Rebecca. 'You're this sort of drifter who never imposes himself on life.'

So much is interpretation, isn't it? The emotional climate in which we experience things. Nine months ago, when Rebecca and I began living together, she thought my drifting a positive thing: a refusal to be hog-tied by the conventional. She would lie bare-breasted beside me in the midday sun and eat hard-boiled eggs. Small pieces of yolk, their outer surface gun metal blue, shimmied on her warm skin. Now she has her arms tight about her knees and she rocks impatiently on the window sill above the kitchen showroom. Even her smile has a slight constraint of impatience. 'Anyway,' she says.

We have spent a good deal of the night on it — Our Relationship — and in that

exposition I have realised how unsatisfactory she considers it to be. Most of her grievances cut so deep that I've no reply, but I offer to do something about not having a
car. 'I could buy one,' I tell her. 'I could get together the deposit. I think Richie
Tomlinson is wanting to sell the veedub.'

'It's not just that, although I'm sick of not having a decent set of wheels. This flat
here, four rooms stuck above the shops and still with the cruddy student furniture.
A toilet cistern which won't flush properly, yet never stops running.'

What we're talking about hasn't anything to do with cars, or sofas, or the warm
aromas from the Chinese takeaway, nothing to do with red diamonds worn from the
lino around the stove, or the ice cream pottle substituting for the missing bottom
louvre. What we're talking about is the failure of our infatuation with each other.
Ambition is a loveless thing. As long as Rebecca was in love she was content to lie
eternally naked in the sun and eat boiled eggs; a concern for her future as a television
frontperson signalled a change of heart. As soon as she let me go then she saw that I
was drifting.

'We can still see each other around,' she says. Everything about this woman is
admirable, except her opinion of me. Her big front teeth, the muscles of her shoulders, the faintest stubble of her armpits, are part of the wonder. 'No reason at all we
can't still see each other around,' Rebecca says. There is an advertising blimp floating
behind her in the blue sky above the city. DOOLEY'S TOYOTA. The moment is there for
me to say something that will undercut triviality and strike her soul like an arrow.

'You're right. We're bound to still see each other around.'

I feel hard done by, that's the truth of it. I have established the pleasures of my life
on her without thought for any future and now she wishes to be free. What is the use
of talking of the north wind when the southerly is blowing?

Rebecca sits in the frame of the window and, although we continue to talk, I can
see so clearly that there is a past now, and a future, in her conception. We have separated, she and I, as the holistic present has divided.

'Don't think that I regret any of it, though,' she says.

'Nor I.'

As we talk we are separate and there is the past, the present and the future once
again. A consciousness of those divisions is with us when we are out of love, so that
in a sensible fashion we order things in the hope of consequences to our benefit.

'I just have to give more time to my work,' she says. 'I've got to get ahead.' What
she has to get ahead of is lying in bed until the afternoon sun is in our eyes, not
answering the phone because we know we've done nothing deserving of good news,
spending the rent money on a Hello Dolly Masquerade Ball.

'Do you remember the Hello Dolly Masquerade Ball?' I ask her.

'So what?'

They had a terrace at the ballroom, just like in the movies, and Rebecca and I went
out and looked over a carpark, but also, in the moonlight, a line of concrete tubs with
ornamental conifers. The cooler air made me realise that my shirt was wet with sweat

and Rebecca's hair had started to come down. She was one of the best-looking women there, by anyone's assessment. An older woman who had argued with her partner came out and fell over the small balustrade into the carpark. She broke her collar bone and was in the papers. It happened after Rebecca and I had been standing together with the breeze on our flushed faces, but because I was only a few minutes from being there and have seen the photograph, it has become part of my experience — this heavy woman with puffed sleeves and tears on her cheeks, the thud of her on the asphalt.

'Look,' says Rebecca. 'If it's better for you I can stay for another day or two. I want you to feel that we've talked it through, not just that I'm walking out or something.' The blimp bobs as if in agreement with such counsel. Every time I kissed her I was excited by the smooth, white keys of those two front teeth. 'People are changing, growing all the time.' All such generalisations are perfectly true, but I see no connection between them and what is happening to us. Rebecca drums with the knife on the window sill, holding it loosely in her fingers so that it can reverberate.

'I'd rather not draw it out,' I say.

Less than a year ago I first met her at the final of theatresports in the old town hall. She had a lovebite on her neck and neither of us made any mention of it then, or since. She told me that she'd been invited to apply for the Drama School in Wellington, but wanted to go into journalism. As she goes down the stairs what we have between us is drawn tight for the last time and then parts. We will indeed see each other around, as she says; will see each other here as she comes for her things. Nothing will be the same. From the window I see her walk past the display of whiteware, microwaves, dual sinks and cupboard units that we live above. We have talked a great deal over two days and the more intimate the discussion, the more certain was the outcome. When a glance, a kiss, a hand on the shoulder, an old joke half told, can't do the job, then recourse to analysis is bound to fail.

Rebecca doesn't look up and I see, in contrast to a Chinese girl she passes, that her hair isn't black after all, but very dark brown. Maybe in a long time I will find myself, clear of fog, in Dooley's to select a car from the gleaming new models there and I will get an odd snag in my breathing, unaccountable, as I see the Dooley's sign. Maybe I will sign a contract and think of boiled egg crumbs on her warm skin, her slightly buck teeth, whole glamorous kitchens beneath us as we slept.

Prairie Nights

⁓

SOME PEOPLE, SO I'm told, dream always of the sea, an endless flux and an exhilaration that is part liberation and part threat. The year I worked at the agency in Auckland and still had some residue of imagination, I dreamt of endless prairie under a cheesy moon. Nothing but flowing grasses between the earth and the sky and the unrestricted wind of the night.

Sure, it was an escape. I could even feel it coming on when I was talking with clients about extrusion plumbing fittings, or listening to Simone Proctor giving her staff ra-ra sessions. I would drift away from myself until I stood knee-deep in all that endless, moonlit prairie grass. Sometimes the passing wind bore snatches of Simone's inanities, or my own.

Never neglect the enduring small client base.

There's a useful angle in that your grandfather founded the firm.

Animals, for example, are big, very big, at the moment.

Doco footage can be a sweet thing.

A very exciting prospect, Mr Whirler.

When the Spaniards first pushed northwards from Mexico they were at a loss as to how to navigate in so vast a sea of grass.

I had a three-roomed flat in Mount Eden. The house was an old one on the slope of the volcano. In some small caves in the scoria beneath the garden bluff the owner's father had discovered Maori relics and refused to give them up, although there was nothing impressive, or particularly valuable.

How happily we enter our own tombs. I can still remember my joy when the agency took me on and the mixture of envy and congratulation with which I was received by my fellow graduates. Broglioli's was the best restaurant in Palmerston North. I invited my friends to a farewell dinner and a good many came, although they had to pay for themselves. I had been the editor of the varsity magazine and in my speech said that I expected to bring a new thrust to advertising. Blow winds beneath a cheesy moon.

What I lacked was a conceptualisation of product. Simone Proctor pointed that out to me after I'd been with the agency six months. I knew on that occasion even before she spoke that she'd given up on me, because she stayed behind her desk rather than moving around to take a chair on my side. You've done the management courses yourself. Conceptualisation of product was her jargon, of course, but it was quite true. There wasn't anybody in that office who could manage alliteration, cadence, associative imagery, assonance, the way that I could, but increasingly I just couldn't relate them to almond moisture crème, or long-run colour-baked roofing iron. She said that my talent had an inward orientation and lacked market coupling points. Maybe I had something of a knack for brochures, she said. Not even a wolf moves across the albino grasses of the prairie night.

It's clear to me now how predictable was my response to comparative failure. I became the office hard case; all the best laughs and an inventory of weekend successes to disparage anything between Monday and Friday. If I had little to say at Simone's brain-storming sessions on Tuesday and Thursday, then I made up for it in the wine bar on Friday after work. Who wants the indignity of taking such a job seriously and still not being able to do it? Mike Dermott won a national award for his mime ad for Zeus Acoustics. It was funny and novel and I knew that I would never have come up with it.

In October I resigned from the agency to take up a position with Statsfact Polling Agency as a survey question writer. I told the people in the agency office that the new job paid more, that I was suited to it, that I'd been invited by management to apply. The first two were correct, the third an excusable lie in the circumstances. In a material sense I've never looked back, though question writing was only the first step. That first failure, that first painful inadequacy, became the goad for a conventional success. Think of a night on the old prairie, not a tree beneath the moon. Have you any idea of the sound the wind makes over a thousand miles of natural grassland?

I invited the others to come to the wine bar after my last day at the agency. Mike Dermott had a special client briefing to attend with Simone Proctor but he made a point of wishing me well during the afternoon and Simone left a bon voyage card on my desk. Of the rest, David Lymes and Estelle Hargreaves came. They were an item and later almost married. With such a modest number at my staff farewell I felt able to shout and we had three bottles of a good Gisborne chardonnay. I had the item in stitches on several occasions over recollections of my meetings with more unusual clients and professional differences with Simone, but after I was held up at the bar by Bernie Kinsman, who wanted to talk about varsity days, I got back to the table to find that David and Estelle had gone.

From the Mount Eden bus I could see a grey and white sky and although the traffic had worn shower water from the roads, the trees, the grass, the flowers and weeds of October had a fresh glisten to them in the evening.

A very exciting prospect, Mr Whirler.

I thought of climbing the mountain at dusk — just a hill really — and looking at the grassy crater again, at the remains of the old kumara pits along the rim. It would have been quiet at that time of the day, but Miss Hoddie, who had the better flat downstairs, invited me in for a drink. It was, I suppose, the eighth or ninth time I had spoken to her in as many months. She was very sharply black and white, and the white of her skin was just beginning to infiltrate the black of her hair.

'I've resigned too,' she said, 'and I'll be in Europe by Christmas.' Miss Hoddie taught French at a boys' school and was tired of their muscular dim-wittedness. She must have been almost thirty years older than me, yet had been no more successful in gathering close friends to celebrate such an important decision. 'I haven't heard a decent French accent in years,' she said. Appropriately enough, she opened French brandy and even from her lower flat we could see over a great many houses towards Herne Bay. Hoddie was thin, wiry. She even looked French, though the language was the only connection she had. 'It's mainly a lack of courage,' she said, 'that makes us put up with lives other than those we wish for ourselves.'

Her decision seemed so much more dramatic than my own. After all, I wasn't changing countries, cities, tongues, not even flats perhaps; just moving away from my inability to conceptualise product. But how the moon and clouds and wind combine to send dark vessels sweeping and dipping across the infinite prairie, and how the pelt of the world flows on for ever.

'Did you get a good degree?' Hoddie asked me, as we drank brandy on the window seat. 'It's so much more difficult to be reconciled to mediocrity if you've got a good degree.' Good degree or not, she had the wiry forearms of a French seamstress and the dark hairs lay all the same way on the pale skin. I would like to use her first name for I remember that she offered it, but it has succumbed to time, along with my imagination. 'No one gives a damn for excellence,' she said with a fine emphatic flourish. It occurred to me that maybe I had given up on advertising one chance too soon, that I could make something of Hoddie's black and white tautness, her given damn for excellence, that would double brandy sales in the land of the long white cloud.

'The problem with my generation of women was that it couldn't be selfish enough,' she said. 'You recognise too late that there isn't anyone else worth pleasing.' It was dark outside Miss Hoddie's bay window and the houses, gardens, streets below us, all of sensible and calculable dimension, had been replaced by a shimmer of lights.

Hoddie didn't become drunk in any way that led to a loss of composure, but after a time she spoke only in French and I couldn't respond, so I thanked her and went up to my own three rooms. We were both making something of a bolt for it, Hoddie and I. From my flat I could look down into hers and see her still on the window seat, talking, although the words were now inaudible as well as unintelligible.

Think of the effortless power of the wind across the land of grasses and wildflowers, the gliding shadows and the cool linen of the moon over the dips and long upward sweeps of the high plains. Think of the tremors you might feel from the ground as, far out of sight, the vast herds of bison rush through the night with the white wolves of the moon in silent pursuit.

Peacock Funeral

~

A RETURN TO the place made Hammond think of life, you see, and death, which is necessary at least to highlight life. And the cry of the peacocks across the grass courts from the gardens, and the small children's cases, almost phosphorescent green, or pink, bobbing like marshmallows to keep the cars away. The hospital on the hill where Hammond had worked, the perfumed gardens between it and the town; enduring trees with name tags to introduce themselves to passing generations, a clearing, too, with Humpty on a wall to supervise the swings and regard with an eternal smile the great plaster bum of the elephant slide. The peacocks strode through the paths; tails rich and dark swept in the leaves, but the cries had always an empty truculence.

The mood was self-imposed, of course. Despite having given no warning, Hammond was well received at the hospital. The one departmental colleague who still recalled him made time to greet him, to reminisce, to introduce him to the head of the unit, with whom they had herbal tea. Ginny had been fond of such drinks. She had small packs of them, each with a name more wondrously aromatic than the contents could hope to be, and there were always a few small, discarded bags clustered at the plughole of the sink. His mother once told him that the only thing from her childhood which could still move her was the recollection of the blue sky seen through the branches of a yellow plum tree in Motueka.

An offer was made to accompany him around the place, but Hammond knew the pressures of their work, how much of a nuisance the passer by can be in a busy day. The colleague had become intensely interested in the hospital grounds as an unofficial extension of the gardens; the unit chief, on the other hand, was curious, he said, as to how funding was controlled in Hammond's existing job. There were condolences as well.

Structurally there had been little change; it wasn't large as hospitals go. A new ambulance put-down bay at casualty admission, an internal décor of lighter pastels, a lot more signs outside informing people of possible destinations. It had all seemed common sense before. There were still the rose plots before the main block and still they seemed in half bloom, unable to provide a full show at any time of the year. The grass was stiff with drought, the garden clods ash grey. Hammond could see the third-floor window from which Mr Neilson, with good reason, did a header to the carpark. A wind from the sea was persistent on the hill, bowling in from a horizon always flat and far and sad.

Hammond followed the exact way he had always taken to the house in Liebers Street. Some of the mundane landmarks were still there. A plaster lighthouse on the

Seddon Street corner; the paua shell porch further on; the home of a woman who was once the mistress of an ex-mayor. At the Bidewell Boarding House there was no old garage any more with a hole cut so that the door could be closed and just the front bumper stick out like a moustache at the other end. The dairy had become gaudy and its produce spilled out into makeshift displays on the footpath. Hammond caught a glimpse of the high counter where his children would wait to hear Mrs Lee say, 'Hokey-pokey, or plain?'

He had been filled with confidence then, believing that, having achieved the qualifications for a professional career, he had passed the greatest test and everything else would come naturally. That experience proved it almost true was the greatest danger.

The house was too far from the gardens for the peacocks to be heard except in the still of night. Then, when the children were asleep and Hammond and his wife lay together, sometimes they had heard those urgent calls. At first Hammond thought them exotic, but as his own life soured the notes became more discordant. Why, after all, should a creature's beauty be any indication at all of benevolence?

The brick house was part of the archaeology of his life and even without going in, he could see things as significantly and trivially vital as the ossifications, shards and simple beads in site strata. The cracks in the roughcast beneath the main ridge facing he had twice filled with sealant, and once fallen from to lie painfully winded in the hydrangeas. The golden elm that shook leaves into the gutterings, he had heeled in and sequestered with sacking. There was a false bolt hole in the letter-box that perpetuated one of his lesser mistakes, and the concrete lip to the basement garage was never quite enough to prevent water running in during the worst rains of winter.

The things he recognised were overlaid by the habitation of other people and as he stood on the sunny footpath the house was both painfully intimate and painfully strange to him and he had a slight taste of copper at the back of his throat. In one year, inspired by some neighbour since forgotten, they'd had a street party — well, a sort of their end of the street party. Trestles, barbecues, lights strung in the trees and the access denied to vehicles by coloured ropes that depended on toleration for obedience. Ginny had been one of the prime movers responsible for a great success, and people had eaten, laughed and talked in the street well into the night. Everyone was filled with neighbourly bonhomie and vowed to do it again.

And it was never done again.

Hammond walked on back to the church where he had left his car. At the service there had been several invitations to visit people before he left, but the hospital and the house were all he wanted to meet. At the crematorium Michael and Rae had rested their hands on his shoulder to show they understood that not every father was able to make a success of marriage, but they told him little about their own lives and he was too proud to ask. The three of them had perhaps become accustomed to the detachment of correspondence. Lynley Grath had glanced at Hammond coldly at the crematorium. She had been Ginny's friend and he'd fucked her just once from behind at a midwinter party in the Tilbury Rooms. He remembered the sharp moon like a searchlight and the sharp pleasure. Lynley had remained a loyal friend to Ginny and sent Hammond a letter of contempt after the divorce.

Despite all that, the crematorium meant the least to him of all the things of the day. It was a new place with much stained glass and blond wood. It overlooked some sloping paddocks that must have been close to the farm on which Bruce Mulherron fell from his tractor and had his legs so badly injured in the discs. Bruce told him that as he lay there at first, in the shock before the pain, he was aware how sweet the fresh soil smelled. After the rare rains towards the end of summer the mushrooms would come, especially around the gateways and the tops of mounds. Hammond and Ginny often went to Mulherrons' and other farms to gather them. Real mushrooms, not the designer ones sold in the supermarkets. Large and quickly black on the underside: sudden of growth and strong and dank and black and white. The kids wouldn't eat them. Ginny would bake them with bacon and onion in a pastry shell and Hammond would bring up a bottle of pinot noir. The plots at the crematorium were mainly roses. They seemed to do better there than on the high ground of the hospital.

The cost of life is everything you have. Hammond was glad that Michael and Rae were making their way independently north. He looked forward to their company for a day or two. More than he could express, he looked forward to having them with him, but for the moment, driving away from the church, driving past the peacock gardens, the associations and reproaches of the small city, he wanted only his own admonitions.

Maybe at last you can be happy, Ginny had once said. I truly believe that you meant the best for us all, but you weren't willing to forgo anything yourself to make sure it happened. At the time he had assumed that it was requitable malice in the guise of reasonableness. Later he had admitted it as honesty. Thinking of it again after the peacocks and the crematorium, he decided it was truth. How does one find out all the heartfelt emotions that masquerade as love?

How many couples had held each other in the summer nights, in the arbours and ardours of the ratepayers' gardens, and thought the peacocks cried just for them.

Hammond's face itched. He found it necessary to draw the flat of his hand down his cheek again and again. The sun, still powerful, was at an unkind angle and made him sneeze. Sometimes in the summer, after a big blow, the kelp would lie in caramel heaps, rotting on the stones, and the stench would drift into the town centre. Hammond thought he had a whiff of it as he drove north. Sometimes his wife had read Larkin to him while he ate a late supper on his return from the hospital.

Had Hammond stayed until dusk he would have heard the empty truculence of the peacocks although they had been taken from the perfumed gardens years before. Their phantom cries were exactly as the pain a man feels in an amputated leg.

Genesis

$\sim$

IT WAS ONE of those long centuries at the Creations Bureau, during which the front office staff had so little to do, and such small hope of promotion, that they sat open mouthed in a number of suns, or gossiped with enervated malice concerning the goings on at the last Seraphim executive training conference.

There were some magnificent and imaginative projects on the go in other areas of Heavenly Administration: Resources had a plan to harness the parakinetic energy of time if it could be bent into a full circle and Onus and Obligation proposed a voluntary depletion of personal vanity in all choirs below Cherubim.

In Creations, though, things were rather ho-hum and ho-hum wasn't good enough in Heaven. G.O.D.'s foremost corporate slogan consisted of the Three Vs — Vision, Vigour and Versatility. Archangel Lucifer was Creations Chief, however, and for longer than most heavenly memories he had received the trust and confidence of G.O.D. Creations was the senior executive portfolio below G.O.D. — well, equal with Resources anyway. Many in Heaven thought Lucifer the obvious angel for the top job in due course. A brilliant mind, absolutely, even if he was resting on his laurels somewhat. Who else could have originated the expanding universes concept and overseen the immense detailed planning required for implementation? Who but Lucifer could come up with a plan of such imaginative symmetry as a standardised set of wave velocities — light, sound, thought, matter. Oh, you could hear the comments about austerity and pride, about ruthless efficiency, but no one denied Lucifer's ability.

Gabriel was pretty bright too. He had been a senior echelon executive in the Creations Bureau and pushing for all six wings. His flair was for personnel and PR, but he'd found himself increasingly out of sympathy with Archangel Lucifer's management style and policy direction for Creations. So Gabriel resigned, devoted all his time to his best idea and then presented it directly to G.O.D., whom he knew quite well socially and through a common interest in metaphysics.

G.O.D. told Lucifer that he thought the project should be considered and the Creations Chief said that he didn't want to and that he resented Gabriel not going through channels. G.O.D. insisted.

How do such things happen? In even the best run and most successful corporations, tremendous consequences can result from nuances of personality. Perhaps Gabriel was too ambitious and presumptuous; perhaps Lucifer was too proud; maybe old G.O. still felt the necessity to demonstrate his power from time to time.

Gabriel received a curt request for a full documentation of his proposal, but no invitation to make a personal presentation on it before the Chief of Creations. Lucifer and his 2IC, the great Baal, read it separately and then met in Lucifer's domed office with the distinctive ornamental flames casting images into reflection.

Lucifer drew the heavy documentation towards him on the desk. 'Another world,' he said contemptuously. 'Always another world.'

'Earth, this time,' said Baal. His face was heavy and yellow.

'Since G.O.D. made the first one — how many applications for worlds!' continued Lucifer. 'A good idea flogged to death. They're so limiting, so concrete. And you and I know that if G.O.D.'s best idea had been synchronous entities then not many people would be bothering with world projects.'

'Does one more matter then? One more world. Is it worth a stink?' said Baal loyally. 'Is it worth jeopardising your position with G.O.D.?'

Lucifer understood the value of the point; every successful administrator has to be something of a politician as well. Yet he considered that there were principles at stake concerning both standards of project excellence and the proper channels for submission.

'It's a bad project, a badly realised world. Isn't it?' asked Lucifer. Baal nodded. 'Then we must say so. I can't believe that G.O.D. will go for it. Not when all the defects are pointed out to him in an objective way. G.O. and I go way back.'

Lucifer and Baal, a pair who respected each other's abilities and were renowned as a team, began to prepare their critical report. There was the provision for free will, for example. It made Lucifer very angry. Gabriel knew quite well that intrinsic loyalty to revelatory guidance was a prime ordinance of the Creations Manual. And allowing the highest beings of Earth a knowledge of their own mortality when it was so obviously beyond their emotional capacity to bear! It must become a cause of melancholia and unhappiness. Even the science sections were faulty. The basic instability of the gaseous spectrum, for instance, so that within a few million years atmospheric breakdown was highly likely. 'Oh, there's so much that doesn't hang together in so many ways,' said Lucifer testily. 'A continuous creation period of seven days! I ask you. Imagine the Lower Choirs Guild's reaction to that.'

'Then there's all that about instincts,' said Baal.

'Instincts?'

'The whole section about instincts and logical intelligence is muddled. There's no clear established dominance for either mode of behaviour. The wretched folk proposed here wouldn't know if they were Arthur or Martha. Gabriel's always been indecisive on that sort of thing.'

'Exactly. He's a generalities man, but he doesn't think things right through and isn't scrupulous about the practical details. The anatomical visuals, for example; apart from the bizarre gender division, which is sheer gimmickry, even at a quick glance I picked up that he'd placed the defecatory and procreative organs side by side. It's a small enough thing, but so typically slipshod.'

Baal was pleased that Lucifer had mentioned the visuals of the proposed beings. He brought them up in greater definition and colour on the display screen. He made them rotate. 'Look at them closely,' he said. 'Of Whom do they remind you?'

Archangel Lucifer leant over the desk. There was something, yes.

'Gabriel's made them look somewhat like G.O.D.,' said Baal softly.

'The cheeky, ingratiating little bastard!' Lucifer very rarely laughed, yet both he and Baal did so. It was so Gabriel, so calculatingly PR. Of course it only hardened their resolve to oppose the creation of Earth.

G.O.D. set a time for both parties to make their submissions to him personally. The project of Earth, minor in itself, was becoming an arena for powerful political forces in Heaven. Lucifer and Baal waited outside G.O.D.'s office and Gabriel and Raphael sat just a squab away. When the time came for them all to be ushered into the haloed room, Lucifer went and stood beside Gabriel for a moment. 'Reconsider,' he said genuinely. 'You won't win and think how divisive such an argument could be.'

But Gabriel, of course, saw Earth as his best shot.

Cass Robbins

~

ANGIE BRUIN WAS used to people coming down from the North Island looking for cheap accommodation. It had become a trend over several years. After all, if you had no work to go to and a fixed welfare benefit irrespective of location, then why not have a better house at least and not such a distance to walk to the shops. The populations of places like Oamaru and Waimate and Palmerston were becoming used to such people, even if they weren't sure whether they wanted them.

Cass Robbins, though, was a bit different right from the start: a single and middle-aged guy who said in his letter to the agency that he didn't much care about the size, condition or location of the place as long as it was cheap and had a view of the sea. He was buried somewhere in a boarding house in Hamilton. Angie Bruin was in the rural real estate side of Kelly and Tarrowe, but in practice that included fringes and clusters of settlement: one-garage towns on the main south road, fishing huts at the estuaries, the obsolete hydro village, old baches and farmhouses hidden about the headlands. If he wasn't fussy about mod cons and appearances other than a view, then she had plenty to show him.

Cass couldn't afford to take a trip just to look; when Angie wrote to him with some examples, he just packed his two cardboard suitcases and took a bus down to the ferry. On board he was candid enough to strike up acquaintance with a group of stilt walkers and clowns who were doing a tour of the South Island in a van and so he came to Angie Bruin's office only a day or two after he'd said to expect him. Angie was out negotiating an irrigated block for a switch to dairy use so Cass left his two old cases in the office and wandered about the main street putting up stilt and clown posters. 'What a great place this is,' he told the Kelly and Tarrowe receptionist after being in town for eleven minutes. 'You know, I really believe there's something in the air down here we don't get north of the strait.'

'This is the place to be all right.' The receptionist was regularly applying for secretarial jobs in Wellington where there was some night life, for God's sake.

'People here have the courtesy to look at you when you're speaking with them,' said Cass, 'and there are still animals to be seen going about their own business rather than ours.'

It was on five when Angie got back, but Cass Robbins had been waiting contentedly at the office. He remarked cheerfully on the shimmer of the late afternoon sun on the poplar tree behind the town hall. But he was keen to see the real estate she'd picked out for him and at that time of year there were still hours of daylight. 'I mean I could come back in an hour when you've had a chance to eat,' said Cass. 'Don't let me push you. I guess you get sick of houses just as a teacher gets fed up with kids

357

and a driver loses the thrill of the road.' He took his cases with him to Angie's car, because he had nowhere else to leave them. He said it was deplorable the way people would nick your stuff given half a chance.

Cass decided on the very first place Angie Bruin showed him: an old farm cottage on clay cliffs between Kakanui and Moeraki. There was a vast, half burnt out macrocarpa hedge on the south side and across the gravel road some crouching boxthorns worn into green riffles and tunnels by the sea wind. Not another place in sight; just the rolling, close cropped paddocks of dry summer grass on the one side and the cliff and the ocean on the other. Some of the weatherboards were off and the timbers showed beneath, and clumps of bird nest straw. The road and the hedge formed two rough boundaries and there was a solitary waratah with a splash of blue paint at its head to mark the junction of the other two. The sheep had found the unlocked laundry for shade and shelter and the pebbles of their shit were thick on the floor.

'Marvellous,' said Cass. 'There's not one window broken. Do you notice that?'

'Some of them might be a bit stiff, mind,' said Angie, which in agent speak meant they were nailed up.

'I reckon that old table's totara.'

'You realise the power isn't on, not even connected now any further than Jamiesons' at the corner.' Angie was slightly disconcerted by the reversal of the usual roles. Cass enthused about everything he saw, while she felt obliged to make the realistic comment. However, the change was almost liberating after a while.

'A whole acre you say. One acre.'

'The macrocarpa must cover half of that,' said Angie.

'Ah, what a sweet smelling tree it is, despite its ordinary appearance.'

She watched him cross the road and stand in a gap among the boxthorn on the cliff top. His brown trousers looked as if they might once have been the bottom of a suit and he wore a tartan shirt with the sleeves rolled up on arms surprisingly muscular for a short, pale man. 'Listen to the stones going up and down the beach with the swell, Mrs Bruin,' he said.

'Be careful there. The cliff gets undermined and comes down every so often.'

'I'll bet you could sit in the kitchen and see all of the horizon if a bit of this thorn was knocked back.'

They stood in the kitchen for, despite the farm table, there were no chairs and they could see the broken line of the ocean horizon through the boxthorn.

'I'll take it,' said Cass Robbins. 'Twelve thousand dollars for the freehold to a house with an acre of good land and a view of the sea. It makes you wonder, doesn't it? You know in the city you could hardly put a deposit on a section with that.'

'Cash,' said Angie. 'The Jamiesons were clear about that. And everything as is, where is.'

'I always feel,' he said, 'that the coast is alive in a special way. Anywhere that's a meeting of the land and the air and the sea.'

Cass didn't want to go back to town for the paperwork. He decided that he wanted to take possession that night and cheerfully opposed anything that Angie said to the contrary. He handed over five hundred dollars as a sign of good intent and said he would appreciate it a great deal if she could bring out the papers the next day. 'I don't mind what time,' he said. 'I'll be making a start tidying here and getting a list together.' He turned on one of the taps above the yellowed sink and was overjoyed when, after some spluttering, the water began to run reasonably clean. He got down on his hands and knees outside and pointed out that the piles were concrete and not wood. Some homecoming magpies started squawking in the macrocarpa and he told Angie that birdsong always reminded him of his happy childhood in the Wairarapa. He stood on the narrow, gravel road in the dusk and waved to her as she left.

Angie had been long enough in the business not to bring it home with her at night, and with a husband and three teenage children she had plenty to occupy her thoughts, yet she wondered about Cass Robbins — whether it would work out, whether he was as happy as he seemed, or if he was one of those dreamers about life in the country and the reality of it would be a bitter awakening. 'Well, he can certainly get away from it all down there,' said her husband. 'Jesus! Now that old Jamieson place was one I thought you'd never sell for sure. I've got to hand it to you.'

After lunch the next day, Angie took the papers down and a carton with corned beef sandwiches, some apples, a toilet roll, a tin of coffee and a plastic mug, an old scrubbing brush and some cleaning gear. Cass had rested his best trousers and tartan shirt and wore corduroys and a baggy blue jersey direct on his skin. She expected that if his enthusiasm had survived the night, then he would have made a start in the house, but he was giving the boxthorn a hiding with a slasher and saw borrowed from the Jamiesons. Short, pale and middle-aged, he wasn't an impressive man in appearance, but he plied the slasher with considerable strength and balance. He was thickset without being fat and his chest stood out more than his stomach.

'You shouldn't have gone to all this trouble.' Cass put a towel on the mottled verandah edge for Angie to sit on so that they could share the sun and the view of the sea as he had the sandwiches. There they sat, Angie as tall and thin as a heron and Cass with his neck and hairy chest showing from the vee of the loose jersey. Some Romney sheep, seemingly unaggrieved at being denied the laundry for the first time, fossicked along the side of the building. 'One thing I don't need to buy is a lawn-mower,' Cass said. The sheep themselves, and the verandah that had often been a camp for them, were aromatic with the oil-wool smell the hot sun releases. The sky above the macrocarpas was a pale, burnished blue; the loess at their roots a pale yellow; the sea darker and flowing in the gap Cass had cleared in the boxthorn. Apart from their own voices, the unhurried movement and cropping of the Romneys, the shingle sliding on the steep beach out of sight, there was no other noise at all. Angie was bound to agree that there were a lot worse places to be.

Cass paid the balance for the house in hundred-dollar notes. 'It's going to be my asset, though, isn't it,' he said stoutly. 'Could I ask for one more favour, that you give me a ride back to town? We can see the lawyer together if it suits you and then I can buy the things I need. It's urgent I get some wheels of my own and some bits of furniture and so on. I bet you could recommend the best second-hand places.' And so she could, of course. She also had an inclination to ask him how he intended to make a living, how he was going to spend his time once the house was fixed and the boxthorn on the cliff was cleared to give him his sea horizon, but she didn't, because after all what business was it of hers and would she ever see him again anyway. 'Last night I had a dream about the pioneers who built this house,' said Cass. 'Fine people they were.'

Cass bought a second-hand farm bike and trailer and that was his sum total of transport. He picked up his furniture and pot and pans, bare essentials, at garage sales and second-hand shops; ferried them back to the old Jamieson place above the sea, bit by bit in the trailer behind the farm bike.

Old Gideon Jamieson maintained a traditional rural reserve for a few months, but when none of the Romneys went missing, he didn't find any odd plants among his shelter belts and the police didn't come with any enquiries, then he unbent a little and was a helpful enough neighbour. For his part, Cass Robbins wasn't selfish with his acre. The sheep wandered happily outside his windows to seek shade in the day and a wall at night, kept only from the verandah by a strip of netting nailed to the supports and from the laundry by the closed door.

Cass did some casual work for old Gideon Jamieson: help in the yards and the shearing shed, a bit of painting, potato picking. Through Gideon's laconic endorsement he began to get work from other local cockies and so the sound of his farm bike and the sight of his short, compact body became customary in the district. 'One thing,' old Gideon would say, 'he never whines, does he? You've got to give him that. Always the cheerful bugger.'

It came as a surprise to Angie Bruin when Cass rang her from a town phone box and wanted her and her husband to come out to his place. 'I owe you a meal,' he said, 'and I bet you'd like to have a look at how I've got the place and enjoy the view of the sea again. All that thorn's cleared, you know.' Angie had seen more ocean views than hot dinners, but she was interested to view the old place again, and very few clients had ever invited her back to a house she'd sold them. She insisted on bringing a salad, though, and a six pack for her husband, who felt the heat after a day in the woollen mills.

'What am I going to talk to him about?' Ross said dubiously.

The cottage hadn't undergone any transformation. Cass had replaced the missing weatherboards and given them an undercoat and taken off the rusted guttering that had been such an eyesore, but the place still looked what it was — an old wooden cottage in a paddock bare except for the macrocarpa. Inside was clean and tidy enough to suit a single guy, though Angie was appalled at the strange assortment of furniture and she could see he'd been keeping the farm bike in the laundry. Cass still thought the place was just Christmas, however, and took them round it and gestured at the sea view as if he owned a place in Kohimarama. 'Imagine how my asset's increasing,' he said. 'What do you reckon?'

'Well, certainly I don't think you've lost any of your twelve thousand dollars. On the other hand, being this far out of town isn't everybody's cup of tea.'

'It's quiet and no one to bother you,' said Ross, who had to put up with the noise of the woollen mills day after day. A beer in his hand, he found a comfortable canvas chair on Cass Robbins' sagging verandah and he sat there looking over the netting surround at the glitter of the sea out from the clay cliff.

'You know,' said Cass, 'overseas I reckon only a millionaire could afford this sort of privacy and this sort of view.'

'You could be right there,' said Ross, and though he winked at Angie, he could appreciate Cass's enthusiasm.

'For most people it's a question of job prospects rather than views of the ocean, though, isn't it?' said Angie. 'I mean, think of a family living out here. That's the problem.'

From his second-hand rock gas stove on top of the old coal range, Cass got a meal of sorts and they sat around the heavy, plain table, which had proved not to be totara after all. 'But all solid timber, absolutely throughout,' said Cass. 'Gideon Jamieson reckons it's been sitting right where it is since well before the First World War.'

'Old Gideon probably remembers when it arrived,' said Angie.

'What sort of work did you do in the North Island, Cass?' asked Ross. Angie was surprised how naturally he came out with it, while she had often wanted an opportunity for the same question. 'Palmerston North, was it?' continued her husband.

'Hamilton,' said Angie.

'I was a bright sign electrician,' said Cass. 'Twenty-five years in bright sign work and had a business employing three men.'

'Bright signs?' said Ross.

'Neon signs, you'd say, that sort of thing, though most of them these days aren't neon at all. Marching and flashing signs, colour alternates, running codes. I've done everything from major theatres to nudes above a massage parlour.'

'Jesus,' said Ross, 'and this place hasn't even got electricity. Now that's ironic, or poetic justice, or something.'

'I got so tied up with making a go of the business that it was my marriage which folded. When all that was over I had no business either. Then for a while I just did jobbing work. All in all I pretty much went off city life, and that's when you came in, Angie.'

'All that special knowledge,' she said. 'It seems such a waste really. There's always a call for a good electrician.'

Cass was serious, but not downcast, as he told them his reasons for coming south. He leant back in his ill-matched chair and watched the movement of his ocean. Far to the south, where the long beach was visible, the setting sun caught a roll of fine mist or sea spray, where the ocean met the land, and out of sight they could hear

Gideon's tractor going home for the day and his dogs barking him in. 'The whole thing made me pull up and take stock,' said Cass. 'My marriage and my business gone, most of the complacent assumptions that stood for any real thought — gone. Your confidence suffers, you know. I could hardly choose between white and brown bread without my hands starting to shake.'

'A clean break was best then, I suppose,' said Ross. He hoped Cass wasn't going to get maudlin and embarrass him with a need for emotional support. 'Well, you've got a great little place here.'

'That's for sure, but it's not primarily a matter of a new place, is it? It's a new outlook yourself. That's what I've found. It seems to me now that happiness is the absence of pain, rather than something positive in its own right. Almost all of us in this country are better off in so many ways than ninety percent of the people in the world, but we never twig to it, do we? We're always worried by seeing someone who's doing just a bit better than us.'

'That's the motivation for capitalism, I suppose,' said Ross.

'All by yourself out here, though. You think that's the best way?' asked Angie. Two or three of the duller sheep still stood round by the laundry and one was giving a very human cough.

'I've never seen things so clearly. I've never before been able to make better personal judgements.'

'Personal judgements?' said Angie, and Ross popped the top of another beer.

'Think of it this way,' said Cass. 'All those people you meet who ask you what you do, and never a one that asks you why you do it.'

'I hadn't thought of it,' said Ross.

'You need to forget yourself a bit and be open to the existence of other things. The other day I saw a falcon hunting. How many people can say they've seen a falcon?'

It was dark by the time Cass saw them off, but warm on the headland road in the time between the sea breeze and the land one. Cass could taste the dust left in the air by the Bruins' car and see the soft Tilly light from the window of his cottage. The Romneys had a soft, dimmed luminosity in their movement. There was a bird calling below the cliff and the lights of Kakanui showed on the coast to the north. Cass stood on the headland to see over his night ocean and think for a while. He could feel the ash of the boxthorn fires beneath his sneakers.

Ross and Angie talked about him, of course, on their way home. 'What do you think he'll do then?' said Angie as they reached the town.

'He's licking his wounds, isn't he? Self-assessment can be a dangerous thing; maybe he'll become a bit of a weirdo out there. Who knows.'

'A bright signs expert, eh, and now he lives in a farm cottage and watches the sea.'

There's always work for a good electrician and Ross assumed that because Cass Robbins had run his own bright signs firm then he was no slug. As a day foreman, Ross had some initiative in things at the woollen mills and when various electrical jobs built up on their own staff, he had a word with the manager and then wrote a note to Cass saying there might be a few days' casual work if he wanted it.

Ross was prepared to give a chance to any reasonable chap who was up against it. 'We'll see what he makes of it,' he told Angie.

He made a good deal of it, as things turned out. Cass came in every day for a fortnight on his farm bike and wearing his best tartan shirt. Even the maintenance engineer said quite openly that the little guy certainly knew his onions. 'Well, once you've sighted his qualifications then offer him a fulltime position,' said the manager.

On the day he started full time, Cass made a point of seeking Ross out and thanking him for putting him in the way of a job. Cass stopped in at the Bruins' after work with beer for Ross and a chardonnay for Angie. He had a new denim shirt and told them that the farm bike wouldn't be ideal for coming in and out each day in the winter. 'You're still happy out there, though?' asked Angie.

'Look, I found my real self in that place,' said Cass. 'After what happened to me up north I knew I had to get a grip on the things that really matter. There's too great a chance of losing yourself in a complicated existence. A good deal of what passes for necessary activity in everyday life is futile.'

'Tell that to the taxman,' said Ross.

Cass Robbins was senior electrician within three months and he started wearing an orange work coat with the company logo. He bought an almost new Honda Prelude, which he parked by the cottage and carefully covered from the frost. Ross told Angie he'd heard that Cass had started going out with Rebecca Levitt, who worked in accounts and whose husband had been accidentally shot while hunting wallaby in the Hunter Hills.

The next spring the company offered Cass Robbins promotion in Dunedin as maintenance manager. He came to see Angie about putting the old Jamieson place on the market. 'A nice enough little place,' he said, 'but I'm finding it a real nark to have no phone, or electricity. What with the shift callouts and everything I'll need to have something pretty central in Dunedin.'

'I know a couple of good people in real estate down there. I'll give you their names. Would you like a drink?'

'Thanks, but no. Time's money and as a matter of fact I've got someone waiting in the car.' Cass was wearing fashionable twill trousers and had begun a new look by combing his hair back from his forehead. 'I wanted you to have sole agency,' he said.

'You'll be looking for another place by the sea.'

'By the sea?'

'For your ocean view,' said Angie.

'Haven't much time to admire a view these days,' said Cass. 'A modern, low maintenance, all convenience place is what I'm after. As a matter of fact the firm's offering generous mortgage facilities, but don't tell your agent friends that.'

Angie rather expected that Cass would go on to say that he was going to be married. She hoped he might invite her to come out to the car and meet Rebecca Levitt, but he didn't. He shook hands almost formally and gave Angie his temporary Dunedin address. 'You know,' he said, 'I'm quite looking forward to the greater challenge of the city. Maybe Ross mentioned the scope of my responsibilities with the company?'

A few weeks later Angie Bruin had reason to be not far from the old Jamieson place and she turned off the main road and drove down to the coast. She wanted to have an up-to-date impression of Cass Robbins' cottage when she spoke of it to any possible buyers. It sat in the bare paddock on the headland above the sea; the high, half burnt out macrocarpas on the south side, the sheep with the run of the verandah and laundry again, the immensely powerful yet subdued sound of the swell and shingle up and down the steep beach. The paddocks had a tinge of green because of the season and the repaired weatherboards were still pink with undercoat. Otherwise it was much as it had been when Cass Robbins came to the place the summer before.

Angie Bruin looked from the empty cottage out across the gravel road and the headland. A new crop of boxthorn was already sprouting from the ash and stumps of Cass's onslaught, but for a time at least there was that complete and wind-raw view of sea and sky and the meeting of one blue with another which was the horizon.

This Man's Army

~

WHAT I REMEMBER about leaving for National Service is having my photo taken for the local paper, along with the five or six other guys who were also going to Waiouru. The photograph itself I never saw, but I remember standing on the platform with the wooden wall of the railway station behind us on which was hanging a row of empty buckets, God knows why. And this hugely pregnant girl who had come to see her husband off, and who discomforted the rest of us because of her condition. Maybe even before we were quite in the army we considered that she added a non-military element; maybe it was a misgiving as to which of us in the photograph would seem most likely to be responsible for her condition. I can't put a face to any of the other guys: we got split up in basic training. Just the grouping of us before the buckets I recall, and our disinclination to press towards the pregnant girl who was the centre-piece. She had a summer smock, large, white legs and straight, girl-next-door hair. Her meaty features quivered at the farewells, and I'll bet National Service was worse for her than any of us who left for the army that day.

On the train to Picton and on the ferry across the strait I could almost forget the destination, and the origin of my travel warrant, but at Wellington there were enough of us from that intake to fill a special bus to go north in the evening. A corporal with a clip-board, too, whose uniform was the unsought indication of things to come. I had a biro in the inside pocket of my sportscoat and body heat must have made it burst, for when I roused myself from lolling on the seat back and window I had a purple stain on the lining, my shirt, my chest. 'Now listen up, cocksuckers,' the corporal said, 'when you debus for Intake and Documentation I don't want nothing left on board. Nothing, right?' That stain went from my skin after a week or so, but much later when I collected my civvy gear to go home for the first time, there it was on my shirt and coat lining, and I heard that first corporal telling us cocksuckers to listen up.

Plain loneliness is what you feel most in National Service, for the first weeks anyway. After you make friends and realise that a good deal of all the hoopla is just show, then you move on to complex loneliness. You look forward to rec time playing table tennis, or sinking a few in the wet canteen, but at the centre of it all there's still loneliness that arises from not being in command of your own life, or among people of your own choice. Maybe loneliness isn't so much what I mean: futility perhaps.

Mail was brought to the barracks in the afternoons. When we got back from train-ing, the letters would be lying on the right beds. They would lie at all angles, just as flipped on to the army blanket of perfect tension, and the bedrolls would look down on them. The blankets and sheets of the bedroll had to make perfect and alternate layers. Any crease at morning inspection meant a charge. When we came back from the butts, the gas hut, the confidence course, the lecture rooms, the bivvies, the first thing we looked for was mail. Guys read their letters in all sorts of ways and many places. The letters were part of our life on the outside, the only bits getting through to us. If I was first into the barrack room I always noticed the pale envelopes with their stamps, lying on the smooth grey of the army blankets. Some beds would have several; some beds never had any, no matter how many weeks passed.

At the end of each bed was a large wooden box for issue gear, and down the centre of the barrack room was a rifle rack for the Browning SLRs. The rifles had to be cleaned before mess parade in the evening, then the corporal for the day checked them in, drew a long chain through all the trigger guards down the rack and padlocked it.

The best letters I got were the few from Debra Eastcliff who was doing law at Canterbury. They weren't passionate letters because we'd been seeing each other for only a few weeks before the exams of the year before, and she lived in Nelson. Her life seemed to have so much more freedom than my own. Almost everything she talked about was familiar to me; almost everything around me as I read her letters, or replied, or thought about her, was incomprehensible to someone not living it. That particular sound of the chain through the trigger guards, the two guys who had started bumming in the showers, the MPs' Land Rover at three or four in the morning so that the barrack room was briefly lit with flashes through the windows. Miles Procter, who was cheerful all day, cried in his sleep at night. Benny Wesley tried to steal a live hand grenade to blow up his old school. There was a tin slide that you put under your brass coat buttons when you cleaned them that some guys could use as a bottle opener. Where else, I wonder, would this be considered a useful knack?

In certain circumstances you shut down some of your emotional responses, as a form of defence, in the same way that some animals slow their metabolism to get through winter. I could sit in the back of a truck coming back from exercises and for half an hour just watch the dust suck in under the canopy, stick to the sweat on the faces opposite and darken gradually as a make-up. The padre came into the barrack room one morning before parade, and our instructing NCOs discreetly, yet derisively, withdrew. He talked to a platoon of bland faces, and both he and we knew that none of us would go to see him.

Each barrack block looked much the same. All were wooden and one-storeyed and each had a letter on the end so that one could be proved distinct from another. Each block had its orderly room, its parade ground, its mess. In summer the heat shimmered across the parade grounds, and in winter the snow lay in the tussock slopes above the butts.

Debra Eastcliff had this vacation job ringing just about everyone in Nelson as part of a survey on newspaper reading habits. Every day she got offered dates from guys who liked the sound of her voice. I liked the sound of her voice very much myself — from recollection and the few calls that I made while other servicemen stood waiting. I liked the way she wrote, too: candidly, and with no reference to the excessive familiarity to which I was driven by my unnatural life.

Sergeant Neke was a regular army man. He regarded the responsibility for the basic training of our platoon as a form of penance, and so bore all the humiliation of it with sorrow rather than rage. The sarcasm and spurious intimidation were left to Lance Corporal Dellmer, who was also regular army, but limited enough to draw satisfaction from shouting at thirty people who had their own talents, yet were certainly ignorant concerning Corporal Dellmer's army. But don't imagine that he was a man of any real malice: all he required was our acceptance that there was no higher aspiration in life than to be a fighting man.

Sundays were designated non-training days, but we found that even recreation was compulsory. There was a choice of sports, but no alternative to participation. The monotony of softball on the brown summer grass I remember, and the cross-country winter runs that gave privacy at least. The combination of external chill and internal heat on those winter runs used to mottle my legs and shoulders brick red and white. We were convinced that the army authorities put kill-cock in our drink, but I think a policy of physical exertion was enough. Nevertheless, it was strange that the homely women who served in the canteen were transformed into beauties by the passage of time. Noeline had the best pair on her and consequently worked a very popular shift, but it was all a hopeless and muted lust.

There was a hot day when we sat in a dry creekbed while Sergeant Neke explained to us the logic and formation of a dispersed infantry advance across open country. He had taken off his beret, and his straight hair was in quills because of the sweat, which also darkened his jungle greens in an arc that reached well down his ribs. There was a damp clay bank behind him, grey as pencil lead, and a mass of small, lilac butterflies swooped and quivered there. Nothing of Neke's instruction has remained, but there is the memory of him talking there and all the while the lilac butterflies a shifting aura behind him. It was a brief, random beauty and not one of us made mention of it.

Occasionally there were training films, with Corporal Dellmer quite pumped up with the novelty of such instructional aids, and Sergeant Neke providing a resigned introduction, his large, dark eyes glossy with despair. *Why Things Are Seen* we watched in a room inadequately blacked out, and with a platoon of B Company square bashing outside. The film's narrator told us all about shape, movement, colour and silhouette in a very English voice and in a very English landscape, while a light drizzle twisted in shrouds across the parade ground and clotted on the windows. Sergeant Neke left us after his introduction; the corporal stood at one of the windows, looked into the drifting rain and moved his lips exactly to make the drill commands his own. See the English hedgerow with a red triangle set among its amorphous green; see awkward Tutty a row in front with, behind his left ear, a mulberry birthmark that an army haircut doesn't conceal; see the B Company platoon fall in on its marker. The projector ran on with a clicking repetition that was a clichéd anachronism even then. We moved our shoulders, gaped like baboons, in some unconscious protest at the passing of our lives.

Our company did a five-day field exercise shortly before we completed basic training. Combat conditions, they said, and so we slogged around the hills with full gear, dug slitties, stood sentry, kept moving out at some Godforsaken hour of the night. The enemy were a group of officer cadets who had a fondness for extravagant camouflage, and lobbing thunder-flashes into our perimeter. As our section moved across this bush creek after midnight, Kyle MacDonald slumped down on the cool boulders and couldn't go on. We got his pack off and stood among the ferns of the bank listening to his forced breathing. The medic thought he'd had a heart attack, and at first light we carried him up to a tussock ridge and he went out by helicopter. We were impressed by something as solemn as a heart attack. It seemed the real thing among so much simulation. Our sympathy for Kyle MacDonald, and the unspoken regard for our own fortitude, were destroyed when we got back to Waiouru to find that he'd been diagnosed as having hyperventilated and was discharged after one night. After that we considered him a bit of a prick.

There were friends made, of course, whether of convenience, or necessity, we didn't stop to consider. Guy Wynn, who had a subversive humour that attracted me, and breath that repelled us all. Peter Evans who, because he was both lazy and powerful, had an easy disposition. 'She'll be jake,' he'd say of fatigues duty, or a charge for not being back in barracks. 'She'll be jake.' With all of that platoon I lived more closely than I ever did with my brothers — we were shackled together by the army squad mentality, by identical daily programmes, and an obligation of duty. We recognised it, and didn't blame one another for our predicament. Like porkers in a pen, we knew about enforced familiarity.

We had one big snowfall on Waiouru itself before I left. It started in the evening when we were coming back from the mess hall. In the dusk the snowflakes were almost invisible until they passed before the windows, doorways or large lights mounted on the street end of the barrack blocks. Like Lux flakes the snow passed almost horizontally before the light sources, yet I wasn't conscious of a wind. For a long time there was no sign that any snow ever touched the ground, but overnight it silently reached up along the sides of the barrack blocks as if to disguise their ugliness. When we formed up in the half-light of a winter morning, the tread pattern of our boots was minted over and over in the snow.

What I remember about leaving from National Service is just the green, covered trucks drawn up at the barracks to take us to the station. Northbound and southbound at different times, and the laughter and the relief and the pledges to keep in touch with mates that were never redeemed. And the things that had been invested with special power and significance, shrunk to objective appreciation. The empty rifle rack, and the beds revealed scarred and plain once the immaculate blankets had gone. A CSM's parade square cry become irrelevant, the cracked and dust-dappled windows of the wet canteen. 'Get out of here, you useless bastards,' said Corporal Dellmer, and stood smiling, flattered by our jeers of farewell.

Day One

IN THE MID-60S I finished my thesis on extruded igneous dykes of Banks Peninsula and sat back to receive the plaudits and post-graduate study offers of the academic world. The academic world remained strangely mute and I accepted a job as assistant housemaster at a traditional boys' college. All the physical possessions that I owned in the world were crammed into my series E Morris and I drove up the day before the start of term one.

The great sycamore trees stirred like galleons on the expansive lawns beyond the stone gates and the side parking area by the boiler house was full of boarder parent cars. Those boys who already knew the school immediately abandoned their parents lest they be shamed by association with family. In threes and fours and anthropoidal amble they drifted back to old haunts. Only the third formers, bright as reef fish in their new uniforms, kept close to the adults as they wandered about to forestall farewell. The new mothers of the school maintained a despairing cheerfulness, smiling fiercely and commenting on the stained glass window in the chapel, and all the time hoping to see a familiar face. The fathers, whose minds had thankfully suppressed their own experience as new boys, patted shoulders with inarticulate support and murmured the bastard Latin of the school song.

I was a new boy again myself in a way and a little humbled to be seated by the secretary outside the head's study until he could see me. There was a box with a frosted glass front mounted by the door, which displayed COME IN, WAIT or ENGAGED, at the direction of the person inside.

Ian Villier was the headmaster. I got a first glimpse of him as a father with an expensive tweed jacket was shown out, but Villier didn't want to meet my eye just then and turned back, closed the door, looked over my application and CV again perhaps. COME IN was then displayed in a shimmer of letters on the frosted glass. I did so, and walked a surprising stretch of opulent, heraldic carpet before I could reach the headmaster's desk. Villier had a great jutting face, with a nose large enough to saddle, and his grey hair was swept back directly from his face. His features were both exaggerated and impressive, like those of an aristocratic baboon. He had an expression as if he were about to be photographed, which he maintained over the several years that I knew him.

'A sound enough degree,' he said, while pointing emphatically to a chair with a cloth seat of paisley pattern as if he wanted some comment on it, or from it. 'The profession is stuffed with geographers, however. Still, it could have been history. I could have had two firsts in history sitting in your place and one of them played for Manawatu.' I knew enough of the school to realise that any official reference to sport pertained to rugby. 'There's not a lot of advancement possible through the humanities, I'm afraid. I'd advise you to make the most of housemastering. A good housemaster now, there's progress in a career that way. Most of the principals I know proved themselves on the boarding side.'

He began each sentence with sufficient volume and clarity of enunciation to command the assembly hall and then, as if realising the talk was more personal, allowed his voice to drop away. It reminded me of Anzac days long ago. He wore an academic gown slightly greened with age and ran his fingers down the heavy, dark edges of it on his chest. He made a good deal of eye contact, tilting his head up so that the trajectory of his great nose altered and the large nostrils came level with my vision like the muzzles of a shotgun.

'You'll soon settle to it. Routine is the secret of efficiency. We have a full staff meeting early tomorrow.' The head passed over a folder containing my teaching timetable, a staff list, fire drill and a discount voucher from the local takeaway. His fingers rustled on the edges of his gown and he leant back in his chair, turning his eyes to watch the returning boarders in the grounds beyond his office. 'The team,' he said ringingly. 'The team is everything. Do your bit and it'll carry you along.' The inner door opened and the secretary mouthed a name at him and then withdrew. Villier spread his hands palms uppermost in mock exasperation at the need to end the meeting and I stood up to leave.

'Ontology,' boomed the head as we moved to the door. I could think of no reply. 'That's why I chose you. I rang the dean at the college and she said that you had it recorded as a major interest. I'm always drawn to a thinking man — and a man who appreciates the needs of a team, of course. Anyway, ontology swung it for you.' I had no idea what ontology was, had met the dean only twice, but I wasn't going to question the grounds of my appointment. Rather I took it as an omen of the sort of place that I had come to. Villier posed briefly in the doorway to farewell me; his great shoes of burnished oxblood leather shone like the hooves of a show horse. 'Ontology,' he said and tilted his head to suggest this would remain a secret between us, and to present his better profile to the camera.

Across the lower quad and furthest from the noise of traffic was the old hostel building known as the Gables, although they had been removed years before because of earthquake risk. The wooden building was dwarfed by modern, two-storeyed hostel blocks close to it, but still held the housemasters' study, matron's office, the sickbay, lost and found, and a display case of transfixed and mouldering native birds presented by the first dux of the school on his return thirty years later.

Already boys were coming and going at the Gables and they looked at me with a mixture of curiosity and derision as I went into the housemasters' study. Chink McMahon was duplicating dorm lists and not surprised by my arrival because the secretary had rung. Chink was head of hostel and got his name not from any oriental appearance, but because he resembled some general of the desert campaign who had the name. Chink had been there himself and after that time of trial seemed to find all of life trivial and fit only for grim burlesque. The fewer people about him who were returned soldiers, the greater his disregard for the present became. Beneath all was a bitterness that the epic world he had experienced was fading and that more and more of the Lilliputians around him had no understanding, no regard, for what had happened in the desert. Chink himself was far too proud to tell them and kept the flame alive by drinking whisky from a glass at the RSA and from a flask when he was off duty within the school grounds. It was said that his name was mentioned fifty-seven times in the battalion history.

'Seen the head then?' shouted Chink above the noise of the gestetner he was cranking. His wry grin showed the gap between his front teeth typical of his name-sake. From time to time sheets stuck to the roller longer than they should, and shot high into the air. Chink snatched them down with the reflexes of a praying mantis while still cranking with the other hand. 'No need for a great deal of patter,' he said as he finished with the machine. He gestured to the long notice boards, so festooned with ageing papers, many six deep to a pin, that they resembled soiled tutus. 'Duty rosters, bell routines, leave provisions, extension numbers, team lists, and so on. There when you need it. Learn the job by doing it, I always say.' He looked at me with his eyebrows up as if askance that one so young should be given even the least command.

'Oh,' and Chink took a couple of steps towards the quad window and patted a large, well-used book that had pride of place on a table there. 'Caning book. Caning book. Never forget it. See.' He flicked it open and, with a pencil attached to the spine with twine, pointed out the headed columns that he had ruled in — date, name, strokes, reason, staff signature. 'Never forget it. The senior housemasters find it essential for their term reports.' I could see at a glance that the last boy had been punished for dumb insolence and imitating a hyena during prep.

Chink told me which house I was attached to and a few other administration things. There was no garage available, but Chink said that I could nose my car into the lean-to behind the boiler house where the figure targets were kept. 'No military service, I suppose?' asked Chink. I attempted to inject a degree of disappointment into my voice when replying that I'd missed out on National Service. 'Sport, though?' Chink knew that no one would be appointed to the college without some physical qualification and was barely mollified by my recital of considerable participation and notably less achievement.

When I was at the door again, about to leave in the direction of my house, Stanways, Chink made his one effort in pastoral guidance. 'Advice,' he said. I halted, wishing to show no disinclination to listen. 'Are you interested in advice?' asked Chink diffidently. I nodded.

Chink drew himself up and protected himself with an added formality of tone. 'Six things,' he said, 'in the school and in the hostel. Always be prepared, never permit insolence, never court popularity, cane severely and therefore rarely, never introduce a topic dear to your heart and never expect gratitude.'

I said that I would bear all of them in mind. Such precepts were far from those I had recently been introduced to at teachers' college, yet Chink's were easier to hold in the mind and experience was to prove them also more valuable.

Stanways was one of the new hostel blocks, built largely through the generosity of old boys who were determined that a new generation have things no easier than they themselves had found them. Change other than expansion was anathema to them, while demonstrative progress was even worse. Had it been possible, they would have insisted on the identical prescriptions, an equivalent number of wet Sundays and bullies, the very same teachers even, revitalised as caricatures generation after generation.

The housemaster of Stanways was John Roffery, known by the boys as Pecker because of his nodding head when stressed, which was ever the case. Pecker was in the second-storey fourth form dorm making copies of the wall graffiti in a scrapbook of low-quality paper. 'The little bastards keep telling me that it's already there from the year before, but now I'll have them, have the little bastards.' I had barely introduced myself before he had me counter-signing the sketches as a true record and then numbering the light bulb in each fourth former's cubicle with a green felt pen. Pecker couldn't have been more than thirty-five and had a soft, jellied face that quivered with high emotion because of the onset of another term. He taught French despite a temperament quite unsuited to the profession. Rage is the emotion in a teacher which most delights all students and once they recognise that it can be provoked, they'll go to any lengths to do so.

Pecker was not a fool and understood that he'd made the wrong choice of profession. He was a housemaster as well as a teacher at the college so that he could amass the greatest amount of money in the least time and then resign. 'A mussel farm in Queen Charlotte Sound,' he told me as we confiscated beer that incoming boarders had stashed in the lavatory cisterns. 'You go out in the boat with a few select companions,' he said, 'and no one else can come near you all day.' Some weeks later I was with Pecker in the Collar and Tie Bar and, when a visitor asked his job, he replied that he demeaned himself for a living. Pecker could see his own situation even if unable to rectify it immediately.

Pecker went into the third form dorm and rounded up several red-eyed, small boys to help me bring in my gear. After I had parked the Morris among a mass of Hun target flats like protest placards, and as the laden new boys and I trekked back to Stanways, I could see in the growing dusk and at the periphery of vision, skulking figures drift towards the car. The third formers piled my stuff outside my room and, despite the agony of their homesickness and the brief time we had been together, it later proved that they had got off with six bottles of Australian shiraz, my running shoes, a flashing works lamp, all my love letters from Molly Parmenter and several male-oriented magazines.

The room was well appointed and quite new, with a view over the fives courts and the ramps behind the kitchens where the pig drums were rumbled out each morning. Unfortunately during the vacation a starling had blundered in somehow and shat on almost all the furniture before dying at last behind the wall heater. 'Just heap your stuff in for the moment,' said Pecker, 'and I'll take you down to the house prefects' room so that you can get to know a face or two.' Four or five of them were there, all uncouthly large and hairy and with knuckled hands that seemed to gravitate naturally to the crotch — their own in the first instance, at least — or to the destruction of what furniture hadn't already been unravelled. Pecker rattled through their names and said it was important, as a housemaster, to carry the prefects with you — vital in fact. An exhausting task judging by the size of them.

The head of house had just got in and still wore his school blazer with his achievements scrolled beneath the crest like campaign medals. 'We shall find a name for you, sir,' he said to me kindly, 'but it may take a few weeks' observation.'

'Maybe prickface,' I heard another say as Pecker and I went back down the corridor.

As it was the boarders' in day, the meal was a good deal later than usual and the lights were needed in the dining room by the time nearly three hundred boys were seated and Chink led in the staff. There were just six of us that first night: Chink, Pecker, a large marshmallow who was the nurse, Jetarse Munns who was head of Chivers, and Neville Gillespie who was, like myself, new to the school.

Our table was a little raised, presumably to allow masters to exercise a supervisory function as they ate. It was rather like having a meal on a crowded railway platform; no awareness of individual speakers, but a disconcerting general roar of voices and occasional surges to the kitchen slides. From time to time Chink stood up from his meal, showed his gapped teeth like an old lion, and paced down a few aisles.

'Dining room supervision begins for one of you tomorrow,' Pecker told Neville and me. During the rice pudding course Jetarse Munns suddenly sprang into the throng and dragged from the room a mid-sized boy with a continuous eyebrow. 'Marriage collapsed last year,' said Pecker. He tapped his forehead. 'I give him a term, that's all.' I presumed that the description applied to Jetarse rather than the boy.

'I don't believe I caught your name,' said the nurse to Neville and, after being given it, turned and asked the same question of me. She had the softest flesh I have ever seen, palely luminous and so unresisting to gravitational forces that when she rested her arm on the table it spread out like cake mixture. 'Treat me as a confidante,' she said.

'Notices,' roared Chink and the noise in the dining hall gradually fell to a menacing rumble. Chink sucked his teeth and seemed to be contemplating a bayonet charge. Pecker motioned to us and we quietly filed away while Chink read the list of outstanding detentions from the year before. As we passed into the quad, Jetarse was there in the shadows, still haranguing the mid-sized boy with the never-ending eyebrow. The boy's body language suggested to me exactly the term dumb insolence that I had read in the caning book, though Jetarse was contributing the animal noises.

Neville and I grouped together for support, as is always the way of newcomers in a unknown environment. We had little in common apart from our profession and our predicament, but it was weeks before our mutual antipathy developed. For that first night we were the best of friends and sat in his room, which was starlingless, drinking vodka and lime as the school whirled around us. Neville was a five foot five mathematician with a penchant for savage sarcasm and a complete tolerance to alcohol. We assured each other that we were born teachers. We got drunk by the window open to the summer night, ignoring the strange cries and jostling shadows of an educational Serengeti. We watched the moon and stars, and a line of glowing, red dots closer to the horizon that were the cigarettes of seniors sitting on the back field.

Even very drunk, I retained an odd, ambivalent reaction to the new world in which I found myself — part exhilaration and part apprehension. I had commenced a career.

Goodbye, Stanley Tan

~

WE DIDN'T SEE the Raffles Hotel; it was closed for renovations. Isn't that always the way and now if ever the trip comes up in conversation with other people, they expect us to have been to Raffles. We saw the merlion at the harbour, though, and the useless gun emplacements on Sentosa Island. We climbed to Fort Canning on the site of the ancient royal palace. We had our photo taken with a black snake at the cable-car terminal and in the Tiger Balm Gardens and in the Orchid Gardens and with pygmy hippos only a fence away. We have a photo emphasising my bulk as I board a bum boat, a photo of my wife boarding the bum boat, a photo of a woman from Tuttle, North Dakota, who for an hour was our best friend in the world, disembarking from a bum boat. We have photos of our hotel bed covered with a day's purchases from plazas twenty storeys high. We have photos in which we can identify nothing, not even ourselves, and for which there seems no earthly or unearthly reason. These photographs tend to cause disagreement as to whether they even belong to the Singapore album, or whether they are of Hong Kong, or Penang, or Bangkok. As if there were any real connection between the settings and ourselves.

But you know all of that. It is part of collective tourist folklore, so let me give you three things that come from a working visit, when I was twenty-seven and had a larger appetite for experience and a smaller perception of its whereabouts, than my own country suited. Flotillas of scooters and motorbikes at the very start of the day, with riders wearing their jackets back to front as a windbreak; lizards on the walls where the first sun strikes; Thais, muffled like gangsters, spraying weeds and verges and, unmuffled, doing many of the other menial jobs. From that time I have only one photo. Dog-eared and monochrome, it shows me with Stanley Tan outside the illegal pig abattoir in which we worked. Strangely enough, it was my farming background which provided for me in that close pressed city. That more intimate knowledge of Singapore is like a dream now and provides no link with the present place. For some months I lived closely with Stanley Tan as a friend, but even then we knew that it was the fortuitous friendship of circumstance and not something that could survive once we left the squeals of the abattoir and the concrete room by the old harbour where we slept with the continual noise and smell of the city through the metal bars of the door. There is a sense of free fall in the relationships of youth that is lost in a later regard for security.

The woman from Tuttle, North Dakota, is a different story. An hour on an Asian bum boat seems to have cemented our lives together. She has since sent postcards from Nepal, Denmark, Egypt, Timor and Tuttle, North Dakota. She is planning a trip to New Zealand with her husband largely on our unsuspecting praise of the country.

Her husband, she told my wife, is six foot three and was legal counsel to the previous Governor of North Dakota.

My wife and I stayed at a hotel in Orchard Road that had an atrium designed by the Pharaohs and a labyrinth of soft, air-conditioned corridors. I slept more poorly there than I had years before in the barred, concrete room by the estuarine harbour. My wife likes hotels, but I lay listening through much of the night to the shouts from the streets. It was as if gangs still fought there, which, Stanley Tan said, was the regular thing before Lee took over.

So safe a city did he make it that Stanley and I, my wife and I, years apart, could wander late at night and feel quite at ease. My wife is a perceptive traveller, whereas I am merely a bewildered one. She pointed out to me that although people drove on the left in Singapore, they tended to walk on the right. Nobody whistles as they go about their business, she said, and she was right. I guess that it's some cultural thing between Singaporeans and ourselves.

Orchard Road was like a drying room into which a community had been herded. The cries began with intensity, but were rendered languid by the hot, moist air as they rose towards our hotel room. When we had finished work, Stanley Tan sometimes took a shower in the flush room where the gutted pigs were given a final hose down and their bristles shaved if the buyers preferred them that way. The naked pigs were similar in colour to the naked Stanley, but carried more fat. If he jostled them as he held the hose with one hand and washed with the other, the carcasses would sway coyly away, then back again. Occasionally I showered there myself; it was cooling, but I disliked the feel of blood clots and fat between my feet and the concrete floor. If he showered at the abattoir, Stanley usually took a head he could buy cheaply and exchanged it for the favours of a very short, smiling mother of two who had a calligraphy stall in the direction of our room.

My wife said that I should attempt to find the places I was accustomed to from those far off months in Singapore. Long hours and little money had reduced my view of the city. After more than twenty years how was I to find the site of an illegal pig abattoir smaller than a New Zealand family home, the barred apartment cell Stanley Tan and I shared, the parasol shop that twice a day served fried rice and vegetable ends among the umbrellas to a few regulars who worked close at hand? The owner of the abattoir saw no reason for breaks of longer than twenty minutes. I could still find my way to Raffles, of course, although my wife and I couldn't go in. Twice I had been there before. Once with a Canadian girl whom I met lost by the parasol shop; once to have a gin sling with Eddie Gilmore who supervised my thesis. There were the ceiling fans and a good deal of dark wood. There was also an air of self-conscious history. Eddie Gilmore was to give a plenary address at the three-day conference, but knew he wasn't well. 'Would that I were in the abattoir with you,' he said with feeling. 'Killing pigs and young again, or better still that I were here and young again.'

Our American friend from Tuttle told my wife and me on the bum boat that of all the places she had visited, and she seemed well through the places of the world,

Singapore was the cleanest and the most orderly. She said that they had the sense to teach everyone English in Singapore and so put them in the ballgame with everyone else. Certainly it's comforting to have foreign people speak your language in their country. The friend from Tuttle, North Dakota said that she found it easier to understand the Singaporeans than she did us, though we also were in the same ballgame, I guess.

One morning of lurid skies when Stanley and I arrived for work, the old wooden door was still closed and the cobbled pen at the back empty of porkers. Mr Ng stood with a police officer by the wooden door, but what was going on had nothing to do with the abattoir being illegal: in the whole incident that didn't arise. The police in Singapore were busy people with strict priorities. Two people had fallen, or been pushed, from the top of the old building that had the parasol shop on its ground floor. It had happened in the darkness, but the bodies still lay uncovered, though watched by another policeman with folded arms. Mr Ng was impatient with the time taken by police procedure; he wanted to truck in his pigs, but could hardly do so under the very noses of the authorities.

Gold is very special to the Chinese and my wife had heard of a manufacturing jeweller in Bukit Timah Road who had lovely stuff, and all twenty-two carat or better. We went there in a taxi and, sure enough, the bracelet chains and necklaces were superb, but my wife wasn't the only one to have heard of them and there were whole busloads of people, from all over the world it seemed to me, crowded into a small showroom. Our friend from Tuttle, North Dakota, seemed the only tourist in Singapore at the time who wasn't there.

After a while I went out and sat on the parapet above the carpark on the shady side. I sweated quietly there and watched an employee from the pottery next door working a pug mill for reconstituted clay. I wished my wife good fortune in finding just the gold chain that she wanted within her budget and I had a sudden foresight that thereafter, whenever she wore it, whenever it was remarked on, I would again be on that parapet in the hot shade, watching the boy working the pug mill. The clay made a glistening cream right up to his elbows. Several times he looked up and smiled; once he raised an arm richly gloved in clay. I felt a whim to explain to him that years before I had lived in the city, worked with Stanley Tan killing and gutting pigs, eaten in the parasol shop, covered the cheerful woman calligrapher with some considerable goodwill myself while her younger child watched with religious solemnity, been taken by the police to see if I could identify the bodies in the street.

Stanley Tan and I had been regulars for the cheap meals at the parasol shop and it was thought that we might recognise the dead men, but we didn't. One man was quite plump and much of his chest and stomach was showing from a shirt completely open at the front. There was no sign of injury, but his body was an odd purple-grey that I recall unpleasantly well. Mr Ng was quite sure that they were gamblers who had brought death on themselves and told the police so.

Goodbye, Stanley Tan ~ 377

As we went by taxi to the airport my wife and I talked of what we had done in Singapore, so that we could reach agreement on the things to be considered high points and the incidents of disappointment and bad service that we would retain as criticism. So much experience in between had to be discarded as transient to make room for the next destination. As we talked I half recognised the area through which we moved. Stanley Tan and I had driven out towards Changi sometimes to collect pigs, years before the new airport was built there. We had travelled in an old Bedford truck and usually at night. There had been fish farms down Tampines Road then and the moon and few artificial lights would flick and scud from the heavy surface of one pond after another.

Stanley Tan had a smile that was all in the eyes and in the crinkles around them, while his mouth stayed the same. As we came back past the fish farm pools one night, the crate sides of the Bedford tight with pigs from the small holdings, he told me very dirty jokes that I've forgotten and talked as well about the tigers which his grandfather could remember in the area. 'Forget the lions,' said Stanley. 'Singapore was tiger country and the Chinese owners of the pepper and gambier plantations had no end of trouble getting coolie workers because of the attacks. You, now, has your family given up anyone to the tigers?'

I began to tell my wife about the tigers and the Tans, but the heat, the noise of the many aircraft overhead and our provincial anxiety to do everything right at the airport distracted us and so there wasn't much pleasure in the telling, or the listening. A kind attendant in the flight lounge, though, took a photo of us both. We are standing close together, both in affection and in accordance with subject grouping, and we have smiles fit for a new destination.

Flute and Chance

~

RABBER WAS, LIKE ourselves, something of a smart-arse and lived, though not by choice, in an all-male flat on the steepest street in the world. He was beginning that year a PhD thesis on nasal wind instruments in traditional Pacific communities and most days he carefully descended the steepest street in the world in crêpe-soled shoes and walked down North East Valley and through the gardens into Castle Street. That was his most direct route to the anthropology department at the university. Rabber liked to see the ducks in the park and the rose gardens out in summer. He was rather dapper, with a cloth cap and a briefcase. In the department he shared a small room on the south side with three other post-graduate students. They had a phone and their own extension number.

After a tough day, Rabber decided to amuse himself with non sequiturs on his way home. He had spent several hours reading catalogue printouts from the Pacific collections at two Australian museums and had failed to turn up even one Melanesian single-stop resonance conch nose flute. He needed a diversion. The departmental secretary saw him on his way from the south side. All agreed that she was a lovely woman and unjustly afflicted with a broken marriage and a son who would never make anything of himself. 'Oh, Rabber, there's a note from computers.' Rabber pirouetted in the corridor, his briefcase extended. He swayed his head back towards the entrance to her office.

'Leap year is a propitious time for alpine cheeses,' he said.

On the bank past the staff club a group of Japanese clustered to take photos of the clock tower on the other side of the stream. Rabber climbed a modest stone wall and gestured to them with exaggerated familiarity. Several, including the interpreter, came towards him. They were bowed down with cameras. 'Pardon?' said the interpreter, though Rabber had said nothing.

'Who rescues the tiger from the pit?' whispered Rabber.

In Castle Street, Rabber came across a student from his stage one tutorial group. 'Hi,' he said. She was a large girl from the Rai Valley near Blenheim. Everything about her was smooth and copious except the short spikes of her hair — 'Hi,' she said — and her conversation.

'Prorogation is rarely an easy constitutional option,' Rabber told her. He looked into her face and raised his eyebrows as a sign he expected a response. She shrugged the backpack uneasily, lifted her smooth face to the sky in a simulation of thought. From that pose she was able to take several steps backwards, turn with her face still full to the sky and escape without meeting Rabber's eye. He had a recollection of the sides of the Rai Valley clothed with pig fern and he imagined his student standing there, her smooth bulk rising from the green and brown of the fern and her eyes fixed on the blue heavens.

Rabber crossed the footbridge and began his walk through the gardens. There were great trees bearing name tags on their chests and lowly, but more colourful, beds of annuals welling up from the lawns. But Rabber knew better than to leave the path because the grass was mined with duck shit.

Two men by the hothouses were putting up netting to keep the ducks from an assault on flowers already bruised purple. One man was pale and old, with all the weight of him seemingly slumped to the swollen, grey gardening boots he wore. The other man was young and had his overalls folded down to his waist so that his square, brown chest was in the sun. Rabber examined the netting of the roll. 'In the Devonian period,' he said, 'the brachiopod was a prevalent mollusc.' Both men stopped work as Rabber spoke. A conversation was preferable to hammering the waratahs and attaching the netting. 'Nothing that the Hubble telescope descried was conclusive proof that after the big bang the galaxies condensed from the outside in, or the inside out,' Rabber told them.

'Well, hell, you got me there, mate, I must say,' said the young man.

Rabber left the gardens by the main gates and entered the supermarket, which was among the shops at the mouth of North East Valley. There were one or two things he needed for the flat. The checkout girl had a very long, sinuous neck, and a very small, even-featured head. She looked like a white swan in a company smock. 'Have a good day,' she said.

'Despite its name, the arum lily isn't a true lily. Not in strict botanical terms it's not. The floozie of the funeral parlours is really *Zantedeschia*,' said Rabber.

'Eh?'

'The secret of humour is irrationality. That's why sex is so amusing,' said Rabber. The white swan arched her neck away.

The supermarket bag was a handy counterpoise to his briefcase, and Rabber strolled up the North East Valley. He had only another two or three years of research into the place of nasal wind instruments in traditional Pacific societies and then the world would be his oyster.

Ahead, Rabber saw some sort of stooping misfit in a long coat of blue cloth despite the sun, and heels scuffed away. As he drew level with the man, Rabber was aware of a smell compounded of soot, sweat, steam, silverside sandwiches and leather. 'The Jesuits were founded in 1534 by St Ignatius,' said Rabber blithely. 'Not a lot of people know that, or care.'

'Precisely,' said the misfit eagerly, turning his face to see and be seen. Rabber had half expected a dingy beard, but the man's tight, narrow face had the gun-metal shine that is imparted only by a cut-throat razor. 'Precisely.'

'A Barsac though, eh?' murmured Rabber. 'A child of the true and noble rot.'

'My words exactly,' said the misfit. He put his left hand into an inside pocket, produced and unfolded a cut-throat razor, rested the blade below Rabber's jawline. No doubt it was the razor that had given him such a smooth complexion himself. With his other hand he assumed a fond grip on Rabber's arm not far above the briefcase.

'Whoa. Now hang on,' said Rabber, but the misfit kept them both walking up the North East Valley.

'The darkest blood flows back to the heart,' the misfit said. 'You and I talk the same language, amigo.'

Rabber and the misfit were exactly in step: Rabber made sure of it for that way the blade had the least pressure at his throat. The North East Valley seemed remarkably quiet. There were just two uniformed schoolgirls who passed engrossed in their own shrieking conversation. Rabber made a quick prayer in which he gave God carte blanche over his life in return for its continuation.

'Lucifer doesn't need an arsehole. Can you work that one out?' said the misfit. He guided them round a left turn and down two blocks to where the houses ended at the Lindsay Stream and a hill thick with trees rose beyond it. Across a small bridge a dirt track led to a wooden farmhouse high above. 'No kingfisher here today,' said the misfit. 'Ah, what burning colour has old *Alcedinidae*.'

'Now look here,' said Rabber weakly. The misfit jostled him down the bank and motioned beneath the bridge with the cut-throat razor. 'I've nothing against you,' said Rabber. The motion was repeated more insistently, closer to his face. Rabber waded beneath the planks and stooped there, still holding the briefcase and the supermarket bag. The misfit hunkered down on the grass alongside, undoing all the buttons of his long, blue coat so that he wasn't constricted. He had no shirt underneath, just a tight, leather jerkin, and the hair of his chest showed between the buttons. Rabber began to shiver, though the water wasn't inordinately cold.

'I saw a pig stuck under there once,' said the misfit. 'In the flood and all jammed in with branches and that. It had started to swell.' He leant forward and tugged gently at the shopping bag until Rabber released his grip. The misfit held the ivory handle of the cut-throat razor in his mouth while he looked through Rabber's purchases. He put a tin of marmalade and a packet of Oddfellow mints in the pocket of his coat; the five other things he guided into the stream. He took the razor from his mouth. 'You would have hated my Aunt Rosie,' he said. 'The bitch gave me fruit for Christmas presents.'

The misfit leant forward again and patiently prodded Rabber with the cut-throat until they had exchanged the empty plastic shopping bag for the briefcase. Rabber had sunk somewhat in the slush beneath the small bridge. The water was up to his groin, and his head free of the underside of the wooden planks stained with asphalt from above. The misfit let all of Rabber's papers float away, but he was delighted with the two-stop West Irian nose flute that Rabber's thesis supervisor had lent him two days before. Still on his haunches, the misfit held the flute aloft and said, 'See with this sceptre I absolve you.' He then turned the razor very close to Rabber's face so that, even beneath the bridge, Rabber could see the white glint of the blade. 'Bow your head,' the misfit said and he cut Rabber vertically on both cheeks. Rabber hunched, pulling his chin down to protect his throat. The cuts were very thin and the blood came almost unwillingly.

The misfit stood up and buttoned his coat. He folded the razor and put it away. 'Justice is a privilege,' he said. Not for a moment was the nose flute a mystery to him; it was almost as if he had reclaimed something of his own. He put the flute to his tight, clean-shaven, gun-metal face and walked back to the North Road, playing a few exploratory notes. Rabber came cautiously from under the bridge and put his head above the bank to make sure that the misfit was really on his way. The two cuts on his cheeks were narrow, but brilliant in the last of the sun, glistening as did his tears. The misfit didn't look back.

The Birthday Boy

~

THE WOODEN HOUSE on the corner had been built for a successful grocer, long dead and with no later generations remaining. The big house had all the chapters of a slow decline and was eventually divided into three flats so that the place became a mixture of cheap, ad hoc alterations and solid, original carpentry. Gazz and Vicky had four rooms at the front of the house; three were self-contained, but to reach their bathroom they crossed the communal hall with its central strip of raddled carpet, flanking floorboards of mahogany stain, and the dim green-yellow glow from the front door leadlights.

Gazz was sleeping in the mid-morning. A pink sheet was held across the window with drawing pins. The corner nearest to the bed was often used by Gazz as a napkin. He didn't snore, but lay very quietly with a damp patch by his mouth and the scar showing in the hairs of his left eyebrow. There was a tartan rug over the wall side of him. The other side was naked apart from his blue underpants. A thin, hairy leg, an arm with no tattoos, a soft stomach, one nipple in the straggling hair of his chest. Gazz was thirty-seven years old that very day, but he'd forgotten it and no one else would jog his memory with a celebration.

His eyes opened quite suddenly; nothing else changed as a result. Gazz lay just the same except that he took in what he could see of the room. There was someone knocking on the front door, but Gazz was neither interested, nor alarmed. He knew there would never be any good news, that any of his few acquaintances would come again, that Vicky had her own key. It would be the landlord, or a man about starting your life anew with Christ, or a kid selling chocolate eggs out of season.

When Gazz sat up, his clothes were to hand where he had left them on the floor. It took him forty seconds to put them on and to run his fingers through his hair. He then stood by the side of the window, pulled the sheet back a little with one hand, picked his nose with the other. The twitch was almost up to the window sill; the chestnut that the grocer had imagined one day shading his entrance was a broad stump; a large japonica, though, made a blaze of pink. None of these things was of the slightest interest to Gazz.

Vicky came up the path. Her head was like a pear, heavy cheeks and chin towards the bottom of it. A fine, big, white arse, though, when he could get the clothes off it. Their eyes met without message as she passed.

'So you're up at last,' said Vicky.

'Yeah.'

'No joy with dorkface down there. He won't give any credit.'

'Shit.'

'I had to use more rent money.'

'Shit.' Gazz screwed his face right up for a moment as if he had a belly pain. He made a hissing sound through his teeth. 'Shit, another week behind. Any fags?'

Vicky offered him the packet she had already opened.

'Maybe if you went back to Gabites Plywood and told them that you're not sick any more. You're just so slack.'

'Someone was hammering on the bloody door before. That prick for the rent, I reckon.'

Gazz went from the bedroom, across the hall to the bathroom. Further down the hall, Turtle was about to go into his door.

'Morning, Gazz.'

'Yeah.'

Gazz left the bathroom door open so that if he spoke up, Vicky and he could keep talking. He washed his face with his fingers and cold water, brushed his teeth without paste.

'Hey, don't you use my bloody brush,' said Vicky.

'Eh?' said Gazz, as he did just that.

'Do you want to eat soon?' she called.

'What time is it?'

'After eleven.'

'I don't mind.'

'What?'

'I don't care.'

'Eh?'

Gazz turned the water off with a sudden wrench. 'I don't bloody care,' he shouted.

'Well, fuck you too.'

Gazz stood in the hall for a time after he left the bathroom. He listened, then moved through the diminishing green-yellow light towards the back of the house where Turtle and the Tierneys had their flats. He listened at Turtle's door, then the Tierneys'. The Tierneys had external access to their larger flat through the back door, but sometimes they left their hall door unlocked and Gazz could get down on some fags, a few dollars, or a bit of booze. Enough to be useful without stirring up the Tierneys too much. He listened and decided they were at work. He tried the handle. 'Shit.'

He went back into the bedroom and took his electric shaver from the water-stained and lifting walnut veneer of the duchess. He could hear Vicky in the kitchen, so he had a quick flick around the room in search of her cigarettes. 'Shit.' Gazz left the bedroom, eternally darkened by the pink sheet, and went through into the kitchen, which was half an original room with a particle board partition between it and the Tierneys' kitchen. Less plumbing and electrics that way. Gazz stood behind Vicky to shave; he could see a sufficient reflection of his face in that part of the microwave front not covered with insulating tape. Vicky was heating a spring roll. He stretched the thumb and fingers of his left hand apart so that he could get a grip of her backside through the leather skirt. It seemed a long time since he had last had that big arse.

'Bugger off.'

'Come on, Vick. Just a quick one.' Gazz put his other hand, with the razor still buzzing, around her waist and pulled her back.

'No,' she said. 'I've had a shower and I'm not going to work this afternoon all smelly.'

'Aw, come on, Vick.'

'Bugger off.' Taking his hand from her waist, she took her spring roll from the microwave, sat down at the laminated table by the window and cleared some space for her plate. Gazz was left with his reflection and his shaver.

'I might have one of those,' he said later. She told him to make sure that there was one left for her at night. 'So how long you going to be?' he asked.

'I've got three hours' cleaning at the Richmond. Maybe four at the most, Tracey says.'

'Where's that?'

'By the hospital, Tracey says. Used to be called Aspern, Aspen, something.'

'So you'll be back pretty early.'

'Yeah, I guess so,' said Vicky. 'What about you?'

'I might see if the guys in the mart want a hand. Humping stuff off the trucks.'

Vicky was idly looking at the newspapers in front of her, but then it was as if she remembered some decision that applied immediately. 'Yeah,' she said and put down her fork to concentrate. Her face was made up for the day: blue eye shadow, heavy powder over her orange peel complexion. Her gloss lipstick was worn away by eating, except at the corners of her mouth. 'Yeah. It's getting pretty shitty around here without even the rent money,' she said. 'It's not on, really.'

'All right,' said Gazz.

'You reckoned you were happy to pay the rent and then we'd share all the other stuff — food and that. You were dead keen then.'

'So I've been short. Jesus, no need to make a thing about it.'

'It's just getting all shitty, that's all I'm saying.'

Tracey leant on the horn when Vicky was touching up her face and Gazz looked out of the window to check. 'It's that Tracey,' he said. Vicky took her clutch purse and went down the hall, through the leadlighted front door, down the concrete path that was tilted to the side among the weeds because of subsidence over the many years since the grocer's death. The noon sun glinted on the chrome buckles of her leather skirt and her solid leg muscles showed as she went warily over the camber. Gazz watched her from the top of the path by the door; Tracey watched her from the car.

'See you then,' said Gazz as she went further away.

'Haven't you ditched that loser yet?' said Tracey as she came closer. 'Has he got a feather on the end of it, or bloody something?' It was the direct humour that Vicky liked about working with Tracey.

'Don't tempt me,' she said. 'I've just been giving him a bloody razz-up.'

Gazz stayed outside in the sun while he finished the last cigarette Vicky had given him. He took in the smoke with a very long breath and then allowed it to ease out. He looked over the rank lawn, the chestnut stump, the coral of the japonica, the section of fence that had come down. 'Well, shit,' he said mildly to himself. The smoke drifted with his breath as he spoke.

Back inside, Gazz continued down the hall to Turtle's. Turtle had been quite a successful commercial artist until he developed arthritis. With the loss of his one talent he went quickly downhill, but Gazz found that he always seemed to have a few dollars stashed away.

'It's me. Gazz,' he said after knocking. He could hear soft noises. 'Hey, Turtle.' The noises became even softer. 'Open the bloody door, Turt. I know you're in there.'

'What is it?' Turtle's voice came from so close, just behind the door. He must have been standing right there with his face to the wood.

'Let us in,' said Gazz. 'I've got to go to town soon — to work.' Turtle didn't answer, but Gazz could hear him unhooking the safety lock.

Turtle didn't have a hell of a lot going for him once he couldn't draw. He was into his sixties, small, fat, a very slow mover and with a few freckles so big on his pasty face that they were like birthmarks. He once told Gazz that he'd spent a fortune on gold injections. Turtle tried to make up for his delay in opening the door by swaying, smiling, offering coffee.

'Nah,' said Gazz. 'The thing is, see, I need a few bucks to tide me over until the eagle shits.'

'I saw Vicky going off somewhere.' Turtle looked at the vinyl furniture in his living room. It was a tidy room, but not a clean one. He knew that neither changing the subject, nor avoiding Gazz's eyes, would save his money.

'She's got a few hours' work on.' Gazz knew that Turtle was soft on Vicky, that he talked to her when he had a chance, that he would wait with his door ajar for her to walk across the hall in knickers and a top. It was pathetic, wasn't it.

'Aw, come on, Turtle. You won't miss a twenty for a day or two. You can come in later for a drink. I'm late as it is.'

Turtle went through to his bedroom and drew the door behind him. Gazz listened to the slow, soft noises there, imagining Turtle getting the money. Turtle was pretty much a creep, but he had his uses. When Turtle came back he held the twenty out as if he were surprised to discover it and could think of no better use for it than subsidising Gazz. 'Hey, I hope I can help out a friend,' said Turtle, with his voice jollied up.

'Good on you,' said Gazz. 'Well, things to do.'

Gazz walked in the sun for fifteen minutes to reach the Norfolk Hotel, but he thought of nothing around him as he walked, remembered nothing of it, assumed it the same as all the other times he had walked there to save drinking money. He had no curiosity concerning people who walked or drove by, no expectation of recognition. He wore soiled, white sports shoes that were copies of a good brand and a hip-length grey jacket with a black plastic cat hanging from the zip. He spat occasionally, without any shame to make him look around before doing so. Gazz was known to the barman in the Oakleaves Bar of the Norfolk. Not that the barman could remember Gazz's name, but he knew the combination of grey jacket and the scar over Gazz's left eye. 'How you going?' he asked.

'Getting by,' said Gazz.

'That's the ticket.'

'Yeah.'

'Keeping you busy?'

'So, so,' said Gazz.

He took his jug to a blue-topped stool by one of the windows that had a striped awning outside. He passed Norman Rouse, who had worked with him for several weeks on the Parks and Reserves gardening staff. Neither appreciated the other sufficiently to give up his solitude. Gazz settled down to spend his afternoon the best way he knew how. He took a mouthful of his bitter, letting it flush into his cheeks and eddy in his mouth. He looked around the bar to see if anyone had left the day's paper on a stool or table.

Two hours later Gazz stood at the back door of the Norfolk after coming from the lavatory. He enjoyed the sun on his face.

He gave a long yawn without raising a hand to his mouth and so his slightly yellow side teeth and the dark line of fillings on his lower back ones were plain. He adjusted his trousers at the crotch, moving his cock to the left as he preferred.

A tall man in a brown suit was leaving his Camry in the carpark. When he put the keys into his coat pocket the tag still hung outside so that when he pulled the coat at the front and jerked his shoulders for comfort before walking away the keys flipped from his pocket to the ground. Gazz saw the quick glint of them, but he made no sound, or movement. His yawn continued to close. He stood by the door and watched the tall man walk through the archway and into Gordon Street.

When the carpark had been quiet for a full minute, Gazz walked over to the Camry, picked up the keys and let himself in. He drove slowly into Gordon Street and then Marsden Road. From there he drove to the old cemetery and parked inside the gates long enough to check the back seat and the boot — only two packets of photocopy paper and a cake mixer with a repair ticket from Nimrod Electrics. Gazz headed into Riverside until he reached the panelbeating shop at the far end of the service lane behind the bakery. He parked the car behind a Telstar that had suffered a nasty frontal.

Gazz walked across the oil-stained gravel to the main building and looked at the two men working there. He didn't know them and they didn't know him, so he went around the side of the building to a tin, tilt-door garage that served as an office. Bernie Thompson was sorting through files in a carton that had once held twenty-four 190 gram packets of Nacho Style Corn Chips. It took Bernie a while to remember Gazz, but then he smiled and said, 'Gazz. How's things, Gazz?'

'I've got a Camry I don't need.'

Bernie became very matter of fact, very business-like. He pushed the Nacho carton aside and came out with Gazz and they walked over behind the Ford to look at the car. Bernie assessed it for a full thirty seconds, then he said, 'Nice car.'

'It's yours for five.'

'Come off it, Gazz.'

'Four on the fucken knocker, or I'm off,' said Gazz. 'You know that's fair.'

'It's a nice car,' said Bernie. 'One thing is, we got to get it away pronto and then I'll bring the money. You know I don't have four thou here.'

'Yeah, okay,' said Gazz. He gave Bernie the keys and then went and sat in the garage office. He had no curiosity about Bernie's business; just sat quietly on the office chair and heard the considerable noise that Bernie's two men were making in the panel shop. Bernie Thompson was back in twenty minutes so Gazz took his envelope of money, walked out of the service lane and began looking for a taxi rank. It was well under an hour since he had left the hotel carpark. 'Well bugger me,' he said as he walked. 'How about that.' A little imagination started up in him as happened in the few times he scored. Money provided options in his life.

When Vicky returned from the Richmond — opened the front door, entered the green-yellow world of that long hall — she could hear Gazz and Turtle laughing. Turtle's laugh was infectious, eager and appeasing at the same time. Gazz's laugh was harsh, short, almost as if he were jeering at himself and all else beside. Both of them had been into the hard stuff. Gazz had an impressive collection on the living room table, including two bottles of gin, which was Vicky's favourite. 'What's all this then?' she said.

'I came across this guy at the mart who owed me a few hundred,' said Gazz. 'I'd just about given up on it.'

Vicky hadn't much enjoyed four hours of cleaning rooms at the Richmond. She was in the mood for welcome news and relaxation. She let Turtle pour her a really stiff one as an opener before she went through and changed her shoes. She had cleared the letter-box and still carried the bundle in her hand. She dealt the pieces quickly like cards on to the duchess. Supermarket coupons, householder circulars, pre-paid donation envelopes from Corso and the blind, a flyer concerning the Mad Mitch Show in the RSA Hall, a civic explanation of the new refuse scheme, a photocopied slip to let them know that Partietime home caterers was under new management. 'Jesus.'

'What?' said Gazz from the other room.

'Just once. Just once I'd like to get a friggin personal letter. Just once a bloody letter asking how I was and that. Is that so much?'

'Turtle'll write you a letter. Won't you Turt?'

'Sure, if you like.' For a small, soft guy, Turtle could put away a fair bit. Maybe he calculated it the only way he was likely to recoup the money that Gazz chiselled out of him. Vicky, too, drank as if there were a pot of gold at the end of it, but Gazz was steady, persistent, as though it were just the best way he could find to pass the time. By summer nightfall the three of them were kicking up a fair din. Turtle was attempting a falsetto for 'Bridge Over Troubled Water' when the Tierneys banged on the kitchen partition. Gazz went through and beat on the wall with a pan, yelled 'Shut your fucken hole' seven times. There was no more trouble after that.

Turtle became quite talkative. He kept drinking although he was soon brimful of it: his eyes swam, his lips gleamed wetly, as did his pale face with its great, blotched freckles. Vicky encouraged him to describe some of the odd-ball characters he'd come across in the boarding houses. A woman who had an imaginary husband and did both voices, even arguments. A retired gold miner who was caught having sex with a pony. Vicky straddled the sofa arm and shrieked. Gazz wondered how Turtle could remember it all, but his reaction was not admiration, only derision. What was the point of anything once it was done with? Turtle's shirt ends had come out the way they usually did; something to do with his belly. They hung outside the green corduroys that he wore even in summer.

Gazz interrupted their laughter. 'Hey, Turtle. I'd say it's about time for a feed.'

'Sure. You're right.' Turtle was reminded not to get above himself.

'That outfit closes at ten, that's all. You don't mind getting some greasies, do you?'

'Right,' said Turtle. 'May I have your order, madam?'

'Why don't you bloody go?' Vicky asked Gazz.

'I don't mind, but Turtle's got a bike. Haven't you, mate? You want to see Turt on that bike. Fucken hell. He's up and down like a whore's drawers.'

Turtle gave an appreciative and lengthy laugh and tried to tuck his shirt in. He wiped his damp face with his hands as he worked out with the others what to buy, then he went into the hall and down to his own room. 'Give him some money,' said Vicky.

'He's into my grog, isn't he?'

'Stop being a tight-arse and give him the money. He shouldn't pay for us.'

'Yeah, okay,' said Gazz. He had a particular reason for wanting Vicky friendly while Turtle was away. He walked down to Turtle's hall door. Turtle had assumed that he was alone and so hadn't fully closed the bedroom door. From the hall doorway, looking across the living room, Gazz could see all of the bedhead and chest of drawers and Turtle wasn't in sight. The soft noise of Turtle retrieving money came from the other end of the room. Gazz stepped back into the hall and didn't show himself until Turtle was on the way out. He walked with Turtle to the front door, stood on the darkening verandah while Turtle unlocked the chain from his wheel. 'No need to rip your guts getting back,' said Gazz. 'Know what I mean?' Turtle wheeled his bike away on the concrete path. Gazz couldn't make out his expression in the dark.

Vicky wasn't all that ready to fall in with Gazz's plans, even though she kept the gin bottle busy and allowed Gazz to have his hand between her broad thighs in a companionable sort of way. Gazz tried to push her back on the sofa. 'Get off,' she said languidly.

'Aw, come on, Vick.'

'We can have it in bed later on, for Christ's sake.'

'Aw, come on.'

'Turtle will be back in a minute.'

'So what,' said Gazz. He wished that he'd never invited Turtle anyway. He was just an old sod. No use at all.

'Yeah, you'd get a buzz out of that, wouldn't you? Turtle coming back and seeing us. Well, forget it. Did you give him some money?'

'Yeah,' said Gazz. He made the most of feeling her up and drew her head on to his shoulder with the other hand, but he felt irritation not tenderness. And Vicky had used some sort of hair spray that was unpleasant on his cheek and left a smell that reminded him of the floral air freshener in the staff cafeteria at Gabites Plywood.

'We'll be able to pay some of the back rent, won't we?' said Vicky.

'I suppose so,' said Gazz.

Turtle was something of a gentleman and made a noise coming in the door and down the hall. He looked sillier than usual, with his corduroys tucked into very short, white socks. 'My hero,' said Vicky and she went into the kitchen to fetch plates and tomato sauce.

'Good one,' said Gazz. He noticed that Turtle put his keys on the mantelpiece of the walled-up fireplace before sorting the food. Gazz handed the second gin bottle to Turtle. 'Get some of this down you while it lasts,' he said.

It was Vicky's habit to become girlish when drunk, giggling and pretending to be shocked by behaviour that she'd exceeded for years. Not that there was anything to shock her about Gazz and Turtle. Gazz drank slowly, saying less and less; Turtle was the reverse on both counts. Vicky and Turtle had a butting contest on the sofa. After the first bout or two, Turtle caught Gazz's eye before starting again, but Gazz gave no sign that he cared. 'Playing silly buggers,' he said. The scar above his eye seemed accentuated by the drinking and he tipped his head right back to blow smoke at the single light bulb. Turtle began to sing 'Lili Marlene'. He said his father had been an artillery colonel in the war. Vicky joined in, her voice high, penetrating and unmusical.

Vicky was the first to fall asleep and Turtle pretended to be, because he wanted to stay there on the sofa with his face pushed close to her chest. Gazz went quietly into their bedroom and packed the best of his stuff into the large duffle bag he used instead of a case. When he came out again he could tell that Turtle was really asleep, because his head had rolled out from Vicky's breast a little and his breathing was wheezy. His worn, but oddly boyish face had a sweat of drunkenness on it and his shirt was rucked up to expose the tunnel of his belly button in the roll of his stomach. Vicky slept with a fatuous but good-humoured smile on the large pear of her face. Gazz could stare at their unprotected faces, which seemed in relaxation to be lumpish, functionally organic — like a head of cauliflower, or a canker on the bole of a cherry tree. 'Completely out the monk,' said Gazz softly to himself and he made a noise in his nose that sounded like a succession of sniffs, but was a reduced laugh.

Gazz took Turtle's keys from the mantelpiece and closed the door behind himself as he went into the hall. The light there was no longer green-yellow, but almost grey from the one small bulb at the Tierneys' end. Gazz unlocked Turtle's door and went through to the bedroom. It was drab, but tidy, with just one large Toulouse Lautrec poster as a sign of any other life that Turtle may have had. Gazz knew which end to search, even though it appeared unlikely. There was only a two-bar cabinet heater and Gazz soon found the envelope hidden in the back. He counted at least seven hundred dollars. 'Cunning old bugger,' said Gazz. His tone was half admiration, half contempt. He added Turtle's notes to his own and was so intrigued by the bulk he had in the wallet that he squeezed it several times to feel the wad expand again within the leather. 'Shit,' he said.

On his way to the front door, Gazz didn't check on Turtle and Vicky. He put his duffle bag on his left shoulder and walked carefully down the subsided concrete path past the stump of the grocer's chestnut tree and the japonica blooms that were colourless in the night. He made no pause at the gateway; he marked his departure in no way whatsoever, not even a glance up at the house. He walked steadily away along the dark, quiet street. What reason was there to look back? There were just the two lights showing. The white light from the room where Vicky and Turtle were sleeping and the pink light through the sheet pinned over the bedroom window.

A Late Run

~

'SPRUIKER?' CALLED THE attendant. No one moved, or replied, and the man looked at the slip of paper again. His lips shaped the name to check pronunciation. 'Spruiker?' he said more coarsely.

Reece Spruiker had been watching through the foyer window as a southerly came up. There'd be a fair blow and cold rain as the front moved through. 'That's me,' he said. It was no longer of any real concern to him what the weather did.

'Well, come on, come on.' The attendant took Spruiker's two suitcases that showed cardboard through the wear on their cheap mottled surfaces. He carried them to the mini-van and slid the door open for them and the old man who followed.

'Now, Mr Spruiker,' said the attendant loudly. 'I'll put you on at the depot, right, and your daughter will meet you in Dunedin. Right? Don't wander off at any stop in between except for a quick piss.'

'I know all that.'

'Then why have you been in the bin?'

The attendant didn't find a park close to the depot and had to carry both cases a fair way. 'Jesus,' he said. 'What you got in here? You murdered somebody or something?'

'Not lately,' said Spruiker.

The attendant didn't feel any need to wait around until the bus left. 'Remember you stay put until Dunedin,' he said and leant forward for the next few words. 'Watch yourself, you old prick,' he said.

'Soft bugger,' replied Spruiker. He waited to make sure that his suitcases were loaded, then climbed into the bus and took a seat as far back as possible.

Some faces are as if carved from soap — sanitised, opaque, all of a part. Others are wonderfully physical, animalistic even, with veins, sprouting hair, blemishes, folds and stains, gleams of linings and liquids and the stench of life. Spruiker's head would look at home on the body of a goat. He watched a woman board who must have been barely forty. She had excellent tits, but instead of taking pride in them her expression was one of discontent.

As the bus journeyed south into the evening, Reece Spruiker watched the farmland and assessed the crops and stock without being aware that he did it. An old man is mainly conditioning. Only the thistles were green in the dry, autumn paddocks. Eventually he could see no more than his own reflection in the dark window. He had been accustomed to sit on the step of his hut at Erewhon in the evenings with a beer and his dog, watching the shadows close in on the Rangitata headwaters, but a new owner can't be expected to inherit goodwill towards an old shepherd who's well past it. Spruiker saw no reason for self-pity in that, or in the fact that, out of five children, only his eldest daughter could be bothered with him. He hadn't gone out of his way for them and expected nothing in return. You had to be prepared to take in life what you dished out.

June and Keith were waiting for him and took him home to the small, weatherboard cottage by the old Caversham shops. 'Is any other stuff coming down?' asked June.

'I sold the dogs,' he said.

'Just two cases then,' said Keith, 'and June was wondering where we'd put a load of stuff. Jesus! Good on you.' Keith put the cases in the small, south-facing room. It had a high ceiling and a built-in dark varnished wardrobe with leadlight glass in the door to the hat compartment. Tricky, bubbled paper gave the walls a strange sinuosity.

'A pretty flash place,' said Spruiker, and meant it. He could even catch sight of trees on the hill above the motorway.

'You can't be knocking about by yourself at your age, Dad. You can't do for yourself for ever.' June didn't mention the memory problems he had, the hospital assessment. Spruiker had forgotten all about it.

He wasn't any great trouble, both June and Keith were quick to say that. She did grit her teeth when she heard him spitting phlegm into the basin and she had to raid his room to get clothes for the wash. He was good at preparing vegetables, doing shopping for her, taking in the washing by four during the winter when she was still at work. Mostly he walked, often down to the various grounds to watch sports teams practising — any sport. Also he liked television; mainly sport again, but also films that often had women's legs and breasts bared for him.

Apart from money for a beer in the evening, he gave his modest universal super to June. In his own odd, selfish way he was a proud man and, faced with the realisation that he might live a good while longer and not be able to maintain his independence, he wondered if he might end up being a nuisance to the only one of his children who didn't treat him with the same cheerful disregard with which he had treated them. Maybe his physical toughness would rebound on him in the end, if the mental side went first. There were special homes, he knew, which charged hundreds a week.

'Dad's always gone his own way. You know that,' Alec had said. 'Tough as old rope.'

'He never interfered; that was the good thing,' Margie had said.

'The bad thing was that he never cared.'

'He wouldn't thank you for doing anything for him. Not a bit of it,' Nigel had said. 'Old people set in their ways are best left alone. I read this article on it somewhere.'

'I've got commitments closer to home, that's for sure,' Louise had said.

But June reckoned that, with nowhere to go and being seventy, her dad needed some help, at least until the latest memory problem sorted itself out. Keith was very fond of his own parents. He could see that June needed to make something of an effort.

'I'm fine. I'm fine,' said Spruiker. 'Jesus, I've looked after myself all my life just about.'

Of the five children, June had the fewest resources to assist her father. Nigel was actually rich, but was cautious about admitting it. June worked in a bakery and Keith did part time in the Civic Information Centre, after suffering a breakdown while teaching.

Quite often Keith had time to sit with his father-in-law during the day and watch television, or endeavour to keep up with him as he walked about the city. Keith held no grudge that Spruiker hadn't bothered to give June and him a wedding present years before, though his own parents were very different. He rather enjoyed the old guy's earthy directness, his contempt for his fellows, his emotional reticence.

In the spring a veterans' athletic series from America was shown on afternoon television. Wrinkled people with necks full of tendons, taking themselves seriously in a whole range of events. Some of them were has-beens who couldn't give up gracefully; some were never-beens who found that they could foot it at the end of their lives. Spruiker laughed until his eyes watered at such people making goats of themselves; rejoicing in twilight victories and medal ceremonies; confiding in the interviewers as to their training programmes; sporting their monogrammed gear and warm-up exercises. 'What a load of wankers,' he told Keith. 'A bunch of bloody nellies.'

He stopped laughing when Keith pointed out to him the size of the crowds there to watch and the size of the cash purses. 'It's a fad thing in America at present,' said Keith. 'Something to do with their determination to empower the old and enhance their sociological profile. And money's no problem over there, you know.'

'How much did that old coot get for winning the hurdles?' asked Spruiker.

'Fifteen thousand dollars US. Nearer thirty in our money.'

'Eh!' said Spruiker incredulously.

'Nearly thirty thousand dollars. And that's a regional meet.'

'Jesus George! What about that spindly, hatchet-faced bint who won the long women's race?'

'I think it said not all that much less.'

Spruiker watched the series with less contempt after that. He was amazed that there was a market for all those old people aping the athletics of excellence. He asked Keith to keep a record of the winning fifteen hundred metres times.

'Why, do you think you'll have a go?'

'Don't you tell any bugger.' Spruiker was quite sensitive to ridicule, although he didn't show it.

'There's no money in veterans' athletics here anyway,' said Keith.

'Never you mind.'

On a September Sunday morning when the sun was bright, but without heat, old Spruiker asked Keith to go with him down to the Caversham Oval. 'Don't say anything to any bugger, not even June. I'm not going to be made a laughing stock. Has your watch got a second hand?' Spruiker carried a cheap and new pair of tennis shoes in a supermarket bag. 'I haven't the skills for the specialist events,' he told Keith, 'but I reckon I can run as fast as those old bastards there on the television.'

'I think you underestimate them.'

'I was mustering until just a few years ago,' said Spruiker. 'I've never smoked. I've had years and years of high-country air, not like those poor city buggers. And I haven't talked, shagged, boozed, or molly-coddled myself into weakness.'

There wasn't anyone else at the Oval and that suited Spruiker just fine. He put on the tennis shoes and tucked his trouser cuffs into his grey socks. He took off his green woollen jersey to reveal a grey workshirt with a blue stain at the pocket where a biro had burst. He spat on the ground where the track was marked and lifted his arms rather awkwardly a few times as a suggestion of limbering up exercises. He was of only average height and he was thin, ugly and seventy years old. He had lines so deep running from both sides of his nose and down past his mouth that his face seemed to have been put together in segments. Years of sun had created a blossom of small cancers on his weathered skin. 'Say go when you're ready,' he told Keith, who tried not to smile. 'Four times around. That's what you said?'

'That's right.'

'Okay then,' said Spruiker.

'Get set, go,' said Keith. He made a show for the old guy by looking keenly at the watch. Spruiker kept his arms low while he ran and his shoulders turned from side to side in what seemed to Keith a poor action. Spruiker's knees didn't come up far either, but he had a surprisingly long stride. He ran round the Caversham Oval four times without any apparent variation in pace, or action, and when he'd finished he'd come within nine seconds of the man from Wabash, Indiana, who had won fifteen thousand dollars at the regional veterans' meet at Tulsa.

'Jesus,' said Keith. 'Jesus, Reece, you did just fine. But maybe I made some cock-up with the watch.'

'No,' said Spruiker. 'As soon as I saw those old pricks on the telly I knew I'd do almost as well. All my life I've had good wind. For years and years I was the top beat musterer on every station I worked on. I reckon there's an opportunity to take some easy money from those soft American buggers who've got so much of it they'll spend it watching geriatrics rupturing themselves.'

'It's not a bad idea, I suppose.'

'It's got to be done in the next year or two, though,' said Spruiker. He put his jersey on again, replaced the tennis shoes in the plastic bag. Keith waited in the cool sun. A tall woman with imperiously piled grey hair was walking a King Charles spaniel that was sorely in need of exercise. A young guy, cutting across the Oval, had stopped to comb his hair, using the club house window as a mirror. Keith knew that Spruiker was most comfortable when coming out with things in his own way and his own time.

'The first reason,' said Spruiker, 'is that I'm seventy. I'll be among the youngest in the seventy to seventy-five age group. That's a real plus, I reckon. You can go down hill bloody quick at my age. The other thing is that the old grey matter is getting a bit dicey. I could be making chicken noises to myself in the corner any time now.'

Keith and Spruiker talked a good deal about the first point on their way home. The other thing was never mentioned between them again.

'Maybe,' said Keith to June that night, for, as a good husband he told his wife everything in secret, 'maybe your dad's really on to something.'

'One way and another he's been running all his life,' she said.

Keith, who considered that his teaching experience fitted him for both tasks, became coach and manager. As coach he insisted that Spruiker buy some first-rate running shoes; as manager he corresponded with the United States Pan Veterans' Athletics Association and boned up on all the rules and requirements. He began to read a good many books about motivation and metabolism and budget travel, which increased his confidence, but had no other benefit.

Spruiker ran three afternoons a week — around the Oval if it was free, or into the hill suburbs. June pretended to know nothing about it; Keith paced him on the bike if it was road work. 'There's no hills on those athletic tracks,' he said.

'Hills are good for your wind,' said Spruiker. And he enjoyed seeing his son-in-law suffer a bit.

The television series was long over, but Keith was getting all the meet times sent out to him. He even built up files on the most consistent fifteen hundred metre winners and the nature of the different venues. 'Yours is a glamour event,' he told the old guy. 'Top prizes for it.'

Within three months Spruiker was recording times that would have put him in the money if he were running in the States. Keith had spent a lot of time talking to him also about tactics and motivation. 'Visualise yourself passing Dan Swarfest of Shadow Man Falls, Montana; visualise yourself breasting the tape,' he told his father-in-law. Spruiker never bothered to answer. He did agree, however, that he should have the best steak twice a week, and his legs massaged regularly by Mrs Drummhagen who lived next door and used to be a district nurse.

Keith and Spruiker had a meeting after a tea of curried sausages one night. Spruiker said that it was time to go to the States and take some money from the Americans. June pretended to be surprised by the project, but she and Keith had already decided that it was worth while backing the old guy to have a go. What else did he have? June said. It would take all of Spruiker's small savings and the bulk of June's and Keith's. 'I'll win enough to set us up nicely, to more than pay my way in the family, but I don't want anyone getting wind of it. You understand. If anyone asks, it's just a holiday.' Spruiker never overcame a certain self-consciousness, almost shame, about the whole thing. A lot of silly old people flogging themselves in games, taking their laughable performances seriously.

Keith and Spruiker flew to Los Angeles on a Big Top from Christchurch. Spruiker first ran at a qualifying race at the Wachumpba spring festival in Fresno. His first prize barely covered expenses, but enabled him to enter the Pan Veteran indoor event at Sac City, Iowa. He came fourth in the final because he was elbowed in the face at the final turn, but it was a lesson learned. He was never less than third in the thirteen regional meets he competed in after that. He won at Savannah, Lubback, Seattle, St Cloud, Saratoga Springs and Troy in Alabama and was a close second to Dan Swarfest in the national final of the United States Pan Veterans' Athletics fifteen hundred metres at Glameen Park, Chicago. He received forty thousand dollars and a citation and his name was entered on a copper plaque above the members' cocktail bar at Glameen Park, between that of Dan Swarfest and Wesley Boist Smith, who was third.

Keith was amazed and grateful and interested in all around him. He wanted Spruiker to take it easier, to see something of the country and the people while they had the opportunity, but his father-in-law saw it all as a vast sham that might collapse at any minute. Spruiker insisted they stay in modest motels and the only friend he made was a seventy-six-year-old ex-miner from West Virginia who was doing all right in the hammer throw. They used to watch blue movies and drink Hills pinball beer together after the meets.

One week after Glameen Park, in unit nineteen of the Saddle Sore Motels on the east side of Beaumont, Texas, Reece Spruiker told Keith that it was time to get out, time for a reckoning.

'One of my legs is going,' said Spruiker, 'and I'm fed up with the people. I reckon I've done my dash.' From the motel window they could see a group of young hoods trashing cars in the park of the El Pecho Diner and Bar. The neons were starting to brighten in the dusk. 'What have we got clear?' he asked Keith. 'What can we get back home with?'

Keith got out the laptop that he had purchased from their winnings for managerial purposes. 'In the vicinity of one two five New Zealand,' he said.

'What vicinity? How much clear when we're back home?'

'I'd say a hundred and twenty-six thousand dollars,' said Keith.

'Half for June and half for me,' said Spruiker. Keith assumed charitably that June and himself were seen as indivisible. 'And I don't want any bugger to know more than he needs to.'

In Caversham Spruiker slipped back into his pre-athletic role as if all the rest had never happened. He was happier, though, because he was certain that he wasn't beholden to any bugger, that he wasn't a drag on his daughter. Nothing that the rest of the family could bitch about. He let Keith keep his last pair of expensive running shoes in case his son-in-law developed talent in old age himself. Spruiker reduced his exercise to walking again, watched a lot of television, drank rather more beer — all the same sort of things as before. But he decided that he needed to keep on with the massages from Mrs Drummhagen and just occasionally came out with a turn of phrase which betrayed his American career and friendship with the West Virginian.

Like when he told the plumber that the new bath was as smooth as a prom queen's thigh.

If anyone ever bothered to ask him what was the best thing he'd managed in his life, he always recalled the time he and Buck had won the Canterbury Huntaway Championship at the Windwhistle dog trials. That dog could walk on water, he said.

Coming Home in the Dark

~

WINDSWEPT TO A bowl of peerless blue, the sky arched above it all; not oppressive on the landscape, but rather an insistent suction that offered to remove everything into the endless, spun abstraction. The lake had a chop on its milk green opaqueness. The mountains of black and white rose up ahead. There was a fixed intensity in the delineation of shapes and colours; no compromise, no merging.

'We'll see Cook again soon, I think,' said Hoaggie.

'It's the boys' first time up here,' said Jill.

'So it is, and it should be a view today that they'll remember. I hope that all their lives they can think back to this trip — their first sight of Mount Cook.'

'I wish we were going to ski, though,' said Mark.

At the head of Lake Pukaki was the flat outwash of the glaciers and the cold, braided streams milky with rock flour. Hoaggie noticed how the sun caught and glittered from surfaces and turns of the water as he drove. For a selfish moment he was without family, and felt a pack on his back, boots on his feet, and heard the skirl of the wind on the rock faces.

Jill was telling the boys what the Hermitage was like, based on somewhat hazy recollection of a visit well before she and Hoaggie had shifted to Auckland. Her sons were more interested in the outside opportunities of the place. 'Well, make sure you don't lose anything today. We can't come back. Check your stuff.' She didn't believe in having the twins dressed the same. She said the modern thinking was to encourage a natural growth of separate identity. Both the boys wore linen shorts, but Mark had a jersey and light, suede boots, while Gordon had a ribbed, blue jacket and sneakers. Gordon had more to say, but Mark was more stubborn.

They passed Bush Creek and Hoaggie recalled for his wife a climb that he and Tony Bede made to the saddle from there. He experienced as he talked a quick reprise of the euphoria of youth, but had no words to articulate it. They passed Fred's Creek and saw a Mercedes abandoned on its side in a ditch of stones.

'Look at that. Yeah, wipeout,' enthused Gordon. He and Mark scrabbled to see more from the back window as they went on.

'Someone overdid it there,' said Hoaggie.

'And can't have had any help for miles,' said Jill.

'You remember when Bruce Trueno broke down on the Desert Road last Christmas and when he came back with the tow-truck he found the wheels stolen.'

The outwash was mainly an expanse of shingle, but those parts not recently swept by the channels had rough pasture and matagouri, briar, clumped lichens. Beef cattle were feeding by the road. There was oddity in the sight, because of the close proximity, although distinct by altitude, of ice and snow and screes. The inside of the car was more comfortable still: the sun warmed it and the breeze was excluded.

'Moira wants to nominate me as the Regional Arts Council rep on the Grants Board,' said Jill.

'Who better if you've got the time. Go for it.' Hoaggie was always gratified when his wife proved her competence in her own right. Successful himself, he felt no threat from the achievement of others. He realised also, that because of his own focus on work, his wife had given up much of her own time to the family. 'They would be lucky to have someone of your ability,' he said in all sincerity.

'Flatterer.' She rested her hand on his arm. 'You won't say that if you're left to cope when I'm away.'

They came up the final slope to the head of the alpine valley beyond the lake's expanse. Scenery has little intrinsic appeal to the young, but even the twins, accustomed only to the landscape of the North Island, gazed quietly for a few moments at the sheer valley sides, and the towering bulk of Cook and Tasman among their barely less impressive fellows. Then Gordon elbowed his brother. 'Now those suckers are big,' he said.

'I had a talk with Athol Wells at Rotary a while back,' said Hoaggie. 'Did I tell you that?'

'Athol Wells?'

'He's the deputy principal at Westpark. You must remember; I said that maybe he'd have an angle on a school for the boys.'

'I don't want them to go to a boarding school. You know that.'

'Well, neither do I personally. It's what's best for them in the long run though, isn't it?'

'What better environment can you have than your own family?'

'Roddy Sinclair says he's going to Wanganui Collegiate,' put in Gordon.

'Spastic,' said his brother. Hoaggie had almost forgotten that they were in the back. He dropped the subject.

Hoaggie turned off the Hermitage road and on to the track that led them to the area where camping was allowed. He was pleased to see almost as few amenities, as few small climbing tents, as he remembered.

When the family stood on a knoll not far from the car, prepared for their walk up the Hooker Valley towards the glacier, they could see over the way they had come and the end of the road. Hoaggie noted that the Hermitage had been developed a good deal, but even so the view was almost entirely unspoiled. He hadn't been to Cook for more than fourteen years and he refreshed himself with all the defiant angles and peaks, the low alpine vegetation, the mutual touch of bright sun and sweet, cold breeze.

'Come on, come on,' shouted Gordon, and as if it were a consequence almost immediately there was the shivering rumble of an avalanche on Mount Cook, although not on the faces they could see.

'Let's hope no one's under that lot,' said Hoaggie.

'No one would be climbing where that's likely to happen, would they?' asked Jill.

'Sometimes I guess it's just luck.'

The four of them started on the walking track to the Hooker, which wound through the tussock and thorns of the old, heaped moraines. They were out of the breeze from the snowfields for a while and it was pleasantly warm. Jill put her hand on Hoaggie's collar. She ran her nails up and down the back of his neck as they walked behind the twins. 'Maybe you're right,' she said. 'About the secondary school thing.'

'Maybe not,' said Hoaggie. 'What the hell. We can work it out among us all. It's about giving them the right start, isn't it?'

Mark had found a stick, discarded by a previous walker. He flourished it proudly, and Gordon began questing on both sides of the track as they went on, searching for a stick that would restore his equality. They could hear the sound of the swift stream from the little lake at the glacier's snout and the track began to wind over heaped greywacke shingle and boulders.

Below them two other people were climbing up to join the track. The man in the lead was thin and pale; he shrugged his shoulders as he walked. The man behind was immensely solid, the features of his full face seeming indented like those of a snow-man. He wore a denim jacket so tight that it pulled his arms back, accentuating the bulge of chest and stomach. Neither of them was old, but men nevertheless, not boys. The big man behind was singing a song from *Phantom of the Opera*, but only the tune was an identification; the words had been replaced by ta and la. The one in front wore a denim top as well, but of a much darker blue against which light stitching stood out. The stoop of his thin shoulders made the sides of the jacket hang below his waist, while the back rode up showing the grubby white of his T-shirt.

Having ta-laed himself to the end of the music of the night as he reached the path ahead of Hoaggie and his family, the big man followed his friend with a gait grown suddenly shambling without a melody. Neither man looked back; neither waved.

Gordon sniggered and was joined by Mark. 'Don't be rude,' said Jill.

'What a geek,' said Gordon, doing a quick, chesty imitation of the man's walk. It was true they seemed unlikely nature lovers.

'It takes all sorts,' said Jill.

The two men were soon lost in the turns of the track through the moraine and when the family reached the swingbridge there was no sign of them. Hoaggie was happy to share the surroundings with no one but his wife and children: he had delib-erately planned on being there before the school holidays began and in that had been very loyally supported by Gordon and Mark. Such feelings of exclusivity were selfish, Hoaggie knew, but part of his response to beauty.

There was the small lake among the shingle and boulders at the glacier's end. Etched icebergs floated there, freed from the rocks that covered the ice flow. Some of them had seams of dirt, or stones, some had the flat tints of very old milk. Other ice showed in the banks where the overlay of shingle kept it from the sun. Impressive though it was, Hoaggie knew it to be only the remnant of the ice-age days and he pointed out the ledges and striations hundreds of feet up the valley sides where the great rivers of ice had been thousands of years before. 'Hey, yeah,' said Gordon. 'Next time, Mark and I'll climb up there and roll stuff down.'

They walked for an hour up the Hooker and then sat for a while before beginning a return. In the clarity of the mountain air the soaring ridges and coruscating sweeps of snow were deceptively near at hand, and even the stunted olearia, hebe and cotton-wood where they rested seemed to have a special sharpness of form. Just occasionally they were caught by the edge of a passing breeze and drew their shoulders in for warmth.

On the way back, shortly before the carpark, Hoaggie took a snap of his wife and the twins just below a cairn that commemorated the death of mountaineers many years before. As he lined it up through the viewfinder he had a sudden sense of image within image, of time within time: the shot as it would be with all the others in the album, the wider freeze frame, transient, but stronger just for that instant, showing the four of them together there at the foot of the mountains with the grasses and flowers, the spiked matagouri and the sheen of the great snow slopes in the distance. Hoaggie had no god to pray to, but he offered a sort of prayer nevertheless, which was part gratitude for what he had, and part plea for continuance.

'Take another one and let me hold the stick in it,' called Gordon.

The brown grasses were ungrazed and high as Hoaggie's knee. Where the moraine was exposed the grey stones bore badges of lichens — green, yellow, silver and silver-blue. Some puffed out a little from the rock like the frilled head of a lizard; others were so fine, so delicate, they seemed more like fossils within the rock than anything that grew on its surface. The small white and pink flowers glistened on the humped bushes among the stones, and flies, quick and colourful, were in a euphoria of pollination.

As the family went on to their car and the grassy clearing where camping was allowed, the sounds from the Hermitage carried clearly to them, but subdued in that great natural space. No wind at all in the low clearing, and just a toss of cloud at Cook's summit to show the westerly at work.

The boys wanted to eat at once, but Jill didn't wish to have their picnic near the tents and within sight of the small toilet block. 'There's always red sleeping bags and socks out to air,' she said. 'Always someone with an empty, unpleasant laugh.'

So Hoaggie drove back down the valley just a short distance, and took the turn-off to the Blue Lakes and ventured into the tussock grass along its side. There was a bridge not much further on, and on the high side of that a cluster of alpine beech as a feature in the treeless area around them. Hoaggie nosed the Volvo between two matagouri bushes so that the boot was ideally placed to service a grassy area behind it. Jill took out the tartan rugs and told the twins to sort out a good place without stones. The long, dry stalks held up the rugs at first, but Gordon and Mark rolled over and over on them to crush them flat.

'I hope you checked for any stuff under there,' said Hoaggie.

'You mean poop,' said Gordon delightedly.

'Anything,' said Hoaggie.

'But especially crap,' said Gordon.

'Crap,' repeated Mark.

'That's enough,' said Hoaggie.

Hoaggie and Jill ate on the rugs there, propped on their elbows like Romans, and looking down because of the late-afternoon sun. The boys grappled and snorted through their food, pursued grasshoppers, collected chrysalids, scratched themselves, claimed to see skinks beneath the stones they lifted. Eventually they, too, lay on the rugs, talking in their own close language.

Hoaggie relaxed on his back, his hand across his face as a shield from the sun. He could smell chlorine from the swim a day ago, and the sultanas from the muffin he'd held, and also a scent from the hair on his wrists that had something of tobacco although he didn't smoke.

He was wondering if it was time to consider buying a bach in the Coromandel, and thinking of the joy the twins would have there, when they stopped arguing with each other and in the pause he heard Jill say, 'Hoaggie.' Her voice wasn't loud, but had an odd formality. He took his hand away and squinted up into the sun. Two men were standing close to them, among the briars. The same men that the boys had laughed at on the track.

The big man put on a silly smile when he realised the family were watching, as if he wanted to appear friendly, but had never checked the expression to ensure that it accorded with his intention. He cracked his knuckles and looked at the food on the rugs. The other man was more interested in the twins. He took several long steps to bring himself up to them, and as they sat up he pushed them down again with his foot. Mark still had something of a smile, as though he thought the men might turn out to be part of a joke his father was playing on them, and he didn't want to be too easily taken in. 'Oh, my God,' said Jill. She put her hands to her face. Hoaggie stood up, clumsy after lying in the sun all that time.

'Okay, Tub,' said the thin man in the darker denims, and Tub reached Hoaggie at the same time as Jill stood up to help. Neither Hoaggie nor his wife knew much about hurting people, but Tub did. He ignored Jill, who was tugging at him, and concentrated on pushing Hoaggie back on to the boot of the car and then abruptly breaking his right forearm on the curve of the metal. He slammed it a second time, which caused a great deal more pain, and Hoaggie slumped down by the car. The dry grass rustled as he slid into it, and he crushed a spray of tiny white flowers.

Jill was left pulling at Tub and yet trying to back off at the same time. Tub's large hand encompassed her wrist as a precaution against the latter inclination winning out.

'Mandrake?' he said, in a voice both surprisingly high-pitched and equable.

'Enough of this shit,' said Mandrake. He had a sawn-off .22 and he held it to

Gordon's head. 'Now that you know we're the bad guys, no one else needs to get hurt, okay. You there, Dad, you give these kids the message just to lie still.'

'It's okay,' said Hoaggie. 'It's all right, boys. Just lie still.'

'There you go then,' said Mandrake. 'Easy as fucking pie.'

Hoaggie was still slumped in the grass with his back to the side of the car. With the pressure of his hand, Tub made Jill sit down again beside the twins. Only Tub and Mandrake were standing. Tub started eating sultana muffins and neenish tarts from one of Jill's oblong, green containers. Mandrake looked off among the grass and stunted bushes towards the road. 'Just a little old family picnic here, folks,' he said loudly, and then grinning, and almost at a shout, 'Nothing to see here.' There was no response. The sun was all brilliance in the high, clear air. Mandrake shifted his grip on the rifle so that it hung more comfortably.

A long way off the height of a bus showed itself on the way to the Hermitage, and a pair of paradise duck gave their tuneless call from the flats at the head of the lake. The olearia had fresh and fragrant flowers that glowed like coral amid the leaves, and the burnished thorns of matagouri. Cicadas, briefly subdued by the flurry about the car, came back as a chorus. Above everything was the great, sharp angle of Cook with a nightcap of cloud streaming from its peak.

Mandrake jiggled his foot playfully on Gordon's back. 'This is some place,' he said. 'What a strange thing bloody privacy is. We could be a world apart here, yet radio waves are going right through us this very instant, aren't they? Full of ski reports and talkbacks and government promises and music from Memphis, Tennessee. We hear nothing of it at all, though, and they've no idea we're even alive. Things can be so close, yet have no point of contact.'

'My husband's hurt,' said Jill. 'I need to help him.'

'Tub's just broken his arm,' said Mandrake, 'so he doesn't think he's a fucking hero. Take his jacket there and wrap it tightly round his arm. That way it won't jar.'

'He needs a doctor,' she said.

'You play the doctor then,' said Mandrake. 'Go on then. Tub will help you.'

Tub took hold of Jill by her hair in a matter-of-fact way and forced her around to Hoaggie at the side of the car. Her face looked very young because of the skin being pulled upwards. With his free hand, Tub kept a grip on the muffin box. Jill wrapped the jacket around Hoaggie's broken arm and, while attention was on that, Mandrake shot Mark and Gordon. Mark died almost immediately, with only a bubbling sound and the shaking of his suede boots, but Gordon struggled to get up from beneath Mandrake's foot and called out piercingly, 'Look at this. Look at this,' until he was shot several times. He arched powerfully in his death, and his face had one last primitive, instinctual expression before it relaxed.

The shots were not loud, but sufficient to quiet the cicadas briefly again and startle goldfinches, which fled in an alternating series of violent wing-bursts and dipping glides. The sun flashed on the bright feathers of their head-dress. A patch of tussock fluffed up suddenly in a gust of wind, as an animal's fur rises for an instant in alarm.

Jill was held back by her hair as she tried to reach her sons, calling loudly. Hoaggie tried to move towards them too, but Mandrake stepped to the car and put the short barrel of the .22 into Hoaggie's left eyesocket to push him back. The crudely sawn muzzle made a cut beneath Hoaggie's eyebrow and blood ran, diluted with tears, as a pink wash on his cheek.

'Enough of this shit,' said Mandrake. 'Get into the car. Open the door, Tub, and get them into the car.' When both of them were in the back seat, holding to each other for some comfort, Mandrake reloaded the small magazine of the rifle. 'Go out towards the road and look around,' he told Tub. 'See if anybody's about. Make sure everything's okay.'

'I'm still hungry,' said Tub calmly.

'Better still,' said Mandrake, 'wrap the kids in a rug first and find a place for them somewhere. There's tons of stuff you can eat here when you come back. We won't be leaving until it's pretty much dark.' Tub wrapped the boys in a rug of red tartan and took them away through the high grass and low bushes. He experimented to find the most comfortable carrying position as he went.

'It's actually better for them this way,' said Mandrake at the window. 'Nothing drawn out at all. You know what kids are; as time went on they'd be getting in our way more and more. Jesus yes. Were they twins?' Jill and Hoaggie didn't answer. They hardly heard what he said. 'I reckon they were. I reckon they were twins,' Mandrake said. He checked the fuel gauge at the dash of the Volvo. From the picnic things he took up a wedge of egg and bacon pie and ate it carefully, lifting his lips at each bite so that his teeth were visible.

Mandrake leant on the car in the sunlight while he ate and looked in at Jill and Hoaggie from time to time as if he quite fancied a yarn while they all waited for Tub to come back. 'I don't suppose there's any booze,' he said, partly to himself. He yawned in the sun and ran his free hand over his face as he watched Tub return alone.

The big man settled down very deliberately among the picnic food and began to eat. As he ate one thing, he fossicked for others, saying 'yes' to himself at the most welcome discoveries. He was scrupulous to replace the lids of each container when he'd had enough, in case the bright, darting flies might join the feast.

Jill tried to concentrate on what she had left to love.

'How do you feel, Hoaggie?' she said. He just gazed at her wet face.

'What did she call you?' said Mandrake. 'Speak up.'

'Hoaggie,' he said.

'A special name, is it? Something intimate between husband and wife? Hoaggie, Poaggie, Boaggie.'

'It's short for Hoaganraad. That's my name — Hoaganraad.'

'I like it,' said Mandrake, lifting his head, and his lip to show his upper teeth, in a posture of contemplation and assessment. 'It's friendly and fucking informal. Hoaggie, yes.' His face lifted to the sun again and he shaped the word several times more. 'Wasn't there a Hoagy Carmichael?' he said.

'You may be right,' said Hoaggie. A conversation so unreal was more a blessing than the reverse.

'I am right, old son. A musician, wasn't he? What did he play?' He stooped in to look at Jill. 'Come on, I'm sure you're a bright woman.'

'The trumpet?' she said.

'You may be right,' said Mandrake. 'What do you think, Tub? Is Hoaggie a name that takes your fancy?'

'Sounds like shit to me.' Tub lay on his back amid the picnic things with his arms and legs spread like a starfish. He had a stalk of grass in his mouth and he switched it back and forth with his tongue, or puffed his cheeks and made a succession of small, poofing sounds that caused the stem to tremble. Maybe the poofing sounds had something in them of the music of the night.

'And what sort of a name is Mandrake?' asked Hoaggie. All he wanted was an opportunity to show his contempt. What he saw, though, even as they spoke, was Tub carrying away his sons in the tartan picnic rug.

'I'm a bloody magician, aren't I. It doesn't take all that much with the people I spend my time with.' Mandrake's contempt was equal to Hoaggie's and the object much the same.

'How's your philosophy, old son?' he asked Hoaggie.

'It's not my line,' said Hoaggie. The tears, pink on one side of his face, shone on his skin. He thought of the twins: their affection and abilities, all the opportunities that had been before them. He wondered who would ever find them. He thought of them lying all alone in the coming night.

'The big fucking mistake, Hoaggie, is to imagine that evil and beauty are antithetical. Don't you think? That's where people go wrong despite one experience after another. There's no natural affinity, but no mutual exclusion either. Don't you think, Hoaggie? Anyway, I've pretty much thought that one out to my own satisfaction.'

'What you did to Mark and Gordon. What you did,' cried Jill. She looked away from him, through the window on the other side, where the thorns of the matagouri and the alpine briar made a lattice against the sky. While mentioning her sons she had thought for a moment that the deaths were contestable, that what had happened could be overturned, then her head and shoulders sagged down.

'There's nothing you could've done,' said Mandrake. 'Nothing to be done now. Just one thing impinging on another, as the philosophers tell us. The whole thing is bad luck on your part: just a matter of timing. It's like going out driving, and hitting two, or even three, birds when it hasn't happened for bloody ages, and when you get back and have a look, there they are, packed tight into the grille by the impact.'

'I wish we hadn't come. I wish we hadn't come. I wish we hadn't come.' Her voice was muffled by the seat back, but rising almost to hysteria.

'Shut it,' shouted Mandrake, but almost immediately he was reasonable again. His hand steadied her shoulder through the open window. 'It's best for us all if we do things quietly. A fucking uproar gets nobody anywhere. You've no reason to blame yourself for anything. Take it easy. Bad luck is really just bringing forward what's bound to happen.'

The sun was going down over Cook; different shadows were at play over the rock buttresses, screes and snowfields of the mountains. With the dropping of the sun came an obvious dropping of temperature. The sound of the river became more distinct; the briar and matagouri bushes took on a tinge of purple; the cicadas ceased their song. Tub stood up and tried to pull the sides of his jacket together so that more of his front would be covered. Mandrake still leant on the side of the car. He held the rifle loosely, and partly disguised by the line of his leg. Hoaggie and Jill sat silently in the back seat. Hoaggie cradled his broken arm with the good one and his wife's sobs had subsided to a wide-mouthed, heavy breathing.

'Let's piss off,' said Tub.

'In just a bit,' said Mandrake. 'Better that no one gets a clear look at us on the road.'

'It's got cold.'

'Yeah, but tonight we won't have to be out in it. That's the difference,' said Mandrake. Tub nodded to that. 'I think we should check on the playmates,' said Mandrake, 'to take care of stuff that might get lost.'

'Bloody right,' said Tub.

Mandrake already had the keys; he took Hoaggie's wallet and Jill's handbag with just a motion of the .22 and gave both to Tub, who went through them with the single-minded curiosity occasioned by the unfamiliar. All the money, Tub put in his trouser pocket; something of a struggle because of the tautness of his belly and backside against the cloth. He gave the credit cards to Mandrake, who was saying how he was looking forward to getting back into the city — not the fucking sticks he said. An urgency seized him and he broke off, opened the car door and put the rifle to the back of Jill's head. 'It occurs to me, old son,' he said to Hoaggie, 'that you're just the sort of yuppie bastard to have a cellphone, and just silly enough to keep it hidden.'

'I haven't. We're on holiday, for God's sake. There's nothing at all.' Mandrake looked carefully at him, at the same time lifting the short barrel of the .22 through Jill's fair hair, which parted noiselessly, brushing the metal and falling into place again with its own smooth weight.

'No, of course you haven't,' said Mandrake. 'Silly fucking me, eh. You know, I'm prone to an odd, paranoid notion that people are out to get me. Funny, that.' He closed the door again and stood in the last of the light, laughing. Hoaggie and Jill could see only the contrast stitched denim jacket, but they could hear the laugh which was subdued, like that of a panting dog. Tub joined in for a time on a higher and less controlled note.

Mandrake decided that he would do the driving. He had Jill come into the front seat beside him, and Tub sit with Hoaggie in the back. 'This is a class car,' he said as he nosed from the grasses on to the road. The flat outwash before the lake was becoming an indiscriminate mix of dark evening shades, and only Mount Cook and its fellows were still sharp against a westward edge of sky, ember lit by the sun. 'Tub and I recently had an unfortunate experience with a Mercedes,' he said. 'It was a great car, too, but I don't think we quite had time to get used to it. Eh, Tub?'

'Bummer,' said Tub. He confined Hoaggie to a small portion of the Volvo's generous squab as he settled down to rest. His obvious feeling that neither Hoaggie nor Jill could pose any threat whatsoever increased Hoaggie's sense of helplessness.

For a time, as they drove in the gathering darkness with the steep hills on one side and the leaden expanse of glacier-fed lake on the other, Mandrake quizzed his captives about their lives for information that might be helpful to him. He was disappointed to find they had no home in the South Island. Soon, though, he indulged his fondness for speculative, even intellectual talk. 'You wouldn't know it, but I'm a bugger for the reading. I reckon I would have done all right at university had things been different,' he said, 'but sooner or later the point of every lesson that you can be told about occurs in the course of your life anyway. It's the capacity to see to the core of things, to put aside that fucking self-deceit, that's the important thing. Don't you think?'

'You're a murderer, a senseless bastard,' said Hoaggie. The great, dimly seen platter of Tub's sleeping face was close to his shoulder and the man's breathing had become an adenoidal whine.

'You are a murderer,' said Jill distantly and she wept for the proof of it. Mandrake drove on beside Pukaki, which was assuming a pale luminosity as the mountains around it retreated into darkness.

'As to a bastard,' he said. 'You're right there in any way you like.'

'You're not right in the head,' said Hoaggie. 'Who kills people for the sake of it?'

'I'm on the outside, Hoaggie. Don't you fucking get it? I'm on the outside of this whole thing that the rest of you have got going. Nothing connects me with it except bringing it down. That's all an outsider has, you see. What the books call a negative capability.'

'You'll get caught.'

'Wonderful, Hoaggie, but what's that to me now? Don't you see? I've always been caught, so there's no difference. I'm teaching a few people, and you're one of them, that I'm determined to have all the things I can't claim within your rules. Get it? You never asked me to any dinner party, old son, yet here I am with my hand warmed by your wife's thighs and my heart by this philosophic discussion. Boredom and truth, they're the two things that have done for me. I tend to break down if my life's too flat. Yes, Hoaggie, boredom's a killer and so is truth.'

Mandrake's long, mulish face came alive when he talked, and he was his own best listener. 'I reckon truth is the worst affliction that anyone can have. Most people are shielded by stupidity, convention, or privilege, but I wasn't lucky enough. By the time I was fourteen I was on my own and could see what a fucking, rat-arsed world we've got here and entirely rigged against pricks like me. Everything comes to nothing, Hoaggie, soon enough. Nothing that anyone does ever matters.'

'None of that's an excuse for the things you do. It's pointless, it's horrifying.'

'You know sometimes I horrify myself. Can you believe that?' Mandrake gave his panting laugh. 'But the more you get into it the more you need the kicks. You get so far down the line that there's no way back even if you wanted it. You're fucked one way or another.'

Jill was stiff and quiet, her head turned away from Mandrake and against the glass of the window. Hoaggie wept for a while, the sound of that conjoining within the car with the noise made by sleeping Tub. Hoaggie attempted to adjust the coat twisted as a support for his fractured arm. The Volvo swept on past the lake towards the Tekapo road. 'Did I tell you that Tub and I spent last night in the open?' said Mandrake. 'Well, near enough. Jesus, it got cold. You wouldn't think it at this time of the year so much, but I suppose it's the height and being so far inland.'

They met only one or two other cars in the night. The Volvo headed back towards Tekapo through the desolate Mackenzie Country. The lights on full swept the thin avenue of seal before them or, on the bends, caught the barren undulation of the landscape beyond, with not enough vegetation to hide the rabbits that moved there. Just the fierce spaniards made profiles and a few, small pines wind-sown across the stony ground. In the dark felt of the sky hung a gibbous moon and the bright barbs of stars.

Mandrake took his free hand from Jill's leg and marvelled at it all. 'Look how there's light on some of the peaks,' he said. 'White on white until they glow. I wonder if any bastard climbs there at night, do you think. Jesus. I remember, oh years ago, when I spent a few weeks in the Hokianga and some nights, after we'd had a fair bit of shit, we'd row this old dinghy out and just sit and talk and watch the lights of Rawene down the harbour. We'd smoke and lie back, rocked by the swell. It always seems to me that the sky is closer when you're out on the water.'

Jill had begun weeping and to Mandrake it made her less attractive: it also distracted him from his conversation. 'Quit all the blubbing,' he said. 'It gets on my nerves.' But she was past the point of caring even for the things that Mandrake could do.

'Leave her alone,' said Hoaggie.

'All this fucking snivelling,' said Mandrake. 'What's the point.'

They came down past the few shops and the hotel at Tekapo. A brief oasis of lights in the night and the lake like a pale carpet spread into the mountains. Tub woke and said that he wanted to get some booze, but Mandrake said maybe at the next pub, Burke's Pass. 'Jesus,' he said to Jill, 'haven't I been telling you to shut up?' On a long, climbing straight with not a house for miles, he pulled abruptly to the side of the road, cut the lights and, leaving the driver's seat, went round the front of the Volvo and pulled Jill from her place. He held her among the low lupins as a shearer holds a sheep, steadied in a crouch with one hand and a knee. Her crying altered not at all in intensity; without resistance she held any position into which he forced her. Hoaggie managed to get his door open before Tub reacted.

Mandrake shot Jill twice beneath the ear and then Hoaggie once in the flesh of his upper leg. 'Get that prick back inside,' he told Tub, and he rolled Jill through the soft, rustling lupins into the grassed ditch flanking the road. She lay there very low, very relaxed, almost as if she was pressing herself into the scented earth. The noise of her weeping had been with them for so long that the silence which succeeded it was a noticeable release. Mandrake walked back to the driver's side and had a stretch there, his long arms reaching up as if for a hold among the stars. Tub quietly held Hoaggie in the back seat; nothing seemed to disturb the equanimity of the big man's life.

'That's a whole lot better,' said Mandrake. He made himself comfortable in the car and placed the .22 carefully at his feet again. He shrugged his shoulders in the denim jacket as he had done on the track to the Hooker Glacier when Hoaggie had first seen him, and then began driving again up the lonely road through the tussock to the pass. 'Women have a tendency to whine, don't you think, Hoaggie? And besides, I've been quite considerate. The worst thing for you would be to go first, imagining me at play on your wife. Aren't I right?'

'Bugger you,' cried Hoaggie. What else could Mandrake threaten him with once Jill and the boys were dead. 'You're nothing — nothing at all,' he said in a voice that had become almost a whisper again.

'The odd fucking thing is that I can't get it up these days! Your wife's okay for looks. I took to her voice and the way her hair was done, but I can't get it up anymore. Some sort of punishment I suppose, Hoaggie, and you'll be pleased to hear that. Yet I can still sleep like a baby.' Mandrake bounced his head on his chest and gave his panting laugh.

'You're nothing,' said Hoaggie harshly. He rocked a bit. 'Jesus,' he said. With his good hand he tried to hold his handkerchief to the wound in his thigh.

'Come on, Hoaggie,' said Mandrake. 'Be a man. No one dies from a fucking .22 in the leg. Most likely you'll hardly even bleed.' At the crest of the pass the lights for a moment pointed up to nothingness and then the car dipped over the highest place and the beam caught again the sealed road, the median white dashes, the treeless hills above.

'Does it look any different out there, Hoaggie, than when you came up? I often think that's the thing, how little connection there is. Indifference, Hoaggie, that's all there is in nature. In a community, a family too, I suppose, people can babble on to conceal it, but when you're on your own, when you come down to it, then it stares you in the face if you've any brains at all. No wonder so many people get pissed, or turn to religion.'

'Your apple barrel meditations are rubbish,' said Hoaggie. 'You've killed people for no reason, no reason at all.'

'Well, you're an educated man, Hoaggie. I'm just a fucking bum trying to get some share of the action and make sense of things. But I reckon that I have reasons: it's just that for you they're not good enough.'

'You could've had the money, the car, without hurting any of us.'

'But that's not it, Hoaggie. I want you to see me, to take me seriously. Get it? From time to time I need intelligent conversation. I will have attention paid to me, see?' Mandrake struck the wheel in his vehemence.

Before the Burke's Pass Hotel and the three or four other buildings, isolated a little higher on the slope, there is a graveyard with wooden gates and a line of oak trees facing the road. Consecrated ground no bigger than three or four urban house sections. Mandrake pulled into the dirt track of the entrance and stopped there. He cut the lights and told Hoaggie that they were going to take a breather. 'Tub will give you a hand,' he said solicitously. 'What with your arm and leg the way they are.'

It seemed very dark at first, as if there was nothing present but themselves, and then, as Hoaggie's eyes adjusted to the absence of the headlights, his surroundings gradually came up before him. First the sky as a sheen with hump-backed moon and a scatter of stars, then the dark but individual masses of the oak trees and the pines on the other boundaries, with a glimmer among them in one quarter from the hotel.

It was a lawn cemetery or, rather, a rough pasture one, with the older monuments at the higher end catching enough light to show the symmetry of their shapes. Mandrake walked in further from the road and Tub took a good deal of Hoaggie's weight as they followed. 'Jesus, what a life you have,' Hoaggie said to him, but Tub just turned his great, flat snowman's face to him and said nothing. Hoaggie felt and heard dry acorns beneath his shoes as he went through the gateway and the night breeze drew through the trees of the cemetery with an easy sigh.

'I could stay here all night talking, just about,' said Mandrake. 'I love the night. It's the other side of the coin, isn't it? People think that it's just some sort of pit that separates one day from another, but there are sights and sounds and smells that exist only then: there's animals and all sorts that have their whole life when most of us are sleeping. It's an alternative, Hoaggie, isn't it, and that's always a good thing. I always feel uneasy when there's only one choice, one way of looking at things.'

Tub had drawn off towards the trees and was having a piss, which cascaded long and loud into the rank grass. It reminded Mandrake that time was passing. 'The thing is,' he told Hoaggie, 'that Tub's keen to get down to the pub and that's fair enough. He doesn't ask much. He's a fucking natural man and doesn't pretend to love his fellows, but he's very loyal.'

Hoaggie sat down on the cold, concrete bed of one of the graves. His arm ached, his leg ached, but the real anguish was that of loss. It occurred to him, quite without irony, that he would like to read the inscription on the headstone, so he would know his companion for the night. He could see the graves more clearly then, and realised that the night was their natural time — cold and quiet and peaceful. No matter what Mandrake, Tub and Hoaggie could do there, the place was one of serenity. The trees, the old stones, the wrought iron surrounds of some of the oldest plots, caught the more subtle light of the night. Hoaggie was amazed by the coherent detail that formed about him.

Mandrake looked at the shadowed graves with interest. 'Everyone living must be considered an optimist, for they've had the alternative of suicide after all,' he said. 'Hold on to your philosophy, old son. That's the bloody thing to do,' and he lifted the hand which held the sawn off .22 and began the gasping that was his laugh.

New Work

People We Know

~

TO COME ACROSS an old acquaintance after many years is to find that one physical characteristic has won through, become emphatic. Doreen Gallagher's fullness of jaw had been relatively subdued when she was eighteen, but was positively mulish when Dylan met her in the Koru Lounge of Wellington airport thirty years later. The third Webb boy, best squash player of them all, once had limp, sandy hair, a scatter of American freckles, a wry grin and hands so large, so powerful, that they always seemed closer to you than the rest of his body. When Dylan heard Webb speak at an Auckland seminar on individual contracts, the hair was gone, the freckles faded quite away, wryness replaced by non-commital sardonicism, but the throttling hands, so useful in business no doubt, were large as ever.

And what is observable in regard to the physical, remains true also of the personality, so that from the rich possibilities, even contradictions, of the early psyche, some prevailing trait comes through. This man is rancorous, another full of self-doubts: one woman is all shrill conceit, and her neighbour given up utterly to motherliness. The conventional wisdom, that people grow more devious, subtle and maturely complex, is false. Time and fortune weather us, so that the most resistant seam juts out above all else.

All of this was in Dylan's mind again at Elspeth and Albie Bailey's party, and it came to him because, although apparently listening to someone close who was talking of coalition politics, he was watching Peter Unser in another group by the patio doors.

Peter was one of those old acquaintances, you see; known from school and university days, and then ceasing to exist for many years, before reappearing to be an acquaintance again — nothing more. Peter and Dylan had been exact contemporaries at school, they were for a year at the same university hostel, they continued in the same loose group of students during all their years of study. Yet they were never quite friends, although having friends in common. Quite comfortable in that wider group, they rarely contacted each other directly. Without antagonism, or specific incident, their personalities seemed to sheer away from each other, as if recognising some incompatibility in anything apart from casual company.

Dylan had enjoyed sport, foolery and efficient study: Peter had a reputation for wit, was a Thespian and, despite being a commerce student, worked on the campus newspaper. He had worn paisley waistcoats, smoked a curved Peterson, and been dark, lounging, and with an expressive face.

Dylan looked at him across the eddies of the party. No paisley and no pipe, but still the shambling man with his dark hair slicked back from his Humphrey Bogart face — the ugly smile which ushered in cynicism when he spoke. He held his brandy bulb up as emphasis to some point made, and his tight, Bogart smile came again.

After university, Dylan hadn't seen him for a good part of his life, then Unser came south with his firm on promotion, and they met up again. Occasionally these meetings were to do with business, rather more often they were social, but neither form of contact led to any deepening of it. There remained a passive apathy between them. Dylan and his wife never invited the Unsers to their home, and were never invited to the Unser's, yet quite often, as at the Baileys' party, the couples saw each other, greeted each other, stood in the same groups easily enough to talk of real estate, news presenters, or Zoe Aspen who stumbled bringing in the cheese board at her own New Year's party and ran a knife through her cheek and tongue.

Nothing brought Dylan and Peter any closer. Earlier in the evening while Dylan had been telling a group, which included Peter, that his daughter had a brush with pneumonia, Unser burst into laughter at something said across the room.

It was strange, surely, that after so many years their understanding of each other should have made no progress whatsoever, while for Susan Unser, Dylan felt admiration and camaraderie, although her life was almost completely unknown to him. She was a large, luminously pale woman: not at all vivacious, but with equable sympathy, good sense and grace. Promotions director for a firm which provided corporate management seminars, she quite often used Dylan on the panels she assembled.

He had never seen her in a bathing costume, but he imagined her full, white body in black, or red, with not a single wrinkle to hint at inadequacy of flesh. At a party not dissimilar to the Baileys', but months before, and on the shadowed end of a verandah over garages, he had felt drawn as they talked to slide his hand down the low front of her dress. Susan had relaxed her shoulders for a moment to allow her breast the freedom to be cupped, for Dylan to feel its agile weight, the prominent nipple, to hold for a second, all, there. But then she smiled and took his hand away without indignation, or alarm, but ultimate resolve. 'Please, Dylan, please,' she said, meaning of course not please, but don't please, and he had immediately complied and they had stayed there talking, hands still lightly clasped on the verandah rail. He was repulsed so gently and with such completely non-provocative affection that an innocent and never mentioned understanding was created between them.

He saw her close to the Baileys' stairs, with her full, pale shoulders and calm smile. Why such a woman would choose Peter Unser was a mystery to Dylan. It was bewilderment he felt rather than jealousy, for he was himself fortunate and happy in his marriage. What woman of discrimination would choose a man like Peter Unser, whose skin seemed as if soaked in walnut juice, and who had no pity for the confusion of others.

Dylan looked for his wife, saw her with the Sansoms and slim Nicola Dowd who kept flicking her head as she talked, like a bird trying to stun the fish in its beak. As always, Sharon knew that he was looking across at her. She glanced back at once, giving a smile compounded of intimacy for him alone, and mockery of all others in the room. He knew it so well yet, as always felt, the pleasure of such exclusive flattery. Why did they bother with such evenings, when they knew the glib bonhomie and small personal aggrandisements were always the same, small offences inevitable, the supper a predictable delight, and that the invitations created obligations of hospitality in their turn.

Dylan was on the fringe of a coterie gathered to listen to stories of the Olympic Village. The revelations were unfolded with mock understatement and perfunctory reluctance by a supremely bald man who had been an official with the rowing team, the small bore marksmen, maybe the electronic timekeepers? The prompter, intermediary, master of supporting leers, chortles and half-suppressed and wondering incredulity, was Alain Judd: a hapless bore who could never command attention himself, but had developed a knack as servile facilitator for more interesting people, so that he could at least manage to be something more than just another listener.

The truth was that Dylan was melancholy. He had been melancholy all evening though well-mannered enough to disguise it. He had talked with some wit and presence, and listened to others in his turn. Yet he was held again in a familiar malaise. Not the kitchen sink bitterness of the poor, or the unemployed, but the derided, yearning desolation of the middle class, which isn't a fit subject for sympathy, or sociological study. What was the value of the activities and incidents that filled his days? Robustness of emotional response was bled out of his life, and he moved as though through a world of those semi-translucent, trembling aquatic creatures whose organs can be seen, hearts pumping fluids to pale extremities

The image reminded him that his glass was empty. 'Ah, come on, come on. You can give us the real oil. All friends together aren't we?' Judd paused on a high note, palms out disarmingly. Maybe he would slide, showman like, on to one knee. The ex-Olympic official was persuaded, and Dylan eased away towards the drinks table. Albie Bailey kept a good brandy, and Dylan found it among the cheaper stuff brought by guests. He was easy on the ginger ale.

His wife came behind him, took his free hand, ran a finger down the palm in the small intimacy she employed in company. 'Don't overdo it,' she said. 'Remember the foursomes tomorrow. I'd hate to be beaten by the Normans, and only in the second round. Let's deny them historical right of conquest.'

'Two or three brandies?'

'Just a thought,' she said.

'I'll get some sporting tips from the Olympic guy.' But she was away, with a clump of full wine glasses carefully held in front of her.

Tragedy isn't a necessary prelude for sadness, which, like any season, will have its turn. Dylan wondered if his sorrow arose from realisation that, at his age, life could offer only repetitions of known joys, and that the only novel prospect was of death. What are the sounds of melancholy? An unknown woman's sobs in an adjacent motel room, the train whistle from the long, night curve of departure, the slow, irrevocable intake of the bank manager's breath, the tone of unconscious dismissal in a daughter's voice.

Dylan eased his way towards the patio and the garden, gently disengaging from Simpson Stewart who, while talking to the babysitter on the telephone, put a friendly hand on Dylan's arm. And he stayed just long enough with the Smiths and Hopkirks to pay small compliments to each. He went over the brick-coloured tiles of the patio, down two steps into the summer night of the garden, and found, behind the bougainvillaea, a seat ingeniously fashioned from a tree stump. Even across those few metres of the Baileys' garden he had absently plucked traces from the growing things he passed. As a boy he had trailed his hands everywhere he walked, strolling on to flick berries, petals, seed heads, shredded leaves, behind him. As a man he was still the same, and colleagues were accustomed to see him at the board table fiddling with botanical loot. He might have a cypress nut from the main door tub, a leaf like a frog's back from the rubber plant by the lift entrance, a large thorn snapped expertly in the moment of passing from the post-coital roses on Samantha McDougall's desk.

On the comfortable stump seat behind the Baileys' bougainvillaea, he had his brandy glass in one hand and, in the other, a sprig of rosemary which he crushed and brought to his nose. Dylan felt no more optimistic in the garden, but more resigned. He could still hear the party, even pick out voices at times, but he need neither pay attention, nor make reply. He slipped the top button of his shirt: the collar was damp with the sweat of fellowship. He smelled the brandy and rosemary he held, the more general fragrance of the summer garden with a trace of the cigarettes some guests had smoked on the patio. He was still there, alone, relaxed, mellow, when the Unsers came to leave, Peter spilling out on to the path haphazardly, Susan thanking Elspeth Bailey on the steps. Dylan could barely see Peter through the lattice of bougainvillaea, but glimpses of Susan's white shoulders were clear. He had the inclination to cool his hands on them, as you do on the smooth balustrade marble as you leave the theatre.

When Peter thought himself alone with his wife, he spat into the roses and gave the even rattle of his laugh. 'Why do we come?' he said. 'Why do we come?'

'Well, we're off home now,' said Susan.

'A charade,' he said. 'An utter hoax, and we're all going down to the grave. The people here are the people anywhere — braying and milling around, setting store on their footling achievements and illusionary slights. We're dying, Susan.'

'But not right now I hope,' she said cheerfully.

But Dylan, listening, was riven by the open despair and bitterness in Peter's voice: a private voice that he hadn't heard before, even when they had been drunk together as students. 'Where is the joyousness of the world?' said Peter, and Dylan, out of sight, shaped the words after him. Peter Unser began a quick, unkind caricature of those at the party, and yes, Dylan was one of the first. 'Bloody old Dylan Grainger, eh, sucking at the best brandy, and with his great face of hang dog superiority. All condescension and muted affability. How does Sharon put up with such a po-faced bastard?'

'Maybe he doesn't talk too much,' said Susan mildly, keeping Peter on the way towards the gate on which the Baileys had a replica gig lamp for a light. 'Maybe he's kind and unassuming as well as successful.'

As she fiddled with the latch, Peter Unser said, 'Remember Ezekiel, "Behold with a stroke I take away from thee the desire of thine eyes"' and then finished with a cough, a laugh, perhaps it was a sob.

'Don't, please don't,' she said. 'Not tonight, Peter.'

Dylan sat quietly in the warm, still shadows of the garden when the Unsers had gone. The noise from the Baileys' lounge seemed far off and inconsequential. He wasn't in the least bothered by Peter's opinion of him: he'd known it long before any expression in words, but the candidness, the futility, the yearning, in other things said, were a revelation.

Dylan had assumed his old acquaintance to be full of glib and casual complacency, but heard instead a new voice. He felt ashamed that, despite many opportunities, he'd never communicated with the man in any way that was meaningful. Ezekiel, Ezekiel, he repeated to himself.

And when he and Sharon were home that night he went at once to the bookcases, pulling his damp collar away from his neck with one hand, while he trailed the other along the shelves. 'Have we no Bible in this house?' he shouted in astonishment, having not noticed the lack in twenty-five years.

'In the morning, Dylan,' said his wife. She was already upstairs and taking off her make-up.

'Nothing, nowhere?' he shouted again, as bewildered as if the taps wouldn't run, or the phone give a dial tone.

'Anna's is probably still in her dresser.'

Sure enough, it was: the soft, dark cover of leather and the three sides of golden zip. The Bible given to their daughter by a Christian radio station when she was the second best soloist in the young people's singing competition. He stood in his daughter's room, with the desk lamp catching the gloss on the posters of pop stars, and he skimmed Ezekiel. There it was, 24:16. 'Behold, I take away from thee the desire of thine eyes with a stroke.' Dylan turned off the downstairs lights and went up to the main bedroom. The word was zipped up again and he felt the comfort of the soft leather in his palm. Sharon was changed, and it was warm enough for her to sit before the mirror as she brushed her hair.

'Why should Peter Unser be so unhappy?' he said.

'Is he?' Sharon said. Dylan opened the compact, soft Bible again and read aloud from it.

Sharon held the brush steady by her left ear for a time, giving all her concentration to the words. 'They lost an only child didn't they? A daughter when she was nine or ten.' She began brushing her hair again.

'I never knew that.'

'Yes, what an appalling thing,' she said softly. They were both thinking of their own daughter, giving thanks for her.

'I never knew,' said Dylan. Was it likely that Unser would have told him anything as terrible and personal of all those years during which they had lost track of each other. Dylan remembered Unser's inattention and discourtesy at the party when he'd talked of Anna's pneumonia scare, and the ugly, Bogart face as Unser in the Baileys' garden spoke ill of others at the party. How could someone not be maimed by the loss of a child.

'I think I'll go out for a while,' he said. 'Just walk around a bit before coming to bed.'

'It's nearly one o'clock.'

'I'll be hardly any time at all. It's warm and quiet and my head needs clearing after the party.'

Sharon wasn't surprised. He often went walking by himself. 'Remember you've had a fair bit to drink, and there's winning to be done tomorrow.'

'Won't be long,' he said, 'but I'll lock the door and take the key with me.'

A summer night expands, so that the streets and lawns and lights and stars seem flung far back and quiet. Dylan had walked three blocks before he was sure in his mind that he was deliberately heading for the Unsers' place. He and Sharon had passed it often, and although they had never been invited there, they had admired the Monier tiles, the unfenced American-style frontage with established silver birches and sycamores; they had declared it a shame that the north-facing rooms were overlooked by a neighbour's house of dark brick. After all these years, why shouldn't he walk to Peter Unser's and offer him sympathy, manly consolation, despite whatever casualness there'd been in the past. He had a daughter too; wasn't she still at risk in the world?

Dylan walked up the slope of the road which led to Unsers' and he recalled times when he had listened to his daughter — talking to Sharon perhaps, or even on occasion sharing with him — and he had been almost overcome with the hope, eagerness, trust and ribald innocence of his child. His wife was worldly wise and tolerant of behaviour in Anna's young men that she still rebuked in him after twenty-five years.

Peter Unser's daughter was dead at ten, so he and Susan were cut off from her love.

Three dark cats sat like chess pieces on the Unsers' even lawn. Each kept its distance from the others, but when Dylan began to walk up the paved path beneath the sycamores, they all vanished. He smoothed his hair back and tugged his open collar, as proof of his intention to go right on up to the front door beneath the columned portico, but he turned aside without any break in his step and went to stand beneath the large silver birch across the lawn from the main windows. Maybe his compassion would be misunderstood because there was so little history of it in their acquaintanceship. Maybe Unser's dark and narrow face was already on the pillow

No, there he was, standing behind the large bay window and before a lounge suite of polished wood and embroidered fabric. The two old acquaintances could look directly at each other, but Dylan knew that Unser, with the light behind him, couldn't see into the garden. Unser was wearing glasses, the belt of his trousers was undone to allow him comfort in his home, and he moved his shoulders up and down, up and down, to ease the muscles. He was talking to Susan in some other part of the house, but as he continued to face the window, it was as if he were speaking to Dylan. Dylan could hear nothing, but watching Unser mouthing in that yellow aquarium, staring forward as he spoke to his wife behind, he remembered what Unser had said when leaving the Baileys' about going down to the grave.

And Dylan had memories of Anna when she was ten, with braces on her teeth and a blue bike for Christmas: her dry, warm scalp as he would rest his hand in her hair while they stood together deciding where to pitch the plastic play tent. And she would pick the winged sycamore seeds like those about him in the Unsers' garden, spike them with pins, set them in a straw, and run with the whirling propellers through the amber of the autumn air. On both sides of ten all the memories were there, and they continued in a sequence until they linked up with the Anna, who was doing post-graduate work on alpine grasses at Canberra.

Even so long after midnight it was warm in the Unsers' garden. The air moved from the west and was fragrant with lavender from the plots by the house, and with the less readily identified essences transpired by the birches and sycamores. Brown beetles whirled in the air, estatic in enjoyment of a new, brief life. Several headed for the light of the window, tapped the glass in front of Unser's face, and tumbled bewildered into the lavender. Dylan had small, strong birch leaves in his hand, and he tore them, as was his habit.

Peter Unser stopped talking and stood staring out into the garden. It seemed Dylan's opportunity to go forward into the light, or say something even if Peter was unable to hear him, but Dylan had nothing to say. Anything at all would be a parade of his riches. Some relationships go past the point at which it's appropriate to express a personal sympathy. The two old acquaintances stood facing each other: one oblivious to their physical proximity, the other with the realisation that there was no way of bridging the gap between them. Dylan listened to the winged beetles in the heavy air, the drawing of the night breeze through the weakening leaves of autumn, then walked back towards the road, and this time the chess pieces on the soft lawn made no change.